U.S.

D0392389

MESHED•

AFGHANISTAN

IRAN

AGROS THREE

MOUNTAINS

ZAHEDAN•

PAKISTAN

LENGEH

Strait of
Hormuz

SIRI

ulf

OMAN

AL SHARGAZ

Gulf of Oman

CHAH BAHAR

Arabian

Sea

U.A.E.

OMAN

WHIRLWIND

Volume 1

WHIRLWIND
is the fifth novel in the Asian Saga
that so far consists of:

James Clavell's

WHIRLWIND

Volume 1

WILLIAM MORROW AND COMPANY, INC.
New York

This adventure story is set in revolutionary Iran, between February 9 and March 4, 1979, long before the hostage crisis began. I've tried to make it seem as real as possible—but it is fiction, with imaginary characters and many imaginary places. No reference to any living person or company that was or is part of the era is intended. Of course, the shadows of the opposing giants, HIH Shah Mohammed Pahlavi (and his father Reza Shah) and Imam Khomeini, that are cast upon my imaginary characters are a vital part of this story, though the leaders personally are not portrayed. I have tried to present an accurate but fictional picture of those times, of the different kinds of people who endured them, the sorts of opinions that existed and would have been expressed, but nothing herein is meant by me in disrespect.

This is a story, not as things really happened, but as I imagined they came to pass within those twenty-four days. . . .

For
Shigatsu

They have sown the wind,
and they shall reap the whirlwind

—Hosea 8:7

BOOK ONE

FRIDAY
February 9, 1979

IN THE ZAGROS MOUNTAINS: SUNSET. Now the sun touched the horizon and the man reined in his horse tiredly, glad that the time for prayer had come.

Hussain Kowissi was a powerfully built Iranian of thirty-four, his skin light and his eyes and beard very dark. Over his shoulder was a Soviet AK47 assault rifle. He was bundled against the cold and wore a white turban and travel-stained dark robes with a rough, nomad Kash'kai sheepskin jacket belted over them, and well-used boots. Because his ears were muffled he did not hear the distant scream of the approaching jet helicopter. Behind him his weary pack camel tugged at the halter, impatient for food and rest. Absently he cursed her as he dismounted.

The air was thin at this height, almost eight thousand feet, and cold, very cold, a heavy snow on the ground that the wind took into drifts, making the way slippery and treacherous. Below, the little-known track curled toward distant valleys, at length to Isfahan where he had been. Ahead the path wound dangerously upward through the crags, then to other valleys facing the Persian Gulf and to the town of Kowiss where he had been born, where he now lived and from which he had taken his name when he had become a *mullah.*

He did not mind the danger or the cold. The danger felt clean to him as the air was clean.

It's almost as though I was once more a nomad, he thought, my grandfather leading us as in the old days when all our tribes of the Kash'kai could roam from winter pasture to summer pasture, a horse and a gun for every man and herds to spare, our flocks of sheep and goats and camels a multitude, our women unveiled, our tribes living free as our forefathers had done for tens of centuries, subject to no one but the Will of God—the old days that were ended barely sixty years ago, he told himself, his anger rising, ended by Reza Khan, the upstart soldier who with the help of the vile British usurped the throne, proclaimed himself Reza Shah, first of the Pahlavi Shahs, and then, with the support of his Cossack regiment, curbed us and tried to stamp us out.

God's work that in time Reza Shah was humiliated and exiled by his foul British masters to die forgotten, God's work that Mohammed Shah was forced to flee a few days ago, God's work that Khomeini has returned to lead His revolution, the Will of God that tomorrow or the next day I will be martyred, God's pleasure that we're swept by His whirlwind and that now there will be a final reckoning on all Shah lackeys and all foreigners.

The helicopter was closer now but still he did not hear it, the whine of the gusting wind helping to bury the sound. Contentedly he pulled out his prayer rug and spread it on the snow, his back still aching from the weals that the whip had caused, then scooped up a handful of snow. Ritually he washed his hands and face, preparing for the fourth prayer of the day, then faced southwest toward the Holy City of Mecca that lay a thousand miles away in Saudi Arabia, and put his mind to God.

"Allah-u Akbar, Allah-u Akbar. La illah illa Allah . . ." As he repeated the *Shahada* he prostrated himself, letting the Arabic words embrace him: God is most Great, God is most Great. I testify there is no other God but God and Mohammed is His Prophet. God is most Great, God is most Great, I testify there is no other God but God and Mohammed is His Prophet. . . .

The wind picked up, colder now. Then through his earmuffs he caught the pulse of the jet engine. It grew and grew and went into his head and drove away his peace and ruined his concentration. Angrily he opened his eyes. The approaching helicopter was barely two hundred feet above the ground, climbing straight toward him.

At first he thought it might be an army aircraft and a sudden fear went into him that they were searching for him. Then he recognized the British red, white, and blue colors and familiar markings of the bold S-G around the red lion of Scotland on the fuselage—the same helicopter company that operated from the air base at Kowiss and all over Iran—so his fear left him but not his rage. He watched it, hating what it represented. Its course was almost directly overhead but it presented no danger to him—he doubted if those aboard would notice him, here in the lee of an outcrop—even so, with all of his being, he resented the intrusion into his peace, and destruction of his prayers. And as the ear-shattering scream increased, his anger soared.

"La illah illa Allah . . ." He tried to go back into prayer but now the thrust of the blades whirled the snow into his face. Behind him his horse whinnied and cavorted in sudden panic, the hobble making him slip and slide. The pack camel, jerked by the halter, equally in panic, reeled to her feet, bellowing, and stumbled this way and that on three legs, shaking her load and fouling the bindings.

His rage burst. "Infidel!" he bellowed at the airplane that now was almost over the lip of the mountain, leaped to his feet, and grabbed his gun, slipped the safety and let off a burst, then corrected and emptied the magazine.

"SATAN!" he shrieked in the sudden silence.

When the first bullets splashed the chopper, the young pilot, Scot Gavallan, was momentarily paralyzed and he stared stupidly at the holes in the plastic canopy ahead. "Christ Almighty . . ." he gasped, never having been fired on before, but his words were drowned by the man in the front seat beside him whose reactions were honed and battle fast: "Hit the deck!" The command roared in his headphones.

"Hit the deck," Tom Lochart shouted again into his boom mike, then, because he had no controls of his own, he overrode the pilot's left hand and shoved the collective lever down, cutting lift and power abruptly. The chopper reeled drunkenly, instantly losing height. At that moment the second burst sprayed them. There was an ominous crack above and behind, somewhere else a bullet howled off metal, the jets coughed, and the chopper fell out of the sky.

She was a 206 Jet Ranger, one pilot, four passengers, one in front, three in the back and she was full. An hour ago Scot had routinely picked up the others back from a month's home leave at Shiraz Airport, fifty-odd miles southeast, but now routine was nightmare and the mountain rushed at them until just over a ridge the earth tumbled away miraculously and the chopper sank into a depression, giving him a split second of respite to get back air power and partial control.

"Watch out for crissake!" Lochart said.

Scot had seen the hazard but not as quickly. Now his hands and feet slid the plane into a shuddering swerve around the jutting outcrop, the left skid of the undercarriage caught the rocks a glancing blow, howled in protest, and once more they plunged away barely a few feet above the uneven surface of rocks and trees that fell and reeled up again.

"Low and fast," Lochart said, "that way, Scot—no, that way, over there, down that crest into the ravine. . . . Are you hit?"

"No, no, I don't think so. You?"

"No, you're fine now, drop into the ravine, come on, hurry!"

Scot Gavallan banked obediently and fled, too low and too fast and his mind not quite normal yet. There was still the taste of bile in his mouth and his heart was pumping. From behind the partition he could hear the shouts and curses of the others in the back above the roar of the engines, but he could not risk turning and said anxiously into the intercom, "Anyone hurt back there, Tom?"

"Forget them, concentrate, watch the ridge, I'll deal with them!" Tom Lochart said urgently, his eyes searching everywhere. He was forty-two, Canadian, ex-RAF, ex-mercenary, and now chief pilot of their base, Zagros Three. "Watch the ridge and get ready to evade again. Hug the deck and keep her low. Watchittt!"

The ridge was slightly above them and it came at them too fast. Gavallan saw the fang of rocks directly in his path. He just had time to lurch around it when a violent gust shoved him perilously near to the sheer side of the ravine. He overcorrected and heard the obscenity in his earphones, got back control. Then ahead he saw the trees and the rocks and the sudden end to the ravine and he knew they were lost.

Abruptly everything seemed to slow down for him. "Christ Al—"

"Hard aport . . . watch the rock!"

Scot felt his hands and feet obey and saw the chopper pirouette the rocks by inches, slam for the trees, ride over them, and escape into free air.

"Set her down over there, fast as you can."

He gaped at Lochart, his insides still churning. "What?"

"Sure. We better take a look, check her out," Lochart said urgently, hating not having the controls. "I heard something go."

"So did I, but what about the undercart, it might be torn off?"

"Just keep her weight off. I'll slip out and check it, then if it's all right, set her down and I'll make a quick inspect. Safer to do that; Christ only knows if the bullets chopped an oil line or nicked a cable." Lochart saw Scot take his eyes off the clearing to glance around at his passengers. "The hell with them for crissake, I'll deal with them," he said sharply. "You concentrate on the landing." He saw the younger man flush but obey, then, trying to contain his sudden nausea, Lochart turned around expecting blood splashed everywhere and entrails and someone screaming—screams drowned by the jet engines—knowing there was nothing he could do until they reached sanctuary and landed, always the first duty to land safely.

To his aching relief the three men in the backseat—two mechanics and another pilot—were seemingly unhurt though they were all hunched down, and Jordon, the mechanic directly behind Scot, was white-faced, holding his head with both hands. Lochart turned back.

They were about fifty feet now, on a good approach, coming in fast. In the clearing the surface was stark and white and flat with no tufts of grass showing through, the snow banked high at the sides. Seemingly a good choice. Easily enough room to maneuver and land. But how to judge the depth of snow and the hidden level of the earth beneath? Lochart knew what he would do if he had the controls. But he did not have control, he was not the captain though he was senior. "They're okay in the back, Scot."

"Thank God for that," Scot Gavallan said. "You set to get out?"

"How's the surface look to you?"

Scot heard the caution in Lochart's voice, instantly aborted the landing, put on power and went into a hover. Christ, he thought, almost in panic at his stupidity, if Tom hadn't nudged me I'd've put down there and Christ knows how deep the snow is or what's underneath! He steadied at a hundred feet and searched the mountainside. "Thanks, Tom. What about over there?"

The new clearing was smaller, a few hundred yards away across the other side of the valley, lower down with a good escape route if they needed one, and protected from the wind. The ground was almost clear of snow, rough but serviceable.

"Looks better to me too." Lochart slid one earphone away and looked back. "Hey, Jean-Luc," he shouted over the engines, "you all right?"

"Yes. I heard something go."

"So did we. Jordon, you all right?"

"Course I'm all effing right, for Gawd's sake," Jordon shouted back sourly. He was a lean, tough Australian and he was shaking his head like a dog. "Just banged my bleeding head, didn't I? Bloody effing bullets! I thought Scot said things were getting bleeding better with the bleeding Shah gone and

Khomeini bleeding back. Better? Now they're bleeding firing at us! They've never done that before—what the eff's going on?"

"How the hell do I know? Probably just a trigger-happy nutter. Sit tight, I'm going to take a quick look. If the undercart's okay we'll set down and you and Rod can make a check."

"How's the effing oil pressure?" Jordon shouted.

"In the Green." Lochart settled back, automatically scanning the dials, the clearing, the sky, left, right, overhead, and below. They were descending nicely, two hundred feet to go. Through his headset he heard Gavallan humming tonelessly. "You did very well, Scot."

"The hell I did," the younger man said, trying to sound matter-of-fact. "I'd've pranged. I was bloody paralyzed when the bullets hit, and if it hadn't been for you I'd've gone in."

"Most of it was my fault. I bashed the collective without warning. Sorry about that but I had to get us out of the bastard's line of fire fast. I learned that in Malaya." Lochart had spent a year there with the British Forces in their war against Communist insurgents. "No time to warn you. Set down as fast as you can." He watched approvingly as Gavallan went into a hover, searching the terrain carefully.

"Did you see who fired at us, Tom?"

"No, but then I wasn't looking for hostiles. Where you going to land?"

"Over there, well away from the fallen tree. Okay?"

"Looks fine to me. Quick as you can. Hold her off about a foot."

The hover was perfect. A few inches above the snow, as steady as the rocks below though the wind was gusting. Lochart opened the door. The sudden cold chilled him. He zipped up his padded flight jacket, slid out carefully, keeping his head well down from the whirling blades.

The front of the skid was scraped and badly dented and a little twisted but the rivets holding it to the undercarriage mounts were firm. Quickly he checked the other side, rechecked the damaged skid, then gave the thumbs-up. Gavallan eased off the throttle a hair and set her down, soft as thistledown.

At once the three men in the back piled out. Jean-Luc Sessonne, the French pilot, ducked out of the way to let the two mechanics begin their inspection, one port, the other starboard, working back from nose to tail. The wind from the rotors tore at their clothes, whipping them. Lochart was under the helicopter now looking for oil or gasoline seepage but he could find none, so he got up and followed Rodrigues. The man was American and very good —his own mechanic who, for a year now, had serviced the 212 he normally flew. Rodrigues unclipped an inspection panel and peered inside, his gray-flecked hair and clothes tugged by the airflow.

S-G safety standards were the highest of all Iranian helicopter operators, so the maze of cables, pipes, and fuel lines was neat, clean, and optimum. But suddenly Rodrigues pointed. There was a deep score on the crankcase where a bullet had ricocheted. Carefully they backtracked the line of the bullet. Again he pointed into the maze, this time using a flash. One of the oil lines was nicked. When he brought out his hand it was oil heavy. "Shit," he said.

"Shut her down, Rod?" Lochart shouted.

"Hell no, there may be more of those trigger-happy bastards around, an' this's no place to spend the night." Rodrigues pulled out a piece of waste and a spanner. "You check aft, Tom."

Lochart left him to it, uneasily looked around for possible shelter in case they had to overnight. Over the other side of the clearing, Jean-Luc was casually peeing against a fallen tree, a cigarette in his mouth. "Don't get frostbite, Jean-Luc!" he called out and saw him wave the stream good-naturedly.

"Hey, Tom."

It was Jordon beckoning. At once he ducked under the tail boom to join the mechanic. His heart skipped a beat. Jordon also had an inspection panel off. There were two bullet holes in the fuselage, just over the tanks. Jesus, just a split second later and the tanks would have blown, he thought. If I hadn't shoved the collective down we'd all've bought it. Absolutely. But for that we'd be sprayed over the mountainside. And for what?

Jordon tugged him and pointed again, following the line of the bullets. There was another score on the rotor column. "How the effer missed the effing blades I'm effed if I know," he shouted, the red wool hat that he always wore pulled down over his ears.

"It wasn't our time."

"Wot?"

"Nothing. Have you found anything else?"

"Not effing yet. You all right, Tom?"

"Sure."

A sudden crash and they all whirled in fright, but it was only a huge tree limb, overloaded with snow, tumbling earthward.

"*Espèce de con,*" Jean-Luc said and peered up into the sky, very conscious of the falling light, then shrugged to himself, lit another cigarette, and wandered off, stamping his feet against the cold.

Jordon found nothing else amiss on his side. The minutes ticked by. Rodrigues was still muttering and cursing, one arm reaching awkwardly into the bowels of the compartment. Behind him the others were huddled in a group, watching, well away from the rotors. It was noisy and uncomfortable, the light good but not for long. They still had twenty miles to go and no guidance systems in these mountains other than the small homer at their base which sometimes worked and sometimes didn't. "Come on, for Christ's sake," someone muttered.

Yes, Lochart thought, hiding his disquiet.

At Shiraz the outgoing crew of two pilots and two mechanics they were replacing had hurriedly waved good-bye and rushed for their company 125— an eight-place, twin-engined private jet airplane for transportation or special freighting—the same jet that had brought them from Dubai's International Airport across the Gulf and a month's leave, Lochart and Jordon in England, Jean-Luc in France, and Rodrigues from a hunting trip in Kenya. "What the hell's the hurry?" Lochart had asked as the small twin jet closed its doors and taxied off.

"The airport's only still partially operational, everyone's still on strike, but not to worry," Scot Gavallan had said. "They've got to take off before the officious, bloody little burk in the tower who thinks he's God's gift to Iranian Air Traffic Control cancels their bloody clearance. We'd better get the lead out too before he starts to sod us around. Get your gear aboard."

"What about Customs?"

"They're still on strike, old boy. Along with everyone else—banks're still closed. Never mind, we'll be normal in a week or so."

"*Merde*," Jean-Luc said. "The French papers say Iran is *une catastrophe* with Khomeini and his mullahs on one side, the armed forces ready to stage a coup any day, the Communists winding everyone up, the government of Bakhtiar powerless, and civil war inevitable."

"What do they know in France, old boy?" Scot Gavallan had said airily as they loaded their gear. "The Fr—"

"The French know, *mon vieux*. All the papers say Khomeini'll never cooperate with Bakhtiar because he's a Shah appointee and anyone connected with the Shah is finished. Finished. That old fire-eater's said fifty times he won't work with anyone Shah-appointed."

Lochart said, "I saw Andy three days ago in Aberdeen, Jean-Luc, and he was bullish as hell that Iran'll come back to normal soon, now that Khomeini's back and the Shah gone."

Scot beamed. "There, you see. If anyone should know it's the Old Man. How is he, Tom?"

Lochart grinned back at him. "In great shape, his usual ball of fire." Andy was Andrew Gavallan, Scot's father, chairman and managing director of S-G.

"Andy said Bakhtiar has the army, navy, and air force, the police, and SAVAK, so Khomeini's got to make a deal somehow. It's that or civil war."

"Jesus," Rodrigues said, "what the hell we doing back here anyway?"

"It's the money."

"Bullmerde!"

They had all laughed, Jean-Luc the natural pessimist, then Scot said, "What the hell does it matter, Jean-Luc? No one's ever bothered us here, have they? All through the troubles here no one's really ever bothered us. All our contracts are with IranOil which's the government—Bakhtiar, Khomeini or General Whoever. Doesn't matter whoever's in power, they've got to get back to normal soon—any government'll need oil dollars desperately, so they've got to have choppers, they've got to have us. For God's sake, they're not fools!"

"No, but Khomeini's fanatic and doesn't care about anything except Islam —and oil's not Islam."

"What about Saudi? The Emirates, OPEC, for God's sake? They're Islamic and they know the price of a barrel. The hell with that, listen!" Scot beamed. "Guerney Aviation have pulled out of all the Zagros Mountains and are cutting all their Iranian ops to zero. To zero!"

This caught the attention of all of them. Guerney Aviation was the huge American helicopter company and their major rival. With Guerney gone, work would be doubled and all expat S-G personnel in Iran were on a bonus system that was tied to Iranian profits.

"You sure, Scot?"

"Sure, Tom. They had a helluva row with IranOil about it. The upshot was that IranOil said, If you want to leave, leave, but all the choppers are on license to us so they stay—and all spares! So Guerney told them to shove it, closed their base at Gash, and put all the choppers in mothballs and left."

"I don't believe it," Jean-Luc said. "Guerney must have fifty choppers on contract; even they can't afford to write off that lot."

"Even so, we've already flown three missions last week which were all Guerney exclusives."

Jean-Luc broke through the cheers. "Why did Guerney pull out, Scot?"

"Our Fearless Leader in Tehran thinks they haven't the bottle, can't stand the pressure, or don't want to. Let's face it, most of Khomeini's vitriol's against America and American companies. McIver thinks they're cutting their losses and that's great for us."

"Madonna, if they can't take out their planes and spares, they're in dead trouble."

"Ours not to reason why, old boy, ours just to do and fly. So long as we sit tight we'll get all their contracts and more than double our pay this year alone."

"Tu en parles mon cul, ma tête est malade!"

They had all laughed. Even Jordon knew what that meant: speak to my backside, my head is sick. "Not to worry, old chap," Scot said.

Confidently, Lochart nodded to himself, the cold on the mountainside not hurting him yet. Andy and Scot're right, everything's going to be normal soon, has to be, he thought. The newspapers in England were equally confident the Iranian situation'd normalize itself quickly now. Provided the Soviets didn't make an overt move. And they had been warned. It was hands off, Americans and Soviets, so now Iranians can settle their affairs in their own way. It's right that whoever's in power needs stability urgently, and revenue —and that means oil. Yes. Everything's going to be all right. She believes it and if she believed everything would be wonderful once the Shah was overthrown and Khomeini back, why shouldn't I?

Ah, Sharazad, how I've missed you.

It had been impossible to phone her from England. Phones in Iran had never been particularly good, given the massive overload of too-fast industrialization. But in the past eight months since the troubles began, the almost constant telecommunication strikes had made internal and external communication worse and worse and now it was almost nonexistent. When Lochart was at Aberdeen HQ for his biannual medical he had managed to send her a telex after eight hours of trying. He had sent it care of Duncan McIver in Tehran where she was now. You can't say much in a telex except see you soon, miss you, love.

Not long now, my darling, and th—

"Tom?"

"Oh, hi, Jean-Luc? What?"

"It's going to snow soon."

"Yes."

Jean-Luc was thin-faced, with a big Gallic nose and brown eyes, spare like all the pilots who had serious medicals every six months with no excuses for overweight. "Who fired at us, Tom?"

Lochart shrugged. "I saw no one. Did you?"

"No. I hope it was just one crazy." Jean-Luc's eyes bored into him. "For a moment I thought I was back in Algiers, these mountains are not so different, back in the air force fighting the fellagha and the FLN, may God curse them forever." He ground the cigarette stub out with his heel. "I've been in one civil war and hated it. At least then I had bombs and guns. I don't want to be a civilian caught in another with nothing to rely on except how fast I can run."

"It was just a lone crazy."

"I think we're going to have to deal with a lot of crazies, Tom. Ever since I left France I've had a bad feeling. It's worse since I got back. We've been to war, you and I, most of the others haven't. We've a nose, you and I, and we're in for bad trouble."

"No, you're just tired."

"Yes, that's true. Andy was really bullish?"

"Very. He sends his best and said to keep it up!"

Jean-Luc laughed and stifled a yawn. "Madonna, I'm starving. What's Scot planned for our homecoming?"

"He's got a WELCOME HOME sign up over the hangar."

"For dinner, *mon vieux*. Dinner."

"Scot said he and some villagers went hunting so he's got a haunch of venison and a couple of hares ready for your tender mercies—and the barbecue'll be all set to go."

Jean-Luc's eyes lit up. "Good. Listen, I've brought Brie, garlic, a whole kilo, smoked ham, anchovies, onions, also a few kilos of pasta, cans of tomato puree, and my wife gave me a new *amatriciana* recipe from Gianni of St. Jean that is merely incredible. And the wine."

Lochart felt his juices quicken. Jean-Luc's hobby was cooking and he was inspired when he wanted to be. "I brought cans of everything I could think of from Fortnums and some whisky. Hey, I've missed your cooking." And your company, he thought. When they had met at Dubai they had shaken hands and he had asked, "How was leave?"

"I was in France," Jean-Luc had said grandly.

Lochart had envied him his simplicity. England had not been good, the weather, food, leave, the kids, her, Christmas—much as he had tried. Never mind. I'm back and soon I'll be in Tehran. "You'll cook tonight, Jean-Luc?"

"Of course. How can I live without proper food?"

Lochart laughed. "Like the rest of the world." They watched Rodrigues still working hard. The sound of the jets was muted, the rotors whipping him. Lochart gave a thumbs-up to Scot Gavallan waiting patiently in the cockpit. Scot returned the signal, then pointed at the sky. Lochart nodded, shrugged, then put his attention back on Rodrigues, knowing there was nothing he could do to help but wait stoically.

"When do you go to Tehran?" Jean-Luc asked.

Lochart's heart quickened. "Sunday, if it doesn't snow. I've a report for

McIver and mail for them there. I'll take a 206; it'll take all tomorrow to check everything. Scot said we're to stand by to start up full operations."

Jean-Luc stared at him. "Nasiri said full ops?"

"Yes." Nasiri was their Iranian liaison and base manager, an employee of IranOil—the government monopoly that owned all oil above and below the ground—that channeled and authorized all their flights. S-G worked under contract to this company, surveying, supplying personnel, supplies, and equipment to the oil rigs that were scattered over the mountain range, and dealing with the inevitable CASEVACs—casualty evacuations—accidents and emergencies. "I doubt if we'll be doing much flying over the next week because of the weather, but I should be able to get out in the 206."

"Yes. You will need a guide. I will come too."

Lochart laughed. "No way, old friend. You're next in command and on duty for the next two weeks."

"But I will not be needed. For three days, eh? Look at the sky, Tom. I must see that our apartment is all right." In normal times Tehran was where all pilots with families would be based, who would fly two weeks on, one week off. Many pilots opted for two months on and one month off on leave at home, particularly the English. "It's very important I get to Tehran."

"I'll check out your apartment if you like, and if you promise to cook three nights a week, I'll sneak you two days when I get back. You've just had a month's leave."

"Ah, but that was at home. Now I must think of *mon amie*. Of course she is desolate without me in Tehran, it's been a whole month for her without me. Of course." Jean-Luc was watching Rodrigues. Then again he looked at the sky. "We can wait ten minutes more, Tom, then we should prepare a camp while there is light."

"Yes."

"But back to more important things. Tom, w—"

"No."

"Madonna, be French and not Anglo-Saxon. A whole month, consider her feelings!"

Rodrigues clipped the panel back in place and wiped his hands. "Let's get the hell outta here," he called out and climbed aboard. They followed quickly. He was still fastening his seat belt, his back and head and neck aching, when they were airborne and scudding for their base over the next range. Then he saw Jordon staring at him. "What's with you, Effer?"

"How'd you fix that effing pipe, sport? She was effing holed to bust."

"Gum."

"Wot?"

"Chewing gum. Sure, goddamnit. It worked in goddamn Vietnam, so it'll goddamn work here. Maybe. Because it was only a goddamn little bit but it was all I got so start goddamn praying. Can't you stop cursing for crissake?"

They landed safely at their base, snow just beginning. The ground staff had switched on the landing lights, just in case.

Their base consisted of four trailer huts, a cookhouse, hangar for the 212—a fourteen-place passenger transport, or freight helicopter—and two 206s and landing pads. Storage sheds for oil-drilling spares, sacks of cement, pumps, generators, and all manner of support equipment for the rigs, along with drilling pipe. It was on a small plateau at seventy-five hundred feet, wooded and very picturesque, in a bowl half surrounded by snowcapped peaks that soared to twelve thousand feet and more. Half a mile away was the village of Yazdek. The villagers were from a minor tribe of nomad Kash'kai who had settled here a century ago around this crossroads of two of the minor caravan routes that had crisscrossed Iran for three, perhaps four thousand years.

S-G had had a base here for seven years under contract to IranOil, first to survey a pipeline and make topographical maps of the area, then to help build and service the rigs of the rich oil fields nearby. It was a lonely, wild, and beautiful place, the flying interesting and good, the hours easy—throughout Iran only daylight flying allowed by Iranian regulations. Summers were wonderful. Most of the winter they were snowed in. Close by were crystal lakes with good fishing, and in the forests game was plentiful. Their relations with the villagers of Yazdek were excellent. Apart from mail they were well supplied, usually, and wanted for nothing. And, important for all of them, they were well away from HQ in Tehran, out of radio contact most of the time, and left happily to their own devices.

The moment the rotors had stopped and the airplane shut down, Rodrigues and Jordon unclipped the panel again. They were aghast. The floor of the compartment was awash with oil. With it was the heavy smell of gasoline. Shakily Rodrigues searched, then pointed the flash. In one of the seams at the edge of a gasoline tank was a tiny rupture they could not possibly have detected on the mountainside. A thin stream of fuel came out to mix with the oil below.

"Jesus, Effer! Lookit, she's a goddamn time bomb," he croaked. Behind him, Jordon almost fainted. "One spark and . . . Effer, get me a hose for crissake, I'll flood her out now before we go sky-high. . . ."

"I'll get it," Scot said, then added queasily. "Well, I guess that's one of our lives gone. Eight more to go."

"You musta been born lucky, Captain," Rodrigues said, feeling very sick.

"Yeah, you must've been born lucky. This baby . . ." He stopped abruptly, listening. So did everyone nearby—Lochart and Jean-Luc, near the HQ hut with Nasiri, the half-dozen Iranian ground staff, cooks, and laborers. It was very quiet. Then again came a burst of machine-gun fire from the direction of the village.

"Goddamn!" Rodrigues muttered. "What the hell'd we come back to this lousy dump for?"

CHAPTER 2

ABERDEEN, SCOTLAND—McCLOUD HELIPORT: 5:15 P.M.
The great helicopter came down out of the gloaming, blades thrashing, and landed near the Rolls that was parked near one of the rainswept helipads—the whole heliport busy, other helicopters arriving or leaving with shifts of oil riggers, personnel, and supplies, all airplanes and hangars proudly displaying the S-G symbol. The cabin door opened and two men wearing flight overalls and Mae Wests came down the hydraulic steps, leaning against the wind and the rain. Before they reached the car the uniformed chauffeur had opened the door for them.

"Smashing ride, wasn't it?" Andrew Gavallan said happily, a tall man, strong and very trim for his sixty-four years. He slipped out of his Mae West easily, shook the rain from his collar and got in beside the other man. "She's marvelous, everything the makers claim. Did I tell you we're the first outsiders to test-fly her?"

"First or last, makes no difference to me. I thought it was bloody bumpy and bloody noisy," Linbar Struan said irritably, fighting off the Mae West. He was fifty, sandy-haired, and blue-eyed, head of Struan's, the vast conglomerate based in Hong Kong, nicknamed the Noble House, that secretly owned the controlling interest in S-G Helicopters. "I still think the investment is too much per aircraft. Much too much."

"The X63's as good a bet economically as you can get; she'll be perfect for the North Sea, Iran, and anywhere we have heavy loads, particularly Iran,"

Gavallan said patiently, not wanting his hatred of Linbar to spoil what had
been a perfect test ride. "I've ordered six."

"I haven't approved the buy yet!" Linbar flared at him.

"Your approval isn't necessary," Gavallan said and his brown eyes hardened. "I'm a member of Struan's Inner Office; you and the Inner Office
approved the buy last year, subject to the test ride, if I recommended it
an—"

"You haven't recommended it yet!"

"I am now so that's the end to it!" Gavallan smiled sweetly and settled
back in the seat. "You'll have contracts at the board meeting in three weeks."

"There's never an end to it, Andrew, you and your bloody ambition, is
there?"

"I'm not a threat to you, Linbar, let's l—"

"I agree!" Angrily Linbar picked up the intercom to speak to the driver on
the other side of the soundproofed glass partition. "John, drop Mr. Gavallan
at the office, then head for Castle Avisyard." At once the car moved off for
the three-story office block the other side of a group of hangars.

"How is Avisyard?" Gavallan asked strangely.

"Better than in your day—so sorry you and Maureen weren't invited for
Christmas, perhaps next year." Linbar's lips curled. "Yes, Avisyard is much
better." He glanced out the window and jerked a thumb at the jumbo helicopter. "And better you don't fail with that. Or anything else."

Gavallan's face tightened; the jibe about his wife had slipped under his
constant guard. "Talking about failure, what about your disastrous South
American investments, your stupid fracas with Toda Shipping over their
tanker fleet, what about losing the Hong Kong tunnel contract to Par-Con/
Toda, what about betraying our old friends in Hong Kong with your stock
manipul—"

"Betray, bullshit! 'Old friends,' bullshit! They're all over twenty-one and
what've they done for us recently? Shanghainese are supposed to be smarter
than us—Cantonese, mainlanders, all of them, you've said it a million times!
Not my fault there's an oil crisis or the world's in turmoil or Iran's up the
spout or the Arabs are nailing us to the cross along with the Japs, Koreans,
and Taiwanese!" Linbar was suddenly choked with rage. "You forget we're in
a different world now, Hong Kong's different, the world's different! I'm
taipan of Struan's, I'm committed to look after the Noble House, and every
taipan has had reverses, even your God cursed Sir bloody Ian Dunross, and
he'll have more with his delusions of oil riches China. Ev—"

"Ian's right ab—"

"Even Hag Struan had reverses, even our bloody founder, the great Dirk himself, may he rot in hell too! Not my fault the world's sodded up. You think you can do better?" Linbar shouted.

"Twenty times!" Gavallan slammed back.

Now Linbar was shaking with rage. "I'd fire you if I could but I can't! I've had you and your treachery, you tired, old, out-of-date burk. You married into the family, you're not a real part of it, and if there's a God in heaven you'll destroy yourself! I'm taipan and by God you'll never be!"

Gavallan hammered on the glass partition and the car stopped abruptly. He tore the door open and got out. "*Dew neh loh moh*, Linbar!" he said through his teeth and stormed off into the rain.

Their hatred stemmed from the late fifties and early sixties when Gavallan was working in Hong Kong for Struan's, prior to coming here at the secret order of the then taipan, Ian Dunross, the brother of Gavallan's late wife, Kathy. Linbar had been frantically jealous of him because he had had Dunross's confidence while Linbar had not, and mostly because Gavallan had always been in the running to succeed as taipan one day, whereas Linbar was considered to have no chance.

It was Struan's ancient company law for the taipan to have total, undisputed executive power, and the inviolate right to choose the timing of his own retirement and successor—who had to be a member of the Inner Office and therefore in some way, family—but once the decision was made, to relinquish all power. Ian Dunross had ruled wisely for ten years then had chosen a cousin, David MacStruan to succeed him. Four years ago, in his prime, David MacStruan—an enthusiastic mountaineer—had been killed in a climbing accident in the Himalayas. Just before he died and in front of two witnesses he had, astonishingly, chosen Linbar to succeed him. There had been police inquiries into his death—British and Nepalese. His ropes and climbing gear had been tampered with.

The inquiries finalized with "accident." The mountain face they had been climbing was remote, the fall sudden, no one knew exactly what had happened, neither climbers nor guides, conditions were only fair, and, yes, the sahib was in good heath and a wise man, never one to take a foolish risk, "But, sahib, our mountains in the High Lands are different from other mountains. Our mountains have spirits and get angry from time to time, sahib, and who can foretell what a spirit may do?" No finger was pointed at any one man, the rope and gear "might" not have been tampered with, just badly serviced. Karma.

Apart from Nepalese guides all twelve climbers in the party were men from Hong Kong, friends and business associates, British, Chinese, one American, and two Japanese, Hiro Toda, head of Toda Shipping Industries—

a longtime personal friend of David MacStruan's—and one of his associates, Nobunaga Mori. Linbar was not among them.

At great personal risk two men and a guide climbed down the fault and reached David MacStruan before he died, Paul Choy, an enormously wealthy director of Struan's, and Mori. Both testified that, just before he died, David MacStruan had formally made Linbar Struan his successor. Shortly after the distraught party had returned to Hong Kong, MacStruan's executive secretary going through his desk had found a simple typewritten page signed by him, dated a few months before, witnessed by Paul Choy, that confirmed it.

Gavallan remembered how shocked he had been, they all had—Claudia Chen, who had been executive secretary to the taipan for generations, cousin to his own executive secretary, Liz Chen, most of all. "It wasn't like the taipan, Master Andrew," she had told him—an old lady but still sharp as a needle. "The taipan would never have left such an important piece of paper here, he would have put it in the safe in the Great House along with . . . with all the other private documents."

But David MacStruan had not. And the dying command and the supporting paper had made it legal and now Linbar Struan was taipan of the Noble House and that was the end of it but *dew neh loh moh* on Linbar even so, his foul wife, his devil Chinese mistress, and his rotten friends. I'll still bet my life if David wasn't murdered, he was manipulated somehow. But why should Paul Choy lie, or Mori, why should they—they've nothing to gain by that. . . .

A sudden rain squall battered him and he gasped momentarily, brought out of his reverie. His heart was still pumping and he cursed himself for losing his temper and letting Linbar say what should not have been said. "You're a bloody fool, you could have contained him like always, you've got to work with him and his ilk for years—you were also to blame!" he said aloud, then muttered, "Bastard shouldn't've jibed about Maureen . . ." They had been married for three years and had a daughter of two. His first wife, Kathy, had died nine years ago of multiple sclerosis.

Poor old Kathy, he thought sadly, what bad luck you had.

He squinted against the rain and saw the Rolls turn out of the heliport gate and vanish. Damn shame about Avisyard, I love that place, he thought, remembering all the good times and the bad that he had lived there with his Kathy and their two children, Scot and Melinda. Castle Avisyard was the ancestral estate of Dirk Struan, left by him to succeeding taipans during their tenure. It was rambling and beautiful, more than a thousand hectares in Ayrshire. Shame we'll never go there, Maureen and I and little Electra, certainly as long as Linbar's taipan. Pity, but that's life.

"Well, the sod can't last forever," he said to the wind and felt all the better for the saying of it aloud. Then he strode into the building and into his office.

"Hi, Liz," he said. Liz Chen was a good-looking Eurasian woman in her fifties who had come with him from Hong Kong in '63 and knew all the secrets of Gavallan Holdings—his original cover operation—S-G, and Struan's. "What's new?"

"You had a row with the taipan, never mind." She offered him the cup of tea, her voice lilting.

"Dammit, yes. How the hell did you know?" When she just laughed he laughed with her. "The hell with him. Have you got through to Mac yet?" This was Duncan McIver, head of S-G's Iran operations and his oldest friend.

"We've a laddie dialing from dawn to dusk but the Iran circuits are still busy. Telex isn't answering either. Duncan must be just as anxious as you to talk." She took his coat and hung it on the peg in his office. "Your wife called —she's picking up Electra from nursery school and wanted to know if you'd be home for dinner. I told her I thought yes but it might be late—you've the conference call with ExTex in half an hour."

"Yes." Gavallan sat down behind his desk and made sure the file was ready. "Check if the telex to Mac's working yet, would you, Liz?"

At once she began to dial. His office was large and tidy, looking out on the airfield. On the clean desk there were some framed family photographs of Kathy with Melinda and Scot, when they were small, the great Castle Avisyard behind them, and another of Maureen holding up their baby. Nice faces, smiling faces. Just one oil painting on the wall by Aristotle Quance of a corpulent Chinese mandarin—a gift from Ian Dunross to celebrate their first successful landing on a North Sea rig that McIver had done, and the start of an era.

"Andy," Dunross had said, beginning it all, "I want you to take Kathy and the kids and leave Hong Kong and go home to Scotland. I want you to pretend to resign from Struan's—of course you'll still be a member of the Inner Office but that'll be secret for the time being. I want you to go to Aberdeen and quietly buy the best property, wharfs, factory areas, a small airfield, potential heliports—Aberdeen's still a backwater so you can get the best cheaply. This's a secret operation, just between us. A few days ago I met a strange fellow, a seismologist called Kirk who convinced me the North Sea's over an enormous oil field. I want the Noble House to be ready to supply the rigs when they're developed."

"My God, Ian, how could we do that? The North Sea? Even if there's oil there, which sounds impossible, those seas are the worst in the world for most of the year. Wouldn't be possible, all the year round—and anyway the expense'd be prohibitive! How could we do it?"

"That's your problem, laddie."

Gavallan remembered the laugh and the brimming confidence and, as always, he was warmed. So he had left Hong Kong, Kathy delighted to leave, and he had done everything asked of him.

Almost at once, like a miracle, North Sea oil began to blossom and the major U.S. companies—headed by ExTex, the enormous Texas oil conglomerate, and BP, British Petroleum—rushed in with huge investments. He had been superbly positioned to take advantage of the new El Dorado and the first to recognize that the only efficient way to service the vast discoveries in those violent waters was by helicopter, the first—with Dunross's power—to raise the massive funds needed for helicopter leasing, the first to shove major helicopter manufacturers into size, safety, instrumentation, and performance standards undreamed of, and the first to prove that all-weather flying in those foul seas was practical. Duncan McIver had done that for him, the flying and developing the necessary techniques quite unknown then.

The North Sea had led to the Gulf, Iran, Malaysia, Nigeria, Uruguay, South Africa—Iran the jewel in his crown, with its enormous potential, vastly profitable, with the very best connections into the ultimate seat of power, the Court, that his Iranian partners had assured him would be equally powerful enough, even though the Shah had been deposed. "Andy," General Javadah, the senior partner, stationed in London, had told him yesterday, "there's nothing to worry about. One of our partners is related to Bakhtiar and, just in case, we've the highest level of contracts with Khomeini's inner circle. Of course, the new era will be more expensive than before. . . ."

Gavallan smiled. Never mind the added expense and that each year the partners become a little more greedy, there's still more than enough left over to keep Iran as our flagship—just so long as she gets back to normal quickly. Ian's gamble paid off a thousandfold for the Noble House—pity he resigned when he did, but then he'd carried Struan's for ten years. That'd be enough for any man—even me. Linbar's right that I want that slot. If I don't get it, by God, Scot will. Meanwhile, onward and upward, the X63s'll put us way out ahead of Imperial and Guerney and make us one of the biggest helicopter-leasing companies in the world. "In a couple of years, Liz, we'll be the biggest," he said with total confidence. "The X63's a smash! Mac'll be fractured when I tell him."

"Yes," she said and put down the phone. "Sorry, Andy, the circuits are still busy. They'll let us know the very moment. Did you tell the taipan the rest of the good news?"

"It wasn't exactly a perfect moment, never mind." They laughed together. "I'll reserve that for the board meeting." An old ship's clock on a bureau began to chime six o'clock. Gavallan reached over and switched on the multi-band radio that was on the filing cabinet behind him. Sound of Big Ben tolling the hour. . . .

TEHRAN—McIVER'S APARTMENT: Last of the chimes dying away, radio reception minimal, heavy with static. "This is the BBC World Service, the time is 1700 Greenwich Mean Time . . ." 5:00 p.m. London time was 8:30 p.m. local Iranian time.

The two men automatically checked their watches. The woman just sipped her vodka martini. The three of them were huddled around the big short-wave battery radio, the broadcast signal faint and heterodyning badly. Outside the apartment the night was dark. There was a distant burst of gunfire. They took no notice. She sipped again, waiting. Inside the apartment it was cold, the central heating cut off weeks ago. Their only source of warmth now was a small electric fire that, like the dimmed electric lights, was down to half power.

". . . at 1930 GMT there will be a special report on Iran 'From Our Own Correspondent' . . ."

"Good," she muttered and they all nodded. She was fifty-one, young for her age, attractive, blue-eyed and fair-haired, trim, and she wore dark-rimmed glasses. Genevere McIver, Genny for short.

". . . but first a summary of the world news: in Britain nineteen thousand workers again struck the Birmingham plant of British Leyland, the country's largest automobile manufacturer, for higher pay: union negotiators representing public-service workers reached an agreement for pay increases of 16 percent though Prime Minister Callaghan's Labour Government wants to maintain 8.8 percent: Queen Elizabeth will fly to Kuwait on Monday to begin a three-week visit of the Persian Gulf states: in Washington, Pres—"

The transmission faded completely. The taller man cursed.

"Be patient, Charlie," she said gently. "It'll come back."

"Yes, Genny, you're right," Charlie Pettikin answered. Another burst of machine-gun fire in the distance.

"A bit dicey sending the queen to Kuwait now, isn't it?" Genny said. Kuwait was an immensely wealthy oil sheikdom just across the Gulf, flanking Saudi Arabia and Iraq. "Pretty stupid at a time like this, isn't it?"

"Bloody stupid. Bloody government's got its head all the way up," Duncan McIver, her husband, said. "All the bloody way to Aberdeen."

She laughed. "That's a pretty long way, Duncan."

"Not far enough for me, Gen!" McIver was a heavyset man of fifty-eight, built like a boxer, with grizzled gray hair. "Callaghan's a bloody twit and th—" He stopped, hearing faint rumbles of a heavy vehicle going past in the street below. The apartment was on the top floor, the fifth, of the modern residential building in the northern suburbs of Tehran. Another vehicle passed.

"Sounds like more tanks," she said.

"They are tanks, Genny," Charlie Pettikin said. He was fifty-six, ex-RAF, originally from South Africa, his hair dark and gray-flecked, senior pilot, Iran, and chief of S-G's Iranian Army and Air Force helicopter training program.

"Perhaps we're in for another bad one," she said.

For weeks now every day had been bad. First it was martial law in September when public gatherings had been banned and a 9:00 P.M. to 5:00 A.M. curfew imposed by the Shah had only further inflamed the people. Particularly in the capital Tehran, the oil port of Abadan, and the religious cities of Qom and Meshed. There had been much killing. Then the violence had escalated, the Shah vacillating, then abruptly canceling martial law in the last days of December and appointing Bakhtiar, a moderate, prime minister, making concessions, and then, incredibly, on January 16 leaving Iran for "a holiday." Then Bakhtiar forming his government and Khomeini—still in exile in France—decrying it and anyone who supported it. Riots increasing, the death toll increasing. Bakhtiar trying to negotiate with Khomeini, who refused to see him or talk to him, the people restive, the army restive, then closing all airports against Khomeini, then opening them to him. Then, equally incredibly, eight days ago on February 1, Khomeini returning.

Since then the days have been very bad, she thought.

That dawn she, her husband, and Pettikin had been at Tehran's International Airport. It was a Thursday, very cold but crisp with patches of snow here and there, the wind light. To the north the Elburz Mountains were white-capped, the rising sun blooding the snow. The three of them had been beside the 212 that was standing on the airport apron, well away from the tarmac in front of the terminal. Another 212 was on the other side of the airfield, also ready for instant takeoff—both ordered here by Khomeini's supporters.

This side of the terminal was deserted, except for twenty or so nervous airport officials, most of whom carried submachine guns, waiting near a big black Mercedes and a radio car that was tuned to the tower. It was quiet here —in violent contrast to the inside of the terminal and outside the perimeter fence. Inside the terminal building was a welcoming committee of about a thousand specially invited politicians, *ayatollahs*, mullahs, newsmen, and hundreds of uniformed police and special Islamic Guards with green armbands—nicknamed Green Bands—the mullahs' illegal revolutionary private army. Everyone else had been kept away from the airport, all access roads blocked, guarded, and barricaded. But just the other side of these barricades were tens of thousands of anxious people of all ages. Most women wore the *chador*, the long, shroudlike robe that covered them from head to foot. Beyond these people, lining the ten-mile route, all the way to Behesht-Zahra Cemetery where the Ayatollah was to make his first speech, were five thousand armed police, and around them, crammed together on balconies, in windows, on walls, and in the streets was the biggest gathering of people Iran had ever known, a sea of people—most of Tehran's population. Nearly five million lived in and around the city. All anxious, all nervous, all afraid that there would be a last-moment delay or that perhaps the airport would be closed once more against him or that perhaps the air force would shoot him down—with or without orders.

Prime Minister Shahpur Bakhtiar, his cabinet, and the generals of all the armed services were not at the airport. By choice. Nor were there any of their officers or soldiers. These men waited in their barracks or airfields or ships— all equally anxious and impatient to move.

"I wish you'd stayed at home, Gen," McIver had said uneasily.

"I wish we'd all stayed at home," Pettikin said, equally ill at ease.

A week before, McIver had been approached by one of Khomeini's supporters to supply the helicopter to take Khomeini from the airport to Behesht-Zahra. "Sorry, that's not possible, I haven't the authority to do that," he had said, aghast. Within an hour the man was back with Green Bands, McIver's office and the outer offices jammed with them, young, tough, angry-looking men, two with Soviet AK47 automatic rifles over their shoulders, one with a U.S. M16.

"You will supply the helicopter as I have said," the man told him arrogantly. "In case crowd control becomes too difficult. Of course all Tehran will be there to greet the Ayatollah, the Blessings of God be upon him."

"Much as I would like to do that, I can't," McIver had told him carefully, trying to buy time. He was in an untenable position. Khomeini was being allowed to return, but that was all; if the Bakhtiar government knew that S-G was supplying their archenemy with a chopper for a triumphal entry into their capital, they would be very irritated indeed. And even if the government agreed, if anything went wrong, if the Ayatollah was hurt, S-G would be blamed and their lives not worth a bent farthing. "All our aircraft are leased and I don't have the necessary authority to g—"

"I give you the necessary authority on behalf of the Ayatollah," the man had said angrily, his voice rising. "The Ayatollah is the only authority in Iran."

"Then it should be easy for you to get an Iranian Army or Air Force helicopter t—"

"Quiet! You have had the honor to be asked. You will do as you are told. In the Name of Allah, the *komiteh* has decided you will supply a 212 with your best pilots to take the Ayatollah to where we say, when we say, as we say."

This was the first time McIver had been confronted by one of the komitehs—small groups of young fundamentalists—that had appeared, seemingly miraculously, the moment the Shah had left Iran, in every village, hamlet, town, and city to seize power, attacking police stations, leading mobs into the streets, taking control wherever they could. Most times a mullah led them. But not always. In the Abadan oil fields the komitehs were said to be left-wing *fedayeen*—literally "those who are prepared to sacrifice themselves."

"You will obey!" The man shook a revolver in his face.

"I'm certainly honored by your confidence," McIver had said, the men crowding him, the heavy smell of sweat and unwashed clothes surrounding him. "I will ask the government for perm—"

"The Bakhtiar government is illegal and not acceptable to the People," the man had bellowed. At once the others took up the shout and the mood became ugly. One man unslung his automatic rifle. "You will agree or the komiteh will take further action."

McIver had telexed Andrew Gavallan in Aberdeen, who gave immediate approval provided S-G's Iranian partners approved. The partners could not be found. In desperation McIver contacted the British embassy for advice: "Well, old boy, you can certainly ask the government, formally or informally, but you'll never get an answer. We're not even certain they'll really allow Khomeini to land, or that the air force won't take matters into their own hands. After all the bloody fellow's an out-and-out revolutionary, openly calling for insurrection against the legal government that everyone else recognizes—Her Majesty's Government to boot. Either way, if you're silly enough to ask, the government will certainly remember you embarrassed them and you're damned either way."

Eventually McIver had worked out an acceptable compromise with the komiteh. "After all," he had pointed out with enormous relief, "it would look very strange if a British aircraft ferried your revered leader into town. Surely it would be better if he was in an Iranian Air Force plane, flown by an Iranian. I'll certainly have one of ours standing by, two in fact, in case of accidents. With our best pilots. Just call us on the radio, call for a CASEVAC and we'll respond at once. . . ."

And now he was here, waiting, praying that there was no CASEVAC to which they would have to respond.

The Air France 747 jumbo jet appeared out of the pink haze. For twenty minutes she circled, waiting for clearance to land.

McIver was listening to the tower on the 212's radio. "Still some problem about security," he told the other two. "Wait a minute . . . she's cleared!"

"Here we go," Pettikin muttered.

They watched her come on to final. The 747 was gleaming white, the French colors sparkling. She inched her way earthward on a perfect approach, then, at the last moment, the pilot put on full power, aborting the landing. "What the hell's he playing at?" Genny said, her heart fluttering.

"Pilot says he wanted to take a closer look," McIver told her. "I think I would too—just to make sure." He looked at Pettikin who would fly any CASEVAC call from the komiteh. "I hope to Christ the air force don't do anything crazy."

"Look!" Genny said.

The jet came on to final and touched down, smoke belched from the tires, her massive engines roaring into reverse thrust to slow her. At once a Mercedes rushed to intercept her, and as the news spread to those in the terminal, thence to the barricades, thence to the streets, the multitudes went berserk with joy. The chant began: "Allah-u Akbar . . . Agha uhmad," God is Great . . . the Master has returned. . . .

It seemed to take forever for the steps to arrive and the doors to open and the stern-faced, black-turbaned, heavily bearded old man to come down the steps, helped by one of the French stewards. He walked through the hastily assembled honor guard of a few mullahs and the Iran Air France crew, to be surrounded by his top aides and the nervous officials and quickly bundled into the car which headed for the terminal. There he was greeted by bedlam as the cheering, screaming, frenzied guests fought with one another to get near him, to touch him, newspapermen from all the world fighting each other for the best position with their barrage of flash cameras, TV cameras—everyone shouting, Green Bands and police trying to protect him from the crush. Genny could just see him for a moment, a graven statue among the frenzy, then he was swallowed up.

* * *

Genny sipped her martini, remembering, her eyes fixed on the radio, trying to will the broadcast to continue, to blot out the memory of that day and Khomeini's speech at Behesht-Zahra Cemetery, chosen because so many of those massacred on Bloody Friday—martyrs he called them—were buried there.

To blot out the TV pictures they had all seen later of the raging sea of bodies surrounding the motorcade as it inched along—all ideas of security gone—tens of thousands of men, women, and young people shouting, struggling, shoving to get closer to him, scrambling all over the Chevy van that he was in, trying to reach him, to touch him, the Ayatollah sitting in the front seat in seeming serenity, occasionally raising his hands at the adulation. People clambering on the hood and on the roof, weeping and shouting, calling to him, fighting to keep others off—impossible for the driver to see, he at times braking hard to shake people off, at others simply accelerating blindly. To blot out the memory of a youth in a rough brown suit who had scrambled onto the hood but could not get a proper grip and slowly rolled off and under the wheels.

Dozens like the youth. Eventually Green Bands had fought their way around and onto the van and called down the helicopter and she remembered the way the helicopter carelessly plummeted down onto the mob that scattered from the blades, bodies everywhere, injured everywhere, then the Ayatollah walking in the center of his pack of Islamic Guards to be helped into the copter, stern-faced, impassive, then the helicopter taking off into the skies to the never-ending torrent of "Allah-uuuuu Akbar . . . Agha uhmad . . ."

"I need another drink," she said and got up to hide a shiver. "Can I fix yours, Duncan?"

"Thanks, Gen."

She went toward the kitchen for some ice. "Charlie?"

"I'm fine, Genny, I'll get it."

She stopped as the radio came back strongly: ". . . China reports that there have been serious border clashes with Vietnam and denounces these attacks as further evidence of Soviet hegemony: In Fran—" Again the signal vanished, leaving only static.

After a moment Pettikin said, "I had a drink at the club on the way here. There's a rumor amongst the journalists that Bakhtiar's readying a showdown. Another was that there's heavy fighting in Meshed after a mob strung up the chief of police and half a dozen of his men."

"Terrible," she said, coming back from the kitchen. "Who's controlling the mobs, Charlie, really controlling them? Is it the Communists?"

Pettikin shrugged. "No one seems to know for certain but the Communist Tudeh've got to be stirring it up, outlawed or not. And all the leftists, particularly the *mujhadin-al-khalq*, who believe in a sort of marriage between the religions of Islam and Marx, Soviet sponsored. The Shah, the U.S., and most Western governments *know* it's them, aided and heavily abetted by the Soviets north of the border, so of course all the Iranian press agree. So do our Iranian partners, though they're scared out of their pants, not knowing which way to jump, trying to support the Shah and Khomeini equally. I wish to God they'd all settle down. Iran's a great place and I don't plan to move."

"What about the press?"

"The foreign press're mixed. Some of the Americans agree with the Shah as to who is to blame. Others say it's pure Khomeini, purely religious, and led by him and the mullahs. Then there're those who blame the left-wing fedayeen, or the hard-core fundamentalist Muslim Brotherhood—there was even one sport, I think he was French, who claimed Yasir Arafat and the PLO're . . ." He stopped. The radio came in for a second then went back to emitting static. "It must be sunspots."

"Enough to make you want to spit blood," McIver said. Like Pettikin, he was ex-RAF. He had been the first pilot to join S-G, and now as director of Iran operations, he was also managing director of IHC—Iran Helicopter Company—the fifty-fifty joint venture with the obligatory Iranian partners that S-G leased their helicopters to, the company that got their contracts, made their deals, held the money—without whom there would be no Iranian operations. He leaned forward to adjust the tuning, changed his mind.

"It'll come back, Duncan," Genny said confidently. "I agree Callaghan's a twit."

He smiled at her. They had been married thirty years. "You're not bad, Gen. Not bad at all."

"For that you can have another whisky."

"Thanks, but this time put some in with the wat—"

"—partment of Energy spokesman says that the new 14 percent OPEC hike will cost the U.S. $51 billion for imported oil next year. Also in Washington, President Carter announced, because of the deteriorating situation in Iran, a carrier force has been ordered to proceed from the Philip—" The announcer's voice was drowned by another station, then both faded.

In silence they waited, very tense. The two men glanced at each other, trying to hide their shock. Genny walked over to the whisky bottle that was on the sideboard. Also on the sideboard, taking up most of the space, was the

HF radio, McIver's communicator with their helicopter bases all over Iran—conditions permitting. The apartment was big and comfortable, with three bedrooms and two sitting rooms. For the last few months, since martial law and the subsequent escalating street violence, Pettikin had moved in with them—he was single now, divorced a year ago—and this arrangement pleased them all.

A slight wind rattled the windowpanes. Genny glanced outside. There were a few dim lights from the houses opposite, no streetlamps. The low rooftops of the huge city stretched away limitlessly. Snow on them, and on the ground. Most of the five to six million people who lived here lived in squalor. But this area, to the north of Tehran, the best area, where most foreigners and well-to-do Iranians lived, was well policed. Is it wrong to live in the best area if you can afford it? she asked herself. This world's a very strange place, whichever way you add it up.

She made the drink light, mostly soda, and brought it back. "There's going to be a civil war. There's no way we can continue here."

"We'll be all right, Gen. Carter won't let . . ." Abruptly the lights died and the electric fire went out.

"Bugger," Genny said. "Thank God we've the butane cooker."

"Maybe the power cut'll be a short one." McIver helped her light the candles that were already in place. He glanced at the front door. Beside it was a five-gallon can of gasoline—their emergency fuel. He hated the idea of having gasoline in the apartment, they all did, particularly when they had to use candles most evenings. But for weeks now it had taken from five to twenty-four hours of lining up at a gas station and even then the Iranian attendant would more than likely turn you away because you were a foreigner. Many times their car had had its tank drained—locks made no difference. They were luckier than most because they had access to airfield supplies, but for the normal person, particularly a foreigner, the lines made life miserable. Black-market gasoline cost as much as 160 rials a liter—$2 a liter, $8 a gallon, when you could get it. "Mind the iron rations," he said with a laugh.

"Mac, maybe you should stand a candle on it, just for old times' sake," Pettikin said.

"Don't tempt him, Charlie! You were saying about Carter?"

"The trouble is if Carter panics and puts in even a few troops—or planes —to support a military coup, it will blow the top off everything. Everyone'll scream like a scalded cat, the Soviets most of all, and they'll have to react and Iran'll become the set piece for World War Three."

McIver said, "We've been fighting World War Three, Charlie, since '45 . . ."

A burst of static cut him off, then the announcer came back again. ". . . for illicit intelligence work: It is reported from Kuwait by the chief of staff of the armed forces that Kuwait has received shipments of arms from the Soviet Union. . . ."

"Christ," both men muttered.

". . . In Beirut, Yasir Arafat, the PLO leader, declared his organization will continue to actively assist the revolution of Ayatollah Khomeini: At a press conference in Washington, President Carter reiterated the U.S. support for Iran's Bakhtiar government and the 'constitutional process': And finally from Iran itself, Ayatollah Khomeini has threatened to arrest Prime Minister Bakhtiar unless he resigns, and has called on the people to 'destroy the terrible monarchy and its illegal government,' and on the army 'to rise up against their foreign-dominated officers and flee their barracks with their weapons.' Throughout the British Isles exceptionally heavy snow, gales, and floods have disrupted much of the country, closing Heathrow Airport and grounding all aircraft. And that ends the news summary. The next full report will be at 1800, GMT. You're listening to the World Service of the BBC. And now a report from our international farm correspondent, 'Poultry and Pigs.' We begin . . ."

McIver reached over and snapped it off. "Bloody hell, the whole world's falling apart and the BBC gives us pigs."

Genny laughed. "What would you do without the BBC, the telly, and the football pools? Gales and floods." She picked up the phone on the off chance. It was dead as usual. "Hope the kids are all right." They had a son and a daughter, Hamish and Sarah, both married now and on their own and two grandchildren, one from each. "Little Karen catches cold so badly and Sarah! Even at twenty-three she needs reminding to dress properly! Will that child never grow up?"

Pettikin said, "It's rotten not being able to phone when you want."

"Yes. Anyway, it's time to eat. The market was almost empty today for the third straight day. So it was a choice of roast ancient mutton again with rice, or a special. I chose the special and used the last two cans. I've corned beef pie, cauliflower au gratin, and treacle tart, and a surprise hors d'oeuvre." She took a candle and went off to the kitchen and shut the door behind her.

"Wonder why we always get cauliflower au gratin?" McIver watched the candlelight flickering on the kitchen door. "Hate the bloody stuff! I've told her fifty times . . ." The nightscape suddenly caught his attention. He walked over to the window. The city was empty of light because of the power cut. But southeastward now a red glow lit up the sky. "Jaleh, again," he said simply.

On September 8, five months ago, tens of thousands of people had taken to the streets of Tehran to protest the Shah's imposition of martial law. There was widespread destruction, particularly in Jaleh—a poor, densely populated suburb—where bonfires were lit and barricades of burning tires set up. When the security forces arrived, the raging, milling crowd shouting "Death to the Shah" refused to disperse. The clash was violent. Tear gas didn't work. Guns did. Estimates of the death toll ranged from an official 97 to 250 according to some witnesses, to 2,000 to 3,000 by the militant opposition groups.

In the following crackdown to that "Bloody Friday," a vast number of opposition politicians, dissidents, and hostiles were arrested and detained— later the government admitted 1,106—along with two ayatollahs, which further inflamed the multitudes.

McIver felt very sad, watching the glow. If it weren't for the ayatollahs, he thought, particularly Khomeini, none of it would have happened.

Years ago when McIver had first come to Iran he had asked a friend in the British embassy what *ayatollah* meant. "It's an Arabic word, ayat'Allah, and means 'Reflection of God.' "

"He's a priest?"

"Not at all, there are no priests in Islam, the name of their religion—that's another Arabic word, it means 'submission,' submission to the Will of God."

"What?"

"Well," his friend had said with a laugh, "I'll explain but you've got to be a little patient. First, Iranians are not Arabs but Aryans, and the vast majority are Shi'ite Muslims, a volatile sometimes mystical breakaway sect. Arabs are mostly orthodox Sunni—they make up most of the world's billion Muslims— and the sects are somewhat like our Protestants and Catholics and they've fought each other just as viciously. But all share the same overarching belief, that there is one God, Allah—the Arabic word for God—that Mohammed, a man of Mecca who lived from A.D. 570 to 632 was His Prophet, and the words of the Koran proclaimed by him and written down by others over many years after his death came directly from God and contain all instruction that is necessary for an individual or society to live by."

"Everything? That's not possible."

"For Muslims it is, Mac, today, tomorrow, forever. But 'ayatollah' is a title peculiar to Shi'ites and granted by consensus and popular acclaim by the congregation of a *mosque*—another Arabic word meaning 'meeting place,' which is all it is, a meeting place, absolutely not a church—to a mullah who exhibits those characteristics most sought after and admired amongst the Shi'ites: piety, poverty, learning—but only the Holy Books, the Koran and the Sunna—and leadership, with a big emphasis on leadership. In Islam there's no separation between religion and politics, there can be none, and the Shi'ite mullahs of Iran, since the beginning, have been fanatic guardians of the Koran and Sunna, fanatic leaders and whenever necessary fighting revolutionaries."

"If an ayatollah or mullah's not a priest, what is he?"

"Mullah means 'leader,' he who leads prayers in a mosque. Anyone can be a mullah, providing he's a man, and Muslim. Anyone. There's no clergy in Islam, none, no one between you and God, that's one of the beauties of it, but not to Shi'ites. Shi'ites believe that, after the Prophet, the earth should be ruled by a charismatic, semidivine infallible leader, the *Imam,* who acts as an intermediary between the human and the divine—and that's where the great split came about between Sunni and Shi'ite, and their wars were just as bloody as the Plantagenets. Where Sunnis believe in consensus, Shi'ites would accept the Imam's authority if he were to exist."

"Then who chooses the man to be Imam?"

"That was the whole problem. When Mohammed died—by the way he never claimed to be anything other than mortal although last of the Prophets —he left neither sons nor a chosen successor, a *Caliph.* Shi'ites believed leadership should remain with the Prophet's family and the Caliph could only be Ali, his cousin and son-in-law who had married Fatima, his favorite daughter. But the orthodox Sunnis, following historic tribal custom which applies even today, believed a leader should only be chosen by consensus. They proved to be stronger, so the first three Caliphs were voted in—two were murdered by other Sunnis—then, at long last for the Shi'ites, Ali became Caliph, in their fervent belief the first Imam."

"They claimed he was semidivine?"

"Divinely guided, Mac. Ali lasted five years, then he was murdered— Shi'ites say martyred. His eldest son became Imam, then was thrust aside by a usurping Sunni. His second son, the revered, twenty-five-year-old Hussain, raised an army against the usurper but was slaughtered—martyred—with all his people, including his brother's two young sons, his own five-year-old son, and suckling babe. That happened on the tenth day of Muharram, in A.D. 650 by our counting, 61 by theirs, and they still celebrate Hussain's martyrdom as their most holy day."

"That's the day they have the processions and whip themselves, stick hooks into themselves, mortify themselves?"

"Yes, mad from our point of view. Reza Shah outlawed the custom but

Shi'ism is a passionate religion, needing outward expressions of penitence and mourning. Martyrdom is deeply embedded in Shi'ites, and in Iran venerated. Also rebellion against usurpers."

"So the battle is joined, the Faithful against the Shah?"

"Oh, yes. Fanatically on both sides. For the Shi'ites, the mullah is the sole interpreting medium which therefore gives him enormous power. He is interpreter, lawgiver, judge, and leader. And the greatest of mullahs are ayatollahs."

And Khomeini is the Grand Ayatollah, McIver was thinking, staring at the bloody nightscape over Jaleh. He's it, and like it or not, all the killing, all the bloodshed and suffering and madness, have to be laid at his doorstep, justified or not. . . .

"Mac!"

"Oh, sorry, Charlie," he said, coming back to himself. "I was miles away. What?" He glanced at the kitchen door. It was still closed.

"Don't you think you should get Genny out of Iran?" Pettikin asked quietly. "It's getting pretty smelly indeed."

"She won't bloody go. I've told her fifty times, asked her fifty times, but she's as obstinate as a bloody mule—like your Claire," McIver replied as quietly. "She just bloody smiles and says: 'When you go, I go.' " He finished his whisky, glanced at the door, and hastily poured himself another. Stronger. "Charlie, you talk to her. She'll listen to y—"

"The hell she will."

"You're right. Bloody women. Bloody obstinate. They're all the bloody same." They laughed.

After a pause, Pettikin said, "How's Sharazad?"

McIver thought a moment. "Tom Lochart's a lucky man."

"Why didn't she go back with him on leave and stay in England until Iran settles down?"

"There's no reason for her to go—she has no family or friends there. She wanted him to see his kids, Christmas and all that. She said she felt she'd stir things up and be in the way if she went along. Deirdre Lochart's still very pissed off with the divorce, and anyway Sharazad's family's here and you know how strong Iranians are on family. She won't leave until Tom goes and even then I don't know. And as for Tom, if I tried to post him I think he'd quit. He'll stay forever. Like you." He smiled. "Why do you stay?"

"Best posting I've ever had, when it was normal. Can fly all I want, ski winters, sail summers. . . . But let's face it, Mac, Claire always hated it here. For years she spent more time in England than here so she could be near Jason and Beatrice, her own family, and our grandchild. At least the parting of the ways was friendly. Chopper pilots shouldn't be married anyway, have to move about too much. I'm born expatriate, I'll die one. Don't want to go back to Cape Town—hardly know that place anyway—and can't stand those bloody English winters." He sipped his beer in the semidarkness. "Insha'Allah," he said with finality. In God's hands. The thought pleased him.

Unexpectedly the telephone jangled, startling them. For months now the phone system had been unreliable—for the last few weeks impossible and almost nonexistent, with perpetually crossed lines, wrong numbers, and no dial tones that miraculously cleared for no apparent reason for a day or an hour, to fall back like a shroud again, equally for no reason.

"Five pounds it's a bill collector," Pettikin said, smiling at Genny who came out of the kitchen, equally startled at hearing the bell.

"That's no bet, Charlie!" Banks had been on strike and closed for two months in response to Khomeini's call for a general strike, so no one—individuals, companies, or even the government—had been able to get any cash out and most Iranians used cash and not checks.

McIver picked up the phone not knowing what to expect. Or who. "Hello."

"Good God, the bloody thing's working," the voice said. "Duncan, can you hear me?"

"Yes, yes, I can. Just. Who's this?"

"Talbot, George Talbot at the British embassy. Sorry, old boy, but the stuff is hitting the fan. Khomeini's named Mehdi Bazargan prime minister and called for Bakhtiar's resignation or else. About a million people are in the streets of Tehran right now looking for trouble. We've just heard there's a revolt of airmen at Doshan Tappeh—and Bakhtiar's said if they don't quit he'll order in the Immortals." The Immortals were crack units of the fanatically pro-Shah Imperial Guards. "Her Majesty's Government, along with the U.S., Canadian, et al., are advising all nonessential nationals to leave the country at once. . . ."

McIver tried to keep the shock out of his face and mouthed to the others, "Talbot at the embassy."

". . . Yesterday an American of ExTex Oil and an Iranian oil official were ambushed and killed by 'unidentified gunmen' in the southwest, near Ahwaz"—McIver's heart skipped another beat—". . . you're operating down there still, aren't you?"

"Near there, at Bandar Delam on the coast," McIver said, no change in his voice.

"How many British nationals do you have here, excluding dependents?"

McIver thought for a moment. "Forty-five, out of our present complement of sixty-seven, that's twenty-six pilots, thirty-six mechanic/engineers, five admin, which's pretty basic for us."

"Who're the others?"

"Four Americans, three German, two French, and one Finn—all pilots. Two American mechanics. But we'll treat them all as British if necessary."

"Dependents?"

"Four, all wives, no children. We got the rest out three weeks ago. Genny's still here, one American at Kowiss and two Iranians."

"You'd better get both the Iranian wives into their embassies tomorrow—with their marriage certificates. They're in Tehran?"

"One is, one's in Tabriz."

"You'd better get them new passports as fast as possible."

By Iranian law all Iranian nationals coming back into the country had to surrender their passports to Immigration at the point of entry, to be held until they wished to leave again. To leave they had to apply in person to the correct government office for an exit permit for which they needed a valid identity card, a satisfactory reason for wanting to go abroad, and, if by air, a valid prepaid ticket for a specific flight. To get this exit permit might take days or weeks. Normally.

"Thank God we don't have that problem," McIver said.

"We can thank God we're British," Talbot went on. "Fortunately we don't have any squabbles with the Ayatollah, Bakhtiar, or the generals. Still, any foreigners are liable for a lot of flak so we're formally advising you to send dependents off, lickety-split, and cut the others down to basic—for the time being. The airport's going to be a mess from tomorrow on—we estimate there are still about five thousand expats, most of them American—but we've asked British Airways to cooperate and increase flights for us and our nationals. The bugger of it is that all civilian air traffic controllers are still totally out on strike. Bakhtiar's ordered in the military controllers and they're even more punctilious if that's possible. We're sure it's going to be the exodus over again."

"Oh, God!"

A few weeks ago, after months of escalating threats against foreigners—mostly against Americans because of Khomeini's constant attacks on American materialism as "the Great Satan"—a rampaging mob went berserk in the industrial city of Isfahan, with its enormous steel complex, petrochemical refinery, ordnance and helicopter factories, and where a large proportion of the fifty thousand-odd American expats and their dependents worked and lived. The mobs burned banks—the Koran forbade lending money for profit

—liquor stores—the Koran forbade the drinking of alcohol—and two movie houses—places of "pornography and Western propaganda," always particular targets for the fundamentalists—then attacked factory installations, peppered the four-story Grumman Aircraft HQ with Molotov cocktails, and burned it to the ground. That precipitated the "exodus."

Thousands converged on Tehran Airport, mostly dependents, clogging it as would-be passengers scrambled for the few available seats, turning the airport and its lobbies into a disaster area with men, women, and children camping there, afraid to lose their places, barely enough room to stand, patiently waiting, sleeping, pushing, demanding, whining, shouting, or just stoic. No schedules, no priorities, each airplane overbooked twenty times, no computer ticketing, just slowly handwritten by a few sullen officials—most of whom were openly hostile and non-English-speaking. Quickly the airport became foul and the mood ugly.

In desperation some companies chartered their own airplanes to pull out their own people. United States Air Force transports came to take out the military dependents while all embassies tried to play down the extent of the evacuation, not wanting to further embarrass the Shah, their stalwart ally of twenty years. Adding to the chaos were thousands of Iranians, all hoping to flee while there was still time to flee. The unscrupulous and the wealthy jumped the lines. Many an official became rich and then more greedy and richer still. Then the air traffic controllers struck, shutting down the airport completely.

For two days no flights came in or left. The crowds streamed away or stayed. Then some of the controllers went back to work and it began again. Rumors of incoming flights. Rushing to the airport with the kids and the luggage of years, or with no luggage, for a guaranteed seat that never was, back to Tehran again, half a thousand waiting in the taxi rank ahead of you, most taxis on strike—back to the hotel at length, your hotel room long since sold to another, all banks closed so no money to grease the ever-open hands.

At length most foreigners who wanted to leave left. Those who stayed to keep the businesses running, the oil fields serviced, airplanes flying, nuclear plants abuilding, chemical plants working, tankers moving—and to protect their gigantic investments—kept a lower profile, particularly if they were American. Khomeini had said, "If the foreigner wants to leave, let him leave; it is American materialism that is the Great Satan . . ."

McIver held the phone closer to his ear as the volume slipped a fraction, afraid that the connection would vanish. "Yes, George, you were saying?"

Talbot continued: "I was just saying, Duncan, we're quite sure everything's going to work out eventually. There's no way in the world the pot will completely blow up. An unofficial source says a deal's already in place for the Shah to abdicate in favor of his son Reza—the compromise HM Government advocates. The transition to constitutional government may be a bit wobbly but nothing to worry about. Sorry, got to dash—let me know what you decide."

The phone went dead.

McIver cursed, jiggled the connectors to no avail, and told Genny and Charlie what Talbot had said. Genny smiled sweetly. "Don't look at me, the answer's no. I agr—"

"But, Gen, Tal—"

"I agree the others should go but this one's staying. Food's almost ready." She went back to the kitchen and closed the door, cutting off further argument.

"Well she's bloody going and that's it," McIver said.

"My year's salary says she won't—until you leave. Why don't you go for God's sake? I can look after everything."

"No. Thanks, but no." Then McIver beamed in the semidarkness. "Actually it's like being back in the war, isn't it? Back in the bloody blackout. Nothing to worry about except get with it and look after the troops and obey orders." McIver frowned at his glass. "Talbot was right about one thing: we're bloody lucky to be British. Tough on the Yanks. Not fair."

"Yes, but you've covered ours as best you can."

"Hope so." When the Shah had left and violence everywhere increased, McIver had issued British IDs to all Americans. "They should be all right unless the Green Bands, police, or SAVAK check them against their licenses." By Iranian law all foreigners had to have a current visa, which had to be canceled before they could leave the country, a current ID card giving their corporate affiliate—and all pilots a current annual Iran pilot's license. For a further measure of safety McIver had had corporate IDs made and signed by the chief of their Iranian partners in Tehran, General Valik. So far there had been no problems. To the Americans, McIver had said, "Better you have these to show if necessary," and had issued orders for all personnel to carry photographs of both Khomeini and the Shah. "Make sure you use the right one if you're stopped!"

Pettikin was trying to call Bandar Delam on the HF with no success. "We'll try later," McIver said. "All bases'll be listening out at 0830—that'll give us time to decide what to do. Christ, it's going to be bloody difficult. What do you think? Status quo, except for dependents?"

Very concerned, Pettikin got up and took a candle and peered at the operations map pinned to the wall. It showed the status of their bases, crew, ground staff, and aircraft. The bases were scattered over Iran, from air force and army training bases at Tehran and Isfahan, to high-altitude oil-rig support in the Zagros, a logging operation in Tabriz in the northwest, a uranium survey team near the Afghan border, from a pipeline survey on the Caspian, to four oil operations on or near the Gulf, and the last, far to the southeast, another at Lengeh on the Strait of Hormuz. Of these only five were operational now: Lengeh, Kowiss, Bandar Delam, Zagros, and Tabriz. "We've fifteen 212s, including two nonoperational on their two-thousand-hour checks, seven 206s, and three Alouettes, all supposed to be working at the moment. . . ."

"And all leased on binding legal contracts, none of which have been rescinded, but none of which we're being paid for," McIver said testily. "There's no way we can base them all at Kowiss—we can't even legally remove any one of them without the approval of the contractor, or our dear partners' approval—not unless we could declare force majeure."

"There isn't any yet. It has to be status quo, as long as we can. Talbot sounded confident. Status quo."

"I wish it was status quo, Charlie. My God, this time last year we had almost forty 212s working and all the rest." McIver poured himself another whisky.

"You'd better go easy," Pettikin said quietly. "Genny'll give you hell. You know your blood pressure's up and you're not to drink."

"It's medicinal, for Christ's sweet sake." A candle guttered and went out. McIver got up and lit another and went back to staring at the map. "I think we'd better get Azadeh and the Flying Finn back. His 212's on its fifteen-hundred-hour so he could be spared for a couple of days." This was Captain Erikki Yokkonen and his Iranian wife, Azadeh, and their base was near Tabriz in East Azerbaijan Province, to the far northwest, near the Soviet border. "Why not take a 206 and fetch them? That'd save him three hundred and fifty miles of lousy driving and we've got to take him some spares."

Pettikin was beaming. "Thanks, I could do an outing. I'll file a flight plan by HF tonight and leave at dawn, refuel at Bandar-e Pahlavi, and buy us some caviar."

"Dreamer. But Gen'd like that. You know what I think of the stuff." McIver turned away from the map. "We're very exposed, Charlie, if things got dicey."

"Only if it's in the cards."

McIver nodded. Absently his eyes fell on the telephone. He picked it up. Now there was a dial tone. Excitedly he began to dial: 00, international; 44,

British Isles; 224, Aberdeen in Scotland, 765-8080. He waited and waited, then his face lit up. "Christ, I'm through!"

"S-G Helicopters, hold the line, please," the operator said before he could interrupt and put him on hold. He waited, fuming. "S-G Helico—"

"This's McIver in Tehran, give me the Old Man, please."

"He's on the phone, Mr. McIver." The girl sniffed. "I'll give you his secretary."

"Hello, Mac!" Liz Chen said almost at once. "Hang on a tick, I'll get Himself. You all right? We've been trying to get you for days; hang on."

"All right, Liz."

A moment, then Gavallan said happily, "Mac? Christ, how did you get through? Wonderful to hear from you— I've got a laddie permanently dialing you, your office, your apartment, ten hours a day. How's Genny? How did you get through?"

"Just luck, Andy. I'm at home. I'd better be fast in case we're cut off." McIver told him most of what Talbot had said. He had to be circumspect because rumor had it that SAVAK, the Iranian secret police, often tapped telephones, particularly of foreigners. It was standing company procedure for the last two years to presume someone was listening—SAVAK, CIA, MI5, KGB, someone.

There was a moment's silence. "First, obey the embassy and get all our dependents out at once. Alert the Finnish embassy for Azadeh's passport. Tell Tom Lochart to expedite Sharazad's—I got him to apply two weeks ago, just in case. He's, er, got some mail for you, by the way."

McIver's heart picked up a beat. "Good, he'll be in tomorrow."

"I'll get on to BA and see if I can get them guaranteed seating. As backup, I'll send our company 125. She's scheduled for Tehran tomorrow. If you've any problem with BA, send all dependents and spare bods out by her, starting tomorrow. Tehran's still open, isn't it?"

"It was today," McIver said carefully.

He heard Gavallan say equally carefully, "The authorities, thank God, have everything under control."

"Yes."

"Mac, what do you recommend about our Iranian ops?"

McIver took a deep breath. "Status quo."

"Good. All indications here, up to the highest levels, say it should be business as usual soon. We've got lots of face in Iran. And future. Listen, Mac, that rumor about Guerney was correct."

McIver brightened perceptibly. "You're sure?"

"Yes. A few minutes ago I got a telex from IranOil confirming we'll get all

Guerney contracts at Kharg, Kowiss, Zagros, and Lengeh to begin with. Apparently the order to squeeze came from on high, and I did have to make a generous *pishkesh* contribution to our partners' slush fund." A pishkesh was an ancient Iranian custom, a gift given in advance for a favor that might be granted. It was also ancient custom for any official legitimately to keep pishkesh given him in the course of his work. How else could he live? "But never mind that, we'll quadruple our Iranian profits, laddie."

"That's wonderful, Andy."

"And that's not all: Mac, I've just ordered another twenty 212s and today I confirmed the order for six X63s—she's a smasher!"

"Christ, Andy, that's fantastic—but you're pushing it, aren't you?"

"Iran may be, er, in temporary difficulties, but the rest of the world's scared fartless about alternate sources of oil. The Yanks have their knickers in a twist, laddie." The voice picked up another beat. "I've just confirmed another huge deal with ExTex for new contracts in Nigeria, Saudi, and Borneo, another with All-Gulf Oil in the Emirates. In the North Sea it's just us, Guerney, and Imperial Helicopters." Imperial Helicopters was a subsidiary of Imperial Air, the second semi-government airline in opposition to British Airways. "It's paramount you keep everything stable in Iran—our contracts, aircraft, and spares're part of our collateral for the new aircraft. For God's sake keep our dear partners on the straight and narrow. How are the dear sweet people?"

"Just the usual."

Gavallan knew this meant rotten as usual. "I've just had a session with General Javadah in London myself." Javadah had left Iran with all his family a year ago, just before the troubles became overt. For the past three months two of their other Iranian partners, and families, had been visiting London "for medical reasons," four others were in America also with their families. Three remained in Tehran. "He's bullish—though expensive."

McIver put him away for more important problems. "Andy, I've got to have some money. Cash."

"It's in the post."

McIver heard the rich laugh and felt the warmer for it. "Up yours, Chinaboy!" he said. Chinaboy was his private nickname for Gavallan who, before going to Aberdeen, had spent most of his previous life as a China trader, based first in Shanghai, then with Struan's in Hong Kong where they had first met. At that time McIver had had a small, struggling helicopter service in the colony. "For God's sake, we're way behind paying our ground crews, there's all the pilots' expenses, almost everything's got to be bought on the . . ." He stopped himself in time. In case someone was listening. He was going to say black market. "The bloody banks are still closed and the little cash I've left is for *heung yau*." He used the Cantonese expression, literally meaning "fragrant grease," the money used to grease palms.

"Javadah's promised that General Valik in Tehran'll give you half a million rials tomorrow. I've got a telex confirming."

"But that's barely $6,000 and we've bills for twenty times that amount."

"I know that, laddie, but he says both Bakhtiar and the Ayatollah want the banks open so they'll open within the week. As soon as they're open he swears IHC will pay us everything they owe."

"Meanwhile has he released A stock yet?" This was a code that McIver and Gavallan used for funds held outside Iran by IHC, almost $6 million. IHC was almost $4 million behind on payments to S-G.

"No. He claims that he has to have the partners' formal approval. The standoff stays."

Thank God for that, McIver thought. Three signatures were needed on this account, two from the partners, one from S-G, so neither side could touch this particular fund without the other. "It's pretty dicey, Andy. With the down payment on the new aircraft, lease payments on our equipment here, you're on the edge, aren't you?"

"All life's on the edge, Mac. But the future's rosy."

Yes, McIver thought, for the helicopter business. But here in Iran? Last year the partners had forced Gavallan to assign real ownership of all S-G helicopters and spares in Iran to IHC. Gavallan had agreed, providing he could buy everything back at a moment's notice, without a refusal on their part, and provided they kept up the lease payments on the equipment on time and made good any bad debts. Since the crisis began and the banks closed, IHC had been in default and Gavallan had been making the lease payments on all Iranian-based helicopters from S-G funds in Aberdeen—the partners claiming it was not their fault the banks had closed, Javadah and Valik saying as soon as everything's normal of course we'll repay everything—don't forget, Andrew, we've got you all the best contracts for years; we got them, we did; without us S-G can't operate in Iran. As soon as everything's normal . . .

Gavallan was saying, "Our Iranian contracts're still very profitable, we can't fault our partners on that, and with Guerney's we'll be like pigs in wallah!" Yes, McIver thought, even though they're squeezing and squeezing and each year our share gets smaller and theirs fatter. ". . . They've a lock on the country, always have had, and they swear by all that's holy, it'll all settle down. They have to have choppers to service their fields. Everyone here says it'll blow over. The minister, their ambassador, ours. Why shouldn't it? The Shah did his best to modernize, the people's income's up, illiteracy down. Oil revenues are huge—and'll go higher once this mess's over, the minister says. So do my contacts in Washington, even old Willie in ExTex, for God's sake, and he should know if anyone does. The betting's fifty to one it'll all be normal in six months, with the Shah abdicating in favor of his son Reza and a constitutional monarchy. Meanwhile I think we sh—"

The line went dead. McIver jigged the plunger anxiously. When the line came back it was just a constant busy signal. Angrily he slammed the receiver down. The lights came on suddenly.

"Bugger," Genny said, "candlelight's so much prettier."

Pettikin smiled and switched the lights off. The room was prettier, more intimate, and the silver sparkled on the table she had laid earlier. "You're right, Genny, right again."

"Thanks, Charlie. You get an extra helping. Dinner's almost up. Duncan, you can have another whisky, not as strong as the one you sneaked—don't look so innocent—but after speaking to our Fearless Leader even I need extra sustenance. You can tell me what he said over dinner." She left them.

McIver told Pettikin most of what Gavallan had said—Pettikin was not a director of S-G or IHC so, of necessity, McIver had to keep his own counsel on much of it. Deep in thought, he wandered over to the window, glad to have talked to his old friend. It's been a lot of years, he thought. Fourteen.

In the summer of '65 when the Colony was poised on revolution with Mao Tse-tung's Red Guards rampaging all over Mainland China, tearing the motherland apart and now spilling over into the streets of Hong Kong and Kowloon, Gavallan's letter had arrived. At that time McIver's helicopter business was on the edge of disaster, he was behind on lease payments on his small chopper, and Genny was trying to cope with two teenage children in a tiny, noisy flat in Kowloon where the riots were the worst.

"For God's sake, Gen, look at this!" The letter said: "Dear Mr. McIver, You may remember we met once or twice at the races when I was with Struan's a few years back—we both won a bundle on a gelding called Chinaboy. The taipan, Ian Dunross, suggested I write to you as I have great need of your expertise immediately—I know that you taught him to fly a chopper, and he recommends you highly. North Sea oil is a fait accompli. I have a theory that the only way to supply the rigs in all weather conditions is by helicopter. That is presently not possible—I think you'd call it Instrument Flight Rules, IFR. We could make it possible. I've got the weather, you've got the skill. One thousand pounds a month, a three-year contract to prove or disprove, a bonus based on success, transportation for you and your family back to Aberdeen, and a case of Loch Vay whisky at Christmas. Please phone as soon as possible. . . ."

Without saying a word Genny had casually handed him back the letter and started out of the room, the constant noise of the great city—traffic, Klaxons, street vendors, ships, jets, blaring discordant Chinese music through the windows that rattled in the wind.

"Where the hell're you going?"

"To pack." Then she laughed and ran back and hugged him. "It's a gift from heaven, Duncan, quick, call him, call him now. . . ."

"But Aberdeen? IFR in all weather? My God, Gen, it's never been done. There isn't the instrumentation, I don't know if it's poss—"

"For you it is, my lad. Of course. Now, where the devil have Hamish and Sarah gone?"

"Today's Saturday, they've gone to the movies an—"

A brick crashed through one of the windows, and the tumult of a riot began again. Their apartment was on the second floor and faced a narrow street in the heavily populated Mong Kok area of Kowloon. McIver pulled Genny to safety then cautiously looked out. In the street below, five to ten thousand Chinese, all shouting, Mao, Mao, *Kwai Loh! Kwai Loh*—Foreign Devil, Foreign Devil—their usual battle cry, were surging toward the police station a hundred yards away where a small detachment of uniformed Chinese police and three British officers waited silently behind a barricade.

"My God, Gen, they're armed!" McIver gasped. Usually the police just had batons. Yesterday the Swiss consul and his wife had been burned to death nearby when a mob had overturned their car and set it on fire. Last night on radio and television the governor had warned that he had ordered the police to take whatever steps necessary to stop all rioting. "Get down, Gen, out of the way. . . ."

His words were drowned by police loudspeakers as the superintendent commanded the massed rioters in Cantonese and English to disperse. The mob paid no attention and attacked the barricade. Again the order to stop was disregarded. Then the firing began and those in front panicked and were trampled as others fought to get away. Soon the street was clear except for the dozen or so bodies lying in the dirt. It was the same on Hong Kong Island. The next day the whole Colony was once more at peace; there were no more serious riots, only a few pockets of hard-core Red Guards trying to whip up the crowds who were quickly deported.

Within the week McIver sold his interest in his helicopter business, flew to Aberdeen ahead of Genny, and hurled himself into his new job with gusto. It had taken her a month to pack, settle their apartment, and sell what they didn't need. By the time she arrived he had found an ideal apartment near the McCloud heliport that she promptly declined: "For goodness' sake, Duncan, it's a million miles away from the nearest school. An apartment in Aberdeen? Now that you're as rich as Dunross, we, my lad, we are renting a house. . . ."

He smiled to himself, thinking about those early days, Genny loving being back in Scotland—she had never really liked Hong Kong, life so difficult there with little money and children to care for—he loving his work, Gavallan a great man to work for and with, but hating the North Sea, all the cold and the wet and the aches that the salt-heavy air brought. But the five-odd years there had been worth it, renewing and increasing his old contacts in the still tiny international helicopter world—most of the pilots ex-RAF, -RCAF, -RAAF, -USAF, and all the allied services—against the day they could expand. Always a generous bonus at Christmas, carefully put away for retirement, and always the case of Loch Vay: "Andy, that was the one condition that really got me!" Gavallan always the driving force, living up to his motto for the company, Be Bold. In East Scotland nowadays, Gavallan was known as "the Laird," from Aberdeen to Inverness and south as far as Dundee, with tentacles reaching to London, New York, Houston—wherever there was oil power. Yes, old Chinaboy's great and he can also wrap you and most men around his little finger, McIver thought without rancor. Look how you got here. . . .

"Listen, Mac," Andrew Gallavan had said one day in the late sixties, "I've just met a top general in the Iranian General Staff at a shoot. General Beni-Hassan. Great shot, he got twenty brace to my fifteen! Over the weekend I spent a lot of time with him and sold him on close-support helicopters for infantry and tank regiments along with a whole program for training their army and air force—as well as helicopters for their oil business. We, laddie, are in like Flynn."

"But we're not equipped to do half of that."

"Beni-Hassan's a smashing fellow and the Shah's a really go-ahead monarch—with great plans for modernization. You know anything about Iran?"

"No, Chinaboy," McIver had said, suspiciously, recognizing the twinkling exuberance. "Why?"

"You're booked on Friday for Bahrain, you and Genny . . . now wait a moment, Mac! What do you know about Sheik Aviation?"

"Genny's happy in Aberdeen, she doesn't want to move, the kids are finishing school, we've just put the down payment on a house, we're not moving and Genny'll kill you."

"Of course," Gavallan said airily. "Sheik Aviation?"

"It's a small but good helicopter company that services the Gulf. They've three 206s and a few fixed-wing feeder planes, based in Bahrain. Well thought of and they do a lot of work for ARAMCO, ExTex, and I think IranOil. Owned and operated by Jock Forsyth, ex-paras and pilot who formed the company in the fifties with an old chum of mine, Scrag Scragger, an Aussie. Scrag's the real owner, ex-RAAF, AFC and Bar, DFC and Bar, now a chopper fanatic. First they were based in Singapore where I first met Scrag. We, er, we were on a bender and I don't remember who started it but the others said it was a draw. Then they moved to the Gulf with an ex-ExTex executive who happened to have a great contract to launch them there. Why?"

"I've just bought them. You take over as managing director on Monday. Scragger and all their pilots and personnel will stay on or not, as you suggest, but I think we'll need their knowledge—I found them all good fellows—Forsyth's happy to retire to Devon. Curious, Scragger didn't mention he knew you, but then I only spent a few moments with him and dealt with Forsyth. From now on we're S-G Helicopters Ltd. Next Friday I want you to go to Tehran . . . listen, for Christ's sake . . . on Friday to set up an HQ there. I've made a date for you to meet Beni-Hassan and sign the papers for the air force deal. He said he'd be glad to introduce us to the right people, all over. Oh, yes, you've 10 percent of all profits, 10 percent of the stock in the new Iran subsidiary, you're managing director of Iran—which includes the rest of the Gulf for the time being . . ."

Of course McIver had gone. He could never resist Andrew Gavallan and he had enjoyed every moment, but he had never found out how Gavallan had persuaded Genny. When he had gone home that night she had his whisky and soda ready and wore a sweet smile. "Hello, dear, did you have a nice day?"

"Yes, what's up?" he asked suspiciously.

"You're what's up. Andy says there's a wonderful new opportunity for us in some place called Tehran in some place called Persia."

"Iran. It used to be called Persia, Gen, modern word's Iran. I, er, I th—"

"How exciting! When are we leaving?"

"Er, well, Gen, I thought we'd talk it over and if you like I've fixed it so that I could do two months on and one month off back here an—"

"And what do you plan to do for the two months, nights and Sundays?"

"I, er, well I'll be working like the devil and there wo—"

"Sheik Aviation? You and old Scragger east of Suez together drinking and cavorting?"

"Who, me? Come on there'll be so much to do we won't ha—"

"No, you won't, my lad. Huh! Two on and one off? Over Andy's dead body and I mean dead. We go as a family by God or we don't go by God!" Even more sweetly, "Don't you agree, darling heart?"

"Now look here, Gen—"

Within a month they were once more starting afresh, but it had been exciting and the best time he had ever had, meeting all sorts of interesting people, laughing with Scrag and the others, finding Charlie and Lochart and Jean-Luc and Erikki, making the company into the most efficient, the safest flying operation in Iran and the Gulf, molding it the way he alone decided. His baby. His alone.

Sheik Aviation was the first of many acquisitions and amalgamations Gavallan made. "Where the hell do you get all the money, Andy?" he had once asked.

"Banks. Where else? We're a triple-A risk and Scots to boot."

It wasn't until much later that he discovered, quite by chance, that the S of S-G Helicopters really stood for Struan's that was also the secret source of all their financing and civilian intelligence, and S-G their subsidiary.

"How did you find out, Mac?" Gavallan had asked gruffly.

"An old friend in Sydney, ex-RAF, who's in mining, wrote to me and said he'd heard Linbar spouting about S-G being part of the Noble House—I didn't know but it seems Linbar's running Struan's in Australia."

"He's trying to. Mac, between us, Ian wanted Struan's involvement kept quiet—David wants to continue the pattern so I'd prefer you to keep it to yourself," Gavallan had said quietly. David was David MacStruan, the then taipan.

"Of course, not even Genny. But it explains a lot and gives me a grand feeling to know the Noble House's covering us. I often wondered why you left."

Gavallan had smiled but not answered. "Liz knows about Struan's, of course, the Inner Office, and that's all."

McIver had never told anyone. S-G had thrived and grown as the oil business had grown. So had his profits. So had the value of his stock in the Iran venture. When he retired in six or seven years he would be comfortably well off. "Isn't it time to quit?" Genny would say every year. "There's more than enough money, Duncan."

"It's not the money," he would always say. . . .

* * *

McIver was staring at the red glow to the southeast over Jaleh that now had deepened and spread. His mind was in turmoil. Jaleh's got to make it hit the fan again all over Tehran, he thought.

He sipped his whisky. No extra need to be nervous, he thought, the weight of it all bearing down. What the devil was Chinaboy going to say when we were cut off? He'll get me word if it was important—he's never failed yet. Terrible about Stanson. That's the third civilian, all American, to be murdered by "unknown gunmen" in the last few months—two ExTex and one from Guerney. Wonder when they'll start on us—Iranians hate the British just as much as the Yanks. Where to get more cash? We can't operate on half a million rials a week. Somehow I'll have to lean on the partners, but they're as devious as anyone on earth and past masters at looking after number one.

He took the last swallow of his whisky. Without the partners we're stymied, even after all these years—they're the ones who know who to talk to, which palm to touch with how much or what percentage, who to flatter, who to reward. They're the Farsi speakers, they've the contacts. Even so, Chinaboy was right: whoever wins, Khomeini, Bakhtiar, or the generals, they have to have choppers. . . .

In the kitchen Genny was almost in tears. The secret can of haggis that she had kept hidden so carefully for half a year and had just opened was defective and the contents ruined. And Duncan loves it so. How could he, a mess up of minced sheep heart and liver and lungs and oatmeal, onion, suet, seasonings, and stock, all stuffed into a bag made from the poor bloody sheep's stomach, then boiled for several hours. "Ugh! Bugger everything!" She had had young Scot Gavallan—sworn to secrecy—bring the can back after his last leave for this special occasion.

Today was their wedding anniversary and this was her secret surprise for Duncan. Sod everything!

It's not Scot's fault the bloody tin's defective, she thought in misery. Even so, shit shit shit! I've planned this whole bloody dinner for months and now it's ruined. First the bloody butcher lets me down even though I'd paid twice as much as usual in advance, sod his "Insha'Allah," and then because the bloody banks are closed I've no cash to bribe the rotten sod's rival to sell me the leg of good fresh lamb not old mutton he'd promised, then the grocery store pulls a sudden strike, then . . .

The window of the small kitchen was half open and she heard another burst of machine-gun fire. Closer this time. Then wafted on the wind came the distant, deep-throated sound of the mobs: "Allahhh-u Akbarrr . . . Allahhh-u Akbarrr . . ." repeated over and over. She shivered, finding it curiously menacing. Before the troubles began she used to find the muezzin's call to prayer five times daily from the minarets reassuring. But not now, not from the throats of the mobs.

I hate this place now, she thought. Hate the guns and hate the threats. There was another in the mailbox, their second—like the other, badly typed and copied on the cheapest of paper: "On December 1 we gave you and family one month to leave our country. You are still here. You are now our enemies and we will fight you categorically." No signature. Almost every expat in Iran got one.

Hate the guns, hate the cold and no heat and no light, hate their rotten toilets and squatting like an animal, hate all the stupid violence and destruction of something that was really very nice. Hate standing in queues. Sod all queues! Sod the rotten bugger who screwed up the tin of haggis, sod this rotten little kitchen and sod corned beef pie! For the life of me I can't understand why the men like it. Ridiculous! Canned corned beef mixed with boiled potatoes, a little onion butter and milk if you have it, bread crumbs on top, and baked till it's brown. Ugh! And as for cauliflower, the smell of it cooking makes me want to puke but I read it's good for diverticulitis and anyone can see Duncan's not as well as he should be. So silly to think he can fool me. Has he fooled Charlie? I doubt it. And as for Claire, what a fool to leave such a good man! I wonder if Charlie ever found out about the affair she had with that Guerney pilot. No harm in that I suppose if you're not caught—difficult being left so much alone and if that's what you want. But I'm glad they parted friends though I thought she was a selfish bitch.

She caught sight of herself in the mirror. Automatically she straightened her hair and stared at her reflection. Where's all your youth gone? I don't know, but it's gone. At least mine has, Duncan's hasn't, he's still young, young for his age—if only he'd look after himself. Damn Gavallan! No, Andy's all right. So glad he remarried such a nice girl. Maureen'll keep him in line and so will little Electra. I was so afraid he was going to marry that Chinese secretary of his. Ugh! Andy's all right and so was Iran. Was. Now it's time to leave and to enjoy our money. Definitely. But how?

She laughed out loud. More of the same, I suppose.

Carefully she opened the oven, blinked against the heat and smell, then shut the door again. Can't stand corned beef pie, she told herself irritably.

Dinner was very good, the corned beef pie golden brown on top, just as they liked it. "Will you open the wine, Duncan? It's Persian, sorry, but it's the last bottle." Normally they were well stocked with both French and

Persian wines but the mobs had smashed and burned all Tehran's liquor shops, encouraged by the mullahs, following Khomeini's strict fundamentalism—drinking any form of alcohol being prohibited by the Koran. "The man in the bazaar told me there's none officially on sale anywhere and even drinking in the Western hotels is officially forbidden now."

"That won't last, the people won't stand for it—or fundamentalism—for long," Pettikin said. "Can't, not in Persia. Historically, the Shahs've always been tolerant and why not? For almost three thousand years Persia's been famous for the beauty of its women—look at Azadeh and Sharazad—and their vineyards and wines. What about the *Rubáiyát of Omar Khayyám*, isn't that a hymn to wine, women, and song? Persia forever, I say."

" 'Persia' sounds so much better than 'Iran,' Charlie, so much more exotic, as it used to be when we first came here, so much nicer," Genny said. For a moment she was distracted by more firing, then went on, talking to cover her nervousness. "Sharazad told me they've always called it Iran, or Ayran themselves. Seems that Persia was what the ancient Greeks called it, Alexander the Great and all that. Most Persians were happy when Reza Shah decreed Persia was to be henceforth Iran. Thank you, Duncan," she said and accepted the glass of wine, admiring its color, and smiled at him.

"Everything's grand, Gen," he said and gave her a little hug.

The wine had been savored. And the pie. But they were not merry. Too much to wonder about. More tanks going by. More firing. The red glow over Jaleh spreading. The chant of distant mobs. Then halfway through the dessert—trifle, another McIver favorite—one of their pilots, Nogger Lane, staggered in, his clothes badly torn, his face deeply bruised, helping a girl. She was tall and dark-haired and dark-eyed, rumpled and in shock, mumbling pathetically in Italian, one sleeve almost ripped out of her coat, her clothes and face and hands and hair filthy, as though she had fallen in the gutter.

"We got caught between . . . between the police and some bastard mobs," he said in a rush, almost incoherently. "Some bugger'd siphoned my tank so . . . but the mob, there were thousands of them, Mac. One moment the street was normal, then everyone else started running and they . . . the mobs, they came out of a side street and a lot had guns . . . it was the God cursed chanting over and over, Allah-u Akbar, Allah-u Akbar, that made your blood curdle . . . I'd never . . . then stones, firebombs, tear gas —the lot—as the police and troops arrived. And tanks. I saw three, and I thought the bastards were going to open up. Then someone started firing from the crowd, then there were guns everywhere and . . . and bodies all over the place. We ran for our lives, then a swarm of the bastards saw us and started shrieking 'American Satan' and charged after us and cornered us in an alley. I tried to tell 'em I was English and Paula, Italian, and not . . . but they were crowding me and . . . and if it hadn't been for a mullah, a big bastard with a black beard and black turban, this . . . this bugger called them off and Christ, they let us go. He cursed us and told us to piss off. . . ." He accepted the whisky and gulped it, trying to catch his breath, his hands and knees shaking uncontrollably now, quite unnoticed by him. McIver, Genny, and Pettikin were listening aghast. The girl was sobbing quietly.

"Never, never been in the middle of a nightmare like that, Charlie," Nogger Lane continued shakily. "Troops were all as young as the mobs and they all seemed scared shitless, too much to take night after night, mobs screaming and throwing stones. . . . A Molotov cocktail caught a soldier in the face and he burst into flames, screaming through the flames with no . . . and then those bastards cornered us and started manhandling Paula, trying to get at her, pawing her, tearing at her clothes. I went a bit mad myself and got hold of one bastard and smashed his face in, I know I hurt him because his nose went into his head and if it hadn't been for this mullah . . ."

"Take it easy, laddie," Pettikin said worriedly, but the youth paid no attention and rushed onward.

". . . if it hadn't been for this mullah who pulled me off I'd've gone on smashing until that bugger was pulp; I wanted to claw out his eyes, Jesus Christ, I tried to, I know I did . . . Jesus Christ, I've never killed anything with my hands, never wanted to until tonight but I did and would have. . . ." His hands were trembling as he brushed his fair hair out of his eyes, his voice edged now and rising. "Those bastards, they had no right to touch us but they were grabbing Paula and . . . and . . ." The tears began gushing, his mouth worked but no words came out, a fleck of foam was at the corners of his lips, "and . . . and . . . kill . . . I wanted to killllll—"

Abruptly Pettikin leaned over and belted the young man backhanded across the face, knocking him spread-eagled on the sofa. The others almost leaped out of themselves at the suddenness. Lane was momentarily stunned, then he groped to his feet to hurl himself at his attacker.

"Hold it, Nogger!" Pettikin roared. The command stopped the youth in his tracks. He stared at the older man stupidly, fists bunched. "What the bloody hell'sthematterwithyou, youdamn near broke my bloodyjaw," he said furiously. But the tears had stopped and his eyes were clean again. "Eh?"

"Sorry, lad, but you were going, flipping, I've seen it aco—"

"The bloody hell I was," Lane said menacingly, his senses back, but it took them time to explain and to calm him and calm her. Her name was Paula Giancani, a tall girl, a stewardess from an Alitalia flight.

"Paula, dear, you'd better stay here tonight," Genny said. "It's past curfew. You understand?"

"Yes, understand. Yes, I speak English, I th—"

"Come along, I'll lend you some things. Nogger, you take the sofa."

Later Genny and McIver were still awake, tired but not sleepy, gunfire somewhere in the night, chanting somewhere in the night. "Like some tea, Duncan?"

"Good idea." He got up with her. "Oh, damnit, I forgot." He went over to the bureau and found the little box, badly wrapped. "Happy anniversary. It's not much, just a bracelet I got in the bazaar."

"Oh, thank you, Duncan." As she unwrapped it she told him about the haggis.

"What a bugger! Never mind. Next year we'll have it in Scotland."

The bracelet was rough amethysts set in silver. "Oh, it's so pretty, just what I wanted. Thank you, darling."

"You too, Gen." He put his arm around her and kissed her absently.

She didn't mind about the kiss. Most kisses nowadays, hers as well, were just affectionate, like patting a beloved dog. "What's troubling you, dear?"

"Everything's fine."

She knew him too well. "What—that I don't know yet?"

"It's getting hairier and hairier. Every hour on the hour. When you were out of the room with Paula, Nogger told us they'd come from the airport. Her Alitalia flight—it'd been chartered by the Italian government to evacuate their nationals and had been grounded for two days—had got clearance to leave at midday, so he'd gone to see her off. Of course takeoff was delayed and delayed, as usual, then just before dusk the flight was grounded again, the whole airport closed down, and everyone was told to leave. All Iranian staff just vanished. Then almost immediately a group of heavily armed, and he meant heavily armed revolutionaries, started spreading out all over the place. Most of 'em were wearing green armbands, but some had IPLO on them, Gen, the first Nogger'd seen. 'Iranian Palestine Liberation Organization.' "

"Oh, my God," she said, "then it's true that the PLO's helping Khomeini?"

"Yes, and if they're helping, it's a different game, civil war's just started, and we're in the bloody middle."

AT TABRIZ ONE: 11:05 P.M.   Erikki Yokkonen was naked, lying in the sauna that he had constructed with his own hands, the temperature 107 degrees Fahrenheit, the sweat pouring off him, his wife Azadeh nearby, also lulled by the heat. Tonight had been grand with lots of food and two bottles of the best Russian vodka that he had purchased black market in Tabriz and had shared with his two English mechanics, and their station manager, Ali Dayati. "Now we'll have sauna," he had said to them just before midnight. But they had declined, as usual, with hardly enough strength to reel off to their own cabins. "Come on, Azadeh!"

"Not tonight, please, Erikki," she had said, but he had just laughed and lifted her in his great arms, wrapped her fur coat around her clothes, and carried her through the front door of their cabin, out past the pine trees heavy with snow, the air just below freezing. She was easy to carry, and he went into the little hut that abutted the back of their cabin, into the warmth of the changing area and then, unclothed, into the sauna itself. And now they lay there, Erikki at ease, Azadeh, even after a year of marriage, still not quite used to the nightly ritual.

He lay on one arm and looked at her. She was lying on a thick towel on the bench opposite. Her eyes were closed and he saw her breast rising and falling and the beauty of her—raven hair, chiseled Aryan features, lovely body, and milky skin—and as always he was filled with the wonder of her, so small against his six foot four.

Gods of my ancestors, thank you for giving me such a woman, he thought. For a moment he could not remember which language he was thinking in. He was quadrilingual, Finnish, Swedish, Russian, and English. What does it matter? he told himself, giving himself back to the heat, letting his mind waft with the steam that rose from the stones he had laid so carefully. It satisfied him greatly that he had built his sauna himself—as a man should— hewing the logs as his ancestors had done for centuries.

This was the first thing he had done when he was posted here four years ago—to select and fell the trees. The others had thought him crazy. He had shrugged good-naturedly. "Without a sauna life's nothing. First you build the sauna, then the house; without sauna a house is not a house; you English, you know nothing—not about life." He had been tempted to tell them that he had been born in a sauna, like many Finns—and why not, how sensible when you think of it, the warmest place in the home, the cleanest, quietest, most revered. He had never told them, only Azadeh. She had understood. Ah, yes, he thought, greatly content, she understands everything.

Outside, the threshold of the forest was silent, the night sky cloudless, the stars very bright, snow deadening sound. Half a mile away was the only road through the mountains. The road meandered northwest to Tabriz, ten miles away, thence northward to the Soviet border a few miles farther on. Southeast it curled away over the mountains, at length to Tehran, three hundred and fifty miles away.

The base, Tabriz One, was home for two pilots—the other was on leave in England—two English mechanics, the rest Iranians: two cooks, eight day laborers, the radio op, and the station manager. Over the hill was their village of Abu Mard and, in the valley below, the wood-pulp factory belonging to the forestry monopoly, Iran-Timber, they serviced under contract. The 212 took loggers and equipment into the forests, helped build camps and plan the few roads that could be built, then serviced the camps with replacement crews and equipment and flew the injured out. For most of the landlocked camps the 212 was their only link with the outside, and the pilots were venerated. Erikki loved the life and the land, so much like Finland that sometimes he would dream he was home again.

His sauna made it perfect. The tiny, two-room hut at the back of their cabin was screened from the other cabins, and built traditionally with lichen between the logs for insulation, the wood fire that heated the stones well ventilated. Some of the stones, the top layer, he had brought from Finland. His grandfather had fished them from the bottom of a lake, where all the best sauna stones come from, and had given them to him on his last home leave eighteen months ago. "Take them, my son, and with them surely there'll go a good Finnish sauna tonto"—the little brown elf that is the spirit of the sauna—"though what you want to marry one of those foreigners for and not your own kind, I really don't know."

"When you see her, Grandfather, you'll worship her also. She has blue-green eyes and dark dark hair an—"

"If she gives you many sons—well, we'll see. It's certainly long past the time you should be married, a fine man like you, but a foreigner? You say she's a schoolteacher?"

"She's a member of Iran's Teaching Corps, they're young people, men and women, volunteers as a service to the state, who go to villages and teach villagers and children how to read and write, but mostly the children. The Shah and the empress started the corps a few years ago, and Azadeh joined when she was twenty-one. She comes from Tabriz where I work, teaches in our village in a makeshift school and I met her seven months and three days ago. She was twenty-four then. . . ."

Erikki glowed, remembering the first time he ever saw her, neat in her uniform, her hair cascading, sitting in a forest glade surrounded by children, then her smiling up at him, seeing the wonder in her eyes at his size, knowing at once that this was the woman he had waited his life to find. He was thirty-six then. Ah, he thought, watching her lazily, once more blessing the forest tonto—spirit—that had guided him to that part of the forest. Only three more months then two whole months of leave. It will be good to be able to show her Suomi—Finland.

"It's time, Azadeh, darling," he said.

"No, Erikki, not yet, not yet," she said half asleep, drowsed by the heat but not by alcohol, for she did not drink. "Please, Erikki, not y—"

"Too much heat isn't good for you," he said firmly. They always spoke English together, though she was also fluent in Russian—her mother was half Georgian, coming from the border area where it was useful and wise to be bilingual. Also she spoke Turkish, the language most used in this part of Iran, Azerbaijan, and of course Farsi. Apart from a few words, he spoke no Farsi or

Turkish. He sat up and wiped the sweat off, at peace with the world, then leaned over and kissed her. She kissed him back and trembled as his hands sought her and hers sought him back. "You're a bad man, Erikki," she said, then stretched gloriously.

"Ready?"

"Yes." She clung to him as he lifted her so easily into his arms, then walked out of the sauna into the changing area, then opened the door and went outside into the freezing air. She gasped as the cold hit her and hung on as he scooped up some snow and rubbed it over her, making her flesh tingle and burn but not painfully. In seconds she was glowing within and without. It had taken her a whole winter to get used to the snow bath after the heat. Now, without it, the sauna was incomplete. Quickly she did the same for him, then rushed happily back into the warm again, leaving him to roll and thrash in the snow for a few seconds. He did not notice the group of men and the mullah standing in a shocked group up the rise, half hidden under the trees beside the path, fifty yards away. Just as he was closing the door he saw them. Fury rushed through him. He slammed the door.

"Some villagers are out there. They must have been watching us. Everyone knows this is off limits!" She was equally enraged and they dressed hurriedly. He pulled on his fur boots and heavy sweater and pants and grabbed the huge ax and rushed out. The men were still there and he charged them with a roar, his ax on high. They scattered as he whirled at them, then one of them raised the machine gun and let off a burst into the air that echoed off the mountainside. Erikki skidded to a halt, his rage obliterated. Never before had he been threatened with guns, or had one leveled at his stomach.

"Put ax down," the man said in halting English, "or I kill you."

Erikki hesitated. At that moment Azadeh came charging between them and knocked the gun away and began shouting in Turkish: "How dare you come here! How dare you have guns—what are you, bandits? This is our land —get off our land or I'll have you put in jail!" She had wrapped her heavy fur coat over her dress but was shaking with rage.

"This is the land of the people," the mullah said sullenly, keeping out of range. "Cover your hair, woman, cover y—"

"Who're you, mullah? You're not of my village! Who are you?"

"I'm Mahmud, mullah of the Hajsta mosque in Tabriz. I'm not one of your lackeys," he said angrily and jumped aside as Erikki lunged at him. The man with the gun was off balance but another man, safely away, cocked his rifle: "By God and the Prophet, stop the foreign pig or I'll blow you both to the hell you deserve!"

"Erikki, wait! Leave these dogs to me!" Azadeh called out in English, then shouted at them, "What do you want here? This is our land, the land of my father Abdollah Khan, Khan of the Gorgons, kin to the Qajars who've ruled here for centuries." Her eyes had adjusted to the darkness now and she peered at them. There were ten of them, all young men, all armed, all strangers, all except one, the *kalandar*—chief—of their village. "Kalandar, how dare you come here!"

"I'm sorry, Highness," he said apologetically, "but the mullah said I was to lead him here by this trail and not by the main path and so—"

"What do you want, parasite?" she said, turning on the mullah.

"Show respect, woman," the mullah said even more angrily. "Soon we'll be in command. The Koran has laws for nakedness and loose living: stoning and the lash."

"The Koran has laws for trespass and bandits and threatening peaceful people, and rebellion against their chiefs and liege lords. I'm not one of your frightened illiterates! I know you for what you are and what you've always been, the parasites of the villages and the people. *What do you want?*"

From the base, people were hurrying up with flashlights. At their head were the two bleary-eyed mechanics, Dibble and Arberry, with Ali Dayati carefully in tow. All were sleep ruffled, hastily dressed, and anxious. "What's going on?" Dayati demanded, thick glasses on his nose, peering at them. His family had been protected by and had served the Gorgon Khans for years.

"These dogs," Azadeh began hotly, "came out of the nigh—"

"Hold your tongue, woman," the mullah said angrily, then turned on Dayati. "Who're you?"

When Dayati saw the man was a mullah, his demeanor changed and at once he became deferential. "I'm . . . I'm Iran-Timber's manager here, Excellency. What's the matter, please, what can I do for you?"

"The helicopter. At dawn I want it for a flight around the camps."

"I'm sorry, Excellency, the machine is in pieces for an overhaul. It's the foreigner's policy an—"

Azadeh interrupted angrily, "Mullah, by what right do you dare to come here in the middle of the night to—"

"Imam Khomeini has issued ord—"

"Imam?" she echoed, shocked. "By what right do you call Ayatollah Khomeini that?"

"He is Imam. He has issued orders an—"

"Where does it say in the Koran or the Sharia that an ayatollah can claim to be Imam, can order one of the Faithful? Where does it sa—"

"Aren't you Shi'ite?" the mullah asked, enraged, conscious of his followers listening silently.

"Yes, I'm Shi'ite, but not an illiterate fool, mullah!" The way she used the word it was a curse. "Answer!"

"Please, Highness," Dayati said, pleading with her. "Please leave this to me, please, I beg you."

But she began to rage and the mullah to rage back, and the others joined in, the mood becoming ugly, until Erikki raised his ax and let out a bellow of rage, infuriated that he could not understand what was being said. The silence was sudden, then another man cocked his machine pistol.

"What's this bastard want, Azadeh?" Erikki said.

She told him.

"Dayati, tell him he can't have my 212 and to get off our land now or I'll send for the police."

"Please, Captain, please allow me to deal with it, Captain," Dayati said, sweating with anxiety, before Azadeh could interrupt. "Please, Highness, please leave now." Then turned to the two mechanics. "It's all right, you can go back to bed. I'll deal with it."

It was then that Erikki noticed Azadeh was still barefoot. He scooped her up into his arms. "Dayati, you tell that *matyeryebyets* and all of them if they come here again at night I'll break their necks—and if he or anyone touches one hair of my woman's head I'll crawl into hell after him if need be." He went off, massive in his rage, the two mechanics following.

A voice in Russian stopped him. "Captain Yokkonen, perhaps I could have a word with you in a moment?"

Erikki looked back. Azadeh, still in his arms, was tense. The man stood at the back of the pack, difficult to see, seemingly not very different from the others, wearing a nondescript parka. "Yes," Erikki told him in Russian, "but don't bring a gun into my house, or a knife." He stalked off.

The mullah went closer to Dayati, his eyes stony. "What did the foreign devil say, eh?"

"He was rude, all foreigners are rude, Her High—the woman was rude too."

The mullah spat in the snow. "The Prophet set laws and punishments against such conduct, the People have laws against hereditary wealth and stealing lands, the land belongs to the People. Soon correct laws and punishments will govern us all, at long last, and Iran will be at peace." He turned to the others. "Naked in the snow! Flaunting herself in the open against all the laws of modesty. Harlot! What are the Gorgons but lackeys of the traitor Shah and his dog Bakhtiar, eh?" His eyes went back to Dayati. "What lies are you telling about the helicopter?"

Trying to hide his fear, Dayati said at once that the fifteen-hundred-hour check was according to foreign regulations imposed upon him and the aircraft and further ordered by the Shah and the government.

"Illegal government," the mullah interrupted.

"Of course, of course illegal," Dayati agreed at once and nervously led them into the hangar and lit the lights—the base had its own small generating system and was self-contained. The engines of the 212 were laid out neatly, piece by piece, in regimented lines. "It's nothing to do with me, Excellency, the foreigners do what they like." Then he added quickly, "And although we all know Iran-Timber belongs to the people, the Shah took all the money. I've no authority over them, foreign devils or their regulations. There's nothing I can do."

"When will it be airworthy?" the Russian-speaking man asked in perfect Turkish.

"The mechanics promise two days," Dayati said and prayed silently, very afraid, though he tried hard not to show it. It was clear to him now that these men were leftist *mujhadin* believers in the Soviet-sponsored theory that Islam and Marx were compatible. "It's in the Hands of God. Two days; the foreign mechanics are waiting for some spares that're overdue."

"What are they?"

Nervously he told him. They were some minor parts and a tail rotor blade.

"How many hours do you have on the rotor blade?"

Dayati checked the logbook, his fingers trembling. "One thousand seventy-three."

"God is with us," the man said, then turned to the mullah. "We could safely use the old one for fifty hours at least."

"But the life of the blade . . . the airworthy certificate's invalidated," Dayati said without thinking. "The pilot wouldn't fly because air regulations requi—"

"Satan's regulations."

"True," the Russian speaker interrupted, "some of them. But laws for safety are important to the People, and even more important, God laid down rules in the Koran for camels and horses and how to care for them, and these rules can apply equally to airplanes which also are the gift of God and also carry us to do God's work. We must therefore care for them correctly. Don't you agree, Mahmud?"

"Of course," the mullah said impatiently and his eyes bore into Dayati who began to tremble. "I will return in two days, at dawn. Let the helicopter be ready and the pilot ready to do God's work for the People. I will visit every camp in the mountains. Are there other women here?"

"Just . . . just two wives of the laborers and . . . my wife."

"Do they wear chador and veil?"

"Of course," Dayati lied instantly. To wear the veil was against the law of Iran. Reza Shah had outlawed the veil in 1936, made the chador a matter of choice and Mohammed Shah had further enfranchised women in '64.

"Good. Remind them God and the People watch, even in the foreigner's vile domain." Mahmud turned on his heel and stomped off, the others going with him.

When he was alone, Dayati wiped his brow, thankful that he was one of the Faithful and that now his wife would wear the chador, would be obedient, and act as his mother acted with modesty and not wear jeans like Her Highness. What did the mullah call her to her face? God protect him if Abdollah Khan hears about it . . . even though, of course, the mullah's right, and of course Khomeini's right, God protect him.

IN ERIKKI'S CABIN: 11:23 P.M. The two men sat at the table opposite each other in the main room of the cabin. When the man had knocked on the door, Erikki had told Azadeh to go into the bedroom but he had left the inner door open so that she could hear. He had given her the rifle that he used for hunting. "Use it without fear. If he comes into the bedroom, I am already dead," he had said, his *pukoh* knife sheathed under his belt in the center of his back. The pukoh knife was a haft knife and the weapon of all Finns. It was considered unlucky—and dangerous—for a man not to carry one. In Finland it was against the law to wear one openly—that might be considered a challenge. But everyone carried one, and always in the mountains. Erikki Yokkonen's matched his size.

"So, Captain, I apologize for the intrusion." The man was dark-haired, a little under six feet, in his thirties, his face weather-beaten, his eyes dark and Slavic—Mongol blood somewhere in his heritage. "My name is Fedor Rakoczy."

"Rakoczy was a Hungarian revolutionary," Erikki said curtly. "And from your accent you're Georgian. Rakoczy's not Georgian. What's your real name —and KGB rank?"

The man laughed. "It is true my accent is Georgian and that I am Russian from Georgia, from Tbilisi. My grandfather came from Hungary but he was no relation to the revolutionary who in ancient times became prince of Transylvania. Nor was he Muslim, like my father and me. There, you see, we both know a little of our history, thanks be to God," he said pleasantly. "I'm an engineer on the Iran-Soviet natural gas pipeline, based just over the border at

Astara on the Caspian—and pro-Iran, pro-Khomeini, blessings be upon him, anti-Shah and anti-American."

He was glad that he had been briefed about Erikki Yokkonen. Part of his cover story was true. He certainly came from Georgia, from Tbilisi, but he was not a Muslim, nor was his real name Rakoczy. His real name was Igor Mzytryk and he was a captain in the KGB, a specialist attached to the 116th Airborne Division that was deployed just across the border, north of Tabriz, one of the hundreds of undercover agents who had infiltrated northern Iran for months and now operated almost freely. He was thirty-four, a KGB career officer like his father, and he had been in Azerbaijan for six months. His English was good, his Farsi and Turkish fluent, and although he could not fly, he knew much about the piston-driven Soviet Army close-support helicopters of his division. "As to my rank," he added in his most gentle voice, "it is friend. We Russians are good friends of Finns, aren't we?"

"Yes, yes, that's true. Russians are—not Party members. Holy Russia was a friend in the past, yes, when we were a grand duchy of Russia. Soviet Russia was friendly after '17 when we became independent. Soviet Russia is now. Yes, now. But not in '39. Not in the Winter War. No, not then."

"Nor were you in '41," Rakoczy said sharply. "In '41 you went to war against us with the stinking Nazis; you sided with them against us."

"True, but only to take back our land, our Karelian, our province you'd stolen from us. We didn't walk on to Leningrad as we could have done." Erikki could feel the knife in the center of his back and he was very glad of it. "Are you armed?"

"No. You said not to come armed. My gun is outside the door. I have no pukoh knife nor need to use one. By Allah, I'm a friend."

"Good. A man has need of friends." Erikki watched the man, loathing what he represented: the Soviet Russia that, unprovoked, had invaded Finland in '39 the moment Stalin had signed the Soviet-German nonaggression pact. Finland's little army had fought back alone. They had beaten off the Soviet hordes for one hundred days in the Winter War and then they had been overrun. Erikki's father had been killed defending Karelian, the southern and eastern province, where the Yokkonens had lived for centuries. At once Soviet Russia had annexed the province. At once all Finns left. All of them. Not one would stay under a Soviet flag, so the land became barren of Finns. Erikki was just ten months old then and in that exodus thousands died. His mother had died. It was the worst winter in living memory.

And in '45, Erikki thought, bottling his rage, in '45 America and England betrayed us and gave our lands to the aggressor. But we've not forgotten. Nor have the Estonians, Latvians, Lithuanians, East Germans, Czechs, Hungarians, Bulgars, Slavs, Romanians—the list endless. There will be a day of reckoning with the Soviets, oh, yes, one day there will surely be a day of reckoning with the Soviets—most of all by Russians who suffer their lash most of all.

"For a Georgian you know a lot about Finland," he said calmly.

"Finland is important to Russia. The détente between us works, is safe, and a lesson to the world that anti-Soviet American imperialistic propaganda is a myth."

Erikki smiled. "This is not the time for politics, eh? It's late. What do you want with me?"

"Friendship."

"Ah, that's easily asked, but as you would know, for a Finn, given with difficulty." Erikki reached over to the sideboard for an almost empty vodka bottle and two glasses. "Are you Shi'ite?"

"Yes, but not a good one, God forgive me. I drink vodka sometimes if that's what you ask."

Erikki poured two glasses. "Health." They drank. "Now, please come to the point."

"Soon Bakhtiar and his American lackeys will be thrown out of Iran. Soon Azerbaijan will be in turmoil, but you will have nothing to fear. You are well thought of here, so is your wife and her family, and we would like your . . . your cooperation in bringing peace to these mountains."

"I'm just a helicopter pilot, working for a British company, contracted to Iran-Timber, and I'm without politics. We Finns have no politics, don't you remember?"

"We're friends, yes. Our interests of world peace are the same."

Erikki's great right fist slammed down on the table, the sudden violence making the Russian flinch as the bottle skittered away and fell to the floor. "I've asked you politely twice to come to the point," he said in the same calm voice. "You have ten seconds."

"Very well," the man said through his teeth. "We require your services to ferry teams into the camps within the next few days. We . . ."

"What teams?"

"The mullahs of Tabriz and their followers. We requ—"

"I take my orders from the company, not mullahs or revolutionaries or men who come with guns in the night. Do you understand?"

"You will find it is better to understand us, Captain Yokkonen. So will the Gorgons. All of them," Rakoczy said pointedly, and Erikki felt the blood go into his face. "Iran-Timber is already struck and on our side. They will provide you with the necessary orders."

"Good. In that case I will wait and see what their orders are." Erikki got up to his great height. "Good night."

The Russian got up too and stared at him angrily. "You and your wife are too intelligent not to understand that without the Americans and their fornicating CIA, Bakhtiar's lost. That motherless madman Carter has ordered U.S. Marines and helicopters into Turkey, an American war fleet into the Gulf, a task force with a nuclear carrier and support vessels, with marines and nuclear-armed aircraft—a war fleet an—"

"I don't believe it!"

"You can. By God, of course they're trying to start a war, for of course we have to react, we have to match war game with war game, for of course they'll use Iran against us. It's all madness—we don't want nuclear war. . . ." Rakoczy meant it with all his heart, his mouth running away with him. Only a few hours ago his superior had warned him by code radio that all Soviet forces on the border were on Yellow Alert—one step from Red— because of the approaching carrier fleet, all nuclear missiles on equal alert. Worst of all, vast Chinese troop movements had been reported all along the five thousand miles of shared border with China. "That motherfucker Carter with his motherfucking Friendship Pact with China's going to blow us all to hell if he gets half a chance."

"If it happens, it happens," Erikki said.

"Insha'Allah, yes, but why become a running dog for the Americans, or their equally filthy British allies? The People are going to win, we are going to win. Help us and you won't regret it, Captain. We only need your skills for a few da—"

He stopped suddenly. Running footsteps were approaching. Instantly Erikki's knife was in his hand and he moved with catlike speed between the front door and the bedroom door as the front door burst open.

"SAVAK!" a half-seen man gasped, then took to his heels.

Rakoczy jumped for the doorway, scooped up his machine pistol. "We require your help, Captain. Don't forget!" He vanished into the night.

Azadeh came out into the living room. With the gun ready, her face white. "What was that about a carrier? I didn't understand him."

Erikki told her. Her shock was clear. "That means war, Erikki."

"Yes, if it happens." He put on his parka. "Stay here." He closed the door after him. Now he could see lights from approaching cars that were racing along the rough dirt road that joined the base to the main Tabriz-Tehran road. As his eyes adjusted to the darkness, he could make out two cars and an army truck. In a moment the lead vehicle stopped and police and soldiers fanned out into the night. The officer in charge saluted. "Ah, Captain Yokkonen, good evening. We heard that some revolutionaries were here, or Communist Tudeh—firing was reported," he said, his English perfect. "Her Highness is all right? There's no problem?"

"No, not now, thank you, Colonel Mazardi." Erikki knew him quite well. The man was a cousin of Azadeh, and chief of police in this area of Tabriz. But SAVAK? That's something else, he thought uneasily. If he is, he is, and I don't want to know. "Come in."

Azadeh was pleased to see her cousin and thanked him for coming and they told him what had occurred.

"The Russian said his name was Rakoczy, Fedor Rakoczy?" he asked.

"Yes, but it was obviously a lie," Erikki said. "He had to be KGB."

"And he never told you why they wanted to visit the camps?"

"No."

The colonel thought a moment, then sighed. "So the mullah Mahmud wishes to go flying, eh? Foolish for a so-called man of God to go flying. Very dangerous, particularly if he's an Islamic-Marxist—that sacrilege! Flying helicopters, you can easily fall out, so I'm told. Perhaps we should accommodate him." He was tall and very good-looking, in his forties, his uniform immaculate. "Don't worry. These rabble-rousers will soon be back in their flea-bitten hovels. Soon Bakhtiar'll give the orders for us to contain these dogs. And that rabble-rouser Khomeini—we should muzzle that traitor quickly. The French should have muzzled him the moment he arrived there. Those weak fools. Stupid! But then they've always been weak, meddling, and against us. The French've always been jealous of Iran." He got up. "Let me know when your aircraft is airworthy. In any event we'll be back just before dawn in two days. Let's hope the mullah and his friends, particularly the Russian, return."

He left them. Erikki put the kettle on to boil for coffee. Thoughtfully he said, "Azadeh, pack an overnight bag."

She stared at him. "What?"

"We're going to take the car and drive to Tehran. We'll leave in a few minutes."

"There's no need to leave, Erikki."

"If the chopper was airworthy we'd use that but we can't."

"There's no need to worry, my darling. Russians have always coveted Azerbaijan, always will, tsarist, Soviet, it makes no difference. They've always wanted Iran and we've always kept them out and always will. No need to worry about a few fanatics and a lone Russian, Erikki."

He looked at her. "I'm worried about American marines in Turkey, the

American task force, and why the KGB think 'you and your wife are much too intelligent,' why that one was so nervous, why they know so much about me and about you and why they 'require' my services. Go and pack a bag, my darling, while there's time."

SATURDAY
February 10

AT KOWISS AIR BASE: 3:32 A.M. Led by the mullah, Hussain Kowissi, the shouting mob was pressing against the barred, floodlit main gate and the nearby barbed-wire fence that surrounded the huge base, the night dark, very cold, with snow everywhere. There were three to four thousand of them, youths mostly, a few armed, some young women in chadors well to the front, adding their cries to the tumult: "God is Great . . . God is Great . . ."

Inside the gate, facing the mob, platoons of nervous soldiers were spread out on guard, their rifles ready, other platoons in reserve, all officers with revolvers. Two Centurion tanks, battle ready, waited in the center of the roadway, engines growling, the camp commander and a group of officers nearby. Behind them were trucks filled with more soldiers, headlights trained on the gate and the fence—soldiers outnumbered twenty or thirty to one. Behind the trucks were the hangars, base buildings, barracks, and the officers' mess, knots of milling, anxious servicemen everywhere, all hastily dressed, for the mob had arrived barely half an hour ago demanding possession of the base in the name of Ayatollah Khomeini.

Again the voice of the camp commander came over the loudspeakers. "You will disperse at once!" His voice was harsh and threatening, but the mob's chant overpowered him, "Allah-u Akbarrr . . ."

The night was overcast, obscuring even the southern foothills of the snow-capped Zagros Mountains that towered behind the base. The base was S-G's main HQ in southern Iran as well as home for two Iranian Air Force squadrons of F4s and, since martial law, a detachment of Centurions and the soldiers. Outside the fence, eastward, the giant oil refinery sprawled over hundreds of acres, the tall stacks belching smoke, many sending jets of flame into the night as the excess gas was burned off. Though the whole plant was struck and shut down, parts were floodlit: a skeleton staff of Europeans and Iranians were permitted by the strike komiteh to try to keep the refinery and its feeder pipelines and storage tanks safe.

"God is Great . . ." Hussain shouted again, and at once the mob took up the cry and again the cry went into the heads and hearts of the soldiers. One of those in the front rank was Ali Bewedan, a conscript like all the others, young like all the others, not so long ago a villager like all the others and those outside the fence. Yes, he thought, his head hurting, heart pounding, I'm on the side of God and ready to be martyred for the Faith and for the Prophet, whose Name be praised! Oh, God, let me be a martyr and go straight to Paradise as promised to the Faithful. Let me spill my blood for Islam and Khomeini but not for protecting the evil servants of the Shah!

The living words of Khomeini kept pounding in his ears, words from the cassette their mullah had played in the mosque two days ago: ". . . Soldiers: join with your brothers and sisters doing God's work, flee your barracks with your arms, disobey the illegal orders of the generals, tear down the illegal government! Do God's work, God is Great . . ."

His heart picked up tempo as he heard the voice again, the rich, deep peasant voice of the leader of leaders, that made everything clear. "God is Great, God is Great . . ."

The young soldier did not realize that now he was shouting with the mob, his eyes fixed on his mullah who was outside the gate, on God's side, outside, clawing at the gate, leading what he knew were his brothers and sisters, trying to break it down. His brother soldiers nearby shifted, even more nervously, staring at him, not daring to say anything, the baying going into their heads and hearts equally. Many of those inside the fence wished to open the gate. Most would have done so if it were not for their officers and sergeants and the inevitable punishments, even death, that all knew was the reward for mutiny.

"On God's side, *outside* . . ."

The young man's brain seemed to explode with the words and he did not hear the sergeant shouting at him, nor see him, but only the gate that was closed against the Faithful. He flung down his rifle and ran for the gate, fifty yards away. For an instant there was a vast silence, all eyes within and without riveted on him, transfixed.

Colonel Mohammed Peshadi, the camp commander, stood near his lead tank, a lithe man with graying hair, his uniform immaculate. He watched the youth screaming, "Allahhhh-u Akkbarrr . . ." the only voice now.

When the youth was five yards from the fence, the colonel motioned to the senior sergeant beside him. "Kill him," he said quietly.

The sergeant's ears were filled with the battle cry of the youth who now was tearing at the bolts. In one fluid motion, he jerked the rifle from the nearest soldier, cocked it, leaned momentarily on the side of the tank, put the sights on the back of the youth's head, and pulled the trigger. He saw the face blow outward, showering those on the other side of the gate. Then the body slumped and hung obscenely on the barbed wire.

For a moment there was an even vaster silence. Then, as one, Hussain leading, the mob surged forward, a roaring, senseless, mindless being. Those in front tore at the wires, careless of the barbs that ripped their hands to shreds. Urged on by those behind, they began to climb the wires.

A submachine gun began to chatter among them. At that moment the colonel stabbed a finger at the officer in the tank.

At once a tongue of flame leaped from the barrel of the four-inch gun that was aimed just over the heads of the crowd and loaded with a blank charge, but the suddenness of the explosion sent attackers reeling from the gate in panic, half a dozen soldiers dropped their rifles in equal shock, a few fled, and many of the unarmed watchers scattered in fright. The second tank fired, its barrel closer to the ground, the shaft of flame lower.

The mob broke. Men and women fled from the gate and the fence, trampling one another in their haste. Again the lead tank fired and again the tongue of flame and again the earsplitting detonation and the mob redoubled its effort to get away. Only the mullah Hussain remained at the gate. He reeled drunkenly, momentarily blinded and deafened, then his hands caught the stanchions of the gate and he hung on. Immediately, instinctively, many went forward to help him, soldiers, sergeants, and one officer.

"Stay where you are!" Colonel Peshadi roared, then took the microphone on the long lead and switched to full power. His voice blasted the night. "All soldiers stay where you are! Safety catches on! SAFETY CATCHES ON! All officers and sergeants take charge of your men! Sergeant, come with me!"

Still in shock, the sergeant fell into step beside his commander who went forward toward the gate. Scattered in front of the gates were thirty or forty who had been trampled on. The mass of rioters had stopped a hundred yards away and was beginning to re-form. Some of the more zealous began to charge. Tension soared.

"STOP! Everyone STAND STILL!"

This time the commander was obeyed. At once. He could feel the sweat on his back, his heart pumping in his chest. He glanced briefly at the corpse impaled on the barbs, glad for him—hadn't the youth been martyred with the Name of God on his lips, and wasn't he therefore already in Paradise?— then spoke harshly into the mouthpiece. "You three . . . yes, you three, help the mullah. NOW!" Instantly, the men outside the fence he had pointed at rushed to do his bidding. He jerked an angry thumb at some soldiers. "You! Open the gate! You, take the body away!"

Again he was obeyed instantly. Behind him, some groups of men began to move, and he roared, "I said, STAND STILL! THE NEXT MAN WHO MOVES WITHOUT MY ORDER'S A DEAD MAN!" Everyone froze. Everyone.

Peshadi waited a moment, almost daring someone to move. No one did. Then he glanced back at Hussain whom he knew well. "Mullah," Peshadi said quietly, "are you all right?" He was standing beside him now. The gate was open. A few yards away the three villagers waited, petrified.

There was a monstrous ache in Hussain's head and his ears hurt terribly. But he could hear and he could see and though his hands were bloody from the barbs, he knew he was undamaged and not yet the martyr he had expected and had prayed to be. "I demand . . ." he said weakly, "I demand this . . . this base in the name of Khomeini."

"You will come to my office at once," the colonel interrupted, his voice and face grim. "So will you three, as witnesses. We will talk, mullah. I will listen and then you will listen." He turned on the loudspeaker again and explained what was going to happen, his voice even grimmer, the words echoing, cutting the night apart. "He and I will talk. We will talk peacefully and then the mullah will return to the mosque and you will all go to your homes to pray. The gate will remain open. The gate will be guarded by my soldiers and my tanks, and, by God and the Prophet on whose Name be praised, if one of you sets foot inside the gate or comes over the fence uninvited, my soldiers will kill him. If twenty or more of you charge into my base I will lead my tanks into your villages and I will burn your villages with you in them! Long live the Shah!" He turned on his heel and strode off, the mullah and the three frightened villagers following slowly. No one else moved.

And on the veranda of the officers' mess, Captain Conroe Starke, leader of the S-G contingent, sighed. "Good sweet Jesus," he muttered with vast admiration to no one in particular, "what *cojones!*"

5:21 A.M. Starke stood at the window of the officers' mess, watching Peshadi's HQ building across the street. The mullah had not yet come out. Here in the main lounge of the officers' mess it was very cold. Freddy Ayre hunched deeper into his easy chair, pulling his flight jacket closer around him, and looked up at the tall Texan who rocked gently on his heels. "What do you think?" he asked wearily, stifling a yawn.

"I think it'll be dawn in an hour odd, old buddy," Starke said absently. He also wore a flight jacket and warm flying boots. The two pilots were in a corner window of the second-floor room overlooking most of the base. Scattered around the room were a dozen of the senior Iranian officers who had also been told to stand by. Most were asleep in easy chairs, bundled in their flight jackets or army greatcoats—heating throughout the base had been off for weeks to conserve fuel. A few weary orderlies, also in overcoats, were clearing up the last of the debris from the party that the mob had interrupted.

"I feel wrung out. You?"

"Not yet, but how come I always seem to draw duty on high days and holidays, Freddy?"

"It's the Fearless Leader's privilege, old chum," Ayre said. He was second-in-command of the S-G contingent, ex-RAF, a good-looking man of twenty-eight, with sloe-blue eyes, his accent Oxford English. "Sets a good example to the troops."

Starke glanced toward the open main gate. No change: it was still well guarded. Outside, half a thousand of the villagers still waited, huddled together for warmth. He went back to staring at the HQ building. No change there either. Lights were on in the upper floor where Peshadi had his offices. "I'd give a month's pay to be kibitzing on that one, Freddy."

"What? What's that mean?"

"To be listening to Peshadi and the mullah."

"Oh!" Ayre looked across the street at the offices. "You know, I thought we'd had it when those miserable buggers started climbing the wire. Bloody hell! I was all set to hare off to old Nellie, crank her up, and say farewell to

Kublai Khan and his Mongol hordes!" He chuckled to himself as he imagined himself running for his 212. "Of course," he added dryly, "I'd have waited for you, Duke." He used their nickname for Starke who was Texan like John Wayne and built like John Wayne and just as handsome.

Starke laughed. "Thanks, old buddy. Come to think of it, if they'd bust in I'd've been ahead of you." His blue eyes crinkled with the depth of his smile, his accent slight. Then he turned back to the window, hiding his concern. This was the base's third confrontation with a mob, always led by the mullah, each more serious than the last. And now the first deliberate death. Now what? That death'll lead to another and to another. If it hadn't been for Colonel Peshadi someone else would have gone for the gate and been shot and now there'd be bodies all over. Oh, Peshadi would've won—this time. But soon he won't, not unless he breaks the mullah. To break Hussain he'll have to kill him—can't jail him, the mob'll bust a gut, and if he kills him, they'll bust a gut, if he exiles him, they'll bust a gut, so he's onto a no-win play. What would I do?

I don't know.

He looked around the room. The Iranian officers didn't seem concerned. He knew most of them by sight, not one of them intimately. Though S-G had shared the base since it was built some eight years before, they had had little to do with the military or air force personnel. Since Starke had taken over as chief pilot last year, he had tried to expand S-G's contacts with the rest of the base but without success. The Iranians preferred their own company.

That's okay too, he thought. It's their country. But they're tearing it apart and we're in the middle and now Manuela's here. He had been overjoyed to see his wife when she had arrived by helicopter five days ago—McIver not trusting her to the roads—though a little angry that she had talked her way onto a lone incoming BA flight that had slipped back into Tehran. "Damnit, Manuela, you're in danger here!"

"No more than in Tehran, Conroe darlin'. Insha'Allah," she had said with a beam.

"But how'd you talk Mac into letting you come down here?"

"I just smiled at him, honey, and promised to go on the first available flight back to England. Meanwhile, darlin', let's go to bed."

He smiled to himself and let his mind drift. This was his third two-year tour in Iran and his eleventh year with S-G. Eleven good years, he thought. First Aberdeen and the North Sea, then Iran, Dubai, and Al Shargaz just across the Gulf, then Iran again where he'd planned to stay. The best years here, he thought. But not anymore. Iran's changed since '73 when the Shah quadrupled the price of oil—from $1 to $4 or thereabouts. It was like B.C. and A.D. for Iran. Before, they were friendly and helpful, good to live among and to work with. After? Increasingly arrogant, more and more puffed up by the Shah's constant overriding message about the "inherent superiority of Iranians" because of their three thousand years of civilization and how within twenty years Iran would be a world leader as was her divine right—would be the fifth industrial power on earth, sole guardian of the crossroads between East and West, with the best army, the best navy, the best air force, with more tanks, helicopters, refrigerators, factories, telephones, roads, schools, banks, businesses than anyone else here in the center of the world. And based on all of this, with the rest of the world listening attentively, Iran under his leadership would be the real arbiter of East and West, and real fountain of all wisdom—his wisdom.

Starke sighed. He had come to understand the message, loud and clear over the years, but he blessed Manuela for agreeing to hurl themselves into the Iranian way of life, learning Farsi, going everywhere and seeing everything—new sights and tastes and smells, learning about Persian carpets and caviar, wines and legends and making friends—and not living their life out like many of the expat pilots and engineers who elected to leave their families at home, to work two months on and one off and sat on their bases on days off, saving money, and waiting for their leaves home—wherever home was.

"Home's here from now on," she had said. "This's where we'll be, me and the kids," she had added with the toss of her head he admired so much, and the darkness of her hair, the passion of her Spanish heritage.

"What kids? We haven't got any kids and we can't afford them yet on what I make."

Starke smiled. That had been just after they were married, ten years ago. He had gone back to Texas to marry her as soon as his place with S-G was firmed. Now they had three children, two boys and a girl, and he could afford them all, just. Now? Now what's going to happen? My job here's threatened, most of our Iranian friends've gone, there're empty shops where there was plenty—and fear where there'd only been laughter.

Goddamn Khomeini and these goddamn mullahs, he thought. He's certainly messed up a great way of life and a great place. I wish Manuela'd take the kids and leave London and fly home to Lubbock until Iran stabilizes. Lubbock was near the Panhandle of Texas where his father still ran the family ranch. Eight thousand acres, a few cattle, some horses, some farming, enough for the family to live comfortably. I wish she was there already, but then there'd be no mail for weeks and the phones're sure to be out. Goddamn Khomeini for frightening her with his speeches—wonder what he'll say to God and God'll say to him when they meet, as they will.

He stretched and sat back in the easy chair. He saw Ayre watching him, his eyes bleary. "You really hung one on."

"It was my day off, my two days in fact, and I hadn't planned on the hordes. Actually I had intended to drink to oblivion, I miss my Better Half, bless her, and anyway Hogmanay's important to us Scots an—"

"Hogmanay was New Year's Eve and today's February tenth and you're no more Scots than I am."

"Duke, I'll have you know the Ayres are an ancient clan and I can play the bagpipes, old boy." Ayre yawned mightily. "Christ, I'm tired." He burrowed deeper into the chair, trying to settle himself more comfortably, then glanced out of the window. At once his tiredness dropped away. An Iranian officer was hurrying out of the HQ entrance, heading across the street toward them. It was Major Changiz, the base adjutant.

When he came in, his face was taut. "All officers will report to the commandant at seven o'clock," he said in Farsi. "All officers. There will be a full parade of all military and air force personnel at eight o'clock in the square. Anyone absent—anyone," he added darkly, "except for medical reasons approved by me in advance—can expect immediate and severe punishment." His eyes searched the room until he found Starke. "Please follow me, Captain."

Starke's heart skipped a beat. "Why, Major?" he asked in Farsi.

"The commandant wants you."

"What for?"

The major shrugged and walked out.

Starke said quietly to Ayre, "Better alert all our guys. And Manuela. Huh?"

"Got it," Ayre said, then muttered, "Christ."

As Starke walked across the street and up the stairs, he felt the eyes on him as a physical weight. Thank God I'm a civilian and work for a British company and not in the U.S. Army anymore, he thought fervently. "Goddamn," he muttered, remembering his year's stint in Vietnam in the very early days when there were no U.S. forces in Vietnam, "only a few advisers." Shit! And that sonofabitching spit-and-polish meathead Captain Ritman who ordered all our base's helicopters—in our jungle base a million miles from anywhere, for crissake—to be painted with bright red, white, and blue stars and stripes: "Yes, goddamnit, all over! Let the gooks know who we are and they'll rush their asses all the way to goddamn Russia." The Viet Cong could see us coming from fifty miles and I got peppered to hell and back and we lost three

Hueys with full crews before the sonofabitch was posted to Saigon, promoted and posted. No wonder we lost the goddamn war.

He went into the office building and up the stairs, past the three petrified villagers who had been banished to the outer office, into the camp commandant's lair. "Morning, Colonel," he said cautiously in English.

"Morning, Captain Starke." Peshadi switched to Farsi. "I'd like you to meet the mullah, Hussain Kowissi."

"Peace be upon you," Starke said in Farsi, very conscious of the speckles of blood from the dead youth that still marred the man's white turban and black robe.

"Peace be upon you."

Starke put out his hand to shake hands as was correct custom. Just in time he noticed the coagulated rips in the man's palms that the barbed wire had caused. He made his grip gentle. Even so he saw a shaft of pain go across the mullah's face. "Sorry," he said in English.

The mullah just stared back and Starke felt the man's hatred strongly.

"You wanted me, Colonel?"

"Yes. Please sit down." Peshadi motioned at the empty chair opposite his desk. The office was Spartan, meticulously tidy. A photograph of the Shah and Farah, his wife, in court dress was the only wall decoration. The mullah sat with his back toward it. Starke took the chair facing the two men.

Peshadi lit another cigarette and saw Hussain's disapproving eyes drop to the cigarette, then glare into his face. He stared back. Smoking was forbidden in the Koran—according to some interpretation. They had argued this point for over an hour. Then he had said with finality, "Smoking is not forbidden in Iran, not yet. I am a soldier. I have sworn to obey orders. Ir—"

"Even the illegal ord—"

"I repeat: the orders of His Imperial Majesty, Shahinshah Mohammed Pahlavi or his representative, Prime Minister Bakhtiar, are still legal according to the law of Iran. Iran is not yet an Islamic state. Not yet. When it is I will obey the orders of whoever leads the Islamic state."

"You will obey the Imam Khomeini?"

"If Ayatollah Khomeini becomes our legal ruler, of course." The colonel had nodded agreeably, but he was thinking: before that day comes there's going to be a lot of blood spilled. "And me, if I'm elected leader of this possible Islamic state, will you obey me?"

Hussain had not smiled. "The leader of the Islamic state will be the Imam, the Whirlwind of God, and after him another ayatollah, then another."

And now the stony, uncompromising eyes still glared at him, and Peshadi wanted to smash the mullah into the ground and take his tanks and smash everyone else who would not obey the orders of the Shahinshah, their God-given ruler. Yes, he thought, our God-given leader who like his father stood against you mullahs and your grasp for power, who curbed your archaic dogmatism and brought Iran out of the Dark Ages into our rightful greatness, who single-handedly bulldozed OPEC to stand up to the enormous power of the foreign oil companies, who slung the Russians out of Azerbaijan after World War II and has kept even them at bay, licking his hands like lapdogs.

By God and the Prophet, he told himself, enraged, staring back at Hussain, I cannot understand why fornicating mullahs don't recognize the truth about that senile old man Khomeini who screams lies from his deathbed, won't realize that the Soviets are sponsoring him, feeding him, protecting him, to stir them up to enflame the peasants to wreck Iran and make it a Soviet protectorate?

We only need one single order: Stamp out rebellion forthwith!

With that order, by God, within three days I'd have Kowiss and a hundred miles around quiet, peaceful, and prosperous, mullahs happily in the mosques where they belong, the Faithful praying five times a day—within a month the armed forces'd have all Iran as it was last year and Khomeini solved permanently. Within minutes of the order I'd arrest him, publicly shave off half his beard, strip him naked, and trundle him through the streets in a dung cart. I'd let the people see him for what he is: a broken, beaten old man. Make him a loser and all the people would turn their faces and ears from him. Then accusers would come from the ayatollahs who adore life and love and power and land and talking, accusers would come from the mullahs and *bazaaris* and from the people and together they would snuff him out.

So simple to deal with Khomeini or any mullah—by God if I'd been in charge I'd've dragged him from France months ago. He puffed his cigarette and very carefully kept his thoughts off his face and out of his eyes. "Well, mullah, Captain Starke is here." Then he added, as though it was unimportant. "You can speak to him in Farsi or English, as you wish—he speaks Farsi as you speak English. Fluently."

The mullah turned on Starke. "So," he said, his English American accented, "you are CIA."

"No," Starke said, instantly on his guard. "You were at school in the States?"

"I was a student there, yes," Hussain said. Then, because of his pain and tiredness, his temper snapped. He switched to Farsi and his voice harshened. "Why did you learn Farsi if not to spy on us for the CIA—or your oil companies, eh?"

"For my interest, just for my interest," Starke replied politely in Farsi, his knowledge and accent good, "I'm a guest in your country, invited here by your government to work for your government in partnership with Iranians. It's polite for guests to be aware of their hosts' taboos and customs, to learn their language, particularly when they enjoy the country and hope to be guests for many years." His voice edged. "And they're not my companies."

"They're American. You're American. The CIA's American. All our problems come from America. The Shah's greed's American. All our problems come from America. For years Iran's been spat on by Americans."

"Bullshit," Starke said in English, now equally angry, knowing the only way to deal with a bully was to come out swinging. At once. He saw the man flush. He looked back, unafraid, letting the silence hang. The seconds ticked by. His eyes held the mullah's. But he couldn't dominate him. Unsettled but trying to appear calm, he glanced at Peshadi who waited and watched, smoking quietly. "What's this all about, Colonel?"

"The mullah has asked for one of your helicopters to visit all the oil installations in our area. As you're aware we don't plan your routes or participate in your operations. You will arrange for one of your best pilots to do this. Today, starting at midday."

"Why not use one of your airplanes? Perhaps I could supply a navig—"

"No. One of your helicopters with your personnel. At midday."

Starke turned to the mullah. "Sorry, but I only take orders from IranOil, through our base manager and their area rep, Esvandiary. We're under contract to them and they're exclus—"

"The airplanes you fly, they're Iranian," the mullah interrupted harshly, his exhaustion and pain welling up again, wanting a finish. "You will provide one as required."

"They're Iranian registry, but owned by S-G Helicopters Ltd of Aberdeen."

"Iranian registry, in Iranian skies, filled with Iranian gasoline, authorized by Iranians, servicing Iranian rigs pumping Iranian oil, by God. They're Iranian!" Hussain's thin mouth twisted. "Esvandiary will give the necessary flight orders by noon. How long will it take to visit all your sites?"

After a pause Starke said, "Airtime, maybe six hours. How long do you plan to spend at each setdown?"

The mullah just looked at him. "After that I want to follow the pipeline to Abadan and land where I choose."

Starke's eyes widened. He glanced at the colonel but saw that the man was still pointedly watching the spirals of smoke from his cigarette. "That one's more difficult, mullah. We'd need clearances. Radar's not working, most of that airspace's controlled by Kish Air Traffic Control and that's, er, air force controlled."

"Whatever clearance is needed you will get," Hussain said with finality and turned his eyes inflexibly on Peshadi. "In the Name of God, I come back at noon: if you stand in my way, the guns begin."

Starke could feel his heart pumping and the mullah could feel his heart pumping and so could Peshadi. Only the mullah was content—there was no need for him to worry, he was in the Hands of God, doing God's work, obeying orders: "Press the enemy in every way. Be like water flowing down-hill to the dam. Press against the dam of the usurper Shah, his lackeys, and the armed forces. We have to win them over with courage and blood. Press them in every way, you do God's work. . . ."

A wind rattled the window and, involuntarily, they glanced at it and at the night beyond. The night was still black, the stars brilliant, but to the east there was the glimmer of dawn, the sun just under the rim of the sky.

"I will return at noon, Colonel Peshadi, alone or with many. You choose," Hussain said quietly, and Starke felt the threat—or promise—with all of his being. "But now, now it is time for prayer." He forced himself to his feet, his hands still burning with pain, his back and head and ears still aching mon-strously. For a moment he felt he was going to faint but he fought off the giddiness and the pain and strode out.

Peshadi got up. "You will do as he asks. Please," he added as a great concession. "It is a temporary truce and temporary compromise—until we have final orders from His Imperial Majesty's legal government when we will stop all this nonsense." Shakily he lit a cigarette from the butt of the last. "You have no problem. He will provide the necessary permissions so it will be a routine VIP flight. Routine. Of course you must agree because of course I can't allow one of my military airplanes to service a mullah, particularly Hussain who's renowned for his sedition! Of course not! It was a brilliant finesse on my part and you will not destroy it." Angrily he stubbed out the cigarette, the ashtray full now, the air nicotine-laden, and he almost shouted, "You heard what he said. At noon! Alone or with many. Do you want more blood spilled? Eh?"

"Of course not."

"Good. Then do what you're told!" Peshadi stormed off.

Grimly Starke went to the window. The mullah had taken his place near the gate, raised his arms, and, like every muezzin from every minaret at every dawn in Islam, called the Faithful to first prayer in the time-honored Arabic: "Come to prayer, come to progress, prayer is better than sleep. There is no other God but God . . ."

And as Starke watched, Peshadi devoutly took his place at the head of all the men of the base, all ranks, who obediently, and with obvious gladness, had streamed out of their barracks, soldiers laying down their rifles on the ground beside them, villagers outside the fence equally devout. Then, following the lead of the mullah, they all turned toward Mecca, and began the obligatory movements, prostrations, and Shahada litany: "I testify there is no other God but God, and Mohammed is the Prophet of God . . ."

When the prayer was finished there was a great silence. Everyone waited. Then the mullah called out loudly: "God, the Koran, and Khomeini." Then he went through the gates toward Kowiss. Obediently, the villagers followed him.

Starke shivered in spite of himself. That mullah's so full of hate it's coming out of his pores. And so much hate's got to blow something or someone to hell. If I fly him maybe it'll make him worse. If I assign someone or ask for a volunteer that's ducking it because it's my responsibility.

"I have to fly him," he muttered. "Have to."

OFF LENGEH: 6:42 A.M.   The 212, with two pilots and a full load of thirteen passengers, was on a routine flight, outward bound into the Strait of Hormuz from her S-G base at Lengeh, heading over the placid water of the Gulf for the French-developed Siri oil field. The sun just over the horizon with the promise of another fine cloudless day, though haze, routine over the Gulf, brought visibility down to a few miles.

"Chopper EP-HST, this is Kish radar control, turn to 260 degrees."

Obediently, she went on to her new heading. "260 at one thousand," Ed Vossi answered.

"Maintain one thousand. Report overhead Siri." Unlike most of Iran, radar here was good, with stations at Kish Island and Lavan Island, manned by excellent USAF-trained Iranian Air Force operators—both ends of the Gulf were equally strategic and equally well serviced.

"HST." Ed Vossi was an American—ex-USAF, thirty-two, and built like a linebacker. "Radar's jumpy today, huh, Scrag?" he said to the other pilot.

"Too right. Must be their piles."

Ahead now was the small island of Siri. It was barren, desolate, and low-lying, with a small dirt airstrip, a few barracks for oil personnel, and a cluster of huge storage tanks that were fed by pipes laid on the seabed from rigs that were westward in the Gulf. The island lay about sixty miles off the Iranian coast, just inside the international boundary that bisected the Strait of Hormuz and separated Iranian waters from those of Oman and the United Arab Emirates.

Directly over the oil tanks, the chopper banked smoothly, heading westward, her first stop some miles away on the oil rig called Siri Three. At present the field had six working rigs, all operated by the French semigovernment consortium, EPF, that had developed the field for IranOil against future shipments of oil. "Kish radar control, HST over Siri at one thousand feet," Ed Vossi said into the boom mike.

"Roger HST. Maintain one thousand," came back instantly. "Report before you let down. You have outbound traffic ahead of you at ten o'clock, climbing."

"We have them in sight." The two pilots watched the flight of four closely packed fighter jets soaring into the high skies, going past them for the mouth of the strait.

"They're in a hurry," the older man said and shifted in his seat.

"You can say that again. Lookit! Jesus, they're USAF, F15s!" Vossi was astonished. "Shit, I didn't know any were in this area. You seen any before, Scrag?"

"No, mate," Scrag Scragger said, equally concerned, making a slight adjustment to the volume of his headset. At sixty-three, he was the oldest pilot in S-G, senior pilot at Lengeh, a wizened little man, very thin, very tough, with grizzled gray hair and deep-set, light-blue Australian eyes that always seemed to be searching the horizon. His accent was interesting. "I'd like to know wot the hell's up. Radar's as itchy as a roo in a twiddle and that's the third flight we've seen since we got airborne, though the first Yankee."

"Gotta be a task force, Scrag. Or maybe they're escort fighters the U.S. sent to Saudi Arabia, with the AWACs."

Scragger was sitting in the left seat, acting as training captain. Normally the 212 used a single-pilot configuration, the pilot in the right seat, but Scragger had had this airplane fitted with dual controls for training purposes. "Well," he said with a laugh, "so long as we don't spot MIGs we're in good shape."

"The Reds won't send equipment down here, much as they want the strait." Vossi was very confident. He was barely half Scragger's age and almost twice his size. "They won't so long as we tell them they'd better the hell not—and have airplanes and task forces and the will to use them." He squinted down through the haze. "Hey, Scrag, lookit."

The huge supertanker was heavily burdened, low in the water, steaming ponderously outward bound toward Hormuz. "I'll bet she's five hundred thousand tons or more." They watched her for a moment. Sixty percent of the free world's oil went through this shallow, narrow waterway between Iran and Oman, barely fifteen miles across where the neck was navigable. Twenty million barrels a day. Every day.

"You think they'll ever build a million-ton tanker, Scrag?"

"Sure. Sure they'll build her if they want, Ed." The ship passed below them. "She was flying a Liberian flag," Scragger said absently.

"You got eyes like an eagle."

"It's all my clean living, sport." Scragger glanced around into the cabin. All the passengers were in their seats, belts on, regulation Mae West life jackets on, ear protectors on, reading or looking out of the windows. Everything normal, he thought. Yes, and instruments're normal, sounds're normal, I'm normal and so's Ed. Then why'm I itchy? he asked himself, turning back once more.

Because of the task force, because of Kish radar, because of the passengers, because it's your birthday, and most of all because you're airborne and the only way you stay alive airborne is to be itchy. Amen. He laughed out loud.

"What's up, Scrag?"

"You're up, that's wot. So you think you're a pilot, right?"

"Sure, Scrag," Vossi said cautiously.

"Okay. You've pegged Siri Three?"

Vossi grinned and pointed at the distant rig that was barely visible in the haze, slightly east of the cluster.

Scragger beamed. "Then close your eyes."

"Aw c'me on, Scrag, sure this's a check flight but how about le—"

"I got control," Scragger said happily. Instantly Vossi relinquished the controls. "Now close your eyes 'cause you're under training." Confidently the young man took a last careful look at the target rig, adjusted his headset, took off his dark glasses, and obeyed.

Scragger handed Vossi the special pair of dark goggles he had had made. "Here, put 'em on and don't open your eyes till I say. Get ready to take control."

Vossi put on the goggles, and smoothly, still with his eyes closed, his hands

and feet reached out, barely touching the controls as he knew Scragger liked.
"Okay. Ready, Scrag."

"You got her."

At once Vossi took over the controls, firmly and lightly, and was pleased
that the transition was smooth, the airplane staying straight and level. He was
flying now with only his ears to guide him, trying to anticipate the slightest
variation in engine note—slowing down or speeding up—that would indicate
he was climbing or descending. Now a small change. He anticipated nicely,
almost sensing it before it happened, that the pitch was rising, therefore the
engines were gathering speed and therefore the chopper was diving. He made
the correction and brought her level again.

"Good on you, sport," Scragger said approvingly. "Now open your eyes."

Vossi had expected the usual training glasses that excluded outside visibility but allowed you to see the instruments. He found himself in total blackness. In sudden panic, his concentration vanished and with it his coordina-
tion. For a split second he was totally disoriented, his stomach reeling as he
knew the airplane would reel. But it didn't. The controls stayed rock firm in
Scragger's hands that he had not felt on the controls.

"Jesssus," Vossi gasped, fighting his nausea, automatically reaching up to
tear off the goggles.

"Keep 'em on! Ed, this's an emergency, you're the pilot, the only pilot
aboard and you're in trouble—you can't see. Wot're you going to do? Take
the controls! Come on! Emergency!"

There was bile in Vossi's mouth and he spat it out, his hands and feet
nervous. He took the controls, overcorrected, and almost cried out in panic as
they lurched, for he was expecting that Scragger would still be monitoring
them. But he wasn't. Again Vossi overcorrected, totally disoriented. This
time Scragger minimized the mistake.

"Settle down, Ed," he ordered. "Listen to the bloody engine! Get your
hands and feet in tune." Then more gently: "Steady now, you're doing fine,
steady now. You can vomit later. You're in an emergency, you've got to put
her down, and you got thirteen passengers aft. Me, I'm here beside you but
I'm not a bleeding pilot, now wot you going to do?"

Vossi's hands and feet were together again and his ears listening to the
engine. "I can't see but you can?"

"Right."

"Then you can talk me down!"

"Right!" Scragger's voice edged. "Course you got to ask the right questions. Kish Control, HST leaving one thousand for Siri Three."

"Roger, HST."

Scragger's voice became different. "My name's Burt from now on. I'm a roustabout off one of the rigs. I know nothing about flying but I can read a dial—if you tell me proper where to look."

Happily Vossi hurled himself into the game and asked the right questions, "Burt" forcing him to use the limits of his knowledge of flight control, cockpit control, where the dials were, making him ask what only an amateur could understand and answer. From time to time when he was not accurate enough, Burt, with rising hysteria would screech, "Jesus, I can't find the dial, which dial for Christ's sake, they're all the bloody same! Explain again, explain slower, oh, God we're all going to die. . . ."

For Vossi the darkness fed on darkness. Time became stretched, no friendly dials or needles to reassure him, nothing but the voice forcing him to his own utmost limits.

When they were at fifty feet on their approach, Burt calling out landing advice, Vossi was nauseous, terrified in the darkness, knowing that the tiny landing circle on the oil rig was coming up to meet him. You've still time to abort, to put on power and get to hell out of here and wait it out aloft, but for how long?

"Now you're ten feet up and ten yards away just like you wanted."

At once Vossi put her into hover, the sweat pouring off him.

"You're perfect, just over the dead center, just like you wanted."

The blackness had never been more intense. Nor his fear. Vossi muttered a prayer. Gently he eased off power. It seemed to take a lifetime and another and another and then the skids touched and they were down. For an instant he didn't believe it. His relief was so intense that he almost wept for joy. Then, from a great distance, he heard Scragger's real voice and felt the controls taken over. "I got her, sport! That was bloody good, Ed. Ten out of ten. I'll take her now."

Ed Vossi pulled off the goggles. He was soaking, his face chalky, and he slumped in his seat, hardly seeing the activity on the working rig before him, the heavy rope net spread over the landing pad that was a bare thirty yards in diameter. Jesus, I'm down, we're down and safe.

Scragger had put the engines to idle; no need to shut down as this was a short stop. He was humming "Waltzing Matilda" which he did only when he was very pleased. The lad did very well, he thought, his flying's bonzer. But how fast will he recover? Always wise to know, and where his balls are—when you fly with someone.

He turned and gave the thumbs-up to the man in the side front seat of the cabin, one of the French engineers who had to check electrical pumping equipment that had just been installed on this rig. The rest of the passengers waited patiently. Four were Japanese, guests of the French officials and engineers from EPF. Scragger had been disquieted about carrying Japanese—pulled back to memories of his war days, memories of Australian losses in the Pacific war and the thousands who died in the Japanese POW camps and on the Burma railway. Murders more like, he told himself darkly, then turned his attention to the off-loading.

The engineer had opened the door and was now helping Iranian deck laborers take packing cases from the cargo hatch. It was hot and humid on the deck, enervating, and the air stank of oil fumes. In the cockpit it was scorching as usual, humidity bad, but Scragger was comfortable. The engines were idling and sounding sweet. He glanced at Vossi, still slumped in his seat, his hands behind his neck, gathering himself.

He's a good lad, Scragger thought, then the dominating voice in the cabin behind him attracted his attention. It was Georges de Plessey, chief of the French officials and EPF's area manager. He was sitting on the arm of one of the seats, delivering another of his interminable lectures, this time to the Japanese. Better them'n me, Scragger told himself amused. He had known de Plessey for three years and liked him—for the French food he provided and the quality of his bridge which they both enjoyed, but not for his conversation. Oil men're all the same, oil's all they know and all they want to know, and as far as they're concerned all the rest of us are here on earth to consume the stuff, pay through the bloody nose for it till we're dead—and even then most crematoriums're oil fired. Bloody hell! Oil's skyrocketed to $14.80 a barrel, $4.80 a couple of years ago, and $1.80 a few years before that. Bloody highway robbers, the bloody lot, OPEC, the Seven Sisters, and even North Sea oil!

"All these rigs're on legs that sit on the sea floor," de Plessey was saying, "all French built and operated, serving one well each . . ." He wore khakis, and had sparse sandy hair, his face sunburned. The other Frenchmen were chattering and arguing among themselves—and that's all they do, Scragger thought, except eat and drink wine and romance the pants off any sheila without so much as a by-your-leave. Like that old bugger Jean-Luc, king cocksman of them all! Still, they're all individualists, every one of them—not like those other buggers. The Japanese were all short, lithe, and well groomed, all dressed the same: short-sleeved white shirt and dark tie and dark trousers and dark shoes, same digital watches, dark glasses; the only difference was in their ages. Like sardines in a can, Scragger thought.

". . . The water here, as in all of the Gulf is very shallow, M'sieur Kasigi," de Plessey was saying. "Here it's just about a hundred feet—oil's easy to reach at about a thousand feet. We've six wells in this part of the field we call

Siri Three, they're all on stream, that is connected by pipes and pumping oil into our storage tanks on Siri island—tank capacity is 3 million barrels and all tanks are full now."

"And the docking on Siri, M'sieur de Plessey?" Kasigi, the graying Japanese spokesman asked, his English clear and careful. "I could not see when we were over the island."

"We load offshore at the moment. A wharf's planned for next year. Meanwhile there'll be no problem to load your medium tankers, M'sieur Kasigi. We guarantee quick service, quick loading. After all, we are French. You'll see tomorrow. Your *Rikomaru* hasn't been delayed?"

"No. She will be there at noon. What's the final capacity of the field?"

"Limitless," the Frenchman said with a laugh. "We're only pumping 75,000 barrels a day now but, *mon Dieu*, under the seabed here is a lake of oil."

"Capit'an Excellency!" At Scragger's side window was the beaming face of young Abdollah Turik, one of the fire crew. "I very good, ver very good. You?"

"Tip-top, young feller. How're things?"

"I pleased you to see, Capit'an Excellency."

About a year ago Scragger's base at Lengeh had been alerted by radio there was a CASEVAC on this rig. It was in the middle of a dirty night and the Iranian manager said perhaps the fireman had a burst appendix and could they get there as quick as possible after dawn—night flying being forbidden in Iran except for emergencies. Scragger had been duty officer and he had gone at once—it was company policy to go immediately, even in minimum conditions, and part of their special service. He had fetched the young man, taken him direct to the Iranian Naval Hospital at Bandar Abbas and talked them into accepting the youth. But for that the youth would have died.

Ever since then the young man would be there to welcome him, and once a month there was a haunch of fresh goat meat at the base, much as Scragger tried to prevent it, because of the expense. Once he had visited the village in the hinterland of Lengeh where the youth had come from. It was usual: no sanitation, no electricity, no water, dirt floors, mud walls. Iran was very basic outside the cities but, even so, better than most of the Gulf states outside the cities. Abdollah's family was like all the others, no better no worse. Many children, clouds of flies, a few goats and chickens, a few scrubby acres and soon, his father had said, one day soon we'll have our own school, Excellency pilot, and our own water supply and one day electricity, and yes it is true we are much better off with work from our oil that foreigners exploit—thanks be to God for giving us oil. Thanks be to God that my son Abdollah lived. It was the Will of God that Abdollah lived, the Will of God that persuaded the Excellency pilot to take so much trouble. Thanks be to God!

"How're things, Abdollah?" Scragger repeated, liking the youth who was modern, not like his father.

"Good." Abdollah came closer, put his face almost into the window. "Capit'an," he said haltingly, no longer smiling, his voice so soft Scragger had to bend forward to hear. "Soon much trouble . . . Communist Tudeh, mujhadin, perhaps fedayeen. Guns and explosives—perhaps a ship at Siri. Danger. Please please say not anything who says, yes?" Then he put back the smile on his face and called out loudly, "Happy landings and come again soon, Agha." He waved once and, hiding his nervousness, went back to join the others.

"Sure, sure, Abdollah," Scragger muttered. There were a number of Iranians watching but that was usual. Pilots were appreciated because they were the only link on a CASEVAC. He saw the landing master give him the thumbs-up. Automatically he turned around and rechecked that all was locked and everyone back in his place. "Shall I take her, Ed?"

"Yeah, sure, Scrag."

At a thousand feet Scragger leveled off, heading for Siri One where the rest of the passengers were due to disembark. He was very perturbed. Stone the crows, he thought. One bomb could blow Siri island into the Gulf. This was the first time there had been any whisper of trouble. The Siri field had never been subjected to any of the strikes that had closed down all other fields, mostly, expats believed, because the French had given sanctuary to Khomeini.

Sabotage? Didn't the Jap say he's got a tanker due tomorrow? Yes, he did. Wot to do? Nothing at the moment, just put Abdollah aside for later—now's not the time, not when you're flying.

He glanced at Vossi. Ed did good, very good, better than . . . better than who? His mind ranged over all the pilots he had helped train over the years. Hundreds. He had been flying since he was fifteen, Royal Australian Air Force at seventeen in '33, Spitfires in '39 and flight lieutenant, then converting to choppers in '45. Korea '49, and out after twenty years' service, still a flight lieutenant, still ornery, and only thirty-seven. He laughed. In the air force he was always on the mat.

"For Christ's sake, Scragger, why pick on the air vice-marshal? You've done it this time. . . ."

"But, Wingco, the Limey started it, the bastard said all us Aussies were thieves, had chain marks around our wrists, and were descended from convicts!"

"He did? Fucking Limeys're all the same, Scrag, even though in your case he was probably right as your family's been Down Under forever, but even so you're still busted a rank again and if you don't behave I'll ground you forever!"

But they never did. How could they? DFC and Bar, AFC and Bar, sixteen kills, and three times as many missions, happily, as anyone in the whole RAAF. And today still flying which was all he wanted in the world, still trying to be the best and safest, and still wanting to walk away from a prang, all passengers safe. If you fly choppers you can't not have equipment failures, he thought, knowing he had been very, very lucky. Not like some, equally good pilots, whose luck ran out. You've got to be lucky to be a good pilot.

Again he glanced across at Vossi, glad there wasn't a war on which was a pilot's great testing ground. I wouldn't like to lose young Ed, he's one of the best in S-G. Now who's better that you've flown with? Charlie Pettikin, of course, but then he should be, he's been a bush pilot and through the wringer too. Tom Lochart the same. Dirty Duncan McIver's still the best of the lot even though he's grounded, may he rot with his bleeding three-month medicals—but I'd be just as mean and just as careful with him if I was grounded and he was flying around at sixty-three like a junior birdman. Poor bugger.

Scragger shuddered. If the CAA brings in the new regs about age and enforced retirement, I've had it. The day I'm grounded I'm for the pearly gates and no doubt about it.

Siri One was still well ahead. He had landed there three times a week for a year or more. Even so he was planning his approach as though it were the first time. "Safety's no accident, it has to be prepared." Today we'll do a nice gentle low approach an—

"Scrag."

"Yes, me son?"

"You scared the bejesus outta me."

He chuckled, "You scared the bejesus out've yourself, that's lesson number one. Wot else did you learn?"

"I guess how goddamn easy it is to panic, how lonely you feel, helpless, and to bless your eyes." Vossi almost burst out, "I guess I learned how mortal I am, goddamnit. Jesus, Scrag, I was scared—shit-scared."

"When it happened t'me I did it in my pants."

"Huh?"

"I was flying out of Kuwait, a 47G2 in the old days, the sixties." The 47G2 was the small, three-seat, bubble-shaped, piston-engined Bell, now the workhorse of most traffic control and police forces. "The charter was for a doc and an engineer in ExTex. They wanted to go out to an oasis, past Wafrah, where they had a CASEVAC—some poor sod mixed his leg up with the drill. Well, we were flying with the doors off's usual 'cause it was summer, about a hundred and twenty degrees, and dry and rotten for man and chopper as only the desert can be—worse'n our Outback by a long shot. But we'd been promised double charter and a bonus, so my old pal Forsyth volunteered me. It wasn't a bad day as desert days go, Ed, though the winds were red-hot'n gusting'n playing tricks, you know, the normal: sudden eddies whipping the sand into dust clouds, the usual whirlwinds in the eddies. I was at around three hundred feet on the approach when we hit the dust cloud—the dust so fine you couldn't see it. How it got through my goggles God only knows but one moment we were okay and the next coughing and spluttering and I had both eyes full and was as blind as an old Pegleg Pete."

"You're kidding me!"

"No. It's true, swear to God! Couldn't see a bleeding thing, couldn't open my eyes, and I'm the only pilot with two passengers aboard."

"Jesus, Scrag. Both eyes?"

"Both eyes and we swung all over the sky to hell until I got her more or less even and my heart back in me chest. The doc couldn't get the dust out, and every time he tried or I tried we near turned belly-up—you know how twitchy the G2 is. They were as panicked as me and that didn't help a bleeding bit. That's when I figured the only chance we got was to set her down blind. You said you was shit-scared, well, when I got our skids on the sand there wasn't a dribble left to come out, not even a dribble."

"Jesus, Scrag, you got her down for real? Just like today but for real, both eyes full of dust? No shit?"

"I got 'em to talk me down, just like I did to you—'least the doc did, the other poor sod'd fainted." Scragger's eyes had never left his landfall. "How's she look to you?"

"No sweat." Siri One was dead ahead, the landing pad esplanaded over the water. They could see the landing master and his obligatory fire crew standing by. The wind sock was half full and steady.

Normally Scragger would report into radar and begin their gradual descent. Instead he said, "We'll stay high today, sport, a high-angle approach and let her settle in."

"Why, Scrag?"

"Make a change."

Vossi frowned but said nothing. He rescanned the dials, seeking something amiss. There was nothing. Except a slight strangeness about the old man.

When they were in position high over the rig, Scragger clicked on the transmit: "Kish radar, HST, leaving one thousand for Siri One."

"Okay, HST. Report when ready for takeoff."

"HST."

They were set up for a steep-angle approach, normally used when high buildings or trees or pylons surrounded the point of touchdown. Scragger took off the exact amount of power. The chopper began to settle nicely, perfectly controlled. Nine hundred, eight seven six five . . . four . . . three . . . They both felt the vibration in the controls at the same time.

"Jesus," Vossi gasped, but Scragger had already put her nose down sharply and floored the collective lever. Immediately she began to go down very fast. Two hundred feet, one fifty, one, vibrations increasing. Vossi's eyes leaped from dial to dial to landing point and back again. He was rigid in his seat, his mind shouting, Tail rotor's gone or tail rotor gearbox. . . .

The landing pad was rushing at them, the ground crew scattering in panic, passengers hanging on in sudden fright at the untoward steepness, Vossi holding on to the side of his seat to steady himself. Now the whole instrument panel was vibrating, the engine pitch different. Any second he expected them to lose the tail rotor completely and then they'd be lost. The altimeter read sixty feet . . . fifty . . . forty . . . thirty . . . twenty, and his hands reached to grab the controls to begin the flare but Scragger anticipated him by a fraction of a second, gave her full power and flared perfectly. For a second she seemed poised motionless three feet up, engines screaming, then she touched down hard but not too hard on the near edge of the circle, skidded forward, and came to rest six feet off center.

"Fuck," Scragger muttered.

"Jesus, Scrag." Vossi was hardly able to talk. "That was perfect."

"Oh, no, no, it wasn't. I'm off six feet." With an effort Scragger unlocked his hands from the controls. "Shut her down, Ed, quick as you can!" Scragger opened his door and slid out fast, the airflow from the blades whipping him, and went back to the cabin door, opening it. "Stay where you are a moment," he shouted over the dying scream of the jets, wet with relief that everyone was still belted in and no one hurt. Obediently they stayed put, two of them pasty gray. The four Japanese stared at him impassively. Cold bloody lot, he thought.

"*Mon Dieu*, Scrag," Georges de Plessey called out. "What happened?"

"Don't know, think it's the tail rotor—soon's the rotors slow we c—"

"What the hell are you playing at, Vossi!" It was Ghafari, the Iranian landing manager, and he had shoved his face near the pilot's window, taut with rage. "How dare you pull a practice engine out on this rig? I'll report you for dangerous flying!"

Scragger whirled on him. "I was flying, not Capt'n Vossi!" Abruptly,

Scragger's enormous relief that he had got down safely, mixed with his long-standing detestation of this man snapped his temper. "Piss off, Ghafari, piss off, or I'll thump you once and for all!" His fists bunched and he was ready. "PISS OFF!"

The others watched, appalled. Vossi blanched. Ghafari, bigger and heavier than Scragger, hesitated then shook his fist in Scragger's face, cursing him in Farsi, then shouted in English, wanting to provoke him: "Foreign pig! How dare you swear at me, threaten me? I'll have you grounded for dangerous flying and thrown out of Iran. You dogs think you own our skies . . ."

Scragger lunged forward but Vossi was suddenly between them and he blocked the lunge with his great chest. "Well, what you know, old buddy? Hey, sorry, Scrag," he said easily, "but we'd better look at the tail rotor. Scrag, Scrag, old buddy, the tail rotor, huh?"

It took a few seconds for Scragger's eyes to clear. His heart was pumping and he saw them all staring at him. With a great effort he fought down his rage. "You're . . . you're right, Ed. Yes." Then he turned on Ghafari. "We had a . . . we had an emergency." Ghafari began to scoff and Scragger's rage soared but this time he controlled it.

They went aft. Many of the oil riggers, European and Iranian, were crowding around. The tail rotor stopped. About four inches were missing from one blade, the break jagged. When Vossi tried the main bearing, it was completely loose—the enormous torque caused by the imbalance of the blades had wrecked it. Behind him one of the passengers went to the side of the rig and was violently sick.

"Jesus," Vossi muttered, "I could break it off with two fingers."

Ghafari broke the silence with his bluster. "Clearly bad servicing, endangering the li—"

"Shut up, Ghafari," de Plessey said angrily. "*Merde*, we are all alive and we owe our lives to Captain Scragger. No one could forecast this, S-G's standards are the highest in Iran."

"It will be reported, Mr. de Plessey, an—"

"Yes, please do that and remember that I will be commending him for his airmanship." De Plessey was imposing in his rage. He loathed Ghafari, considering him a rabble-rouser, openly pro-Khomeini one moment, inciting the workers to strike—provided there were no pro-Shah military or police nearby —the next fawningly pro-Shah and punishing the riggers for a minor infraction. Foreign pig, eh? "Remember, too, this is a French-Iranian coventure and France is not, how shall I put it, France has not been unfriendly to Iran in her hour of need."

"Then you should insist Siri be serviced only by Frenchmen and not by old men! I will report this incident at once." Ghafari walked off.

Before Scragger could say or do anything, de Plessey put his hands on his shoulders and kissed him on both cheeks and shook his hand with equal warmth. "Thank you, *mon cher ami!*" There were loud cheers from the French as they congratulated themselves and crowded Scragger, formally embracing him. Then Kasigi stepped forward. *"Domo,"* he said formally, and to Scragger's further acute embarrassment, the four Japanese bowed to him in unison to more French cheers and much backslapping.

"Thank you, Captain," Kasigi said formally. "Yes, we understand and thank you." He smiled and offered his card with both hands and another little bow. "Yoshi Kasigi, Toda Shipping Industries. Thank you."

"It wasn't a bad one, Mr. er, Mr. Kasigee," Scragger said, trying to get over his embarrassment—over his rage now and back in control though he promised himself that one day soon he'd get Ghafari alone ashore. "We've, er, we've flotation gear, we'd plenty of space and we could have put her down in the water. It's our job, our job to get her down safely. Ed here." He beamed at Vossi genially, knowing that by getting in the way the young man had saved him from a matting he would not have won. "Captain Vossi would've done the same. Easy. It wasn't a bad one—I just wanted to save you getting wet though the water's nice and warm but you never know about Jaws. . . ."

The tension broke and they all laughed, albeit a little nervously, for most of the Gulf and the mouths of the rivers that fed it were shark-infested. The warm waters and the abundance of food waste and untreated sewage that the Gulf nations poured into it for millennia encouraged fish of all kinds. Particularly sharks. And because all food waste and human waste from the rigs went overboard, sharks would usually be nearby.

"Have you ever seen a big one, Captain?"

"Too right. There's a hammerhead that lurks off Kharg Island. I was stationed there for a couple of years and I'd spot him, oh, once or twice every few months. He's maybe twenty-five, maybe thirty feet. I've seen plenty of giant stingrays but he's the only big one."

De Plessey shuddered. *"Merde* on all sharks. I was almost caught once on Siri and I was, how do you say it, ah, yes, I was only paddling but the shark came racing at me in the shallows and going so fast it beached itself. It was about eight feet long. We shot it six times but it still thrashed around and tried to get us and took hours to die and even then not one of us wanted to get within range of it. Eh, sharks!" He glanced back at the broken blade. "Me, I am very happy to be on the rig."

They all agreed. The Frenchmen started chattering among themselves, gesticulating, two went to unload some hampers and another went to help the man who was still being sick. Riggers wandered off. The Japanese waited and watched.

Superstitiously Vossi touched the blade. "Just for luck, huh, Scrag?"

"Why not? So long as you and the passengers walk away, it was a good landing."

"What caused it?" de Plessey asked.

"Don't know, mate," Scragger said. "There was a flock of small seabirds, terns I think, at Siri Three. One of them might have gone into the rotor and caused a stress point—I never felt anything, but then you wouldn't. I know the rotor was perfect this morning because we both checked her as routine." He shrugged. "Act of God."

"*Oui. Espèce de con!* Me, I don't like to be that close to an Act of God." He frowned at the landing pad. "Can a 206 or Alouette get in to take us out by stages?"

"We'll send for another 212 and park our bird over there." Scragger pointed to the inside of the landing pad near the tall stack of the working derrick. "We've wheels in the baggage compartment, so it'll be no sweat, and no delay for you."

"Good. Good, then we'll leave you to it. Come along the rest of you," de Plessey said importantly. "I think we all need some coffee and then a glass of iced Chablis."

"I thought all rigs were dry," Kasigi said.

De Plessey's eyebrows soared. "They are, m'sieur. Of course. For Iranians and non-French. Of course. But our rigs are French and subject to the Code Napoleon." He added grandly, "We should celebrate our safe arrival, and today you are guests of la Belle France so we can be civilized and bend the rules—what are rules for if not to be bent? Of course. Come along, then we'll begin the tour and have the briefing."

They all followed him, except Kasigi. "And you, Captain?" he asked. "What will you do?"

"We'll wait. The chopper'll bring out spares and mechanics," Scragger said, ill at ease, not liking to be so near to any Japanese, unable to crush the memory of so many friends lost in the war so young with him still alive, and the constant, nagging question why them and not me? "We'll wait till she's repaired, then we'll go home. Why?"

"When will that be?"

"Before sundown. Why?"

Kasigi glanced back at the blade. "With your permission I would like to fly back with you."

"That's . . . that's up to Capt'n Vossi. He's formally captain on this flight."

Kasigi turned his attention to Vossi. The young pilot knew Scragger's dislike for Japanese but could not understand it. Just before takeoff he had said, "Hell, Scrag, World War Two was a million years ago. Japan's our ally now—the only big one we've got in Asia." But Scragger had said, "Just leave it, Ed," so he had left it.

"You'd, er, best go back with the others, Mr. Kasigi, there's no telling how long we'll be."

"Choppers make me nervous. I'd prefer to fly with you, if you don't mind." Kasigi looked back at Scragger, hard eyes in a lived-in face. "It was a bad one. You had almost no time, yet you autorotate at barely three hundred feet to make a perfect setdown on this flyspot. That was incredible flying. Incredible. One thing I don't understand: why were you high angle, on a high-angle approach?" He caught Vossi glance at Scragger. Ah, he thought, you're wondering too. "There's no reason on a day like today, is there?"

Scragger stared at him, even more unsettled. "You fly choppers?"

"No, but I've been in enough to know when there's bad trouble. My business is tankers, so oil fields, here in the Gulf, Iraq, Libya, Alaska, everywhere—even Australia." Kasigi let the hatred pass over him. He was used to it. He knew the reason, for he did a great deal of business now in Australia, a very great deal. Some of the hatred's merited, he thought. Some. Never mind, Australians will change, they'll have to. After all, we own a considerable section of her raw materials for years to come and soon we'll own more. Curious that we can do economically so easily what we failed to do militarily. "Please, why did you choose a high-angle approach today? On a normal approach we'd be under the sea right now, on the bottom. Why?"

Scragger shrugged, wanting to end it.

"Skipper," Vossi said, "why did you?"

"Luck."

Kasigi half smiled. "If you'll allow me I would like to fly back with you. A life for a life, Captain. Please keep my card. Perhaps one day I can be of service to you." He bowed politely and left.

11:56 A.M.   "Explosives on Siri, Scrag?" De Plessey was shocked.

"There might be," Scragger replied, equally softly. They were on the far side of the platform, well away from everyone, and he had just told him what Abdollah had whispered.

The second 212 was long since there, waiting for de Plessey to give the word to start up and take him and his party on to Siri where they were due to have lunch. Mechanics had already stripped most of the tail section of Scragger's 212 and were well into repairs, Vossi watching attentively. The new rotor and gearbox were already in place.

After a moment, de Plessey said helplessly, "Explosives could be anywhere, anywhere. Even a little explosive could wreck our whole pumping system. Madonna, it would be a perfect ploy to further wreck Bakhtiar's chances—or Khomeini's—of getting back to normal."

"Yes. But be careful how you use the info—and for God's sake keep it to yourself."

"Of course. This man was on Siri Three?"

"At Lengeh."

"Eh? Then why didn't you tell me this morning?"

"There was no time." Scragger glanced around, making sure they were still not overheard. "Be careful, whatever you do. Those fanatics don't give a twopenny damn for anything or anyone and if they think there's been a leak, that someone's ratted . . . there'll be bodies floating from here to Hormuz."

"I agree." De Plessey was very worried. "Did you tell anyone else?"

"No, cobber."

"*Mon Dieu*, what can I do? Security is . . . how can you have security in Iran? Like it or not we're in their power." Then he added, "Thank you a second time. I must tell you I've been expecting major sabotage on Kharg, and at Abadan, it's to the leftist advantage to create even more chaos, but I never thought they'd come here."

Moodily he leaned on the rail and looked down at the sea sluggishly washing the legs of the platform. Sharks were circling and feeding. Now we've terrorists threatening us. Siri's tanks and pumps are a good target for sabotage. And if Siri's interfered with, we lose years of planning, years of oil that France desperately needs. Oil we may have to buy from the shit-stenched English and their shit-stenched North Sea oil fields—how dare they be so lucky with their 1.3 million barrels a day and rising!

Why isn't there oil off our coasts or off Corse? God-cursed English with their two-faced, two-hearted approach to life! De Gaulle was right to keep them out of Europe, and now that we, out of the goodness of our hearts, have accepted them, even though we all know they're lying bastards, they care nothing to share their windfall with us, their partner. They only pretend to

be with us in the EEC—they've always been against us and always will be.
The Great Charles was right about them but incredibly wrong about Algeria.
If we still had our Algeria, our soil and therefore our oil, we'd be rich,
content, with Britain and Germany and all the rest licking the grime from
between our toes.

Meanwhile, what to do?

Go to Siri and have lunch. After lunch you will think better. Thank God
we can still get supplies from sensible, civilized Dubai, Sharjah, and Al Shargaz: Brie, Camembert, Boursin, fresh garlic and butter from France daily,
and real wine without which we might as well be dead. Well, almost, he
added cautiously and saw Scragger staring at him. "Yes, *mon brave?*"

"I said, wot're you going to do?"

"Order a security exercise," he said majestically. "It seems that I had
forgotten clause 56/976 of our original French-Iran contract that says every
six months for a period of several days security must be checked against any
and all intruders for . . . for the great glory of France and, er, Iran!" De
Plessey's fine eyes lit up with the beauty of his ruse. "Yes. Of course my
subordinates forgot to remind me but now we will all hurl ourselves into the
exercise with perfect French enthusiasm. Everywhere, on Siri, on the rigs,
ashore, even at Lengeh! *Les crétins!* How dare they think they could sabotage
the work of years." He glanced around. There was still no one near. The rest
of the party was assembled now near the second 212. "I'll have to tell Kasigi
because of his tanker," he said quietly. "That might be the target."

"Can you trust him? I mean to do everything quietly."

"Yes. We will have to, *mon ami.* We will have to warn him, yes, we'll have
to do that." De Plessey felt his stomach rumbling. My God, he thought, very
perturbed, I hope it's just hunger and that I'm not in for a bilious attack—
though I wouldn't wonder with all that's happened today. First we almost
have an accident, then our top pilot almost has a fight with that barrel full of
dung Ghafari, and now the revolution may come to us. "Kasigi asked if he
could fly back with you. When will you be ready?"

"Before sundown, but there's no need for him to wait for us, he can go
back with you."

De Plessey frowned. "I understand why you don't like Japanese—me, I
still can't stand the Germans. But we must be practical. He's a good customer and since he asked, I'd appreciate it if you'd, you'd, er, ask Vossi to fly
him, *mon cher ami.* Yes, now we are intimate friends, you saved our lives, and
we shared an Act of God! And he is one of our very good customers," he
added firmly. "Very good. Thank you, *mon ami.* I'll leave him at Siri. When
you're ready, pick him up there. Tell him what you told me. Excellent, then

that's decided, and rest assured I will commend you to the authorities and to the Laird Gavallan himself." He beamed again. "We'll be off and I'll see you tomorrow."

Scragger watched him go. He cursed silently. De Plessey was the top man so there was nothing he could do and that afternoon on the way to Siri he sat back in the cabin, sweating and hating it.

"Jesus, Scrag," Vossi had said, in shock, when he had told him he was riding in the back. "Passenger? You all right? You sure y—"

"I just want to see what it feels like," Scragger had said irritably. "Get your arse in the captain's seat, fetch that bugger from Siri, and set her down like a bleeding feather at Lengeh or it's in your bleeding report."

Kasigi was waiting at the helipad. There was no shade and he was hot, dusty, and sweating. Dunes stretched back to the pipelines and tank complex, all dirty brown from the dust. Scragger watched the dust devils, little whirlwinds, dance over the ground, and he thanked his stars that he could fly and didn't have to work in such a place. Yes, choppers are noisy and always vibrating and maverick, he thought, and yes, I miss flying the high skies, flying fixed wing alone in the high skies, diving and turning over and falling like an eagle to rise up again—but flying is flying and I still hate sitting in the bleeding cabin. For God's sake, here it's even worse than a regular aircraft! He hated flying without the controls and never felt safe and this added to his discomfort as he beckoned Kasigi to sit beside him and slammed the door shut. The two mechanics were dozing in their seats opposite, their white overalls stained with sweat. Kasigi adjusted the Mae West and snapped his seat belt tight.

Once airborne Scragger leaned closer to him. "There's no way to tell you but quickly so here it is: there may be a terrorist attack on Siri, one of the rigs, perhaps even your ship. De Plessey asked me to warn you."

The air hissed out of Kasigi's mouth. "When?" he asked over the heavy cabin noise.

"I don't know. Nor does de Plessey. But it's more than possible."

"How? How will they sabotage?"

"No idea. Guns or explosives, maybe a time bomb, so you'd better tighten security."

"It is already optimum," Kasigi replied at once, and then saw the flash of anger in Scragger's eyes. For a second he could not fathom the why, then he remembered what he had just said. "Ah, so sorry, Captain, I did not mean to be boastful. It is just that we have always very high standards and in these waters my ships're . . ." He had almost said "on a war footing" but stopped himself in time, containing his irritation at the other's sensitivity. "In these waters everyone is more than careful. Please excuse me."

"De Plessey wanted you to know. And also to keep the tip mum—to keep it to yourself—and not get any Iranian backs up."

"I understand. The tip is safe with me. Again, thank you." Kasigi saw Scragger nod briefly then settle back in his seat. The bigger half of him also wanted to nod briefly and end everything there, but because the Australian had saved his companions' lives as well as his own, therefore enabling them to give further service to the company and their leader, Hiro Toda, he felt it his duty to attempt a healing.

"Captain," he said as quietly as he could over the thunder of the jets, "I understand why we Japanese are hated by Australians and I apologize for all the Changis, all the Burma Roads, and all the atrocities. I can only tell you the truth: these happenings are well taught in our schools and not forgotten. It is to our national shame that these things happened."

It's true, he thought angrily. To commit those atrocities was stupid even though those fools did not understand they were committing atrocities—after all, the enemy were cowards, most of them, and meekly surrendered in tens of thousands and so forfeited their rights as human beings according to our Bushido, our code, that stipulates for a soldier to surrender is the worst dishonor. A few mistakes by a few sadists, a few ill-educated peasants of prison guards—most of whom were the garlic eaters, Koreans—and all Japanese have to suffer forever. It is a shame of Japan. And another, the worst of all shames, that our supreme war-leader failed in his duty and so forced the emperor into the shame of having to terminate the war. "Please accept my apology for all of us."

Scragger stared at him. After a pause he said simply, "Sorry, but I can't. For one thing my ex-partner Forsyth was the first man into Changi; he never got over what he saw; for another too many of my cobbers, not just POWs, bought it. Too many. I can't forget. An' more than that, I won't. I won't because if I did, that'd be their last betrayal. We've betrayed them in the peace—wot peace? We've betrayed 'em all, that's what I think. Sorry, but there it is."

"I understand. Even so we can make a peace, you and I. No?"

"Maybe. Maybe in time."

Ah, time, Kasigi thought, bemused. Today I was again on the edge of death. How much time do we have, you and I? Isn't time an illusion and all life just illusions within illusions. And death? His revered samurai ancestor's death poem had summed it up perfectly: What are clouds,/But an excuse for the sky?/What is life,/But an escape from Death?

The ancestor was Yabu Kasigi, daimyo of Izu and Baka and supporter of Yoshi Toronaga, first and greatest of the Toronaga shoguns who, from father to son, ruled Japan from 1603 until 1871 when the Meiji emperor finally obliterated the shogunate and outlawed the entire samurai class. But Yabu Kasigi was not remembered for his loyalty to his liege lord or his courage in battle—as was his famous nephew Omi Kasigi, who fought for Toronaga at the great battle of Sekigahara, had his hand blown off but still led the charge that broke the enemy.

Oh, no, Yabu betrayed Toronaga, or tried to betray him, and so was ordered by him to commit seppuku—ritual death by disembowelment. Yabu was revered for the calligraphy of his death poem, and his courage when he committed seppuku. On that day, kneeling before the assembled samurai, he contemptuously dispensed with the second samurai who would stand behind him with a long sword to end his agony quickly by cutting off his head and so preventing the shame of crying out. He took the short knife and plunged it deep into his stomach, then leisurely made the four cuts, the most difficult seppuku of all—across and down, across again and up—then lifted out his own entrails to die at length, never having cried out.

Kasigi shivered at the thought of having to do the same, knowing he would not have the courage. Modern war's nothing to those days when you could be ordered to die thus at the whim of your liege lord. . . .

He saw Scragger watching him.

"I was in the war, too," he said involuntarily. "Fixed wing. I flew Zeros in China, Malaya, and Indonesia. And New Guinea. Courage in war is different from . . . from courage alone. . . . I mean, not in war, isn't it?"

"I don't understand."

I haven't thought about my war for years, Kasigi was thinking, a sudden wave of fear going through him, remembering his constant terror of dying or being maimed, terror that had consumed him—like today when he was certain they were all going to die and he and his companions had been frozen with fear. Yes, and we all did today what we did all those war years: remembered our heritage in the Land of the Gods, swallowed our terror as we had been taught from childhood, pretended calm, pretended harmony so as not to shame ourselves before others, flew missions for the emperor against the enemy as best we could and then, when he said lay down your arms, thankfully laid down our arms, however much the shame.

A few found the shame unbearable and killed themselves in the ancient way with honor. Did I lose honor because I didn't? Never. I obeyed the emperor who ordered us to bear the unbearable, then joined my cousin's firm as was ordained and have served him loyally for the greater glory of Japan.

From the ruins of Yokohama I helped rebuild Toda Shipping Industries into one of Japan's greatest firms, constructing great ships, inventing the super-tankers, bigger every year—soon the keel of the first million-tonner to be laid. Now our ships are everywhere, carrying bulk raw materials into Japan and finished goods out. We Japanese are rightly the wonder of the world. But, oh, so vulnerable—we must have oil or we perish.

Out of one of the windows he noticed a tanker steaming up the Gulf, another going toward Hormuz. The bridge continues, he thought. At least one tanker every hundred miles all the way from here to Japan, day in day out, to feed our factories without which we starve. All OPEC knows it, they're gouging us and gloating. Like today. Today it took all my willpower to pretend outward calm dealing with that . . . that odious Frenchman, stink-ing of garlic and that revolting, stinking, oozing vomit mess called Brie, blatantly demanding $2.80 over and above the already outrageous $14.80, and me, of ancient samurai lineage, having to haggle with him like a Hong Kong Chinese.

"But, M'sieur de Plessey, surely you must see that at that price, plus freight an—"

"So sorry, m'sieur, but I have my instructions. As agreed the 3 million barrels of Siri oil are on offer to you first. ExTex have asked for a quote and so have four other majors. If you wish to change your mind . . ."

"No, but the contract specifies 'the current OPEC price' and w—"

"Yes, but you surely know that all OPEC suppliers are charging a pre-mium. Don't forget the Saudis plan to cut back production this month, that last week all the majors ordered another sweeping wave of *force majeure* cutbacks, that Libya's cutting her production too. BP's increased its cutback to 45 percent. . . ."

Kasigi wanted to bellow with rage as he remembered that when at length he had agreed, provided he could have all 3 million barrels at the same price, the Frenchman had smiled sweetly and said, "Certainly, provided you load within seven days," both of them knowing it was impossible. Knowing too that a Romanian state delegation was presently in Kuwait seeking 3 million tons of crude, let alone 3 million barrels, to compensate for the cutoff of their own Iranian supplies that came to them through the Iran-Soviet pipelines. And that there were other buyers, dozens of them, waiting to take over his Siri option and all his other options—for oil, liquid natural gas, naphtha, and other petrochemicals.

"Very well, $17.60 a barrel," Kasigi had said agreeably. But inside he swore to even the score somehow.

"For this one tanker, m'sieur."

"Of course for this tanker," he had said even more agreeably.

And now this Australian pilot whispers to me that even this one tanker may not be safe. This strange old man, far too old to be flying yet so skilled, so knowledgeable, so open, and so foolish—foolish to be so open, for then you put yourself into another's power.

He looked back at Scragger. "You said we could make a peace maybe in time. We both ran out of time today—but for your skill, and luck, though we call that karma. I truly don't know how much time we have. Perhaps my ship is blown up tomorrow. I will be aboard her." He shrugged. "Karma. But let us be friends, just you and I—I don't think we betray our war comrades, yours and mine." He put out his hand. "Please."

Scragger looked at the hand. Kasigi willed himself to wait. Then Scragger conceded, half nodded and shook the hand firmly. "Okay, sport, let's give it a go."

At that moment he saw Vossi turn and beckon him. At once Scragger went forward to the cockpit. "Yes, Ed?"

"There's a CASEVAC, Scrag, from Siri Three. One of the deck crew's fallen overboard. . . ."

They went at once. The body was floating near the legs of the rig. They winched it aboard. Sharks had already fed on the lower limbs and one arm was missing. The head and face were badly bruised and curiously disfigured. It had been Abdollah Turik.

NEAR BANDAR DELAM: 4:52 P.M. Shadows were lengthening. Beyond the road the land was scrubby, and beyond that stony foothills rose to snowcapped mountains—the northern end of the Zagros. This side, beside the stream and marshes that led at length to the port a few miles away, was one of the numerous oil pipelines that crisscrossed this whole area. The pipeline was steel, twenty inches in diameter, and set on a concrete trestle that led down into a culvert under the road, then went underground. A mile or so to the east was a village—low-lying, dust-covered, earth-colored, made from mud bricks—and coming from that direction was a small car. It was old and battered and traveled slowly, the engine sounding good, too good for the body.

In the car were four Iranians. They were young and clean-shaven and better dressed than usual, though all were sweat stained and very nervous. Near the culvert the car stopped. One young man wearing glasses got out from the front seat and pretended to urinate on the side of the road, his eyes searching all around.

"It's all clear," he said.

At once the two youths in the back came out swiftly, a rough, heavy bag between them, and ducked down the dirt embankment into the culvert. The young man with glasses fastened his buttons, then casually went to the trunk of the car and opened it. Under a piece of torn canvas he saw the snub nose of the Czech-made machine pistol. A little of his nervousness left him.

The driver got out and urinated into the ditch, his stream strong.

"I wanted to, Mashoud, but couldn't," the youth with glasses said, envying him. He wiped the sweat off his face and pushed at his glasses.

"I can never do it before an exam," Mashoud said and laughed. "God grant university will open again soon."

"God! God's the opiate of the masses," the youth with glasses said witheringly, then turned his attention to the road. It was still empty as far as they could see in both directions. South a few miles away, the sun reflected off the waters of the Gulf. He lit a cigarette. His fingers trembled. Time passed very slowly. Flies swarmed, making the silence seem more silent. Then he noticed a dust cloud on the road, the other side of the village. "Look!"

Together they squinted into the distance. "Are they lorries—or trucks, army trucks?" Mashoud said anxiously, then ran to the side of the culvert and shouted, "Hurry up, you two. There's something coming!"

"All right," a voice called from below.

"We're almost done," another voice said.

The two youths in the culvert had the sack open and were already packing the flat bags of explosive haphazardly against the welded steel pipe and along its length. The pipe was covered with a sheath of canvas and pitch to protect it from erosion. "Give me the detonator and fuse, Ali," the older one said throatily. Both of them were filthy now, the dirt streaked with sweat.

"Here." Ali handed it to him carefully, his shirt clinging to his skin. "Are you sure you know how to do it, Bijan?"

"We've studied the pamphlet for hours. Didn't we practice doing it with our eyes closed?" Bijan forced a smile. "We're like Robert Jordan in *For Whom the Bell Tolls*. Just like him."

The other shivered. "I hope the bell's not tolling for us."

"Even if it does, what does that matter? The party will conquer, and the Masses will have victory." Bijan's inexperienced fingers awkwardly jammed the highly volatile, nitroglycerin detonator against one of the explosives, connected one end of the fuse beside it, and piled the last of the bags on top to hold it in place.

Mashoud's voice called out even more urgently, "Hurry, they're . . . we think they're army trucks with soldiers!"

For a moment both young men were paralyzed, then they unreeled the length of fuse, tripping over each other in their nervousness. Unnoticed, the fuse end near the detonator came away. They laid the ten-foot length along the ground, lit the far end, and took to their heels. Bijan glanced back to check everything, saw that one end was spluttering nicely, and was aghast to notice the other end dangling free. He rushed back, shakily stuffed it near the detonator, slipped, and slammed the detonator against the concrete.

The nitroglycerin exploded and blew the bag of explosives next to it and that blew the next and the next and they all went and tore Bijan to pieces with twenty feet of the pipe, blowing off the culvert roof and overturning the car, killing two of the other youths and ripping a leg off the last.

Oil began gushing from the pipe. Hundreds of barrels a minute. The oil should have ignited but it did not—the explosives had been wrongly placed and detonated—and by the time the two army trucks had stopped cautiously a hundred yards away, the oil slick had already reached the stream. The lighter oils, gaseous, volatile, floated on the surface, and the heavier crude began to seep into the banks and marshes and soil, making the whole area highly dangerous.

In the two commandeered trucks were some twenty of Khomeini's Green Bands, most of them bearded, the rest unshaven, all wearing their characteristic armbands—peasants, a few oil-field workers, a PLO-trained leader, and a mullah—all armed, all battle-stained, a few wounded, the uniformed police captain bound and gagged and still alive lying on the floor. They had just attacked and overwhelmed a police station to the north and were now heading into Bandar Delam to continue the war. Their assignment was to help others subdue the civilian airport that was a few miles to the south.

The mullah leading, they came to the edge of the blown-up culvert. For a moment they watched the oil gushing, then a moaning attracted them. They unslung their guns and went carefully to the overturned car. The youth missing a leg was lying half under it, dying fast. Flies swarmed and settled and swarmed again, blood and entrails everywhere.

"Who are you?" the mullah asked, shaking him roughly. "Why did you do this?"

The youth opened his eyes. Without his glasses everything was misted. Blindly he groped for them. The terror of dying engulfed him. He tried to say the Shahada but only a petrified scream came forth. Blood welled into his throat, choking him.

"As God wants," the mullah said, turning away. He noticed the broken glasses in the dirt and picked them up. One lens was fractured, the other missing.

"Why should they do this?" one of the Green Bands asked. "We've no orders to sabotage the pipes—not now."

"They must be Communists, or Islamic-Marxist carrion." The mullah tossed the glasses away. His face was bruised and his long robe torn in places and he was starving. "They look like students. May God kill all His enemies as quickly."

"Hey, look at these," another called out. He had been searching the car and found three machine pistols and some grenades. "All Czech made. Only leftists are so well armed. These dogs're enemy all right."

"God be praised. Good, we can use the arms. Can we get the trucks around the culvert?"

"Oh, yes, easily, thanks be to God," his driver, a thickset bearded man said. He was a worker in one of the oil fields and knew about pipelines. "We'd better report the sabotage," he added nervously. "This whole area could explode. I could phone the pumping station if there's a phone working —or send a message—then they can cut the flow. We'd better be fast. This whole area's deadly and the spill will pollute everything downstream."

"That's in the Hands of God." The mullah watched the oil spreading. "Even so it's not right to waste the riches God gave us. Good, you will try to phone from the airport." Another bubbling scream for help came from the youth. They left him to die.

BANDAR DELAM AIRPORT: 5:30 P.M. The civilian airport was unguarded, abandoned, and not operational except for the S-G contingent that had come here a few weeks ago from Kharg Island. The airport had two short runways, a small tower, some hangars, a two-story office building, and some barracks, and now a few modern trailers—S-G's property—for temporary housing and HQ. It was like any one of the dozens of civilian airports that the Shah had had built for the feeder airlines that used to service all Iran: "We will have airports and modern services," he had decreed and so it was done. But since the troubles had begun six months ago and all internal feeder airlines struck, airplanes had been grounded throughout Iran and the airports closed down. Ground crews and staff had vanished. Most of the aircraft had been left in the open, without service or care. Of the three twin jets that were parked on the apron, two had flat tires, one, a cockpit window broken. All had had their tanks drained by looters. All were filthy, almost derelict. And sad.

In great contrast to these were the five sparkling S-G helicopters, three 212s and two 206s lined up meticulously, being given their daily bath and final check of the day. The sun was low now and cast long shadows.

Captain Rudiger Lutz, senior pilot, moved to the last helicopter and inspected it as carefully as he had the others. "Very good," he said at length. "You can put them away." He watched while the mechanics and their Iranian ground crew wheeled the airplanes back into the hangars that were also spotless. He knew that many of the crew laughed at him behind his back for his meticulousness, but that didn't matter—so long as they obeyed. That's our most difficult problem, he thought. How to get them to obey, how to operate in a war situation when we're not governed by army rules and just noncombatants in the middle of a war situation whether Duncan McIver wants to admit it openly or not.

This morning Duke Starke at Kowiss had relayed by HF McIver's terse message from Tehran about the rumored attack on Tehran Airport and the revolt of one of the air bases there—because of distance and mountains Bandar Delam could not talk direct to Tehran or to their other bases, only to Kowiss. Worriedly Rudi had assembled all his expat crew, four pilots, seven mechanics—seven English, two Americans, one German, and one Frenchman—where they could not be overheard and had told them. "It wasn't so much what Duke said but the way he said it—kept calling me 'Rudiger' when it's always 'Rudi.' He sounded itchy."

"Not like Duke Starke to be itchy—unless it's hit the fan," Jon Tyrer, Rudi's American second-in-command, had said uneasily. "You think he's in trouble? You think maybe we should go take a look at Kowiss?"

"Perhaps. But we'll wait till I talk to him tonight."

"Me, I think we'd better get ready to do a midnight skip, Rudi," mechanic Fowler Joines had said with finality. "Yes. If old Duke's nervous . . . we'd best be ready to scarper, to get lost."

"You're crazy, Fowler. We've never had trouble," Tyrer said. "This whole area's more or less quiet, police and troops disciplined and in control. Shit, we've five air force bases within twenty miles and they're all elite and pro-Shah. There's bound to be a loyalist coup soon."

"You ever been in the middle of a coup for crissake? They bloody shoot each other and I'm a civilian!"

"Okay, say the stuff hits the fan, what do you suggest?"

They had discussed all sorts of possibilities. Land, air, sea. Iraq's border was barely a hundred miles away—and Kuwait within easy range across the Gulf.

"We'll have plenty of notice." Rudi was very confident. "McIver'll know if there's a coup coming."

"Listen, old son," Fowler had said, more sourly than usual, "I know companies—same as bloody generals! If it gets really tough we'll be on our tod—on our bloody own—so we'd better have a plan. I'm not going to get my head shot off for the Shah, Khomeini, or even the Laird-god Gavallan. I say we just scarper—fly the coop!"

"Bloody hell, Fowler," one of the English pilots had burst out, "are you suggesting we hijack one of our own planes? We'd be grounded forever!"

"Maybe that's better than the pearly gates!"

"We could get shot down, for God's sake. We'd never get away with it—you know how all our flights are monitored, how twitchy radar is here—bloody sight worse than at Lengeh! We can't get off the ground without asking permission to start engines. . . ."

At length Rudi had asked them to give him contingency suggestions in case sudden evacuation was necessary, by land, by air, or by sea, and had left them arguing.

All day he had been worrying what to do, what was wrong at Kowiss, and at Tehran. As senior pilot he felt responsible for his crew—apart from the dozen Iranian laborers and Jahan, his radio op, none of whom he had been able to pay for six weeks now—along with all the aircraft and spares. We were damned lucky to get out of Kharg so well, he thought, his stomach tightening. The withdrawal had gone smoothly with all airplanes, all important spares, and some of their transport brought here over four days without interfering with their heavy load of contract flying and CASEVACs.

Getting out of Kharg had been easy because everyone had wanted to go. As quickly as possible. Even before the troubles, Kharg was an unpopular base with nothing to do except work and look forward to R and R in Tehran or home. When the troubles began everyone knew that Kharg was a prime target for revolutionaries. There had been a great deal of rioting, some shooting. Recently more of the IPLO armbands had been seen among the rioters and the commander of the island had threatened that he'd shoot every villager on the island if the rioting didn't stop. Since they had left a few weeks ago the island had been quiet, ominously quiet.

And that retreat wasn't a real emergency, he reminded himself. How to operate in one? Last week he had flown to Kowiss to pick up some special spares and had asked Starke how he planned to operate at Kowiss if there was real trouble.

"The same as you, Rudi. You'd try to operate within company rules which won't apply then," the tall Texan had said. "We got a couple of things going for us: just about all of our guys're ex-service of some sort so there's a kinda chain of command—but hell, you can plan all you want and then you still won't sleep nights because when the stuff hits the fan, it'll be the same as ever: some of the guys'll fall apart, some won't, and you'll never know in advance who's gonna do what, or even how you'll react yourself."

Rudi had never been in a shooting war, though his service with the German army in the fifties had been on the East German borders, and in West Germany you're always conscious of the Wall, the Curtain, and of all your brothers and sisters behind it—and of the waiting, brooding Soviet legions and satellite legions with their tens of thousands of tanks and missiles also behind it, just yards away. And conscious of German zealots on both sides of the border who worship their messiah called Lenin and the thousands of spies gnawing at our guts.

Sad.

How many from my hometown?

He had been born in a little village near Plauen close to the Czechoslovakian border, now part of East Germany. In '45 he had been twelve, his brother sixteen and already in the army. The war years had not been bad for him and his younger sister and mother. In the country there was enough to eat. But in '45 they had fled before the Soviet hordes, carrying what they could, to join the vast German migrations westward: two million from Prussia, another two from the north, four from the center, another two from the south—along with other millions of Czechs, Poles, Hungarians, Romanians, Austrians, Bulgarians, of all Europe—all starving now, all petrified, all fighting to stay alive.

Ah, staying alive, he thought.

On the trek, cold and weary and almost broken, he remembered going with his mother to a garbage dump, somewhere near Nürnberg, the countryside war-ravaged and towns rubbled, his mother frantic to find a kettle—their own stolen in the night—impossible to buy one, even if they had had the money. "We've got to have a kettle to boil water or we'll all die, we'll get typhus or dysentery like the others—we can't live without boiled water," she had cried out. So he had gone with her, in tears, convinced it was a waste of time, but they had found one. It was old and battered, the spout bent, and the handle loose but the top was with it and it did not leak. Now the kettle was clean and sparkling and in a place of honor on the mantelpiece in the kitchen of their farmhouse near Freiburg in the Black Forest where his wife and sons and mother were. And once a year, each New Year's Eve, his mother would still make tea from water boiled in the kettle. And, when he was there, they would smile together, he and she. "If you believe enough, my son, and try," she would always whisper, "you can find your kettle. Never forget, you found it, I didn't."

* * *

There were sudden warning shouts. He whirled around to see three army trucks burst through the gate, one racing for the tower, the other toward his hangars. The trucks skidded to a halt and Green Band revolutionaries fanned out over the base, two men charging at him, their guns leveled, screaming Farsi which he did not understand, as others started rounding up his men in the hangar. Petrified, he raised his hands, his heart pounding at the suddenness. Two Green Bands, bearded and sweating with excitement-fear shoved gun barrels at his face and Rudi flinched.

"I'm not armed," he gasped. "What do you want? Eh?"

Neither man answered, just continued to threaten him. Behind them he could see the rest of his crew being herded out of their barrack trailers onto the apron. Other attackers were jumping in and out of the helicopters, searching them, carelessly overturning gear, one man hurling neatly rolled life jackets out of their seat pockets. His rage overcame his terror. "Hey, *Sie verrückte Dummköpfe,*" he shouted. "*Lass'n Sie meine verrückten Flugzeuge allein!*" Before he knew what he was doing he had brushed the guns aside and rushed toward them. For a moment it looked as though the two Iranians would shoot, but they just went after him, caught up with him, and pulled him around. One lifted a rifle by the butt to smash his face in.

"Stop!"

The men froze.

The man who shouted out the command in English was in his early thirties, heavyset, wearing rough clothes, with a green armband, a stubbled beard, dark wavy hair, and dark eyes. "Who is in charge here?"

"I am!" Rudi Lutz tore his arms out of his assailants' grasp. "What are you doing here? What do you want?"

"We are possessing this airport in the name of Islam and the revolution." The man's accent was English. "How many troops are here, air staff?"

"There're none. No troops—there's no tower staff, there's no one here but us," Rudi said, trying to catch his breath.

"No troops?" The man's voice was dangerous.

"No, none. We've had patrols here since we came here a few weeks ago— they come from time to time. But none are stationed here. And no military airplanes." Rudi stabbed a finger at the hangar. "Tell those . . . those men to be careful of my airplanes, lives depend on them, Iranian as well as ours."

The man turned and saw what was happening. He shouted another command, cursing them. The men shouted back at him carelessly, then after a moment came out into the sunset, leaving chaos in their wake.

"Please excuse them," the man said. "My name is Zataki. I am chief of the Abadan komiteh. With the Help of God, we command Bandar Delam now."

Rudi's stomach was churning. His expats and Iranian staff were in a frozen group beside the low office building, guns surrounding them. "We're working for a British comp—"

"Yes, we know about S-G Helicopters." Zataki turned and shouted again. Reluctantly, some of his men went to the gate and began to take up defensive positions. He looked back at Rudi. "Your name?"

"Captain Lutz."

"You have nothing to fear, Captain Lutz, you and your men. Do you have arms here?"

"No, except Very light pistols, aircraft stores. For signaling, distress signaling."

"You will fetch them." Zataki turned and went nearer to the S-G group and stood there, examining faces. Rudi saw the fear of his Iranians, cooks, ground staff, fitters, Jahan, and Yemeni, the IranOil manager.

"These are all my people," he said trying to sound firm. "All S-G employees."

Zataki looked at him, then came very close, and Rudi had to steel himself not to flinch again. "Do you know what mujhadin-al-khalq means? Fedayeen? Tudeh?" he asked softly, heavier than Rudi, and with a gun.

"Yes."

"Good." After a pause, Zataki went back to staring at the Iranians. One by one. The silence grew. Suddenly he stabbed a finger at one man, a fitter. The man sagged, then began to run frantically, screaming in Farsi. They caught him easily and beat him senseless.

"The komiteh will judge him and sentence him in God's name." Zataki glanced at Rudi. "Captain," he said, his lips a thin line, "I asked you to fetch your Very pistols."

"They're in the safe, and quite safe," Rudi said, just as toughly, not feeling brave inside. "You may have them whenever you want. They're only in the airplane during a mission. I . . . I want that man released!"

Without warning, Zataki reversed his machine gun and slammed the butt at Rudi's head but Rudi caught it with one hand, deflecting it, tore it out of the man's grasp, his reflexes perfect, and before the gun crashed to the ground, the hardened edge of his other, open hand was axing into Zataki's unprotected throat. But he stopped the death blow, barely touching the man's skin. Then he stepped back, at bay now. All guns were trained on him.

The silence grew. His men watched, appalled. Zataki was staring at Rudi enraged. The shadows were long, and a slight wind toyed with the wind sock, crackling it slightly.

"Pick up the gun!"

In the bigger silence, Rudi heard the threat and the promise and he knew that his life—all of theirs—was in balance. "Fowler, do it!" he ordered and prayed that he had chosen correctly.

Reluctantly Fowler came forward. "Yessir, coming right up!" It seemed to take a long time for him to cover the twenty yards, but no one stopped him and one of the guards moved out of his way. He picked the gun up, automatically put the safety on, carefully handed it back to Zataki, butt first. "It's not bent and, er, good as new, me son."

The leader took the gun and slipped the safety off and everyone heard the click as though it were a thunderclap. "You know guns?"

"Yes . . . oh, yes. We . . . all mechanics were . . . we all had to have a course in the RAF . . . Royal Air Force," Fowler said, keeping his eyes on the man's eyes and he thought, What the fuck am I doing here, standing up to this smelly son of a whore's left tit? "Can we dismiss? We're civilians, me son, we're noncombatants, begging your pardon. Neutral."

Zataki jerked a thumb at the line. "Go back there." Then he turned to Rudi. "Where did you learn karate?"

"In the army—the German army."

"Ah, German. You're German? Germans have been good to Iran. Not like the British, or Americans. Which are your pilots, their names and their nationalities?"

Rudi hesitated, then pointed. "Captain Dubois, French, Captains Tyrer, Block, and Forsyth, English."

"No Americans?"

Rudi had another great sinking in his stomach. Jon Tyrer was American and had false identity cards. Then his ears heard the sound of the approaching chopper, recognized the thrunk-thrunk of a 206, and automatically he searched the skies, along with all of them. Then one of the Green Bands let out a cry and pointed as others rushed into defensive positions, everyone scattering except the expats. They had recognized the markings.

"Everyone into the hangar," Zataki ordered. The chopper came over the airfield at a thousand feet and began to circle. "It's one of yours?"

"Yes. But not from this base." Rudi squinted into the sun. His heart picked up when he read the markings. "It's EP-HXT, from Kowiss, from our base in Kowiss."

"What's he want?"

"Obviously to land."

"Find out who's aboard. And don't try any tricks."

Together they went to the UHF in his office. "HXT, do you read?"

"HXT, loud and clear. This is Captain Starke of Kowiss." A pause, then, "Captain Lutz?"

"Yes, it's Captain Lutz, Captain Starke," he said, knowing by the formality that there must be hostiles aboard, as Starke would know something was wrong here.

"Request permission to land. I'm low on gas and require refueling. I'm cleared by Abadan radar."

Rudi glanced at Zataki. "Ask who's in that airplane?" the man said.

"Who've you got aboard?"

There was a pause. "Four passengers. What's the problem?"

Rudi waited. Zataki did not know what to do. Any of the military bases might be listening in. "Let him land . . . near the hangar."

"Permission to land, HXT. Set her down near the east hangar."

"HXT."

Zataki leaned over and switched off the set. "In future you will only use the radio with permission."

"There are routine reports to give to Abadan and Kharg radar. My radio op's been with us f—"

Blood soared into Zataki's face and he shouted, "Until further orders your radio's only to be used with one of us listening in. Nor will any planes take off, nor land here without permission. You are responsible." Then the rage evaporated as quickly as it had arrived. He lifted his gun. The safety was still off. "If you'd continued the blow you would have broken my neck, my throat, and I would have died. Yes?"

After a pause, Rudi nodded. "Yes."

"Why did you stop?"

"I've . . . I've never killed anyone. I did not want to start."

"I've killed many—doing God's work. Many—thanks be to God. Many. And will kill many more enemies of Islam, with God's help." Zataki clicked on the safety. "It was the Will of God the blow was stopped, nothing more. I cannot give you that man. He is Iranian, this is Iran, he is an enemy of Iran and Islam."

They watched from the hangar as the 206 came in. There were four passengers aboard, all civilians, all armed with submachine guns. In the front seat was a mullah and some of Zataki's tension left him, but not his anger. The moment the chopper touched down his revolutionaries swarmed out of hiding, guns leveled, and surrounded her.

The mullah Hussain got out. His face tightened seeing Zataki's hostility. "Peace be with you. I am Hussain Kowissi of the Kowiss komiteh."

"Welcome to my area in the Name of God, mullah," Zataki said, his face even grimmer. "I am Colonel Zataki of the Abadan komiteh. We rule this area and do not approve of men putting themselves between us and God."

"Sunnis and Shi'as are brothers, Islam is Islam," Hussain said. "We thank our Sunni brethren of the Abadan oil fields for their support. Let us go and talk, our Islamic revolution is not yet won."

Tautly Zataki nodded and called his men off and beckoned the mullah to follow him out of earshot.

At once Rudi hurried under the rotors.

"What the hell's going on, Rudi?" Starke said from the cockpit, his shoulders aching, finishing shutdown procedures.

Rudi told him. "What about you?"

As rapidly Starke told him what had happened during the night and in Colonel Peshadi's office. "The mullah and these thugs came back at midday and they near bust a gut when I refused to fly armed men. Man, I liked to die, but I'm not flying armed men, that makes us accessories to revolution, and the revolution's nowhere near settled yet—we saw hundreds of troops and roadblocks coming here." His hard eyes went over the base and the pockets of Green Bands here and there, the rest of the crew still standing near their barracks under guard, and the fitter still senseless. "Bastards," he said and got out. He stretched against the ache in his back and felt better. "Eventually we compromised. They kept their weapons but I kept their magazines and stowed them in the baggage compart—" He stopped. The tall mullah, Hussain, was approaching them, the blade above circling leisurely now.

"The baggage key please, Captain," Hussain said.

Starke gave it to him. "There's no time to get back to Kowiss and no time to get to Abadan."

"Can't you night fly?"

"I can but it's against your regulations. You had a headset, you heard how radar is here. You'll have military choppers and airplanes buzzing us like hornets before we're halfway airborne. I'll refuel and we'll overnight here— least I will. You can always grab some transport from your buddies here if you need to go into town."

Hussain flushed. "Your time is very short, American," he said in Farsi. "You and all your imperialist parasites."

"If it is the Will of God, mullah, if it's the Will of God. I'll be ready to leave after first prayer. Then I leave, with or without you."

"You will take me to Abadan and wait and then return to Kowiss as I wish and as Colonel Peshadi ordered!"

Starke snapped in English, "If you're ready to leave after first prayer! But Peshadi didn't order it—I'm not under his orders, or yours—IranOil asked me to fly you on this charter. I'll have to refuel on the way back."

Hussain said irritably, "Very well, we will leave at dawn. As to refueling . . ." He thought a moment. "We will do that at Kharg."

Both Starke and Rudi were startled. "How we going to get cleared into Kharg? Kharg's loyal, er, still air force controlled. You'd have your heads blown off."

Hussain just looked at them. "You will wait here until the komiteh has decided. In one hour I want to talk to Kowiss on the HF." He stormed off.

Starke said quietly, "These bastards're too well organized, Rudi. We're up shit creek."

Rudi could feel the weakness in his legs. "We'd better get ourselves organized, prepare to get to hell out of here."

"We'll do that after food. You okay?"

"I thought I was dead. They're going to kill us all, Duke."

"I don't think so. For some reason we're VIPs to them. They need us and that's why Hussain backs off, your Zataki too. They might rough us up to keep us in line but I figure at least for the short haul we're important in some way." Again Starke tried to ease the tiredness out of his back and shoulders. "I could use one of Erikki's saunas." They both looked off at a burst of exuberant gunfire into the air from some Green Bands. "Crazy sonsofbitches. From what I overheard this operation's part of a general uprising to confront the armed forces—guns against guns. How's your radio reception? BBC or Voice of America?"

"Bad to very bad and jammed most days and nights. Of course Radio Free Iran's loud and clear as always." This was the Soviet station based just over the border at Baku on the Caspian Sea. "And Radio Moscow's like it was in your back garden, as always."

NEAR TABRIZ: 6:05 P.M. In the snow-covered mountains far to the north, not far from the Soviet border, Pettikin's 206 came over the rise fast, continuing to climb up the pass, skimming the trees, following the road.

"Tabriz One, HFC from Tehran. Do you read?" he called again.

Still no answer. Light was closing in, the late afternoon sun hidden by deep cloud cover that was only a few hundred feet above him, gray and heavy with snow. Again he tried to raise the base, very tired now, his face badly bruised and still hurting from the beating he had taken. His gloves and the broken skin over his knuckles made it awkward for him to press the transmit button. "Tabriz One. HFC from Tehran. Do you read?"

Again there was no answer but this did not worry him. Communication in the mountains was always bad, he was not expected, and there was no reason for Erikki Yokkonen or the base manager to have arranged a radio watch. As the road climbed, the cloud cover came down but he saw, thankfully, that the crest ahead was still clear, and once over it, the road fell away and there, half a mile farther on, was the base.

This morning it had taken him much longer than expected to drive to the small military air base at Galeg Morghi, not far from Tehran's international airport, and though he had left the apartment before dawn, he did not arrive there until a bleak sun was well into the polluted, smoke-filled sky. He had had to divert many times. Street battles were still going on with many roads blocked—some deliberately with barricades but more with burned-out wrecks of cars or buses. Many bodies sprawled on the snow-covered sidewalks and roadways, many wounded, and twice, angry police turned him back. But he persevered and took an even more circuitous route. When he arrived, to his surprise the gate to their section of the base where they operated a training school was open and unguarded. Normally air force sentries would be there. He drove in and parked his car in the safety of the S-G hangar but found none of the day skeleton crew of mechanics or ground personnel on duty.

It was a cold brisk day and he was bundled in winter flight gear. Snow covered the field and most of the runway. While he waited he ground-checked the 206 that he was going to take. Everything was fine. The spares that Tabriz needed, tail rotor and two hydraulic pumps, were in the baggage compartment. Tanks were full which gave it two and a half to three hours' range—two to three hundred miles depending on wind, altitude, and power settings. He would still have to refuel en route. His flight plan called for him to do this at Bandar-e Pahlavi, a port on the Caspian. Without effort he wheeled the airplane onto the apron. Then all hell let loose and he was on the edge of a battle.

Trucks filled with soldiers raced through the gate and headed across the field to be greeted with a hail of bullets from the main part of the base with its hangars, barracks, and administration buildings. Other trucks raced down the perimeter road, firing as they went, then a tracked armored Bren carrier joined the others, its machine guns blazing. Aghast, Pettikin recognized the shoulder badges and helmet markings of the Immortals. In their wake came armored buses filled with paramilitary police and other men who spread out over his side of the base, securing it. Before he knew what was happening, four of them grabbed him and dragged him over to one of the buses, shouting Farsi at him.

"For Christ's sake, I don't speak Farsi," he shouted back, trying to fight out of their grasp. Then one of them punched him in the stomach and he retched, tore himself free, and smashed his attacker in the face. At once another man pulled out a pistol and fired. The bullet went into the neck of his parka, ricocheted violently off the bus, speckles of burning cordite in its wake. He froze. Someone belted him hard across the mouth and the others started punching and kicking him. At that moment a police officer came over. "American? You American," he said angrily in bad English.

"I'm British," Pettikin gasped, the blood in his mouth, trying to free himself from the men who pinioned him against the hood of the bus. "I'm from S-G Helicopters and that's my—"

"American! Saboteur!" The man stuck his gun in Pettikin's face and Pettikin saw the man's finger tighten on the trigger. "We SAVAK know you Americans cause all our troubles!"

Then through the haze of his terror he heard a voice shout in Farsi and he felt the iron hands holding him loosen. With disbelief he saw the young British paratroop captain, dressed in a camouflage jumpsuit and red beret, two small, heavily armed soldiers with Oriental faces, grenades on their shoulder belts, packs on their backs, standing in front of them. Nonchalantly the captain was tossing a grenade up and down in his left hand as though it were an orange, the pin secured. He wore a revolver at his belt and a curiously shaped knife in a holster. Abruptly he stopped and pointed at Pettikin and then at the 206, angrily shouted at the police in Farsi, waved an imperious hand, and saluted Pettikin.

"For Christ's sake, look important, Captain Pettikin," he said quickly, his Scots accent pleasing, then knocked a policeman's hand away from Pettikin's arm. One of the others started to raise his gun but stopped as the captain jerked the pin out of his grenade, still holding the lever tight. At the same time his men cocked their automatic rifles, held them casually but very ready. The older of the two beamed, loosened his knife in its holster. "Is your chopper ready to go?"

"Yes . . . yes it is," Pettikin mumbled.

"Crank her up, fast as you can. Leave the doors open and when you're ready to leave, give me the thumbs-up and we'll all pile in. Plan to get out low and fast. Go on! Tenzing, go with him." The officer jerked his thumb at the chopper fifty yards away and turned back, switched to Farsi again, cursed the Iranians, ordering them away to the other side where the battle had waned a little. The soldier called Tenzing went with Pettikin who was still dazed.

"Please hurry, sahib," Tenzing said and leaned against one of the doors, his gun ready. Pettikin needed no encouragement.

More armored cars raced past but paid no attention to them, nor did other groups of police and military who were desperately intent on securing the base against the mobs who could now be heard approaching. Behind them the police officer was angrily arguing with the paratrooper, the others nervously looking over their shoulders at the advancing sound of "Allah-uuuu Akbarrrr!" Mixed with it was more gunfire now and a few explosions. Two hundred yards away on the perimeter road outside the fence, the vanguard of the mob set fire to a parked car and it exploded.

The helicopter's jet engines came to life and the sound enraged the police officer, but a phalanx of armed civilian youths came charging through the gate from the other direction. Someone shouted, "Mujhadin!" At once everyone this side of the base grouped to intercept them and began firing. Covered by the diversion, the captain and the other soldier rushed for the chopper, jumped in, Pettikin put on full power and fled a few inches above the grass, swerved to avoid a burning truck, then barreled drunkenly into the sky. The captain lurched, almost dropped his grenade, couldn't put the pin back in because of Pettikin's violent evading action. He was in the front seat and hung on for his life, held the door open, tossed the grenade carefully overboard, and watched it curve to the ground.

It exploded harmlessly. "Jolly good," he said, locked the door and his seat belt, checked that the two soldiers were okay, and gave a thumbs-up to Pettikin.

Pettikin hardly noticed. Once clear of Tehran he put her down in scrubland, well away from any roads or villages, and checked for bullet damage. When he saw there was none, he began to breathe. "Christ, I can't thank you enough, Captain," he said, putting out his hand, his head aching. "I thought you were a bloody mirage at first. Captain . . . ?"

"Ross. This's Sergeant Tenzing and Corporal Gueng."

Pettikin shook hands and thanked both of them. They were short, happy men, yet hard and lithe. Tenzing was older, in his early fifties. "You're heaven sent, all of you."

Ross smiled, his teeth very white in his sunburned face. "I didn't quite know how we were going to get out of that one. Wouldn't have been very good form to knock off police, anyone for that matter—even SAVAK."

"I agree." Pettikin had never seen such blue eyes in a man, judging him to be in his late twenties. "What the hell was going on back there?"

"Some air force servicemen had mutinied, and some officers, and loyalists were there to put a stop to it. We heard Khomeini supporters and leftists were coming to the help of the mutineers."

"What a mess! Can't thank you enough. How'd you know my name?"

"We'd, er, got wind of your approved flight plan to Tabriz via Bandar-e Pahlavi and wanted to hitch a ride. We were very late and thought we'd missed you—we were diverted to hell and gone. However, here we are."

"Thank God for that. You're Gurkhas?"

"Just, er, odd bods, so to speak."

Pettikin nodded thoughtfully. He had noticed that none of them had shoulder patches or insignias—except for Ross's captain's pips and their red berets. "How do 'odd bods' get wind of flight plans?"

"I really don't know," Ross said airily. "I just obey orders." He glanced around. The land was flat and stony and open, and cold with snow on the ground. "Don't you think we should move on? We're a bit exposed here."

Pettikin got back into the cockpit. "What's on in Tabriz?"

"Actually, we'd like to be dropped off just this side of Bandar-e Pahlavi, if you don't mind."

"Sure." Automatically Pettikin had begun start-up procedures. "What's going on there?"

"Let's say we have to see a man about a dog."

Pettikin laughed, liking him. "There're lots of dogs all over! Bandar-e Pahlavi it is, then, and I'll stop asking questions."

"Sorry, but you know how it is. I'd also appreciate it if you'd forget my name and that we were aboard."

"And if I'm asked—by authority? Our departure was a little public."

"I didn't give any name—just ordered you," Ross grinned, "with vile threats!"

"All right. But I won't forget your name."

Pettikin set down a few miles outside the port of Bandar-e Pahlavi. Ross had picked the landing from a map that he carried. It was a duned beach, well away from any village, the blue waters of the Caspian Sea placid. Fishing boats dotted the sea, great cumulus clouds in the sunny sky. Here the land was tropical and the air humid with many insects and no sign of snow though the Elburz Mountains behind Tehran were heavily covered. It was highly irregular to land without permission, but twice Pettikin had called Bandar-e Pahlavi Airport where he was to refuel and had got no answer so he thought that he would be safe enough—he could always plead an emergency.

"Good luck, and thanks again," he said and shook all their hands. "If you ever need a favor—anything—you've got it." They got out quickly, shouldered their packs, heading up the dunes. That was the last he had seen of them.

"Tabriz One, do you read?"

He was circling uneasily at the regulation seven hundred feet, then came lower. No sign of life—nor were any lights on. Strangely disquieted he landed close to the hangar. There he waited, ready for instant takeoff, not knowing what to expect—the news of servicemen mutinying in Tehran, particularly the supposedly elite air force, had disturbed him very much. But no one came. Nothing happened. Reluctantly, he locked the controls with great care and got out, leaving the engines running. It was very dangerous and against regulations—very dangerous because if the locks slipped it was possible for the chopper to ground-loop and get out of control.

But I don't want to get caught short, he thought grimly, rechecked the locks and quickly headed for the office through the snow. It was empty, the hangars empty except for the disemboweled 212, trailers empty, with no sign of anyone—or any form of a battle. A little more reassured, he went through the camp as quickly as he could. On the table in Erikki Yokkonen's cabin was an empty vodka bottle. A full one was in the refrigerator—he would dearly have loved a drink but flying and alcohol never mix. There was also bottled water, some Iranian bread, and dried ham. He drank the water gratefully. I'll eat only after I've gone over the whole place, he thought.

In the bedroom the bed was made but there was a shoe here and another there. Gradually his eyes found more signs of a hasty departure. The other trailers showed other clues. There was no transport on the base and Erikki's red Range Rover was gone too. Clearly the base had been abandoned somewhat hastily. But why?

His eyes gauged the sky. The wind had picked up and he heard it whine through the snow-laden forest over the muted growl of the idling jet engines. He felt the chill through his flying jacket and heavy pants and flying boots. His body ached for a hot shower—even better, one of Erikki's saunas—and food and bed and hot grog and eight hours' sleep. The wind's no problem yet, he thought, but I've got an hour of light at the most to refuel and get back through the pass and down into the plains. Or do I stay here tonight?

Pettikin was not a forest man, not a mountain man. He knew desert and bush, jungle, veld, and the Dead Country of Saudi. The vast reaches on the flat never fazed him. But cold did. And snow. First refuel, he thought.

But there was no fuel in the dump. None. Many forty-gallon drums but they were all empty. Never mind, he told himself, burying his panic. I've enough in my tanks for the hundred and fifty miles back to Bandar-e Pahlavi. I could go on to Tabriz Airport, or try and scrounge some from the ExTex depot at Ardabil, but that's too bloody near the Soviet border.

Again he measured the sky. Bloody hell! I can park here or somewhere en route. What's it to be?

Here. Safer.

He shut down and put the 206 into the hangar, locking the door. Now the silence was deafening. He hesitated, then went out, closing the hangar door after him. His feet crunched on the snow. The wind tugged at him as he walked to Erikki's trailer. Halfway there he stopped, his stomach twisting. He sensed someone watching him. He looked around, his eyes and ears searching the forest and the base. The wind sock danced in the eddies that trembled the treetops, creaking them, whining through the forest, and abruptly he remembered Tom Lochart sitting around a campfire in the Zagros on one of their skiing trips, telling the Canadian legend of the Wendigo, the evil demon of the forest, borne on the wild wind, that waits in the treetops, whining, waiting to catch you unawares, then suddenly swoops down and you're terrified and begin to run but you can't get away and you feel the icy breath behind you and you run and run with bigger and ever bigger steps until your feet are bloody stumps and then the Wendigo catches you up into the treetops and you die.

He shuddered, hating to be alone here. Curious, I've never thought about it before but I'm almost never alone. There's always someone around, mechanic or pilot or friend or Genny or Mac or Claire in the old days.

He was still watching the forest intently. Somewhere in the distance dogs began to bark. The feeling that there was someone out there was still very strong. With an effort he dismissed his unease, went back to the chopper, and found the Very light pistol. He carried the huge-caliber, snub-nosed weapon openly as he went back to Erikki's cabin and felt happier having it with him. And even happier when he had bolted the door and closed the curtains.

Night came quickly. With darkness animals began to hunt.

TEHRAN: 7:05 P.M.   McIver was walking along the deserted, tree-lined residential boulevard, tired and hungry. All streetlights were out and he picked his way carefully in the semidarkness, snow banked against the walls of fine houses on both sides of the roadway. Sound of distant guns and, carried on the cold wind, "Allahhh-u Akbarrr." He turned the corner and almost stumbled into the Centurion tank that was parked half on the sidewalk. A flashlight momentarily blinded him. Soldiers moved out of ambush. "Who're you, Agha?" a young officer said in good English. "What're you doing here?"

"I'm Captain . . . I'm Captain McIver, Duncan . . . Duncan McIver, I'm walking home from my office, and . . . and my flat's the other side of the park, around the next corner."

"ID please."

Gingerly McIver reached into his inner pocket. He felt the two small photos beside his ID, one of the Shah, the other of Khomeini, but with all the day's rumors of mutinies, he could not decide which would be correct so produced neither. The officer examined the ID under the flashlight. Now that McIver's eyes had adjusted to the darkness, he noticed the man's tiredness and stubble beard and crumpled uniform. Other soldiers watched silently. None were smoking which McIver found curious. The Centurion towered over them, malevolent, almost as though waiting to pounce.

"Thank you." The officer handed the well-used card back to him. More firing, nearer this time. The soldiers waited, watching the night. "Better not be out after dark, Agha. Good night."

"Yes, thank you. Good night." Thankfully McIver walked off, wondering if they were loyalist or mutineers—Christ, if some units mutiny and some don't there's going to be hell to pay. Another corner, this road and the park also dark and empty that, not so long ago, were always busy and brightly lit with more light streaming from windows, servants and people and children, all happy and lots of laughter among themselves, hurrying this way and that. That's what I miss most of all, he thought. The laughter. Wonder if we'll ever get those times back again.

His day had been frustrating, no phones, radio contact with Kowiss bad, and he had not been able to raise any of his other bases. Once again none of his office staff had arrived which further irritated him. Several times he had tried to telex Gavallan but could not get a connection. "Tomorrow'll be better," he said, then quickened his pace, the emptiness of the streets unpleasant.

Their apartment block was five stories and they had one of the penthouses. The staircase was dimly lit, electricity down to half power again, the elevator out of action for months. He went up the stairs wearily, the paucity of light making the climb more gloomy. But inside his apartment, candles were already lit and his spirits rose. "Hi, Genny!" he called out, relocked the door, and hung up his old British warm. "Whisky time!"

"Duncan! I'm in the dining room, come here for a minute."

He strode down the corridor, stopped at the doorway, and gaped. The dining table was laden with a dozen Iranian dishes and bowls of fruit, candles everywhere. Genny beamed at him. And so did Sharazad. "Bless my soul! Sharazad, this's your doing? How nice to see you wh—"

"Oh, it's nice to see you too, Mac, you get younger every day, both of you are, so sorry to intrude," Sharazad said in a rush, her voice bubbling and joyous, "but I remembered that yesterday was your wedding anniversary because it's five days before my birthday, and I know how you like lamb *horisht* and *polo* and the other things, so we brought them, Hassan, Dewa, and I, and candles." She was barely five foot three, the kind of Persian beauty that

Omar Khayyám had immortalized. She got up. "Now that you're back, I'm off."

"But wait a second, why don't you stay and eat with us an—"

"Oh but I can't, much as I'd like to, Father's having a party tonight and I have to attend. This is just a little gift and I've left Hassan to serve and to clean up and oh I do hope you have a lovely time! Hassan! Dewa!" she called out, then hugged Genny and hugged McIver and ran down to the door where her two servants were now waiting. One held her fur coat for her. She put it on, then wrapped the dark shroud of her chador around her, blew Genny another kiss, and, with the other servant, hurried away. Hassan, a tall man of thirty, wearing a white tunic and black trousers and a big smile, relocked the door. "Shall I serve dinner, madam?" he asked Genny in Farsi.

"Yes, please, in ten minutes," she replied happily. "But first the master will have a whisky." At once Hassan went to the sideboard and poured the drink and brought the water, bowed, and left them.

"By God, Gen, it's just like the old days," McIver said with a beam.

"Yes. Silly, isn't it, that that's only a few months ago?" Up to then they had had a delightful live-in couple, the wife an exemplary cook of European and Iranian food who made up for the lighthearted malingering of her husband whom McIver had dubbed Ali Baba. Both had suddenly vanished, as had almost all expat servants. No explanation, no notice. "Wonder if they're all right, Duncan?"

"Sure to be. Ali Baba was a grafter and had to have enough stashed away to keep them for a month of Sundays. Did Paula get off?"

"No, she's staying the night again—Nogger isn't. They went to dinner with some of her Alitalia crew." Her eyebrows arched. "Our Nogger's sure she's ripe for nogging, but I hope he's wrong. I like Paula." They could hear Hassan in the kitchen. "That's the sweetest sound in the world."

McIver grinned back at her and raised his glass. "Thank God for Sharazad and no washing up!"

"That's the best part." Genny sighed. "Such a nice girl, so thoughtful. Tom's so lucky. Sharazad says he's due tomorrow."

"Hope so, he'll have mail for us."

"Did you get hold of Andy?"

"No, no, not yet." McIver decided not to mention the tank. "Do you think you could borrow Hassan or one of her other servants for a couple of days a week? It'd help you tremendously."

"I wouldn't ask—you know how it is."

"I suppose you're right, bloody annoying." Now it was almost impossible for any expats to find help, whatever you were prepared to pay. Up to a few months ago it had been easy to get fine, caring servants and then, with a few words of Farsi and their help, running a happy home, shopping was usually a breeze.

"That was one of the best things about Iran," she said. "Made such a difference—took all the agony out of living in such an alien country."

"You still think of it as alien—after all this time?"

"More than ever. All the kindness, politeness, of the few Iranians we'd meet, I've always felt it was only on the surface—that their real feelings are the ones out in the open now—I don't mean everyone, of course, not our friends: Annoush, for instance, now she's one of the nicest, kindest people in the world." Annoush was the wife of General Valik, the senior of the Iranian partners. "Most of the wives felt that, Duncan," she added, lost in her musing. "Perhaps that's why expats flock together, all the tennis parties and skiing parties, boating, weekends on the Caspian—and servants to carry the picnic baskets and clean up. I think we had the life of Riley, but not anymore."

"It'll come back—hope to God it does, for them as well as us. Walking home I suddenly realized what I missed most. It was all the laughter. No one seems to laugh anymore, I mean on the streets, even the kids." McIver was drinking his whisky sparingly.

"Yes, I miss the laughter very much. I miss the Shah too. Sorry he had to go—everything was well ordered, as far as we were concerned, up to such a short time ago. Poor man, what a rotten deal we've given him now, him and that lovely wife of his—after all the friendship he gave our side. I feel quite ashamed—he certainly did his best for his people."

"Unfortunately, Genny, for most of them it seems it wasn't good enough!"

"I know. Sad. Life is very sad sometimes. Well, no point in crying over spilt milk. Hungry?"

"I'll say."

Candles made the dining room warm and friendly and took the chill off the apartment. Curtains were drawn against the night. At once Hassan brought the steaming bowls of various horisht—literally meaning soup but more like a thick stew of lamb or chicken and vegetables, raisins and spices of all kinds—and polo, the delicious Iranian rice that is parboiled, then baked in a buttered dish until the crust is firm and golden brown, a favorite of both of them. "Bless Sharazad, she's a sight for sore eyes."

Genny smiled back at him. "Yes, she is, so's Paula."

"You're not so bad either, Gen."

"Get on with you, but for that you can have a nightcap. As Jean-Luc would say, *Bon appétit!*" They ate hungrily, the food exquisite, reminding both of them of meals they had had in the houses of their friends.

"Gen, I ran into young Christian Tollonen at lunch, you remember Erikki's friend from the Finnish embassy? He told me Azadeh's passport was all ready. That's good, but the thing that shook me was he said, in passing, about eight out of every ten of his Iranian friends or acquaintances are no longer in Iran and if it kept up in the new exodus, pretty soon there'd only be mullahs and their flocks left. Then I started counting and came up with about the same proportion—those in what we'd call the middle and upper class."

"I don't blame them leaving. I'd do the same." Then she added involuntarily, "Don't think Sharazad will."

McIver had heard an undercurrent and he studied her. "Oh?"

Genny toyed with a little piece of the golden crust and changed her mind about not telling him. "For the love of God don't say anything to Tom who'd have a fit—and I don't know how much is fact and how much a young girl's idealistic make-believe—but she happily whispered she'd spent most of the day at Doshan Tappeh where, she says, there's been a real insurrection, guns, grenades, the lot . . ."

"Christ!"

". . . militantly on the side of what she called 'our Glorious Freedom Fighters' who turn out to be mutinying air force servicemen, some officers, Green Bands supported by thousands of civilians—against police, loyalist troops, and the Immortals. . . ."

AT BANDAR DELAM AIRPORT: 7:50 P.M. With the going down of the sun, more armed revolutionaries had arrived and now there were guards on all hangars and approaches to the airport. Rudi Lutz had been told by Zataki that no S-G personnel could leave the field without permission and they were to continue as usual and one or more of his men would accompany every flight. "Nothing will happen providing you all obey orders," Zataki had said. "This is a temporary situation during the change from the Shah's illegal government to the new government of the people." But his nervousness and that of all his ill-disciplined rabble belied his attempt at confidence.

Starke had heard mutterings among them and told Rudi they expected troops loyal to the Shah to arrive any moment and the counterattack to begin. By the time he, Rudi, and the other American pilot, Jon Tyrer, had managed to get to the radio in Rudi's trailer, most of the news was over. The little they heard of it was all bad.

". . . and the Saudi, Kuwait, and Iraqi governments fear that the political turmoil in Iran will destabilize the entire Persian Gulf, with the Sultan of Oman reported as saying the problem is more than just a contagion, it's another convenient umbrella for Soviet Russia to use its string of client states to create nothing less than a colonial empire in the Gulf with the end goal of possessing the Strait of Hormuz . . ."

"In Iran it is reported that there was heavy fighting during the night between mutinying, pro-Khomeini air cadets at the Tehran air base of Doshan Tappeh—supported by thousands of armed civilians—against police, loyalist troops, and units of the Immortals, the Shah's elite Imperial Guard. Joining the insurgents later were over five thousand leftists of the Saihkal Marxist Group, some of whom broke into the base's armory and carried away its weapons . . .

"Jesus!" Starke said.

". . . Meanwhile Ayatollah Khomeini again demanded total resignation of the whole government and called on the people to support his choice of prime minister, Mehdi Bazargan, exhorting all soldiers, airmen, and navy personnel to support him. Prime Minister Bakhtiar discounted rumors of an imminent military coup, but confirmed a big buildup of Soviet forces on the border. . . .

"Gold went to an all-time high of $254 per ounce and the dollar slumped sharply against all currencies. That is the end of the news from London."

Rudi switched the set off. They were in the sitting room of his trailer. In one of the cabinets was a spare HF that, like the radio, he had built in himself. On the sideboard was a telephone that was hooked up to the base system. The telephone was not working.

"If Khomeini wins at Doshan Tappeh, then the armed forces will have to choose," Starke said with finality. "Coup, civil war, or concede."

"They won't concede, that'd be suicide, why the hell should they?" Tyrer said. He was a loose-limbed American from New Jersey. "And don't forget the air force elite, the ones we've met, for crissake. The mutiny's just a bunch of local meathead discontents. The real kicker's about the Marxists joining in, five thousand of them! Jesus! If they're out in the open now with guns! We're goddamn crazy to be here right now, huh?"

Starke said, "Except we're here by choice; the company says no one loses seniority if they want out. We've got it in writing. You want out?"

"No, no, not yet," Tyrer said irritably. "But what we gonna do?"

"Stay out of the way of Zataki for one thing," Rudi said. "That bastard's psycho."

"Sure," Tyrer said, "but we've gotta make a plan."

There was an abrupt knock and the door opened. It was Mohammed Yemeni, their IranOil base manager—a good looking, clean-shaven man in his forties who had been in their area for a year. With him were two guards. "Agha Kyabi is on the HF. He wants to speak to you at once," he said with an untoward imperiousness. Kyabi was IranOil's senior area manager and most important official in southern Iran.

At once Rudi switched on the HF which interlinked them with Kyabi's HQ near Ahwaz, north of Bandar Delam. To his astonishment the set did not activate. He jiggled the switch a few times, then Yemeni said with an open sneer, "Colonel Zataki ordered the current cut off and the set disconnected. You will use the main office set. At once."

None of them liked the tone of voice. "I'll be there in a minute," Rudi said.

Yemeni scowled and said to the guards in coarse Farsi, "Hurry the dog of a foreigner!"

Starke snapped in Farsi, "This is our ruler's tent. There are very particular laws in the Holy Koran about defending the leader of your tribe in his tent against armed men." The two guards stopped, nonplussed. Yemeni gaped at Starke, not expecting Farsi, then backed a pace as Starke got up to his full height and continued: "The Prophet, whose Name be praised, laid down rules of manners amongst friends, and also amongst enemies, and also that dogs are vermin. We are People of the Book and not vermin."

Yemeni flushed, turned on his heel, and left. Starke wiped the sweat from his hands on his trousers. "Rudi, let's see what's with Kyabi."

They followed Yemeni across the tarmac, the guards with them. The night was clean and the air tasted good to Starke after the closeness of the little office.

"What was all that about?" Rudi asked.

Starke explained, his mind elsewhere, wishing he was back at Kowiss. He had hated leaving Manuela but thought she was safer there than in Tehran. "Honey," he had said, just before he had left, "I'll get you out the soonest."

"I'm safe here, darlin', safe as Texas. I've got lots of time, the kids are safe in Lubbock—I didn't leave England till I knew they were home—and you know Granddaddy Starke won't let them come to harm."

"Sure. The kids'll be fine, but I want you out of Iran as soon as possible."

He heard Rudi saying, "Who're 'People of the Book'?"

"Christians and Jews," he replied, wondering how he could get the 125 into Kowiss. "Mohammed considered our Bible and the Torah as Holy Books too—a lot of what's in them's also in the Koran. Many scholars, our scholars, think he just copied them, though Muslim legend says that Mohammed couldn't read or write. He recited the Koran, all of it, can you imagine that?" he said, still awed by the accomplishment. "Others wrote it all down—years after he was dead. In Arabic it's fantastically beautiful, his poetry, so they say."

Ahead now was the office trailer, guards outside smoking, and Starke felt good within himself and pleased that he had dealt satisfactorily with Yemeni and all day with the mullah Hussain—fifteen landings, all perfect, waiting at the rigs while the mullah harangued the workers for Khomeini with never a soldier or policeman or SAVAK in sight, expecting them any second and always at the next setdown. Yemeni's chicken shit compared to Hussain, he thought.

Zataki and both mullahs were waiting in the office trailer. Jahan, the radio op, was on the HF. Zataki sat behind Rudi's desk. The office had been very neat. Now it was a mess, with files open and papers spilled everywhere, dirty cups, cigarette stubs in the cups and on the floor, half-eaten food on the desk —rice and goat meat. And the air stank of cigarette smoke.

"*Mein Gott!*" Rudi said, enraged. "It's a *verrückte* pigsty and y—"

"SHUT UP!" Zataki exploded. "This is a war situation, we need to search," then added, more quietly, "You . . . you can send one of your men to clean up. You will not tell Kyabi about us. You will act normally and take my instructions, you will watch me. Do you understand, Captain?"

Rudi nodded, his face set. Zataki motioned to the radio op who said into the mike, "Excellency Kyabi, here is Captain Lutz."

Rudi took the mike. "Yes, Boss?" he said, using their nickname for him. Both he and Starke had known Yusuf Kyabi for a number of years. Kyabi had been trained at Texas A&M, then by ExTex before taking over the southern sector, and they were on good terms with him.

"Evening, Rudi," the voice said in American English. "We've a break in one of our pipelines, somewhere north of you. It's a bad one—it's only just shown up in our pumping stations. God knows how many barrels have been pumped out already, or how much is left in the pipe. I'm not calling for a CASEVAC but want a helicopter at dawn to find it. Can you pick me up early?"

Zataki nodded in agreement so Rudi said, "Okay, Boss. We'll be there as soon after dawn as possible. Would you want a 206 or 212?"

"A 206, there'll be me and my chief engineer. Come yourself, will you? It may be sabotage—may be a break. You had any problems at Bandar Delam?"

Rudi and Starke were very conscious of the guns in the room. "No, no more than usual. See you tomorrow," Rudi said, wanting to cut him off because Kyabi was usually very outspoken about revolutionaries. He did not

approve of insurrection or Khomeini's fanaticism, and hated the interference
with their oil complex.

"Hold on a moment, Rudi. We heard there're more riots in Abadan, and
we could hear shooting in Ahwaz. Did you know that an American oilman
and one of our own people were ambushed and killed near Ahwaz, yesterday?"

"Yes, Tommy Stanson. Lousy."

"Very. God curse all murderers! Tudeh, mujhadin, fedayeen, or whom the
hell ever!"

"Sorry, Boss, got to go, see you tomorrow."

"Yes. Good, we can talk tomorrow. Insha'Allah, Rudi. Insha'Allah!"

The transmission went dead. Rudi breathed a sigh of relief. He did not
think that Kyabi had said anything that could harm him. Unless these men
were secretly Tudeh—or one of the other extremists—and not Khomeini
supporters as they claimed. "All our extremists use mullahs as a cover, or try
to use them," Kyabi had told him. "Sadly most mullahs are impoverished,
dull-witted peasants, and easy prey for trained insurgents. God curse
Khomeini. . . ."

Rudi felt the sweat on his back.

"One of my men will go with you, and this time you will not remove his
magazine," Zataki said.

Rudi's jaw came out and tension in the room soared. "I will not fly armed
men. It is against all company rules, air rules, and particularly Iranian CAA
orders. Disobeying ICAA rules invalidates our licenses," he said, loathing
them.

"Perhaps I will shoot one of your men unless you obey." Furiously Zataki
slammed a cup off his desk and it skittered across the room.

Starke came forward, as angry. Zataki's gun covered him. "Are the followers of Ayatollah Khomeini murderers? Is this the law of Islam?"

For a moment Starke thought Zataki was going to pull the trigger, then
the mullah Hussain got up. "I will go in the airplane." Then to Rudi, "You
swear you will play no tricks and return here without tricks?"

After a pause Rudi said shakily, "Yes."

"You are Christian?"

"Yes."

"Swear by God you will not cheat us."

Again Rudi paused. "All right. I swear by God I won't cheat you."

"How can you trust him?" Zataki asked.

"I don't," Hussain said simply. "But if he cheats God, God will punish him. And his companions. If we don't return or if he brings back trouble . . ." He shrugged.

ABERDEEN—GAVALLAN'S MANSION: 7:23 P.M. They were in the TV room watching on a big screen a replay of today's rescheduled Scotland versus France rugby match—Gavallan, his wife Maureen, John Hogg who normally flew the company 125 jet, and some other pilots. The score was 17–11 in France's favor deep in the second half. All the men groaned as a Scot fumbled, a French forward recovered and gained forty yards. "Ten pounds that Scotland still wins!" Gavallan said.

"I'll take that," his wife said and laughed at his look. She was tall and red-haired and wore elegant green that matched her eyes. "After all I'm half French."

"A quarter—your grandmother was Norman, *quelle horreur*, and sh—" An enormous cheer that was echoed in the room drowned his pleasantry as the Scottish scrum half grabbed the ball from the scrimmage, threw it to a wing half who threw it to another who broke loose of the pack, smashed two enemy out of his way, and hurtled for the goal line fifty yards away, weaving, brilliantly changing direction to rush onward again, then stumble but somehow stay upright, then charge in a last, chest-heaving glorious run to dive over the line—to be buried at once by bodies and thunderous applause. Touchdown! 17 to 15 now. A successful goal kick will make it 17 all. "Scotland foreverrrr . . ."

The door opened and a manservant stood there. At once Gavallan got up, achingly watched the kick that was good and breathed again. "Double or nothing, Maureen?" he asked over the pandemonium, grinning at her as he hurried off.

"Taken!" she called out after him.

She's down twenty quid, he thought, very pleased with himself, and crossed the corridor of the big, rambling old house that was well furnished with old leather and good paintings and fine antiques, many of them from Asia, and went into his study opposite. In it, his chauffeur, also gun bearer and trusty, who had been dialing McIver in Tehran for three hours and monitoring his incoming calls, held up one of the two phones. "Sorry to interrupt, sir, th—"

"You got him, Williams? Great—score's seventeen all."

"No, sir, sorry, circuits're still busy—but I thought this one was important enough—Sir Ian Dunross."

Gavallan's disappointment vanished. He took the phone. Williams went out and closed the door. "Ian, how wonderful to hear from you—this is a pleasant surprise."

"Hello, Andy, can you speak up, I'm phoning from Shanghai?"

"I thought you were in Japan; I can hear you very well. How's it going?"

"Grand. Better than I expected. Listen, have to be quick but I heard a buzz, two in fact, the first that the taipan needs some financial success to get himself and Struan's out of the hole this year. What about Iran?"

"Everyone advises that it will cool down, Ian. Mac's got things under control, as much as possible; we've been promised all of Guerney's contracts so we should be able to more than keep our end up, even double our profits, presuming there's no Act of God."

"Perhaps you should presume there might be."

Gavallan's bonhomie vanished. Time and again his old friend had privately given him a warning or information that had later proved to be astonishingly correct—he never knew where Dunross obtained the information, or from whom, but he was rarely wrong. "I'll do that right away."

"Next, I've just heard that a secret, very high-level—even perhaps cabinet level—shuffle has been ordered, financial as well as management, for Imperial Air. Will that affect you?"

Gavallan hesitated. Imperial Air owned Imperial Helicopters, his main competition in the North Sea. "I don't know, Ian. In my opinion they squander taxpayers' money; they could certainly use reorganization—we beat them hands down in every area I can think of, safety, tenders, equipment—I've ordered six X63s by the way."

"Does the taipan know?"

"The news almost broke his sphincter." Gavallan heard the laugh, and for a moment he was back in Hong Kong in the old days when Dunross was taipan and life was hairy but wildly exciting, when Kathy was Kathy and not sick. Joss, he thought, and again concentrated. "Anything to do with Imperial's important—I'll check at once. Other business news from here is very good—new contracts with ExTex—I was going to announce them at the next board meeting. Struan's isn't in danger, is it?"

Again the laugh. "The Noble House is always in danger, laddie! Just wanted to advise you—got to go—give my love to Maureen."

"And to Penelope. When do I see you?"

"Soon. I'll call when I can; give my best to Mac when you see him, bye."

Lost in thought, Gavallan sat on the edge of his fine desk. His friend always said "soon" and that could mean a month or a year, even two years. It's over two years since I last caught up with him, he thought. Pity he's not taipan still—damn shame he retired, but then we all have to move on and move over sometime. "I've had it, Andy," Dunross had said, "Struan's is in cracking good shape, the '70s promise to be a fantastic era for expansion and . . . well, now there's no excitement anymore." That was in '70, just after his hated main rival, Quillan Gornt, taipan of Rothwell-Gornt, had drowned in a boating accident off Sha Tin in Hong Kong's New Territories.

Imperial Air? Gavallan glanced at his watch, reached for the phone, but stopped at the discreet knock. Maureen stuck her head in, beamed when she saw he wasn't on the phone. "I won—twenty-one to seventeen—busy?"

"No, come in, darling."

"Can't, have to check dinner's ready. In ten minutes? You can pay me now if you like!"

He laughed, caught her in his arms, and gave her a hug. "After dinner! You're a smashing bird, Mrs. Gavallan."

"Good, don't forget." She was comfortable in his arms. "Everything all right with Mac?"

"It was Ian—he just called to say hello. From Shanghai."

"Now there's a lovely man too. When do we see him?"

"Soon."

Again she laughed with him, dancing eyes and creamy skin. They had first met seven years ago at Castle Avisyard where the then taipan, David Mac-Struan, was giving a Hogmanay Ball. She was twenty-eight, just divorced, and childless. Her smile had blown the cobwebs from his head and Scot had whispered, "Dad, if you don't drag that one off to the altar, you're crazy." His daughter Melinda had said the same. And so, somehow, three years ago it had happened, and every day since then a happy day.

"Ten minutes, Andy? You're sure?"

"Yes, just have to make one call." Gavallan saw her frown and added quickly, "Promise. Just one and then Williams can monitor the calls."

She gave him a quick kiss and left. He dialed. "Good evening, is Sir Percy free—this is Andrew Gavallan." Sir Percy Smedley-Taylor, director of Struan's Holdings, an MP, and slated as the probable minister for defence if the Conservatives won the next election.

"Hello, Andy, nice to hear from you—if it's about the shoot next Saturday, I'm on. Sorry not to have told you before but things have been rather busy with the so-called government shoving the country up the creek, and the poor bloody unions as well, if they only knew it."

"I quite agree. Am I disturbing you?"

"No, you just caught me—I'm off to the House for another late-night vote. The stupid twits want us out of NATO, amongst other things. How did the X63 test out?"

"Wonderful! Better than they claimed. She's the best in the world!"

"I'd love a ride in her if you could fix it. What can I do for you?"

"I heard a buzz that there's a secret, high-level reorganization of Imperial Air going on. Have you heard anything?"

"My God, old man, your contacts are bloody good—I only heard the rumor myself this afternoon, whispered in absolute secrecy by an unimpeachable Opposition source. Damn curious! Didn't mean much to me at the time —wonder what they're up to. Have you anything concrete to go on?"

"No. Just the rumor."

"I'll check. I wonder . . . I wonder if the burks might be positioning Imperial to formally nationalize it, therefore Imp Helicopters, therefore you and all the North Sea?"

"God Almighty!" Gavallan's worry increased. This thought had not occurred to him. "Could they do that if they wanted?"

"Yes. Simple as that."

SUNDAY
February 11

U.S.S.R.

Caspian Sea

U.S.S.R.

TURKEY

KHOI
TABRIZ

MOUNT
SABALAN

BANDAR-E
PAHLAVI

QAZVIN

★ TEHRAN

IRAQ

AFGHANISTAN

IRAN

BAGHDAD

DEZ DAM

ZAGROS

• ISFAHAN

BANDAR DELAM

Shatt-
al-Arab
Estuary

ABADAN

• ZAGROS THREE

KOWISS

MOUNTAINS

KUWAIT

KHARG

JELLET

Persian Gulf

LENGEH

Strait of
Hormuz

PAKISTAN

BAHRAIN

SAUDI
ARABIA

QATAR

SÎRI

Gulf of Oman

AL SHARGAZ

OUTSIDE BANDAR DELAM: 6:55 A.M. It was just after dawn and Rudi had landed away from the culvert and now the four of them were standing on the lip. The early sun was good, and so far no problems. Oil still poured out of the pipe but it was no longer under pressure. "It's just what's left in the line," Kyabi said. "It should stop entirely in an hour." He was a strong-faced man in his fifties, clean-shaven with glasses, and he wore used khakis and a hard hat. Angrily he looked around. The earth was soaked with oil and the fumes almost overpowering. "This whole area's lethal." He led the way to the overturned car. Three bodies were twisted in or near the wreckage and already beginning to smell.

"Amateurs?" Rudi said, waving away the flies. "Premature explosion?"

Kyabi did not answer. He went below into the culvert. It was hard to breathe but he searched the area carefully, then climbed back onto the road. "I'd say you were right, Rudi." He glanced at Hussain, his face set. "Yours?"

The mullah took his eyes off the car. "It is not the Imam's orders to sabotage pipelines. This is the work of enemies of Islam."

"There are many enemies of Islam who claim to be Followers of the Prophet, who have taken his words and twisted them," Kyabi said bitterly, "betraying him and betraying Islam."

"I agree, and God will seek them out and punish them. When Iran is ruled according to Islamic law we will seek them out and punish them for Him." Hussain's dark eyes were equally hard. "What can you do about the oil spill?"

It had taken them two hours backtracking to find the break. They had circled at a few hundred feet, appalled at the extent of the spill that had inundated the small river and its marshlands and carried by the current was already some miles downstream. A thick black scum covered the surface from bank to bank. So far only one village was in its path. A few miles south there were many others. The river supplied drinking water, washing water, and was the latrine.

"Burn it off. As soon as possible." Kyabi glanced at his engineer. "Eh?"

"Yes, yes, of course. But what about the village, Excellency?" The engineer was a nervous, middle-aged Iranian who watched the mullah uneasily.

"Evacuate the villagers—tell them to leave until it's safe."

"And if the village catches fire?" Rudi asked.

"It catches fire. The Will of God."

"Yes," Hussain said. "How will you burn it off?"

"One match would do most of it. Of course you'd burn up too." Kyabi thought a moment. "Rudi, you've your Very pistol aboard?"

"Yes." Rudi had insisted on taking the pistol, saying it was essential equipment in case of an emergency. All the pilots had backed him though all knew it was not essential. "With four signal flares. Do yo—"

They all looked into the sky at the scream of approaching jets. Two fighters, low and very fast, slashed over the terrain heading out into the Gulf. Rudi judged their path as leading directly to Kharg. They were attack fighters and he had seen the air-to-ground missiles in their racks. Are the missiles for Kharg Island? he asked himself, a new tightness in his throat. Has the revolution hit there too? Or is it just a routine flight?

"What do you think, Rudi? Kharg?" Kyabi asked.

"Kharg's that way, Boss," Rudi said, not wanting to be involved. "If so it'd be a routine flight. We'd have dozens of takeoffs and landings a day when we were there. You want to use flares to set the fire?"

Kyabi hardly heard him. His clothes were stained with sweat, his desert boots black with the oil ooze. He was thinking about the air force revolt at Doshan Tappeh. If those two pilots are also in revolt and attack Kharg and sabotage our facilities there, he thought, almost choked with rage and frustration, Iran will go back twenty years.

When Rudi had come to collect him early this morning, Kyabi had been astonished to see the mullah. He had demanded an explanation. When the mullah angrily said that Kyabi should close down all facilities and declare for Khomeini at once, he was almost speechless. "But that's revolution. That means civil war!"

Hussain had said, "It is the Will of God. You're Iranian, not a foreign lackey. The Imam has ordered confrontation with the armed forces to subdue them. With God's help, the first true Islamic republic on earth since the days of the Prophet, the Blessings of God be upon him, begins in a few days."

Kyabi had wanted to say what he had said privately many times: "It's a madman's dream, and your Khomeini's an evil, senile old man, driven by a personal vendetta against the Pahlavis—Reza Shah whose police he believes murdered his father, and Mohammed Shah whose SAVAK he believes murdered his son in Iraq a few years ago; he's nothing but a narrow-minded fanatic who wants to put us, the people, and particularly women, back into the Dark Ages. . . ."

But he had said none of this today to this mullah. Instead, he put his mind back onto the problem of the village. "If the village catches fire, they can easily rebuild it. Their possessions are the important things." He hid his hatred. "You can help, if you want, Excellency. I would appreciate your help. You can talk to them."

The villagers refused to go. For the third time Kyabi explained that fire was the only way to save their water and to save the other villages. Then Hussain talked to them, but still they would not go. By now it was time for the midday prayer and the mullah led them in prayer and again told them to leave the banks of the river. The elders consulted with one another and said, "It is the Will of God. We will not leave."

"It is the Will of God," Hussain agreed. He turned on his heel and led the way back to the helicopter.

Once more they landed near the culvert. Now oil just seeped out of the pipe, no more than a trickle. "Rudi," Kyabi said, "go upwind, far as you can, and put a flare into the culvert. Then put one smack in the middle of the stream. Can you do that?"

"I can try. I've never fired a Very pistol before." Rudi plodded out into the scrub desert. The others went back to the chopper which he had parked safely away. When he was in position he put the large cartridge into the pistol, aimed, and pulled the trigger. The gun kicked, more than he expected. The burning phosphorus signal flare arced low over the ground, bounced as it came down short, then skipped into the air again and fell into the culvert. For a moment nothing happened, then the earth exploded and fire gushed upward and outward, making the overturned car into a funeral pyre. The superheated shock wave enveloped him but passed by safely. Acrid black smoke billowed skyward. Fire began spreading, racing toward the stream.

The second red flare arced high and then went into the river. The river caught fire. They knew it more from the sound than sight, but when they were airborne once more, skirting the river upwind, they saw the fire spreading rapidly downstream. Vast clouds of black smoke marked its path. Near the village they circled. Men, women, and children were fleeing with what they could carry. As they watched, the village was consumed.

The four men flew home.

Home for Kyabi was the area HQ of IranOil just outside Ahwaz, a neat complex of white concrete buildings with well-watered lawns and a helipad, enclosed by a tall fence.

"Thanks, Rudi," he said, sick at heart. Around the chopper was a ring of armed men who had rushed out of hiding the moment they had landed, shouting and pointing their guns. Behind Kyabi the mullah toyed with his string of prayer beads.

Kyabi unbuckled his seat belt. The Will of God, he thought. I've done what I could, prayed correctly, and know that there is no other God but God and Mohammed is the Prophet of God. When I die I will die cursing the enemies of God, chief among them, Khomeini, False Prophet, murderer, and all those who follow him.

He turned around. His engineer was gray-faced and rigid in his seat beside Hussain. "Mullah, I commend you to God's vengeance." Kyabi got out.

They shot Kyabi and dragged the engineer away. Then, because the mullah asked it, they allowed the chopper to leave.

AT KOWISS AIR BASE: 5:09 P.M.   Manuela was hurrying across the S-G compound toward the one-story office building that was tidy under the afternoon sun, the radio tower jutting above as a second floor. She wore flight overalls with the S-G emblem on the back and her auburn hair was bundled into a long peaked flight cap, but her walk shouted her femininity.

In the outer office were three of their Iranian staff. Politely they got up and smiled, watching her under heavy-lidded eyes.

"Good afternoon, Excellency Pavoud," she said in Farsi with a smile. "Captain Ayre wanted to see me?"

"Yes, Madam Lady. His Excellency's in the tower," the chief clerk replied. "May I have the honor of escorting you?" She declined with thanks, and when she had gone along the corridor and up the spiral staircase, Pavoud said contemptuously, "Scandalous the way she flaunts herself at us—she does it just to taunt us."

"Worse than a public woman from the Old Quarter, Excellency," another said, equally disgusted. "By God, of all Infidels, Americans are the worst and their women the worst. And that one, that one's asking, that one's begging for trouble. . . ."

"She's begging for a good Iranian cock," a small man said, scratching himself.

Pavoud said, "She should wear a chador and cover herself and walk modestly. We are all men here. We've all sired children. Does she think we're eunuchs?"

"She should be whipped for taunting us."

Pavoud picked his nose delicately. "With God's help, soon she will be—publicly. Everyone will be subject to Islamic law, and punishments."

"They say that American women have no pubics."

"No, it's just that they shave those parts."

"Pubics or no, Excellency Chief Clerk, I'd like to thrust it into her, until she squealed—with joy," the small man said, and they laughed together.

"That great oaf of her husband has every night since she's been here." The chief clerk's eyes glittered. "I've heard them moaning in the night." He lit a cigarette from the butt of the last, then got up and looked out of the window. He wore glasses and peered into the sky until he saw the distant chopper turn on to final. Death to all foreigners, he thought, then added in his most secret heart: And death to Khomeini and his parasites! Long live the Tudeh and the revolution of the Masses!

The tower was small with glass windows on all sides and well equipped. This had been their permanent base for many years, so S-G had had time to fit it out with some modern air safety and all-weather landing aids. Freddy Ayre, senior pilot in Starke's absence, was waiting for Manuela.

"HXB's on final," he said as she came up the stairs. "He—"

"Oh, wonderful," she interrupted happily. They had been trying to contact Starke all day without success: "Not to worry," Ayre had told her, "their HF often goes out, same's ours." Since last night, just after dark, the only communication had been Starke's terse report that he was overnighting at Bandar Delam and would contact them today.

"Sorry, Manuela, but Duke's not aboard. Marc Dubois's flying her."

"There's been an accident?" she burst out, her world tumbling. "He's hurt?"

"Oh, no, nothing like that. When Marc reported in a few minutes ago, he said Duke had stayed behind at Bandar Delam and he'd been told to fly the mullah and his team on the return trip."

"Is that all? You're sure?"

"Yes. Look," Ayre said, pointing out of the window, "there she is."

The 206 was coming out of the sun nicely. Behind her the Zagros Mountains reached skyward. Below were the chimney stacks of the vast refinery, plumes of fire from waste gases perpetually burning off. She touched down in the exact center of Landing Pad One. "HXB shutting down," Marc Dubois said over the radio.

"Roger, HXB," S-G's duty tower operator, Massil Tugul, a Palestinian and longtime employee, replied. He switched to the main base frequency. "Base, we have no birds in the system now. I confirm HVU and HCF will return before sunset."

"Okay, S-G." There was a moment of quiet, then over the main base channel, they heard a voice cut in harshly in Farsi, transmitting from the 206. It went on for half a minute, then ceased.

Massil muttered, "Insha'Allah!"

"Who the hell was that?" Ayre said.

"The mullah Hussain, Agha."

"What the hell did he say?" Ayre asked him, forgetting Manuela could speak Farsi.

Massil hesitated. Manuela answered for him, her face white. "The mullah said, 'In the Name of God and in the Name of the Whirlwind of God, strike!' over and over, just ov—" She stopped.

From the other side of the airfield came the muted sound of gunfire. At once Ayre took the mike. *"Marc, à la tour, vite, immédiatement,"* he ordered, his accent excellent, then squinted at the base, half a mile away. Men were running from their barracks now. Some carried guns. Several fell as other men opposed them. Ayre opened one of the windows to hear better. Faint shouts of "Allah-u Akbarr" mixed with the coarse thrangg-thrangg-thrangg of automatic rifles.

"What's that? Near the gate, the main gate?" Manuela said, Massil on his feet beside her, equally shocked and not a little frightened.

Ayre reached for the binoculars and focused them. "Christ Almighty, soldiers're firing into the base and . . . and trucks're storming the gate . . . half a dozen of them . . . Green Bands and mullahs and soldiers jumping out of them . . ."

Over the base channel came an excited voice shouting in Farsi that was abruptly cut off. Again Manuela translated: " 'In the Name of God, kill all officers who oppose Imam Khomeini and take possession—' It's revolution!"

Below they saw the mullah Hussain and his two Green Bands pile out of the 206, guns unslung. The mullah motioned Dubois out of the cockpit, but the pilot just shook his head and pointed at the whirling blades, continued shutdown procedure. Hussain hesitated.

All over the S-G compound work had stopped. People were leaning out of windows or had come out onto the tarmac and were standing there in silent little groups, looking across the field. Sounds of gunfire increased. Nearby, the jeep and fuel truck that were to service the 206 had skidded to a halt the moment the guns had started. Hussain had hailed the jeep, left one man to guard the chopper. The driver saw him coming, jumped out, and took to his heels. The mullah cursed him and, with a Green Band, got into the driving seat, gunned the engine, and tore off down the boundary road, heading for the far barracks.

Dubois came up the steps, three at a time. He was thirty-six, tall and skinny, with dark hair and a roguish smile. At once he stuck out his hand and shook with Ayre. "Madonna, what a day, Freddy! I . . . Manuela!" He kissed her fondly on both cheeks. "The Duke is fine, *chérie*. He just had a row with the mullah who told him that he would no longer fly with him. Bandar Delam's not . . ." He stopped, very conscious now of Massil, not trusting him. "I need a drink, eh? Let's go to the mess, eh?"

They did not go to the mess. Marc led them out onto the tarmac and into the lee of a building where they could watch with safety and not be overheard. "There's no way of telling which side Massil's on, eh, or even most of our staff—if they even know themselves, poor people."

On the other side of the field there was a loud explosion. Fire gushed from one of the sheds and smoke billowed. "*Mon Dieu*, is that the fuel dump?"

"No, just near it." Ayre was filled with disquiet. Another explosion distracted him, then mixed with sporadic gunfire came the heavy, deep-throated detonation of a tank's big gun.

The jeep with the mullah in it had disappeared behind the barracks. Near the main gate, the army trucks had stopped haphazardly; their attacking soldiers and Green Bands vanished into hangars and barracks. A few bodies lay in the dust. Tank soldiers guarding Camp Commandant Peshadi's office block crouched near the doorway, their guns ready. Others waited at the second-floor windows. One of the men there let off a burst of automatic fire as half a dozen screaming soldiers and airmen charged in attack across the square. Another burst of fire and they were all dead or dying or badly wounded. One of the wounded half crawled, half scrambled for safety. The tank guards let him get almost to safety. Then they filled him with bullets.

Manuela moaned and they both took her deeper into the lee of their building. "I'm all right," she said. "Marc, when's Duke coming back?"

"Rudi or Duke will call tonight or tomorrow, guarantee it. *Pas problème!* Le Grand Duke is fine. *Mon Dieu,* now I am ready for a drink!"

They waited a moment, the firing lessening. "Come on," Ayre said, "we'll be safer in the bungalows."

They scurried across the compound into one of the fine bungalows surrounded by whitewashed fences and tidy gardens. There were no married quarters at Kowiss. Usually two pilots shared the two-bedroom bungalows.

Manuela left them to get the drinks. "Now, what really happened?" Ayre asked softly.

Rapidly the Frenchman told him about the attack and Zataki and Rudi's bravery. "That old Kraut really deserves a medal," he said admiringly. "But listen, last night the revs shot one of our day laborers. They tried him and shot him in four minutes for being fedayeen. This morning other bastards shot Kyabi."

Ayre was appalled. "But why?"

Dubois told him about the pipeline sabotage, then added, "When Rudi and the mullah got back, Zataki paraded us all and said it was correct Kyabi had been shot as 'a supporter of the Shah, a supporter of satanic Americans and British who had despoiled Iran for years and was therefore an enemy of God.' "

"Poor old Boss. Christ, I liked him a lot, he was a good fellow!"

"Yes. And openly anti-Khomeini, and now those bastards have guns—never seen so many guns and they're all *stupides,* crazy." Dubois tightened. "Old Duke began raving in Farsi at them all; he'd already had a confrontation with Zataki and the mullah last night. We don't know what he said but it all became ugly, the bastards fell on him, started to kick and scream at him. Of course we all began to charge, then there was an explosion of automatic fire and we froze. Them too, because it was Rudi. Somehow he'd taken a gun from one of them and let another short burst into the air. He shouted, 'Leave him alone or I'll kill you all,' keeping the gun trained on Zataki and the group near Duke. They left him. After cursing them—*ma foi, quel homme*—he made a deal; they leave us alone, we leave them to their revolution, I was to fly the mullah here and Duke was to stay, and Rudi keeps the gun. He made Zataki and the mullah swear by Allah not to break the contract, but I still wouldn't trust them. *Merde,* they're all *merde, mon ami.* But Rudi, Rudi was fantastic. He should be French, that one. I tried to call them all day but no answer. . . ."

The other side of the field, a Centurion tank came charging out of one of the streets in the far barracks complex, whirled across the open, and went into the main street opposite base HQ and the officers' mess. It stopped there, engines growling, fat, squat, and deadly. The long gun swiveled, seeking a target. Then suddenly the tracks spun, the tank twirled on its axis and fired and the shell decimated the second floor where Colonel Peshadi had his offices. The defenders reeled from the sudden treachery. Again the tank fired. Great slabs of masonry tore off and half the roof collapsed. The building began to burn.

Then from the ground floor and part of the second story a fusillade of bullets surrounded the tank. At once two of the loyalists charged out of the main door with grenades, tossed them through the tank slits, and fled for cover. Both men crumpled under a hail of automatic fire from across the roadway, but there was a terrible explosion inside the tank and flames and smoke gushed forth. The metal top flipped open and a burning man tried to clamber out. His body was almost ripped out of the tank by the hail of automatic fire from the broken building. On the wind that blew from across the base there was the smell of cordite and fire and meat burning.

The battle continued for more than an hour, then ended. The lowering sun cast a bloody hue and there were dead and dying throughout the base, but the insurrection had failed because they had not killed Colonel Peshadi or his chief officers in the first sneak attack, because not enough of the airmen and soldiers went over to their side—and only one of three tank crews.

Peshadi had been in the lead tank, and he held the tower and all radio communications. He had gathered loyal forces and led the ruthless drive that gouged the revolutionaries out of the hangars and out of the barracks. And once the cautious majority, the fence-sitting, unsure—in this case airmen and troops—perceived that the revolt was lost, they hesitated no longer. Immediately and zealously they declared their undying and historic loyalty to Peshadi and the Shah, picked up discarded weapons, and, equally zealously, in the Name of God, began firing at the "enemy." But few fired to kill and though Peshadi knew it, he left an escape route open and allowed a few of the attackers to escape. His only secret order to his most trusted men was, Kill the mullah Hussain.

But, somehow, Hussain escaped.

"This is Colonel Peshadi," came over the main base frequency and all loudspeakers. "Thanks be to God the enemy is dead, dying, or captured. I thank all loyal troops. All officers and men will collect our glorious dead who died doing God's work and report numbers, and also numbers of enemy killed. Doctors and medics! Attend to all wounded without favor. God is Great . . . God is Great! It is almost the time for evening prayer. Tonight I am mullah and I will lead it. All will attend to give thanks to God."

In Starke's bungalow, Ayre, Manuela, and Dubois were listening on the base intercom. She finished translating Peshadi's Farsi. Now there was just static. Smoke hung over the base and the air was heavy with the smell. The two men were sipping vodka and canned orange juice, she mineral water. A portable butane gas fire warmed the room pleasantly.

"That's curious," she said thoughtfully, steeling herself not to think of all the killing or about Starke at Bandar Delam. "Curious that Peshadi didn't end: Long live the Shah. Surely it's a victory for him? He must be scared out of his wits."

"I would be too," Ayre said. "He's g—" They all jumped as the base intercom telephone jangled. He picked it up. "Hello?"

"This is Major Changiz. Ah, Captain Ayre, did they come your side of the base? What happened with you?"

"Nothing. No insurgents came over here."

"Praise be to God. We were all worried for your safety. You're sure there are no dead or wounded?"

"None—to my knowledge."

"Thanks be to God. We've plenty. Fortunately there're no enemy wounded."

"None?"

"None. You won't mind if I mention that you will not report or relate this incident to anyone on the radio—to no one, Captain. Top security. Do you understand?"

"Loud and clear, Major."

"Good. Please listen out on our base frequency—as for safety we will monitor yours. Please do not use your HF radio until first clearing it with us during the emergency." Ayre felt the blood in his face but he said nothing. "Please stand by for a briefing by Colonel Peshadi at eight o'clock, and now send Esvandiary and all your Faithful to evening prayers—at once."

"Certainly, but Hotshot—Esvandiary's on leave for a week." Esvandiary was their IranOil station manager.

"Very well. Send the rest with Pavoud in charge."

"Right away." The phone went dead. He told them what had been said, then went to pass the word.

In the tower Massil was very uneasy. "But, Captain, Excellency. I'm on duty till sunset. We've our two 212s to come home yet and the—"

"He said all Faithful. At once. Your papers are in order, you've been in Iran for years. He knows you're here so you'd better go—unless you've something to fear?"

"No. No, not at all."

Ayre saw the sweat on the man's forehead. "Don't worry, Massil," he said, "I'll see the lads in. No sweat. And I'll stay here until you get back. It won't take you long."

He saw his two 212s to bed, waiting with growing impatience, Massil long overdue now. To pass the time he had tried to do some paperwork but gave up, his mind in turmoil. The only thought that cheered him was that his wife and infant son were safe in England—even with the lousy weather there, the gales and blizzards and rains and lousy cold and lousy strikes and lousy government.

The HF came to life. It was just after dark. "Hello, Kowiss, this is McIver in Tehran . . ."

TEHRAN—AT THE S-G OFFICE: 6:50 P.M. McIver said again, "Hello, Kowiss, this is McIver in Tehran, do you read?"

"Tehran, this is Kowiss, Standby One"—one minute—vernacular for "Please wait a moment."

"All right, Freddy," McIver said and put the HF mike back on the desk. He and Tom Lochart, who had arrived from Zagros that afternoon, were in his office on the top floor of the building that had been HQ for S-G ever since it had opened operations in Iran almost ten years before. The building had five stories with a flat roof where Genny had made a delightful, screened roof garden with chairs and tables and barbecue. General Beni-Hassan, Andrew Gavallan's friend, had recommended the building highly: "Nothing but the best for Andy Gavallan's company. There's space for half a dozen offices, the price's reasonable, you've space on the roof for your own generator and radio antenna, you're near the main highway that goes to the airport, bazaar's convenient, my HQ's around the corner, parking's convenient, projected hotels convenient, and here's the pièce de résistance!" Proudly the general had shown McIver the toilet. It was ordinary and not very clean.

"What's so special about that?" McIver had asked, nonplussed.

"It's the only one in the building, the rest are squatters—just a hole in the floor over a sewer—and if you're not used to squatting it's a tricky operation —in fact it's a pain in the ass, particularly for the ladies, who've been known to slip into the hole with messy results," the general had said jovially. He was a fine-looking man, very strong, very fit.

"Squatters are everywhere?"

"Even in the best houses, everywhere outside of modern hotels. When you think about it, Mac, squatting's more hygienic, nothing sensitive touches anything alien. Then there's this." The general had pointed to a small hose attached to the toilet spigot. "We use water to clean ourselves—always use the left hand, that's the shit hand, the right's for eating, which is why you never offer anything with your left hand. Very bad manners, Mac. Never eat or drink with your left hand in the Islamic world, and don't forget most toilets and squatters don't have hoses so you have to use water from a bucket, if there happens to be one. As I said it's a tricky op, but a way of life. By the way we've no lefthanded people in Islam." Again the good-natured chuckle. "Most Muslims can't perform comfortably unless they squat—it's the muscles—so a lot will squat on the Western seat when they relieve themselves. Strange, isn't it, but then outside of most cities, even in them, throughout most of Asia, the Middle East, China, India, Africa, South America, there's not even running water. . . ."

"A penny for your thoughts, Mac?" Lochart said. The tall Canadian sat opposite him, both of them in old easy chairs. Their electric light and fire were at full power from their own generator.

McIver grunted. "I was thinking about squatters. Hate squatters and bloody water. Just can't get used to them."

"Doesn't bother me now, hardly notice it. We've squatters in our apartment—Sharazad said she'd have a 'Western' toilet put in if I wanted it as a wedding present, but I said I could deal with it." Lochart smiled wryly. "Doesn't bother me now but, my God, that was the one thing that sent Deirdre around the bend."

"Same for all the wives. That's their biggest bitch, all of them, Genny too. Not my bloody fault most of the world does it that way. Thank God we've a real loo in the flat. Gen'd mutiny otherwise." McIver fiddled with the volume on the receiver. "Come on, Freddy," he muttered. There were many charts on the walls, no pictures, though there was the heavy dust mark of one

taken down recently—the obligatory photograph of the Shah. Outside, the
night sky was lit with fires that dotted the skyline of the darkened city, no
lights or streetlamps anywhere except here. Gunfire, rifle and automatic,
mixed with the ever-present sound of the city—mobs roaring "Allahhh-u
Akbarrrrrr . . ."

Now over the loudspeaker: "This is Kowiss, Captain Ayre speaking. I read
you loud and clear, Captain McIver."

Both men were startled and Lochart sat upright. "Something's wrong,
Mac, he can't talk openly—someone's listening."

McIver clicked on the send switch. "You're doing your own radio,
Freddy," he said deliberately to make sure there was no mistake, "as well as
putting in the hours?"

"Just happened to be here, Captain McIver."

"Everything five by five?" This meant maximum radio signal strength, or
in the vernacular of pilots, Everything okay?

After a deliberate pause that told them no, "Yes, Captain McIver."

"Good, Captain Ayre," McIver said, to tell him at once that he understood. "Put Captain Starke on, will you?"

"Sorry, sir, I can't. Captain Starke's still at Bandar Delam."

McIver said sharply, "What's he doing there?"

"Captain Lutz ordered him to stop over and ordered Captain Dubois to
complete the VIP journey requested by IranOil—and approved by you."

Starke had managed to get through to Tehran before taking off to explain
the problem of the mullah Hussain to McIver. McIver had approved the trip
as long as Colonel Peshadi okayed it, and told him to keep him advised.

"Is the 125 due in Kowiss tomorrow, Captain McIver?"

"It's possible," McIver replied, "but you never know." The 125 had been
scheduled for Tehran yesterday, but because of the insurrection surrounding
the airport, all inbound traffic had been provisionally canceled until tomorrow, Monday. "We're working on getting clearances for a direct into Kowiss.
It's dicey because military air traffic control are . . . are undermanned. The
airport at Tehran is, er, jammed so we can't get any of our dependents out.
Tell Manuela to stand by in case we can get a clearance." McIver grimaced,
trying to decide how much he should say over the open airwaves, then saw
Lochart motioning to him.

"Let me, Mac. Freddy can speak French," Lochart said softly.

McIver brightened and gratefully leaned over and gave him the mike.
"*Écoute,* Freddy," Lochart began in Canadian French that he knew even
Ayre, whose French was excellent, had difficulty in understanding. "Marxists
still hold the International Airport, helped by Khomeini insurgents, suppos-

edly with some PLO, and still hold the tower. Tonight's major rumor is that
there's going to be a coup, that the prime minister's approved it, that troops
are finally on the move all over Tehran with orders to quell the riots and
shoot to kill. What's your problem down there? Are you all right?"

"Yes, no sweat," they heard him reply in gutter French and innuendo;
"I'm under orders to say nothing, but no real problems here, bet on it, but
they're listening. At Smelly"—their nickname for Bandar Delam where the
air stank constantly of gasoline—"lots of problems and Boss was sent upward
before his allotted span . . ."

Lochart's eyes widened. "Kyabi's been shot," he muttered to McIver.

". . . but old Rudi's got everything under control and the Duke's okay.
We'd better stop this, old one. They're listening."

"Understand. Sit tight and tell the others if you can; also that we're okay,"
adding in English without missing a beat, "and I repeat we'll be sending
down cash for your people tomorrow."

Ayre's voice brightened. "No shit, old chap?"

Involuntarily Lochart laughed. "No shit. Keep a duty radio op on and we'll
call back progress. Here's Captain McIver again. Insha'Allah!" He handed
the mike back.

"Captain, have you heard from Lengeh, yesterday or today?"

"No, we tried them but couldn't raise them. Might be the sunspots. I'll try
again now."

"Thanks. Give my regards to Captain Scragger and remind him his medi-
cal's due next week." McIver smiled grimly, then added, "Make sure Captain
Starke calls the moment he returns." He signed off. Lochart told him what
Ayre had said. He poured himself another whisky.

"What about me, for God's sake?" McIver said irritably.

"But, Mac, you kn—"

"Don't you start. Make it a light one." As Lochart poured, McIver got up,
went to the window, and stared out, seeing nothing. "Poor old Kyabi. Now
there was a good man if ever there was one, good for Iran and fair to us.
What'd they murder him for? Madmen! Rudi 'ordering' Duke and 'ordering'
Marc—what the hell does that mean?"

"Only that there was trouble but Rudi's got it in control. Freddy would
have told me if Rudi hadn't—he's very sharp and his French's good so he
could've found a way. There was plenty of time, even though 'they' were
listening, whoever the hell 'they' were," Lochart said. "Maybe it was like at
Zagros."

At Zagros the villagers from Yazdek had come at dawn the day after
Lochart had arrived back from leave. Their village mullah had received

Khomeini's orders to begin the insurrection against "the illegal government of the Shah," and to take control of his area. The mullah had been born in the village and was wise in the ways of the mountains that were snow-locked in winter and only accessible with great difficulty the rest of the year. And, too, the chief of police against whom he should lead the revolt was his nephew, and Nasiri, the base manager who was also a target, was married to his wife's sister's daughter who now lived in Shiraz. Even more important, they were all Galezan, a minor tribe of the nomad Kash'kai who had settled protectively—centuries ago—athwart this tiny crossroads, and the chief of police whose name was Nitchak Khan was also their kalandar, their elected tribal leader.

So, correctly, he had consulted Nitchak Khan and the Khan had agreed that a revolt should take place against their hereditary enemy the Pahlavi Shah, that to celebrate the revolution any who cared to could fire their arms at the stars and that, at dawn, he would lead the necessary investiture of the foreigners' airfield.

They had arrived at dawn. Armed. Every man in the village. Nitchak Khan no longer wore his police uniform but tribal clothes. He was much shorter than Lochart, a hard-bodied man, spare, with hands of iron and legs of steel, a cartridge belt over his chest and rifle in his hands. By prearrangement, Lochart, accompanied by Jean-Luc Sessonne—at the Khan's request—met them at two hastily erected columns of stones that symbolized the gate to the base. Lochart saluted and agreed that Nitchak Khan had jurisdiction over the base, the two tiers of stones were formally knocked down, there were loud cheers from all sides and many guns were fired into the air. Then Nitchak Khan presented bouquets of flowers to Jean-Luc Sessonne as a representative of France, thanking him on behalf of all the Galezan-Kash'kai for succoring and helping Khomeini who had rid them of their enemy, the Pahlavi Shah. "Thanks be to God that this self-dubbed Great King of Kings who dared sacrilege to try to connect his line back to Kings Cyrus and Darius the Great, men of courage and pride—this Light of the Aryans, this lackey of foreign devils—fled like a painted paramour from his Iraqi pasha!"

Then there were brave speeches from both sides and the feast began and Nitchak Khan, the mullah beside him, had asked Tom Lochart, tribal chief of the foreigners at Zagros Three, to continue as before under the new regime. Lochart had gravely agreed.

"Let's hope Rudi and his lads're as lucky as you at Zagros, Tom." McIver turned back to the windows, knowing there was nothing he could do to help them. "Things get worse and worse," he muttered. Kyabi's murder's terrible, and a very bad sign for us, he thought. How the hell can I get Genny out of Tehran and where the hell's Charlie?

They had not heard from Pettikin since he had left yesterday morning for Tabriz. From their ground staff at Galeg Morghi they had had garbled reports—that Pettikin had been kidnapped and forced to fly off with "three unknown persons," or that "three Iranian Air Force pilots hijacked the 206 and fled for the border," or that "the three passengers were high-ranking officers fleeing the country." Why three passengers in every story? McIver had asked himself. He knew Pettikin must have got to the airfield safely because his car was still there, though the tanks were dry, the radio torn out, and the car vandalized. Bandar-e Pahlavi, where he was to have refueled, was silent—Tabriz was hardly ever in range. He cursed silently. It had been a bad day for McIver.

All day irate creditors had arrived to harass him, the phones weren't working, the telex got jammed and took hours to clear, and his meeting at noon with General Valik who Gavallan had promised would supply cash weekly, was a disaster.

"As soon as the banks open we'll pay what is owed."

"For God's sake, you've been saying that for weeks," McIver said coldly, "I need money now."

"So do we all," the general had hissed back, shaking with rage, but very conscious of the Iranian employees in the outer office who would be sure to be listening. "There's civil war going on and I can't open the banks. You'll have to wait." He was a rotund man, balding, with darkish skin, an ex-army general, his clothes expensive, his watch expensive. He dropped his voice even lower. "If it wasn't for stupid Americans who betrayed the Shah and persuaded him to curb our glorious armed forces, we wouldn't be in this mess!"

"I'm British as you well know and you brought the mess on yourself."

"British, American, what's the difference? It's all your fault. You both betrayed our Shah and Iran and now you're going to pay for it!"

"With what?" McIver asked sourly. "You've got all our money."

"If it wasn't for your Iranian partners—me particularly—you wouldn't have any money. Andy's not complaining. I had a telex from my revered colleague, General Javadah, that Andy was signing the new Guerney contracts this week."

"Andy said he had a telex from you confirming that you promised him you'd provide us with cash."

"I promised I'd try." The general curbed his rage with an effort, for he needed McIver's cooperation. He mopped his forehead and opened his briefcase. It was stuffed with high-denomination rials but he held the top carefully so it was impossible for McIver to see inside, then brought out a small sheaf of notes, closing the briefcase. With great deliberation he counted out 500,000 rials—about $6,000. "There," he said with a great flourish, putting the rials on the table and the rest away again. "Next week I or one of my colleagues will bring some more. A receipt, please."

"Thank you." McIver signed the receipt. "When can we exp—"

"Next week. If the banks open we can settle everything. We're always good as our word. Always. Haven't we arranged the Guerney contracts?" Valik leaned forward and dropped his voice even more. "Now, I have a special charter. Tomorrow I want a 212, to leave sometime in the morning."

"To go where?"

"I need to inspect some facilities at Abadan," Valik said and McIver noticed the sweat.

"And how will I get the necessary permissions, General? With all your airspace controlled by the military and w—"

"Don't bother with permission, just hav—"

"Unless we've a flight plan, approved by the military in advance, it's an illegal flight."

"You can always say you asked for permission and it was given verbally. What's so difficult about that?"

"First it's against Iranian law, General, your law, second even if cleared verbally and the aircraft got out of Tehran airspace, you've still got to give the next military air traffic controller your recorded number—all flight plans are recorded at your air force HQ and they're even more twitchy about helicopters than civilians—and if you don't have one the controller will say get your tail down at the next military base and report to the tower. And when you land, they'll meet you very irritably—and correctly—in force, my aircraft will be impounded, and the passengers and crew put in jail."

"Then find a way. It's a very important charter. The, er, the Guerney contracts depend on it. Just have the 212 ready at nine o'clock, say at Galeg Morghi."

"Why there? Why not at the International Airport?"

"It's more convenient . . . and quiet now."

McIver frowned. It was well within Valik's authority to ask for and authorize such a flight. "Very well, I'll try." He pulled out the pad of blank flight plan forms, noticed that the last copy referred to Pettikin's flight to Tabriz and again his anxiety mounted—where the devil is he? Under "passengers" he put General Valik, chairman of IHC, and handed it to him. "Please sign under authority."

Valik shoved the form back imperiously. "There's no need for my name to be put on it—just put four passengers—my wife and two children will be with me, and some luggage. We will be staying in Abadan for a week, then returning. Just have the 212 ready at 9:00 A.M. at Galeg Morghi."

"Sorry, General, the names have to be on the clearance or the air force won't even accept the flight plan. All passengers have to be named. I'll apply for clearance but I don't hold out much hope for you." McIver began to add the other names.

"No, stop! No need to give our names. Just put down the trip's to send some spares to Abadan. Surely there are some spares you need to send there." The sweat was beading him.

"All right, but first please sign the authority, with the name of all passengers and your final destination."

The general's face reddened. "Just arrange it without involving me. At once!"

"I can't." McIver was becoming equally impatient. "I repeat, the military will want to know all the 'who' and the 'where'—they're as sticky now as flypaper. We'll get even more searching enquiries than usual because we haven't had any traffic in weeks going that way. Tehran's not like in the south where we're flying all day."

"This is a special flight for spares. Simple."

"It isn't simple at all. Sentries at Galeg Morghi wouldn't let you aboard without papers, nor would the tower. They'd see you going aboard, for God's sake." McIver stared at him exasperated. "Why don't you arrange the clearance yourself, General? You've the best connections in Iran. You've certainly made that clear. For you it should be simple."

"They're all our planes. We own them—own them!"

"Yes, you do," McIver said as grimly. "When you've paid for them—you owe us almost 4 million U.S. in back payments. If you want to go to Abadan that's your business, but if they catch you doing it in an S-G chopper with false papers which I must countersign, you'll land in jail, your family'll be in jail along with me and the pilot, and they'll impound our aircraft and close us down forever." Just the thought of jail made him feel bilious. If a tenth of the stories about SAVAK and Iranian jails were true, they were no places to be.

Valik choked back his rage. He sat down and put a sickly smile on his face. "There's no need for us to quarrel, Mac, we've been through too much together. I, I will make it very worthwhile, eh? Both to you and the pilot." He opened the briefcase. "Eh? 12 million rials—between you."

McIver looked at the money blankly. 12 million was about $150,000—over 100,000 pounds sterling. Numbly, he shook his head.

At once Valik said, "All right, 12 million each—and expenses—half now and half when we're safe at Kuwait Airport, eh?"

McIver was in shock, not only because of the money but because Valik had openly said "Kuwait" which McIver had suspected but had not wished to think about. This was a complete 180-degree turn from everything that Valik had been saying for months: for months he had been bullish about the Shah crushing the opposition, then Khomeini. And even after the Shah's unbeliev-able departure and Khomeini's astonishing return to Tehran—my God, was that only ten days ago?—Valik had said a dozen times that there was nothing to worry about, for Bakhtiar and the generals of the Imperial Staff held the complete balance of power and would never permit "this Khomeini–covert Communist revolution to succeed." Nor would the United States permit it. Never. At the right time the services would seize power and take over. Only yesterday Valik had confidently repeated it and said he'd heard that any hour the army was going to move in force and that the Immortals at Doshan Tappeh, putting down the small air force mutiny, was the first sign.

McIver tore his gaze off the money and looked at the eyes of the man opposite. "What do you know that we don't know?"

"What're you talking about?" Valik began to bluster. "I don't know an—"

"Something's happened, what is it?"

"I've got to get out, with my family," Valik said, on the edge of despera-tion now. "Rumors are terrible—coup or civil war, Khomeini or not, I'm, we're, we're marked. Do you understand? It's my family, Mac, I've got to get out, until things quiet down. 12 million each, eh?"

"What rumors?"

"Rumors!" Valik almost spat at him. "Get the clearance any way you can. I pay in advance."

"However much money you offer I won't do it. It has to be straight."

"You stupid hypocrite! Straight? How have you been operating all these years in Iran? Pishkesh! How much have you yourself paid under the counter —or to customs men? Pishkesh! How do you think we get contracts, eh? The Guerney contracts? Pishkesh! By putting cash, quietly, into the right hands. Are you so stupid you still don't know Iranian ways?"

McIver said as grimly, "I know pishkesh, I'm not stupid, and I know Iran has its own ways. Oh, yes, Iran has its own ways. The answer's no."

"Then the blood of my children and my wife are on your head. And mine."

"What're you talking about?"

"Are you afraid of the truth?"

McIver stared at him. Valik's wife and two children were favorites of Genny's and his. "What makes you so sure?"

"I've . . . I've a cousin in the police. He saw a . . . a secret SAVAK list. I am to be arrested the day after tomorrow along with many other prominent persons as a sop to the . . . the opposition. And my family. And you know how they treat . . . how they can treat women and children in front of the . . ." Valik's words trailed off.

McIver's defenses crumbled. They had all heard horrendous stories of wives and children being tortured in front of the arrested man to force his compliance with whatever they wanted, or just for devilment. "All right," he said helplessly, feeling rotten, knowing he was trapped. "I'll try, but don't expect to get a clearance, and you shouldn't go south to Abadan. Your best bet would be Turkey. Perhaps we could chopper you to Tabriz, then you could buy your way over the border in a truck. You must have friends there. And you can't make the pickup Galeg Morghi—there's no way you could sneak aboard with Annoush and the children or even get into that military field without being stopped. You'd . . . you'd have to be picked up outside of Tehran. Somewhere off the roads and out of sight of radar."

"All right, but it has to be Abadan."

"Why? You lessen your chances by half."

"Has to be. My family . . . my father and mother got there by road. Of course you're right about Galeg Morghi. We could be picked up outside Tehran at . . ." Valik thought for a moment, then rushed on: "at the junction of the pipeline south and the river Zehsan . . . it's away from the road and safe. We'll be there in the morning at eleven o'clock. God will thank you, Mac. If . . . if you apply for a clearance for spares, I . . . I will arrange that it's approved. Please, I beg you."

"But what about refueling? When you land for refueling, the landing officer's bound to spot you and you'll be arrested in seconds."

"Request refueling at the air force base at Isfahan. I . . . I will arrange Isfahan." Valik wiped the sweat off his face.

"And if anything goes wrong?"

"Insha'Allah! You'll apply for clearance for spares—no names on the clearance or I'm dead or worse and so are Annoush, Jalal, and Setarem. Please?"

McIver knew it was madness. "I'll apply for clearance: spares only for Bandar Delam. I should know by midnight if it's approved—I'll send someone to wait for it and bring it to me at the apartment. Phones are out so you'll have to come to me for confirmation. That'll give me time to think this out and decide yes or no."

"But y—"

"Midnight."

"Yes, very well, I shall be there."

"What about the other partners?"

"They—they know nothing of this. Emir Paknouri or one of the others will act for me."

"What about weekly monies?"

"They will provide it." Again Valik wiped his forehead. "The Blessings of God on you." He put on his overcoat and walked for the door. The briefcase stayed on the desk.

"Take that with you."

Valik turned back. "Ah, you want me to pay in Kuwait? Or Switzerland? In what currency?"

"There's no payment. You can authorize a charter. Maybe we can get you to Bandar Delam—then you're on your own."

Valik stared at him with disbelief. "But . . . but even so, you'll need expense money to pay for the, er, pilot or whatever."

"No, but you can give me an advance of 5 million rials against the money the partnership owes which we desperately need." McIver scrawled out a receipt and handed it to him. "If you're not here, the Emir or the others may not be so generous."

"The banks will open next week, we're sure of it. Oh, yes, quite sure."

"Well, let's hope so and we can be paid what's owing." He saw Valik's expression, saw him count out the money, knowing that Valik thought him mad not to have accepted the pishkesh, knowing also that inevitably the man would try to bribe the pilot, whoever the pilot was, to take them the last stretch if the chopper ever got out of Tehran airspace—and that would be a disaster.

And now, in his office, staring blankly out of the window at the night, not hearing the gunfire or seeing the occasional flare light the darkened city, he thought, My God, SAVAK? I have to try to help him, have to. Those poor bloody kids and poor woman. I have to! And when Valik offers the pilot a bribe, even though I'll warn the pilot in advance, will he resist? If Valik offered 12 million now, at Abadan it would be doubled. Tom could use that money, Nogger Lane, so could I, anyone. Just for a short trip across the Gulf —short but one way and no return. Where the hell did Valik get all that cash anyway? Of course from a bank.

For weeks there had been rumors that for a fee certain well-connected people could get monies out of Tehran even though the banks—formally— were closed. Or for an even larger fee get monies transferred to a numbered account in Switzerland, and that now Swiss banks were groaning under the weight of money fleeing the country. Billions. A few million in the right palm and anything's possible. Isn't that the same over the whole of Asia? Be honest, why just Asia? Isn't it true over the whole world?

"Tom," he said wearily, "try military air traffic control and see if the 212's cleared, will you?" As far as Lochart was concerned, this was just a routine delivery—McIver had told him only that he had seen Valik today and that the general had given him some cash, but nothing else. He still had to decide the pilot he would send, wishing he could do it himself and so put no one else at risk. God cursed medical! God cursed rules!

Lochart went to the HF. At that moment there was a scuffle in the outer office, and the door swung open. Standing there was a youth with an automatic rifle over his shoulder and a green band on his arm. Half a dozen other youths were with him. The Iranian staff waited, paralyzed. The young man stared at McIver and Lochart then consulted a list.

"Salaam, Agha. Capta'n McIver?" he asked Lochart, his English hesitant and heavily accented.

"Salaam, Agha. No, I am Captain McIver," McIver said uneasily, his first thought, Are these more of the same group who murdered poor Kyabi? His second thought, Gen should have left with the others, I should have insisted, his third about the stacks of rials in his open attaché case on the floor beside the hatstand.

"Ah, good," the young man said politely. There were dark rings under his eyes, his face strong, and though McIver judged him to be twenty-five at the most, he had an old man's look about him. "Danger here. For you here. Now. Please to go. We are komiteh for this block. Please you to go. Now."

"All right. Certainly, er, thank you." Twice before, McIver had thought it prudent to evacuate the offices because of riots and mobs in the streets around them even though, astonishingly, considering their vast numbers, the mobs had been very disciplined with little damage to property or to Europeans—except for cars parked on the streets. This was the first time anyone had come here to warn him personally. Obediently McIver and Lochart put on their overcoats, McIver closed his attaché case, and, with the others, began to leave. He switched off the lights.

"How lights when no one else?" the leader asked.

"We've our own generator. On the roof."

The youth smiled strangely, his teeth very white. "Foreigners have generators and warm, Iranians not."

McIver was going to answer but thought better of it.

"You got message? Message about leaving? Message today?"

"Yes," McIver said. One message in the office, one at the apartment that Genny had found in their letter box. They just said, "On December 1 you were warned to leave: Why are you still here if not as an enemy? You have little time left. [signed] The university supporters for Islamic Republic in Iran."

"You, er, you are representatives of the university?"

"We are your komiteh. Please to leave now. Enemies better not come back ever. No?"

McIver and Lochart walked out. The revolutionaries followed them down the stairs. For weeks the elevator had not worked.

The street was still clear, no mobs, or fires, and all gunfire distant.

"Not come back. Three days."

McIver stared at them. "That's not possible. I've got many th—"

"Danger." The young man and the others, equally young, waited silently and watched. Not all were armed with guns. Two had clubs. Two were holding hands. "Not come back. Very bad. Three days, komiteh says. Understand?"

"Yes, but one of us has to refuel the generator or the telex will stop and then we'll be out of touch an—"

"Telex unimportant. Not come back. Three days." The youth patiently motioned them to leave. "Danger here. Not forget, please. Good night."

McIver and Lochart got into their cars that were locked in the garage below the building, very conscious of the envious stares. McIver was driving his '65 four-seat Rover coupe that he called Lulu and kept in mint condition. Lochart had borrowed Scot Gavallan's car, a small battered old Citroën that was deliberately low key though the engine was souped up, the brakes perfect, and if need be, she was very fast. They drove off, and around the second corner stopped alongside one another.

"Those buggers really meant it," McIver said angrily. "Three days? I can't stay out of the office three days!"

"Yes. What now?" Lochart glanced into his rearview mirror. The young men had rounded the far corner and stood watching them. "We better get going. I'll meet you at your apartment," he said hurriedly.

"Yes, but in the morning, Tom, nothing we can do now."

"But I was going to go back to Zagros—I should have left today."

"I know. Stay tomorrow, go the next day. Nogger can do the charter, if the clearance comes through, which I doubt. Come around ten."

McIver saw the youths begin to walk toward them. "Around ten, Tom," he said hurriedly, let in the clutch, and drove off cursing.

*   *   *

The youths saw them go and their leader, Ibrahim, was glad, for he did not want to clash with foreigners or to kill them—or to bring them to trial. Only SAVAK. And guilty police. And enemies of Iran, inside Iran, who wanted to bring back the Shah. And all traitorous Marxist totalitarians who opposed democracy and freedom of worship and the freedom of education and universities.

"Oh, how I'd like that car," one of them said, almost sick with envy. "It was a sixty-eight, wasn't it, Ibrahim?"

"A sixty-five," Ibrahim answered. "One day you'll have one, Ali, and the gasoline to put in it. One day you'll be the most famous writer and poet in all Iran."

"Disgusting of that foreigner to flaunt so much wealth when there's so much poverty in Iran," another said.

"Soon they'll all be gone. Forever."

"Do you think those two will come back tomorrow, Ibrahim?"

"I hope not," he said with a tired laugh. "If they do I don't know what we'll do. I think we scared them enough. Even so, we should visit this block at least twice a day."

A young man holding a club put his arm around him affectionately. "I'm glad we voted you leader. You were our perfect choice."

They all agreed. Ibrahim Kyabi was very proud, and proud to be part of the revolution that would end all of Iran's troubles. And proud too of his father who was an oil engineer and important official in IranOil who had patiently worked over the years for democracy in Iran, opposing the Shah, who now would surely be a powerful voice in the new and glorious Iran. "Come along, friends," he said contentedly. "We've several more buildings to investigate."

CHAPTER 12

AT SIRI ISLAND: 7:42 P.M. A little over seven hundred miles southwest from Tehran, the loading of the 50,000-ton Japanese tanker, the *Rikomaru,* was almost complete. A good moon lit up the Gulf, the night was balmy with many stars above and Scragger had agreed to join de Plessey and go aboard for dinner with Yoshi Kasigi. Now the three of them were on the bridge with the captain, the deck floodlit, watching the Japanese deckhands and the chief engineer near the big intake pipe that led overboard to the complex of valves on the permanently anchored, floating oil-loading barge that was alongside and also floodlit.

They were about two hundred yards off the low-lying Siri island, the tanker anchored securely with her two bow chains fixed to buoys ahead and two anchors aft from the stern. Oil was pumped from the shore storage tanks through a pipe laid on the seabed up to the barge, thence aboard through their own pipe system into their tanks. Loading and unloading were dangerous operations because volatile, highly explosive gases built up in the tanks in the space over the crude—emptied tanks being even more dangerous until they were washed out. In the most modern tankers, for increased safety, nitrogen—an inert gas—was pumped into the space built up in the tanks, to be expelled at leisure. The *Rikomaru* was not so equipped.

They heard the chief engineer shout down to the men on the barge, "Close the valve," then turn to the bridge and give a thumbs-up that the captain acknowledged and said to Kasigi in Japanese, "Permission to sail as soon as we can?" He was a thin, taut-faced man in starched white shirt and shorts, with white socks and shoes, epaulets, and a naval style, peaked cap.

"Yes, Captain Moriyama. How long will that be?"

"Two hours at the most—to clean up and to cat the moorings." This meant sending out their motorboat to unshackle their bow anchor chains that were bolted to the permanent buoys, then reattach them to the ship's anchors.

"Good." To de Plessey and Scragger, Kasigi said in English, "We're full now and ready to leave. About two hours and we'll be on our way."

"Excellent," de Plessey said, equally relieved. "Now we relax."

The whole operation had gone very well. Security had been tightened throughout the island and throughout the ship. Everything that could be checked was checked. Only three essential Iranians had been allowed aboard. Each had been searched and were being carefully monitored by a Japanese crewman. There had been no signs of any hostiles among any of the other Iranians ashore. Every likely place had been searched that could hide explosives or arms. "Perhaps that poor young man off Siri One was mistaken, Scrag, *mon ami.*"

"Perhaps," Scragger replied. "Even so, cobber, I think young Abdollah Turik was murdered—no one gets face and eye mutilation like that from falling off a rig in a calm sea. Poor young bugger."

"But the sharks, Captain Scragger," Kasigi said, equally disquieted, "the sharks could have caused those wounds."

"Yes, they could. But I'll bet my life it was because of wot he told me."

"I hope you're wrong."

"I'll bet we'll never know the truth," Scragger said sadly. "Wot was your word, Mr. Kasigi? Karma. That poor young bugger's karma was short and not sweet."

The others nodded. In silence they watched the ship being detached from the barge's umbilical cord.

To see better, Scragger went to the side of the bridge. Under more flood-lights oilmen were laboriously unscrewing the twelve-inch pipe from the barge's complex of valves. Six men were there. Two Japanese crew, three Iranians, and a French engineer.

Ahead of him was the expanse and length of the flat deck. In the middle of the deck was his 206. He had landed there at de Plessey's suggestion and with Kasigi's permission. "Beaut," Scragger had told the Frenchman; "I'll fly you back to Siri, or Lengeh, just as you want."

"Yoshi Kasigi suggests we both stay overnight, Scrag, and return in the morning. It'll make a change for you. We can leave at dawn and return to Lengeh. Come aboard. I'd appreciate it."

So he had landed on the tanker at sunset, not sure why he had accepted the invitation but he had made a pact with Kasigi and felt he should honor it. Too, he felt sickeningly responsible for young Abdollah Turik. The sight of the youth's corpse had rocked him badly and made him want to be at Siri until the tanker left. So he had arrived and had tried to be a good guest, halfheartedly agreeing with de Plessey that perhaps, after all, the youth's death was just a coincidence and that their security precautions would stop any sabotage attempt.

Since the loading had begun the day before, they had all been edgy. Tonight more so. The BBC news had again been very bad with reports of greatly increased confrontations in Tehran, Meshed, and Qom. Added to this was McIver's report that Ayre had carefully relayed from Kowiss in French—news of the continuing investiture of Tehran's International Airport, of the possible coup and about Kyabi. Kyabi's murder had also shocked de Plessey. And all of this, along with the floods of rumors and counterrumors among the Iranians had made the evening somber. Rumors of imminent U.S. military intervention, of imminent Soviet intervention, of assassination attempts on Khomeini, on Bazargan his chosen prime minister, on Bakhtiar the legal prime minister, on the U.S. ambassador, rumors that the military coup d'état would happen in Tehran tonight, that Khomeini was arrested already, that all the armed services had capitulated and Khomeini was already de facto ruler of Iran and that General Nassiri, chief of SAVAK, had been captured, tried and shot.

"All the rumors can't be true," Kasigi had said for all of them. "There's nothing we can do except wait."

He had been a fine host. All the food was Japanese. Even the beer. Scragger had tried to hide his distaste for the hors d'oeuvre of sushi but he greatly enjoyed the barbecued chicken in a salty sweet sauce, the rice, and the deep-fried prawns and vegetables in batter. "Another beer, Captain Scragger?" Kasigi had offered.

"No, thanks. One's all I allow myself though I'll admit it's good. Maybe not as good as Foster's but close."

De Plessey had smiled, "You don't know what a compliment that is, Mr. Kasigi. For an Australian to say a beer's 'close to Foster's' is praise indeed."

"Oh, yes, indeed I know, Mr. de Plessey. Down Under I prefer Foster's."

"You spend a lot of time there?" Scragger had asked him.

"Oh, yes. Australia's one of Japan's main sources of all kinds of raw materials. My company has bulk cargo freighters for coal, iron ore, wheat, rice, soya bean," Kasigi had said. "We import huge amounts of your rice though much of that goes into the manufacture of our national drink, sake. Have you tried sake, Captain?"

"Yes, yes I did once. But warm wine . . . sake's not to my taste."

"I agree," de Plessey said, then added hurriedly, "except in winter, like hot toddy. You were saying about Australia?"

"I enjoy the country very much. My eldest son goes to Sydney University too, so we visit him from time to time. It's a wonderland—so vast, so rich, so empty."

Yes, Scragger had thought grimly. You mean so empty and just waiting to be filled up by your millions of worker ants? Thank the Lord we're a few thousand miles away and the U.S.'ll never allow us to be taken over.

"Bollocks!" McIver had said to him once during a friendly argument, when he, McIver, and Pettikin were on a week's leave two years ago in Singapore. "If some time in the future Japan picked the right time, say when the U.S. was having at Russia, the States wouldn't be able to do a thing to help Australia. I think they'd make a deal an—"

"Dirty Duncan's lost his marbles, Charlie," Scragger had said.

"You're right," Pettikin had agreed. "He's just needling you, Scrag."

"Oh, no, I'm not. Your real protector's China. Come hell or strawberries, China's always going to be there. And only China will always be in a position to stop Japan if ever Japan got militant and strong enough to move south. My God, Australia's the great prize in the whole Pacific, the treasure chest of the Pacific, but none of you buggers down there care to plan ahead or use your loaf. All you bloody want's three days' holiday a week, with more pay for less bloody work, free bloody school, free medical, free welfare, and let some other bugger man the ramparts—you're worse than poor old bloody England who's got nothing! The real tr—"

"You've got North Sea oil. If that's not the luck of the devil I do—"

"The real trouble is you bloody twits Down Under don't know your arse from a hole in the wall."

"Sit down, Scrag!" Pettikin had said warningly. "You agreed no fighting.

None. You try and thump Mac when he's not smashed you'll end up in the sewer. He may have high blood pressure but he's still a black belt."

"Me thump Dirty Duncan? You must be joking, cobber. I don't pick on old buggers. . . ."

Scragger smiled to himself, remembering their bender to end all benders. Singapore's a good place, he thought, then turned his attention back to the ship, feeling better now, well fed and very glad that the loading was done.

The night was grand. Far above him he saw the blinking navigation lights of an airplane heading westward and wondered briefly where its landfall was, what airline it was and how many passengers were aboard. His night vision was excellent and he could see that now the men on the barge had almost unscrewed the pipe. Once it had been winched aboard, the tanker could leave. At dawn the *Rikomaru* would be in the Strait of Hormuz and he would take off and fly home to Lengeh with de Plessey.

Then his sharp eyes saw some men running away from the semifloodlit pumping junction just ashore. His attention zeroed on them.

There was a small explosion, then a gush of flame as the oil caught fire. Everyone aboard watched aghast. The flames began to spread, and they heard shouting—Iranian and French—ashore. Men were running down from the barracks and storage tanks area. A sudden flicker of a machine gun in the darkness, the sharp ugly crackle following. Over the ship's loudspeaker system came the captain's voice in Japanese: "Action stations!"

At once the men on the barge redoubled their efforts, petrified that somehow the fire might spread through the pipe to the barge and blow it up. The moment the nozzle fell away from the valve, the Iranians hastily jumped into their small motorboat and fled, their work completed. The French engineer and Japanese seamen ran up the gangplank as the tanker's deck winch rattled into life, dragging the pipe aboard.

Belowdecks the crew had scurried to emergency positions, some to the engine room, some to the bridge, others to the main gangways. Momentarily the three Iranians monitoring the fuel flow in various parts of the ship were left alone. They rushed for the deck.

One of them, Saiid, pretended to stumble and fall near the main tank inlet. When he was sure he was not observed he hastily opened his trousers and brought out the small plastic explosive device that had been missed in the body search when he had come aboard. It had been taped to the inside of a thigh, high up between his legs. Hastily he activated the chemical detonator that would explode in about one hour, stuck the device behind the main valve, and ran for the gangway. When he came on deck he was appalled to find that the men on the barge had not waited and that now the motorboat was almost ashore. The other two Iranians were chattering excitedly, equally enraged to be left aboard. Neither were members of his leftist cell.

Onshore the oil spill was blazing out of control but the oil supply had been cut and the break isolated. Three men had been badly burned, one French and two Iranians. The mobile fire-fighting truck poured seawater into the flames, sucking it up from the Gulf. There was no wind and the choking black smoke made fire fighting even more difficult.

"Get some foam onto it," Legrande, the French manager, shouted. Almost beside himself with rage, he tried to get order, but everyone was still milling about in the floodlights not knowing what to do. "Jacques, round up everyone and let's count heads. Fast as you can." Their full complement was seven French and thirty Iranians on the island. The security force of three men hurried off into the darkness, unarmed except for hastily made batons, not knowing what further sabotage to expect or from where.

"M'sieur!" The Iranian medic was beckoning Legrande.

He went down toward the shore to the complex of pipes and valves that joined the tanks to the barge. The medic was kneeling beside two of the injured men who lay on a piece of canvas, unconscious and in shock. One of them had had his hair completely singed off and most of his face severely burned; the other had been sprayed with oil in the initial explosion that had instantly conflagrated his clothes, causing first-degree burns over most of the front of his body.

"Madonna," Legrande muttered and crossed himself, seeing the ugly charred skin, barely recognizing his Iranian foreman.

One of his French engineers sat hunched over and was moaning softly, his hands and arms burned. Mixed with his agony was a constant stream of expletives.

"I'll get you to the hospital, fast as I can, Paul."

"Find those fornicators and burn them," the engineer snarled, then went back into his pain.

"Of course," Legrande said helplessly, then to the medic, "Do what you can, I'll call for a CASEVAC." He hurried away from the shore for the radio room that was in one of the barracks, his eyes adjusting to the darkness. Then he noticed two men on the far side of the tiny airstrip, running up the track on the slight bluff. Over that bluff was a cove with a small wharf used for sailing and swimming. I'll bet the bastards have a boat there, he thought at once. Then, almost berserk with rage, he shouted after them into the night, "Bastardsssss!"

When the first explosion had occurred de Plessey had rushed for the ship-to-shore radio that was on the bridge. "Have you found that machine gun yet?" he asked the base submanager in French. Behind him, Scragger, Kasigi, and the captain were equally grim. Lights on the bridge were dimmed. Outside, the moon was high and strong.

"No, m'sieur. After the first burst, the attackers vanished."

"What about the damage to the pumping system?"

"I don't know. I'm waiting for a . . . ah, just a moment, here's M'sieur Legrande." After a moment again in French: "This's Legrande. Three burned, two Iranians very badly, the other's Paul Beaulieu, hands and arms—call for a CASEVAC at once. I saw a couple of men heading for the cove—probably the saboteurs, and they've probably a boat there. I'm assembling everyone so we can see who's missing."

"Yes, at once. What about the damage?"

"Not major. With luck we'll have that fixed in a week—certainly by the time the next tanker arrives."

"I'll come ashore as soon as I can. Wait a moment!" De Plessey looked at the others and told them what Legrande had said.

Scragger said at once, "I'll take the CASEVAC, no need to call for one."

Kasigi said, "Bring the injured aboard—we've a surgery and a doctor. He's very skilled, particularly with burns."

"Good on you!" Scragger rushed off.

Into the mike de Plessey said, "We'll deal with the CASEVAC from here. Get the men onto stretchers. Captain Scragger will bring them aboard at once. There's a doctor here."

A young Japanese deck officer came and spoke briefly to the captain who shook his head and replied curtly, then explained in English to de Plessey: "The three Iranians who were left aboard when the others on the barge fled want to be taken ashore at once. I said they could wait." Then he called down to the engine room preparing to make way.

Kasigi was staring at the island. And at the tanks there. I need that oil, he thought, and I need the island safe. But it's not safe and nothing I can do to make it safe.

"I'm going ashore," de Plessey said and left.

Scragger was already at the 206, unhooking the rear doors.

"What're you doing, Scrag?" de Plessey said, hurrying up to him.

"I can lay the stretcher on the backseat and lash it safe. Quicker than rigging an outside carry sling."

"I'll come with you."

"Hop in!" They glanced around at the noise behind them. The three Iranians had run over and were jabbering at him. It was clear they wanted to go ashore in the helicopter. "Shall we take them, Scrag?"

Scragger was already in the pilot's seat, his fingers dancing over the switches. "No. You're an emergency, they're not. Get in, old sport." He pointed at the right seat then waved the Iranians away. *"Nah, ajaleh daram"* —No, I'm in a hurry—he said, using one of the few expressions in Farsi he knew. Two of them backed off obediently. The third, Saiid, slid into the backseat and started to buckle up. Scragger shook his head, motioning him to get out. The man took no notice and spoke rapidly and forced a smile and pointed at the shore.

Impatiently Scragger motioned him out, one finger pressing the Engine Start button switch. The whine began instantly. Again the man refused and, angry now, pointed at the shore, his voice drowned by the cranking engine. For a moment Scragger thought, Okay, why not? Then he noticed the sweat dripping off the man's face, his sweat-soaked overalls, and seemed to smell his fear. "Out!" he said, studying him very carefully.

Saiid paid no attention to him. Above them the blade was turning slowly, gaining speed.

"Let him stay," de Plessey called out over. "We'd better hurry."

Abruptly Scragger aborted the engine start, and with very great strength for such a small man, had Saiid's belt unbuckled and the man out on the deck, half unconscious, before anyone knew what was happening. He cupped his hands around his mouth and shouted up at the bridge. "Hey there, aloft! Kasigi! This joker's too bloody anxious to go ashore—wasn't he belowdecks?" Without waiting for an answer, he jumped back into the cockpit and jabbed Engine Start.

De Plessey watched him silently. "What did you see in that man?"

Scragger shrugged. Long before the engine came to full power, seamen had grabbed the man and the other two and were herding them up to the bridge.

The 206 went like an arrow for the shore. The two injured men were already on stretchers. Rapidly a spare stretcher was lashed in place across the backseat and the first stretcher lashed to this. Scragger helped the injured Frenchman, arms and hands bandaged, into the front seat alongside him, and trying to close his nostrils to the stench, eased her airborne and flew back, landing like gossamer. Medics and the doctor were waiting, plasma ready, morphine hypodermic ready.

In seconds Scragger darted shoreward again. In more seconds the last stretcher was in place and he was away, again to land delicately. Once more the doctor was waiting, needle ready, and again he ducked down and ran for the stretcher under the whirling blades. This time he did not use the needle.

"Ah so sorry," he said in halting English. "This man dead." Then, keeping his head low, he scurried for his surgery. Medics took the body away.

When Scragger had shut down and had everything locked and safe, he went to the side of the ship and was violently sick. Ever since he had seen and heard and smelled a pilot in a crashed, burning biplane, years upon years ago, it had been an abiding horror of his to be caught in the same way. He had never been able to stomach the smell of burned human hair and skin.

After a while he wiped his mouth, breathing the good air, and blessed his luck. Three times he had been shot down, twice in flames, but each time he had got out safely. Four times he had had to autorotate to save himself and his passengers, twice over jungle and into the trees, once with an engine on fire. "But my name wasn't on the list," he muttered. "Not those times." Footsteps were approaching. He turned to see Kasigi walking across the deck, an ice-cold bottle of Kirin beer in each hand.

"Please excuse me, but here," Kasigi said gravely, offering the beer. "Burns do the same for me. I was sick too. I . . . I went down to the surgery to see how the injured were and . . . I was very sick."

Scragger drank gratefully. The cool, hops-flavored liquid, bubbles tingling as he swallowed, rebirthed him. "Christ Jesus that was good. Thanks, cobber." And having said it once it became easier to say it the second time. "Thanks, cobber." Kasigi heard it both times and considered it a major victory. Both of them looked at the seaman hurrying up to them with a teleprinter message in his hand. He gave it to Kasigi who went to the nearest light, put on his glasses, and peered at it. Scragger heard him suck in his breath and saw him become even more ashen.

"Bad news?"

After a pause Kasigi said, "No—just, just problems."

"Anything I can do?"

Kasigi did not answer him. Scragger waited. He could see the turmoil written in the man's eyes though not his face, and he was sure Kasigi was trying to decide whether to tell him. Then Kasigi said, "I don't think so. It's . . . it's about our petrochemical plant at Bandar Delam."

"The one Japan's building?" Along with most everyone else in the Gulf, Scragger knew about the enormous $3.5 billion endeavor that, when completed, would easily be the biggest petrochemical complex in Asia Minor and the Middle East, with a 300,000-ton ethylene plant as its heart. It had been building since '71 and was almost finished, 85 percent complete. "That's some plant!"

"Yes. But it's being built by Japanese private industry, not by the Japanese government," Kasigi said. "The Iran-Toda plant's privately financed."

"Ah," Scragger said, the connection falling into place. "*Toda* Shipping—Iran-*Toda*! You're the same company?"

"Yes, but we're only part of the Japanese syndicate that put up the money and technical advice for the Shah . . . for Iran," Kasigi corrected himself. All gods great and small curse this land, curse everyone in it, curse the Shah for creating all the oil crises, curse OPEC, curse all the misbegotten fanatics and liars who live here. He glanced at the message again and was pleased to see his fingers were not shaking. It was in private code from his chairman, Hiro Toda.

It read: "URGENT. Due to absolute and continuous Iranian intransigence, I have finally had to order all construction at Bandar Delam to cease. Present cost overruns total $500 million and would probably go to 1 billion before we could begin production. Present interest payments are $495,000 daily. Due to infamous secret pressure by 'Broken Sword,' our Contingency Plan 4 has been rejected. Go to Bandar Delam urgently and give me a personal report. Chief Engineer Director Watanabe is expecting you. Please acknowledge."

It's impossible to get there, Kasigi thought crestfallen. And if Plan 4 is rejected, we're ruined.

Contingency Plan 4 called for Hiro Toda to approach the Japanese government for low-interest loans to take up the shortfall, and at the same time, discreetly, to petition the prime minister to declare the Iran-Toda complex at Bandar Delam a "National Project." "National Project" meant that the government formally accepted the vital nature of the endeavor and would see it through to completion. "Broken Sword" was their code name for Hiro Toda's personal enemy and chief rival, Hideyoshi Ishida, who headed the enormously powerful group of trading companies under the general name of Mitsuwari.

All gods curse that jealous, lying son of vermin, Ishida, Kasigi was thinking, as he said, "My company is only one of many in the Syndicate."

"I flew over your plant once," Scragger said, "going from our base to Abadan. I was on a ferry, ferrying a 212. You've trouble there?"

"Some temporary . . ." Kasigi stopped and stared at him. Pieces of a plan fell into place. "Some temporary problems . . . important but temporary. As you know we've had more than our fair share of problems since the beginning, none of them our fault." First there was February '71 when twenty-three oil producers signed the OPEC price agreement, formed their cartel, and doubled the price to $2.16 . . . then the Yom Kippur War of '73 when OPEC cut shipments to the United States and raised the price to $5.12. Then the catastrophe of '74 when OPEC shipments were resumed but again at over double the price, $10.95, and the world recession began. "Why the U.S. allowed OPEC to wreck the economy of the world when they alone had the power to smash it, we'll never know. *Baka!* And now we're all in a perpetual pawn to OPEC, now our major supplier Iran is in revolution, oil's almost $20 a barrel and we have to pay it, have to." He bunched his fist to smash it on the gunnel, then unclenched, disgusted with his lack of control. "As to Iran-Toda," he said, forcing outward calm, "like everyone else we found Iranians very . . . very difficult to deal with in recent years." He motioned at the message. "My chairman asked me to go to Bandar Delam."

Scragger whistled. "That's going to be dicey—difficult."

"Yes."

"Is it important?"

"Yes. Yes, it is." Kasigi left that hanging in the air, sure that Scragger would suggest the solution. Ashore the oil-soaked earth around the sabotaged valve complex still burned brightly. The fire truck was spreading foam now. They could see de Plessey nearby, talking to Legrande.

Scragger said, "Listen, old sport, you're an important client of de Plessey, eh? He could fix a charter for you. We've a spare 206. If he agreed, all our aircraft are contracted to IranOil but to him in truth, perhaps we could get permission from air traffic control to fly you up the coast—or if you could clear Immigration and Customs at Lengeh, maybe we could nip you across the Gulf to Dubai or Al Shargaz. From there perhaps you could get a flight into Abadan or Bandar Delam. Whichever, old sport, he could let us get you started."

"Do you think he would?"

"Why not? You're important to him."

Kasigi was thinking, Of course we're very important to him and he knows it. But I'll never forget that iniquitous $2-a-barrel premium. "Sorry? What did you say?"

"I said, wot made you start the project anyway? It's a long way from home and had to be nothing but trouble. Wot started you?"

"A dream." Kasigi would like to have lit a cigarette but smoking was only allowed in certain fireproofed areas. "Eleven years ago, in '68, a man called Banjiro Kayama, a senior engineer working for my company and kinsman of our president, Hiro Toda, was driving through the oil fields around Abadan. It was his first visit to Iran and everywhere he went he saw jets of natural gas being flared off. He had a sudden thought: why can't we turn that wasted gas into petrochemicals? We've the technology and the expertise and a long-range-planning attitude. Japanese skill and money married to Iranian raw materials that presently are totally wasted! A brilliant idea—unique and another first! The feasibility planning took three years, quite long enough, though jealous rivals claimed we went too quickly, at the same time they tried to steal our ideas and tried to poison others against us. But the Toda plan correctly went forward and the $3.5 billion raised. Of course, we're only a part of the Gyokotomo-Mitsuwari-Toda Syndicate, but Toda ships will carry Japan's share of the products that our industries desperately need." If ever we can finish the complex, he thought disgustedly.

"And now the dream's a nightmare?" Scragger asked. "Didn't I hear . . . wasn't it reported that the project was running out of money?"

"Enemies spread all sorts of rumors." Under the ever-present drone of the ship's generators, his ears heard the beginning of a scream that he had been expecting—surprised it had been so long arriving. "When de Plessey comes back aboard, will you help me?"

"Glad to. He's the man who c—" Scragger stopped. Again the thin edge of the scream. "Burns must be terrible painful."

Kasigi nodded.

Another gush of flame took their attention to the shore. They watched the men there. Now the fire was almost under control. Another scream. Kasigi dismissed it, his mind on Bandar Delam and the teleprinter reply he should make at once to Hiro Toda. If anyone can solve our problem it's Hiro Toda. He has to solve it—if he doesn't, I'm ruined, his failure becomes mine.

"Kasigi-san!" It was the captain calling from the bridge.

"*Hai?*"

Scragger listened to the stream of Japanese from the captain, the sound of the Japanese not pleasing to his ears.

Kasigi gasped. "*Domo,*" he shouted back, then, urgently to Scragger all else forgotten, "Come on!" He led the rush to the gangway. "The Iranian— you remember, the one you threw out of the chopper? He's a saboteur and he's planted an explosive device below."

Scragger followed Kasigi through the hatchway, down the gangway two steps a time, rushed along the corridor, and down another deck and another and then he remembered the screams. I thought they came from the bridge and not from below! he told himself. Wot did they do to him?

They caught up with the captain and his chief engineer. Two angry seamen half shoved, half dragged the petrified Saiid ahead of them. Tears ran down his face and he was jabbering incoherently, one hand holding his pants up. He stopped, trembling and moaning, and pointed at the valve. The captain squatted on his haunches. Very carefully he reached behind the huge valve. Then he stood up. The plastic explosive just covered his hand. The timing device was chemical, a vial embedded in it and taped strongly in place.

"Turn it off," he said angrily in hesitant Farsi and held it out to the man who backed off, jabbering and screaming, "You can't turn it off. It's overdue to explode . . . don't you understand!"

The captain froze. "He says it's overdue!"

Before he could move, one of the seamen grabbed it out of his hand and half dragging Saiid with him, half smashing him ahead, rushed for the gangway—there were no portholes on this deck but there were on the next. The nearest porthole was in a corner of the corridor, clamped shut by two heavy metal wing nuts. He almost flung Saiid at it, shouting at him to open it. With his free hand he began unscrewing one of them. The swing bolt fell away, then Saiid's. The seaman swung the port open. At that second the device exploded and blew both his hands off and most of his face and tore Saiid's head apart and splattered the far bulkhead with blood.

The others charging up from below were almost blown backward down the gangway. Then Kasigi went forward and knelt beside the bodies. Numbly he shook his head.

The captain broke the silence. "Karma," he muttered.

CHAPTER 13

AT TEHRAN: 8:33 P.M. After Tom Lochart had left McIver near their office he had driven home—a few diversions, some angry police but nothing untoward. Home was a fine penthouse apartment in a modern six-story building, in the best residential area—a wedding present from his father-in-law. Sharazad was waiting for him. She threw her arms around him, kissed him passionately, begged him to sit in front of the fire and take his shoes off, rushed to fetch some wine that was iced exactly as he liked, brought him a snack, told him that dinner would be ready soon, ran into the kitchen and in her lilting, liquid voice, urged their maid and the cook to hurry for the Master was home and hungry, then came back and sat at his feet—the floor beautifully and heavily carpeted—her arms around his knees, adoring him. "Oh, I'm so happy to see you, Tommy, I've missed you so much," her English lovely. "Oh, I've had such an interesting time today and yesterday."

She wore light silk Persian trousers and a long loose blouse and was, for

him, achingly beautiful. And desirable. Her twenty-third birthday was in a
few days. He was forty-two. They had been married almost a year and he had
been spellbound from the first moment he had seen her.

That had been a little over three years before, at a dinner party in Tehran
that was given by General Valik. It was early September then, just at the end
of English school summer vacations, and Deirdre, his wife, was in England
with their daughter, holidaying and partying, and only that morning he had
had another irate letter from her, insisting he write to Gavallan for an immediate transfer: "I hate Iran, don't want to live there anymore, England's all I
want, all that Monica wants. Why don't you think of us for a change instead
of your damned flying and damned company? All my family's here, all my
friends are here, and all Monica's friends are here. I'm fed up with living
abroad and want my own house, somewhere near London, with a garden, or
even in town—there are some super bargains going in Putney and Clapham
Common. I'm totally fed up with foreigners and foreign postings, and absolutely chocker with Iranian food, the filth, the heat, the cold, their foul-
sounding language, their foul loos and squatting like an animal, and foul
habits, manners—everything. It's time we sorted out things while I'm still
young . . ."
"Excellency?"
The smiling, starched waiter had deferentially offered him a tray of drinks,
soft drinks mostly. Many middle- and upper-class Muslims drank in the privacy of their homes, a few in public—liquor and wine of all sorts being on
sale in Tehran, and also in bars in all modern hotels. There were no restric-
tions on foreigners drinking openly or privately, unlike in Saudi Arabia—and
some of the Emirates—where anyone caught, anyone, was subject to Koranic
punishment of the lash.
"*Mamoonan,*" thank you, he said politely and accepted a glass of the white
Persian wine that had been sought after for almost three millennia, hardly
noticing the waiter or the other guests, unable to shake off his depression and
irritated that he agreed to join this party tonight, substituting for McIver
who had had to go to their HQ base at Al Shargaz, the other side of the Gulf.
"But, Tom, you can talk Farsi," McIver had said airily, "and someone's got to
go . . ." Yes, he thought, but Mac could just as easily have asked Charlie
Pettikin.
	It was almost nine o'clock, still before dinner, and he had been standing
near one of the open doorways that led to the gardens, looking out at the
candlelights and at the lawns that were spread with fine rugs on which guests
were sitting and reclining, others standing in groups under trees or near the

little pond. The night was star-filled and kind, the house rich and spacious—in the district of Shemiran at the foot of the Elburz Mountains—and the party like most of the others that, because he could speak Farsi, he was usually welcomed to. All the Iranians were very well-dressed, there was much laughter and much jewelry, tables piled with an abundance of food, both European and Iranian, hot and cold, the conversation about the latest play in London or New York or "Are you going to St. Moritz for the skiing or Cannes for the season," and about the price of oil and gossip about the Court and "His Imperial Majesty this or Her Imperial Majesty that," all of it spiced with the politeness and flattery and extravagant compliment so necessary in all Iranian society—preserving a calm, polite, and gentle surface rarely penetrated by an outsider, let alone by a foreigner.

At the time he was stationed at Galeg Morghi, a military airfield in Tehran, training Iranian Air Force pilots. In ten days he was due to leave for his new posting at Zagros, well aware that this tour with two weeks in Zagros, one week back in Tehran would further inflame his wife. This morning, in a fit of rage, he had answered her letter and sent it special delivery: "If you want to stay in England, stay in England but stop bitching and stop knocking what you don't know. Get your suburban house wherever you want—but I'm not EVER going to live there. Never. I've a good job and it pays all right and I like it and that's it. We've a good life if you'd open your eyes. You knew I was a pilot when we got married, knew it was the life I'd chosen, knew I wouldn't live in England, knew it's all I'm trained for so I can't change now. Stop bitching or else. If you want to change so be it. . . ."

The hell with it. I've had it. Christ, she says she hates Iran and everything about it but she knows nothing about Iran, has never been outside Tehran, won't go, will never even try the food and just visits with those few Brit wives —always the same ones, the loud and bigoted minority, insular, equally bored and boring with their interminable bridge parties, interminable teas—"But, darling, how can you stand anything that's not from Fortnums or Marks and Sparks"—who preen for an invitation to the British embassy for another stuffy roast beef and Yorkshire pudding dinner or tea party with cucumber sandwiches and seedcake, all of them totally convinced everything English is the best in the world, particularly English cooking: boiled carrots, boiled cauliflower, boiled potatoes, boiled Brussels sprouts, underdone roast beef or overdone lamb as the acme of goddamn perfection. . . .

"Oh, poor Excellency, you don't look happy at all," she had said softly.

He had looked around and his world was different.

"What's the matter?" she asked, a tiny frown on her oval face.

"Sorry," he gasped, for a moment disoriented by her, his heart thumping and a tightness in his throat he had never experienced before. "I thought you were an apparition, something out of *A Thousand and One Nights*, a magical—" He stopped with an effort, feeling like a fool. "Sorry, I was a million miles away. My name's Lochart, Tom Lochart."

"Yes, I know," she said laughing. Tawny brown twinkling eyes. Her lips had a sheen to them, teeth very white, long wavy dark hair, and her skin was the color of Iranian earth, olive brown. She wore white silk and some perfume and she barely came up to his chin. "You're the nasty training captain who gives my poor cousin Karim roastings at least three times a day."

"What?" Lochart found it difficult to concentrate. "Who?"

"There." She pointed across the room. The young man was in civilians, smiling at them, and Lochart had not recognized him as one of his students. Very handsome, dark curly hair, dark eyes, and well built. "My special cousin, Captain Karim Peshadi, of the Imperial Iranian Air Force." She looked back at Lochart, long black lashes. And again his heart turned over.

Get hold of yourself, for crissake! What the hell's wrong with you? "I, er, well, I try not to roast them unless, er, unless they deserve it—it's only to save their lives." He was trying to remember Captain Peshadi's record but couldn't and in desperation switched to Farsi. "But, Highness, if you'll give me the exquisite honor, if you'll stay and talk to me and favor me by telling me your name I promise I will . . ." He groped for the right word, couldn't find it and substituted, "I will be your slave forever and of course I will have to pass His Excellency your cousin one hundred percent before all others!"

She clapped her hands delightedly, "Oh, revered Excellency," she replied in Farsi, "His Excellency my cousin did not tell me you spoke our language! Oh how beautiful the words sound when you say them. . . ."

Almost outside himself, Lochart listened to her extravagant compliments that were normal in Farsi and heard himself replying likewise—blessing Scragger who had told him so many years ago when he had joined Sheik Aviation, after he had left the RAF in '65: "If you want to fly with us, cobber, you'd better learn Farsi 'cause I'm not about to!" For the first time realizing how perfect it was a language of love, of innuendo.

"My name is Sharazad Paknouri, Excellency."

"Then Her Highness is from the *Thousand and One Nights* after all."

"Ah, but I cannot tell you a story even if you swear you will cut off my head!" Then in English, with a laugh, "I was bottom of my class in stories."

"Impossible!" he said at once.

"Are you always so gallant, Captain Lochart?" Her eyes were teasing him.

In Farsi he heard himself say, "Only to the most beautiful woman I have ever seen."

Color came into her face. She dropped her eyes, and he thought, aghast, he had destroyed everything, but when she looked up at him again her eyes were smiling. "Thank you. You make an old married lady happ—"

His glass slipped out of his hand and he cursed and picked it up and apologized but no one had noticed except her. "You're married?" burst out of him, for it hadn't occurred to him, but of course she would be married and anyway he was married with a daughter of eight and what right did he have to get upset? For God's sake you're acting like a lunatic. You've gone mad.

Then his ears and eyes focused. "What? What did you say?" he asked.

"Oh. I said that I *was* married—well, I still am for another three weeks and two days and that my married name is Paknouri. My family name is Bakravan . . ." She stopped a waiter and chose a glass of wine and gave it to him. Again the frown. "Are you sure you're all right, Captain?"

"Oh, yes, oh, yes," he said quickly, "You were saying? Paknouri?"

"Yes. His Highness, Emir Paknouri, was so old, fifty, a friend of my father, and Father and Mother thought it would be good for me to marry him and he consented though I'm skinny, not plump and desirable, however much I eat. As God wants." She shrugged then beamed and the world seemed to light up for him. "Of course I agreed, but only on condition that if I didn't like being married after two years then our marriage would cease. So on my seventeenth birthday we were married and I didn't like it at once and cried and cried and then, as there were no children after two years, or the extra year I agreed to, my husband, my Master, gratefully agreed to divorce me and now he is thankfully ready to remarry and I am free but unfortunately so old an—"

"You're not old, you're as youn—"

"Oh, yes, old!" Her eyes were dancing and she pretended to be sad but he could see that she was not and he watched himself talking to her, laughing with her, then beckoning her cousin to join them, petrified that this was the real man of her choice, chatting with them, learning that her father was an important bazaari, that her family was large and cosmopolitan and well connected, that her mother was sick, that she had sisters and brothers and had been to school in Switzerland but only for half a year because she missed Iran and her family so much. Then eating dinner with them, genial and happy, even with General Valik, and it was the best time he had ever had.

When he had left that night he had not gone home but had taken the road up to Darband in the mountains where there were many cafés in beautiful gardens on the banks of the stream with chairs and tables and sumptuously carpeted divans where you could rest or eat or sleep, some of them esplanaded out over the stream so the water chattered and gurgled below you.

And he lay there, looking up at the stars, knowing that he was changed, knowing he'd gone mad but that he would scale any hurdle, endure any hardship, to marry her.

And he had—though the way had been cruel and many times he had cried out in despair.

"What are you thinking about, Tommy?" she asked now, sitting at his feet on the lovely carpet that had been a wedding gift from General Valik.

"You," he said, loving her, his cares banished by her tenderness. The living room was warm like all of the huge apartment, and delicately lit, the curtains drawn and many rugs and lounging cushions scattered around, the wood fire burning merrily. "But then I think about you all the time!"

She clapped her hands. "That's wonderful."

"I'm not going to Zagros tomorrow but the next day."

"Oh, that's even more wonderful!" She hugged his knees and rested her head against them. "Wonderful!"

He caressed her hair. "You said you had an interesting day?"

"Yes, yesterday and today. I've been to your embassy and got the passport, just as you told me to do, th—"

"Great. Now you're Canadian."

"No, Beloved, Iranian—you're Canadian. Listen, the best part is that I went to Doshan Tappeh," she said proudly.

"Christ," he said, not meaning to, for she did not like to hear him blaspheme. "Sorry, but that's—that was crazy, there's fighting going on there, you're crazy to put yourself in such danger."

"Oh, I wasn't in the fighting," she told him gaily, and got up and rushed out saying, "I'll show you." In a moment she was back in the doorway. She had put on a gray chador that covered her from head to toe and most of her face, and he hated it. "Ah, Master," she said in Farsi, pirouetting in front of him. "You have no need to fear over me. God watches over me, and the Prophet whose Name be praised." She stopped, seeing his expression. "What's the matter?" she asked in English.

"I—I've never seen you in chador. It's—it doesn't suit you."

"Oh, I know it's ugly and I'd never wear it at home, but in the street I feel better wearing one, Tommy. All those awful stares from men. It's time we all went back to wearing them—and the veil."

He was shocked. "What about all the freedoms you've won, freedom to vote, to take off the veil, freedom to go where you please, marry whom you please, no longer the chattel that you used to be? If you agree to the chador, you'll lose everything else."

"Perhaps, perhaps not, Tommy." She was glad that they were talking in English so she could argue a little, unthinkable with an Iranian husband. And so glad that she had chosen to marry this man who, unbelievably, allowed her an opinion, and even more astonishing, allowed her to express it openly to him. This wine of freedom is very heady, she thought, very difficult, very dangerous for a woman to drink—like nectar in the Garden of Paradise.

"When Reza Shah took the veil from our faces," she said, "he should also have taken the obsession from the minds of men. You don't go to market, Tommy, or ride in a car, not as a woman. You've no idea what it's like. Men on the streets, in the bazaar, in the bank, everywhere. They're all the same. You can see the same thoughts, the same obsession, in all of them—thoughts about me which only you should have." She took off the chador, put it neatly on a chair, and sat down at his feet again. "From today on I will wear it on the street, like my mother and hers before me, not because of Khomeini, God protect him, but for you, my beloved husband."

She kissed him lightly and sat at his knee and he knew it was decided. Unless he ordered her not to. But then there would be trouble in the home, for it was truly her right to decide this matter here. She was Iranian, his home Iranian, and always would be in Iran—that was part of his bargain with her father—so the trouble would be Iranian and the solution Iranian: days of vast sighs and soul-filled glances, a little tear, abject, slavelike service, judicious sobs in the night, more tortured sighs, never a word or look in anger and all murderous to a husband's or father's or brother's peace.

Lochart found her so hard to understand sometimes. "Do as you want, but no more Doshan Tappeh," he said, caressing her hair. It was fine and silky and shone as only youth can shine. "What happened there?"

Her face lit up. "Oh, it was so exciting. The Immortals—even them, the Shah's crack troops—couldn't dislodge the Faithful. Guns were going off everywhere. I was quite safe, my sister Laleh was with me, my cousin Ali and his wife. Cousin Karim was there—he's declared for Islam and the revolution with several other officers and he told us where to meet him and how. There were about two hundred other ladies, all of us in chador, and we kept up our chanting, God is Great, God is Great, then some of the soldiers came over to us. Immortals!" Her eyes widened. "Imagine, even the Immortals are beginning to see the Truth!"

Lochart was appalled at the danger of her going there without asking or telling him, even though she was accompanied. Thus far the insurrection and Khomeini had seemingly passed her by, except initially when the real troubles began and she was petrified over the safety of her father and relations who were important merchants and bankers in the bazaar, and well known for their connections at Court. Thankfully her father had dispelled all their concerns when he had whispered to Lochart that he and his brothers were secretly supporting Khomeini and the revolt against the Shah and had been doing so for years. But now, he thought, now if the Immortals are cracking and top-echelon young officers like Karim are openly supporting the revolt the bloodshed will be enormous. "How many came over?" he asked, trying to decide what to do.

"Only three joined us, but Karim said it's a good beginning and any day Bakhtiar and his scoundrels will flee like the Shah fled."

"Listen, Sharazad, today the British and Canadian governments've ordered all dependents out of Iran for a while. Mac's sending everyone to Al Shargaz till things cool down."

"That's very wise, yes, that's wise."

"Tomorrow the 125'll be in. She'll take Genny, Manuela, you, and Azadeh tomorrow so pack a b—"

"Oh, I won't leave, my darling, no need for me to leave. And Azadeh, why should she go either? There's no danger for us—Father would certainly know if there was any danger. No need for you to worry . . ." She saw his wine-glass was nearly empty so she jumped up and refilled it and came back again. "I'm quite safe."

"But I think you'd be safer out of Iran for a wh—"

"It's wonderful of you to think of me, my darling, but there's no reason for me to go and I'll certainly ask Father tomorrow, or you can . . ." A small ember of wood fell without danger into the grate. He started to get up but she was already there. "I'll do it. Rest, my darling, you must be tired. Perhaps you'd have time tomorrow to see Father with me." Deftly she tidied the fire. Her chador was on a nearby chair. She saw him glance at it. The shadow of a smile washed over her.

"What?"

For answer she just smiled again, picked it up, and ran gaily across the room and down the corridor to the kitchen.

Unsettled, Lochart stared at the fire, trying to marshal his arguments, not wanting to order her. But I will if I have to. My God, so many troubles: Charlie vanished, Kowiss in a mess, Kyabi murdered, and Sharazad in the middle of a riot! She's crazy! Mad to take such a risk! If I lost her I'd die. God, whoever you are, wherever you are, protect her . . .

This living room was large. At the far end was a dining-room table and chairs that could seat twelve. Most times, they would use the room in Iranian style, sitting on the floor, a tablecloth spread for the dishes, lounging against cushions. Rarely did they wear shoes and never high heels that could damage the deep carpets. There were five bedrooms, three bathrooms, two living rooms—this one they used generally or with company, the other, much smaller at the far end of the apartment was, as customary, for her to go to when he had business to discuss, or when her sister or girlfriends or relations were visiting so their chatter would not disturb him. Around Sharazad was always movement, always family nearby, children, nannies—except after sunset, though frequently relations or close friends were staying in the guest bedrooms.

He never minded, for they were a happy, gregarious family, in front of him. It was also part of his bargain with her father that he would patiently learn Iranian ways, patiently live Iranian ways for three years and a day. Then he could choose to live outside Iran temporarily with Sharazad if he needed to: "Because by then," her father, Jared Bakravan, had said kindly, "with the Help of the One God and the Prophet of God, may His words live forever, by then you will have enough knowledge to make the correct choice, for surely by then you will have sons and daughters, for though my daughter is thin, divorced, and still childless, I do not think she is barren."

"But she's still so young, we may decide it is too soon to have children."

"It is never too soon," Bakravan had said sharply. "The Holy Books are quite clear. A woman needs children. A home needs children. Without children a woman will get into idle ways. That's the most of my beloved Sharazad's problem, no children. Some modern ways I approve of. Some I do not."

"But if we agree, she and I, that it is too soo—"

"Such a decision would not be her business!" Jared Bakravan had been shocked. He was a small, paunchy man with white hair and beard and hard eyes. "It would be monstrous, an insult, even to discuss it with her. You must think like an Iranian or this possible marriage will never last. Or even begin. Never. Ah, is it that you don't want children?"

"Oh, no, of course I want children, but per—"

"Good, then it's settled thus."

"Then can it be settled thus: for three years and a day may I decide if it is too soon?"

"Such an idea is foolish. If you don't want chil—"

"Oh, but of course I do, Excellency."

At length the old man had said, reluctantly, "One year and a day only—but only if you swear by the One God that you truly want children, that this astonishing request is completely temporary! Your head is truly filled with nonsense, my son. With the Help of God, such nonsense will vanish like the snow on desert sand. Of course women need children . . ."

Absently Lochart smiled to himself. That wonderful old man would bargain with God in the Garden of Paradise. And why not? Isn't that the national pastime of Iranians? But what do I say to him in a few days now—the year and a day almost over? Do I want the burden of children? No, not yet. But Sharazad does. Oh, she went along with my decision, and she's never mentioned it but I don't think she ever approved it.

He could hear the muted sounds of her voice and the maid's voice from the kitchen and the quiet it enhanced was, as always, wonderful—such a contrast to the cockpit that was his other life. His cushions were very comfortable and he watched the fire. There was some gunfire in the night but by now it was so commonplace that they hardly heard it.

I've got to get her out of Tehran, he thought. But how? She'll never leave while her family're here. Maybe she's safer here than anywhere, but not if she joins the riots. Doshan Tappeh! She's crazy, but then they all are at the moment. I wish to God I knew if the army's really been ordered to crush the revolt. Bakhtiar has to move soon or he's finished. But if he does there'll be a bloodbath because Iranians are a violent people, death seekers—providing it's in the service of Islam.

Ah, Islam! And God. Where's the One God now?

In all the hearts and heads of Believers. Shi'ites are Believers. So's Sharazad. And all her family. And you? No, not yet but I'm working on it. I promised him I'd work on it, promised I'd read the Koran and keep an open mind. And?

Now's not the time to think of that. Be practical, think practically. She's in danger. Chador or not she's not going to get involved, but then, why shouldn't she? It's her country.

Yes, but she's my wife and I'll order her to stay out of it. What about her father's place on the Caspian Sea near Bandar-e Pahlavi? Maybe they'd take her there or send her there—the weather's good now, not as rotten cold as it is here, though our home's warm, the oil tank always full, wood for the fire, food in the icebox, thanks to her old man and the family.

My God, I owe him so much, so very much.

A slight noise distracted him. Sharazad was standing in the doorway wearing the chador and a light veil that he had never seen before. Her eyes were never more alluring. The chador was sibilant as she moved closer. Then she let it fall open. She wore nothing underneath. The sight of her made him gasp.

"So." Her voice as always soft and throbbing, the Farsi sweet-sounding. "So, Excellency, my husband, so now my chador pleases you?"

He reached out for her but she darted back a step, laughing. "In the summer the public women of the night wear their chadors thus, so it is said."

"Sharazad . . ."

"No."

This time he caught her easily. The taste of her, the sheen of her, her softness. "Perhaps, Master," she said between kisses, gently taunting him, "perhaps your slave will always wear her chador thus, in the streets, in the bazaar, many women do, so they say."

"No. The thought would drive me mad." He began to pick her up but she whispered, "No, Beloved, let us stay here," and he replied, "But the servants . . ." and again she whispered, "Forget them, they'll not disturb us, forget them, forget everything, I beg you, Beloved, and only remember that this is your house, this is your hearth, and I am your eternal slave."

They stayed. As always her passion equaled his though he could not understand how or why, only that with her he went to Paradise, truly, stayed in the Garden of the Paradise with this nymph of Paradise and then returned with her safe to earth again.

Later, during dinner, the front doorbell disturbed their peace. Her servant Hassan answered it, then came back into the room, closing the door. "Master, it's Excellency General Valik," he said softly. "He apologizes that he arrives so late but it's important and asks if Your Excellency would grant him a few minutes."

Lochart's irritation soared but Sharazad reached over and touched him gently and it went away. "See him, Beloved. I will wait for you in bed. Hassan, bring a fresh plate and heat up the horisht, His Excellency's bound to be hungry."

Valik apologized profusely for arriving so late, refused food twice but of course allowed himself to be persuaded and ate ravenously. Lochart waited patiently, fulfilling his promise to her father to remember Iranian ways—that family came first, that it was good manners to skirt an issue, never to be blunt, never to be direct. In Farsi it was much easier than in English.

As soon as he could, he switched to English. "I'm very pleased to see you, General. What can I do for you?"

"I only heard half an hour ago that you were back in Tehran. This horisht is easily the best I've had in years. I'm so sorry to disturb you so late."

"No trouble." Lochart left the silence to prosper. The older man ate without embarrassment that he ate alone. A piece of lamb attached itself to his mustache and Lochart watched it, fascinated, wondering how long it would remain there, then Valik wiped his mouth. "My compliments to

Sharazad—her cook is well trained. I will tell my favorite cousin, Excellency Jared."

"Thank you." Lochart waited.

Again the silence hung between them. Valik sipped some tea. "Did the clearance for the 212 come through?"

"Not by the time we'd left." Lochart was unprepared for the question. "I know Mac sent a messenger to wait for it. I'd phone him but unfortunately our phone's out. Why?"

"The partners would like you to fly the charter."

"Captain McIver's assigned Captain Lane, presuming there's a clearance."

"It will be granted." Valik wiped his mouth again and helped himself to more tea. "The partners would like you to fly the charter. I'm sure McIver will agree."

"Sorry, but I've got to get back to Zagros, I want to make sure everything's okay." He told him briefly what had happened there.

"I'm sure Zagros can wait a few days. I'm sure Jared would be pleased you thought it important to do what the partners ask."

Lochart frowned. "I'm happy to do anything. What's so important to the partners about this charter, a few spares, a few rials?"

"All charters are important. The partners are very concerned to give the best service. So that's all right, then?"

"I'd . . . first I'd have to take it up with Mac, second I doubt if the 212'll be cleared, third I really should get back to my base."

Valik smiled his nicest smile. "I'm sure Mac will give his approval. You'll have clearance to leave Tehran airspace." He got up. "I'm going to see Mac now and I'll tell him you're agreeable. Thank Sharazad—again a thousand apologies for calling so late but these are troubled times."

Lochart did not move from the table. "I still want to know what's so important about a few spares and a hundred thousand rials."

"The partners have decided it is, and so my dear young friend, hearing you were here and knowing your close relationship with my family, I presumed at once that you would be happy to do this if I asked you personally. We're the same family. Aren't we?" It was said flat now, though the smile remained.

Lochart's eyes narrowed. "I'm glad to do anything to help b—"

"Good, then it's settled. Thank you. I'll see myself out." From the doorway Valik turned and pointedly looked around at the apartment. "You are a very lucky man, Captain. I envy you."

When Valik had gone, Lochart sat by the dying fire, staring at the flames. Hassan and a maid cleaned away the dishes, said good night but he did not hear them—nor Sharazad who came back later, peered at him, then went quietly back to bed, dutifully leaving him to his reverie.

Lochart was sick at heart. He knew that Valik was aware that everything of value in the apartment, along with the apartment itself, had been a wedding gift from Sharazad's father. Jared Bakravan had even given him de facto ownership of the whole building—at least the rents thereof. Few knew of their argument: "As much as I appreciate your generosity I can't accept all this, sir," Lochart had said. "It's impossible."

"But these are material things, unimportant things."

"Yes, but this is too much. I know my pay's not great, but we can manage. Truly."

"Yes, of course. But why shouldn't my daughter's husband live pleasantly? How else can you be at peace to learn Iranian ways and fulfill your promise? I assure you, my son, these represent little value to me. Now you are part of my family. Family is most important in Iran. Family looks after family."

"Yes, but *I* must look after her—I must, not you."

"Of course, and with the Help of God you will, in time, provide for her in the way she is used to. But now this is not possible for you with the support for your ex-wife and child which you must provide. Now it is my wish to arrange matters in a civilized way, our Iranian way. You have promised to live as we live, no?"

"Yes. But please, I cannot accept all this. Give her what you like, not me. I must be allowed to do the best I can."

"I'm sure you will. Meanwhile, this is all my gift to you, not to her. This makes my gift of her to you possible."

"Give it to her not t—"

Jared Bakravan had said sharply, "It is the Will of God that man is the master of the house. If it is not *your* house then you will *not* be the master. I must insist. I am head of the family and Sharazad will do what I say and for Sharazad I must insist, or the wedding cannot take place. I realize your Western dilemma though I don't understand it, my son. But here Iranian ways dominate all else, and family looks after family . . ."

In the vast loneliness of the sitting room Lochart nodded to himself. That's right and I chose Sharazad, chose to accept but . . . but that sonofa-bitch Valik threw it all in my face and made me feel dirty again and I hate him for it, hate not paying for everything, and know the only gift I can give her is freedom she would never otherwise have and my life if need be. At least she's Canadian now and doesn't have to stay.

Don't fool yourself, she's Iranian and always will be. Would she be at home in Vancouver, B.C., with all that rain, no family, no friends, and nothing

Iranian? Yes, yes, I think so; for a time I'd make up for all the other. For a while, of course not forever.

It was the first time he had confronted the real problem looming between them. Our Iran's gone forever, the old one, the Shah one. Never mind that perhaps the new will be better. She'll adapt and so will I. I speak Farsi and she's my wife and Jared's powerful. If we have to leave temporarily, I'll make up for the temporary parting, no problem there. The future's still rosy and good and I love her so very much and bless God for her . . .

The fire was almost finished now and he smelled the comforting, burned wood fragrance and, with it, a thread of her perfume. The cushions still held the indentations where they had lain and though he was totally satisfied and spent, he ached for her. She's really one of the houris, the spirits of Paradise, he thought sleepily. I'm in her spell and that's wonderful, I've no complaints and if I died tonight I know what Paradise is like. She's wonderful, Jared's wonderful, in due course her children will be wonderful and her family . . .

Ah, family! Family looks after family, that's the law, I have to do what Valik asked, like it or not. Have to, her father made that clear.

The last of the embers spluttered and, in dying, momentarily blazed up. "What's so important about a few spares and a few rials?" he asked the flames.

The flames did not answer him.

MONDAY
February 12

On the map: CHAPTER **14**

U.S.S.R.
TURKEY
KHOI
TABRIZ
MOUNT SABALAN
BANDAR-E PAHLAVI
Caspian Sea
U.S.S.R.
IRAQ
QAZVIN ★TEHRAN
BAGHDAD
IRAN
AFGHANISTAN
DEZ DAM •ISFAHAN
ZAGROS
BANDAR DELAM
Shatt-al-Arab Estuary
ABADAN
•ZAGROS THREE
KUWAIT
•KOWISS
MOUNTAINS
KHARG
JELLET
Persian Gulf
LENGEH
Strait of Hormuz
PAKISTAN
BAHRAIN
SAUDI ARABIA
QATAR
SĪRI
Gulf of Oman
AL SHARGAZ

AT TABRIZ ONE: 7:12 A.M. Charlie Pettikin was fitfully asleep, curled up on a mattress on the floor under a single blanket, his hands tied in front of him. It was just dawn and very cold. The guards had not allowed him a portable gas fire and he was locked into the section of Erikki Yokkonen's cabin that would normally be a storeroom. Ice glistened on the inside of the panes of glass in the small window. The window was barred on the outside. Snow covered the sill.

His eyes opened and he jerked upright, startled, not knowing where he was for the moment. Then his memory flooded back and he hunched against the wall, his whole body aching. "What a damned mess!" he muttered, trying to ease his shoulders. With both hands he awkwardly wiped the sleep out of his eyes, and rubbed his face, feeling filthy. The stubble of his beard was flecked with gray. Hate being unshaved, he thought.

Today's Monday. I got here Saturday at sunset and they caught me yester-day morning. Bastards!

On Saturday evening there had been many noises around the cabin that had added to his disquiet. Once he was sure he heard muffled voices. Quietly he doused the lights, slid the bolt back, and stood on the stoop, the Very pistol in his hand. With great care he had searched the darkness. Then he saw, or thought he saw, a movement thirty yards away, then another farther off.

"Who are you?" he called out, his voice echoing strangely. "What do you want?"

No one answered him. Another movement. Where? Thirty forty yards away—difficult to judge distances at night. Look, there's another! Was it a man? Or just an animal or the shadow of a branch. Or perhaps—what was that? Over there by the big pine. "You! Over there! What do you want?"

No answer. He could not make out if it was a man or not. Enraged and even a little frightened he aimed and pulled the trigger. The *banggg* seemed like a clap of thunder and echoed off the mountains and the red flare ripped toward the tree, ricocheted off it in a shower of sparks, sprayed into another to bury itself spluttering and spitting in a snowdrift. He waited.

Nothing happened. Noises in the forest, the roof of the hangar creaking, wind in the treetops, sometimes snow falling from an overladen tree branch that sprang back, free once more. Making a big show he angrily stamped his feet against the cold, switched on the light, loaded the pistol again, and rebolted the door. "You're getting to be an old woman in your old age," he said aloud, then added, "Bullshit! I hate the quiet, hate being alone, hate snow, hate the cold, hate being scared and this morning at Galeg Morghi shook me, God curse it and that's a fact—but for young Ross I know that SAVAK bastard would've killed me!"

He checked that the door was barred and all the windows, closed the curtains against the night, then poured a large vodka and mixed it with some frozen orange juice that was in the freezer and sat in front of the fire and collected himself. There were eggs for breakfast and he was armed. The gas fire worked well. It was cozy. After a while he felt better, safer. Before he went to bed in the spare bedroom, he rechecked the locks. When he was satisfied he took off his flying boots and lay on the bed. Soon he was asleep.

In the morning the night fear had disappeared. After a breakfast of fried eggs on fried bread, just as he liked it, he tidied the room, put on his padded flying gear, unbolted the door, and a submachine gun was shoved in his face, six of the revolutionaries crowded into the room and the questioning began. Hours of it.

"I'm not a spy, not American. I keep telling you I'm British," over and over.

"Liar, your papers say you're South African. By Allah, are they false too?" The leader—the man who called himself Fedor Rakoczy—was tough-looking, taller, and older than the others, with hard brown eyes, his English accented. The same questions over and over: "Where do you come from, why are you here, who is your CIA superior, who is your contact here, where is Erikki Yokkonen?"

"I don't know. I've told you fifty times I don't know—there was no one here when I landed at sunset last night. I was sent to pick him up, him and his wife. They had business in Tehran."

"Liar! They ran away in the night, two nights ago. Why should they run away if you were coming to pick them up?"

"I've told you. I was not expected. Why should they run away? Where're Dibble and Arberry, our mechanics? Where's our manager Dayati and wh—"

"Who is your CIA contact in Tabriz?"

"I haven't one. We're a British company and I demand to see our consul in Tabriz. I dem—"

"Enemies of the People cannot demand anything! Even mercy. It is the Will of God that we are at war. In war people get shot!"

The questioning had gone on all morning. In spite of his protests they had taken all his papers, his passport with the vital exit and residence permits, and had bound him and thrown him in here with dire threats if he attempted to run away. Later, Rakoczy and two guards had returned. "Why didn't you tell me you brought the spares for the 212?"

"You didn't ask me," Pettikin had said angrily. "Who the hell are you? Give me back my papers. I demand to see the British consul. Undo my hands, goddamnit!"

"God will strike you if you blaspheme! Down on your knees and beg God's forgiveness." They forced him to kneel. "Beg forgiveness!"

He obeyed, hating them.

"You fly a 212 as well as a 206?"

"No," he said, awkwardly getting to his feet.

"Liar! It's on your license." Rakoczy had thrown it on the table. "Why do you lie?"

"What's the difference? You believe nothing I say. You won't believe the truth. Of course I know it's on my license. Didn't I see you take it? Of course I fly a 212 if I'm rated."

"The komiteh will judge you and sentence you," Rakoczy had said with a finality that sent a shock wave up his spine. Then they had left him.

At sunset they had brought him some rice and soup and gone away again. He had slept hardly at all and now, in the dawn, he knew how helpless he was. His fear began to rise up. Once in Vietnam he had been shot down and caught and sentenced to death by the Viet Cong but his squadron had come back for him with gunships and Green Berets and they had shot up the village and the Viet Cong with it. That was another time that he had escaped a certainty. "Never bet on death until you're dead. Thataway, old buddy," his young American commander had said, "thataway you sleep nights." The commander had been Conroe Starke. Their helicopter squadron had been mixed, American and British and some Canadian, based at Da Nang. What another bloody mess that was!

Wonder how Duke's doing now? he thought. Lucky bastard. Lucky to be safe at Kowiss and lucky to have Manuela. Now there's one smasher and built like a koala bear—cuddly, with those big brown eyes of hers, and just the right amount of curves.

He let his mind wander, wondering about her and Starke, about where were Erikki and Azadeh, about that Vietnam village—and about the young Captain Ross and his men. But for him! Ross was another savior. In this life you have to have saviors to survive, those curious people who miraculously come into your life for no apparent reason just in time to give you the chance you desperately need, or to extract you from disaster or danger or evil. Do they appear because you prayed for help? At the very edge you always pray, somehow, even if it's not to God. But God has many names.

He remembered old Soames at the embassy with his, "Don't forget, Charlie, Mohammed the Prophet proclaimed that Allah—God—has three thousand names. A thousand are known only to the angels, a thousand only to the prophets, three hundred are in the Torah, the Old Testament, another three hundred in the Zabur, that's the Psalms of David, another three hundred in the New Testament, and ninety-nine in the Koran. That makes two thousand nine hundred and ninety nine. One name has been hidden by God. In Arabic it's called: *Ism Allah ala'zam*: the Greatest Name of God. Everyone who reads the Koran will have read it without knowing it. God is wise to hide His Greatest Name, eh?"

Yes, if there is a God, Pettikin thought, cold and aching.

Just before noon Rakoczy returned with his two men. Astonishingly, Rakoczy politely helped him to his feet and began undoing his bonds. "Good morning, Captain Pettikin. So sorry for the mistake. Please follow me." He led the way into the main room. Coffee was on the table. "Do you drink coffee black or English style with milk and sugar?"

Pettikin was rubbing his chafed wrists, trying to get his mind working. "What's this? The prisoner was offered a hearty breakfast?"

"Sorry, I don't understand."

"Nothing." Pettikin stared at him, still not sure. "With milk and sugar." The coffee tasted wonderful and revived him. He helped himself to more. "So it's a mistake, all a mistake?"

"Yes. I, er, checked your story and it was correct, God be praised. You will leave immediately. To return to Tehran."

Pettikin's throat felt tight at his sudden reprieve—apparent reprieve, he thought suspiciously. "I need fuel. All our fuel's been stolen, there's no fuel in our dump."

"Your aircraft has been refueled. I supervised it myself."

"You know about choppers?" Pettikin was wondering why the man appeared so nervous.

"A little."

"Sorry, but I, er, I don't know your name."

"Smith. Mr. Smith." Fedor Rakoczy smiled. "You will leave now, please. At once."

Pettikin found his flying boots and pulled them on. The other men watched him silently. He noted they were carrying Soviet machine pistols. On the table by the door was his overnight bag. Beside it were his documents. Passport, visa, work permit, and Iranian CAA–issued flying license. Trying to keep the astonishment off his face, he made sure they were all there and stuck them in his pocket. When he went for the refrigerator, one of the men stood in his way and motioned him away. "I'm hungry," Pettikin said, still very suspicious.

"There's something to eat in your plane. Follow me, please."

Outside, the air smelled very good to him, the day crisp and fine with a clean, very blue sky. To the west more snow clouds were building. Eastward, the way over the pass was clear. All around him the forest sparkled, the light refracted by the snow. In front of the hangar was the 206, windshield cleaned, all windows cleaned. Nothing had been touched inside though his map case was now in a side pocket, not beside his seat where he normally left it. Very carefully he began a preflight check.

"Please to hurry," Rakoczy said.

"Of course." Pettikin made a great show of hurrying but he didn't, missing nothing in his inspection, all his senses tuned to find a subtle sabotage, or even a crude one. Gas checked out, oil, everything. He could see and feel their growing nervousness. There was still no one else on the base. In the hangar he could see the 212 with its engine parts still neatly spread out. The spares that he had brought had been put on a bench nearby.

"Now you are ready." Rakoczy said it as an order. "Get in, you will refuel at Bandar-e Pahlavi as before." He turned to the others, embraced both of them hastily, and got into the right seat. "Start up and leave at once. I am coming to Tehran with you." He gripped his machine gun with his knees, buckled himself in, locked the door neatly, then lifted the headset from its hook behind him and put it on, clearly accustomed to the inside of a cockpit.

Pettikin noticed that the other two had taken up defensive positions facing the road. He pressed the Engine Start. Soon the whine and the familiarity—and the fact that "Smith" was aboard and therefore sabotage unlikely—made him light-headed. "Here we go," he said into the boom mike and took off in a scudding rush, banked sweetly, and climbed for the pass.

"Good," Rakoczy said, "very good. You fly very well." Casually he put the gun across his knees, muzzle pointing at Pettikin. "Please don't fly too well."

"Put the safety catch on—or I won't fly at all."

Rakoczy hesitated. He clicked it in place. "I agree it is dangerous while flying."

At six hundred feet Pettikin leveled off, then abruptly went into a steep bank and came back toward the field.

"What're you doing?"

"Just want to get my bearings." He was relying on the fact that though "Smith" clearly knew his way around a cockpit, he couldn't fly a 206 or he would have taken her. His eyes were searching below for a clue to the man's nervousness and his haste to leave. The field seemed the same. Near the junction of the narrow base road with the main road that went northwest to Tabriz were two trucks. Both headed for the base. From this height he could easily see they were army trucks.

"I'm going to land to see what they want," he said.

"If you do," Rakoczy said without fear, "it will cost you much pain and permanent mutilation. Please go to Tehran—but first to Bandar-e Pahlavi."

"What's your real name?"

"Smith."

Pettikin left it at that, circled once, then followed the Tehran road southeast, heading for the pass and biding his time—confident now that somewhere en route his time would come.

AT TEHRAN: 8:30 A.M.   Tom Lochart eased his old Citroën through the debris of the night's battles, heading for Galeg Morghi. The morning was sour and freezing and he was already late though he had started out just after dawn.

He had passed many bodies and wailing mourners, many burned-out wrecks of cars and trucks, some still smoldering—flotsam from the night's riots. Knots of armed or semiarmed civilians still manned balconies or barricades and he had had to make a dozen diversions. Many men wore the Khomeini green armband now. All Green Bands were armed. The streets were ominously empty of traffic. From time to time police trucks screamed past, a few cars and trucks, but they paid no attention to him except to sound their horns, cursing him out of the way. He cursed them back, almost not caring if he ever reached the airport that would be a perfect solution to his dilemma. Only the thought of Valik's wife and their two children in SAVAK hands forced him onward.

How could such a wonderful woman as Annoush, who had been so kind to him since he came into the family, have married such a bastard? And how could the two wonderful kids who adored Sharazad and called him Excellency Uncle . . .

He swerved to avoid a car that charged out of a side street on the wrong side of the road. The car did not stop and he cursed it, and Tehran and Iran and Valik and said, "Insha'Allah," out loud but it did not help him.

Overhead was a dirty, snow-filled overcast that he did not like at all, and he had hated to leave the warmth of his bed and Sharazad. Just before dawn the alarm had startled them awake.

"I thought you weren't going, my darling. I thought you said you were leaving tomorrow."

"I've got a sudden charter, at least I think I have. That's what Valik came about. I've got to see Mac first, but if I go I'll be away for a few days. Go back to sleep, my darling." He had shaved, dressed hurriedly, had a quick cup of coffee, and left. Outside it was still dark with just a sullen wisp of dawn, the air acrid and smoke heavy. In the distance was the inevitable, sporadic gunfire. Suddenly he was filled with foreboding.

McIver lived only a few blocks away. Lochart was surprised to find him fully dressed. "Hello, Tom. Come on in. The clearance came through at midnight, delivered by hand. Valik's got power—I never believed we'd get it. Coffee?"

"Thanks. Did he see you last night?"

"Yes." McIver led the way into the kitchen. Coffee was perking nicely. No sign of Genny, Paula, or Nogger Lane. He poured for Lochart. "Valik told me he'd seen you and that you'd agreed to go."

Lochart grunted. "I said I'd go after you approved it and after I'd seen you —if we got the clearance. Where's Nogger?"

"Back in his flat. I canceled him last night. He's still pretty shook from being involved in that riot."

"I can imagine. What happened to the girl? Paula?"

"She's in the spare room, her Alitalia flight's still grounded, but she'll probably be off today. George Talbot of the embassy dropped by last night and said he heard the airport's been cleared of revolutionaries and today, with any luck, there'll be a few flights in and out."

Lochart nodded thoughtfully. "Then maybe Bakhtiar will win after all."

"Let's hope, eh? The BBC this morning said Doshan Tappeh's still in Khomeini hands and the Immortals are just ringing it, sitting on their tails."

Lochart shuddered at the thought of Sharazad there. She had promised not to go again. "Did Talbot say anything about a coup?"

"Only that the rumor is that Carter's opposed to it—if I was Iranian, and a general, I wouldn't hesitate. Talbot agreed, said the coup'll happen in the next three days, it'll have to, the revs are getting too many guns."

Lochart could almost see Sharazad chanting with the thousands, young Captain Karim Peshadi declaring for Khomeini and three Immortals deserting. "Don't know what I'd do, Mac, if I was one of them."

"Thank God we're not and this's Iran, not England with us at the barricades. Anyway, Tom, if the 125 comes in today I'll put Sharazad on her. She'll be better off in Al Shargaz, at least for a couple of weeks. Did she get her Canadian passport?"

"Yes, but Mac, I don't think she'll go." Lochart told him about her joining the insurrection at Doshan Tappeh.

"My God, she needs her head examined. I'll get Gen to see her."

"Is Genny going to Al Shargaz?"

McIver said testily, "No. If it was up to me she'd've been there a week already. I'll do what I can. Sharazad's all right?"

"Wonderful, but I wish to God Tehran'd settle down. I get worried sick about her here and me in Zagros." Lochart gulped some coffee. "If I'm going I'd better get with it. Keep an eye on her, will you?" He looked at McIver, hard and straight. "What's this charter about, Mac?"

Stonily McIver looked back at him. "Tell me exactly what Valik said to you last night."

Lochart told him. Exactly.

"He's a right bastard to try to make you lose face like that."

"He succeeded very well. Unfortunately he's still family and in Iran—well, you know." Lochart kept the bitterness out of his voice. "I asked him what's so important about a few spares and a few rials and he sloughed me off." He saw that McIver's face was set and seemed older and heavier than he had ever known, yet tougher. "Mac, what *is* so important about a few spares and a few rials?"

McIver finished his coffee and poured some more. He dropped his voice. "Don't want to wake Genny or Paula, Tom. This's between us." He told Lochart what had happened in the office. Exactly.

Lochart felt the sudden rush of blood to his face. "SAVAK? Him and Annoush and little Setarem and Jalal? Jesus wept!"

"That's why I agreed to try. Have to. I'm equally trapped. We're both trapped. But there's more." McIver told him about the money.

Lochart gasped. "12 million rials, cash? Or the equivalent in Switzerland?"

"Keep your voice down. Yes, 12 for me, and another 12 for the pilot. Last night he said his offer still stands and not to be 'naive.'" McIver added grimly, "If Gen hadn't been here, I'd've thrown him out."

Lochart was hardly listening. 12 million rials or cash elsewhere? Mac's right. If Valik offered that here in Tehran what would he really pay when he's in sight of the border? "Christ!"

McIver watched him. "What do you think, Tom? Do you still want to go?"

"I can't refuse. I can't. Not now we've got the clearance." It was on the kitchen table and he picked it up. It read: "EP-HBC cleared to Bandar Delam. Priority flight for urgent spares. Refuel at IIAF Base Isfahan. One crew: Captain Lane." Lane had been crossed out, and marked, "Sick. Substitute pilot ————," then a blank and it was not yet countersigned by McIver.

McIver glanced at the kitchen door that was closed, then back to Lochart. "Valik wants to be picked up outside of Tehran, privately."

"This gets smellier and smellier. Where's the pickup point?"

"If you get to Bandar Delam, Tom, and that's not even probable, he'll pressure you to take them on to Kuwait."

"Of course." Lochart stared back at McIver.

"He'll use any pressure, family, Sharazad, the lot. Particularly money."

"Millions. In cash—which we both know I can use." Lochart's voice was level. "But if I fly on to Kuwait without Iranian clearance, in an Iranian registered chopper, without Iranian or company approval, with unauthorized Iranian passengers trying to escape their still legal government, I'm a hijacker, subject to God knows how many criminal charges here and in Kuwait —the Kuwait authorities'd impound the chopper, shove me in jail, and certainly extradite me to Iran. In any event I'd've blown my future as a pilot and could never come back to Iran and Sharazad—SAVAK might even grab her so I'm not about to do that."

"Valik's a dangerous sod. He'll come armed. He could put a gun to your head and force you to go on."

"That's possible." Lochart's voice stayed but his insides were churning. "I have no option. I've got to help him, and I will—but I'm not goddamn stupid." After a pause, he added, "Does Nogger know about this?"

"No." In the watches of the night, after weighing possible plans, McIver had decided to go himself and not risk Nogger Lane or Lochart. The hell with the medical and that I'd be illegal, he had told himself—the whole flight's mad so a little extra madness won't hurt.

His plan was simple: after talking it out with Tom Lochart he would just say he had decided not to authorize the flight and would not countersign the clearance, that he would drive to the pickup point with enough gasoline for Valik to make the journey by road. Even if Lochart wanted to come with him, it would be easy to fix a rendezvous, then never go to it but just drive to Galeg Morghi, put his own name on the clearance as pilot and take off. At the pickup point . . .

"What?" he asked.

"There are only three possibilities," Lochart said again. "You refuse to authorize the flight, you authorize me or you authorize someone else. You've canceled Nogger, Charlie's not here, so that leaves you or me. You can't go, Mac. You just can't, it's too dangerous."

"Of course I wouldn't go, my license h—"

"You can't go, Mac," Lochart said firmly. "Sorry. You just can't."

McIver sighed, his wisdom overcame his obsession to fly and he decided on his second plan. "Yes. Yes, you're right. I agree. So listen carefully: if you want to do it, that's up to you, I'm not ordering it. I will authorize you if you want but there are conditions. If you get to the pickup point and it seems clean, pick them up. Then go on to Isfahan. Valik said he'd fix that. If Isfahan's okay, go on. Maybe Mr. Fixit Iran can do just that, all the way. That's what we'd have to gamble on."

"That's what I'm gambling on."

"Bandar Delam's the end of the line. You don't go over the border. Agreed?" McIver put out his hand.

"Agreed," Lochart said, shaking hands with a prayer that he could keep his promise.

McIver told him the pickup point, signed the clearance, and noticed his hands were trembling. If anything goes wrong, guess who SAVAK'll come after? Both of us. And even maybe Gen, McIver thought, again filled with dread. He did not tell Lochart that she had overheard Valik last night and figured out the rest. "But I agree, Duncan," she had said gravely. "It's terribly risky but you've got to try to help them, Tom too, he's equally trapped. There isn't any option."

McIver handed Lochart the clearance. "Tom, you're specifically ordered not to go over the border. If you do, I think you really will lose everything, including Sharazad."

"This whole scheme's crackpot, but, there you are."

"Yes. Good luck."

Lochart nodded, smiled back at him, and left.

McIver closed the front door. I hope that's the right decision, he thought, his head aching. Madness to go myself, and yet . . . I wish I was going and not him. I wish . . .

"Oh," he said, startled. Genny was standing by the kitchen door, a warm robe over her nightdress. She was not wearing her glasses and she peered at him.

"I'm . . . I'm awfully glad you didn't go, Duncan," she said in a tiny voice.

"What?"

"Oh, come on, silly, I know you too well. You hardly slept a wink trying to decide—nor did I, worrying about it for you. I know if I'd been you I'd've gone, or wanted to go. But, Duncan, Tom's strong and he'll be all right and I do so hope he takes Sharazad and never comes back . . ." The tears began running down her cheeks. "I'm ever so glad you didn't go." She brushed the tears away and went to the stove and put on the kettle. "Damn, sorry, I really do get into a tizzy sometimes. Sorry."

He put his arms around her. "Gen, if the 125 comes today, will you get on it? Please."

"Certainly, dear. If you get on it too."

"But Gen. You must."

"Duncan, listen a moment, please." She turned and put her arms around him and rested her head against his chest and continued in the same small voice that troubled him greatly, "Three of your partners have already fled with their families and all the money they can, the Shah and his family've gone with all their money, thousands of others, most of the people we know've gone, you said so yourself and now if even the great General Valik's running away, even with all his contacts and they've got to be on both sides of the fence, and . . . and if even the Immortals haven't squashed the little rebellion at Doshan Tappeh of a few air force cadets and badly armed civilians—practically on their home ground—it's time we should close down and leave."

"We can't, Gen," he burst out, and she could hear his heart in his chest and her concern for him increased. "That'd be a disaster."

"It'd only be for a short time, until things get better."

"If I scuttled Iran it'd ruin S-G."

"I don't know about that, Duncan, but surely the decision's up to Andy, not you—he sent us here."

"Yes, but he'd ask me what I thought and I couldn't recommend quitting and leaving $20- to $30-odd million worth of choppers and spares behind—in this mess they wouldn't last a week, they'd be looted or damaged, we'd lose everything, everything—don't forget, Gen, all our retirement money's tied up in S-G, everything."

"But, Duncan, don't you think th—"

"I won't leave our choppers and spares." McIver felt flushed and in momentary panic at the thought. "I just can't."

"Then take them with you."

"For God's sake, we can't get 'em out, we can't get the clearances, can't get off Iranian registry—we can't—we're stuck here until the war's over."

"We're not. Duncan, not you or me or our lads, you've got to think of them too. We have to get out. They'll throw us out anyway, whoever wins, most of all Khomeini." A tremor went through her as she thought of his first speech at the cemetery: "I pray God to cut off the hands of all foreigners . . ."

U.S.S.R.

Caspian Sea

U.S.S.R.

TURKEY

KHOI

◄ TABRIZ

MOUNT
SABALAN

BANDAR-E
PAHLAVI

QAZVIN

★ TEHRAN

IRAQ

BAGHDAD

IRAN

ZAGROS

DEZ DAM

• ISFAHAN

BANDAR DELAM

*Shatt-
al-Arab
Estuary*

ABADAN

• ZAGROS THREE

• KOWISS

MOUNTAINS

KUWAIT

KHARG

JELLET

Persian Gulf

LENGEH

*Strait of
Hormuz*

SAUDI
ARABIA

BAHRAIN

QATAR

SĪRI

AL SHARGAZ

Gulf of Oman

AFGHANISTAN

PAKISTAN

AT TABRIZ ONE: 9:30 A.M. The red Range Rover came out of the gates of the Khan's palace and headed down the rise toward Tabriz and the road for Tehran. Erikki was driving, Azadeh beside him. It had been her cousin, Colonel Mazardi, the chief of police, who had persuaded Erikki not to drive to Tehran on Friday: "The road would be highly dangerous—it's bad enough during the day," he said. "The insurgents won't return now, you're quite safe. Much better to go and see His Highness the Khan and ask his advice. That would be much wiser."

Azadeh had agreed. "Erikki, of course we will do whatever you want but I would really feel happier if we went home for the night and saw Father."

"My cousin's right, Captain; of course you may do as you wish, but I swear by the Prophet, God keep His words safe forever, that Her Highness's safety is just as important to me as to you. If you still feel so inclined, leave tomorrow. I can assure you there's no danger here. I'll post guards. If this so-called

Rakoczy or any other foreigner or this mullah comes within half a mile of here or the Gorgon palace they'll regret it."

"Oh, yes, Erikki, please," Azadeh said enthusiastically. "Of course, my darling, we'll do whatever you like but it might be you would want to consult His Highness, my father, about what you plan to do."

Reluctantly Erikki had agreed. Arberry and the other mechanic, Dibble, had decided to go into Tabriz to the International Hotel and spend the weekend there. "Spares're due Monday, Captain. Old Skinflint McIver knows our 212's got to be working by Wednesday or he'll have to send another one and he won't like that. We'll just sit tight and get the job done and get her airborne. Our apology for a base manager can come and fetch us. We're British, we've nothing to worry about—no one's going to touch us. And don't forget we're working for their guver'ment, whoever's the bleeding guver'ment, and we've no quarrel with any of these bleeding wo—these bleeders, begging your pardon. Now don't you worry about us, you and the Missus. We'll just sit tight and expect you back by Wednesday. Have a fun time in Tehran."

So Erikki had gone in convoy with Colonel Mazardi to the outskirts of Tabriz. The sprawling palace of the Gorgon Khans was set in mountain foothills, in acres of gardens and orchards behind high walls. When they arrived, the whole house awoke and congregated—stepmother, half sisters, nieces, nephews, servants, and children of servants, but not Abdollah Khan, her father. Azadeh was received with open arms and tears and happiness and more tears, and immediate plans were made for a luncheon feast the next day to celebrate their good fortune in having her home at long last—"But, oh, how terrible! Bandits and a rogue mullah daring to come on your land? Hasn't His Highness, our revered father, donated barrels of rials and hundreds of acres of land to various mosques in and around Tabriz!"

Erikki Yokkonen was welcomed politely, and guardedly. All of them were afraid of him, the enormity of his size, his quickness with a knife, the violence of his temper, and could not understand his gentleness toward his friends and the vast love he radiated for Azadeh. She was the fifth of six half sisters, and an infant half brother. Her mother, dead now many years, had been Abdollah Khan's second, concurrent wife. Her own adored blood brother, Hakim, a year older than she, had been banished by Abdollah Khan and was still in disgrace at Khoi to the northwest—banished for crimes against the Khan that both Hakim and Azadeh swore he was not guilty of.

"First a bath," her half sisters said gaily, "and you can tell us all that happened, every detail, *every detail.*" Happily, they dragged Azadeh away. In the privacy of their bathhouse, warm and intimate and luxurious and completely outside the domain of all men, they chatted and gossiped until the dawn. "My Mahmud hasn't made love to me for a week," Najoud, Azadeh's eldest half sister, said with a toss of her head.

"It has to be another woman, darling Najoud," someone said.

"No, it's not that. His erection is giving him trouble."

"Oh, you poor darling! Have you tried giving him oysters . . ."

"Or tried using oil of roses on your breasts . . ."

"Or rubbed him with extract of jacaranda, rhino horn, and musk . . ."

"Jacaranda, musk with rhino horn? I haven't heard of that one, Fazulia."

"It's brand new from an ancient recipe from the time of Cyrus the Great. This is a secret but the Great King's penis was quite small as a young man, but after he conquered the Medes, miraculously it became the envy of the host! It seems that he obtained a magic potion from the Medes that if rubbed on over a period of a month . . . Their high priest gave it to Cyrus in return for his life, providing the Great King swore to keep the secret in his family alone. It's come down from father to son over the centuries and now, dear sisters, the secret's in Tabriz!"

"Oh, who, dearest darling Sister Fazulia, who? The Blessings of God be upon thee forever, who? My rotten husband Abdullah, may his three remaining teeth fall out, he hasn't had an erection for years. Who?"

"Oh, be quiet, Zadi, how can she talk if you talk! Go on, Fazulia."

"Yes, be quiet, Zadi, and bless your good fortune—my Hussan is erect morning, noon, and night and so filled with desire for me he gives me no time to even wash my teeth!"

"Well, the secret of the elixir was bought by the great-great-grandfather of the present owner at a huge cost, I was told for a fistful of diamonds . . ."

"Eeeeeeeeee . . ."

". . . but now you can buy a small vial for fifty thousand rials!"

"Oh, that's too much! Where on earth can I get so much cash?"

"As always you'll find it in his pockets, and you can always bargain. Is anything too much for such a potion when we can't have other men?"

"If it works . . ."

"Of course it works, oh, where do we buy it, dearest dearest Fazulia?"

"In the bazaar, in the shop of Abu Bakra bin Hassan bin Saiidi. I know the way! We'll go tomorrow. Before lunch. You will come with us, darling Azadeh!"

"No thank you, dear sister."

Then there was lots of laughter and one of the young ones said, "Poor Azadeh doesn't need jacaranda and muck—she needs the opposite!"

"Jacaranda and *musk*, child, with rhino horn," Fazulia said.

Azadeh laughed with them. They had all asked her, overtly or covertly, if her husband was equally proportioned and how did she, so skinny and so fragile, deal with it and bear his weight? "By magic," she had told the young ones, "easily," the serious ones, and "with unbelievable ecstasy as it must be in the Garden of Paradise," the jealous ones and those she hated and secretly wanted to taunt.

Not everyone had approved of her marriage to this foreign giant. Many had tried to influence her father against him and against her. But she had won and she knew who her enemies were: her sex-mad half sister, Zadi, lying Cousin Fazulia with her nonsense exaggerations, and, most of all, the honeyed viper of the pack, eldest sister Najoud and her vile husband Mahmud, may God punish them for their evil ways. "Dearest Najoud, I'm so happy to be home, but now it's time for sleep."

And so to bed. All of them. Some happily, some sadly, some angrily, some hating, some loving, some to their husbands and some alone. Husbands could have four wives, according to the Koran, at the same time, provided they treated each with equality in every way—Mohammed the Prophet, alone of all men, had been allowed as many wives as he wished. According to legend, the Prophet had had eleven wives in his lifetime though not all at the same time. Some died, some he divorced, and some outlived him. But all of them honored him forever.

Erikki awoke as Azadeh slipped into bed beside him. "We should leave as early as possible, Azadeh, my darling."

"Yes," she said, almost asleep now, the bed so comfortable, him so comfortable. "Yes, whenever you like, but please not until after lunch because dearest Stepmother will weep buckets. . . ."

"Azadeh!"

But she was asleep now. He sighed, also content, and went back to sleep.

They did not leave Sunday as planned—her father had said it was inconvenient as he wished to talk to Erikki first. At dawn today, Monday, after prayers that her father had led, and after breakfast—coffee and bread and honey and yogurt and eggs—they had been allowed to leave and now swung off the mountainside road on to the main Tehran road and there ahead was the roadblock.

"That's weird," Erikki said. Colonel Mazardi had said he would meet them here but he was nowhere to be seen, nor was the roadblock manned.

"Police!" Azadeh said, with a yawn. "They're never where you want them."

The road climbed up to the pass. The sky was blue and clear and the tops of the mountains already washed with sunlight. Down here in the valley, it was still dark and chill and damp, the road slippery, snow-banked, but this did not worry him as the Range Rover had four-wheel drive and he carried chains. Later, when he came to the base turnoff he passed it by. He knew the base was empty, the 212 safe and waiting for repairs. Before leaving the palace he had tried unsuccessfully to contact his manager, Dayati. But that did not matter. He settled back in his seat, he had full tanks, and six spare five-gallon cans that he had got from Abdollah's private pump.

I can get to Tehran easily today, he thought. And back by Wednesday—if I come back. That bastard Rakoczy's very bad news indeed.

"Would you like some coffee, darling?" Azadeh asked.

"Thanks. See if you can find the BBC or the VOA on the shortwave." Gratefully he accepted the hot coffee from the thermos, listening to the crackle of static and heterodyning and loud Soviet stations and little else. Iranian stations were still strikebound and closed down, except the ones worked by the military.

Over the weekend friends, relations, tradesmen, servants had brought rumors and counterrumors of everything from imminent Soviet invasion to imminent U.S. invasion, from successful military coups in the capital to abject submission of all the generals to Khomeini and Bakhtiar's resignation.

"Asinine!" Abdollah Khan had said. He was a corpulent man in his sixties, bearded, with dark eyes and full mouth, bejeweled and richly dressed. "Why should Bakhtiar resign? He gains nothing so there's no reason, yet."

"And if Khomeini wins?" Erikki had asked.

"It is the Will of God." The Khan was lounging on carpets in the Great Room, Erikki and Azadeh seated in front of him, his armed bodyguard standing behind him. "But Khomeini's victory will be only temporary, if he achieves it. The armed forces will curb him and his mullahs, sooner or later. He's an old man. Soon he will die, the sooner the better, for though he has done God's will and been the instrument to remove the Shah whose time had come, he's vindictive, narrow-sighted, as megalomaniacal as the Shah, if not more so. He will surely murder more Iranians than the Shah ever did."

"But isn't he a man of God, pious and everything an ayatollah should be?" Erikki asked warily, not knowing what to expect. "Why should Khomeini do that?"

"It's the habit of tyrants." The Khan laughed and took another of the halvah, the Turkish sweets he gorged on.

"And the Shah? What will happen now?" As much as Erikki disliked the Khan, he was glad for the opportunity to get his opinion. On him depended much of his and Azadeh's life in Iran and he had no wish to leave.

"As God wants. Mohammed Shah did incredibly well for Iran, like his father before him. But in the last few years he was totally curled up in himself and would listen to no one—not even the Shahbanu, Empress Farah, who was dedicated to him, and wise. If he had any sense he would abdicate at once in favor of his son Reza. The generals need a rallying point, they could train him until he's ready to take power—don't forget Iran's been a monarchy for almost three thousand years, always an absolute ruler, some might say tyrant, with absolute power and removed only by death." He had smiled, his lips full and sensuous, "Of the Qajar Shahs, our legitimate dynasty who ruled for a hundred and fifty years, only one, the last of the line, my cousin, died of natural causes. We are an Oriental people, not Western, who understand violence and torture. Life and death are not judged by your standards." His dark eyes had seemed to grow darker. "Perhaps it is the Will of God that the Qajars will return—under their rule Iran prospered."

That's not what I heard, Erikki had thought. But he held his peace. It's not up to me to judge what has been or what would be here.

All Sunday the BBC and the VOA had been jammed which was not unusual. Radio Moscow was loud and clear, as usual, and Radio Free Iran that broadcast from Tbilisi north of the border also loud and clear as usual. Their reports in Farsi and English told of total insurrection against "Bakhtiar's illegal government of the ousted Shah and his American masters, headed by the warmonger and liar President Carter. Today Bakhtiar tried to curry favor with the masses by canceling a total of $13 billion of usurious military contracts forced on the country by the deposed Shah: $8 billion in the U.S.A., British Centurion tank contracts worth $2.3 billion, plus two French nuclear reactors, and one from Germany worth another $2.7 billion. This news has sent Western leaders into panic and will undoubtedly send capitalist stock markets into a well-deserved crash . . ."

"Excuse me for asking, Father, but will the West crash?" Azadeh had asked.

"Not this time," the Khan had said and Erikki saw his face grow colder. "Not unless the Soviets decide this is the time to renege on the $80 billion they owe Western banks—and even some Oriental banks." He had laughed sardonically, playing with the string of pearls he wore around his neck. "Of course Oriental moneylenders are much cleverer; at least they're not so greedy. They lend judiciously and require collaterals and believe no one and certainly not in the myth of 'Christian charity.' " It was common knowledge that the Gorgons owned enormous tracts of land in Azerbaijan, good oil land, a large part of Iran-Timber, seafront property on the Caspian, much of the bazaar in Tabriz, and most of the merchant banks there.

Erikki remembered the whispers he had heard about Abdollah Khan when he was trying to get permission to marry Azadeh, about his parsimony and ruthlessness in business: "A quick way to Paradise or hell is to owe Abdollah the Cruel one rial, to not pay pleading poverty, and to stay in Azerbaijan."

"Father, please may I ask, cancellation of so many contracts will cause havoc, won't it?"

"No, you may not ask. You've asked enough questions for one day. A woman is supposed to hold her tongue and listen—now you can leave."

At once she apologized for her error and left obediently. "Please excuse me."

Erikki got up to leave too, but the Khan stopped him: "I have not dismissed you yet. Sit down. Now, why should you fear one Soviet?"

"I don't—just the system. That man has to be KGB."

"Why didn't you just kill him then?"

"It would not have helped, it would have hurt. Us, the base, Iran-Timber, Azadeh, perhaps even you. He was sent to me by others. He knows us—knows you." Erikki had watched the old man carefully.

"I know lots of them. Russians, Soviet or tsarist, have always coveted Azerbaijan, but have always been good customers of Azerbaijan—and helped us against the stinking British. I prefer them to British, I understand them." His smile thinned even more. "It would be easy to remove this Rakoczy."

"Good, then do it, please." Erikki had laughed full-throated. "And all of them as well. That would really be doing God's work."

"I don't agree," the Khan said ill-temperedly. "That would be doing Satan's work. Without the Soviets against them, the Americans and their dogs the British would dominate us and all the world. They'd certainly eat up Iran—under Mohammed Shah they nearly did. Without Soviet Russia, whatever her failings, there'd be no check on America's foul policies, foul arrogance, foul manners, foul jeans, foul music, foul food, and foul democracy, their disgusting attitudes to women, to law and order, their disgusting pornography, naive attitude to diplomacy, and their evil, yes, that's the correct word, their evil antagonism to Islam."

The last thing Erikki wanted was another confrontation. In spite of his resolve, he felt his own rage gathering. "We had an agreem—"

"It's true, by God!" Khan shouted at him. "It's true!"

"It's not, and we had an agreement before your God and my spirits that we'd not discuss politics—either of your world or mine."

"It's true, admit it!" Abdollah Khan snarled, his face twisted with rage. One hand went to the ornamental knife at his belt, and at once the guard unslung his machine pistol and covered Erikki. "By Allah, you call me a liar in my own house?" he bellowed.

Erikki said through his teeth, "I only remind you, Highness, by your Allah, what we agreed!" The dark bloodshot eyes stared at him. He stared back, ready to go for his own knife and kill or be killed, the danger between them very great.

"Yes, yes, that's also true," the Khan muttered, and the fit of rage passed as quickly as it had erupted. He looked at the guard, angrily waved him away. "Get out!"

Now the room was very still. Erikki knew there were other guards nearby and spyholes in the walls. He felt the sweat on his forehead and the touch of his pukoh knife in the center of his back.

Abdollah Khan knew the knife was there and that Erikki would use it without hesitation. But the Khan had given him perpetual permission to be armed with it in his presence. Two years ago Erikki had saved his life.

That was the day Erikki was petitioning him for permission to marry Azadeh and was imperiously turned down: "No, by Allah, I want no infidels in my family. Leave my house! For the last time!" Erikki had got up from the carpet, sick at heart. At that moment there had been a scuffle outside the door, then shots, the door had burst open and two men, assassins armed with machine guns, had rushed in, others fighting a gun battle in the corridor. The Khan's bodyguard had killed one, but the other sprayed him with bullets then turned his gun on Abdollah Khan who sat on the carpet in shock. Before the assassin could pull the trigger a second time, he died, Erikki's knife in his throat. At the same moment Erikki lunged for him, ripped the gun out of his hands and the knife out of his throat as another assassin rushed into the room firing. Erikki had smashed the machine gun into the man's face, killing him, almost tearing off his head with the strength of his blow, then charged into the corridor berserk. Three attackers and two of the bodyguards were dead or dying. The last of the attackers took to their heels, but Erikki cut them both down and raced onward. And only when he had found Azadeh and saw that she was safe did the bloodlust go out of his head and he become calm again.

Erikki remembered how he had left her and had gone back to the same Great Room. Abdollah Khan still sat on the carpets. "Who were those men?"

"Assassins—enemies, like the guards who let them in," Abdollah Khan had said malevolently. "It was the Will of God you were here to save my life, the Will of God that I am alive. You may marry Azadeh, yes, but because I do not like you, we will both swear before God and your—whatever you worship—not to discuss religion or politics, either of your world or mine, then perhaps I will not have to have you killed."

And now the same cold black eyes were staring at him. Abdollah Khan clapped his hands. Instantly the door opened and a servant appeared. "Bring coffee!" The man hurried away. "I will drop the subject of your world and go to another we can discuss: my daughter, Azadeh."

Erikki became even more on guard, not sure of the extent of her father's control over her, or his own rights as her husband while he was in Azerbaijan —very much the old man's fief. If Abdollah Khan really ordered Azadeh back to this house and to divorce him, would she? I think yes, I'm afraid yes—she certainly will never hear a word against him. She even defended his paranoiac hatred of America by explaining what had caused it:

"He was ordered there, to university, by his father," she had told him. "He had a terrible time in America, Erikki, learning the language and trying to get a degree in economics which his father demanded before he was allowed home. My father hated the other students who sneered at him because he couldn't play their games, because he was heavier than they which in Iran is a sign of wealth but not in America, and was slow at learning. But most of all because of the hazing that he was forced to endure, forced, Erikki—to eat unclean things like pork that are against our religion, to drink beer and wine and spirits that are against our religion, to do unmentionable things and be called unmentionable names. I would be angry too if it had been me. Please be patient with him. Don't Soviets make a blood film come over your eyes and heart for what they did to your father and mother and country? Be patient with him, I beg you. Hasn't he agreed to our marriage? Be patient with him."

I've been very patient, Erikki thought, more patient than with any man, wishing the interview was over. "What about my wife, Highness?" It was custom to call him that and Erikki did so from time to time out of politeness.

Abdollah Khan smiled a thin smile at him. "Naturally my daughter's future interests me. What is your plan when you go to Tehran?"

"I have no plan. I just think it is wise to get her out of Tabriz for a few days. Rakoczy said they 'require' my services. When the KGB says that in Iran or Finland or even America, you'd better clear the decks and prepare for trouble. If they kidnapped her, I would be putty in their hands."

"They could kidnap her in Tehran much more easily than here, *if* that is their scheme—you forget this is Azerbaijan"—his lips twisted with contempt —"not Bakhtiar country."

Erikki felt helpless under the scrutiny. "I only know that's what I think is best for her. I said I would guard her with my life, and I will. Until the political future of Iran is settled—by you and other Iranians—I think it's the wise thing to do."

"In that case, go," her father had said with a suddenness that had almost frightened him. "Should you need help send me the code words . . ." He thought a moment. Then his smile became sardonic: "Send me the sentence: 'All men are created equal.' That's another truth, isn't it?"

"I don't know, Highness," he said carefully. "If it is or if it isn't, it's surely the Will of God."

Abdollah had laughed abruptly and got up and left him alone in the Great Room and Erikki had felt a chill on his soul, deeply unsettled by the man whose thoughts he could never read.

"Are you cold, Erikki?" Azadeh asked.

"Oh. No, no, not at all," he said, coming out of his reverie, the sound of the engine good as they climbed up the mountain road toward the pass. Now they were just below the crest. There had been little traffic either way. Around the corner they came into sunshine and topped the rise; at once Erikki shifted gears smoothly and picked up speed as they began the long descent, the road—built at the order of Reza Shah, like the railway—a wonder of engineering with cuts and embankments and bridges and steep parts with no railings on the precipice side, the surface slippery, snow-banked. He shifted gears again, driving fast but prudently, very glad they had not driven by night. "May I have some more coffee?"

Happily she gave it to him. "I'll be glad to see Tehran. There's lots of shopping to be done, Sharazad's there, and I have a list of things for my sisters and some face cream for Stepmother . . ."

He hardly listened to her, his mind on Rakoczy, Tehran, McIver, and the next step.

The road twisted and curled in its descent. He slowed and drove more cautiously, some traffic behind him. In the lead was a passenger car, typically overloaded, and the driver drove too close, too fast, and with his finger permanently on the horn even when it was clearly impossible to move out of the way. Erikki closed his ears to the impatience that he had never become used to, or to the reckless way Iranians drove, even Azadeh. He rounded the next blind corner, the gradient steepening, and there on the straight, not far ahead, was a heavily laden truck grinding upward with a car overtaking on the wrong side. He braked, hugging the mountainside. At that moment the car behind him accelerated, swerved around him, horn blaring, overtaking blindly, and hurtled down the wrong side of the curving road. The two cars smashed into each other and both careened over the precipice to fall five hundred feet and burst into flames. Erikki swung closer into the side and stopped. The oncoming truck did not stop, just lumbered past and continued up the hill as though nothing had happened—so did the other traffic.

He stood at the edge and looked down into the valley. Burning remains of the cars were spread over the mountainside down six or seven hundred feet, no possibility of survivors, and no chance to get down there without serious climbing gear. When he came back to the car he shook his head unhappily.

"Insha'Allah, my darling," Azadeh said calmly. "It was the Will of God."

"No, it wasn't, it was blatant stupidity."

"Of course you're right, Beloved, it certainly was blatant stupidity," she said at once in her most calming voice, seeing his anger though not understanding it as she did not understand much that went on in the head of this strange man who was her husband. "You're perfectly right, Erikki. It was blatant stupidity but the Will of God that those drivers' stupidity caused their deaths and the deaths of those who traveled with them. It was the Will of God or the road would have been clear. You were quite right."

"Was I?" he said wearily.

"Oh, yes, of course, Erikki. You were perfectly right."

They went on. The villages that lay beside the road or straddled it were poor or very poor with narrow dirt streets, crude huts and houses, high walls, a few drab mosques, street stores, goats and sheep and chickens, and flies not yet the plague they would become in summer. Always refuse in the streets and in the *joub*—the ditches—and the inevitable scavenging packs of scabrous despised dogs that frequently were rabid. But snow made the landscape and the mountains picturesque, and the day continued to be good though cold with blue skies and cumulus building.

Inside the Range Rover it was warm and comfortable. Azadeh wore padded, modern ski gear and a cashmere sweater underneath, matching blue, and short boots. Now she took off her jacket and her neat woolen ski cap, and her full-flowing, naturally wavy dark hair fell to her shoulders. Near noon they stopped for a picnic lunch beside a mountain stream. In the early afternoon they drove through orchards of apple, pear, and cherry trees, now bleak and leafless and naked in the landscape, then came to the outskirts of Qazvin, a town of perhaps 150,000 inhabitants and many mosques.

"How many mosques are there in all Iran, Azadeh?" he asked.

"Once I was told twenty thousand," she answered sleepily, opening her eyes and peering ahead. "Ah, Qazvin! You've made good time, Erikki." A yawn swamped her and she settled more comfortably and went back into half sleep. "There're twenty thousand mosques and fifty thousand mullahs, so they say. At this rate we'll be in Tehran in a couple of hours . . ."

He smiled as her words petered out. He was feeling more secure now, glad that the back of the journey had been broken. The other side of Qazvin the road was good all the way to Tehran. In Tehran, Abdollah Khan owned many houses and apartments, most of them rented to foreigners. A few he kept for himself and his family, and he had said to Erikki that, this time, because of the troubles, they could stay in an apartment not far from McIver.

"Thanks, thanks very much," Erikki had said and later Azadeh had said, "I wonder why he was so kind. It's . . . it's not like him. He hates you and hates me whatever I try to do to please him."

"He doesn't hate you, Azadeh."

"I apologize for disagreeing with you, but he does. I tell you again, my darling, it was my eldest sister, Najoud, who really poisoned him against me, and against my brother. She and her rotten husband. Don't forget my mother was Father's second wife and almost half Najoud's mother's age and twice as pretty and though my mother died when I was seven, Najoud still keeps up the poison—of course not to our face, she's much more clever than that. Erikki, you can never know how subtle and secretive and powerful Iranian ladies can be, or how vengeful behind their oh so sweet exterior. Najoud's worse than the snake in the Garden of Eden! She's the cause of all the enmity." Her lovely blue-green eyes filled with tears. "When I was little, my father truly loved us, my brother Hakim and me, and we were his favorites. He spent more time with us in our house than in the palace. Then, when Mother died, we went to live in the palace but none of my half brothers and sisters really liked us. When we went into the palace, everything changed, Erikki. It was Najoud."

"Azadeh, you tear yourself apart with this hatred—you suffer, not her. Forget her. She's got no power over you now and I tell you again: you've no proof."

"I don't need proof. I know. And I'll never forget."

Erikki had left it there. There was no point in arguing, no point in rehashing what had been the source of much violence and many tears. Better it's in the open than buried, better to let her rave from time to time.

Ahead now the road left the fields and entered Qazvin, a city like most every other Iranian city, noisy, cramped, dirty, polluted, and traffic-jammed. Beside the road were the joub that skirted most roads in Iran. Here the ditches were three feet deep, in parts concreted, with slush and ice and a little water trickling down them. Trees grew out of them, townsfolk washed their clothes in them, sometimes used them as a source of drinking water, or as a sewer. Beyond the ditches the walls began. Walls that hid houses or gardens, big or small, rich or eyesores. Usually the town and city houses were two floors, drab and boxlike, some brick, adobe, some plastered, and almost all of them hidden. Most had dirt floors, a few had running water, electricity, and some sanitation.

Traffic built up with startling suddenness. Bicycles, motorcycles, buses, trucks, cars of all sizes and makes and ages from ancient to very old, almost all dented and patched, some highly decorated with different-colored paints and small lights to suit the owners' fancy. Erikki had driven this way many times over the last few years and he knew the bottlenecks that could happen. But there was no other way, no detour around the city though one had been planned for years. He smiled scornfully, trying to shut his ears to the noise, and thought, There'll never be a detour, the Qazvinis couldn't stand the quiet. Qazvinis and Rashtians—people from Rasht on the Caspian—were the butts of many Iranian jokes.

He skirted a burned-out wreck, then put in a cassette of Beethoven and turned the volume up to soothe the noise away. But it didn't help much.

"This traffic's worse than usual! Where are the police?" Azadeh said, wide awake now. "Are you thirsty?"

"No, no thanks." He glanced across at her, the sweater and tumbling hair enhancing her. He grinned. "But I'm hungry—hungry for you!"

She laughed and took his arm. "I'm not hungry—just ravenous!"

"Good." They were content together.

As usual the road surface was bad. Here and there it was torn up—partially because of wear, partially because of never-ending repairs and road works though these rarely were signposted or had safety barriers. He skirted a deep hole then eased past another wreck that had been shoved carelessly into the side. As he did so a crumpled truck came from the other direction, its horn blaring angrily. It was brightly decorated, the fenders tied up with wire, the cab open and glassless, a piece of cloth the tank cap. On the flatbed was brushwood, piled high, with three passengers hanging on precariously. The driver was huddled up and wrapped in a ragged sheepskin coat. Two other men were beside him. As Erikki passed he was surprised to see them glaring at him. A few yards farther on a battered, overladen bus lumbered toward him. With great care he went closer to the joub, hugging the side to give the bus room, his wheels on the rim, and stopped. Again he saw the driver and all the passengers stare at him as they passed, women in their chadors, young men, bearded and clothed heavily against the cold. One of them shook his fist at him. Another shouted a curse.

We've never had any trouble before, Erikki thought uneasily. Everywhere he looked were the same angry glances. From the street and from the vehicles. He had to go very slowly because of the swarms of rogue motorcycles, bicycles, among the cars, buses, and trucks, in single lanes that fought for space—obedient to no traffic laws other than those which pleased the individual—and now a flock of sheep poured out of a side street to clutter the road, the motorists screaming abuse at the herdsmen, the herdsmen screaming abuse back and everyone angry and impatient, horns blaring.

"Damned traffic! Stupid sheep!" Azadeh said impatiently, wide awake now. "Sound your horn, Erikki!"

"Be patient, go back to sleep. There's no way I can overtake anyone," he shouted over the tumult, conscious of the unfriendliness that surrounded them. "Be patient!"

Another three hundred yards took half an hour, other traffic coming from both sides to join the stream that got slower and slower. Street vendors and pedestrians and refuse. Now he was inching along behind a bus that took up most of the roadway, almost scraping cars on the other side, most times with one wheel half over the lip of the joub. Motorcyclists shoved past carelessly, banging the sides of the Range Rover and other vehicles, cursing each other and everyone else, pushing and kicking the sheep out of the way, stampeding them. From behind, a small car nudged him, then the driver jammed his hand on his horn in a paroxysm of rage that sent a sudden shaft of anger into Erikki's head. Close your ears, he ordered himself. Be calm! There's nothing you can do! Be calm!

But he found it increasingly difficult. After half an hour the sheep turned off into an alley, and traffic picked up a little. Then around the next corner the whole roadway was dug up and an unmarked ten-foot ditch—some six feet deep and half-filled with water—barred the way. A group of insolent workmen squatted nearby, hurling back abuse. And obscene gestures.

It was impossible to go forward or back, so all traffic had to detour into a narrow side street, the bus ahead not making the turn, having to stop and reverse to more screams of rage and more tumult and when Erikki backed to give it room, a battered blue car behind him swerved around him on the opposite side of the road into the small opening ahead and forced the oncoming car to brake suddenly and skid. One of its wheels sank into the joub and the whole car tipped dangerously. Now traffic was totally snarled.

Enraged, Erikki put on his brake, tore his door open, and went over to the car in the ditch and used his great strength to drag it back on the road. No one else helped, just swore and added to the uproar. Then he strode for the blue car. At that moment the bus made the corner and now there was room to move, the driver of the blue car let in his clutch and roared off with an obscene gesture.

With an effort Erikki unclenched his fists. Traffic on both sides of the road was honking at him. He got into the driver's seat and let in the clutch.

"Here," Azadeh said uneasily. She gave him a cup of coffee.

"Thanks." He drank it, driving with one hand, the traffic slowing again. The blue car had vanished. When he could talk calmly, he said, "If I'd got my hands on him or his car I'd have torn it and him to pieces."

"Yes. Yes, I know. Erikki, have you noticed how hostile everyone is to us? So angry?"

"Yes, yes, I have."

"But why? We've driven though Qazvin twenty tim—" Azadeh ducked involuntarily as refuse suddenly hit her window, then lurched across into his protection, frightened. He cursed and rolled up the windows, then reached across her and locked her door. Dung hit the windshield.

"What the hell's up with these *matyeryebyets?*" he muttered. "It's as though we've an American flag flying and we're waving pictures of the Shah." A stone came out of nowhere and ricocheted off the metal sides. Then, ahead, the bus broke out of the narrow side-street diversion into the wide square in front of a mosque where there were market stalls and two lanes of traffic on either side. To Erikki's relief they picked up some speed. The traffic was still heavy but it was moving and he got into second, heading for the Tehran exit the far side of the square. Halfway around the square the two lanes began to tighten as more vehicles joined those heading for the Tehran road.

"It's never been this bad," he muttered. "What the hell's the holdup for?"

"It must be another accident," Azadeh said, very unsettled. "Or road works. Should we turn back—the traffic's not so bad that way?"

"We've plenty of time," he said, encouraging her. "We'll be out of here in a minute. Once through the town we'll be fine." Ahead everything was slowing again, the din picking up. The two lanes were clogging, gradually becoming one again with much hooting, swearing, stopping, starting again and grinding along at about ten miles an hour, street stores and pushcarts encroaching the roadway and straddling the joub. They were almost at the exit when some youths ran alongside, began shouting insults, some foul. One of the youths banged on his side window. "American dog . . ."

"Pig Amer'can . . ."

These men were joined by others and some women in chador, fists raised. Erikki was bottled in and could not get out of the traffic or speed up or slow down nor could he turn around and he felt rage growing at his helplessness.

Some of the men were banging on the hood and sides of the Range Rover and on his window. Now there was a pack of them and those on Azadeh's side were taunting her, making obscene gestures, trying to open the door. One of the youths jumped on the hood but slipped and fell off and just managed to scramble out of the way before Erikki drove over him.

The bus ahead stopped. Immediately there was a frantic melee as would-be passengers fought to get on and others fought to get off. Then Erikki saw an opening, stamped on the accelerator throwing off another man, got around the bus, just missing pedestrians who carelessly flooded through the traffic, and swung into a side street that miraculously was clear, raced up it and cut into another, narrowly avoided a mass of motorcyclists, and continued on again. Soon he was quite lost, for there was no pattern to the city or town except refuse and stray dogs and traffic, but he took his bearings from the sun's shadows and at length came out onto a wider road, shoved his way into the traffic and around it, and soon came onto a road that he recognized, one that took him into another square in front of another mosque and then back on the Tehran road. "We're all right now, Azadeh, they were just hooligans."

"Yes," she said shakily. "They should be whipped."

Erikki had been studying the crowds near the mosque and on the streets and in the vehicles, trying to find a clue to the untoward hostility. Something's different, he thought. What is it? Then his stomach twisted. "I haven't seen a soldier or an army truck ever since we left Tabriz—none. Have you?"

"No—no, not now that you mention it."

"Something's happened, something serious."

"War? The Soviets have come over the border?" Her face lost even more color.

"I doubt it—there'd be troops going north, or planes." He looked at her. "Never mind," he said, more to convince himself, "we're going to have a fine time in Tehran, Sharazad's there and lots of your friends. It's about time you had a change. Maybe I'll take the leave I'm owed—we could go to Finland for a week or two . . ."

They were out of the downtown area and into the suburbs now. The suburbs were ramshackled, with the same walls and houses and the same potholes. Here the Tehran road widened to four lanes, two each side, and though traffic was still heavy and slow, barely fifteen miles an hour, he was not concerned. A little way ahead, the Abadan-Kermanshah road branched off southwest, and he knew that this would bleed off a lot of the congestion. Automatically his eyes scanned the gauges as he would his cockpit instruments and, not for the first time, he wished he was airborne, over and out of all this mess. The gas gauge registered under a quarter full. Soon he would have to refuel but that would be no problem with plenty of spare fuel aboard.

They slowed to ease past another truck parked with careless arrogance near some street vendors, the air heavy with the smell of diesel. Then more refuse came out of nowhere to splatter their windshield. "Perhaps we should turn around, Erikki, and go back to Tabriz. Perhaps we could skirt Qazvin."

"No," he said, finding it eerie to hear fear in her voice—normally she was fearless. "No," he repeated even more kindly. "We'll go to Tehran and find out what the problem is, then we'll decide."

She moved closer to him and put a hand on his knee. "Those hooligans frightened me. God curse them," she muttered, her other fingers toying nervously with the turquoise beads she wore around her neck. Most Iranian women wore turquoise or blue beads, or a single blue stone against the evil eye. "Those sons of dogs! Why should they be like that? Devils. May God curse them forever!" Just outside the city was a big army training camp and an adjoining air base. "Why aren't soldiers here?"

"I'd like to know too," he said.

The Abadan-Kermanshah turnoff came up on his right. Much of the traffic headed down it. Barbed-wire fences skirted both roads—as on most of the main roads and highways in Iran. The fences were needed to keep sheep and goats and cattle and dogs—and people—from straying across the roads. Accidents were very frequent and mortality high.

But that's normal for Iran, Erikki thought. Like those poor fools who went over the side in the mountains—no one to know, no one to report them or even to bury them. Except the buzzards and the wild animals and packs of rotten dogs.

With the city behind them, they felt better. The country opened up again, orchards once more beyond the joub and the barbed wire. The Elburz Mountains north and undulating country south. But instead of speeding up, his two lanes slowed even more and congested, then reluctantly became one again, with more jostling, hooting, and rage. Wearily he cursed the inevitable roadworks that must be causing the bottleneck, shifted down, his hands and feet working smoothly of their own volition, hardly noticing the stopping and starting, stopping and starting, inching along again, engines grinding and overheating, noise and frustration building in every vehicle. Abruptly Azadeh pointed ahead. "Look!"

A hundred yards ahead was a roadblock. Groups of men surrounded it. Some were armed, all were civilians and poorly dressed. The roadblock was just this side of a nondescript village with street stalls beside the road and in the meadow opposite. Villagers, women and children, mingled with the men.

All the women wore the black or gray chador. As each vehicle stopped, papers were checked and then it was allowed to pass. Several cars had been pulled off the road into the meadow where knots of men interrogated the occupants. Erikki saw more weapons among them.

"They're not Green Bands," he said.

"There aren't any mullahs. Can you see any mullahs?"

"No."

"Then they're Tudeh or mujhadin—or fedayeen."

"Better get your Identity Card ready," he said and smiled at her. "Put on your parka so you won't catch cold when I open the windows, and your hat." It wasn't the cold that worried him. It was the curve of her breasts, proud under the sweater, the delicacy of her waist and her free-flowing hair.

In the glove compartment was a small, sheathed pukoh knife. This he concealed in his right boot. The other one, his big knife, was under his parka, in the center of his back.

When at last their turn came, the surly, bearded men surrounded the Range Rover. A few had U.S. rifles, one an AK47. Among them were some women, just faces in the chador. They peered up at her with beady eyes and grim disapproval. "Papers," one of the men said in Farsi, holding out his hand, his breath reeking, the pervading smell of unwashed clothes and bodies coming into the car. Azadeh stared ahead, trying to dismiss the leers and mutterings and closeness that were totally outside her experience.

Politely Erikki passed over his ID card and Azadeh's. The man accepted them, stared at them, and passed them to a youth who could read. All the others waited silently, staring, stamping their feet in the cold. At length the youth said, his Farsi coarse, "He's a foreigner from somewhere called Finland. He comes from Tabriz. He's not American."

"He looks American," someone else said.

"The woman's called Gorgon, she's his wife . . . at least that's what the papers say."

"I'm his wife," Azadeh said curtly. "Ca—"

"Who asked you?" the first man said rudely. "Your family name's Gorgon which is a landowning name and your accent's high and mighty like your manner and more than likely you're an enemy of the People."

"I'm an enemy of no one. Pl—"

"Shut up. Women are supposed to know manners and be chaste and cover themselves and be obedient even in a socialist state." The man turned on Erikki. "Where are you going?"

"What's he say, Azadeh?" Erikki asked.

She translated.

"Tehran," he said quietly to the thug. "Azadeh, tell him we go to Tehran."
He had counted six rifles and one automatic. Traffic hemmed him in, no way
to break out. Yet.

She did so, adding, "My husband does not speak Farsi."

"How do we know that? And how do we know you're married? Where is
your marriage certificate?"

"I don't have it with me. That I'm married is attested on my Identity
Card."

"But this is a Shah card. An illegal card. Where is your new card?"

"A card from whom? Signed by whom?" she said fiercely. "Give us back
our cards and allow us to pass!"

Her strength had an effect on him and the others. The man hesitated.
"You will understand, please, that there are many spies and enemies of the
People that must be caught . . ."

Erikki could feel his heart pumping. Sullen faces, people out of the Dark
Ages. Ugly. More men joined the group around them. One of them angrily
and noisily waved the cars and trucks behind him ahead to be checked. No
one was honking. Everyone waited their turn. And over the whole traffic jam
was a silent brooding dread.

"What's going on here?" A squat man shouldered his way through the
crowd. The others gave way to him deferentially. Over his shoulder was a
Czechoslovakian machine gun. The other man explained and gave over the
papers. The squat man's face was round and unshaven, his eyes dark, his
clothes poor and filthy. A sudden shot rang out and all heads turned to look
at the meadow.

A man was lying on the ground beside a small passenger car that had been
pulled over by the hostiles. One of these men stood over him with an automatic. Another passenger was pressed against the side of the car with his
hands over his head. Abruptly this man burst through the cordon and dashed
away. The man with the gun raised it and fired, missed and fired again. This
time the running man screamed and fell, writhing in agony, tried to scramble
away, his legs useless now. Leisurely the man with the gun came up to him,
emptied the magazine into him, killing him by stages.

"Ahmed!" the squat man shouted out. "Why waste bullets when your
boots would do just as well. Who are they?"

"SAVAK!" A murmur of satisfaction swept the crowd and villagers and
someone cheered.

"Fool! Then why kill them so quickly, eh? Bring me their papers."

"The sons of dogs had papers claiming they were Tehrani businessmen but
I know a SAVAK man when I see one. Do you want the false papers?"

"No. Tear them up." The squat man turned back to Erikki and Azadeh. "So it is that enemies of the People will be smoked out and done with."

She did not reply. Their own IDs were in the grubby hand. What if our papers are also considered false? Insha'Allah!

When the squat man finished scrutinizing the IDs he stared at Erikki. Then at her. "You claim you're Azadeh Gorgon Yok . . . Yokkonen—his wife?"

"Yes."

"Good." He stuffed their IDs in his pocket and jerked a thumb at the meadow. "Tell him to drive over there. We will search your car."

"But th—"

"Do it. NOW!" The squat man climbed onto the fender, his boots scratching the paintwork. "What's that?" he asked, pointing to the blue cross on a white background that was painted on the roof.

"It's the Finnish flag," Azadeh said. "My husband's Finnish."

"Why is it there?"

"It pleases him to have it there."

The squat man spat, then pointed again toward the meadow. "Hurry up! Over there." When they were in an empty spot, the crowd following them, he slid off. "Out. I want to search your car for arms and contraband."

Azadeh said, "We have no guns or contr—"

"Out! And you, woman, you hold your tongue!" The crones in the crowd hissed approvingly. Angrily he jerked a thumb at the two bodies left crumpled in the trampled slush. "The People's justice is quick and final and don't forget it." He stabbed a finger at Erikki. "Tell your monster husband what I said—if he is your husband."

"Erikki, he says, the People's . . . the People's justice is quick and final and don't forget it. Be careful, my darling. We, we have to get out of the car —they want to search the car."

"All right. But slide over and come out my side." Towering above the crowd, Erikki got out. Protectively, he put his arm around her, men, women, and some children crowding them, giving them little space. The stench of unwashed bodies was overpowering. He could feel her trembling, as much as she tried to hide it. Together they watched the squat man and others clambering into their spotless car, muddy boots on the seats. Others unlocked the rear door, carelessly removing and scattering their possessions, grubby hands reaching into pockets, opening everything—his bags and her bags. Then one of the men held up her filmy underclothes and night things to catcalls and jeers. The crones muttered their disapproval. One of them reached out and touched her hair. Azadeh backed away but those behind her would not give her room. At once Erikki moved his bulk to help but the mass of the crowd did not move though those nearby cried out, almost crushed by him, their cries infuriating the others who moved closer, threateningly, shouting at him.

Suddenly Erikki knew truly, for the first time, he could not protect Azadeh. He knew he could kill a dozen of them before they overpowered and killed him, but that would not protect her.

The realization shattered him.

His legs felt weak and he had an overpowering wish to urinate and the smell of his own fear choked him and he fought the panic that pervaded him. Dully he watched their possessions being defiled. Men were staggering away with their vital cans of gasoline without which he could never make Tehran as all gas stations were struck and closed. He tried to force his legs into motion but they would not work, nor would his mouth. Then one of the crones shouted at Azadeh who numbly shook her head and men took up the cry, jostling him and jostling her, men closing on him, their fetid smell filling his nostrils, his ears clogged with the Farsi.

His arm was still around her, and in the noise she looked up and he saw her terror but could not hear what she said. Again he tried to ease more room for the two of them but again he failed. Desperately he tried to contain the soaring, claustrophobic, panic-savagery and need to fight beginning to overwhelm him, knowing that once he began it would start the riot that would destroy her. But he could not stop himself and lashed out blindly with his free elbow as a thickset peasant woman with strange, enraged eyes pushed though the cordon and thrust the chador into Azadeh's chest, spitting out a paroxysm of Farsi at her, diverting attention from the man who had collapsed behind him, and now lay under their feet, his chest caved in from Erikki's blow.

The crowd was shouting at her and at him, clearly telling her to put on the chador, Azadeh crying out, "No, no, leave me alone . . ." completely disoriented. In her whole life she had never been threatened like this, never been in a crowd like this, never experienced such closeness of peasants, or such hostility.

"Put it on, harlot . . ."

"In the Name of God, put on the chador . . ."

"Not in the Name of God, woman, in the name of the People . . ."

"God is Great, obey the word . . ."

"Piss on God, in the name of the revolution . . ."

"Cover your hair, whore and daughter of a whore . . ."

"Obey the Prophet whose Name be praised . . ."

The shouting increased and the jostling, their feet trampling the dying

man on the ground, then someone tore at Erikki's arm that was around
Azadeh and she felt his other hand go for the big knife and she screamed out,
"Don't, don't, Erikki, they'll kill you . . ."

In panic she pushed the peasant woman away and fought the chador into
place, calling out repeatedly, "Allah-u Akbarrr," and this mollified those
nearby somewhat, their jeers subsiding, though people at the back shoved
forward to see better, crushing others against the Range Rover. In the melee
Erikki and Azadeh gained a little more space around them though they were
still trapped on all sides. She did not look up at him, just clutched him,
shivering like a frozen puppy, enveloped in the coarse shroud. A roar of
laughter as one of the men held her bra against his chest and minced around.

The vandalism went on until, suddenly, Erikki sensed a newness surrounding them. The squat man and his followers had stopped and they were
looking fixedly toward Qazvin. As he watched he saw them begin to melt into
the crowd. In seconds they had vanished. Other men near the roadblock were
getting into cars and heading off down the Tehran road, picking up speed.
Now villagers also stared toward the city, then others, until the whole crowd
was transfixed. Approaching up the road, through the snarled lines of traffic,
was another mob of men, mullahs at their head. Some of the mullahs and
many of the men were armed. "Allah-u Akbar," they shouted, "God and
Khomeiniiiii!" then broke into a run, charging the roadblock.

A few shots rang out, the fire was returned from the roadblock, the opposing forces clashed with staves, stones, iron bars, and some guns. Everyone else
scattered. Villagers rushed for the protection of their homes, drivers and
passengers fled from their cars for the ditches or lay on the ground.

The cries and countercries and shots and noise and screams of this minor
skirmish snapped Erikki's paralysis. He shoved Azadeh toward their car, hastily picking up the nearest of their scattered possessions, throwing them into
the back, and slammed the rear door. Half a dozen of the villagers began
scavenging too but he shoved them out of the way, jumped into the driver's
seat and gunned the engine, jerked the car into reverse, then ahead, then
roared off across the meadow, paralleling the road. Just ahead and to the right
he saw the squat man with three of his followers getting into a car and
remembered that the man still had their papers. For a split second he considered stopping but instantly rejected the thought and held course for the trees
that skirted the road. But then he saw the squat man pull the machine gun
off his shoulder, aim, and fire. The burst was a little high and Erikki's maddened reflexes swung the wheel over and shoved his foot on the accelerator as
he charged the gun. Their massive bumper rammed the man against the car
broadside, crushing him and it, the machine gun firing until the magazine

was spent, bullets howling off metal, splaying through the windshield, the Range Rover now a battering ram. Berserk, Erikki backed off then charged again, overturning the wreckage, killing them, and he would have got out and continued the carnage with his bare hands but then, in the rearview mirror, he saw men running for him and so he reversed and fled.

The Range Rover was built for this sort of terrain, its snow tires gripping the surface of the rough ground. In a moment they were in the trees and safe from capture, and he turned for the road, shifted into low, locked both differentials and clambered over the deep joub, ripping the barbed-wire fence apart. Once on the road he unlocked the differentials, changed gear, and whirled away.

Only when he was well away did the blood clear from his eyes. Aghast, he remembered the howl of the bullets spraying the car, and that Azadeh was with him. In panic he looked across at her. But she was all right though paralyzed with fear and hunched down in the seat, hanging on with both hands to the side, bullet holes in the glass and roof nearby, but all right though he did not recognize her for a moment, saw just an Iranian face made ugly by the chador—like any one of the tens of thousands they had all seen in the mobs.

"Oh, Azadeh," he gasped, then reached over and pulled her to him, driving with one hand. In a moment he slowed and pulled over to the side and held her to him as the sobs tore her. He did not notice that the fuel gauge read near empty, or that the traffic was building up, or the hostile looks of the passersby, or that many cars contained revolutionaries fleeing their roadblock for Tehran.

AT ZAGROS THREE: 3:18 P.M. The four men were lying on toboggans, racing down the slope behind the base, Scot Gavallan slightly in the
lead of Jean-Luc Sessonne who was neck and neck with Nasiri, their base
manager, with Nitchak Khan trailing some twenty yards. This was a challenge match arranged by Jean-Luc, Iran against the World, and all four men
were excitedly trying to maximize their speed. The snow was virgin powder—
very light snow on top of hard pack—and trackless. They had all climbed to
the crest behind the base with Rodrigues and a villager as starting marshals.
The winner's prize was 5,000 rials—about $60—and one of Lochart's bottles
of whisky: "Tom won't mind," Jean-Luc had said grandly. "He's having extra
leave, enjoying the fleshpots of Tehran while we have to stay on base! Me, am
I not in command? Of course. This commander is commandeering the bottle
for the glory of France, the good of my troops, and our glorious overlords, the
Yazdek Kash'kai," he had added to general cheers.

It was a wonderful, sunny afternoon, here at seventy-five hundred feet, the sky cloudless and deep blue, air crisp. In the night the snow had stopped. Ever since Lochart had left to go to Tehran three days before, it had been snowing. Now the base and the bowl of mountains were a fairyland of pine and snow and crests soaring to thirteen thousand feet—with about twenty-four inches of fresh powder.

As the racers came lower, the slope steepened even more, a few unseen moguls bouncing them from time to time. They picked up speed, sometimes almost disappearing under the spray of snowflakes, all exhilarated, flat-out, and determined to win.

Ahead now were clumps of pine trees. Scot braked neatly with the toes of his ski boots, his mittened hands gripping the curved front supports, and arced gracefully around the trees, banked again, and began to swoop down the last great slope toward the finish line far below where the rest of the base and villagers were cheering them on. Nasiri and Jean-Luc braked a fraction later, came around the trees just a fraction faster, banked in a cascade of snow and gained on him, now only inches between the three of them.

Nitchak Khan did not brake at all, or make the diversion. He commended himself to God for the hundredth time, closed his eyes and went barreling into the pines. "Insha'Allahhhh!"

He passed the first tree safely by a foot, the next by half a foot, opened his eyes just in time to avoid a head-on collision by an inch, plowed through a dozen saplings gaining speed, abruptly soared into the air over a bump to clear miraculously a fallen tree, and slam back to earth once more in a chest-aching thump that almost crushed the air out of him. But he hung on, rearing up, heeled over on one runner for a second, got his balance back and now he burst out of the forest faster than the others, straighter than the others, ten yards ahead of the others to a roar from all the villagers.

The four racers were converging now, hugging their toboggans for just that extra little speed, Scot, Nasiri, and Jean-Luc gaining on Nitchak Khan, closer and closer. Here the snow was not so good and some small moguls bounced them, making them hold on tighter. Two hundred yards to go, one hundred —the men from the base and the villagers cheering and begging God for victory—now eighty, seventy, sixty, fifty, and then . . .

The great mogul was well hidden. In the lead Nitchak Khan was the first to sail up out of control and come down broadside, the wind knocked out of him, then Scot and Jean-Luc both whirled into the air to sprawl equally helpless, their toboggans upended in clouds of spray. Nasiri desperately tried to avoid them and the mogul and wrenched his craft into a violent skidding turn but lost it and went tumbling down the mountainside to end up a little ahead of the others, gasping for breath.

Nitchak Khan sat up and wiped the snow out of his face and beard. "Praise be to God," he muttered, astonished that no limbs were broken, and he looked around at the others. They were also picking themselves up, Scot helpless with laughter at Jean-Luc who was also unhurt but still lying on his back letting out a paroxysm of French invective. Nasiri had ended up almost headfirst into a snowdrift and Scot, still laughing, went to help him. He, too, was just a little battered but no damage.

"Hey, you lot up there," someone was shouting from the crowd below. It was Effer Jordon. "What about the bleeding race? It's not over yet!"

"Come on, Scot—come on, Jean-Luc, for crissake!"

Scot forgot Nasiri and started to run for the winning post fifty yards away but he slipped and fell in the heavy snow, lurched up and slipped again, feet leaden. Jean-Luc reeled up and charged in pursuit, closely followed by Nasiri and Nitchak Khan. The cheers of the crowd redoubled as the men fought through the snow, falling, scrambling, getting up and falling again, the going very rough, aches forgotten. Scot was still slightly in the lead, now Nitchak Khan, now Jean-Luc, now Nasiri—mechanic Fowler Joines, red in the face, urging them on, the villagers as excited.

Ten yards to go. The old Khan was three feet in the lead when he tripped and sprawled face forward. Scot took the lead, Nasiri almost beside him, Jean-Luc just inches behind. They were all at a laboring, faltering, stumbling walk, dragging their boots up out of the heavy snow, then there was a mighty cheer as Nitchak Khan began to scuttle forward on all fours the last few yards, Jean-Luc and Scot made one last desperate headlong dive for the line, and they all collapsed in a heap amid cheers and countercheers.

"Scot won . . ."

"No, it was Jean-Luc . . ."

"No, it was old Nitchak . . ."

When he had collected his breath, Jean-Luc said, "As there is no clear opinion and even our revered mullah is not sure, I, Jean-Luc, declare Nitchak Khan the winner by a nostril." There were cheers and even more as he added, "And as the losers lost so bravely, I award them with another of Tom's bottles of whisky which I will commandeer to be shared by all expats at sundown!"

Everyone shook hands with everyone. Nitchak Khan agreed to another challenge match next month and, as he honored the law and did not drink, he haggled voraciously but sold the whisky he had won to Jean-Luc at half its value. Everyone cheered again, then someone shouted a warning.

Northward, far up in the mountains, a red signal flare was falling into the valley. The silence was sudden. The flare vanished. Then another arced up and outward to fall again: SOS Urgent.

"CASEVAC," Jean-Luc said, squinting into the distance. "Must be Rig Rosa or Rig Bellissima."

"I'm on my way." Scot Gavallan hurried off.

"I'll come with you," Jean-Luc said. "We'll take a 212 and make it a check ride for you."

In minutes they were airborne. Rig Rosa was one of the rigs they had acquired from the old Guerney contract, Bellissima one of their regulars. All eleven rigs in this area had been developed by an Italian company for Iran-Oil, and though all were radio linked with Zagros Three, the connection was not always solid because of the mountains and scatter effect. Flares were a substitute.

The 212 climbed steadily, passing through ten thousand feet, snow-locked valleys sparkled in the sunshine, their operational ceiling seventeen thousand, depending on their load. Now Rig Rosa was ahead in a clearing on a small plateau at eleven thousand four hundred seventy. Just a few trailers for housing, and sheds scattered haphazardly around the tall derrick. And a helipad.

"Rig Rosa, this is Jean-Luc. Do you read?" He waited patiently.

"Loud and clear, Jean-Luc!" It was the happy voice of Mimmo Sera, the "company man"—the highest rank on the site, an engineer in charge of all operations. "What you got for us, eh?"

"*Niente*, Mimmo! We saw a red flare and we're just checking."

"Madonna, CASEVAC? It wasn't us." At once Scot broke off his approach, banked, and went on to the new heading, climbing farther into the mountain range. "Bellissima?"

"We're going to check."

"Let us know, eh? We haven't been in contact since the storm came. What's the latest news?"

"The last we heard was two days ago: the BBC said the Immortals at Doshan Tappeh had put down a rebellion of air force cadets and civilians. We haven't heard from our Tehran HQ or anyone. If we do I'll radio you."

"Eh, radio! Jean-Luc, we'll need another dozen loads of six-inch pipe and the usual of cement starting tomorrow. Okay?"

"*Bien sûr!*" Jean-Luc was delighted with the extra business and the opportunity to prove they were better than Guerney. "How's it going?"

"We've drilled to eight thousand feet and everything looks like another bonanza. I want to run the well next Monday, if possible. Can you order up Schlumberger for me?" Schlumberger was the worldwide firm that manufactured and supplied down-hole tools that sampled and electronically measured, with vast accuracy, oil-bearing capabilities and qualities of the various strata, tools to guide the drilling bits, tools to fish up broken bits, tools to perforate, by explosion, the steel casings of the hole to allow oil to flow into the pipe— along with the experts to work them. Very expensive but totally necessary. "To run a well" was the last job before cementing the steel casing in place and bringing the well on stream.

"Wherever they are, Mimmo, we'll bring them Monday—Khomeini willing!"

"Mamma mia, tell Nasiri we have to have them."

Reception was fading rapidly.

"No problem. I'll call you on the way back." Jean-Luc glanced out of the cockpit. They were passing over a ridge, still climbing, the engines beginning to labor. "*Merde*, I'm hungry," he said, and stretched in his seat. "I feel like I've been massaged with a pneumatic drill—but that was a great race!"

"You know, Jean-Luc, you were at the line a second before Nitchak Khan. Easily."

"Of course, but we French are magnanimous, *diplomatique*, and very practical. I knew he'd sell us back our whisky for half price; if he'd been declared the loser, it would have cost us a fortune." Jean-Luc beamed. "But if it hadn't been for that mogul, I would not have hesitated—I would have won easily."

Scot smiled and said nothing, breathing easily, but conscious of his breathing. Above twelve thousand, according to regulations, pilots should be on oxygen if they were to stay up for more than half an hour. They carried none and never, yet, had any of the pilots felt any discomfort other than a headache or two, though it took a week or so to get acclimatized to living at seventy-five hundred feet. It was harder for the riggers at Bellissima.

Their own stopovers at Bellissima were usually very short. Just lumber up with maximum payload, inside or out, of 4,000 pounds. Pipes, pumps, diesel, winches, generators, chemicals, food, trailers, tanks, men, mud—the all-purpose name for the liquid that was pumped into the drill hole to remove waste, to keep the bit lubricated, in due course to tame the oil or gas, and without which deep drilling was impossible. Then lumber out, light, or with a full load of men or equipment for repair or replacement.

We're just a jumped-up delivery van, Scot thought, his eyes scanning the skies, instruments, and all around. Yes, but how grand to be flying and not driving. Below, the crags were quite close, the tree line long since passed. They mounted the last ridge. Now they could see the rig.

"Bellissima, this is Jean-Luc. Do you read?"

Rig Bellissima was the highest of the chain, exactly at twelve thousand four hundred fifty feet above sea level. The base was perched on a ledge just below the crest. The other side of the ledge the mountain fell away seven thousand feet, almost sheer, into a valley ten miles wide and thirty miles long, a vast gash in the surface of the earth.

"Bellissima, this is Jean-Luc. Do you read?"

Again no answer. Jean-Luc switched channels. "Zagros Three, do you read?"

"Loud and clear, Captain," came the immediate answer of their Iranian base radio op Aliwari. "Excellency Nasiri's beside me."

"Stand by on this frequency. The CASEVAC's at Bellissima, but we've no radio contact. We're going in to land."

"Roger. Standing by."

As always at Bellissima, Scot was awed at the vastness of the earth's convulsion that had caused the valley. And, like all who visited this rig, again he wondered at the enormity of the gamble, labor, and wealth necessary to find the oil field, select the site, erect the rig, then to drill the thousands of feet to make the wells profitable. But they were, immensely so, as was this whole area with its huge oil and gas deposits trapped in limestone cones between seventy-five hundred and eleven thousand feet below the surface. And then the further huge investment and more gambling to connect this field to the pipeline that straddled the Zagros Mountains, joining the refineries at Isfahan in the center of Iran to those at Abadan on the Gulf—another extraordinary engineering feat of the old Anglo-Iranian Oil Company, now nationalized and renamed IranOil. "Stolen, Scot, laddie, stolen's the correct word," his father had told him many times.

Scot Gavallan smiled to himself, thinking about his father, feeling a warm glow. I'm bloody lucky to have him, he thought. I still miss Mother but I'm glad she died. Terrible for a lovely, active woman to become a helpless, chair-ridden, palsied shell, still with her mind intact even at the end, the best mother a guy could have. Rotten luck, her death, particularly for Dad. But I'm glad he remarried, Maureen's super, and Dad's super and I've a smashing life and the future's rosy—plenty of flying, plenty of birds and in a couple of years I'll get married: how about Tess? His heart picked up a beat. Bloody nuisance Linbar's her uncle and she his favorite niece, but bloody lucky I don't have anything to do with him, she's only eighteen so there's plenty of time . . .

"Which way will you land, *mon vieux*?" came through his earphones.

"From the west," he said, collecting himself.

"Good." Jean-Luc was peering ahead. No sign of life. The site was heavily covered with snow, almost buried. Only the helipad was cleared. Threads of smoke came up from the trailer huts. "Ah! There!"

They saw the tiny figure of a man, bundled up, standing near the helipad and waving his arms. "Who is it?"

"I think it's Pietro." Scot was concentrating on the landing. At this height and because of the position on the ledge there were sudden gusts, turbulences, and whirlwinds within them—no room for mistakes. He came in over the abyss, the eddies rocking them, then corrected beautifully as he swooped over the land and touched down.

"Good." Jean-Luc turned his attention back to the bundled-up man he now recognized as Pietro Fieri, one of the "tool pushers," next in importance to the company man. They saw him motion with his hand across his throat, the sign to cut engines, indicating the CASEVAC was not an immediate takeoff situation. Jean-Luc beckoned the man to his side window and opened it. "What's up, Pietro?" he shouted over the engines.

"Guineppa is sick," Pietro shouted back—Mario Guineppa was the company man—and thumped the left side of his chest. "We think it may be his heart. And that's not all. Look there!" He pointed aloft. Jean-Luc and Scot craned to see better but could not see what was agitating him.

Jean-Luc unbuckled and got out. The cold hit him and he winced, his eyes watering in the eddies caused by the rotors, his dark glasses helping only a little. Then he saw the problem, and his stomach twisted nastily. A few hundred feet above and almost directly over the camp, just under the crest, was an enormous overhang of snow and ice. "Madonna!"

"If that goes, it'll avalanche the whole mountainside and maybe take us and everything into the valley along with it!" Pietro's face was bluish in the cold. He was thickset and very strong with a dark grizzled beard, his eyes brown and keen but squinting now against the wind. "Guineppa wants to confer with you. Come to his trailer, eh?"

"And that?" Jean-Luc jerked a thumb upward.

"If it goes, it goes," Pietro said with a laugh, his teeth white against the darkness of his oil-stained parka. "Come on!" He ducked away from the rotors and trudged away. "Come on!"

Uneasily Jean-Luc gauged the overhang. It could be there for weeks, or fall any second. Above the crest the sky was peerless, but little warmth came from the afternoon sun. "Stay here, Scot, keep her idling," he called out, then followed Pietro awkwardly, the snow very deep.

Mario Guineppa's two-room trailer was warm and untidy, charts on the walls, oil-stained clothes, heavy gloves, and hard hats on pegs with an oilman's paraphernalia scattered about the office/living room. He was in the bedroom, lying on his bed fully dressed but for his boots, a big tall man of forty-five with an imposing nose, normally ruddy and weathered, but now pallid, a curious bluish tinge to his lips. The tool pusher from the other shift, Enrico Banastasio, was with him—a small, dark man with dark eyes and thin face.

"Ah, Jean-Luc! Good to see you," Guineppa said wearily.

"And you, *mon ami.*" Very concerned, Jean-Luc unzipped his flying jacket and sat beside the bed. Guineppa had been in charge of Bellissima for two years—twelve hours on, twelve off, two months on site, two off—and had brought in three major producing wells here with space to drill another four. "It's the hospital in Shiraz for you."

"That's not important, first there's the overhang. Jean-Luc, I wa—"

"We evacuate and leave that *stronzo* to the Hands of God," Banastasio said.

"Mamma mia, Enrico," Guineppa said irritably, "I tell you again I think we can give God a hand—with Jean-Luc's help. Pietro agrees. Eh, Pietro?"

"Yes," Pietro said from the doorway, a toothpick in his mouth. "Jean-Luc, I was brought up in Aosta in the Italian Alps so I know mountains and avalanches and I th—"

"*Sì, e sei pazzo.*" Yes, and you're crazy, Banastasio said curtly.

"*Nel tuo culo.*" In your ass. Pietro casually made an obscene gesture. "With your help Jean-Luc, it's easy to shift that *stronzo.*"

"What do you want me to do?" Jean-Luc asked.

Guineppa said, "Take Pietro and fly up over the crest to a place he'll show you on the north face. He'll drop a stick of dynamite into the snow from there and that'll avalanche the danger away from us."

Pietro beamed. "Just like that and the overhang will vanish."

Banastasio said even more angrily, his English American-accented, "For crissake, I tell you again it's too goddamn risky. We should evacuate first—then if you must, try your dynamite."

Guineppa's face screwed up as a spasm of pain went through him. One hand went to his chest. "If we evacuate we have to close everything down an—"

"So? So we close down. So what? If you don't care about your own life, think of the rest of us. I say we evacuate pronto. Then dynamite. Jean-Luc, isn't it safer?"

"Of course it's safer," Jean-Luc replied carefully, not wanting to agitate the older man. "Pietro, you say you know avalanches. How long will that hold?"

"My nose says it will go soon. Very soon. There are cracks below. Perhaps tomorrow, even tonight. I know where to blow her—and be very safe." **Pietro** looked at Banastasio. "I can do it whatever this *stronzo* thinks."

Banastasio got up. "Jean-Luc, me and my shift're evacuating. Pronto. Whatever is decided." He left.

Guineppa shifted in his cot. "Jean-Luc, take Pietro aloft. Now."

"First, we'll evacuate everyone to Rig Rosa, you first," Jean-Luc said crisply, "then dynamite. If it works you're back in business, if not there's enough temporary space at Rig Rosa for you."

"Not first, last . . . there's no need to evacuate."

Jean-Luc hardly heard him. He was estimating numbers of men to move. Each of the two shifts contained nine men—tool pusher, assistant, mudman, who monitored the mud and decided on its chemical constituents and weight, driller, who looked after the drilling, motorman, responsible for all winches, pumps, and so on, and four roustabouts to attach or unhook the pipes and drills. "You've seven Iranian cooks and laborers?"

"Yes. But I tell you it's not necessary to evacuate," Guineppa said exhaustedly.

"Safer, *mon vieux.*" Jean-Luc turned to Pietro. "Tell everyone to travel light and be fast."

Pietro glanced down at Guineppa. "Yes or no?"

Disgustedly, Guineppa nodded, the effort tiring him. "Ask for a volunteer crew to stay. If no one will, Mother of God, close down."

Pietro was clearly disappointed. Still picking his teeth, he went out. Guineppa shifted in the cot again, trying to get more comfortable, and began to curse. He seemed more frail than before.

Jean-Luc said quietly, "It's better to evacuate, Mario."

"Pietro is wise and clever but that *porco misero,* Banastasio, he's fart up to his nostrils, always trouble, and it was his fault the radio was smashed, I know it!"

"What?"

"It was smashed on his shift. Now we need a new one, do you have a spare?"

"No, but I'll see if I can get you one. Is it reparable? Perhaps one of our mechanics c—"

"Banastasio said he slipped and fell on it, but I heard he hit it with a hammer when it wouldn't work. . . . Mamma mia!" Guineppa winced and clutched his chest and began to curse again.

"How long have you been having pains?"

"Since two days. Today has been the worst. That *stronzo* Banastasio!" Guineppa muttered. "But what can you expect, it runs in his family. Eh! His family are half-American, no? I heard the American side has mafioso connections."

Jean-Luc smiled to himself, not believing it, half listening to the tirade. He knew that they hated each other—Guineppa, the Portuguese-Roman patrician, and Banastasio, Sicilian-American peasant. But that's not so surprising, he thought, locked up here, twelve hours on, twelve off, day after day, month after month, however good the pay.

Ah, the pay! How I could use their pay! Why even the lowest roustabout gets as much in one week as I get in a month—a miserable 1,200 pounds sterling monthly for me, a senior captain and training captain, with forty-eight hundred hours! Even with the miserly 500 pounds monthly overseas allowance, that's not enough for the kids, school fees, my wife, the mortgage and filthy taxes . . . let alone the best food and wine and my darling Sayada. Ah, Sayada, how I've missed you!

But for Lochart . . .

Piece of shit! Tom Lochart could have let me go with him and I could be in Tehran in her arms right now! My God how I need her. And money. Money! May the balls of all taxmen shrivel into dust and their cocks vanish! I've barely enough as it is and if Iran goes down the sewer, what then? I'll bet S-G won't survive. That's their bad luck—there'll always be chopper work for a pilot as excellent as I am somewhere in the world.

He saw Guineppa watching him. "Yes, *mon vieux?*"

"I'll go with the last load."

"Better to go first, there's a medic at Rosa."

"I'm fine—honestly."

Then Jean-Luc heard his name being called and put on his parka. "Can I do anything for you?"

The man smiled wearily. "Just take Pietro aloft with the dynamite."

"I'll do that, but last, with any luck, before dusk. Don't worry."

Outside the cold hit him again. Pietro was waiting for him. Men were already grouped near the idling helicopter, with packs and duffel bags of various sizes. Banastasio went past leading a big German shepherd.

"The man said to travel light," Pietro told him.

"I am," Banastasio said equally sourly. "I've my papers, my dog, and my shift. The rest's replaceable, on the goddamn company." Then to Jean-Luc, "You've a full load, Jean-Luc, let's get with it."

Jean-Luc checked the men aboard, and the dog, then called Nasiri on the radio and told him what they were going to do. "Okay, Scot, off you go. You take her," he said and got out and saw Scot's eyes widen.

"You mean by myself?"

"Why not, *mon brave.* You've the hours. This's your third check ride. You've got to start sometime. Off you go."

He watched Scot lift off. In barely five seconds the chopper was over the abyss with a clear seventy-five hundred feet below and he knew how eerie and wonderful that first solo takeoff from Bellissima would be, envying the young man the thrill. Young Scot's worth it, he thought, watching him critically.

"Jean-Luc!"

He took his eyes off the distant chopper and glanced around, wondering suddenly what was so different. Then he realized it was the silence, so vast that it almost seemed to deafen him. For a moment he felt weirdly unbalanced, even a little sick, then the whine of the wind picked up and he became whole again.

"Jean-Luc! Over here!" Pietro was in a shadow with a group of men on the other side of the camp, beckoning him. Laboriously, he picked his way over to them. They were strangely silent.

"Look there," Pietro said nervously and pointed aloft. "Just under the overhang. There! Twenty, thirty feet below. You see the cracks?"

Jean-Luc saw them. His testicles heaved. They were no longer cracks in the ice but fissures. As they watched, there was a vast groaning. The whole mass seemed to shift a fraction. A small chunk of ice and snow fell away. It gathered speed and substance and thundered down the steep slope. They were shock-still. The avalanche, now tons of snow and ice, came to rest barely fifty yards away from them.

One of the men broke the silence. "Let's hope the chopper doesn't come barreling back like a kamikaze—that could be the detonator, *amico.* Even a little noise could trigger that whole *stronzo* apart."

IN THE SKIES NEAR QAZVIN: 3:17 P.M. From the moment Charlie Pettikin had left Tabriz almost two hours ago with Rakoczy—the man he knew as Smith—he had flown the 206 as straight and level as possible, hoping to lull the KGB man to sleep, or at least off guard. For the same reason he had avoided conversation by slipping his headset onto his neck. At length Rakoczy had given up, just watched the terrain below. But he stayed alert with his gun across his lap, his thumb on the safety catch. And Pettikin wondered about him, who he was, what he was, what band of revolutionaries he belonged to—fedayeen, mujhadin, or Khomeini supporter—or if he was loyal, gendarmerie, army, or SAVAK, and if so why it was so important to get to Tehran. It had never occurred to Pettikin that the man was Russian not Iranian.

At Bandar-e Pahlavi where refueling had been laboriously slow, he had done nothing to break the monotony, just paid over his last remaining U.S.

dollars and watched while the tanks were filled, then signed the official Iran-Oil chit. Rakoczy had tried to chat with the refueler but the man was hostile, clearly frightened of being seen refueling this foreign helicopter, and even more frightened of the machine gun that was on the front seat.

All the time they were on the ground Pettikin had gauged the odds of trying to grab the gun. There was never a chance. It was Czech. In Korea they had been plentiful. And Vietnam. My God, he thought, those days seem a million years ago.

He had taken off from Bandar-e Pahlavi and was now heading south at a thousand feet, following the Qazvin road. East he could see the beach where he had set down Captain Ross and his two paratroopers. Again he wondered how they had known he was making a flight to Tabriz and what their mission had been. Hope to God they make it—whatever they had to make. Had to be urgent and important. Hope I see Ross again, I'd like that . . .

"Why do you smile, Captain?"

The voice came through his earphones. Automatically on takeoff this time he had put them on. He looked across at Rakoczy and shrugged, then went back to monitoring his instruments and the ground below. Over Qazvin he banked southeast following the Tehran road, once more retreating into himself. Be patient, he told himself, then saw Rakoczy tense and put his face closer to the window, looking downward.

"Bank left . . . a little left," Rakoczy ordered urgently, his concentration totally on the ground. Pettikin put the chopper into a gentle bank—Rakoczy on the low side. "No, more! Make a 180."

"What is it?" Pettikin asked. He steepened the bank, suddenly aware the man had forgotten the machine gun in his lap. His heart picked up a beat.

"There, below on the road. That truck."

Pettikin paid no attention to the ground below. He kept his eyes on the gun, gauging the distance carefully, his heart racing. "Where? I can't see anything . . ." He steepened the bank even more to come around quickly onto the new heading. "What truck? You mean . . ."

His left hand darted out and grabbed the gun by the barrel and awkwardly jerked it through the sliding window into the cabin behind them. At the same time his right hand on the stick went harder left then quickly right and left-right again, rocking the chopper viciously. Rakoczy was taken completely unaware and his head slammed against the side, momentarily stunning him. At once Pettikin clenched his left fist and inexpertly slashed at the man's jaw to put him unconscious. But Rakoczy, karate-trained, his reflexes good, managed to stop the blow with his forearm. Groggily he held on to Pettikin's wrist, gaining strength every second as the two men fought for supremacy, the chopper dangerously heeled over, Rakoczy still on the downside. They grappled with each other, cursing, seat belts inhibiting them. Both became more frenzied, Rakoczy with two hands free beginning to dominate.

Abruptly Pettikin gripped the stick with his knees, took his right hand off it, and smashed again at Rakoczy's face. The blow was not quite true but the strength of it shifted him off balance, destroyed the grip of his knees shoving the stick left, and overrode the delicate balance of his feet on the rudder pedals. At once the chopper reeled onto its side, lost all lift—no chopper can fly itself even for a second—the centrifugal force further throwing his weight askew and in the melee the collective lever was shoved down. The chopper fell out of the sky, out of control.

In panic, Pettikin abandoned the fight. Blindly he struggled to regain control, engines screaming and instruments gone mad. Hands and feet and training against panic, overcorrecting, then overcorrecting again. They dropped nine hundred feet before he got her straight and level, his heart unbearable, the snow-covered ground fifty feet below.

His hands were trembling. It was difficult to breathe. Then he felt something hard shoved in his side and heard Rakoczy cursing. Dully he realized the language was not Iranian but did not recognize it. He looked across at him and saw the face twisted with anger and the gray metal of the automatic and cursed himself for not thinking of that. Angrily he tried to shove the gun away but Rakoczy stuck it hard into the side of his neck.

"Stop or I'll blow your head off, you *matyeryebyets!*"

At once Pettikin put the plane into a violent bank, but the gun pressed harder, hurting him. He felt the safety catch go off and the gun cock.

"Your last chance!"

The ground was very near, rushing past sickeningly. Pettikin knew he could not shake him off. "All right—all right," he said, conceding, and straightened her and began to climb. The pressure from the gun increased and with it, the pain. "You're hurting me for God's sake and shoving me off balance! How can I fly if y—"

Rakoczy just jabbed the gun harder, shouting at him, cursing him, jamming his head against the doorframe.

"For Christ's sake!" Pettikin shouted back in desperation, trying to adjust his headset that had been torn off in the struggle. "How the hell can I fly with your gun in my neck?" The pressure eased off a fraction and he righted the plane. "Who the hell are you, anyway?"

"Smith!" Rakoczy was equally unnerved. A split second later, he thought, and we would have been splattered like a pat of fresh cow dung. "You think

you deal with a *matyeryebyets* amateur?" Before he could stop himself his
reflexes took his hand and backhanded Pettikin across the mouth.

Pettikin was rocked by the blow, and the chopper twisted but came back
into control. He felt the burn spreading over his face. "You do that again and
I'll put her on her back," he said with a great finality.

"I agree," Rakoczy said at once. "I apologize for . . . for that . . . for
that stupidity, Captain." Carefully he eased back against his door but kept
the gun cocked and pointed. "Yes, there was no need. I'm sorry."

Pettikin stared at him blankly. "You're sorry?"

"Yes. Please excuse me. It was unnecessary. I am not a barbarian."
Rakoczy gathered himself. "If you give me your word you'll stop trying to
attack me, I'll put my gun away. I swear you're in no danger."

Pettikin thought a moment. "All right," he said. "If you tell me who you
are and what you are."

"Your word?"

"Yes."

"Very well, I accept your word, Captain." Rakoczy put the safety on and
the gun in his far pocket. "My name is Ali bin Hassan Karakose and I'm a
Kurd. My home—my village—is on the slopes of Mount Ararat on the Iranian–Soviet border. Through the Blessings of God I'm a Freedom Fighter
against the Shah, and anyone else who wishes to enslave us. Does that satisfy
you?"

"Yes—yes it does. Then if y—"

"Please, later. First go there—quickly." Rakoczy pointed below. "Level off
and go closer."

They were at eight hundred feet to the right of the Qazvin–Tehran road.
A village straddled the road a mile back and he could see the smoke whirled
away by a stiff breeze. "Where?"

"There, beside the road."

At first Pettikin could not see what the man pointed at—his mind jumbled
with questions about the Kurds and their historic centuries of wars against
the Persian Shahs. Then he saw the collection of cars and trucks pulled up to
one side, and men surrounding a modern truck with a blue cross on a rectan-
gular white background on the roof, other traffic grinding past slowly. "You
mean there? You want to go over those trucks and cars?" he asked, his face
still smarting and his neck aching. "The bunch of trucks near the one with
the blue cross on its roof?"

"Yes."

Obediently Pettikin went into a descending bank. "What's so important about them, eh?" he asked, then glanced up. He saw the man staring at him suspiciously. "What? What the hell's the matter now?"

"You really don't know what a blue cross on a white background signifies?"

"No. What about it? What is it?" Pettikin had his eyes on the truck that was much closer now, close enough to see it was a red Range Rover, an angry crowd surrounding it, one of the men smashing at the back windows with the butt of a rifle. "It's the flag of Finland" came through his earphones and "Erikki" leaped into Pettikin's mind. "Erikki had a Range Rover," he burst out and saw the rifle butt shatter the window. "You think that's Erikki?"

"Yes . . . yes it's possible."

At once he went faster and lower, his pain forgotten, his excitement over-riding all the sudden questions of how and why this Freedom Fighter knew Erikki. Now they could see the crowd turning toward them and people scattering. His pass was very fast and very low but he did not see Erikki. "You see him?"

"No. I couldn't see inside the cab."

"Nor could I," Pettikin said anxiously, "but a few of those buggers are armed and they were smashing the windows. You see them?"

"Yes. They must be fedayeen. One of them fired at us. If you . . ." Rakoczy stopped, hanging on tightly as the chopper skidded into a 180-degree turn, twenty feet off the ground, and hurtled back again. This time the crowd of men and the few women fled, falling over one another. Traffic in both directions tried to speed away or shuddered to a halt, one overloaded truck skidding into another. Several cars and trucks turned off the road and one almost overturned in the joub.

Just abreast of the Range Rover, Pettikin swung into a sliding 90-degree turn to face it—snow boiling into a cloud—for just enough time to recognize Erikki, then into another 90 degrees to barrel away into the sky. "It's him all right. Did you see the bullet holes in the windscreen?" he asked, shocked. "Reach in the back for the machine gun. I'll steady her and then we'll go and get him. Hurry, I want to keep them off balance."

At once Rakoczy unbuckled his seat belt, reached back through the small intercommunicating window but could not get the gun that lay on the floor. With great difficulty he twisted out of his seat and clambered headfirst, half through the window, groping for it, and Pettikin knew the man was at his mercy. So easy to open the door now and shove him out. So easy. But impossible.

"Come on!" he shouted and helped pull him back into the seat. "Put your belt on!"

Rakoczy obeyed, trying to catch his breath, blessing his luck that Pettikin was a friend of the Finn, knowing that if their positions had been reversed he would not have hesitated to open the door. "I'm ready," he said, cocking the gun, appalled at Pettikin's stupidity. *The British are so stupid the mother-eating bastards deserve to lose.* "Wh—"

"Here we go!" Pettikin spun the chopper into a diving turn at maximum speed. Some armed men were still near the truck, guns pointing at them. "I'll soften them up and when I say 'fire' put a burst over their heads!"

The Range Rover rushed up at them, hesitated, then swirled away drunkenly—no trees nearby—hesitated again and came at them as the chopper danced around it. Pettikin flared to a sudden stop twenty yards away, ten feet off the ground. "Fire," he ordered.

At once Rakoczy let off a burst through the open window, aiming not over heads but at a group of men and women ducked down behind the back end of Erikki's truck, out of Pettikin's line of sight, killing or wounding some of them. Everyone nearby fled panic-stricken—screams of the wounded mingling with the howl of the jets. Drivers and passengers jumped out of cars and trucks scrambling away in the snowdrifts as best they could. Another burst and more panic, now everyone rushing in retreat, all traffic snarled. On the road some youths came from behind a truck with rifles. Rakoczy sprayed them and those nearby. "Make a 360!" he shouted.

Immediately the helicopter pirouetted but no one was near. Pettikin saw four bodies in the snow. "I said over their heads, for God's sake," he began, but at that moment the door of the Range Rover swung open and Erikki jumped out, his knife in one hand. For a moment he was alone, then a chador-clad woman was beside him. At once Pettikin set the chopper down on the snow but kept her almost airborne. "Come on," he shouted, beckoning them. They began to run, Erikki half carrying Azadeh whom Pettikin did not yet recognize.

Beside him Rakoczy unlocked his side door and leaped out, opened the back door, and whirled on guard. Another short burst toward the traffic. Erikki stopped, appalled to see Rakoczy. "Hurry!" Pettikin shouted, not understanding the reason for Erikki's hesitation. "Erikki, come on!" Then he recognized Azadeh. "My God . . ." he muttered, then shouted, "Come on, Erikki!"

"Quick, I've not much ammunition left!" Rakoczy shouted in Russian.

Erikki whirled Azadeh up into his arms and ran forward. A few bullets hummed past. At the side of the helicopter Rakoczy helped bundle Azadeh into the back, suddenly shoved Erikki aside with the barrel of the gun. "Drop your knife and get in the front seat!" he ordered in Russian. "At once."

Half paralyzed with shock, Pettikin watched Erikki hesitate, his face mottled with rage.

Rakoczy said harshly, "By God, there's more than enough ammunition for her, you, and this motherfucking pilot. Get in!"

Somewhere in the traffic a machine gun started to fire. Erikki dropped his knife in the snow, eased his great height into the front seat, Rakoczy slid beside Azadeh, and Pettikin took off and sped away, weaving over the ground like a panicked grouse, then climbed into the sky.

When he could talk he said, "What the hell's going on?"

Erikki did not answer. He craned around to make sure Azadeh was all right. She had her eyes closed and was slumped against the side, panting, trying to get her breath. He saw that Rakoczy had locked her seat belt, but when Erikki reached back to touch her the Soviet motioned him to stop with the gun.

"She will be all right, I promise you." He continued speaking in Russian, "providing you behave as your friend has been taught to behave." He kept his eyes on him as he reached into his small bag and brought out a fresh magazine. "Just so you know. Now face forward, please."

Trying to contain his fury, Erikki did as he was told. He put on the headset. There was no way they could be overheard by Rakoczy—there was no intercom in the back—and it felt strange for both of them to be so free and yet so imprisoned. "How did you find us, Charlie, who sent you?" he said into the mouth mike, his voice heavy.

"No one did," Pettikin said. "What the hell's with that bastard? I went to Tabriz to pick up you and Azadeh, got kidnapped by the sonofabitch in the back, and then he hijacked me to Tehran. It was just luck for Christ's sake—what the hell happened to you?"

"We ran out of fuel." Erikki told him briefly what had happened. "When the engine stopped, I knew I was finished. Everyone seems to have gone mad. One moment it was all right, then we were surrounded again, just like at the roadblock. I locked all the doors but it was only a matter of time . . ." Again he craned around. Azadeh had her eyes open and had pulled the chador off her face. She smiled at him wearily, reached forward to touch him but Rakoczy stopped her. "Please excuse me, Highness," he said in Farsi, "but wait till we land. You will be all right." He repeated it in Russian, adding to Erikki, "I have some water with me. Would you like me to give it to your wife?"

Erikki nodded. "Yes. Please." He watched while she sipped gratefully. "Thank you."

"Do you want some?"

"No, thank you," he said politely even though he was parched, not wishing any favors for himself. He smiled at her encouragingly. "Azadeh, like manna from heaven, eh? Charlie like an angel!"

"Yes . . . yes. It was the Will of God. I'm fine, fine now, Erikki, praise be to God. Thank Charlie for me . . ."

He hid his concern. The second mob had petrified her. And him, and he had sworn that if he ever got out of this mess alive, never again would he travel without a gun and, preferably, hand grenades. He saw Rakoczy watching him. He nodded and turned back again. "*Matyeryebyets,*" he muttered, automatically checking the instruments.

"That bugger's a lunatic—no need to kill anyone, I told him to fire over their heads." Pettikin dropped his voice slightly, uneasy at talking so openly even though there was no way Rakoczy could hear. "The bastard damn near killed me a couple of times. How do you know him, Erikki? Were you or Azadeh mixed up with the Kurds?"

Erikki stared at him. "Kurds? You mean the *matyeryebyets* back there?"

"Yes, him of course—Ali bin Hassan Karakose. He comes from Mount Ararat. He's a Kurd Freedom Fighter."

"He's not a Kurd but a turd, Soviet and KGB!"

"Christ Almighty! You're sure?" Pettikin was openly shocked.

"Oh, yes. He claims he's Muslim but I bet that's a lie too. 'Rakoczy' he called himself to me, another lie. They're all liars—at least why should they tell us, the enemy, anything?"

"But he swore it was the truth and I gave him my word." Angrily Pettikin told him about the fight and the bargain he had made.

"You're the fool, Charlie, not him—haven't you read Lenin? Stalin? Marx? He's only doing what all KGB and committed Communists do: use anything and everything to forward the 'sacred' Cause—absolute world power for the USSR Communist party—and get us to hang ourselves to save them the trouble. My God, I could use a vodka!"

"A double brandy'd be better."

"Both together would be even better." Erikki studied the ground below. They were cruising easily, the engines sounding good and plenty of fuel. His eyes searched the horizon for Tehran. "Not long now. Has he said where to land yet?"

"No."

"Perhaps we'll get a chance then."

"Yes." Pettikin's apprehension increased. "You mentioned a roadblock. What happened there?"

Erikki's face hardened. "We got stopped. Leftists. Had to make a run for it. We've no papers left, Azadeh and I. Nothing. A fat bastard at the road-block kept everything and there wasn't time to get them back." A tremor went through him. "I've never been so scared, Charlie. Never. I was helpless in that mob and almost shitting with fear because I couldn't protect her. That stinking fat bastard took everything, passport, ID, flying licenses, everything."

"Mac'll get you more, your embassy'll give you passports."

"I'm not worried about me. What about Azadeh?"

"She'll get a Finnish passport too. Like Sharazad'll get a Canadian one—no need to worry."

"She's still in Tehran, isn't she?"

"Sure. Tom should be there too. He was due in from Zagros yesterday with mails from home . . ." Strange, Pettikin thought in passing. I still call England home even with Claire gone, everything gone. "He's just back off leave."

"That's what I'd like to do, go on leave. I'm overdue. Perhaps Mac can send a replacement." Erikki punched Pettikin lightly. "Tomorrow can take care of tomorrow, eh? Hey, Charlie, that was a great piece of flying. When I first saw you, I thought I was dreaming or already dead. You saw my Finnish flag?"

"No, that was Ali—what did you call him? Rekowsky?"

"Rakoczy."

"Rakoczy recognized it. If he hadn't I wouldn't have been any the wiser. Sorry." Pettikin glanced across. "What's he want with you?"

"I don't know but whatever it is, it's for Soviet purposes." Erikki cursed for a moment. "So we owe our lives to him too?"

After a moment Pettikin said, "Yes. Yes, I couldn't have done it alone." He glanced around. Rakoczy was totally alert, Azadeh dozing, shadows over her lovely face. He nodded briefly, then turned back. "Azadeh seems okay."

"No, Charlie, no, she's not," Erikki said, an ache inside him. "Today was terrible for her. She said she'd never been that close to villagers ever . . . I mean surrounded, bottled in. Today they got under her guard. Now she's seen the real face of Iran, the reality of her people—that and the forcing of the chador." Again a shiver went through him. "That was a rape—they raped her soul. Now I think everything will be different for her, for us. I think she'll have to choose: family or me, Iran or exile. They don't want us here. It's time for us to leave, Charlie. All of us."

"No, you're wrong. Perhaps for you and Azadeh it's different but they'll still need oil so they'll still need choppers. We're good for a few more years, good years. With the Guerney contracts and all th—" Pettikin stopped, feeling a tap on his shoulder, and he glanced around. Azadeh was awake now. He could not hear what Rakoczy said so he slipped one earphone off. "What?"

"Don't use the radio, Captain, and be prepared to land on the outskirts where I'll tell you."

"I . . . I'll have to get clearance."

"Don't be a fool! Clearance from whom? Everyone's too busy down there. Tehran Airport's under siege—so is Doshan Tappeh and so's Galeg Morghi. Take my advice and make your landfall the small airport of Rudrama after you've dropped me."

"I have to report in. The military insist."

Rakoczy laughed sardonically. "Military? And what would you report? That you landed illegally near Qazvin, helped murder five or six civilians, and picked up two foreigners fleeing—fleeing from whom? From the People!"

Grimly Pettikin turned back to make the call but Rakoczy leaned forward and shook him roughly. "Wake up! The military doesn't exist anymore. The generals have conceded victory to Khomeini! The military doesn't exist anymore—they've given in!"

They all stared at him blankly. The chopper lurched. Hastily Pettikin corrected. "What're you talking about?"

"Late last night the generals ordered all troops back to their barracks. All services—all men. They've left the field to Khomeini and his revolution. Now there's no army, no police, no gendarmes between Khomeini and total power —the People have conquered!"

"That's not possible," Pettikin said.

"No," Azadeh said, frightened. "My father would have known."

"Ah, Abdollah the Great?" Rakoczy said with a sneer. "He'll know by now —if he's still alive."

"It's not true!"

"It's . . . it's possible, Azadeh," Erikki said, shocked. "That'd explain why we saw no police or troops—why the mob was so hostile!"

"The generals'd never do that," she said shakily, then turned on Rakoczy. "It would be suicide, for them and thousands. Tell the truth, by Allah!"

Rakoczy's face mirrored his glee, delighted to twist words and sow dissension to unsettle them. "Now Iran's in the hands of Khomeini, his mullahs, and his Revolutionary Guards."

"It's a lie."

Pettikin said, "If that's true Bakhtiar's finished. He'll nev—"

"That weak fool never even began!" Rakoczy started laughing. "Ayatollah

Khomeini has frightened the balls off the generals and now he'll cut their throats for good measure!"

"Then the war's over."

"Ah, the war," Rakoczy said darkly. "It is. For some."

"Yes," Erikki said, baiting him. "And if what you say is true, it's all over for you too—all the Tudeh and all Marxists. Khomeini will slaughter you all."

"Oh, no, Captain. The Ayatollah was the sword to destroy the Shah, but the People wielded the sword."

"He and his mullahs and the People will destroy you—he's as anti-Communist as he is anti-American."

"Better you wait and see and not further delude yourselves, eh? Khomeini's a practical man and exults in power, whatever he says now."

Pettikin saw Azadeh whiten and he felt an equal chill. "And the Kurds?" he asked roughly, "What about them?"

Rakoczy leaned forward, his smile strange. "I am a Kurd whatever the Finn told you about Soviet and KGB. Can he prove what he says? Of course not. As to the Kurds, Khomeini will try to stamp us out—if he's allowed to— with all tribal or religious minorities, and foreigners and the bourgeoisie, landowners, moneylenders, Shah supporters, and," he added with a sneer, "and any and all people who will not accept his interpretation of the Koran— and he'll spill rivers of blood in the Name of *his* Allah, *his*, not the real One God—if the bastard's allowed to." He glanced out of the window below, checking his bearings, then added even more sardonically, "This heretic Sword of God has served his purpose and now he's going to be turned into a plowshare—and buried!"

"You mean murdered?" Erikki said.

"Buried"—again the laugh—"at the whim of the People."

Azadeh came to life and tried to claw his face, cursing him. He caught her easily and held her while she struggled. Erikki watched, gray-faced. There was nothing he could do. For the moment.

"Stop it!" Rakoczy said harshly. "You of all people should want this heretic gone—he'll stamp out Abdollah Khan and all the Gorgons and you with them if he wins." He shoved her away. "Behave, or I shall have to hurt you. It's true, you of all people should want him dead." He cocked the machine gun. "Turn around, both of you."

They obeyed, hating the man and the gun. Ahead, the outskirts of Tehran were about ten miles away. They were paralleling the road and railway, the Elburz Mountains to their left, approaching the city from the west. Overhead the sky was overcast, the clouds heavy, and no sun showed through.

"Captain, you see the stream where the railway crosses it? The bridge?"

"Yes, I can see that," Pettikin said, trying to make a plan to overcome him, as Erikki was also planning—wondering if he could whirl and grab him but he was on the wrong side.

"Land half a mile south, behind that outcrop. You see it?"

Not far from this outcrop was a secondary road that headed for Tehran. A little traffic. "Yes. And then?"

"And then you're dismissed. For the moment." Rakoczy laughed and nudged the back of Pettikin's neck with the barrel of the gun. "With my thanks. But don't turn around anymore. Stay facing ahead, both of you, and keep your seat belts locked and know that I'm watching you both very closely. When you land, land firmly and cleanly and when I'm clear, take off. But don't turn around or I may become frightened. Frightened men pull triggers. Understand?"

"Yes." Pettikin studied the landing site. He adjusted his headset. "It look all right to you, Erikki?"

"Yes. Watch the snow dunes." Erikki tried to keep the nervousness out of his voice.

"We should have a plan."

"I think he's . . . he's too clever, Charlie."

"Maybe he'll make a mistake."

"I only need one."

The landing was clean and simple. Snow, whipped up by the idling blades, billowed alongside the windows. "Don't turn around!"

Both men's nerves were jagged. They heard the door open and felt the cold air. Then Azadeh screamed, "Erikkiiii!"

In spite of the order both craned around. Rakoczy was already out, dragging Azadeh after him, kicking and struggling and trying to hang on to the door, but he overpowered her easily. The gun was slung over his shoulder. Instantly Erikki jerked his door open and darted out, slid under the fuselage, and charged. But he was too late. A short burst at his feet stopped him. Ten yards away, clear of the rotors, Rakoczy had the gun leveled at them with one hand, the other firm in the neck of her chador. For a moment she was equally still, then she redoubled her efforts, shouting and screaming, flailing at him, catching him unawares. Erikki charged.

Rakoczy grabbed her with both hands, shoved her violently at Erikki, breaking the charge and bringing Erikki down with her. At the same moment he leaped backward, turned, and raced away, whirled again, the gun ready, his finger tightening on the trigger. But there was no need to pull it, the Finn and the woman were still on their knees, half stunned. Beyond them the pilot was still in his seat. Then he saw Erikki come to his senses, and shove her behind him protectively, readying another charge.

"Stop!" he ordered, "or this time I will kill you all. STOP!" He put a warning burst into the snow. "Get back in the plane—both of you!" Now totally alert, Erikki watched him suspiciously. "Go on—you're free. Go!"

Desperately afraid, Azadeh scrambled into the backseat. Erikki retreated slowly, his body shielding her. Rakoczy kept the gun unwavering. He saw the Finn sit on the backseat, the door still open, his feet propped against skid. At once the engines picked up speed. The chopper eased a foot off the ground, slowly swung around to face him, the back door closing. His heart pounded even more. Now, he thought, do you all die or do we live to fight another day?

The moment seemed to him to last forever. The chopper backed away, foot by foot, still so tempting a target. His finger tightened slightly. But he did not squeeze the further fraction. A few more yards then she twisted, hurried away through the snowfields, and went into the sky.

Good, he thought, tiredness almost overcoming him. It would have been better to have been able to keep the woman as a hostage, but never mind. We can grab old Abdollah Khan's daughter tomorrow, or the day after. She can wait and so can Yokkonen. Meanwhile there's a country to possess, generals and mullahs and ayatollahs to kill . . . and other enemies.

AT TEHRAN AIRPORT: 5:05 P.M. McIver was driving carefully along the road that followed the barbed-wire security fence, heading for the gate that led to the freight area. The road was snow banked, slippery, and unplowed. It was just below freezing, the sky heavy and dull, night not more than an hour away. Again he looked at his watch. Not much time, he thought, still seething over the closure of his office last night by the komiteh. Early this morning he had tried to sneak back into the building, but it was still guarded and all of his entreaties to be allowed to check the telex had proved fruitless.

"Damned people!" Genny had said when he had stomped back into their apartment. "There must be something we can do. What about George Talbot? Could he help?"

"I doubt it, but it's worth a try—if Valik was . . ." McIver stopped. "Tom would have refueled by now and be almost there—wherever there is."

"Let's hope," she said with a silent prayer, "hope for the best. Did you see any shops open?"

"None, Gen. It's canned soup for lunch and a bottle of beer."

"Sorry, we're out of beer."

He had tried to call Kowiss and the other bases on his HF but could get no answer from them. Neither could he tune in to the BBC or AFN. He had listened briefly to the inevitable anti-American tirade from Radio Free Iran in Tbilisi and had turned it off in disgust. The phone was dead. He had tried to read, but he could not, his mind beset with worries about Lochart, Pettikin, Starke, and all the others, hating being cut off from his office and telex and, for the moment, out of control. Never happened before, never. Damn the Shah for leaving and letting everything fall apart. Used to be wonderful. Any problem and out to the airport, get on a shuttle to Isfahan, Tabriz, Abadan, Hormuz, Al Shargaz, or wherever, then chopper the rest of the way, wherever you felt like it. Sometimes Genny coming along for the ride—picnic lunches and ice-cold beer.

"Sod everything!"

Just after lunch the HF had crackled into life. It was Freddy Ayre at Kowiss relaying a message that the 125 jet would be at Tehran Airport around 5:00 P.M. today, coming from Al Shargaz, a tiny independent sheikdom eight hundred miles south of Tehran on the other side of the Gulf where S-G had an office.

"Did he say he had clearance, Freddy?" McIver had asked excitedly.

"I don't know. All our HQ in Al Shargaz said: 'ETA Tehran 1700, tell McIver—can't raise him,' repeated several times."

"How're things with you?"

"Five by five," Ayre had said. "Starke's still at Bandar Delam and we've had no contact with them other than a snafu half an hour ago."

"Rudi sent that?" McIver had tried to keep his voice level.

"Yes."

"Keep in touch with them and with us. What happened to your radio op this morning? I tried calling for a couple of hours but no joy."

There had been a long pause. "He's been detained."

"What the hell for?"

"I don't know, Mac—Captain McIver. As soon as I know I'll report it. Also, as soon as I can I'll get Marc Dubois back to Bandar Delam, but, well, it's a bit off here. We've all been confined to base, there's . . . there's a charming and friendly armed guard here in the tower, all flights are grounded except for CASEVACs and even then we've been ordered to take guards along—and no flights're authorized out of our area."

"What's it all about?"

"I don't know. Our revered base commander, Colonel Peshadi, assured me it was temporary, just for today, perhaps tomorrow. By the way, at 1516 hours we had a brief call from Captain Scragger in Charlie Echo Zulu Zulu en route with a special charter for Bandar Delam."

"What the hell's he going there for?"

"I don't know, sir. Old Scr— Captain Scragger said it's been requested by de Plessey at Siri. I, er, I don't think I've much more time. Our friendly guard's getting nervous but if you can get the 125 here Peshadi said he'd clear her to land. I'll try to send Manuela off but don't expect much, she's as nervous as a rabbit in a kennel full of beagles without real news of Starke."

"I can imagine. Tell her I'm sending Gen. I'll sign off now, God knows how long it'll take me to get to the airport." He had turned his attention to Genny. "Gen, pack a b—"

"What do you want to take with you, Duncan?" she had asked sweetly.

"I'm not going, you are!"

"Don't be silly, dear. If you're going to meet the 125 you'd better hurry, but do be careful and don't forget the photos! Oh, by the way, I forgot to tell you that while you were trying to get into your office, Sharazad sent one of her servants over asking us to dinner."

"Gen, you are leaving with the 125 and that's that!"

The argument had lasted no time at all. He had left and had used back roads, most of the main intersections clogged with milling crowds. Every time he was stopped he would hold up the Khomeini photograph with LONG LIVE THE AYATOLLAH in Farsi on the bottom and he would be waved through. He saw no troops, gendarmes, or police so he did not need the photo of the Shah with LONG LIVE GLORIOUS IRAN on the bottom. It still took two and a half hours for a journey that would normally take an hour, his anxiety about being late growing minute by minute.

But the 125 wasn't on either of the parallel runways, or the freight area apron, or near the terminal building across the field. Again he glanced at his watch: 5:17 P.M. Another hour of light. She's cutting it fine, he told himself, if she arrives at all. God knows, they may have already turned her back.

Near the terminal building several civilian jets were still grounded. One of them, a Royal Iranian Air 747, was a twisted wreck, gutted by fire. The others seemed all right—he was too far away to see all their markings but among them would be the still-grounded Alitalia flight. Paula Giancani was still staying with them, Nogger Lane very much in attendance. She's a nice girl that one, he thought absently.

Ahead now was the gate of the freight area and depot. The depot had been closed since last Wednesday—automatically on Thursday and Friday (the Muslim Holy Day) being the Iranian weekend—and there had been no way he or any of his staff could have got there Saturday or Sunday. The gate was open and unguarded. He swung through it into the forecourt. In front of him was the customs freight shed and barriers, signs everywhere in English and Farsi: NO ADMITTANCE, INBOUND, OUTBOUND, KEEP OUT, and company signs of the various international carriers and helicopter companies that had permanent offices here. Normally it was almost impossible to drive into the forecourt. There was work around the clock for half a thousand men, handling the enormous quantity of goods, military and civilian, that poured into Iran in exchange for part of the $90 million daily oil revenue. But now the area was deserted. Hundreds of crates and cartons of all sizes were scattered in the snow—many broken open and looted, most sodden. A few abandoned cars and trucks, some derelict, and one truck burned out. Bullet holes in the sheds.

The customs gate that barred the way to the apron was closed, held only by a bolt. The sign, in English and Farsi, read: NO ENTRY WITHOUT CUSTOMS APPROVAL. He waited, then honked and waited again. No one answered him so he got out, opened the gate wide, and got back into his car. A few yards the other side he stopped, rebolted the gate, then drove down the tarmac to the S-G stores and office shed and allied hangars and repair shop with space for four 212s and five 206s now containing three 206s, and one 212.

To his relief the main doors were still closed and locked. He had been afraid the stores and hangar might have been broken into and looted or wrecked. This was their main depot for repairs and spares in Iran. Over $2 million worth of spares and specialized tools were on the inventory, along with their own refueling pumps and underground tanks containing a highly secret cache of 50,000 gallons of helicopter fuel that McIver had "lost" when the troubles began in earnest.

He scanned the sky. The wind told him the 125 would land from the west on runway 29 left but there was no sign of it. He unlocked the door, closed it after him, and hurried through the chilly foyer to the main office to the telex. It was switched off. "Bloody idiots," he muttered out loud. Standing orders were for it to be on at all times. When he turned it on, nothing happened. He tried the lights but they didn't work either. "Bloody country." Irritably he went over to the HF and UHF receiver-transmitters and switched them on. Both were battery-operated for emergencies. Their hum comforted him.

"Echo Tango Lima Lima," he said crisply into the mike, giving the 125's registration letters: ETLL. "This is McIver, do you read?"

"Echo Tango Lima Lima—we certainly do, old boy," the laconic answer came back at once. "It's rather lonely up here—we've been calling for half an hour. Where are you?"

"At the freight office. Sorry, Johnny," he said, recognizing the voice of their senior fixed-wing captain. "Had a hell of a time getting here—I've just arrived. Where are you?"

"Seventeen miles due south—in the soup—passing through nine thousand on standard approach, expecting final on runway 29 left. What's going on, Mac? We can't raise Tehran Tower—in fact we haven't had a single callback ever since we came into Iran airspace."

"Good God! Not even from Kish radar?"

"Not even from them, old boy. What's amiss?"

"I don't know. The tower was operating yesterday—up to midnight last night. The military gave us a clearance for a flight south." McIver was astonished, knowing Kish radar was punctilious about all traffic inbound or outbound, particularly trans-Gulf. "The whole airfield's deserted which is pretty hairy. Coming here there were crowds all over town, a few roadblocks, but nothing out of the ordinary, no riots or anything."

"Any problem for a landing?"

"I doubt if any landing aids are functional but cloud cover is about four thousand, visibility ten miles. Runway looks all right."

"What do you think?"

McIver weighed the pros and cons of a landing—without tower assistance or approval. "You've enough fuel for the return trip?"

"Oh, yes. You've a no-fuel capability?"

"Unless an emergency—for the moment."

"I'm through the cloud cover at forty-seven hundred and have you in sight."

"Okay, Echo Tango Lima Lima. Wind's from the east at about ten knots. Normally you'd land on 29 left. The military base seems closed down and deserted so there should be no other traffic—all civilian flights in- and outbound have been canceled. Suggest you make a pass and if it looks okay to you, come straight in—don't hang around in the sky, there're too many trigger-happy jokers about. Once you've landed, turn around for a quick takeoff just in case. I'll drive out to meet you."

"Echo Tango Lima Lima."

McIver took out a handkerchief and wiped his hands and forehead. But when he got up, his heart seemed to turn in his chest.

Standing in the open doorway was a customs officer, his hand casually on his holstered gun. His uniform was soiled and crumpled, his roundish face grizzled with three or four days' growth of beard.

"Oh," McIver said, fighting to appear calm. "Salaam, Agha." He did not recognize him as one of their regulars.

The man shifted his gun hand ominously, his eyes going from McIver to the radio sets and back to McIver.

Haltingly, for McIver spoke very little Farsi, he said, *"Inglissi me danid, Agha? Be bahk shid man zaban-e shoma ra khoob nami danam."* Do you speak English, sir? Please excuse me but I don't speak your language.

The customs officer grunted. "What you do here?" he said in halting English, his teeth tobacco-stained.

"I'm . . . I'm Captain McIver, head of S-G Helicopters," he replied, carefully and slowly. "I'm just . . . just checking my telex and here to meet an incoming plane."

"Plane—what plane? Wh—"

At that moment the 125 came directly over the airport at one thousand feet. The Customs man hurried out of the office onto the tarmac, closely followed by McIver. They saw the lovely clean lines of the twin-engined jet against the murky overcast and watched a moment as she hurtled away to go into a steep bank to join the landing pattern.

"What plane? Eh?"

"It's our regular flight—regular flight from Al Shargaz."

The name sent the man into a paroxysm of invective.

"Be bahk shid nana dhan konan." Sorry, I don't understand.

"No land . . . no land, understand?" The man angrily pointed from the plane to the office with the HF. "Tell plane!"

McIver nodded calmly, not feeling calm, and beckoned him back into the office. He counted out 10,000 rials, about $110, and offered it. "Please accept the landing fee—landing money."

The man spurned it with more unintelligible Farsi. McIver put the money on the table, then walked past the man into the storeroom. He unlocked a door. In the small room, put there for just this purpose, were odds and ends of spares, and three full five-gallon cans of gasoline. He picked up one can and put it outside the door, remembering what General Valik had said: a pishkesh was not a bribe but a gift and a good Iranian custom. After a second, McIver decided to leave the door but left it open—three cans would more than guarantee no problem. *"Be bahk shid, Agha."* Please excuse me, Excellency. Then he added in English, "I must meet my masters."

He went out of the building and got into his car and did not look back. "Bloody bastard, damn near gave me a heart attack!" he muttered, then put the man out of his mind, drove on to the taxi runway, and headed for the intercept point. The snow was only a few inches deep and not too bad. His were the only tracks, the main runways equally virgin. The wind had picked up, increasing the chill factor. He did not notice it, concentrating on the airplane.

The 125 came around in a tight turn, gear and flaps down, sideslipping deftly to lose height and cut down the approach distance. John Hogg flared and touched down, letting her roll until it was safe and even then using brakes with great caution. He turned onto the taxi runway and increased power to meet McIver. Near the first access path back to the runway, he stopped.

By the time McIver came alongside, the door was open, the steps down, John Hogg waiting at the foot, bundled in a parka, stamping his feet against the cold.

"Hi, Mac!" he called out—a neat, spare man with a lean face and mustache. "Great to see you. Come on in—it'll be warmer for you."

"Good idea." McIver hastily switched off and followed him up the steps. Inside it was snug, lights on, coffee ready, London newspapers in the rack. McIver knew there would be wine and beer in the refrigerator, a sit-down toilet with soft paper in the back—civilization again. He shook hands warmly with Hogg and waved at the copilot. "I'm so glad to see you, Johnny. His mouth dropped open. Seated in one of the swivel chairs in the eight-place airplane, beaming at him, was Andy Gavallan.

"Hello, Mac!"

"My God! My God, Chinaboy, it's good to see you," McIver said, pummeling his hand. "What the hell are you doing—why didn't you tell me you were coming—what's the id—"

"Slow down, laddie. Coffee?"

"My God, yes." McIver sat opposite him. "How's Maureen—and little Electra?"

"Great—wonderful! Her second birthday coming and already she's a holy terror! Thought we'd better have a chat so I got on the bird and here I am."

"Can't tell you how glad I am. You're looking great," McIver said.

And he was. "Thank you, laddie, you're not so bad yoursel'. How are you, really, Mac?" Gavallan asked more pointedly.

"Excellent." Hogg put down the coffee in front of McIver. With a small tot of whisky and another for Gavallan. "Ah, thanks, Johnny," McIver said, brightening. "Health!" He touched glasses with Gavallan and swallowed the spirit gratefully. "I'm cold as charity. Just had a run-in with a bloody Customs man! Why're you here? Any problem, Andy? Oh, but what about the 125? Both the revs and loyalists are all very twitchy—either of them could arrive in force and impound her."

"Johnny Hogg's keeping an eye out for them. We'll talk about my problems in a minute but I decided that I'd better come and see for myself. We've too much at risk now, here and outside, with all our new, upcoming contracts and aircraft. The X63's a total smash, Mac, everything and better!"

"Great, wonderful. When do we get her?"

"Next year—more about her later. Iran's my top priority now. We have to have some contingency plans, how to keep in touch and so on. Yesterday I spent hours in Al Shargaz trying to get an Iranian clearance for Tehran but no joy on that. Even their embassy was closed; I went to their Al Mullah building myself but it was closed tighter than a gnat's arse. I got our rep to call the ambassador's home but he was out to lunch—all day. Eventually I went to Al Shargaz Air Traffic Control and chatted them up. They suggested we wait but I talked them into clearing us out and having a stab and here we are. First what's the state of our ops?"

McIver related what he knew.

Much of Gavallan's good humor vanished. "So Charlie's vanished, Tom Lochart's risking his neck and our whole Iranian venture—stupidly or bravely depending on your point of view—Duke Starke's up the creek in Bandar Delam with Rudi, Kowiss is in a state of siege, and we've been tossed out of our offices."

"Yes." McIver added gruffly. "I authorized Tom's flight."

"I'd've done the same, probably, if I'd been on the spot, though it doesn't excuse the danger to him, to us, or poor bloody Valik and his family. But I agree, SAVAK's too smelly for anyone's taste." Gavallan was distinctly rattled though he showed none of it on his face. "Ian was right again."

"Ian? Dunross? You saw him? How is the old bugger?"

"He called from Shanghai." Gavallan told him what he had said. "What's the latest on the political situation here?"

"You should know more than we do—we only get real news through the BBC or VOA. There're still no newspapers and only rumors," McIver said, but he was remembering the good times he had had with Dunross in Hong Kong. He had taught him to fly a small chopper the year before joining Gavallan in Aberdeen, and though they had not socialized very much, McIver had enjoyed his company greatly. "Bakhtiar's still top man with the forces behind him, but Bazargan and Khomeini're gnawing at his heels . . . Oh, damn, I forgot to tell you, Boss Kyabi's been murdered."

"Christ Almighty, that's terrible! But why?"

"We don't know the why or how or by whom. Freddy Ayre told us obliqu—"

"Sorry to interrupt, sir," came over the loudspeaker, a thread of urgency under Hogg's placid voice. "There're three cars stuffed with men and guns heading our way, coming from the terminal area."

Both men peered out of the small round windows. They could see the cars now. Gavallan picked up his binoculars and trained them. "Five or six men in each car. There's a mullah in the front of the first car. Khomeini's people!" He slung the binoculars around his neck and was out of his seat quickly. "Johnny!"

Hogg was already at the door. "Yes, sir?"

"Plan B!" At once Hogg gave the thumbs-up to his copilot who immediately started to open the throttles as Gavallan struggled into a parka and picked up a light travel bag on the run. "Come on, Mac!" He led the way down the steps two at a time, McIver just behind him. The moment they were clear, the steps pulled back, the door slammed closed, the engines picked up, and the 125 taxied away, gathering speed. "Put your back to the cars, Mac—don't watch them, watch her leave!"

It had all happened so rapidly McIver hardly had time to zip his parka. One of the cars peeled off to intercept but by now the 125 was careening down the runway. In seconds it took off and was away. Now they faced the oncoming cars.

"Now what, Andy?"

"That depends on the welcoming committee."

"What the hell was Plan B?"

Gavallan laughed. "Better than Plan C, laddie. That was a shit or bust. Plan B: I get out, Johnny takes off at once, and tells no one he had to leave in a hurry, tomorrow he comes back to pick me up at the same time; if there's no contact, visually or by radio, then Johnny skips a day and comes an hour earlier—and so on for four days. Then he sits on his tail in Al Shargaz and waits for further instructions."

"Plan A?"

"That's if we could have safely stayed overnight—them on guard in the plane, me with you."

The cars skidded to a stop, the mullah and Green Bands surrounding them, guns trained on them, everyone shouting. Suddenly Gavallan bellowed, "Allah-u Akbar," and everyone stopped, startled. With a flourish he lifted his hat to the mullah who was also armed, took out an official-looking document —written in Farsi—that was heavily sealed with red wax at the bottom. He handed it to him. "It's permission to land in Tehran from the 'new' ambassador in London," he told McIver airily as men crowded around the mullah peering at the paper. "I stopped off in London to collect it. It says I'm a VIP —on official business and I can arrive and leave without harm."

"How the devil did you manage that?" McIver asked, admiringly.

"Influence, laddie. Influence and a large *heung yau*." He carefully added the Cantonese equivalent of pishkesh.

"You will come with us," a bearded youth near the mullah said, his accent American. "You are under arrest!"

"For what, my dear sir?"

"Illegal landings without permiss—"

Gavallan stabbed at the paper. "Here is an official permission from your very own ambassador in London! Up the revolution! Long live Ayatollah Khomeini!"

The youth hesitated, then translated for the mullah. There was an angry exchange and mutterings among them. "You will together come with us!"

"We will follow in our car! Come on, Mac," Gavallan said firmly and got into the passenger seat. McIver turned on the ignition. For a moment the men were nonplussed, then the man who could speak English and another got into the back. Both carried an AK47.

"Go to terminal! You under arrest."

In the terminal, near the Immigration barrier, were more hostile men and a very nervous Immigration official. At once McIver showed his airport pass, work permit, explained who he and Gavallan were and how they worked under license for IranOil and tried to talk them past but he was imperiously waved into silence. Meticulously and ponderously the official examined the paper and Gavallan's passport—all the while the youths crowding them, the smell of bodies heavy. Then he opened Gavallan's bag and searched it roughly but it contained just shaving gear, a spare shirt, underclothes, and night clothes. And a fifth of whisky. At once the bottle was confiscated by one of the young men, opened, and poured on the floor.

"Dew neh loh moh," Gavallan said sweetly in Cantonese, and McIver nearly choked. "Up the revolution."

The mullah questioned the official, and they could see the sweat and the fear in him. At length the youth who could speak English said, "The authorities will keep paper and passport and you explain more later."

"I will keep my passport," Gavallan said easily.

"The authorities keep. Enemies will suffer. Those who break the laws—illegal landings and comings here—will suffer Islamic punishments. His Excellency wants to know who on the airplane with you?"

"Just my crew of two. They're on the manifest attached to the Permission to Land. Now, my passport, please, and that document."

"The authorities keep. Where you stay?"

McIver gave his address.

The man translated. Again there was a heated discussion. "I am to tell you: now your airplanes may not fly or landings without permissions first. All Iran airplanes—all airplanes now in Iran belong to the state an—"

"Airplanes belong to their legal owners. Legal owners," McIver said.

"Yes," the man said with a sneer, "our Islamic state is owners. You not like laws, leave. Leave Iran. We not ask you here."

"Ah, but you're wrong. We, in S-G Helicopters, were invited here. We work for your government and have served IranOil for years."

The man spat on the floor. "IranOil Shah company. Islamic state owns oil not foreigners. You soon arrested with all others for great crime: stealing Iran oil!"

"Rubbish! We've stolen nothing!" McIver said. "We've helped Iran into the twentieth century! We've b—"

"Leave Iran if you want," the spokesman said again, paying no attention to him. "Now all orders come from Imam Khomeini, Allah protect him! He says no landings or takeoffs without permission. Each time, one Khomeini guard goes with each airplane. Understand?"

"We understand what you say," Gavallan replied politely. "May I ask that we have this in writing, as the Bakhtiar government may not agree."

The man translated this and there was a roar of laughter. "Bakhtiar is gone," the man said through his own laughter. "That dog of a Shah man is in hiding. Hiding, you understand? The Imam is the government! Him alone."

"Yes, of course," Gavallan said, not believing him. "We can go, then?"

"Go. Tomorrow report the authorities."

"Where—and what authorities?"

"Tehran authorities." The man translated for the others and again everyone laughed. The mullah pocketed the passport and paper and strode off importantly. Guards went with him, taking along the sweating Immigration officer. Most of the others wandered off, seemingly aimlessly. A few stayed watching them, lounging against the wall, smoking—their U.S. Army rifles slung carelessly. It was very cold in the terminal. And very empty.

"He's quite right you know," a voice said. Gavallan and McIver looked around. It was George Talbot of the British embassy, a short dry man of fifty-five, wearing a heavy raincoat and a Russian-style fur hat. He stood in the doorway of a customs office. Beside him was a tall, broad-shouldered man of sixty with hard, pale blue eyes, his mustache gray as his hair and clipped, and dressed casually, scarf, soft hat, and an old raincoat. Both were smoking.

"Oh, hello, George, nice to see you." Gavallan went over to him, offering his hand. He had known him over the years, both in Iran and Malaya—

Talbot's previous posting—where S-G also had an extensive oil support operation. "How long have you been here?"

"Just a few minutes." Talbot stubbed out his cigarette, coughed absently. "Hello, Duncan! Well, this is a fine kettle of fish, isn't it?"

"Yes. Yes, it is." Gavallan glanced at the other man. "Ah, may I introduce Mr. Armstrong?"

Gavallan shook hands. "Hello," he said, wondering where he'd seen him before and who he was—the hardness to the eyes and strong face. Fifty pounds to a bent button he's CIA if he's American, he thought. "You're embassy too?" he asked casually to find out.

The man smiled and shook his head. "No, sir."

Gavallan had turned his ears and did not detect a pure English or American accent. Might be either, or Canadian, he thought, difficult to tell on two words.

"You're here on official business, George?" McIver asked.

"Yes and no." Talbot strolled over to the door that led back to the airport apron where McIver's car was parked, guiding them away from prying ears. "Actually the moment we heard your incoming jet on the air, we, er, we hurried out here hoping you could take out some er, some dispatches for Her Majesty's Government. The ambassador would have been most grateful, but, well, we were here just in time to see your plane take off. Pity!"

"I'd be glad to help in any way," Gavallan said as quietly. "Perhaps tomorrow?" He saw the sudden glance between the two men and wondered even more what was amiss.

"Is that possible, Mr. Gavallan?" Armstrong asked.

"It's possible." Gavallan pegged him to be English, though not all English.

Talbot smiled, coughed without noticing it. "You'll leave with or without Iranian permission, an official permit—or a passport?"

"I, er, do have a copy of the paper. And another passport—I applied for a spare, officially, against this eventuality."

Talbot sighed. "Irregular but wise. Yes. Oh, by the way, I would very much like a copy of your Official Permission to Land."

"Perhaps that's not such a good idea—officially. You never know what larceny some people are up to these days."

Talbot laughed. Then he said, "If you, er, do leave tomorrow we would appreciate it if you'd kindly take Mr. Armstrong—I presume Al Shargaz will be your first port of call."

Gavallan hesitated. "This is a formal request?"

Talbot smiled. "Formally informal."

"With or without Iranian permission, permit, or passport?"

Talbot chuckled. "You're perfectly correct to ask. I guarantee that Mr. Armstrong's papers will be perfectly in order." He added pointedly to finish the conversation, "As you so correctly pointed out there's no accounting for the larceny some people will get up to these days."

Gavallan nodded. "Very well, Mr. Armstrong. I'll be with Captain McIver. It'll be up to you to stay in touch. The earliest ETD'd be about 5:00 P.M. but I won't wait around for you. All right?"

"Thank you, sir."

Again Gavallan had been listening carefully but still could not decide. "George, when we started talking, you said of that arrogant little bastard, 'He's quite right, you know.' Right about what? That now I've to find or report to some nebulous authorities in Tehran?"

"No. That Bakhtiar's resigned and in hiding."

Both men gaped at him. "God Almighty, are you sure?"

"Bakhtiar formally resigned a couple of hours ago and has, somewhat wisely, vanished." Talbot's voice was soft and calm, cigarette smoke punctuating his words. "Actually the situation's suddenly rather dicey, hence our, er, anxiety to, er, well, never mind that. Last night the chief of staff, General Ghara-Baghi, supported by the generals, ordered all troops back into their barracks, declaring the armed forces were now 'neutral,' thus leaving their legal prime minister defenseless and the state to Khomeini."

" 'Neutral?' " Gavallan echoed with disbelief. "That's not possible—not possible—they'd be committing suicide."

"I agree. But it is true."

"Christ!"

"Of course, only some of the units will obey, others will fight," Talbot said. "Certainly the police and SAVAK aren't affected; they won't give up though now their battle will be lost eventually. Insha'Allah, old boy. Meanwhile blood will fill the jolly gutters, rest assured."

McIver broke the silence. "But . . . if Bakhtiar . . . doesn't that mean it's over? It's over," he said with growing excitement. "The civil war's over and thank God for that. The generals have stopped the real bloodbath—the total bloodbath. Now we can all get back to normal. The trouble's over."

"Oh, no, my dear chap," Talbot said even more calmly. "The trouble's just begun."

AT RIG BELLISSIMA: 6:35 P.M. The sunset was glorious, red-tinged clouds low on the horizon, clean clear sky, the evening star brilliant, a three-quarter moon. But it was very cold here at twelve thousand five hundred feet, and already dark in the east and Jean-Luc had difficulty in picking out the incoming 212.

"Here she comes, Gianni," Jean-Luc shouted at the driller.

This would complete Scot Gavallan's third round-trip. Everyone—riggers cooks, laborers, three cats and four dogs and a canary belonging to Gianni Salubrio—had already been safely transported to Rig Rosa, with the exception of Mario Guineppa who had insisted on waiting till last, in spite of Jean-Luc's pleadings, and Gianni, Pietro, and two others who were still shutting down the rig.

Jean-Luc kept a wary eye on the overhang that worked from time to time, sending shivers down his spine. When the chopper had come back the first time, everyone had held their breath at the noise even though Pietro had assured them all that was just an old wives' tale—only dynamite would start an avalanche, or an Act of God. And then as if to prove him wrong the overhang shifted again, only a little but enough to nauseate those still left on the rig.

Pietro pulled the last switch and the turbines of the diesel generators began to slow. He wiped his face tiredly and left an oil smear. His back ached and his hands hurt in the cold but the well was sealed and as safe as he could make it. Out over the abyss he saw the chopper beginning her careful approach. "Let's leave," he said to the others in Italian. "There's nothing more that we can do here—nothing more to do except blow that shit roll above to hell!"

The others irritably crossed themselves and trudged off toward the helipad and left him. He looked up at the crest. "You look as though you're alive," he muttered, "a shit-roll monster waiting to get me and my beautiful wells. But you won't, you motherless whore!"

He went to the little dynamite storeroom and picked up the two exploders that he had made—six sticks of dynamite in each, wrapped around a thirty-second fuse. Carefully he put them in a small carrying bag, with a lighter and matches as a backup. "Mother of God," he prayed simply, "make these fornicators work."

"Pietro! Hey, Pietro!"

"I'm coming, I'm coming, there's plenty of time!" Outside he saw the white, pinched face of Gianni. "What's up?"

"It's Guineppa—better take a look!"

Mario Guineppa lay on his back, his breath rattling in his throat, eyelids flickering. Jean-Luc was beside the bed, his hand on the man's pulse. "It's rapid . . . then I can't feel it at all," he said uneasily.

"Mario had a serious medical four weeks ago, his annual—cardiogram, everything. Very serious. He was perfect!" Pietro spat on the floor. "Doctors!"

"He was a fool to insist on waiting," Gianni said.

"He's the boss, he does what he likes. Let's put him on the stretcher and get going." Pietro was grave. "There's nothing we can do for him here. The hell with the dynamite, we'll do it later or tomorrow."

Carefully they lifted him, wrapped him warmly, and carried him out of the trailer, through the snow, toward the waiting helicopter. Just as they reached the helipad, the mountain groaned. They looked up. Snow and ice began tumbling, gathering weight. In seconds the avalance was in full flood. There was no time to run, nothing to do but wait. The roar increased. Snow poured down the mountain to carry the far trailer hut and one of the vast steel mud tanks into the abyss. Then it ceased.

"Mamma mia," Gianni gasped, crossing himself. "I thought we were gone that time."

Jean-Luc, too, had crossed himself. Now the overhang was even more ominous, thousands of tons poised over the site, part of the rock face exposed. Dribbles of snow fell continuously.

"Jean-Luc!" It was Guineppa. His eyes were open. "Don't . . . don't wait . . . dynamite now . . . must . . . must."

Pietro said, "He's right, it's now or never."

"Please . . . I'm fine . . . Mamma mia, do it now! I'm fine."

They hurried for the chopper. The stretcher went across the forward bank of seats and was quickly lashed into place. The others put on their seat belts. Jean-Luc got into the cockpit left seat and put on his headset. "Okay, Scot?"

"Terrific, old chap," Scot Gavallan said. "How's Guineppa?"

"Not good." Jean-Luc checked the instruments. Everything was in the Green and plenty of fuel. "*Merde!* The overhang's going any second; let's watch the up and down drafts, they're liable to be rough. *Allons-y!*"

"Here—I rigged it for Pietro while I was waiting at Rosa." Scot gave Jean-Luc the spare headset that was now linked with theirs.

"I'll give it to him when we're airborne. I don't feel safe here! Take off!"

At once Scot opened the throttles and eased the 212 off the ground, backed off a little, turned, and was over the abyss. As he started to climb, Jean-Luc crawled back into the cabin. "Here, put these on, Pietro, now you're connected with us up front."

"Good, very good." Pietro had taken the seat nearest the door.

"When we begin, for the sake of God, my health, and your mother, don't fall out."

Pietro laughed nervously. Jean-Luc checked Guineppa who seemed more comfortable now, went forward again, and put on his headset. "You hear me, Pietro?"

"*Sì. Sì, amico.*"

The chopper labored in a circling climb. Now they were on a level with the crest. From this angle the overhang did not seem so dangerous. They were beginning to bounce a little. "Go higher, another hundred feet, *amico*," came through the headsets, "and more north."

"Roger, Pietro. You're navigator now," Scot said.

The two pilots concentrated. Pietro showed them the spot on the north face where the dynamite would undercut the overhang and create an avalanche away from the rig. "It might work," Scot muttered.

They circled once to make sure. "*Amico*, when we're over that spot at a hundred feet, hover; I'll light the fuse and throw her out. *Buono?*" They could hear a tremble in Pietro's voice.

"Don't forget to open the door, old chap," Scot said dryly. There was a stream of Italian expletives in reply. Scot smiled, then a downdraft took them fifty feet before he caught it. In a minute they were to altitude and in position.

"Good, *amico*, keep her there."

Jean-Luc turned around to watch. Behind in the cabin the other men stared at Pietro, fascinated. He took out the first charge and caressed the fuse straight, humming *Aida*.

"Mother of God, Pietro," Gianni said. "Are you sure you know what you're doing?"

Pietro clenched his left fist, put his right with the fused dynamite on his left bicep, and gestured with significance. "Get ready, up front," he said into the boom mike, and unlocked his seat belt. He checked the position below, then nodded. "Good, keep her steady. Gianni, ready on the door. Open the fornicator a crack and I'll do the rest."

The airplane was pitching with the gyrating air currents, as Gianni unlocked his belt and went to the door. "Hurry up," he said, feeling very unsafe, then added to the nearest man, "hold on to my belt!"

"Open the door, Gianni!" Gianni fought it open a foot and held it there, the sick man on the stretcher forgotten. A roar of air filled the cabin. The airplane swirled, the added suction from the open door making it more difficult for Scot to control her. Pietro held up the fuse and thumbed the lighter. It failed. Again and again, each time more anxious than the last.

"Mother of God, come on!" Sweat was pouring off Pietro's face when the lighter finally caught. The fuse spluttered into life. Holding on with one hand he leaned toward the door, wind eddies tugging at him. The airplane lurched and both men wished they had had the foresight to bring a safety harness. Carefully Pietro tossed the exploder through the opening. At once Gianni slammed the door closed and locked it. Then he began to swear.

"Bombs away! Let's go!" Pietro ordered, his teeth chattering from the cold, and buckled himself in again. At once the chopper peeled off and he was so relieved that it was done, he started to laugh. Hysterically the others joined him and all happily turned to watch below as he began to countdown: ". . . six . . . five . . . four . . . three . . . two . . . one!" Nothing happened. As quickly as their laughter had arrived, it vanished. "Did you see it fall, Jean-Luc?"

"No. No, we saw nothing," the Frenchman replied gloomily, not wanting to repeat the maneuver. "Perhaps it hit a rock and the fuse got knocked away." But inside he was saying to himself, Stupid Italian anus eater, can't even fix a few sticks of dynamite to a fornicating fuse. "We will do it again, yes?"

"Why not?" Pietro said confidently. "The detonator was perfect. That it did not fire was an Act of the Devil. Yes, without a doubt—it happens many times in snow. Many times. Snow is a whore and you can nev—"

"Don't blame the snow, Pietro, and it was an Act of God, not of the Devil," Gianni said superstitiously, crossing himself. "By my mother, enough of the Devil while we're aloft."

Pietro took out the second charge and examined it carefully. The wire holding the sticks tight was firm and the fuse firm. "There, you see, perfect, just like the other." He tossed it from one hand to the other then banged it hard on his armrest to see if the fuse would dislodge.

"Mamma mia," one of the men said, his stomach turning over. "Are you mad?"

"This's not like nitro, *amico*," Pietro told him and banged it even harder. "There, you see it's tight."

"It's not as tight as my anus," Gianni said angrily in Italian. "Stop it for the love of the Mother of God!"

Pietro shrugged and looked out of the window. The crest was approaching now. He could see the exact spot. "Get ready, Gianni." Then into the boom mike, "Just a little more, Signor Pilot, more to the east. Hold her there . . . steady her . . . can't you keep her steadier? Get ready, Gianni." He held up the fuse, the lighter near to the end. "Open the fornicating door!"

Irritably, Gianni unlocked his seat belt and obeyed, the airplane twisted and he cried out, lost his footing, his weight went against the door, opening it wider, and he pitched out. But the man was holding his belt and he held Gianni there on the brink, half in, half out of the doorway, the wind suction tearing at them. The instant Gianni had opened the door, Pietro had thumbed the lighter and the fuse had caught but in the momentary panic over Gianni, Pietro was distracted. Instinctively he, too, had grabbed for Gianni and the dynamite was knocked out of his hand. They all watched appalled as he scrambled on the floor, reaching under the seats for it as it rolled this way and that, the fuse burning merrily—his headset torn off. Almost fainting with fear, Gianni got one hand firmly on the doorjamb and began to drag himself back, petrified that his belt would give way and cursing himself that he had worn this thin one that his wife had given him for Christmas . . .

Pietro's fingers touched the dynamite. The fuse spluttered against his flesh, burning him, but he did not feel the pain. He got a firm grip then, still on the floor, squirmed around, hung on to a chair support and threw the dynamite and what was left of the fuse past Gianni overboard, then reached forward with his free hand and grabbed one of his friend's legs, helping to drag him back. The other man slammed the door closed and the two of them, Pietro and Gianni, collapsed on the floor.

"Take her away, Scot," Jean-Luc said weakly.

The chopper banked and left the north face two hundred feet below. For a moment the crest was pure and stark and motionless. There was a vast explosion that no one in the chopper felt or heard. Snow spiraled upward and began to settle. Then with a mighty roar, the whole of the north face tumbled away, the avalanche fell into the valley, searing the mountainside with a swath a quarter of a mile wide until it had ceased.

The chopper came around. "My God, look!" Scot said, pointing ahead. The overhang had vanished. Above the Bellissima rig was only a gentle slope, the site untouched except where the trailer and the single mud tank had already been carried away by the first avalanche.

"Pietro!" Jean-Luc called out excitedly. "You've . . ." He stopped. Pietro and Gianni were still on the floor collecting themselves, Pietro's headset vanished. "Scot, they won't be able to see from their windows—go closer and turn so they can see!"

Excitedly, Jean-Luc climbed back into the cabin and began to pummel Pietro, congratulating him. Blankly everyone stared at him and when they understood what he was shouting over the screech of the engines, they forgot their fears and peered out of the windows. And when they saw how perfectly the explosion had cleaned away the danger, they let out a cheer. Gianni embraced Pietro emotionally, swearing eternal friendship, blessing him for saving him, for saving their lives and saving their jobs.

"*Niente, caro,*" Pietro said expansively. "Am I not a man of Aosta?"

Jean-Luc stood over the stretcher and gently shook Mario Guineppa. "Mario! Pietro did it—he did it perfectly. Bellissima's safe . . ."

Guineppa did not answer. He was already dead.

TUESDAY
February 13

ON THE NORTH FACE OF MOUNT SABALAN: 10:00 A.M.

The night was bitterly cold under a cloudless sky, stars abundant, the moon strong and Captain Ross and his two Gurkhas were working their way cautiously under a crest following the guide and the CIA man. The soldiers wore cowled, white snow coveralls over their battle dress, and gloves and thermal underwear, but still the cold tormented them. They were about eight thousand feet, downwind of their target half a mile away the other side of the ridge. Above them the vast cone shape of the extinct volcano soared over sixteen thousand.

"Meshgi, we'll stop and rest," the CIA man said in Turkish to the guide. Both were dressed in rough tribesmen's clothes.

"If you wish it, Agha, then let it be so." The guide led the way off the path, through the snow, to a small cave that none of them had noticed. He was old and gnarled like an ancient olive tree, hairy and thin, his clothes ragged, and still the strongest of them after almost two days' climbing.

"Good," the CIA man said. Then to Ross, "Let's hole up here till we're ready."

Ross unslung his carbine, sat, and rested his pack gratefully, his calves and thighs and back aching. "I'm all one big bloody ache," he said disgustedly, "and I'm supposed to be fit."

"You're fit, sahib," the Gurkha sergeant called Tenzing said with a beam. "On our next leave we go up Everest, eh?"

"Not on your Nelly," Ross said in English and the three soldiers laughed together.

Then the CIA man said thoughtfully, "Must be something to stand on top of that mother."

Ross saw him look out at the night and the thousands of feet of mountain below. When they had first met at the rendezvous near Bandar-e Pahlavi two days ago, if he hadn't been told otherwise he would have thought him part Mongol or Nepalese or Tibetan, for the CIA man was dark-haired with a yellowish skin and Asian eyes and dressed like a nomad.

"Your CIA contact's Rosemont, Vien Rosemont, he's half Vietnamese– half American," the CIA colonel had said at his briefing. "He's twenty-six, been here a year, speaks Farsi and Turkish, he's second-generation CIA, and you can trust him with your life."

"It seems I'm going to have to, sir, one way or another, don't you think?"

"Huh? Oh, sure, yes. Yes, I guess so. You meet him just south of Bandar-e Pahlavi at those coordinates and he'll have the boat. You'll hug the coast until you're just south of the Soviet border, then backpack in."

"He's the guide?"

"No. He, er, he just knows about Mecca—that's our code name for the radar post. Getting the guide's his problem—but he'll deliver. If he's not at the rendezvous, wait through Saturday night. If he's not there by dawn, he's blown and you abort. Okay?"

"Yes. What about the rumors of insurrection in Azerbaijan?"

"Far as we know there's some fighting in Tabriz and the western part— nothing around Ardabil. Rosemont should know more. We, er, we know the Soviets are massed and ready to move in if the Azerbaijanis throw Bakhtiar supporters out. Depends on their leaders. One of them's Abdollah Khan. If you run into trouble go see him. He's one of ours—loyal."

"All right. And this pilot, Charles Pettikin. Say he won't take us?"

"Make him. One way or another. There's approval way up to the top for this op, both from your guys and ours, but we can't put anything into writing. Right, Bob?"

The other man at the briefing, a Robert Armstrong whom he had also never met before, had nodded agreement. "Yes."

"And the Iranians? They've approved it?"

"It's a matter of, er, of national security—yours and ours. Theirs too but they're . . . they're busy. Bakhtiar's, well, he's—he may not last."

"Then it's true—the U.S. are jerking the rug?"

"I wouldn't know about that, Captain."

"One last question: why aren't you sending your fellows?"

Robert Armstrong had answered for the colonel. "They're all busy—we can't get any more here quickly—not with your elite training."

We're certainly well trained, Ross thought, easing his shoulders cut raw by his backpack straps—to climb, to jump, to ski, to snorkel, to kill silently or noisily, to move like the wind against terrorist or public enemy, and to blow everything sky-high if need be, above or under water. But I'm bloody lucky, I've everything I want: health, university, Sandhurst, paratroopers, Special Air Services, and even my beloved Gurkhas. He beamed at both of them and said a Gurkhali obscenity in a vulgar dialect that sent them into silent fits of laughter. Then he saw Vien Rosemont and the guide looking at him. "Your pardon, Excellencies," he said in Farsi. "I was just telling my brothers to behave themselves."

Meshgi said nothing, just turned his attention back to the night.

Rosemont had pulled off his boots and was massaging the chill out of his feet. "The guys I've seen, British officers, they're not friends with their soldiers, not like you."

"Perhaps I'm luckier than others." With the sides of his eyes Ross was watching the guide who had got up and was now standing at the mouth of the cave, listening. The old man had become increasingly edgy in the last few hours. How far do I trust him? he thought, then glanced at Gueng who was nearest. Instantly the little man got the message, nodded back imperceptibly.

"The captain is one of us, sir," Tenzing was saying to Rosemont proudly. "Like his father and grandfather before him—and they were both Sheng'khan."

"What's that?"

"It's a Gurkhali title," Ross said, hiding his pride. "It means Lord of the Mountain. Doesn't mean much outside the Regiment."

"Three generations in the same outfit. That's usual?"

Of course it's not usual, Ross wanted to say, disliking personal questions, though liking Vien Rosemont personally. The boat had been on time, the voyage up the coast safe and quick, them hidden under sacking. Easily ashore at dusk and on their way to the next rendezvous where the guide had been waiting, fast into the foothills, and into the mountains, Rosemont never complaining but pressing forward hard, with little conversation and none of the barrage of questions he had expected.

Rosemont waited patiently, noticing Ross was distracted. Then he saw the guide move out of the cave, hesitate, then come back and squat against the cave mouth, rifle cradled on his lap.

"What is it, Meshgi?" Rosemont asked.

"Nothing, Agha. There are flocks in the valley, goats and sheep."

"Good." Rosemont leaned back comfortably. Lucky to find the cave, he thought, it's a good place to hole up in. He glanced back at Ross, saw him looking at him. After a pause he added, "It's great to be part of a team."

"What's the plan from now on?" Ross asked.

"When we get to the entrance of the cave, I'll lead. You and your guys stay back until I make sure, okay?"

"Just as you like, but take Sergeant Tenzing with you. He can protect your tail—I'll cover you both with Gueng."

After a pause, Rosemont nodded. "Sure, sounds good. Okay, Sergeant?"

"Yes, sahib. Please tell me what you want simply. My English is not good."

"It's just fine," Rosemont said, covering his nervousness. He knew Ross was weighing him like he was weighing them—too much at stake.

"You just blow Mecca to hell," his director had told him. "We've a specialist team to help you; we don't know how good they are but they're the goddamn best we can get. Leader's a captain, John Ross, here's his photo and he'll have a couple of Gurkhas with him, don't know if they speak English but they come recommended. He's a career officer. Listen, as you've never worked close with Limeys before, a word of warning. Don't get personal or friendly or use first names too fast—they're as sensitive as a cat with a feather up its ass about personal questions, so take it easy, okay?"

"Sure."

"Far as we know you'll find Mecca empty. Our other posts nearer Turkey are still operating. We figure to stay as long as we can—by that time the brass'll make a deal with the new jokers, Bakhtiar or Khomeini. But Mecca—goddamn those bastards who've put us at so much risk."

"How much risk?"

"We think they just left in a hurry and destroyed nothing. You've been there, for crissake! Mecca's stuffed with enough top secret gizmos, listening gear, seeing gear, long-range radar, locked in satellite ciphers and codes and computers to get our unfriendly KGB chief Andropov voted Man of the Year —if he gets them. Can you believe it—those bastards just hightailed it out!"

"Treason?"

"Doubt it. Just plain stupid, dumb—there wasn't even a contingency plan at Sabalan, for crissake—anywhere else either. Not all their fault, I guess. None of us figured the Shah'd fold so goddamn quick, or that Khomeini'd get Bakhtiar by the balls so fast. We got no warning—not even from SAVAK . . ."

And now we have to pick up the pieces, Vien thought. Or, more correctly, blow them to hell. He glanced at his watch, feeling very tired. He gauged the night and the moon. Better give it another half an hour. His legs ached, and his head. He saw Ross watching him and he smiled inside: I won't fail, Limey. But will you?

"An hour, then we'll move out," Vien said.

"Why wait?"

"The moon'll be better for us. It's safe here and we've time. You're clear what we do?"

"Mine everything in Mecca you mark, blow it and the cave entrance simultaneously, and run like the clappers all the way home."

Rosemont smiled and felt better. "Where's home for you?"

"I don't know really," Ross said caught unawares. He had never asked himself the question. After a moment, more for himself than the American, he added, "Perhaps Scotland—perhaps Nepal. My father and mother're in Katmandu, they're as Scots as I am but they've been living there off and on since '51 when he retired. I was even born there though I did almost all my schooling in Scotland." Both're home, for me, he thought. "What about you?"

"Washington, D.C.—really, Falls Church, Virginia, which is almost part of Washington. I was born there." Rosemont wanted a cigarette but he knew it might be dangerous. "Pa was CIA. He's dead now but he was at Langley for the last few years, which's close by—CIA HQ's at Langley." He was happy to be talking. "Ma's still in Falls Church, haven't been back in a couple of years. You ever been to the States?"

"No, not yet." The wind had picked up a little and they both studied the night for a moment.

"It'll die down after midnight," Rosemont said confidently.

Ross saw the guide shift position again. Is he going to make a run for it? "You've worked with the guide before?"

"Sure. I tramped all over the mountains with him last year—I spent a month here. Routine. Lotta the opposition infiltrate through this area and we try to keep tabs on 'em—like they do us." Rosemont watched the guide. "Meshgi's a good joe. Kurds don't like Iranians, or Iraqis or our friends across the border. But you're right to ask."

Ross switched to Gurkhali. "Tenzing, watch everywhere and the pathfinder—you eat later." At once Tenzing slipped out of his pack and was gone into the night. "I sent him on guard."

"Good," Rosemont said. He had watched them all very carefully on the climb up and was very impressed with the way they worked as a team, leapfrogging, always one of them flanking, always seeming to know what to do, no orders, always safety catches off. "Isn't that kinda dangerous?" he had said early on.

"Yes, Mr. Rosemont—if you don't know what you're doing," the Britisher had said to him with no arrogance that he could detect. "But when every tree or corner or rock could hide hostiles, the difference between safety on and off could mean killing or being killed."

Vien Rosemont remembered how the other had added guilelessly, "We'll do everything we can to support you and get you out," and he wondered again if they would get in, let alone out. It was almost a week since Mecca had been abandoned. No one knew what to expect when they got there—it could be intact, already stripped, or even occupied. "You know this whole op's crazy?"

"Ours not to reason why."

"Ours but to do or die? I think that's the shits!"

"I think that's the shits too if it's any help."

It was the first time they had laughed together. Rosemont felt much better. "Listen, haven't said it before, but I'm happy you three're aboard."

"We're, er, happy to be here." Ross covered his embarrassment at the open compliment. "Agha," he called out to the guide, "please join us at food."

"Thank you, Agha, but I am not hungry," the old man replied without moving from the cave mouth.

Rosemont put his boots back on. "You got a lot of special units in Iran?"

"No. Half a dozen—we're here training Iranians. You think Bakhtiar will weather it?" He opened his pack and distributed the cans of bully beef.

"No. The word in the hills among the tribes is that he'll be out—probably shot—within the week."

Ross whistled. "Bad as that?"

"Worse: that Azerbaijan'll be a Soviet protectorate within the year."

"Bloody hell!"

"Sure. But you never know"—Vien smiled—"that's what makes life interesting."

Casually Ross offered the flask. "Best Iranian rotgut money can buy."

Rosemont grimaced and took a careful sip, then beamed. "Jesus H. Christ, it's real Scotch!" He prepared to take a real swallow but Ross was ready and he grabbed the flask back.

"Easy does it—it's all we've got, Agha."

Rosemont grinned. They ate quickly. The cave was snug and safe. "You ever been to Vietnam?" Rosemont asked, wanting to talk, feeling the time right.

"No, never have. Almost went there once when my father and I were en route to Hong Kong but we were diverted to Bangkok from Saigon."

"With the Gurkhas?"

"No, this was years ago, though we do have a battalion there now. I was," Ross thought a moment, "I was seven or eight, my father has some vague Hong Kong relations, Dunross, yes that was their name, and there was some sort of clan gathering. I don't remember much of Hong Kong except a leper who lay in the dirt by the ferry terminal. I had to pass him every day—almost every day."

"My dad was in Hong Kong in '63," Vien said proudly. "He was deputy director of station—CIA." He picked up a stone, toyed with it. "You know I'm half-Vietnamese?"

"Yes, they told me."

"What else did they tell you?"

"Just that I could trust you with my life."

Rosemont smiled wryly. "Let's hope they're right." Thoughtfully he began checking the action of his M16. "I've always wanted to visit Vietnam. My pa, my real pa, was Vietnamese, a planter, but he was killed just before I was born—that was when the French owned Indochina. He got clobbered by Viet Cong just outside Dien Bien Phu. Ma . . ." The sadness dropped off him and he smiled. "Ma's as American as a Big Mac and when she remarried she picked one of the greatest. No real pa could've loved me more . . ."

Abruptly Gueng cocked his carbine. "Sahib!" Ross and Rosemont grabbed their weapons, then there was a keening on the wind, Ross and Gueng relaxed. "It's Tenzing."

The sergeant appeared out of the night as silently as he had left. But now his face was grim. "Sahib, many trucks on the road below—"

"In English, Tenzing."

"Yes, sahib. Many trucks, I counted eleven, in convoy, on the road at the bottom of the valley . . ."

Rosemont cursed. "That road leads to Mecca. How far away were they?"

The little man shrugged. "At the bottom of the valley. I went the other side of the ridge and there's a . . ." He said the Gurkhali word and Ross gave him the English equivalent. "A promontory. The road in the valley twists, then snakes as it climbs. If the tail of the snake is in the valley and the head wherever the road ends, then four trucks were already well past tail."

Rosemont cursed again. "An hour at best. We'd bett—" At that moment there was a slight scuffle and their attention flashed to the cave mouth. They just had time to see the guide rushing away, Gueng in pursuit.

"What the hell . . ."

"For whatever reason, he's abandoning ship," Ross said. "Forget him. Does an hour give us a chance?"

"Sure. Plenty." Quickly they got into their packs and Rosemont armed his light machine gun. "What about Gueng?"

"He'll catch us up."

"We'll go straight in. I'll go first—if I run into trouble you abort. Okay?"

The cold was almost a physical barrier they had to fight through but Rosemont led the way well, the snow not bad on the meandering path, the moon helping, their climbing boots giving them good traction. Quickly they topped the ridge and headed down the other side. Here it was more slippery, the mountainside barren, just a few clumps of weeds and plants fighting to get above the snow. Ahead now was the maw of the cave, the road running into it, many vehicle tracks in the snow.

"They could've been made by our trucks," Rosemont said, covering his disquiet. "There's been no snow for a couple of weeks." He motioned the others to wait and went forward, then stepped out on the road and ran for the entrance. Tenzing followed, using the ground for cover, moving as rapidly.

Ross saw Rosemont disappear into the darkness. Then Tenzing. His anxiety increased. From where he was he could not see far down the road, for it curled away, falling steeply. The strong moonlight made the crags and the wide valley more ominous, and he felt naked and lonely and hated the waiting. But he was confident. "If you've Gurkhas with you, you've always a chance, my son," his father had said. "Guard them—they'll always guard you. And never forget, with luck, one day you'll be Sheng'khan." Ross had smiled to himself, so proud, the title given so rarely: only to one who had brought honor to the regiment, who had scaled a worthy Nepalese peak alone, who had used the kookri and had saved the life of a Gurkha in the service of the Great Raj. His grandfather, Captain Kirk Ross, MC, killed 1915 at the Battle of the Somme, had been given it posthumously; his father,

Lieutenant Colonel Gavin Ross, DSO, was given it in Burma, in 1943. And me? Well, I've scaled a worthy peak—K4—and that's all so far but I've lots of time. . . .

His fine-tuned senses warned him and he had his kookri out, but it was only Gueng. The little man was standing over him, breathing hard. "Not fast enough, sahib," he whispered happily in Gurkhali. "I could have taken you moments ago." He held up the severed head and beamed. "I bring you a gift."

It was the first that Ross had seen. The eyes were open. Terror still contorted the face of the old man. Gueng killed him but I gave the order, he thought, sickened. Was he just an old man who was scared fartless and wanted to get out while the going was good? Or was he a spy or a traitor rushing to betray us to the enemy?

"What is it, sahib?" Gueng whispered, his brow furrowed.

"Nothing. Put the head down."

Gueng tossed it aside. The head rolled a little down the slope then stopped. "I searched him, sahib, and found this." He handed him the amulet. "It was around his throat and this"—he gave him the small leather bag—"this hung down around his balls."

The amulet was just a cheap blue stone worn against the evil eye. Inside the little bag was a small card, wrapped in plastic. Ross squinted at it and his heart skipped a beat. At that moment there was another keening on the wind, the note different. Immediately they picked up their guns and ran for the cave mouth, knowing that Tenzing had given them the all-clear signal and to hurry. Inside the throat of the cavern the darkness seemed deeper and then, as their eyes adjusted, they saw a fleck of light. It was a flashlight, the lens partially covered.

"Over here, Captain." Though it was softly said, Rosemont's voice echoed loudly. "This way." He led them farther into the cave and when he was sure it was safe he shone the light on the rock walls and all around to get his bearings. "It's okay to use your flashes." The cave was immense, many tunnels and passages leading off it, some natural, some man-made, the rock dome fifty feet overhead. "This's the unloading area," he said. When he found the tunnel he sought he shone the light down it. At the end was a thick steel door, half open. "It should be locked," he whispered, his voice raw. "I don't know if it was left like that or what, but that's where we have to go."

Ross motioned to Tenzing. At once the kookri came out and the soldier went forward to vanish inside. Automatically Ross and Gueng took up defensive positions. Against whom? Ross asked himself helplessly, feeling trapped. There could be fifty men hidden in any one of those other tunnels.

The seconds dragged. Again there was the keening. Ross led the rush through the doorway, then Gueng, then Rosemont. As Rosemont passed the door he saw that Tenzing had taken up a position nearby and was covering them. He pulled the door to and switched on the lights. The suddenness made the others gasp.

"Hallelujah!" Rosemont said, openly relieved. "The brass figured if the generators were still working, we'd have a good shot. This door's lightproof." He slid heavy bolts into place, hung his flashlight on his belt.

They were in another cave, much smaller, that had been adapted, the floor leveled and carpeted roughly, the walls made more flat. It was a form of anteroom with desks and phones and litter everywhere. "The guys sure didn't waste any time getting the hell out, did they?" he said bitterly, hurrying across the room to another tunnel, down it and into another cave room with more desks, a few radar screens, and more phones, gray and green.

"The grays're internal, greens go to the tower and masts on the crest, from there by satellite to Tehran, our HQ switchboard in the embassy, and various top secret places—they've built-in scramblers." Rosemont picked one up. It was dead. "Maybe the communications guys did their job after all." At the far end of the room was a tunnel. "That goes down to the generator room for this section which has all the gear we've to blow. Living quarters, kitchens, mess halls, repair shops, are in other caves off the unloading area. About eighty guys worked here around the clock."

"Is there any other way out of here?" Ross asked. His feeling of being closed in was greater than ever.

"Sure, topside, where we're going."

Rough steps led upward through the domed roof. Rosemont started climbing them. On the landing was a door: TOP SECURITY AREA—NO ADMITTANCE WITHOUT SPECIAL AUTHORITY. It too was open. "Shit," he muttered. This cave was well-appointed, floor flatter, walls whitewashed. Dozens of computers and radar screens, and banked electronic equipment. More desks and chairs and phones, gray and green. And two red on a central desk.

"What're those for?"

"Direct to Langley by military satellite." Rosemont picked one up. It was dead. So was the other. He pulled out a piece of paper and checked it, then went over to a bank of switches and turned some on. Another obscenity as a soft hum began, computers started chattering, warming up, and three of the radar screens came to life, the central white trace-line turning, leaving a scatter pattern in its wake. "Bastards! Bastards to leave everything like this."

His finger stabbed at four corner computers. "Blow those mothers—they're the core."

"Gueng!"

"Yes, sahib." The Gurkha took off his pack and began to lay out the plastic explosives and detonators.

"Half-hour fuses?" Rosemont said.

"Half-hour fuses it is." Ross was staring at one of the screens, fascinated. Northward he could see most of the Caucasus, all of the Caspian, eastward even part of the Black Sea, all with extraordinary clarity. "That's a lot of space to peer into."

Rosemont went over to its keyboard and turned a switch.

For a moment Ross was dumbfounded. He tore his eyes off the screen. "Now I understand why we're here."

"That's only part."

"Christ! Then we'd better get cracking. What about the cave mouth?"

"We've no time to do a decent job—and the other side of our door's routine junk they've stolen anyways. We'll blow our tunnels after us and use the escapeway."

"Where's that?"

The American went over to a door. This one was locked. He took out a bunch of tagged keys and found the one he wanted. The door swung open. Behind the door a narrow flight of stairs spiraled upward steeply. "It leads out onto the mountain."

"Tenzing, make sure the way's clear." Tenzing went up the stairs two at a time. "Next?"

"Code room and the safes, we'll mine those. Then communications. Generator room last, okay?"

"Yes." Ross liked the incisive strength more and more. "Before we do you'd better look at this." He took out the small, plastic-covered card. "Gueng caught up with our guide. This was on him."

All color left Rosemont's face. On the card was a thumbprint, some writing in Russian script, and a signature. "An ID!" he burst out. "A Commie ID!" Behind them Gueng paused momentarily.

"That's what I thought. What's it say exactly?"

"I don't know, I can't read Russian either but I'll bet my life it's a safe-conduct pass." A wave of sickness came up from his stomach as he remembered all the days and nights he had spent in the old man's company, wandering the mountains, sleeping alongside him in the open, feeling very safe. And all the time he'd been pegged. Numbly he shook his head. "Meshgi was with us for years—he was one of Ali bin Hassan Karakose's band—Ali's an underground leader and one of our best contacts in the mountains. Great guy who even operates as far north as Baku. Jesus, maybe he's been betrayed." He looked at the card again. "Just doesn't figure."

"I think it figures we could have been deliberately set up, sitting ducks," Ross said. "Perhaps the convoy's part of it, full of troops to track us. We'd better hurry it up, eh?"

Rosemont nodded, fighting to dominate the fear that swept through him, helped by the calmness of the other man. "Yes, yes, you're right." Still shattered, he went through a small passage to another door. Locked. As he looked for the key on the tabbed ring of keys he said, "I owe you and your men an apology. I don't know how we—I—got taken in or how that bastard escaped the security check but he did and you're probably right—we're set up. Sorry, but, shit, that doesn't help a goddamn bit."

"It helps." Ross grinned and the fear dropped off both of them. "It helps. Okay?"

"Okay. Thanks, yes, thanks. Gueng killed him?"

"Well," Ross said dryly. "He handed me his head. They usually just bring back ears."

"Jesus. You been with them long?"

"The Gurkhas? Four years."

The key slid into the lock and the door opened. The code room was pedantically neat. Telex and teleprinter and copy machines. A curious computer printer with a keyboard was on its own desk. "That's the decoder—worth any money you'd like to ask the opposition." On the desks pencils were lined up. Half a dozen manuals.

Rosemont picked them up. "Good sweet Jesus . . ." All were codebooks marked MECCA—ONE COPY ONLY. "Well, at least the master code's locked up." He went to the modern safe with its electronic, 0–9 digital lock that was set into one wall, read the combination from his piece of paper and touched the digits. But the Open light didn't come on. "Maybe I missed a number. Read them to me, okay?"

"Sure." Ross began reading out the long series of numbers. Behind them Tenzing came in noiselessly. Neither man heard him. ". . . one twenty-five . . . seven twenty-one." Then both men felt the presence at the same instant and whirled, momentarily panicked.

Tenzing kept the delight off his face and closed his ears to the profanity. Hadn't the Sheng'khan told him to train the son and make him wise in the ways of stealth and killing? Hadn't he sworn to guard him and be his silent teacher? "But, Tenzing, for the love of God don't let my son know I told you to. Keep this secret between us. . . ." It's been very hard to catch the sahib unawares for weeks, he thought happily. But Gueng caught him tonight and so did I. Much better we do than an enemy—and now they surround us like bees and their queen.

"The staircase leads upward for seventy-five steps to an iron door," Tenzing said in his best reporting voice. "The door is rusty but I forced it. Outside is a cave, outside the cave is the night—a good escape route, sahib. Not good is that from there I saw the first of the convoy." He paused, not wanting to be wrong. "Perhaps half an hour of time is left."

"Go back to the first door, Tenzing, the one we barred. Mine the tunnel this side of the door to leave the door unharmed—twenty-minute fuse from now. Tell Gueng to set his fuses the same from now exactly. Tell Gueng what I've ordered."

"Yes, sahib."

Ross turned back. He noticed the sweat on Rosemont's forehead. "Okay?"

"Sure. We got to one hundred three."

"The last two numbers are six sixty and thirty-one." He saw the American touch the numbers. The Open light began winking. Rosemont's right hand went for the lever. "Hold it!" Ross wiped the sweat from his own chin, the golden stubble rasping. "I suppose there's no chance it could be booby-trapped?"

Rosemont stared at him, then at the safe. "It's possible. Sure, it's possible."

"Then let's just blow the bugger and not risk it."

"I—I've gotta check. I've got to check if Mecca's master code's inside or not. That and the decoder're priority." Again he looked at the light winking at him. "You go back in the other room, take cover with Gueng, shout when you're ready. I—it's my shot."

Ross hesitated. Then he nodded, picked up both packs that contained explosives and detonators. "Where's the communications room?"

"Next door."

"Is—is the generator room important?"

"No. Just this one, the decoder and those four mothers back there, though it'd be best if this whole goddamn floor went to hell." Rosemont watched Ross walk away then turned his back and looked back at the lever. There was a bad tightness in his chest. That sonofabitch Meshgi! I'd've bet my life—you did, we all did, even Ali Karakose. "You ready?" he called out impatiently.

"Wait!" Again his stomach surged. Ross was back beside him before he had heard him, in his hands a long, thin, nylon climbing rope that, quickly, he lashed to the lever. "Turn the lever when I say but don't open the door. We'll jerk it open from back there." Ross hurried out. "Now!"

Rosemont took a deep breath to slow his heart and turned the lever to Open then ran through the passage into the other cave. Ross beckoned him down beside the wall. "I sent Gueng to warn Tenzing. Ready?"

"Sure."

Ross tightened the rope, then tugged hard. The rope remained taut. He tugged even harder, then it slackened a foot but came no farther. Silence. Nothing. Both men were sweating. "Well," Ross said, greatly relieved, and got up. "Better safe than sorr—" The explosion obliterated his words, a great cloud of dust and bits of metal blew out of the passage into their cave, jerking the air from their lungs, scattering tables and chairs. All radar screens burst, lights vanished, one of the red phones tore loose and hurtled across the room to smash through the steel casing of a computer. Gradually the dust settled, both men coughing their hearts out in the darkness.

Rosemont was the first to recover. His flashlight was still on his belt. He groped for it.

"Sahib?" Tenzing called out anxiously, rushing into the room, his flash on, Gueng beside him.

"I'm all—all right," Ross said, still coughing badly. Tenzing found him lying in the rubble. A little blood was running down his face but it was only a superficial wound from the flying glass. "Bless all gods," Tenzing muttered and helped him up.

Ross fought to stay upright. "Christalmighty!" Blankly he looked around at the wreckage, then stumbled after Rosemont through the passage into the cipher room. The safe had vanished, with it the decoder, manuals, phones, leaving a huge hole in the living rock. All electronic equipment was just a mess of twisted metal and wires. Small fires had already started.

"Jesus," was all Rosemont could say, his voice little more than a croak, his psyche revolted by the nearness to extinction, mind screaming: run, escape this place of your death . . .

"Christ all bloody mighty!"

Helplessly, Rosemont tried to say something, couldn't, his legs took him into a corner and he was violently sick.

"We'd better—" Ross found it hard to talk, his ears still ringing, a monstrous ache in his head, adrenaline pumping, trying to dominate his own wish to run. "Tenzing, are—are you finished?"

"Two minutes, sahib." The man rushed off.

"Gueng?"

"Yes, sahib. Two minutes also." He hurried away.

Ross went to the other corner and retched. Then he felt better. He found the flask and took a long swig, wiped his mouth on the sleeve of his battle dress, went over and shook Rosemont who was leaning against the wall. "Here." He gave it to him. "You all right?"

"Yes. Sure." Rosemont still felt queasy, but now his mind was working. His mouth tasted foul and he spat the foulness into the rubble. Small fires burned, throwing crazy shadows on the walls and roof. He took a careful sip. After a moment he said, "Nothing on God's earth like Scotch." Another sip and he handed the flask back. "We'd better get the hell out of here."

With the flashlight he made a quick search of the wreckage, found the twisted remains of the all-important decoder, and picked his way carefully into the next cave and laid the remains near the charge at the base of the corner computers. "What I don't understand," he said helplessly, "is why the whole goddamn place didn't go up and blow us all to hell anyway—with all our explosives scattered around."

"I—before I came back with the rope and sent Gueng off to Tenzing, I told Gueng to remove the explosives and the detonators for safety."

"You always think of everything?"

Ross smiled weakly. "All part of the service," he said. "Communications room?"

It was mined quickly. Rosemont glanced at his watch. "Eight minutes to blast-off. We'll forget the generator room."

"Good. Tenzing, you lead."

They went up the escape staircase. The iron hatch creaked as it opened. Once in the cave Ross took the lead. Cautiously he peered out at the night and all around. The moon was still high. Three or four hundred yards away the lead truck was grinding up the last incline. "Which way, Vien?" he asked and Rosemont felt a glow.

"Up," he said, hiding the warmth. "We climb. If there're troops after us, we forget the coast and head for Tabriz. If no troops we circle and go back the way we came."

Tenzing led. He was like a mountain goat, but he picked the easiest path, knowing the two men were still very shaky. Here the slope was steep but not too difficult with little snow to impede them. They had barely started when the ground shook beneath them, the sound of the first explosion almost totally muffled. In quick succession there were other small quakes.

One to go, Rosemont thought, glad of the cold which was clearing his head. The last explosion—the communications room—where they had used all their remaining explosive was much bigger and really shuddered the earth.

Below and to their right, part of the mountain gave way, smoke billowing out of the resulting crater.

"Christ," Ross muttered.

"Probably an air vent."

"Sahib. Look down there!"

The lead truck had stopped at the entrance to the cave. Men were jumping out of it, others staring up at the mountainside, illuminated by the lights of the following trucks. The men all had rifles.

Ross and the others slid deeper into the shadows. "We'll climb up to that ridge," Rosemont said softly, pointing above and to their left. "We'll be out of their sight and covered. Then we head for Tabriz, almost due east. Okay?"

"Tenzing, on you go!"

"Yes, sahib."

They made the ridge and hurried over it to climb again, working their way eastward, not talking, conserving their energy for there were many, many miles to go. The terrain was rough and the snow harried them. Soon their gloves were torn, hands and legs bruised, calves aching but, no longer encumbered by heavy packs, they made good progress and their spirits were high.

They came to one of the paths that crisscrossed the mountains. Whenever the path forked, their choice was always to keep to the heights. There were villages in the valley, very few up this high. "Better we stay up here," Rosemont said, "and . . . and hope we don't run into anyone."

"You think they'll all be hostile?"

"Sure. It's not only anti-Shah country here but anti-Khomeini, anti-everyone." Rosemont was breathing heavily. "It's village against village most of the time and good bandit country." He waved Tenzing onward, thankful for the moonlight and that he was with the three of them.

Tenzing kept up the pace but it was a mountaineer's pace, measured and unhurried and constant and punishing. After an hour Gueng took over the lead, then Ross, Rosemont, and then Tenzing again. Three minutes' rest an hour, then on again.

The moon sank lower in the sky. They were well away now, the going easier, lower down the mountainside. The path meandered but it led generally eastward toward a curiously shaped cleft in the range. Rosemont had recognized it. "Down in that valley's a side road that goes to Tabriz. It's little more than a track in winter but you can get through okay. Let's go on till dawn, then rest up and make a plan. Okay?"

Now they were down below the tree line and into the beginnings of the pine forest, going much slower and feeling the tiredness.

Tenzing still led. Snow muffled their footsteps and the good clean air pleased him greatly. Abruptly he sensed danger and stopped. Ross was just behind him and he stopped also. Everyone waited motionless. Then Ross went forward carefully. Tenzing was peering into the dark ahead, the moon casting strange shadows. Slowly both men used their peripheral vision. Nothing. No sign or smell. They waited. Some snow fell from one of the trees. No one moved. Then a night bird left a branch ahead and to the right and flew noisily away. Tenzing pointed in that direction, motioned Ross to wait, slid his kookri out, and went forward alone, melting into the night.

After a few yards Tenzing saw a man crouched behind a tree fifty yards ahead and his excitement picked up. Closer he could see that the man was oblivious of him. Closer. Then his peripheral vision saw a shadow move to his left, another to his right and he knew. "Ambush!" he shouted at the top of his lungs and dived for cover.

The first wave of bullets passed near him but missed. Part of the second punctured his left lung, ripped a hole out of his back, slamming him against a fallen tree. More guns opened up on the opposite side of the pathway, the crossfire racking Ross and the others, who had scrambled behind tree trunks and into gullies.

For a moment Tenzing lay there helplessly. He could hear the firing but it seemed far away though he knew that it must be near. With a last mighty effort he dragged himself to his feet and charged the guns that had killed him. He saw some of their attackers turn back on him and heard bullets pass him, some tugging at his cowl. One went through his shoulder but he did not feel it, pleased that he was dying as men in the regiment were supposed to die. Going forward. Fearlessly. I am truly without fear. I am Hindu and I go to meet Shiva contentedly, and when I am reborn I pray Brahma, Vishnu, Shiva that I will be born again Gurkha.

As he reached the ambush, his kookri hacked off someone's arm, his legs gave out, a monstrous, peerless light went off in his head and he strode into death without pain.

"Hold all fire," Ross called out, getting his bearings, pulling the strings of battle back into his hands. He pegged two groups of guns against them, but there was no way that he could get at either. The ambush had been well chosen and the crossfire deadly. He had seen Tenzing hit. It had taken all of his willpower not to go to his aid but first there was this battle to win and the others to protect. The shots were echoing and reechoing off the mountainside. He had wriggled out of his pack, found the grenades, made sure his carbine was fully automatic, not knowing how to lead the way out of the trap. Then he had seen Tenzing reel to his feet with a battle cry and charge up the slope, creating the diversion Ross needed. At once he ordered Rosemont,

"Cover me," and to Gueng, "Go!" pointing toward the same group Tenzing was attacking.

Immediately Gueng jumped out of his gully and rushed them, their attention diverted by Tenzing. When he saw his comrade go down, his rage burst, he let the lever on his grenade fly off, hurled it into their midst and hit the snow. The instant the grenade exploded he was up, his carbine spraying the screams, stopping most of them. He saw one man rushing away, another desperately crawling off into the underbrush. One slash of the kookri took off part of the crawler's head. A short burst cut the other to pieces and again Gueng whirled into cover, not knowing where the next danger would come from. Another grenade exploding took his attention to the other side of the path.

Ross had crawled forward out of safety. Bullets straddled him but Rosemont opened up with short bursts, drawing fire, giving Ross the help he needed, and he made the next tree safely, found a deep trough in the snow, and fell into it. For a second he waited, collecting his breath, then scrambled along the hard, frozen snow toward the firing. Now he was out of sight of the attackers and he made good time. Then he heard the other grenade go off and the screaming, and he prayed that Gueng and Tenzing were all right.

The enemy firing was getting closer, and when he judged that he was in position, he pulled the pin out of the first grenade and with his carbine in his left hand went over the top. The instant he was in the open he saw the men but not where he had expected them. There were five, barely twenty yards away. Their rifles turned on him but his reactions were just a little faster and he was on the ground behind a tree, the lever off and counting before the first barrage ripped into it. On the fourth second he reached around the tree and lobbed the grenade at them, buried his head under his arms. The explosion lifted him off the ground, blew the trunk of a nearer tree to pieces, burying him under branches and snow from its limbs.

Down by the path Rosemont had emptied his magazine into where he thought the attackers would be. Cursing in his anxiety, he slapped in a new magazine and fired another burst.

Across the path on the other slope, Gueng was huddled behind a rock waiting for someone to move. Then, near the exploded tree, he saw one man running away, bent double. He aimed and the man died, the shot echoing. Now silence.

Rosemont felt his heart racing. He could wait no longer. "Cover me, Gueng," he shouted and leaped to his feet and rushed for the tree. A flicker of firing to his right, bullets hissed past, then Gueng opened up from the other slope. A bubbling scream and the firing ceased. Rosemont ran onward until he was straddling the ambush point, his carbine leveled. Three men were in pieces, the last barely alive, their rifles bent and twisted. All wore rough tribal clothes. As he watched, the last man choked and died. He turned away and rushed for the other tree, pulling branches away, fighting his way through the snow to Ross.

On the other slope Gueng waited and watched to kill anything that moved. There was a slight stir amid the carnage behind the rocks where his grenade had ripped the three men apart. He waited, hardly breathing, but it was only a rodent feeding. Soon they will clean the ground and make it whole again, he thought, awed by the cycle of the gods. His eyes ranged slowly. He saw Tenzing crumpled to one side of the rock, his kookri still locked in his grasp. Before I leave I will take it, Gueng thought; his family will cherish it and his son will wear it with equal honor. Tenzing Sheng'khan lived and died like a man and will be reborn as the gods decide. Karma.

Another movement. Ahead in the forest. He concentrated.

The other side of the path Rosemont was pulling at the branches, fighting them away, his arms aching. At last he reached Ross and his heart almost stopped. Ross was crumpled on the ground, his arms over his head, his carbine nearby. Blood stained the snow and the back of the white coveralls. Rosemont knelt and turned him over and almost cried out with relief that Ross was still breathing. For a moment his eyes were blank, then they focused. He sat up and winced. "Tenzing? And Gueng?"

"Tenzing got clobbered, Gueng's the other side covering us. He's okay."

"Thank God. Poor Tenzing."

"Test your arms and legs."

Gingerly Ross moved his limbs. Everything worked. "My head hurts like hell, but I'm okay." He looked around and saw the crumpled attackers. "Who are they?"

"Tribesmen. Bandits maybe." Rosemont studied the way ahead. Nothing moved. The night was fine. "We'd better get the hell out of here before more of the bastards jump us. You think you can go on?"

"Yes. Give me a couple of seconds." Ross wiped some snow over his face. The cold helped. "Thanks, eh? You know. Thanks."

Rosemont smiled back. "All part of the service," he said wryly. His eyes went to the tribesmen. Keeping well down he went over to them and searched where he could. He found nothing. "Probably locals—or just bandits. These bastards can be real cruel if they catch you alive."

Ross nodded and another spasm of pain soared. "I'm okay now, I think. We'd better move—the firing must have been heard for miles and this's no place to hang around."

Rosemont had seen the pain. "Wait some more."

"No. I'll feel better moving." Ross gathered his strength, then called out in Gurkhali, "Gueng, we'll go on." He started to get up, stopped as an abrupt keening for danger answered him. "Get down!" he gasped and pulled Rosemont with him.

A single rifle bullet came out of the night and chose Rosemont and buried itself in his chest, mortally wounding him. Then there was firing from the other slope and a scream and silence once more.

In time, Gueng joined Ross. "Sahib, I think that was the last. For the moment."

"Yes." They waited with Vien Rosemont until he died, then did what they had to do for him and for Tenzing. And then they went on.

ISFAHAN MILITARY AIR BASE: 5:40 A.M. To the east the dark night was beginning to lighten with the dawn. The base was quiet now, no one about except for armed Islamic Guards who, with the people of Isfahan in their thousands and led by mullahs, had stormed the base yesterday and now possessed it, all army and air force officers and men confined to their barracks under guard—or free, openly declared now for Khomeini and the revolution.

The sentry Relazi was eighteen and very proud of his green armband and to be on guard outside the shed that contained the traitor General Valik and his family who had been caught yesterday, skulking in the officers' mess with his CIA foreign pilot. God is great, he thought. Tomorrow they will be cast into hell with all foul People of the Left Hand.

For generations the Relazis had been cobblers in one tiny stall of Isfahan's Old Bazaar. Yes, he thought, I was a bazaari until a week ago when our mullah called me and all the Faithful to God's battle, gave me God's armband and this gun and showed me how to use it. How wonderful are the ways of God.

He was sheltered in the lee of the hut, out of the snow, but the damp cold was going through him even though he was wearing all the clothes he possessed in the world—sweatshirt, a coarse shirt over it, a coat and trousers bought secondhand, an old sweater and ancient army coat that once had belonged to his father. His feet felt numb. "As God wants," he said out loud and felt better. "I'll be relieved soon and then I'll eat again—by God, soldiers lived like veritable pashas, at least two meals every day, one with rice, imagine that, and pay every week . . . pay from Satan but pay even so." He coughed badly, his breath wheezing, shifted the U.S. Army carbine to his other shoulder, found the stub of the cigarette he had been saving, and lit it.

By the Prophet, he thought gleefully, who would have imagined that we could take the base so easily, so few of us killed and sent to Paradise before we had overwhelmed the soldiers on the gate and swarmed into the camp—our brothers on the base blocking the runways with trucks, and others seizing the aircraft and helicopters to prevent escape of the Shah traitors. Rushing the bullets of the enemy, the Name of God on our lips. "Join us, brothers," we shouted, "join God's revolution, help do God's work! Come to Paradise . . . don't go to hell . . ."

The young man trembled and began to mouth the words imprinted on him by a dozen mullahs reading from the Koran, then translating: "there to live forever with all sinners and the accursed People of the Left Hand, tasting neither refreshment nor any drink but boiling water or molten metal and decaying filth. And when the fires of hell have burned away the skin, they will grow new ones so that their suffering be never ending . . ."

He closed his eyes with the intensity of his prayers: Let me die with one of God's names on my lips, and so guarantee that I will go straight to the Garden of Paradise with all the People of the Right Hand, to be there forever, never to feel hunger again, never to watch brothers and sisters of the villages with bloated bellies whimper into death, never to cry out in the night at the awfulness of life but to be in Paradise: "there to lie on silken couches adorned with robes of green silk, attended by fresh blooming youths bearing goblets and ewers and cups of flowing wine, with such fruits that please us best and the flesh of such birds as we shall long for. And ours shall be the houris with large dark eyes like pearls hidden in their shells, forever young, forever virgin, amid trees clad with fruit, and in extended shade and by flowing waters, never growing old, forev—"

The rifle butt pulverized his nose and caved in the front of his skull, permanently blinding him and ending forever his normality but not killing him before he tumbled unconscious into the snow. His assailant was a soldier, of an age with him, and this man hastily picked up the carbine—used it to break the lock of the flimsy door and shove it open.

"Hurry," the assailant whispered, sweating with fear. In a moment General Valik poked his head out cautiously. The man grabbed his arm. "Come on, hurry, by God," he snarled.

"May God bless you . . ." Valik said, his teeth chattering, then darted back and came out again with two huge bundles of rials that the man stuffed into his battle dress and vanished as silently as he had arrived. Valik hesitated a moment, his heart driving. He saw the carbine in the snow and picked it up, loaded it, and slung it over his shoulder, then grabbed up the attaché case, blessing God that the revolutionaries had been too hasty in their search to discover its false bottom before they were shoved in here to await the coming of the Tribunals.

"Follow me," he whispered urgently to his family. "But in the Name of God make no noise. Follow me carefully." He pulled his coat closer around him and led the way through the snow. His wife, Annoush, his eight-year-old son, Jalal, and his daughter Setarem, six, hesitated in the doorway. All wore ski clothes—Annoush a mink over hers that the Islamic Guards had taunted her about as an open representation of the wages of sin. "Keep it with you," they had said contemptuously, "that alone damns you!" In the night she had been happy for its warmth, huddled on the dirt floor in the unheated shed, wrapping the children in it. "Come along, my darlings," she whispered, trying to keep her terror from them.

The sentry's body blocked their way as he lay in the snow, moaning softly.

"Mama, why does he sleep in the snow?" the little girl asked in a whisper.

"Never mind, my darling. Let's hurry. Not a sound now!"

Silently she stepped over him. The little girl could not quite make it and had to tread on him, and she stumbled, sprawling in the snow. But she did not cry out, just scrambled to her feet helped by her brother. Together, hand in hand, they hurried onward.

Valik guided them carefully. When they reached the hangar where the 212 was still parked, he breathed a little easier.

This area was well away from the main camp, the other side of the enormous runway. Making sure there were no guards nearby he ran out to the chopper and peered into the cabin. To his enormous relief no guards were asleep inside. He tried the door. It was not locked. He slid it open as quietly as he could, and beckoned the others. Silently they joined him. He helped them up and got in after them, sliding the door to, locking it from the inside.

Quickly he made the children comfortable on some blankets under the jump seats, cautioning them not to make their presence known whatever happened. Then he sat beside his wife, wrapped a blanket around his shoulders, for he was very cold, and held her hand. The tears wet her cheeks.

"Be patient, don't cry. It won't be long now," he whispered, gentling her. "We won't have to wait long. Insha'Allah."

"Insha'Allah," she echoed brokenly, "but the whole world's gone mad . . . thrown into a filthy outhouse like criminals . . . what's going to happen to us . . ."

"With the Help of God we've got this far, so why not all the way to Kuwait?"

They had arrived here yesterday just before noon. The flight from the pickup outside of Tehran had been without incident, all airwaves silent. His trusted chauffeur of fifteen years had driven his car back to Tehran, with orders to tell no one that they had "gone to their house on the Caspian."

"In this escape we trust no one," Valik had told his wife while they were waiting for the chopper to arrive.

She had said, "Of course, but we should have brought Sharazad, that would have helped her and Tom Lochart and guaranteed he would take us onward."

"No, she'd never have left, why should she?" Valik had said. "With or without Sharazad, he is not to be trusted—he's alien and not one of us."

"It would have been wiser to have brought her."

"No," he had said, knowing what would have to be done with Lochart.

All the way from Tehran to Isfahan he had sat in the front with Lochart. They had stayed low, avoiding towns and airfields. When Lochart had called Isfahan Military Base Control they were obviously expected. The tower had given them directions where to land with an order not to call again and to observe radio silence. Air Force Brigadier General Mohammed Seladi, Valik's uncle, who had arranged for them to land and to refuel, met them at the helipad. The general had greeted them somberly. As it was near lunchtime he said they should eat on the base before going on.

"But, Mohammed Excellency, we've enough food here on the aircraft," Valik had told him.

"I must insist," Seladi had said nervously, "I must insist, Excellency. You should pay your respects to the commandant. It is necessary, and, er, we must talk."

It was during this time that the Green Bands and the mob had burst through the gates, swarmed over the station, arrested them all, and had taken Lochart to another part of the base. Sons of dogs, Valik thought angrily, may they all burn in hell! I knew at the time we should have just refueled and gone on at once. Seladi's a blundering fool. It's all his fault . . .

In an upper story of a barrack a quarter of a mile away. Tom Lochart was sleeping fitfully. Suddenly he was awakened by a scuffle outside in the corridor, the door burst open, and he was half blinded by a flashlight.

"Quick," a voice said in American English and two men helped him stand. At once the two half-seen figures turned and ran off. A split second to collect himself then Lochart rushed in pursuit, along the corridor, down three flights of stairs, and into the open. There he stopped with the others, his breathing heavy. He just had time to see that both men were officers, a captain and a major, before they were off again in the semidarkness, running hard. Dawn brightened the eastern sky. Snow fell lightly, helping to hide them, and muffling their footsteps.

Ahead was a guardhouse with a wood fire outside, a few sleepy inattentive revolutionaries huddled around it. The three men diverted and ran down between a line of barracks, diverted again into an alleyway as a truck filled with chanting guards came around a corner, then rushed into the open, along the boundary road for the far hangar and the 212. In the lee of the hangar, they stopped to catch their breath.

"Listen, pilot," the major said, panting, "when I give the word, we run for the chopper and take off. Ready?"

"What about the others?" Lochart asked, a stitch in his side and hardly able to talk. "What about General Valik and his fam—"

"Forget them. Ali," the major jerked his thumb at the other man, "Ali goes in front with you and I'm in the back. How long will it take to get airborne once you start up?"

"Minimum."

"Make it less," the major said. "Come on!"

They rushed for the 212, Lochart and Ali, the captain, heading for the cockpit. At that moment Lochart saw a car without headlights charging along the boundary road toward them and his heart seemed to stop. "Look!"

"In God's name, hurry, pilot!"

Lochart redoubled his efforts, jumped into the pilot's seat, shoved in the circuit breakers, switched on, and began to crank her up. At the same moment the major reached the sliding door and tore it open. He almost fainted when the carbine was shoved in his face by Valik.

"Oh, it's you, Major! Praise be to God . . ."

"Praise be to God you're here and made your escape, Excellency," the major gasped, forced his panic away, and clambered in, the engines already winding the blades but nowhere near airspeed yet. "Praise be to God you made your escape . . . but where's the soldier?"

"He just took the money and fled."

"Did he bring the guns?"

"No, this is all h—"

"Son of a dog!" the major said furiously, then shouted at Lochart, "In the Name of God hurryyyyyyy!" He whirled and looked at the approaching car. It was closing fast. He grabbed the carbine from Valik, kneeled in the doorway, aimed at the driver, and squeezed the trigger. The burst was high—as behind him Annoush and the children cried out in terror—the car hurtled off the road taking evading action and swung behind a row of sheds, came into view for an instant to dart around the hangar and disappear again.

Lochart had his headset on and was watching the needles climbing, willing them to hurry. "Come on, goddamnit," he muttered, hands and feet ready on the controls, the scream of the jets growing, the captain beside him praying openly. He could not hear Annoush sobbing in the back or the petrified children who had scrambled out of their hiding place to bury themselves in her skirts, or Valik and the major raging at him to hurry.

Needles climbing. Still climbing. Still climbing. Almost in the Green. Now! His left hand started to raise the collective lever but the car whirled around the hangar and came at them head-on to stop fifteen yards away. Five men jumped out of it—one rushed directly at the cockpit and pointed an automatic rifle at him, the others went for the cabin door. He was almost airborne but knew he was a dead man if he went the extra inches and he saw the man angrily motion him to stop. He obeyed, then swung around to look into the back. The other men were clambering in. They were all officers, Valik and the major were embracing them and being embraced, then he heard, "Take off, for crissake!" in his headset and felt a shove in the ribs. It was Ali, the captain, beside him.

"Take off!" Ali said again, his English American-accented, and gave a thumbs-up to the man outside still aiming at them. The man rushed for the door, got in, and slammed the door closed. "Hurry, goddamnit, look over there!" He pointed at the other side of the runway. More cars were heading their way. Sparks of machine-gun fire from someone leaning out of a window. In seconds Lochart was airborne, all senses concentrating on escape.

Behind him some of the officers cheered, hung on as the chopper took evading action, and sorted themselves into seats. Most were colonels. Some were shaken, particularly General Seladi who sat between Valik and the major. "I wasn't sure it was you, General Excellency," the major was saying, "so I fired high just as a warning. Praise be to God the plan worked so well."

"But you were going to take off. You were going to leave us! You w—"

"Oh, no, Excellency Uncle," Valik interrupted smoothly, "it was the British pilot, he was panicking and didn't want to wait! They've no balls, Britishers! Never mind him," he added, "we're armed, we've food, and we're safe! Praise be to God! And more praise that I had time to plan." Yes, he thought, if it hadn't been for me and my money we'd all be dead—money to bribe the man who released us and you, and the major and captain to release Lochart whom I need just a little longer.

"If we'd been left we'd've been shot!" General Seladi was enraged, his face purple. "God curse that pilot to hell! Why did you waste time releasing him? Ali can fly a 212!"

"Yes. But Lochart has more experience and we need him to get through the maze."

Valik smiled encouragingly at Annoush who sat across the aisle facing him, the little girl trembling in her arms, his son sitting on the floor dozing, his head in her lap. Weakly she smiled back, shifting the weight of the child to ease the aches that pervaded her. He reached over and touched her, then settled more comfortably in his seat and closed his eyes, very tired but most content. You're a very clever man, he told himself. In his most secret heart he knew that without his stratagem of pretending to McIver that SAVAK was going to arrest him—and particularly his family—neither McIver nor Lochart would have helped them to escape. You measured them perfectly as you have Gavallan.

Fools! he thought contemptuously.

And as for you, Seladi, my stupid and rapacious uncle who bartered safe refueling at Isfahan—which you failed to provide—in return for a safe passage out for yourself and eleven of your friends, you're worse. You're a traitor. If I hadn't had an informant of long standing in the General Staff HQ I would never have heard of the generals' great betrayal in time to escape and we'd've been caught like flies in a honey pot in Tehran. Loyalists may still prevail, the battle's not lost yet, but meanwhile my family and I will watch events from England, St. Moritz, or New York.

He let himself go into the exciting, wonderful power of the jets that were carrying them to safety, to a house in London, a country house in Surrey, another in California, and to Swiss and Bahamian bank accounts. Ah, yes, he told himself happily, and that reminds me about our blocked S-G joint account in the Bahamas, another $4 million to enrich us—and easy now to pry from Gavallan's grubby paws. More than enough to keep me and my family safe whatever happens here—until we can return. Khomeini won't live forever even if he wins—God curse him! Soon we'll be able to return home, soon Iran will be normal again, meanwhile we have everything we need.

His ears heard Seladi still muttering about Lochart and almost being left behind. "Calm yourself, Excellency," he said, and took his arm, gentling him, and thought, You and your running dogs still have a value, a temporary value. Perhaps as hostages, perhaps as bait—who knows? None are family except you and you betrayed us. "Calm yourself, my revered uncle, with the Help of God the pilot will get what he deserves."

Yes. Lochart should not have panicked. He should have waited for my order. Disgusting to panic.

Valik closed his eyes and slept, very satisfied with himself.

CHAPTER 23

AT THE IRAN-TODA REFINERY, BANDAR DELAM: 12:04

P.M. Scragger was whistling tonelessly, hand-pumping fuel into his main tanks from big barrels that were lined up in a small Japanese semi beside the freshly washed 206, sparkling in the sun. Nearby was a young Green Band who squatted in the shade, leaning on his M16, half asleep.

The noonday sun was warm and the light breeze made the day pleasant and took away the constant humidity, here on the coast. Scragger was dressed lightly, white shirt with captain's epaulets, summer-weight black trousers and shoes, the inevitable dark glasses and peaked cap.

Now the tanks were brimming. "That's it, me son," he said to the Japanese assigned to assist him.

"Hai, Anjin-san"—Yes, Mr. Pilot—the man said. Like all employees at the refinery he wore white, spotless overalls and gloves, with Iran-Toda Industries

emblazoned on the back, then the same thing in Farsi politely above, with equivalent in Japanese characters beneath it.

"*Hai*, it is," Scragger said, using one of the words that he had picked up from Kasigi en route from Lengeh yesterday. He pointed. "Next our long-range tanks, and then we'll fill the spares." For the journey that de Plessey had grandly authorized Sunday night—to celebrate their victory over the saboteurs—Scragger had taken out the backseat and lashed in place two 40-gallon drums, "just in case, Mr. Kasigi. I've connected them to the main tanks. We can use a hand pump and can even refuel in the air, if we have to —if you do the pumping. Now we won't have to land for fuel. You can never tell with weather in the Gulf, there's always sudden storms or squalls, fog, winds can play tricks. Our best bet's to stay a little out to sea."

"And Jaws?"

Scragger had laughed with him. "The old hammerhead of Kharg? With any luck we might see him—if we get that far and don't get diverted."

"Still no callback from Kish radar?"

"No, but it doesn't matter. They've cleared us to Bandar Delam. You're sure you can refuel me at your plant?"

"Yes, we've storage tanks, Captain. Helipads, hangar, and repair shop. Those were the first things we built—we had a contract with Guerney."

"Yes, yes, I knew about that, but they've quit, haven't they?"

"Yes, they did, a week or so ago. Perhaps your company would take over the contract? Perhaps you could be put in charge—there's work for three 212s and perhaps two 206s constantly, while we're building."

Scragger had chuckled. "That'd make old Andy and Gav happy as a cat in a barrel of fish sticks and Dirty Dunc fart dust!"

"Please?"

Scragger tried to explain the joke about McIver. But when he was through Kasigi had not laughed, just said, Oh, now I understand.

They're a rum lot, Scragger thought.

When he finished refueling he did another ground check—engine, rotors, airframe—though he did not expect to leave today. De Plessey had asked him to wait for Kasigi, to fly him where he needed to go, and to bring him back to Lengeh on Thursday. The 206 checked out perfectly. Satisfied he glanced at his watch, then he pointed at his stomach and rubbed it. "Grub time, *hai*?"

"*Hai!*" His helper smiled and motioned to the small truck nearby, then pointed at the main, four-story office building two-hundred-odd yards away where the executive offices were.

Scragger shook his head. "I'll walk," he said and waggled his two fingers to parody walking so the young man half bowed and got into the truck and drove off. He stood there for a moment, watching and being watched by the guard. Now that the truck had left and the tanks were closed, he could smell the sea and the rotting debris of the nearby shore. It was near low tide—there was only one tide a day in the Gulf, as in the Red Sea, because it was shallow and landlocked but for the narrow Strait of Hormuz.

He liked the sea smell. He had grown up in Sydney, always within sight of the sea. After the war he had settled there again. At least, he reminded himself, I was there between jobs and the Missus and the kids stayed there and still stay there, more or less. His son and two daughters were married now with children of their own. Whenever he was on home leave, perhaps once a year, he saw them. They had a friendly, distant relationship.

In the early years his wife and children had come to the Gulf to settle. Within a month they had gone home to Sydney. "We'll be at Bondi, Scrag," she had said. "No more foreign places for us, lad." During one of his two-year stints in Kuwait she had met another man. When Scragger had returned the next time, she said, "I think we'll divorce, lad. It's best for the kids—and thee and me," and so they did. Her new husband lived a few years, then died. Scragger and she drifted back into their pattern of friendliness—not that we ever left off, he thought. She's a good sort and the kids're happy and I'm flying. He still sent her money monthly. She always said she didn't need it. "Then put it into savings against a rainy day, Nell," he always told her. So far, touch wood, they've not had rainy days, she and the kids and their kids.

The nearest wood was the butt of the rifle the revolutionary had in his lap. The man was staring at him malevolently from the shade. Shitty bastard, you're not going to spoil my day. He beamed at him, then turned his back, stretched, and looked around.

This's a great site for a refinery, he told himself, close enough to Abadan, to the main pipelines joining the north and south oil fields—great idea to try to save all that gas being burned off, billions of tons of it all over the world. Criminal waste, when you think of it.

The refinery was on a promontory, with its own dredged wharfing setup that stretched out into the Gulf for four hundred yards, that Kasigi had told him would eventually be able to handle two supertankers at the same time of whatever size could be built. Around the helipads were acres of complex cracking plants and buildings, all seemingly interconnected with miles of steel and plastic pipes of all sizes, mazes of them, with huge cocks and valves, pumping stations, and everywhere cranes and earthmovers and vast piles of all manner of construction materials, mountains of concrete and sand, reinforcing steel mesh scattered around—along with neat dumps the size of football fields, of crates and containers protected with plastic tarpaulins—and half-finished roads, foundations, wharves, and excavations. But almost nothing moving, neither men nor machines.

When they had landed, a welcoming committee of twenty or thirty Japanese had been at the helipad, hastily assembled, along with a hundred-odd Iranian strikers and armed Islamic Guards, some wearing IPLO armbands, the first Scragger had ever seen. After much shouting and threatening and examining their papers and the inbound Kish radar clearance, the spokesman had said the two of them could stay but no one could leave or the chopper take off without the komiteh's permission.

En route to the office building, Chief Engineer Watanabe, who could speak English, had explained that the strike komiteh had been, for all intents and purposes, in possession for almost two months. In that time almost no progress had been made and all work had ceased. "They won't even allow us to maintain our equipment." He was a hard-faced, tough, grizzle-haired man in his sixties with very strong working hands. He lit another cigarette from his half-smoked one.

"And your radio?"

"Six days ago they locked the radio room, forbidding its use and took away the key. Phones of course have been out for weeks and the telex for a week or more. We've still about a thousand Japanese personnel here—dependents of course were never permitted—food supplies are very short, we've had no mail for six weeks. We can't move out, we can't work. We're almost prisoners and can do nothing without very great troubles indeed. However, at least we are alive to protect what we have done and wait patiently to be allowed to continue. We are very indeed honored to see you, Kasigi-san, and you, Captain."

Scragger had left them to their business, feeling the tension between the two men, however much they tried to hide it. In the evening he had eaten lightly, as always, allowed himself one ice-cold Japanese beer, "Bugger me, it's not as good as Foster's," then had done his eleven minutes of Canadian Air Force exercises and had gone to bed.

Just before midnight while he was still reading, there had been a soft knock. Kasigi had come in excitedly, apologizing for disturbing him but he felt Scragger should know at once that they had just heard a broadcast from a Khomeini spokesman in Tehran saying that all the armed services had declared for him, Prime Minister Bakhtiar had resigned, that now Iran was totally free of the Shah's yoke, that by Khomeini's personal order, all fighting should cease, all strikes should stop, oil production should commence again, all bazaars and shops should open, all men should hand in their weapons and return to work, and above everything, all should give thanks to God for granting them victory.

Kasigi had beamed. "Now we can start again. Thank all gods, eh? Now things will be normal again."

When Kasigi had left, Scragger had lain there, the light on, his mind racing over the possibilities of what would happen now. Stone the crows, he had thought, how fast everything's been. I'd've bet heavy odds the Shah'd never be shoved out, heavier odds that Khomeini'd never be allowed back, and then my bundle on a military coup.

He had turned off the light. "Just goes to show, Scrag, old chap. You know eff all."

In the morning he had awakened early, accepted Japanese green tea in place of the breakfast tea he usually drank—Indian, very strong, and always with condensed milk—and gone to check, clean, and refuel, and now, everything tidy, he was very hungry. He nodded briefly to the guard who paid no attention to him and strolled off toward the four-story office building.

Kasigi was standing at one of the windows on the top floor where the executive offices were. He was in the boardroom, a spacious corner office with a huge table and seats for twenty and had been watching the 206 and Scragger absently, his mind in turmoil, hard put to contain his rage. Since early this morning he had been going through cost projections, reports, accounts receivable, work projections, and so on, and they all added up to the same result: at least another billion dollars and another year of time to start production. This was only the second time he had visited the refinery which was not in his sphere of responsibility though he was a director and member of the Chairman's Executive Committee that was their conglomerate's highest echelon of decision-making.

Behind him Chief Engineer Watanabe sat alone at the vast table, outwardly patient, chain-smoking as always. He had been in charge for the last two years, deputy chief since the project began in '71—a man of great experience. The previous chief engineer had died here, on-site, of a heart attack.

No wonder, Kasigi thought angrily. Two years ago—perhaps four—it must have been quite clear to him our absolute maximum budget of $3.5 billion would be inadequate, that overruns were already vast and delivery dates totally unrealistic.

"Why didn't Chief Engineer Kasusaka inform us? Why didn't he make a special report?"

"He did, Kasigi-san," Watanabe said politely, "but by direction of the Head Agreements of the joint venture here, all reports have to go through our court-appointed partners. It's an Iranian pattern—it's always supposed to be a joint venture, fifty-fifty, with shared responsibilities, but gradually the Iranians manage to maneuver meetings and contracts and clauses, usually using the court or Shah as an excuse, till they have de facto control and then . . ."

He shrugged. "You've no idea how clever they are—worse than a Chinese merchant, much worse. They agree to buy the whole animal but renege and take only the steak and leave you with the rest of the carcass on your hands." He put out the half-smoked cigarette and lit another. "There was a meeting of the whole board of partners with Gyokotomo-sama—Yoshi Gyokotomo himself, chairman of the Syndicate—here in this office, just before Chief Engineer Kasusaka-san died. I was present. Kasusaka-san cautioned everyone that Iranian bureaucratic delays and harassments—squeeze is the correct word—would put back production dates and cause a vast increase in cost overruns. I was present, I heard him with my own ears, but he was overridden by the Iranian partners who told the chairman everything would be re-arranged, that Kasusaka-san didn't understand Iran or the way they did things in Iran." Watanabe studied the end of his cigarette. "Kasusaka-san even said the same in private to Gyokotomo-sama, begging him to beware, and gave him a written detailed report."

Kasigi's face closed. "Were you present at this meeting?"

"No—but he told me what he had said, that Gyokotomo-sama accepted the report and said that he himself would take it up to the highest level, in Tehran and at home in Japan. But nothing happened, Kasigi-san. Nothing."

"Where is the copy of the report?"

"There isn't one. The next day, before he left for Tehran, Gyokotomo ordered them destroyed." Again the older man shrugged. "Chief Engineer Kasusaka's job, and mine, was and is to get the refinery built, whatever the problems, and not to interfere with the working of the Syndicate." Watanabe lit a fresh cigarette from the half-smoked cigarette, inhaled deeply, stubbed the other out delicately, wanting to smash it and the ashtray and the desk and the building and the plant to smithereens—along with this interloper Kasigi who dared to question him, who knew nothing, had never worked in Iran, and had his position in the company because he was kinsman to the Todas. "Unlike Chief Engineer Kasusaka" he added oh so gently, "over the years I have kept copies of my monthly reports."

"So ka?" Kasigi said, trying to sound matter-of-fact.

"Yes," Watanabe said. And copies of these copies in a very safe place, he thought grimly in his most secret heart, taking a thick file from his briefcase and putting it on the desk, just in case you'll try to make me responsible for the failures. "You may read them if you wish."

"Thank you." With an effort Kasigi resisted the temptation to grab the file at once.

Watanabe rubbed his face tiredly. He had been up most of the night preparing for this meeting. "Once we're back to normal, work will progress quickly. We are 80 percent complete. I'm confident we can complete with the right planning—it's all in my reports, including the matter of the Kasusaka meeting with the partners, and then with Gyokotomo-sama."

"What do you suggest as an overall solution to Iran-Toda?"

"There isn't one until we're back to normal."

"We are now. You heard the broadcast."

"I heard it, Kasigi-san, but normal for me means when the Bazargan government's in full control."

"That will happen within days. Your solution?"

"The solution is simple: get fresh partners who cooperate, arrange the financing we need, and within a year, less than a year, we'll be producing."

"Can the partners be changed?"

Watanabe's voice became as thin as his lips. "The old ones were all court-appointed, or approved, therefore Shah men, therefore suspect and enemies. We haven't seen one since Khomeini returned, or heard from one. We've heard rumors they've all fled but . . ." Watanabe shrugged his great shoulders. "I've no way of checking with no telex, no phones, no transport. I doubt if the new 'partners' will be different in attitude."

Kasigi nodded and glanced back out the window, seeing nothing. Easy to blame Iranians and dead men and secret meetings and destroyed reports. Never had Chairman Yoshi Gyokotomo mentioned any meeting with Kasusaka or any written report. Why should Gyokotomo bury such a vital report? Ridiculous because he and his company are equally at risk as ours. Why? If Watanabe's telling the truth and his own reports could prove it, why?

Then, for an instant that Watanabe noticed, Kasigi's face fell to pieces as the answer came to him: because the immense overrun and management failure of the Iran-Toda complex, added to the disastrous slump in world shipping, will break Toda Shipping Industries, will break Hiro Toda personally and lay us open to a takeover! Takeover by whom? Of course by Yoshi Gyokotomo. Of course by that jumped-up peasant family who has hated us who are highborn, samurai-descended from ancient tim—

Then again Kasigi felt as though his brain was going to explode:

Of course by Yoshi Gyokotomo but aided and abetted of course by our arch rivals, Mitsuwari Industries! Oh, Gyokotomo'll lose a fortune but they can sustain their portion of the loss while they grease the correct palms suggesting that they will jointly absorb Toda's losses, dismember it, and with the benevolence of MITI put it under proper management. With the Todas will go their kinsmen: the Kasigis and the Kayamas. I might as well be dead. *Oh ko!*

And now I am the one who has to bring back the terrible news. Watanabe's reports will prove nothing, for of course Gyokotomo will deny everything, damning me for trying to accuse him and will shout from the rooftops that the Watanabe reports prove conclusively Hiro Toda's mismanagement for years. So I'm in trouble either way. Perhaps it was Hiro Toda's plan to put me in the middle of this mess! Perhaps he wants to replace me with one of his brothers or neph—

At that moment there was a knock and the door burst open. Watanabe's distraught young assistant came in hurriedly, apologizing profusely for disturbing them. "Oh, so sorry, Watanabe-san, oh, yes, so sorr—"

"What is it?" Watanabe said, bringing him up short.

"A komiteh is arriving in strength, Watanabe-san, Kasigi-sama! Look!" The white-faced young man pointed at the other windows that fronted the building.

Kasigi was there first. In front of the main door was a truck filled with revolutionaries, other trucks and cars following. Men jumped out of them, began to collect in haphazard groups.

Scragger was approaching and they saw him stop, then go on again toward the main door, but he was waved away as a big Mercedes drove up. Out of its back came a heavyset man in black robes and a black turban with a white beard, accompanied by another much younger man, mustached, dressed in light clothes with an open-neck shirt. Both wore glasses. Watanabe sucked in his breath.

"Who are they?" Kasigi asked.

"I don't know, but an ayatollah means trouble. Mullahs wear white turbans, ayatollahs wear black." Surrounded by half a dozen guards the two men strode into the building. "Bring them up here, Takeo, ceremoniously." The young man rushed off at once. "We've only had one visit by an ayatollah, last year, just after the Abadan fire. He called a meeting of all our Iranian staff, harangued them for three minutes, then in the name of Khomeini ordered them to strike." His face settled into a mask. "That was the beginning of our trouble here—we expatriates have carried on as best we could ever since."

"What now?" Kasigi asked.

Watanabe shrugged, strode over to a bureau, and lifted up a framed photo of Khomeini that Kasigi had not noticed and hung it on the wall. "Just for politeness," he said with a sardonic smile. "Shall we sit down? They expect formality from us—please take the head of the table."

"No, Watanabe-san. Please, you are in charge. I am only a visitor."

"As you wish." Watanabe took his usual seat, and faced the door. Kasigi broke the silence. "What was that about the Abadan fire?"

"Ah, sorry," Watanabe said apologetically, actually disgusted that Kasigi did not know about that most important event. "It was last August, during their holy month of Ramadan when no Believer may take food or drink from sunup to sunset and tempers are normally thin. At that time there was only a small amount of national protest against the Shah, mostly in Tehran and Qom, but nothing serious then and the clashes easily contained by police and SAVAK. On August fifteenth arsonists set fire to a movie house, the Rex Cinema in Abadan. All the doors 'happened' to be locked or jammed, firemen and police 'happened' to be slow arriving, and in the panic almost five hundred died, mostly women and children."

"How terrible!"

"Yes. The whole nation was outraged. Instantly SAVAK was blamed, and therefore the Shah, the Shah blamed leftists and swore the police and SAVAK had nothing to do with it. Of course he set up an inquiry which went on for weeks. Unfortunately it left the question of responsibility unresolved." Watanabe was listening for the sound of footsteps. "That was the spark that united the warring opposing factions under Khomeini and tore the Pahlavis from their throne."

After a pause Kasigi said, "Who do you think set fire to the cinema?"

"Who wanted to destroy the Pahlavis? So easy to cry SAVAK!" Watanabe heard the elevator stop. "What're five hundred women and children to a fanatic—of any persuasion?"

The door was opened by the assistant Takeo. The ayatollah and the civilian strode in importantly, six armed men crowding after them. Watanabe and Kasigi got up politely and bowed.

"Welcome," Watanabe said in Japanese though he could speak very good Farsi. "I am Naga Watanabe, in charge here, this is Mr. Kasigi from our head office in Japan. Whom do I have the pleasure of addressing please?"

Takeo, who could speak perfect Farsi, began to interpret but the civilian, who had already sat down, cut him short. "*Vous parlez français?*" he said rudely to Watanabe.

"*Iye*"—No—Watanabe said in Japanese.

"*Bien sûr, m'sieur,*" Kasigi said hesitantly, his French mediocre. "*Je parle un peu, mais je parle anglais mieux, et M'sieur Watanabe aussi."* I speak a little French but I speak English better and Mr. Watanabe also.

"Very well," the man said curtly, his English Parisian-accented. "Then we will speak English. I am Muzadeh, deputy minister for the Abadan area for Prime Minister Bazargan an—"

"But Bazargan doesn't make the law, the Imam does," the ayatollah interrupted him sharply. "The Imam appointed Bazargan temporary prime minister until, with the Help of God, our Islamic state is formed." He was in his late sixties, a round-faced man, his eyebrows as white as his beard, his black robe meticulous. "Under the Imam's leadership," he added pointedly.

"Yes, of course," Muzadeh said, then went on as though there had been no interruption, "and I inform you officially that the Iran-Toda is now under our direct control. There will be a meeting in three days to organize controls and future operations. All previous Shah-inspired, therefore illegal, contracts are voided. I will appoint a new controlling board, myself as chairman, workers representatives, one Japanese worker and yourself. You w—"

"And myself, and a mullah from Bandar Delam," the ayatollah said, glaring at him.

Muzadeh angrily switched to Farsi, "We can discuss the makeup of the committee later." There was an edge to his voice. "The important thing is to have the workers represented."

"The important thing is to do the Work of God."

"In this the work of the People and the Work of God is the same."

"Not if the 'work of the People' is a covert name for the work of Satan!"

All six of the Iranian guards shifted uneasily. Unconsciously they had regrouped into four and two. In the silence their eyes went from man to man seated at the table. One of the men quietly eased off a safety catch.

"You were saying?" Watanabe said quickly and almost added, *Banzai,* with relief, as he saw everyone turn their attention back to him. "You wish to form a new committee?"

"Yes." With an effort Muzadeh tore his gaze off the ayatollah and continued, "You will have all books ready for our perusal and you will be held responsible for any—any problems whatsoever, past or future or crimes against Iran, past or future."

"We've been joint partners with the government of Iran since the beg—"

"With the Shah, not with the Iranian people," Muzadeh cut in. Behind him the guards, youths, some teenagers, some hardly bearded, began muttering.

"True, Mr. Muzadeh," Watanabe said, unafraid. He had been through the same sort of confrontation many times in the past few months. "But we are

Japanese. Iran-Toda is being built by Japanese technicians with maximum help from Iranian trainees and workers, it's paid for totally by Japanese money."

"That has noth—"

"Yes, we know," the ayatollah said loudly but agreeably, overriding the other, "we know that and you're welcome in Iran. We know Japanese are not vile Americans or insidious British, and though you're not Muslim, unhappily for yourselves, your eyes not yet open to Allah, we welcome you. But now, now with the Help of God we have possessed our country back, now we must make . . . make new arrangements for future operations. Our people will stay on here, asking questions. Please cooperate with them—you have nothing to fear. Remember, we want the plant finished and operating as much as you. My name is Ishmael Ahwazi, and I am ayatollah of this area." He got up with an abruptness that made some of the men jump. "We will return on the fourth day from now!"

Muzadeh said in Farsi hotly, "There are other orders for these foreign—"

But the ayatollah had already left. Contemptuously Muzadeh got up and stalked out, his men following.

When they were quite alone Kasigi allowed himself to take a handkerchief out and mop his brow. Young Takeo was shock-still. Watanabe searched his pockets for his cigarettes but the pack was empty. He crushed the box. Takeo came to life and hurried to a drawer and found a fresh pack, opened it, and offered it.

"Thank you, Takeo." Watanabe sat and accepted a light. "You can go now." He looked at Kasigi. "So," he said, "now it begins again."

"Yes," Kasigi said, the implications of a new komiteh committed to successful completion possessing him. "That's the best news we could have. That will be very welcome in Japan." In fact, he thought with growing excitement, this news will take the curse off Watanabe's reports and perhaps somehow we—Hiro Toda and I—together we can neutralize Gyokotomo. And if, even better, Hiro retired in place of his brother that would be perfect!

"What?" he asked, seeing Watanabe looking at him.

"I didn't mean work begins again, Kasigi-san," the chief engineer said sharply. "The new komiteh won't be any better than the other—in fact it will be worse. With the partners the inevitable pishkesh opened doors and you knew where you were. But with these fanatics, these amateurs?" Irritably Watanabe ran his hand through his hair. All gods and spirits give me the strength not to curse this fool for his continual stupidity! he thought. Be wise, calm yourself, he's only an ape, not as well born as you who are a direct descendant of the lords of the north.

"The ayatollah lied, then?" Kasigi's happiness vanished.

"No. That poor fool believed what he said but nothing will happen. Police and SAVAK, whatever new name it will have, still control Abadan and this area—the locals are mostly Arab, Sunnis, not Shi'ite Iranians. I meant the killing begins again." Watanabe explained the clash the two men had had in Farsi. "Now it's going to be much worse with every faction maneuvering for power."

"These barbarians won't obey Khomeini? Won't disarm?"

"I'm saying the leftists like Muzadeh will carry on the war, aided and abetted by the Soviets who are desperate to possess Iran, have always wanted Iran, will always want Iran—not for the oil but for the Strait of Hormuz. For with their foot on the strait they possess the Western world—and Japan. As far as I'm concerned the West, America and the rest of the world, can rot, but we *must* go to war if the strait is prohibited to our ships."

"I agree. Of course I agree." Kasigi was equally irritable. "We all know that. Of course it means war—while we depend on oil."

"Yes." Watanabe smiled grimly. "Ten years, no more."

"Yes." Both men were aware of the enormous national effort in research projects, overt and covert, to develop the alternate source of energy that would make the Japanese self-sufficient—*the* National Project. The source: the sun and the sea. "Ten years, yes, for ten years only." Kasigi was confident. "If we have ten years of peace and free access to the U.S. market—then we'll have our alternate and then we'll own the world. But meanwhile," he added, his anger returning, "for the next ten years we have to kowtow to barbarians and bandits of every kind!"

"Didn't Khrushchev say the Soviets didn't have to do anything about Iran because 'Iran's a rotten apple that'll drop into our hands.' " Watanabe was enraged. "I guarantee those dungeaters are shaking the tree with all their might."

"We beat them once," Kasigi said darkly, remembering the Japanese-Russian naval war of 1904 that his grandfather had served in. "We can do it again. That man—Muzadeh? Perhaps he's just a progressive and antimullah —they're not all fanatical Khomeinites."

"I agree, Kasigi-san. But some're equally fanatic for their god Lenin-Marx and equally stupid. But I'd bet long odds Muzadeh is one of those so-called intellectuals, an ex-French university student whose tuition was paid for by Shah grants, who was adopted, trained, and fawned on by left-wing teachers in France. I spent two years in the Sorbonne, doing a postgraduate degree. I know these intellectuals, these cretins and some of the teachers—they tried to induct me. Once wh—"

A short sharp burst of gunfire outside stopped him. For a moment both men were still, then they rushed for the window. Four stories down the ayatollah and Muzadeh were on the front steps. Below them in the forecourt one man was threatening them with an automatic rifle, standing alone in the middle of a semicircle of other armed men, the rest were scattered nearer to the trucks, some of them shouting and all hostile. Scragger was on the outskirts and as they watched they saw him ease into a better defensive position. The ayatollah raised his arms and exhorted them all. Watanabe could not hear what the man was saying. Carefully he opened a window and peered down.

"He's saying, 'In the Name of God give up your weapons, the Imam has ordered it—you've all heard his broadcast and message—I say again, obey him and give up your weapons!' "

There was more angry shouting and countershouting, men shaking their fists at one another. In the confusion they saw Scragger slip away and vanish behind a building. Watanabe leaned farther out, straining to hear better. "The man covering them with the gun . . . I can't see if he's wearing a green armband or not . . . ah, he isn't so he must be fedayeen or Tudeh . . ."

Now in the forecourt there was a great silence. Imperceptibly men began easing for a better position, all weapons armed, everyone eyeing his neighbor, all nerves jagged. The man covering the two of them raised his gun and bellowed at the ayatollah, "Order your men to put down their guns!"

Muzadeh stepped forward, not wanting a confrontation here, knowing he was outnumbered. "Stop it, Hassan! You will st—"

"We didn't fight and our brothers didn't die to give our guns and power to mullahs!"

"The government has power! The government!" Muzadeh raised his voice even more. "Everyone will keep their guns now but hand them into my office as I represent the new government and th—"

"You don't," the ayatollah shouted. "First, in the Name of God, all non-Islamic Guards will put their guns on the ground and go in peace. Second, the government is subject to the Revolutionary Komiteh under the direct guidance of the Imam, and this man Muzadeh is not yet confirmed so has no authority at all! Obey or you will be disarmed!"

"I am the government here!"

"You are not!"

"Allah-u Akbarrr!" someone shouted and pulled his trigger and Hassan, the youth in the center of them all, took the burst in his back and pirouetted in his death dance. At once other guns went off and men dived for cover or turned on their neighbor. The battle was short and vicious. Many died, but the men of Muzadeh were heavily outnumbered. The Green Bands were ruthless. Some of them had seized Muzadeh and now had him on his knees in the dirt, begging for mercy.

On the steps was the ayatollah. A spray of bullets had caught him in the chest and stomach and now he lay in a man's arms, blood marring his robes. A trickle of blood seeped from his mouth into his beard. "God is Great . . . God is Great . . ." he muttered, then let out a dribbling groan as pain took him.

"Master," the man holding him said, tears running down his cheeks, "tell God we tried to protect you, tell the Prophet."

"God . . . is . . . Great . . ." he murmured.

"What about this Muzadeh?" someone else asked. "What shall we do with him?"

"Do God's work. Kill him . . . kill him as you must kill all enemies of Islam. There is no other God but God . . ."

The order was obeyed instantly. Cruelly. The ayatollah died smiling, the Name of God on his lips. Others wept openly—envying him Paradise.

U.S.S.R.

Caspian Sea

U.S.S.R.

TURKEY

KHOI

TABRIZ

MOUNT
SABALAN

BANDAR-E
PAHLAVI

QAZVIN

★ TEHRAN

IRAQ

BAGHDAD

DEZ DAM

ZAGROS

IRAN

AFGHANISTAN

•ISFAHAN

BANDAR DELAM

Shatt-
al-Arab
Estuary

ABADAN

•ZAGROS THREE

◁ **KOWISS**

KUWAIT

KHARG

JELLET

Persian Gulf

ZAGROS

MOUNTAINS

LENGEH

Strait of
Hormuz

PAKISTAN

BAHRAIN

SAUDI
ARABIA

QATAR

SIRI

Gulf of Oman

AL SHARGAZ

AT KOWISS AIR FORCE BASE: 2:32 P.M. Manuela Starke was in the bungalow kitchen making chili. Country music filled the small room from a battery cassette player on the windowsill. On the butane stove was a big stewpot filled with stock and some of the makings, and as it came to a boil she turned the gas to simmer and glanced at her wristwatch to gauge the time. Just right, she thought. We'll eat around 7:00 P.M. and candles will make the table pretty.

There were onions and other things to chop and the goat meat to grind, so she continued happily, absently humming or doing a little dance step in time with the music. The kitchen was small and difficult to work in, unlike the huge, high-beamed kitchen in the lovely, old, sprawling Spanish hacienda in Lubbock that her family had had for almost a century, where she and her brother and sister had grown up. But she did not mind being cramped or cooking without the proper utensils. She was glad for something to do to take her mind off the question of when she would see her husband again.

It was Saturday that Conroe had left to go to Bandar Delam with the mullah, she thought, trying to reassure herself. Today's Tuesday, that's only three days and today's not even over yet. Last night he was on the HF. "Hi, honey, everything's fine here—no need to worry. Sorry, got to go—airtime's restricted for the moment, love you and see you soon," his voice so grand and confident but, even so, she was achingly sure she had heard a nervousness that had filled her mind and permeated her dreams. You're just imagining it. He'll be back soon—leave dreams to the night and work on your daydream that all is very fine. Concentrate on cooking!

She had brought the packets of chili powder with her from London, with extra spices and paprika and cayenne pepper and ginger, fresh garlic and dried chili peppers and dried beans and little else but some night things and toilet paper in the one tote bag that she had been allowed to carry aboard the 747. Chili makings because Starke adored Mexican food and particularly chili, and they both agreed that apart from curry, it was the only way to make goat meat palatable. No need to bring clothes or anything else with her because she still had some in their apartment in Tehran. The only other gift she had brought was a small bottle of Marmite that she knew Genny and Duncan McIver loved on the hot buttered toast made from the bread Genny would bake—when she could get the flour and the yeast.

Today Manuela had baked bread. The three loaves were in their baking dishes, cooling on the counter under muslin to keep the few flies off. Damn all flies, she thought. Flies destroy the summer, even in Lubbock . . . Ah Lubbock, wonder how the kids are.

Billyjoe and Conroe Junior and Sarita. Seven and five and three. Ah, my beauties, she thought happily. I'm so glad I sent you home to my daddy and our ten thousand acres to roam on, Granddaddy Starke nearby: "But wear your snake boots, y'hear now!" in that lovely rough so tender drawl of his.

"Texas forever," she said out loud and laughed at herself, her nimble fingers busy chopping and grinding and spooning, tasting the brew from time to time, adding a little more salt or garlic. Out of the window she saw Freddy Ayre crossing the little square to go up to their radio tower. With him was Pavoud, their chief clerk. He's a nice man, she thought. We're lucky to have loyal staff. Beyond them she could see the main runway and most of the base, snow-covered, the afternoon sky overcast, hiding the mountaintops. A few of their pilots and mechanics were absently kicking a football, Marc Dubois— who had flown the mullah back from Bandar Delam—among them.

Nothing else was going on here, just servicing aircraft, checking spares, painting—no flying since Sunday and the attack on the base. And the mutiny. Sunday evening three mutineers, one airmen and two sergeants from the tank regiment, had been court-martialed and, at dawn, shot. All day yesterday and today the base had been quiet. Once, yesterday, they had seen two fighters rush into the sky but no other flights which was strange as this was a training base and usually very busy. Nothing seemed to move. Just a few trucks, no tanks or parades—or visitors this side. In the night some firing and shouting that had soon died down again.

Critically she peered at herself in the mirror that hung on a hook over the sink that was filled with dirty pans and dishes and measuring spoons and cups. She moved her face this way and that and studied her figure, what she could see of it. "You're fine now, honey," she said to her reflection, "but you better haul ass and go ajogging and quit with the bread and the chili and wine and tostadas, burritos, tacos, and refried beans and Ma's pancakes dripping with homegrown honey, fried eggs, crisp bacon, and pan fries . . ."

The brew began to spit, distracting her. She turned the flame down a fraction, tasted the thickening reddish stew, still fiery from not enough cooking. "Man alive," she said with relish, "that's going to make Conroe happier'n a pig in wallah . . ." Her face changed. It would, she thought, if he was here. Never mind, the boys will like it just fine.

She began the washing up, but she could not divert her thoughts from Bandar Delam. She felt the tears welling. "Oh, shit! Get hold of yourself!"

"CASEVAC!" The faint shout outside startled her and she looked out of the window. The football had stopped. All the men were staring at Ayre who was running down the outside stairs of the tower, calling to them. She saw them crowd around him, then scatter. Ayre headed for her bungalow. Hastily she took off her apron, tidying her hair, brushed away her tears, and met him at the doorway.

"What is it, Freddy?"

He beamed. "Just thought I'd tell you their tower just got me on the blower and told me to ready a 212 for an immediate CASEVAC to Isfahan— they've got approval from IranOil."

"Isn't that kinda far?"

"Oh, no. It's just two hundred miles, a couple of hours—there's plenty of light. Marc'll overnight there and come back tomorrow." Again Ayre smiled. "Good to have something to do. Curiously, they asked for Marc to do it."

"Why him?"

"I don't know. Maybe because he's French and they're the ones who helped Khomeini. Well, got to go. Your chili smells great. Marc's peed off he's missing it." He walked off, heading for the office, tall and handsome.

She stood at the doorway. Mechanics were wheeling out a 212 from the hangar and Marc Dubois, zipping up his winter flight overalls, waved gaily as he hurried over to watch the flight check. Then she saw the procession of four cars approaching along the boundary road. So did Freddy Ayre. He frowned and went into the office. "Have you got the clearance ready, Mr. Pavoud?"

"Yes, Excellency." Pavoud handed it to him.

Ayre did not notice the tension in the man, nor that his hands were shaking. "Thanks. You'd better come too in case it's all in Farsi."

"But, Excell—"

"Come on!" Buttoning his flight jacket against the breeze, Ayre hurried out. Pavoud wiped his sweating palms. The other Iranians watched him, equally anxious.

"As God wants," one of them said, blessing God it was Pavoud, not him.

At the 212 the ground check continued. Ayre arrived as the cars arrived. His smile vanished. The cars were crammed with armed men, Green Bands, and they fanned out around the chopper, a few uniformed airmen among them.

The mullah Hussain Kowissi got out of the front seat of the lead car, his turban very white and his dark robes new, his boots old and well used. Over his shoulder was his AK47. Clearly he was in command. Other men opened the back doors of the first car and half pulled Colonel Peshadi out, then his wife. Peshadi shouted at them, cursing them, and they backed off a little. He straightened his uniform greatcoat and braided, peaked cap. His wife wore a heavy winter coat and gloves and a little hat and shoulder bag. Her face was white and drawn but, like her husband, she held her head high and proudly. She reached back into the car for a small tote bag but one of the Green Bands grabbed it, and after a slight hesitation handed it to her.

Ayre tried to keep the shock off his face. "What's going on, sir?"

"We're . . . we're being sent to Isfahan under guard! Under guard! My base . . . my base was betrayed and is in the hands of mutineers!" The colonel did not keep the fury off his face as he whirled on Hussain, in Farsi: "I say again, what has my wife to do with this? EH?" he added with a roar. One of the nervous Green Bands nearby shoved a rifle into his back. Without looking around the colonel smashed the rifle away. "Son of a whore dog!"

"Stop!" Hussain said in Farsi. "It is orders from Isfahan. I've shown you the orders that you and your wife are to be sent at once t—"

"Orders? A dung filthy piece of paper scrawled in an illegible illiterate handwriting and signed by an ayatollah I've never heard of?"

Hussain walked over to him. "Get aboard, both of you," he warned, "or I'll have you dragged there!"

"When the aircraft is ready!" Contemptuously the colonel took out a cigarette. "Give me a light," he ordered the man nearest to him, and when the man hesitated, he snarled, "Are you deaf? A light!"

The man smiled wryly and found some matches, and all those around nodded approval, even the mullah, admiring courage in the face of death—courage in the face of hell, for surely this man was a Shah man and headed for hell. Of course hell! Didn't you hear him shout, "Long live the Shah," only hours ago when, in the night, we invaded and took possession of the camp and his fine house, helped by all the base's soldiers and airmen and some of the officers, the rest of the officers now in cells? God is Great! It was the Will of God, God's miracle that the generals caved in like the walls of shit the mullahs told us they were. The Imam was right again, God protect him.

Hussain went over to Ayre who was rigid, appalled by what was going on, trying to understand, Marc Dubois beside him, equally shocked, the ground check stopped. "Salaam," the mullah said trying to be polite. "You have nothing to fear. The Imam has ordered everything back to normal."

"Normal?" Ayre echoed angrily. "That's Colonel Peshadi, tank commander, hero of your expeditionary force sent to Oman to help put down a Marxist-supported rebellion and invasion from South Yemen!" That had been in '73 when the Shah was asked for help by Oman's sultan. "Hasn't Colonel Peshadi got the Zolfaghar, your highest medal given only for gallantry in battle?"

"Yes. But now Colonel Peshadi is needed to answer questions concerning crimes against the Iranian people and against the laws of God! Salaam, Captain Dubois, I'm glad that you're going to fly us."

"I was asked to fly a CASEVAC. This isn't a CASEVAC," Dubois said.

"It's a casualty evacuation—the colonel and his wife are to be evacuated to Command Headquarters in Isfahan." Hussain added with a sardonic smile, "Perhaps they are casualties."

Ayre said, "Sorry, our aircraft are under license to IranOil. We can't do what you ask."

The mullah turned and shouted, "Excellency Esvandiary!"

Kuram Esvandiary, or "Hotshot" as he was nicknamed, was in his early thirties, popular with the expats, very efficient, and S-G trained—he had had two years of training at S-G HQ at Aberdeen on a Shah grant. He came from the back and, for a moment, not one of the S-G men recognized their station manager. Normally he was a meticulous dresser and clean-shaven, but now he

had three or four days' growth of heavy beard, and wore rough clothes with a
green armband, slouch hat, an M16 slung over his shoulder. "The trip's
sanctioned, here," he said, giving Ayre the usual forms, "I've signed them
and they're stamped."

"But, Hotshot, surely you realize this isn't a legitimate CASEVAC?"

"My name's Esvandiary—Mr. Esvandiary," he said without a smile and
Ayre flushed. "And it's a legitimate order from IranOil who employ you
under contract here in Iran." His face hardened. "If you refuse a legitimate
order in good flying conditions, you're breaking your contract. If you do that
without cause then we've the right to seize all assets, aircraft, hangars, spares,
houses, equipment, and order you out of Iran at once."

"You can't do that."

"I'm IranOil's chief representative here now," Esvandiary said curtly.
"IranOil's owned by the government. The Revolutionary Komiteh under the
leadership of the Imam Khomeini, peace be upon him, is the government.
Read your IranOil contract—also the contract between S-G and Iran Helicopters. Are you flying the charter or refusing to?"

Ayre held on to his temper. "What about . . . what about Prime Minister Bakhtiar and the gov—"

"Bakhtiar?" Esvandiary and the mullah stared at him. "Haven't you heard
yet? He's resigned and fled, the generals capitulated yesterday morning, the
Imam and the Revolutionary Komiteh are Iran's government now."

Ayre and Dubois and those expats nearby gaped at him. The mullah said
something in Farsi they did not understand. His men laughed.

"Capitulated?" was all Ayre could say.

"It was the Will of God the generals came to their senses," Hussain said,
his eyes glittering. "They were arrested, the whole General Staff. All of them.
As all enemies of Islam will be arrested now. We got Nassiri too—you've
heard of him?" the mullah asked witheringly. Nassiri was the hated head of
SAVAK whom the Shah had arrested a few weeks ago and who was in jail
awaiting trial. "Nassiri was found guilty of crimes against humanity and shot
—along with three other generals, Rahimi, martial law governor of Tehran,
Naji, governor general of Isfahan, Paratrooper Commander Khosrowdad.
You're wasting time. Are you flying or not?"

Ayre was barely able to think. If what they say is true, then Peshadi and his
wife are as good as dead. It's all so fast, all so impossible. "We . . . of course
we will fly a . . . a legal charter. Just exactly what is it you want?"

"To transport His Excellency mullah Hussain Kowissi to Isfahan at once—
with his personnel. At once," Esvandiary interrupted impatiently, "with the
prisoner and his wife."

"They're . . . Colonel and Mrs. Peshadi're not on the manifest."

Even more impatiently Esvandiary ripped the paper out of his hands, wrote on it. "Now they are!" He motioned past Ayre and Dubois to where Manuela was standing in the background, her hair carefully tucked into a hat, wearing overalls. He had noticed her the moment he had arrived—enticing as always, unsettling as always. "I should arrest her for illegal trespass," he said, his voice raw. "She has no right on this base—there are no married quarters, nor're any allowed by base and S-G rules."

Over by the 212, Colonel Peshadi angrily shouted in English, "Are you flying today or not? We're getting cold. Hurry it up, Ayre—I want to spend as little time as possible with these vermin!"

Esvandiary and the mullah flushed. Ayre called back, feeling better for the man's bravery, "Yes, sir. Sorry. Okay, Marc?"

"Yes." To Esvandiary, Dubois said, "Where's my military clearance?"

"Attached to the manifest. Also for your return trip tomorrow." Esvandiary added in Farsi to the mullah: "I suggest you board, Excellency."

The mullah walked off. Guards motioned Peshadi and his wife aboard. Heads high, they went up the steps without faltering. Armed men piled in after them and the mullah took the front left seat beside Dubois.

"Wait a minute," Ayre began, now over the shock. "We're not flying armed men. It's against the rules—yours and ours!"

Esvandiary shouted an order, jerked a thumb at Manuela. At once four armed men surrounded her. Others moved much closer to Ayre. "Now, give Dubois a thumbs-up!"

Grimly aware of the danger, Ayre obeyed. Dubois acknowledged and started up. Quickly he was airborne. "Now into the office," Esvandiary said above the howl of the engines. He called the men off Manuela and ordered them back into the cars. "Leave one car here and four guards—I have more orders for these foreigners. You," he added toughly to Pavoud, "you get an up-to-date on all aircraft here, all spares, all transport, as well as the quantity of gasoline, also numbers of personnel, foreign and Iranians, their names, jobs, passport numbers, residence permits, work permits, flying licenses. Understand?"

"Yes, yes, Excellency Esvandiary. Yes, cert—"

"And I want to see all passports and permits tomorrow. Get busy!"

The man left hurriedly. Esvandiary was bowed through the front door. He led the way into Starke's office and took the main chair and sat behind the desk, Ayre following him. "Sit down."

"Thanks, you're so kind," Ayre said witheringly, taking the chair opposite him. The two men were of an age and they watched each other.

The Iranian took out a cigarette and lit it. "This will be my office from now on," he said. "Now that at long last Iran is back in Iranian hands we can begin to make the necessary changes. For the next two weeks you will operate under my personal guidance until I am sure the new way is understood. I am the top IranOil authority for Kowiss and I'll issue all flight permits; no one takes off without written approval and always with an armed guard an—"

"It's against air law and Iranian law and it's forbidden. Apart from that it's bloody dangerous. Finish!"

There was a big silence. Then Esvandiary nodded. "You will carry guards who will have guns—but no ammunition." He smiled. "There, you see, we can compromise. We can be reasonable, oh, yes. You'll see, the new era will be good for you too."

"I hope it is. For you too."

"Meaning?"

"Meaning every revolution I've ever read about always begins by feeding off itself, friends quickly become enemies and even quicker die."

"Not with us." Esvandiary was totally confident. "It won't be that way with us. Ours was a real people's revolution—of all the people. Everyone wanted the Shah out—and his foreign masters."

"I hope you're right." You poor bastard, Ayre thought, once having liked him. If your leaders can judge, condemn, and shoot four top generals—all good men except for Nassiri—in less than twenty-four hours, can arrest and abuse fine patriots like Peshadi and his wife, God help you. "Are you finished with me for the present?"

"Almost." A shaft of anger went through Esvandiary. Through the windows he noticed Manuela walking back to the bungalow with some of the pilots, and his lust increased his rage. "It would be good to learn manners and that Iran is an Asian, an Oriental country, a world power and never, never again to be exploited by British, Americans, or even Soviets. Never again." He slouched in his chair and put his feet on the desk as he had seen Starke and Ayre do a hundred times, the soles of his feet toward Ayre, always an insult in this part of the world. "British were worse than the Americans. They've caused us national shame for a hundred and fifty years, treating our ancient Peacock Throne and country as their private fief, using the defense of India as an excuse. They've dictated to our rulers, occupied us three times, forced unequal treaties on us, bribed our leaders to grant them concessions. For a hundred and fifty years British and Russians have partitioned my country, the British helped those other hyenas to steal our northern provinces, our Caucasus, and helped put Reza Khan on the throne. They occupied us, with the Soviets, in your world war and only our own supreme efforts broke the chain and threw them out." Abruptly the man's face contorted and he screamed, "Didn't they?"

Ayre had not moved, nor had his eyes flickered. "Hotshot, and I'll never call you that again," he said quietly, "I don't want lectures, just to do the job. If we can't work out a satisfactory method, then that's something else. We'll have to see. If you want this office, jolly good. If you want to act up a storm, jolly good—within reason—you've a right to celebrate. You've won, you've the guns, you've the power, and now you're responsible. And you're right, it is your country. So let's leave it at that. Eh?"

Esvandiary stared at him, his head aching with the suppressed hatred of years that need never be suppressed again. And though he knew it was not Ayre's fault, he was equally certain that a moment ago he would have sprayed him and them with bullets if they had not obeyed and flown the mullah and the traitor Peshadi to the judgment and the hell he deserves. I've not forgotten the soldier Peshadi had murdered—the one who wanted to open the gate to us—or the others murdered two days ago when Peshadi beat us off and hundreds died, my brother and two of my best friends among them. And all the other hundreds, thousands, perhaps tens of thousands who've died all over Iran . . . I've not forgotten them, not one.

A dribble of saliva was running down his chin and he wiped it away with the back of his hand and got his control back, remembering the importance of his mission. "All right, Freddy." He said "Freddy" involuntarily. "All right, and that's . . . that's the last time I'll call you that. All right, we'll leave it at that."

He got up, very tired now but proud of the way he had dominated them and very confident he could make these foreigners work and behave until they were expelled. Very soon now, he thought. I'll have no difficulty putting the partners' long-term plan into effect here. I agree with Valik. We've plenty of Iranian pilots and we need no foreigners here. I can run this operation—as a partner—praise God that Valik was always a secret Khomeini supporter! Soon I'll have a big house in Tehran and my two sons will go to university there, so will my darling little Fatmeh, though perhaps she should also go to the Sorbonne for a year or two.

"I'll return at 9:00 A.M." He did not close the door behind him.

"Bloody hell," Ayre muttered. A fly began battering itself against a windowpane. He did not notice it or the noise it made. At a sudden thought he went into the outer office. Pavoud and the others were at the windows, watching the aliens leave. "Pavoud!"

"Yes . . . yes, Excellency?"

Ayre noticed the man's face had a grayish tinge and he looked much older than usual. "Did you know about the generals, that they've given in?" he asked, feeling sorry for him.

"No, Excellency," Pavoud lied easily, used to lying. He was locked in his own mind, trying to remember, petrified that he might have slipped up in the past three years and given himself away to Esvandiary, never for a moment dreaming that the man could have been a secret Islamic Guard. "We'd . . . we'd heard rumors about their capitulation—but you know how rumors circulate."

"Yes—yes, I suppose you're right."

"I . . . do you mind if I sit down, please?" Pavoud groped for a chair, feeling very old. He had been sleeping badly this last week and the two-mile bicycle ride here this morning from the little four-room house in Kowiss he shared with his brother's family—five adults and six children—had been more tiring than usual. Of course he and all the people of Kowiss had heard about the generals meekly giving up—the first news coming from the mosque, spread by the mullah Hussain who said he had got it by secret radio from Khomeini Headquarters in Tehran so it must be true.

At once their Tudeh leader had called a meeting, all of them astounded at the generals' cowardice: "It just shows how foul the influence of the Americans who betrayed them and so bewitched them that they've castrated themselves and committed suicide, for of course they've all got to die whether we do it or that madman Khomeini!"

Everyone filled with resolve, at the same time frightened of the coming battle against the zealots and the mullahs, the opiate of the people, and Pavoud himself was wet with relief when the leader said they were ordered not to take to the streets yet but to stay hidden and wait, wait until the order came for the general uprising. "Comrade Pavoud, it's vital you keep on the best of terms with the foreign pilots at the air base. We will need them and their helicopters—or will need to inhibit their use to the enemies of the People. Our orders are to lie low and wait, to have patience. When we finally get the order to take to the streets against Khomeini, our comrades to the north will come over the border in legions . . ."

He saw Ayre watching him. "I'm all right, Captain, just worried by all this, and the . . . the new era."

"Just do what Esvandiary asks." Ayre thought a moment. "I'm going to the tower to let HQ know what's happened. Are you sure you're all right?"

"Yes, yes, thank you."

Ayre frowned, then went along the corridor and up the stairs. The astonishing change in Esvandiary who for years had been affable, friendly, with never a glimmer of anti-British had rocked him. For the first time in Iran he felt their future was doomed.

To his surprise the tower room was empty. Since Sunday's mutiny there had been a permanent guard—Major Changiz had shrugged, blood on his uniform, "I'm sure you'll understand, 'national emergency.' We had many loyal men killed here today and we haven't found all traitors—yet. Until further orders you will transmit only during daylight hours, then absolute minimum. All flights are canceled until further notice."

"All right, Major. By the way, where's our radio op, Massil?"

"Ah, yes, the Palestinian. He's being interrogated."

"May I ask what for?"

"PLO affiliation and terrorist activities."

Yesterday he had been informed that Massil had confessed and been shot —without a chance to hear the evidence or question it or to see him. Poor bastard, Ayre thought, closing the tower door now and switching on the equipment. Massil was always loyal to us and grateful for the job, so over-qualified—radio engineering degree from Cairo University, top of the class but nowhere to practice and stateless. Bloody hell! We take our passports for granted—what'd it be like to be without one and to be, say, Palestinian? Must be hairy not to know what's going to happen at every border, with every Immigration man, policeman, bureaucrat, or employer a potential inquisitor.

Thank God in heaven I'm born British and that not even the queen of England can take that away though the bloody Labour Government's changing our overseas heritage. Well the pox on them for every Aussie, Canuck, Kiwi, Springbok, Kenyan, China hand, and a hundred other Britishers who will soon have to have a bloody visa to go home! "Arseholes," he muttered. "Don't they realize those're sons and daughters of men who made the empire and died for it in many cases?"

He waited for the HF and other radios to warm up. The hum pleased him, red and green lights flickering, and he no longer felt locked off from the world. Hope Angela and young Fredrick are okay. Bloody, having no mail or phones and a dead telex. Well, maybe soon everything will be working again.

He reached for the sending switch, hoping that McIver or someone would be listening out. Then he noticed that, by habit, along with the UHF, HF, he had switched on their radar. He leaned over to turn it off. At that moment a small blip appeared on the outer rim—the twenty-mile line—to the north-west, almost obscured among the heavy scatter of the mountains. Startled, he studied it. Experience told him quickly that it was a helicopter. He made sure that he was tuned into all receiving frequencies and when he looked back he saw the blip vanish. He waited. It did not reappear. Either she's down, shot down, or sneaking under the radar net, he thought. Which?

The seconds ticked by. No change, just the revolving, heavy white line of the sweep, in its wake a bird's-eye view of the surrounding terrain. Still no sign of the blip.

His fingers snapped on the UHF sending switch, and he brought the mike closer, hesitated, then changed his mind and switched it off. No need to alert the operators in the base tower, if there're any on duty there, he thought. He frowned at the screen. With a soft, red grease pencil he marked the possible track inbound at eighty knots. Minutes passed. He could have switched to a closer range scan but he did not in case the blip was not inbound but, highly irregularly, sneaking across their area.

Now she should be five or six miles out, he thought. He picked up the binoculars and started to scan the sky, north through west to south. His ears heard light footsteps on the last few stairs. His heart quickening, he snapped the radar off. The screen began dying as the door opened.

"Captain Ayre?" the airman asked, uniform neat, strong good Persian face, clean-shaven, in his late twenties, a standard U.S. Army carbine in his hands.

"Yes, yes, that's me."

"I'm Sergeant Wazari, your new air traffic controller." The man leaned his carbine against a wall, put out his hand, and Ayre shook it. "Hi, I'm USAAF trained, three years, and a military controller. I even did six months at Van Nuys Airport." His eyes had taken in all the equipment. "Nice setup."

"Yes, er, yes, thank you." Ayre fumbled with the binoculars and set them down. "What, er, happens at Van Nuys Airport?"

"It's a nothing little airstrip in the San Fernando Valley in Los Angeles but the third busiest airport in the States and a mother to end all mothers!" Wazari beamed. "The traffic's amateur, most of the jokers're learners who still don't know their ass from a propeller, you've maybe twenty in the system at any one time, eight on final, all wanting to make like Richthofen." He laughed. "Great place to learn traffic controlling but after six months you're ape."

Ayre forced a smile, willing himself not to search the sky. "This place's pretty quiet. Even normally. We've, er, we've no flights out as you know—you've nothing to do here, I'm afraid."

"Sure. I just wanted to take a quick look as we begin bright and early tomorrow." He reached into his uniform pocket and took out a list and gave it to Ayre. "You've three flights scheduled for the local rigs starting 8:00 A.M., okay?" Without thinking he picked up a rag and wiped the inbound track off the radar screen, tidying the desk alongside. The red grease pencil went into its holder with the others.

Ayre looked back at the list. "Are these authorized by Esvandiary?"

"Who's he?"

Ayre told him.

The sergeant laughed. "Well, Captain, Major Changiz personally ordered these so you can bet your ass they're confirmed."

"He's . . . he wasn't arrested with the colonel?"

"Hell, no, Captain. The mullah, Hussain Kowissi, appointed Major Changiz temp base commander, pending confirm from Tehran." Unerringly his fingers switched channels to the MainBase Frequency. "Hello, MainBase, this's Wazari at S-G. Do we need tomorrow's flights countersigned by Iran-Oil's Esvandiary?"

"Negative," came back over the loudspeaker, again American-accented. "Everything okay over there?"

"Yep. The outbound went off without incident. I'm with Captain Ayre now." The sergeant scanned the sky as he talked.

"Good. Captain Ayre, this's the senior traffic controller. Any flights authorized by Major Changiz are automatically approved by IranOil."

"Can I have that in writing please?"

"Sergeant Wazari'll have it for you in duplicate at 8:00 A.M., okay?"

"Thanks—thank you."

"Thanks, MainBase," Wazari said, beginning to sign off, then his eyes fixed. "Hold it, MainBase, we've got a bird inbound! Chopper, 270 degrees. . . ."

"Where? Where . . . I see him! How the hell did he get in under the radar? You switched on?"

"Negative. The sergeant trained the binoculars. "Bell 212, registration . . . can't see it—she's head-on to us." He clicked on the UHF. "This is Kowiss Military Control! Inbound chopper, what is your registration, where are you bound, and what was your point of departure?"

Silence but for the crackle of static. The same call repeated by MainBase. No reply.

"That sonofabitch's in dead trouble," Wazari muttered. Again he trained the binoculars.

Ayre had the second set and his heart was thumping. As the chopper joined the landing pattern, he read the registration: EP-HBX.

"Echo Peter Hotel Boston X-ray!" the sergeant said simultaneously.

"HBX," MainBase agreed. Again they tried radio contact. No reply. "He's

in your regular landing pattern. Is he a local? Captain Ayre, is he one of
yours?"

"No, sir, not one of mine, not based here." Ayre added carefully, "HBX
could be an S-G registration, however."

"Based where?"

"I don't know."

"Sergeant, as soon as that joker lands, arrest him and all passengers, send
them over here to HQ under guard, then give me a quick report who why
and where from."

"Yessir."

Thoughtfully Wazari selected a red grease pencil and traced the same line
on the radar screen that Ayre had drawn and he had wiped out. He stared at
it a moment, knowing Ayre was watching him intently. But he said nothing,
just wiped the glass clean again and put his attention back to the 212.

In silence the two men in the tower watched her make a normal circuit
then break off correctly and head for them. But she made no attempt to land,
just stayed at the correct height and made a much smaller circuit, waggling
from side to side.

"Radio's out—he wants a Green," Ayre said, and reached for a signal light.
"Okay?"

"Sure, give him one—but his ass's still in a wringer."

Ayre checked that the powerful, narrow-beamed signal light was set for
Green, permission to land. He aimed it at the chopper and switched on. The
chopper acknowledged by waggling from side to side and started the approach. Wazari picked up his carbine and went out. Again Ayre trained his
binoculars but still could not recognize the pilot or the man beside him, both
muffled in winter gear and goggles. Then he rushed down the stairs.

Other S-G personnel, pilots and mechanics, had gathered to watch. From
the direction of the main base, a car was speeding their way along the boundary road. Manuela stood in the doorway of the bungalow. The landing pads
were in front of the office building. Crouched in the lee were the four Green
Bands who had stayed behind, Wazari now with them. Ayre noticed that one
was very young, barely a teenager, fiddling with his machine gun. In his
excitement, cocking it, the youth dropped it on the tarmac, the gun pointing
directly at Ayre. But it did not go off. As he watched, the youth picked it up
by the barrel, banged the butt down to knock the snow off, carelessly shoved
more snow away from the trigger guard. Some grenades hung from his belt—
by the pins. Hastily Ayre joined some of the mechanics taking cover.

"Bloody nit!" one of them said queasily. "He'll blow himself to hell and us along with him. You all right, Cap'n? We heard Hotshot's got his knickers in a twist."

"Yes, yes, he has. HBX, where's she from, Benson?"

"Bandar Delam," Benson replied. He was a ruddy-faced, rotund Englishman. "Fifty quid it's Duke."

As the 212 put her skids down and cut her engines, Wazari led the rush, some of the guards shouting, "Allah-u Akbarrr!" They surrounded her, all guns leveled.

"Bloody twits," Ayre said nervously, "they're like Keystone Kops."

He still couldn't see the pilot clearly, so he walked out of cover, praying that it was Starke. The cabin doors slid back. Armed men jumped down, careless of the rotors that still circled, shouting greetings, telling the others to put down their guns. In the pandemonium, someone excitedly fired a welcoming burst into the air. Momentarily everyone began to scatter, then with more shouts, regrouped around the doors as the car arrived and more men rushed to join the others. Hands helped a mullah down. He was badly wounded. Then a stretcher. Then more wounded and Ayre saw Wazari running for him.

"You got medics here?" he said urgently.

"Yes." Ayre turned and cupped his hands around his mouth. "Benson, get Doc and the medic on the double," then to the sergeant, hurrying back with him, "What the hell's going on?"

"They're from Bandar Delam—there was a counterrevolution there, goddamn fedayeen . . ."

Ayre saw the pilot's door open and Starke get out, and he didn't hear the rest of what Wazari said and hurried forward. "Hello, Duke, old chap." Deliberately he kept his face set and his voice flat, though so happy and excited inside that he felt he would burst. "Where've you been?"

Starke grinned, used to the English understatement. "Fishing, old chap," he said. All at once Manuela came charging through the crowd and was in his arms, hugging him. He lifted her easily and whirled her. "Why, honey," he drawled. "Ah guess ya like me after all!"

She was half crying and half laughing and she hung on. "Oh, Conroe, when I saw you I liked to die . . ."

"We damn near did, honey," Starke said involuntarily, but she had not heard him and he hugged her once for luck and put her down. "Just set there for a bitty while I get things organized. Come on, Freddy."

He led the way through the crush. The wounded mullah was on the ground, leaning against a skid, semiconscious. The man on the stretcher was already dead. "Put the mullah on his stretcher," Starke ordered in Farsi. The

Green Bands he had brought in the 212 obeyed at once. Wazari, the only one in uniform here, and the others from the base were astonished—none of them aware of Zataki, the Sunni revolutionary leader who had taken command of Bandar Delam, who now leaned against the helicopter, watching carefully, camouflaged by the S-G flight jacket he wore.

"Let me have a look, Duke," the doctor said, out of breath from hurrying, a stethoscope around his neck, "so happy to have you back." Dr. Nutt was in his fifties, too heavy, with sparse hair and a drinker's nose. He knelt beside the mullah and began examining his chest that was wet with blood. "We'd better get him to the infirmary, quick as poss. And the rest."

Starke told two of those nearby to pick up the stretcher and follow the doctor. Again he was obeyed without question by men he had brought with him—the other Green Bands stared at him. Now there were nine of them, including Wazari and the four who had stayed.

"You're under arrest," Wazari said.

Starke looked at him. "What for?"

Wazari hesitated. "Orders from the brass, Captain, I just work here."

"So do I. I'll be here if they want to talk to me, Sergeant." Starke smiled reassuringly at Manuela who had gone white. "You go back to the house, honey. Nothing to worry about." He turned away and went closer to the side door to look inside.

"Sorry, Captain, but you're under arrest. Get in the car. You're to go to the base pronto."

When Starke turned he was looking into the nozzle of the gun. Two Green Bands jumped him from behind, grabbed his arms, pinioning him. Ayre lunged forward but one of the Green Bands shoved a gun in his stomach, stopping him. The two men started dragging Starke toward the car. Others came to help as he struggled, cursing them. Manuela watched panic-stricken.

Then there was a bellow of rage and Zataki burst through the cordon, dragged the carbine from Sergeant Wazari, and swung it at his head, butt first. Only Wazari's great reflexes, boxing trained, moved his head away just in time and backed him out of reach. Before he could say anything Zataki shouted, "What's this dog doing with a gun? Haven't you fools heard that the Imam ordered all servicemen disarmed?"

Wazari began hotly, "Listen, I'm authorized t—" He stopped in panic. Now there was a pistol at his throat.

"You're not even authorized to shit till the local komiteh clears you," Zataki said. He was neater than before, clean-shaven now, his features well-made. "Have you been cleared by the komiteh?"

"No . . . no bu—"

"Then by God and the Prophet you're suspect!" Zataki kept the gun hard against Wazari's throat, then waved his other hand. "Let the pilot go and put your arms down, or by God and the Prophet I'll kill you all!" The moment he had grabbed Wazari's gun, his men had circled the others and now had them covered from behind. Nervously, the two men pinioning Starke let him go.

"Why should we obey you?" one of them said sullenly. "Eh? Who are you to give us orders?"

"I'm Colonel Zataki, member of the Revolutionary Komiteh of Bandar Delam, thanks be to God. The American helped save us from a fedayeen counterattack and brought the mullah and others who need medical help here." Suddenly his rage broke. He shoved Wazari and the sergeant sprawled helplessly on the ground. "Leave the pilot alone! Didn't you hear?" He aimed and pulled the trigger and the bullet tore through the neck of the sheepskin vest of one of the men beside Starke. Manuela almost fainted and they all scattered. "Next time I'll put it between your eyes! You," he snarled at Wazari, "you're under arrest. I think you're a traitor so we'll find out. The rest of you go with God, tell your komiteh I would be pleased to see them— here."

He waved them away. The men started muttering among themselves, and in the lull Ayre slipped over to Manuela and put his arm around her. "Hang in there," he whispered. "It's all right now." He saw Starke motion them away. He nodded. "Come on, Duke says to leave."

"No . . . please, Freddy, I'm . . . I'm okay, promise." She forced a smile and continued praying that the man with the pistol would dominate the others and all this would end. Please God, let it end.

They all watched in silence while Zataki waited, the pistol loose in his hand, the sergeant on the ground near his feet, those opposing him glaring at him, Starke standing in the middle of them, not at all sure that Zataki would win. Zataki checked the magazine. "Go with God, all of you," he said again, harder this time, getting angrier. "Are you all still deaffff?"

Reluctantly they left. The sergeant got up, pasty-faced, and straightened his uniform. Ayre watched Wazari bravely trying to hide his terror.

"You stand there and stay there till I say to move." Zataki glanced at Starke who was watching Manuela. "Pilot, we should finish the unloading. Then my men must eat."

"Yes. And thank you."

"Nothing. These people did not know—they are not to be blamed." Again he looked at Manuela, dark eyes piercing. "Your woman, pilot?" he asked.

"My wife," Starke replied.

"My wife is dead, killed in the Abadan fire with my two sons. It was the Will of God."

"Sometimes the Will of God is unendurable."

"The Will of God is the Will of God. We should finish the unloading."

"Yes." Starke climbed into the cabin, the danger only over for the moment as Zataki was as volatile as nitroglycerin. Two more wounded were still strapped in their seats as were two stretcher cases. He knelt beside one of them. "How you doing, old buddy?" he said softly in English.

Jon Tyrer opened his eyes and winced, a bloody bandage around his head. "Okay . . . yeah, okay. What . . . what happened?"

"Can you see?"

Tyrer seemed surprised. He peered up at Starke, then rubbed his eyes and forehead. To Starke's relief, he said, "Sure, it's . . . you're a bit soft focus and my head aches like hell but I can see you okay. Course I can see you, Duke. What the hell happened?"

"During the fedayeen counterattack at dawn this morning you were caught in some crossfire, a bullet creased the side of your head, and when you got up you started running around in circles like a headless chicken, crying out, 'I can't see . . . I can't see.' Then you collapsed and you've been out ever since."

"Ever since? Goddamn!" The American peered out of the cabin door. "Where the hell are we?"

"Kowiss—I thought I'd better get you and the rest here fast."

Tyrer was still astonished. "I remember nothing. Nothing. Fedayeens? For crissake, Duke, I don't even remember being brought aboard."

"Hang in there, old buddy. I'll explain later." He turned and called out, "Freddy, get someone to carry Jon Tyrer to the doc," adding, in Farsi, to Zataki who watched from the doorway, "Excellency Zataki, please ask men to carry your men to the infirmary." He paused a moment. "My second-in-command, Captain Ayre, will make arrangements for feeding everyone. Would you like to eat with me—in my house?"

Zataki smiled strangely and shook his head. "Thank you, pilot," he said in English. "I will eat with my men. This evening we should talk, you and I."

"Whenever you wish." Starke jumped out of the cabin. Men began carrying away all the wounded. He pointed at his bungalow. "That is my house, you are welcome there, Excellency."

Zataki thanked him and went away, shoving Sergeant Wazari in front of him.

Ayre and Manuela joined Starke. She took his hand. "When he pulled the trigger, I thought . . ." she smiled weakly, switched to Farsi. "Ah, Beloved, how good the day has become now that you are safe and beside me."

"And thee beside me." Starke smiled at her.

"What happened? At Bandar Delam?" she asked in English.

"There was a goddamn battle between Zataki and his men and about fifty leftists at the base—yesterday Zataki took over our base in the name of Khomeini and the revolution—I had a bit of a run-in with him when I first got there but now he's kinda okay, though he's psycho, dangerous as a rattler. Anyway at dawn the leftist fedayeen rushed the airport in trucks and on foot. Zataki was asleep with the rest of his men, no sentries out, nothing—you heard the generals capitulated and Khomeini's now warlord?"

"Yes, we've just heard actually."

"The first I knew of the attack was all hell let loose, bullets everywhere, coming through the walls of the trailers. Me, you know me, I ducked for cover and scrambled out of the trailer . . . You cold, honey?"

"No, no darlin'. Let's go home—I could use a drink too . . . oh, my God . . ."

"What is it?"

But she was already running for the house. "The chili—I left the chili on the stove!"

"Jesus Christ!" Ayre muttered, "I thought we were about to be shot or something."

Starke was beaming. "We got chili?"

"Yes. Bandar Delam?"

"Not much to tell, Freddy." They started walking for the house. "I evacuated the trailer—I think the attackers figured Zataki and his men would be sleeping in them but Zataki had everyone bedded down in hangars guarding the choppers—Freddy, they're goddamn paranoid about choppers, that we're gonna fly away in them, or use them to fly out SAVAK, generals, or enemies of the revolution. Anyway, old Rudi and me, we had our heads down in back of a spare mud tank, then some of these new bastards—you couldn't tell one from another except Zataki's guys were shouting 'Allah-u Akbar' as they died —some of the fedayeen opened up with a Sten gun on the hangars just as Jon Tyrer was evacuating his trailer. I saw him go down and I got as mad as a sonofabitch—now don't you tell Manuela—and got a gun away from one of them and started my own little war to go get Jon. Rudi . . ." Starke started smiling. "That one's a sonofabitch! Rudi got himself a gun too and we were like Butch Cassidy and the Sundance Kid . . ."

"God Almighty, you must've been crazy!"

Starke nodded. "We were, but we got Jon out of the line of fire and then

Zataki and three of his guys broke out of a hangar and charged the main group, firing like the Wild Bunch. But hell, they ran out of ammo. Poor bastards just stood there and you've never seen anyone nakeder." He shrugged. "Rudi and I thought what the hell, shooting a sitting duck's not fair and Zataki'd been okay once the mullah—Hussain—had left, and we'd, er, come to an agreement. So we let off a burst over the attackers' heads and that gave Zataki and the others time to get to cover." Again he shrugged. "That's about it," he said. They were near the bungalow now. He sniffed the air. "We really got chili, Freddy?"

"Yes—unless it's burned. That's all that happened?"

"Sure, except when the shooting stopped I thought we'd best head for Kowiss and Doc Nutt. The mullah looked rough and I was scared for Jon. Zataki said, 'Sure, why not, I need to go to Isfahan'—so here we are. The radio went out en route—I could hear you but couldn't transmit. No sweat."

Ayre watched him sniff the air again, knowing that a psychopath like Zataki would never give Starke the authority he had given him—or protect him—for so little assistance.

The Texan opened the bungalow door. At once the grand, spicy smell surrounded him, transporting him home to Texas, God's country, and a thousand meals. Manuela had a drink poured for him, the way he liked it. But he did not drink it, just went into the kitchen area and picked up the big wooden spoon and tasted the brew. Manuela watched, hardly breathing. A second taste.

"How 'bout that?" he said happily. The chili was the best he had ever had.

U.S.S.R.

TURKEY

KHOI

TABRIZ

MOUNT
SABALAN

Caspian Sea

BANDAR-E
PAHLAVI

U.S.S.R.

AFGHANISTAN

QAZVIN

★ TEHRAN

IRAQ

BAGHDAD
★

IRAN

ZAGROS

•ISFAHAN

DEZ DAM O

BANDAR DELAM

Shatt-
al-Arab
Estuary

ABADAN

•ZAGROS THREE

•KOWISS

MOUNTAINS

KUWAIT

KHARG

JELLET

Persian Gulf

LENGEH

Strait of
Hormuz

PAKISTAN

BAHRAIN

SAUDI
ARABIA

QATAR

SIRI

Gulf of Oman

AL SHARGAZ

AT THE DEZ DAM: 4:31 P.M.   Lochart's 212 was parked just outside the shed that doubled as a hangar near a well-kept landing pad that was beside the cobbled forecourt of the house. He was standing on the copter's upperworks, checking the rotor column with its multitude of couplings, lockpins—and danger points—but he found nothing untoward. Carefully he clambered down and wiped his hands clean of grease.

"Okay?" Ali Abbasi asked, stretched out in the sun. He was the young and very good-looking Iranian helicopter pilot who had helped release Lochart from detention at Isfahan Air Base just before dawn, and had sat up front in the cockpit with him all the way here. "Everything okay?"

"Sure," Lochart said. "She's clean and all set to go." It was a nice day, cloudless and warm. When the sun went down in an hour or so the temperature would drop twenty or more degrees but that wouldn't matter. He knew that he would be warm because generals always looked after themselves—and those necessary to them for their survival. At the moment I'm necessary to Valik and to General Seladi, but only for the moment, he thought.

Muted laughter came from the house and more from those sunning or swimming in the clear blue waters of the lake below. The house seemed incongruous in such desolation—a modern, single-story, spacious, four-bedroom bungalow with separate servants' quarters. It was set on a slight rise overlooking the lake and the dam, the only habitation in this whole area. Surrounding the lake and the dam was a barren wilderness—small, rock hills jutting from a high plateau devoid of any vegetation. The only ways here were to backpack in or to come by air, by helicopter or light airplane into the very short, narrow, dirt airstrip that had been hacked out of the uneven terrain.

Doubt if even a light twin could get in here, Lochart had thought when he first saw it. Have to be a single engine. And no way to go around again—once you commit you're committed. But it's a great hideaway, no doubt about that —just great.

Ali got up and stretched.

They had arrived here this morning, their flight uneventful. On orders and directions from General Seladi, quietly varied by Captain Ali, Lochart had hugged the ground, weaving through the passes, avoiding all towns and villages. Their radio had been open all the time. The only report they had heard was a venomous broadcast from Isfahan, repeated several times, about a 212 full of traitors that was escaping southward and should be intercepted and shot down. "They didn't give our names—or our registration," Ali had said excitedly. "They must've forgotten to write it down."

"What the hell difference does that make?" Lochart had said. "We must be the only 212 in the sky."

"Never mind. Stay at max a hundred feet and now turn west."

Lochart had been astonished, expecting to head for Bandar Delam that lay almost due south. "Where we heading?"

"Forget compass bearings, I'll guide you from here on in."

"Where're we heading?"

"Baghdad." Ali had laughed.

No one had told him their destination until they were ready to land, and by that time, a little over two hundred miles from Isfahan, flying very low all the way with adverse winds, at maximum consumption and far beyond their expected maximum duration—on empty too long—Ali was openly praying.

"If we put down in this godforsaken wilderness we'll never walk out, what about fuel?"

"There's plenty there when we arrive . . . God be praised!" Ali had said excitedly as they came over the rise to see the lake and the dam. "God be praised!"

Lochart had echoed his thanks and had landed quickly. Beside the helipad was a subterranean 5,000-gallon tank, and the shed hangar. In the shed hangar were some tools and cylinders of air for tires, and racks of water skis and boating equipment.

"Let's put her away," Ali said. Together they wheeled the 212 into the shed where she fitted snugly, putting chocks on her wheels. As Lochart adjusted the rotor tie-down he noticed three hang gliders in a rack overhead. They were dust-covered and in tatters now.

"Whose are those?"

"This used to be the private weekend place of General of the Imperial Air Force, Hassayn Aryani. They were his."

Lochart whistled. Aryani was the legendary head of the air force who, according to rumor, also had been like captain of the Praetorian Guard in Roman times to the Shah, his confidant and married to one of his sisters. He had been killed hang gliding two years ago. "Was this where he was killed?"

"Yes." Ali pointed to the other side of the lake. "They say he got into still-air turbulence and went into those cliffs."

Lochart studied him. " 'They say'? You don't believe that?"

"No. I'm sure he was assassinated. In the air force most of us're sure."

"You mean his hang glider was sabotaged?"

Ali shrugged. "I don't know. Perhaps, perhaps not, but he was much too careful and clever a pilot and flier to get into turbulence. Aryani would never've flown on a bad day." He went out into the sun. Below they could hear the voices and laughter of some of the others, and Valik's children playing down by the lake. "He used a speedboat to take off. He'd wear short water skis, then hold on to a long rope attached to the speedboat that'd go charging down the lake and when he was fast enough he'd drop his skis and go airborne and soar up five hundred, a thousand feet, then cast off and spiral down and land within inches of the raft down there."

"He was that good?"

"Yeah, he was that good. He was too good, that's why he was murdered."

"By whom?"

"I don't know. If I did, then he or they would have died long ago."

Lochart saw the adoration. "You knew him, then?"

"I was his aide, one of his aides, for a year. He was easily the most wonderful man I have ever known—the best general, the best pilot, best sportsman, skier—everything. If he had been alive now the Shah would never have been trapped by foreigners or snared by our archenemy Carter, the Shah'd never have left, Iran would never have been allowed to slide into the abyss, and the generals would never have been allowed to betray us." Ali Abbasi's face twisted with anger. "It's impossible to conceive that we could be so betrayed with him alive."

"Then who killed him? Khomeini's followers?"

"No, not three years ago. He was a famous nationalist, Shi'ite, though a modern. Who? Tudeh, fedayeen or any fanatic of the right, left, or center who wanted Iran weakened." Ali looked at him, dark eyes in a chiseled face. "There are even those who say people in high places feared his growing power and popularity."

Lochart blinked. "You mean the Shah might have ordered his death?"

"No. No, of course not, but he was a threat to those who misguided the Shah. He was *farmandeh*, a commander of the people. He was a threat all over: to British interests, because he supported Prime Minister Mossadegh who nationalized Anglo-Iranian Oil, he supported the Shah and OPEC when they quadrupled the cost of oil. He was pro-Israel though not anti-Arab, so a threat to the PLO and Yasir Arafat. He could have been considered a threat to American interests—to any or all of the Seven Sisters because he didn't give a good goddamn for them or anyone. Anyone. For above all he was a patriot." Ali's eyes had a strange look to them. "Assassination is an ancient art in Iran. Wasn't ibn-al-Sabbah one of us?" His mouth smiled, his eyes didn't. "We're different here."

"Sorry—ibn-al-Sabbah?"

"The Old Man of the Mountains, Hassan ibn-al-Sabbah, the Isma'ili religious leader who invented the Assassins in the eleventh century, and their cult of political assassination."

"Oh, sure, sorry I wasn't thinking. Wasn't he supposed to be a friend of Omar Khayyám?"

"Some legends say so." Ali's face was etched. "Aryani was murdered, by whom, no one knows. Yet." Together they pulled the shed door closed.

"What now?" Lochart asked.

"Now we wait. Then we'll go on." Into exile Ali thought. Never mind, it will only be temporary and at least I know where I'm going, not like the Shah, poor man, who's an outcast. I can go to the States.

Only he and his parents knew that he had a U.S. passport. Goddamn, he thought, how clever of Dad: "You never know, my son, what God has in store," his father had said gravely. "I advise you to apply for a passport while you can. Dynasties never last, only family. Shahs come and go, Shahs feed off each other, and the two Pahlavis together are only fifty-four-year Highnesses —Imperial Majesties! What was Reza Khan before he crowned himself King of Kings? A soldier-adventurer, the son of illiterate villagers from Mazandaran near the Caspian."

"But surely, Father, Reza Khan was a special man. Without him and Mohammed Reza Shah, we'd still be slaves of the British."

"The Pahlavis were of use to us, my son, yes. In many ways. But Reza Shah failed, he failed himself and failed us by stupidly believing the Germans would win the war and tried to support the Axis—and so gave the occupying British an excuse to depose him and exile him."

"But, Father, Mohammed Shah can't fail! He's stronger than his father ever was. Our armed forces are the envy of the world. We've more airplanes than Britain, more tanks than Germany, more money than Croesus, America's our ally, we're the biggest military power and policeman of the Middle and Near East, and the leaders of the outside kowtow to him—even Brezhnev."

"Yes. But we do not yet know what is the Will of God. Get the passport."

"But a U.S. passport could be very dangerous, you know how it's said almost everything goes through SAVAK to the Shah! What if he heard, or General Aryani heard? That'd ruin me in the air force?"

"Why should it—for of course you would tell them proudly you just got the passport, and kept it secret, against the day you could put it to use for the good of the Pahlavis. Eh?"

"Of course!"

"Open your eyes to the ways of the world, my son—the promises of kings have no value, they can plead expedience. If this Shah or the next, or even your great general has to choose between your life and something of more value to them, which would they choose? Put no trust in princes, or generals, or politicians, they will sell you, your family, and your heritage for a pinch of salt to put on a plate of rice they won't even bother to taste. . . ."

And oh how true! Carter sold us out and his generals, then the Shah and his generals, and our generals did the same to us. But how could they be so stupid as to assassinate themselves? he asked himself, shuddering at the thought of how close he had been to death in Isfahan. They must have all gone mad!

"It's cold in the shade," Lochart said.

"Yes, yes, it is." Ali looked back at him and shook off his anxiety. Generals are all the same. My father was right. Even these two bastards Valik or Seladi, they'd have sold us all if need be, still will. They need me because I'm the only one who can fly them—apart from this poor fool who doesn't know he's in dead trouble. "Get rid of this Lochart," Seladi had said. "Why take him to safety? He would have left us at Isfahan, why not leave him here? Dead. We can't leave him alive, he knows us all and he'd betray us all."

"No, Excellency Uncle," Valik had said. "He's more use as a gift to the Kuwaitis, or Iraqis, they can jail him or extradite him. It was he who stole an Iranian helicopter and agreed for money to fly us out. Didn't he?"

"Yes. Even so, he can still give our names to the revolutionaries."

"By that time we will all be safe and our families safe."

"I say dispose of him—he would have sacrificed us. Dispose of him and we will go to Baghdad, not Kuwait."

"Please, Excellency, reconsider. Lochart is the more experienced pilot. . . ."

Ali glanced at his watch. Just thirty minutes to takeoff. He saw Lochart glance at the house where Valik, Seladi were. I wonder who won, Valik or Seladi? Is it the inside of a Kuwaiti or Iraqi jail for this poor joker, or a bullet in the head? I wonder if they'll bury him after they shoot him or just leave him to the vultures.

"What's the matter?" Lochart asked.

"Nothing. Nothing, Captain, just thinking how lucky we were to escape Isfahan."

"Yes, I still think I owe you my life." Lochart was certain that if Ali and the major hadn't released him he would have ended up before a komiteh kangaroo court. And if he was caught now? The same. He had not allowed his mind to think about Sharazad or Tehran or to make a plan. That comes later, he told himself again. Once you see how this turns out and where you end up.

Where're they planning to go? Kuwait? Or maybe just a quick stab over the border into Iraq? Iraq's usually hostile to Iranians so that might be dicey for them. Kuwait's an easy flight from here and most Kuwaitis are Sunni and therefore anti-Khomeini. Against that, to get there, you have to sneak through a lot of sensitive airspace, Iranian and Iraqi, both nervous, jumpy, and trigger-happy. Within fifty miles there must be twenty Iranian air bases, fighter operational, with planes gassed up and dozens of petrified pilots anxious to prove loyalty to the new regime.

And what about your promise to McIver not to fly them the last leg?

Because of Isfahan you're marked now—there's no way the revs will have forgotten your name or the registration of the airplane. Did you see anyone write your name down? No, I don't think so. Even so, you'd better get out while you can, you're implicated in an escape, men were killed at Isfahan—whichever way you stack it you're marked.

What about Sharazad? I can't leave her.

You may have to. She's safe in Tehran.

What if they come looking for you and Sharazad answers the door and they take her away in place of you?

"I could use a cold drink," he said, his mouth suddenly dry. "You think they have a Coke or something?"

"I'll go see." They both looked off as Valik's children came bounding up the path from the lake, Annoush close behind them.

"Ah," she said to them with her happy smile, but dark shadows around her eyes, "it is a wonderful day, isn't it? We're so lucky."

"Yes," both said and wondered how such a woman could marry such a man. She was very good to look at and as beautiful a mother as could be.

"Captain Abbasi, where's my husband?"

"In the house, Highness, with the others," Ali said. "May I escort you, I was just going there?"

"Would you find him for me, please, and ask him to join me?"

Ali did not wish to leave her alone with Lochart, for she had been present when Valik and Seladi had told him of their plans, asking his advice about their destination—though not about Lochart's elimination, that had come later. "I wouldn't want to disturb the general by myself, Highness, perhaps we could go together."

"You will please find him for me." She was as imperious as the general, though kindly and without insult.

Ali shrugged. Insha'Allah, he thought, and went off. When they were quite alone, her two children running around the shed, playing hide-and-seek, Annoush touched Lochart gently. "I haven't thanked you for our lives, Tommy."

Lochart was startled. This was the first time she had ever called him by his first name—he had always been "Captain Lochart" or "my cousin-in-law" or "His Excellency, the husband of Sharazad." "I was glad to help."

"I know that you and dear old Mac did it for the children and me—don't look so surprised, my dear, I know my husband's strengths and . . . and his weaknesses—what wife doesn't?" Tears brimmed in her eyes. "I know what this means for you too—you've jeopardized your life, Sharazad's, your future in Iran, perhaps your company."

"Not Sharazad's. No, she's perfectly safe. Her father, Excellency Bakravan, will keep her safe until she can get out. Of course she's safe." He saw Annoush's brown eyes and read behind her eyes and his soul twisted.

"I pray that with all my heart, Tommy, and beg God to grant that wish." She dabbed her tears away. "I've never been so sad in all my life. I never knew I could be so sad—sad to be running away, sad for that poor soldier dying in the snow, sad for all our families and friends who have to stay, sad because no one's safe in Iran anymore. I'm so afraid most of our circle will be persecuted by the mullahs, we've always been—what shall I say? Too modern and . . . too progressive. No one's safe here anymore—not even Khomeini himself."

Lochart heard himself say, "Insha'Allah," but he wasn't listening to her, suddenly petrified that he would never see Sharazad again, never be able to get back into Iran or her able to get out. "It will be normal again soon, travel permitted and everything okay. Of course it will. In a few months, it's got to be. Of course it will be normal soon."

"I hope so, Tommy, for I love your Sharazad and would hate not being able to see her and the little one."

"Eh?" He gaped at her.

"Oh, but of course you wouldn't know," she said, then brushed the last of her tears away. "It was too soon for you to know. Sharazad told me she's sure she's carrying her firstborn."

"But . . . but, well she . . ." He stopped helplessly, aghast, at the same time ecstatic. "She can't be!"

"Oh, she wasn't sure yet, Tommy, but she felt she was. Sometimes a woman can tell—you feel so different, so very different and so wonderful, so fulfilled," she added, her voice now joyous.

Lochart was trying to get his mind working, completely aware that it would be impossible for her to understand the turmoil she was creating in him. God in heaven, he thought, Sharazad?

"There are still a few days to be certain," she was saying. "I think it's three or four. Let me think. Yes, including today, Tuesday, four more days to be certain. That would make it the day after, after seeing her father," she said delicately. "You were to see him this Holy Day, Friday, the sixteenth, by your counting, weren't you?"

"Yes." Lochart said. As if I could forget. "You knew about that?"

"Of course." Annoush was astonished by his question. "Such an extraordinary request from you, and such an important decision would have to be known by all of us. Oh, wouldn't it be wonderful if she is with child—didn't you tell Excellency Bakravan you wanted children? I so hope she has been blessed by God for that will surely pass the days and nights happily for her until we can get her out. Kuwait's not far. I'm only so sorry she didn't come with us—that would have made everything perfect."

"Kuwait?"

"Yes, but we won't stop there—we'll go on to London." Again the torment showed. "I don't want to leave our home and friends and . . . I don't . . ."

Behind her, Lochart saw the door of the house open. Valik and Seladi came out, Ali with them. He noticed the three of them wore sidearms now. Must have had a cache of weapons here, he thought absently as Ali saluted and hurried down the path toward the lake. Bursting with glee the two children charged from the back of the shed into Valik's arms. He swung the little girl into the air and set her down.

"Yes, Annoush?" he asked his wife.

"You wanted me and the children to be here exactly at this time."

"Yes. Please get Setarem and Jalal ready. We'll be leaving soon." At once the children ran off into the house. "Captain, is the chopper ready?"

"Yes. Yes, it is."

Valik glanced back at his wife. "Please get ready, my dear."

She smiled and did not move. "I just have to fetch my coat. I'm ready to leave." The rest of the officers were approaching now. Several carried automatic rifles.

Lochart tore his mind off Sharazad and Holy Day and four days more and broke the silence. "What's the plan?"

Valik said, "Baghdad. We'll take off in a few minutes."

"I thought we were going to Kuwait," Annoush said.

"We've decided to go to Baghdad. General Seladi thinks it'll be safer than to head south." Valik kept watching Lochart. "I want to be airborne in ten minutes."

"I'd advise you to wait until two or three in the morning and th—"

Seladi interrupted coldly. "We could be trapped here. Soldiers could ambush us—there's an air base nearby, they could send out a patrol. You don't understand military matters. We leave for Baghdad at once."

"Kuwait's better and safer, but in both places the chopper'll be impounded without an Iranian clearance," Lochart said.

"Perhaps, perhaps not," Valik said calmly. "Baksheesh and a few connections will make all the difference." You, interloper into my family, he thought benignly, you along with the gift of the 212 will be a sop to satisfy even the Iraqis, for we certainly agree you have flown it illegally—even the clearance you obtained from Tehran was illegal. The Iraqis will understand and they won't harm us. Most of them hate and fear Khomeini and his version of Islam. With you, the 212 and a little extra on the side, why should they give me trouble?"

He saw Lochart watching him. "Yes?"

"I think Baghdad's a bad choice."

General Seladi said curtly, "We will leave now."

Lochart flushed at the rudeness. Some of the others shifted nervously. "No doubt you'll leave when the aircraft is ready and the pilot ready. Have you flown in these mountains?"

"No . . . no I haven't, but the 212 has the ceiling and Baghdad's where we will go. Now!"

"Then I wish you luck. I still advise Kuwait and waiting, but you do what you want, because I'm not flying you."

There was an even bigger silence. Seladi went red in the face. "You will prepare to leave. Now."

Lochart said to Valik, "On the way to Isfahan I told you I wouldn't be flying the last leg. I'm not flying you onward. Ali can do that—he's fully qualified."

"But you're as wanted as any of us now," Valik said, astonished with his stupidity. "Of course you will fly the last leg."

"No, no I won't. I'll backpack out of here—of course you can't waste time landing me somewhere. Ali can fly you—he's been based in this area and knows the radar. Just leave me a rifle and I'll head for Bandar Delam. Okay?"

The others stared from Lochart to Seladi and Valik. Waiting.

Valik thought through this new problem. So did Seladi. Both men came to the same conclusion: Insha'Allah! Lochart had chosen to stay and therefore Lochart had chosen the consequences. "Very well," Valik said calmly. "Ali will fly us." He smiled and then because he respected Lochart as a pilot, he added quickly, "As we're a very democratic people, I suggest we put it to a vote—Iraq or Kuwait?"

"Kuwait," Annoush said at once, and the others echoed her before Seladi could interrupt.

Good, Valik thought, I allowed myself to be overruled because Seladi claimed to know the chief of police in Baghdad and said that safe passage for me and my family and him would be no more than $20,000 in U.S. notes which would be immeasurably cheaper than Kuwait—how much the others will have to pay will be up to them; I hope they have money with them or the means to get enough quickly. "Of course you agree, Excellency Uncle? Kuwait. Thank you, Captain. Perhaps you'll tell Ali he'll be flying us—he's down by the lake."

"Sure. I'll just get my gear. You'll leave me a rifle?"

"Of course."

Lochart went to the shed and disappeared inside.

Seladi said, "Some of you get the chopper out and we'll be off." They went to obey him. Lochart came out, put his flight bag and carry bag beside the door and walked down the path toward the lake. Seladi watched him go, then impatiently walked over to the 212.

Valik saw his wife watching him. "Yes, Annoush?"

"What's planned for Captain Lochart?" she asked softly though they could not be overheard.

"He's . . . you heard him. He refuses to fly us and wants to stay. He'll walk out."

"I know how your mind works, my dear. Are you going to have him killed?" There was a nice smile on her face. "Murdered?"

"Murder would be the wrong word." His mouth smiled. "I'm sure you'd agree Lochart represents a great danger now. He knows us all, all our names —all our families will suffer when he's caught and tortured and sentenced. It's the Will of God. He made the choice. Seladi wanted it done anyway—a military decision—I said no, that he should fly us onward."

"To be a sacrifice in Kuwait, or Baghdad?"

"Seladi gave orders to Ali, I didn't. Lochart's marked, poor man. It's tragic, but necessary. You agree, don't you?"

"No, my dear, I'm sorry but I don't. So if he's hurt, or touched here, there will be many who live to regret it." Annoush's smile did not change. "You as well, my dear."

His face flushed. Behind him men had pulled the 212 into the open and now they were loading her. He dropped his voice. "Didn't you hear me, Annoush, he's a threat! He's not one of us, Jared barely tolerates him and I promise you he's a great danger to us, to those we've left behind—your family as well as mine."

"Didn't you hear me, husband? I promise you I know only too well the dangers, but if he's killed here—murdered—you will be killed too."

"Don't be ridiculous!"

"Sometime you will sleep and you will not awaken. It will be the Will of God." The smile never changed nor the gentleness of her voice.

Valik hesitated, then his face closed and he hurried down the path. The children barreled out of the house toward her and she said kindly, "Wait here, my darlings, I'll be back in a moment."

Esplanaded over the lake on stilts was an open-sided barbecue area and bar under a neat overhang, with a few steps that went down into the water for skiers, or for the motorboat that was tied up in its shelter nearby.

Lochart was on the water's edge, his hands up.

Ali had the automatic leveled. His orders from Seladi had been clear: go to the lake and wait. We will either call you back or send the pilot to find you. If the pilot comes looking for you, kill him and return at once.

He had hated the order—bombarding or attacking revolutionaries or mutineers from a chopper gunship was not murder as this was murder. His face was ashen, he had never killed before and he asked God's pardon, but an order was an order. "Sorry," he said, hardly able to talk and began to pull the trigger.

At that instant Lochart's legs seemed to collapse and he twisted over the side into the water. Automatically, Ali followed the movement, aimed for the center of the back as though at target practice, knowing he could never miss at this range. Fire!

"Stop!"

The fraction of a second he had hesitated was enough time for his brain to hear the order and obey it thankfully. With shuddering relief, he felt his finger release the pressure on the trigger. Valik rushed up to him and both of them peered into the water, murky here in the shade and quite deep. They waited. Lochart did not appear.

"Perhaps he's under the floor—or under the raft," Ali said, wiping the sweat off his face and hands, and thanking God that the pilot's blood was not on his soul.

"Yes." Valik was also sweating, but mostly with fear. He had never seen that look on his wife's face before, the smile that promised a death in the night. It's her vile ancestors, he thought. She's Qajar, her lineage Qajars who could happily blind or murder rivals to the throne—or children of rivals—didn't only one Qajar Shah in their 146-year dynasty relinquish his throne through natural death? Valik looked around, saw her standing up at the head of the path, then turned back to Ali. "Give me your gun."

Shakily Valik put the gun down on the rough wooden planking, and called out: "Lochart, I've left you a gun. This was all a mistake. The captain was mistaken."

"But, General—"

"Go up to the chopper," Valik ordered loudly. "Seladi's a fool—he should never have given you orders to kill this poor man. We leave at once and we go to Kuwait—not Baghdad. Ali, go and start the aircraft!"

Ali left. As he passed Annoush he eyed her curiously, then hurried onward. She walked down and joined Valik.

"You saw?" he asked.

"Yes."

They waited. No sound here, no tide to lap the pilings. It was beautiful and calm, the surface of the lake glassy and windless. "I . . . I pray he's hiding somewhere," she said, a great void in her soul, but now time to heal the breach. "I'm glad his blood's not on our hands. Seladi's a monster."

"We'd better go back." They were quite hidden from the chopper and the

house. He took out his automatic and fired it once into the ground nearby.
"For Seladi. I, er, think I hit Lochart when . . . when he surfaced. Eh?"

She took his arm. "You're a wise and good man." They walked back up the
rise, arm in arm. "Without you, your cleverness and courage, we would never
have escaped Isfahan. But exile? Wh—"

"Temporary exile," he said jovially, filled with relief that the vile moment
between them had passed. "Then we'll come home again."

"That would be wonderful," she said, forcing herself to believe it. I've got
to or I'll go mad. I've got to for the children! "I'm glad you chose Kuwait—I
never liked Baghdad, and those Iraqis, ugh!" Her eyes still had shadows in
them. "What Lochart said about waiting till after dark was wrong?" -

"There's an air base within a few miles. We could have been seen on radar,
Annoush, or by spotters in the hills. Seladi's right in that—the base will send
a patrol after us." They topped the rise. The children were waiting for them
in the cabin doorway, everyone else aboard. They quickened their pace.
"Kuwait's much safer. I'd already decided to overrule that pompous fool
Seladi—he's never to be trusted."

In minutes they were airborne, heading northward over the rim of these
hills, skirting the crags, hugging the ground to avoid the nearby danger from
the air base. Ali Abassi was a good pilot and knew the area well. Once over
the rim and down into the valley he turned west and scurried through a pass
to avoid the outer perimeter of the airfield, the Iraqi border some fifty miles
farther ahead. Snow covered the heights of the mountains far above them
and parts of the slopes, though the floor of some valleys were green, here and
there, among the rocky wilderness. They thundered over an unexpected and
unknown village, then curled almost due south, again following the water
course, paralleling the border that was far to their right. The whole flight
would take barely two hours, depending on the winds, and the winds were
favorable.

Those in the cabin near the windows happily watched the land rushing
past, the two children given the best positions, the major holding Jalal, Valik,
his daughter beside Annoush. Everyone was content, a few praying silently.
Sunset was not far off and would be good, red-tinged clouds—"red sky at
night, shepherds' delight," Annoush crooned to Setarem in English—and, up
front, the engines sounded good with all needles in the Green.

Ali was glad to be flying, glad that he had not killed Lochart who had stood
there in front of him, saying nothing, not begging for his life or saying
prayers, just standing there with his hands up, waiting. I'm sure he's safe
under the pilings, thanks be to God . . .

He took a quick glance at the map, refreshing his memory. But he did not really need to, he had spent many good years here, flying the passes. Soon he would come down out of the mountains into the marsh plains of the Tigris and Euphrates, staying at ground level, skirting Dezful, then Ahwaz and Khorramshahr, then stab across the Shatt-al-Arab Estuary and the border, into Kuwait and freedom.

Ahead was the ridge with the dominating peak that he had been expecting and he swung upward out of the valley to swoop down into the next, the joy of flying possessing him. Then "HBC, climb to a thousand feet and reduce speed!" filled his headphones and brain. He had been airborne barely six minutes.

The order had been in Farsi and it was repeated in English and then in Farsi and again in English, and all the while he kept her low, desperately trying to get his head working.

"Chopper HBC, you're illegal, climb out of the valley and reduce speed."

Ali Abbasi peered upward, searching the sky, but he saw no airplane. The valley floor was tearing past. Ahead was another rim and then there'd be a succession of rims and valleys that led down to the plains. Westward the Iraqi border was forty-odd miles away—twenty minutes.

"Chopper HBC, for the last time, you're illegal, climb out of the valley and reduce speed!"

His brain shouted, You've three choices: obey and die, try to escape, or put down and wait the night and try at first light—if you survive their rockets or bullets.

Ahead of him to the left he saw trees and the land falling away, the sides of the valley steepening into a ravine, so he cast himself into it, committing them to escape. Now his mind was working well. He pulled off his headset, put himself into the hands of God, and felt the better for it. He slowed as he came nearer the end of the ravine, skirted some trees and ducked into another small valley, reduced speed even more, following the streambed cautiously. More trees and outcrops and he sneaked around them.

Stay low and slow and save gas and ease your way south, he thought with growing confidence. Go nearer the border when you can take your time. They'll never catch you if you use your wits. It'll be dark soon—you can lose them in the dark and you know enough about instrument flying to get to Kuwait. But how did they spot us? It was almost as though they were waiting. Could they have had us on radar going into Dez Dam— Watch ittttt!

The trees were heavier here and he slewed around a scattering of them on the mountainside, went closer to the rocks, and climbed for the ridge and the next valley. Over it safely and down into the protection of the rocks, eyes searching ahead and above and always for a good spot to put down if an engine failed. He was concentrating and confident and doing his job well. All the instruments were in the safety range. Minutes passed and though he searched the sky diligently he saw nothing. At the head of the next valley he put the chopper into a 360 and carefully scanned the sky. Nothing overhead.

Safe! Lost him! Insha'Allah! He took a deep breath and, very satisfied, turned southward again. Over the next ridge. And the next and there ahead were the plains. The two fighters were waiting. They were F14s.

U.S.S.R.

TURKEY

KHOI

TABRIZ

MOUNT
SABALAN

BANDAR-E
PAHLAVI

Caspian Sea

U.S.S.R.

CHAPTER

26

IRAQ

BAGHDAD ★

QAZVIN

TEHRAN

IRAN

AFGHANISTAN

DEZ DAM

ZAGROS

ISFAHAN

BANDAR DELAM

Shatt-
al-Arab
Estuary

ABADAN

ZAGROS THREE

KOWISS

MOUNTAINS

KUWAIT

KHARG

JELLET

BAHRAIN

Persian Gulf

LENGEH

Strait of
Hormuz

PAKISTAN

SAUDI
ARABIA

QATAR

SIRI

Gulf of Oman

AL SHARGAZ

AT TEHRAN AIRPORT—S-G'S OFFICE: 5:48 P.M. ". . . you are not permitted to land!" came over the HF, heavily mixed with static— Gavallan, McIver, and Robert Armstrong grouped around it, listening intently, the vista through the windows dull and brooding, night near.

The breezy voice of John Hogg from the incoming 125 came back again: "Tehran Control, this is Echo Tango Lima Lima, as per yesterday, we have clearance from Kish to land an—"

"ETLL, you are not permitted to land!" The traffic controller's voice was raw and frightened and McIver cursed under his breath. "I say again: negative, all civilian air traffic is grounded and all incoming flights canceled until further orders of the Imam . . ." Behind his voice they could hear other voices chattering in Farsi, a number of mikes open on this frequency. "Return to your point of departure!"

"I say again, we have clearance to land from Kish radar who passed us to

Isfahan air traffic controller who confirmed our clearance. Long live Ayatollah Khomeini and the victory of Islam—I am forty miles south of checkpoint Varamin, expecting runway 29 left. Please confirm your ILS is functioning. Do you have other traffic in your system?"

For a moment Farsi voices dominated the tower, then, "Negative traffic, ETLL, negative ILS but you are not per—" The American English stopped abruptly and an angry, heavily accented voice took over: "Not landings! Komiteh give orders Tehran! Kish not Tehran—Isfahan not Tehran—we give orders Tehran. If landings you arrested."

John Hogg's happy voice replied at once. "EchoTangoLimaLima. Understand you don't want us to land, Tehran Tower, and wish to reject our clearances which I believe is an error according to air traffic regulations— Standby One please." Then at once on their private S-G frequency, mixed with static, came his terse voice, "HQ advise!"

Immediately McIver switched channels and said into the mike, "Three sixty, Standby One," meaning circle and wait for a reply. He glanced up at Gavallan who was grim-faced. Robert Armstrong was whistling tonelessly. "We better wave him off—if he lands they could throw the book at him and impound her," McIver said.

"With official clearances?" Gavallan said. "You told the tower we've the British ambassador's letter approved by Bazargan's office—"

"But not by Bazargan himself, sir," Robert Armstrong said, "and even then for all practical purposes those buggers in the tower are the law in the tower for the moment. I'd suggest th—" He stopped and pointed, his face even grimmer. "Look there!" Two trucks and a radio control car, with its tall aerial waving, were racing along the boundary road. As they watched, the trucks drove directly onto runway 29 left, parked in the middle of it. Armed Green Bands jumped out taking up defensive positions. The control car continued to head their way.

"Shit!" McIver muttered.

"Mac, do you think they'll be monitoring our frequency?"

"Safer to assume so, Andy."

Gavallan took the mike. "Abort. B repeat B."

"EchoTangoLimaLima!" Then, on the tower frequency, kind and friendly: "Tehran Tower: we agree your request to cancel our clearance and formally apply for clearance to land at tomorrow noon to deliver urgent repeat urgent spares required by IranOil, outgoing crew for overdue leave, with immediate turnaround."

McIver grunted. "Johnny always was fast on his feet." Then to Armstrong, "We'll put y—"

"Standby One, EchoTangoLimaLima," from the tower overrode him.

"We'll put you on her passenger list when we can, Mr. Armstrong. Sorry, no joy today. What about your papers?"

Armstrong took his eyes off the approaching car. "I, er, I'd prefer to be a specialist consultant for S-G, going on leave, if you don't mind. Unpaid, of course." He stared back at Gavallan. "What's 'B repeat B'?"

"Try again tomorrow, same time."

"And if they grant ETLL's request?"

"Then it's tomorrow—you'll be a specialist consultant."

"Thanks. Let's hope it's tomorrow." Armstrong looked at the approaching car, and added quickly, "Will you be in about ten tonight, Mr. Gavallan? Perhaps I could drop by—just to chat, nothing important."

"Certainly. I'll expect you. We've met before, haven't we?"

"Yes. If I'm not there by ten-fifteen I've been delayed and can't come—you know how it is—and I'll check in the morning." Armstrong began to leave. "Thanks."

"All right. Where did we meet?"

"Hong Kong." Robert Armstrong nodded politely and walked out, tall and gaunt. They saw him go through the office and take the door that led to the hangar and the back door to the S-G parking lot where he had left his nondescript car—McIver's car was parked in front.

"Almost as though he's been here before," McIver said thoughtfully.

"Hong Kong? Don't remember him at all. Do you?"

"No." McIver frowned. "I'll ask Gen, she has a good memory for names."

"I'm not sure I like or trust Robert bloody Armstrong, whatever Talbot says."

At noon they had gone to see Talbot to find out the who and the why of Armstrong. All George Talbot would say was, "Oh, he's rather decent really, and we'd, er, we'd appreciate your giving him a lift, and er, not asking too many questions. You'll stay for lunch, of course? We've still some rather good Dover sole, fresh frozen, plenty of caviar or smoked salmon if you wish, a couple of La Doucette '76 on ice—or bangers and mash with the house claret which I'd highly recommend if you prefer. Chocolate pudding or sherry trifle, and we've still half of a fairly decent Stilton. The whole world may be on fire, but at least we can watch it burn like gentlemen. How about a pink gin before lunch?"

Lunch had been very good. Talbot had said that Bakhtiar's leaving the field for Bazargan and Khomeini might avert most trouble. "Now that there's no chance of a coup, things should get back to normal, eventually."

"When do you think's 'eventually'?"

"When 'they,' whoever 'they' are, run out of ammunition. But, my dear old boy, whatever I think really doesn't matter. It's what Khomeini thinks that matters, and only God knows what Khomeini thinks."

Gavallan remembered the shrill cackle of laughter that Talbot had let out at his own joke and smiled.

"What?" McIver asked.

"I was just remembering Talbot at lunch."

The car was still a hundred yards away. "Talbot's hiding a mountain of secrets. What do you think Armstrong wants to 'chat' about?"

"Probably to divert us some more—after all, Mac, we did go to the embassy to enquire about him. Curious! Usually I don't forget . . . Hong Kong? Seem to associate him with the races at Happy Valley. It'll come back to me. I'll say one thing for him, he's punctual. I told him five o'clock and he was here—even though he seemed to come out of the woodwork." Gavallan's eyes twinkled under his heavy eyebrows, then went back to the incoming car that was drawing up outside. "Sure as God made Scotland he didn't want to meet our friendly komiteh. I wonder why?"

The komiteh consisted of two armed youths, a mullah—not the same as yesterday—and Sabolir, the perspiring senior Immigration official, still very nervous.

"Good evening, Excellencies," McIver said, his nostrils rebelling against their invading smell of stale sweat. "Would you care for tea?"

"No, no, thank you," Sabolir said. He was still very much on his guard, though he tried to hide it under a mask of arrogance. He sat down in the best chair. "We have new regulations for you."

"Oh?" McIver had had dealings with him over a couple of years, and had provided an occasional case of whisky, fill-ups of gasoline, and, from time to time, free air travel—and accommodation—for him and his family on several summer vacations to Caspian resorts: "We booked rooms for some of our executives and they can't use the space, dear Mr. Sabolir. It's a pity to waste the space, isn't it?" Once he had arranged a week's trip for two to Dubai. The girl had been young and very beautiful, and at Sabolir's blunt suggestion was put on the S-G books as an Iranian expert. "What can we do for you?"

To their surprise Sabolir took out Gavallan's passport and the previous clearance paper and put them on the desk: "Here are your passport and papers, er, approved," he said, his voice automatically oily with officialdom. "The Imam has ordered normal operations to begin at once. The, er, the Islamic State of Iran is back to normal and the airport will reopen in, er, three days, for normal, preagreed traffic. You are to come back to normal now."

"We begin training the Iranian Air Force again?" McIver asked, hard put to keep the glee out of his voice, for this was a very big contract and very profitable.

Sabolir hesitated. "Yes, I presume y—"

"No," the mullah said firmly in good English. "No—not until the Imam or the Revolutionary Komiteh agrees. I will see that you have a firm answer. I do not think this part of your operation will begin yet. Meanwhile your normal business—spares to your bases and their contract flights to assist IranOil resume oil production, or Iran-Timber and so on—provided the flights are approved in advance, may begin the day after tomorrow."

"Excellent," Gavallan said, and McIver echoed him.

"Replacement flight crews and oil rig crews, in and out—if approved in advance and provided their papers are in order," the mullah continued, "will resume the day after tomorrow. Oil production is to be a priority. An Islamic Guard will accompany every internal flight."

"If requested in advance, and the man is on time for the flight. But not armed," McIver said politely, preparing for the inevitable clash.

"Armed Islamic Guards will be carried for your protection to prevent hijacking by enemies of the state!" the mullah said sharply.

"We will be very pleased to cooperate, Excellency," Gavallan interrupted calmly, "very pleased indeed, but I'm sure you won't wish to endanger life or jeopardize the Islamic state. I formally ask you to ask the Imam to agree to no guns whatever—clearly you have immediate access to his presence. Meanwhile all our aircraft are grounded until I have clearance, or clearance from my government."

"You will not ground flights and you will become normal!" The mullah was very angry.

"Perhaps a compromise pending the Imam's agreement: your guards have their guns but the captain holds the ammunition during the flight. Agreed?"

The mullah hesitated.

Gavallan hardened. "The Imam ordered ALL weapons handed in, didn't he?"

"Yes. Very well, I agree."

"Thank you. Mac, prepare the paper for His Excellency to sign and that takes care of it for all our lads. Now, we'll need new flight papers, Excellency, the only ones we've got are the old, er, useless ones from the previous regime. Will you give us the necessary authority? You yourself, Excellency? Clearly you are a man of importance and you know what's going on." He watched as the mullah seemed to grow in stature with the flattery. The man was in his thirties, his beard was greasy and his clothes threadbare. From his accent

Gavallan had pegged him an ex-British student, one of the thousands of Iranians that the Shah had sent abroad on grants for Western education. "You will of course give us new papers at once, to make us legal with the new era?"

"We, er, we will sign new documents for each of our aircraft, yes." The mullah took some papers from his battered briefcase and put on a pair of old glasses, the lenses thick and one of them cracked. The paper he sought was at the bottom. "You have in your trust thirteen Iranian 212s, seven 206s, and four Alouettes in various places, all Iranian registry and owned by Iran Helicopter Company—that's correct?"

Gavallan shook his head. "Not exactly. At the moment they're still actually owned by S-G Helicopters of Aberdeen. Iran Helicopter Company, our joint venture with our Iranian partners, doesn't own the aircraft until they're paid for."

The mullah frowned, then brought the paper closer to his eyes. "But the contract giving ownership to Iran Helicopter, which is an Iranian company, is signed, isn't it?"

"Yes, but it's subject to payments which are . . . are in arrears."

"The Imam has said all debts will be paid so they will be paid."

"Of course, but meanwhile ownership passes on actual payment," Gavallan continued carefully, while hoping against hope the tower would grant Johnny Hogg's clever request for a landing tomorrow. I wonder if this mealy-mouthed bugger could order a clearance? he asked himself. If Khomeini's ordered everything back to normal, it'll go back to normal and I can safely return to London. With any luck I could close the ExTex contract that covers the new X63s' lease payments by the weekend. "For months we've been making payments on behalf of IHC on all these aircraft, with interest, banking charges and so on out of our own funds and w—"

"Islam forbids usury and the paying of interest," the mullah said with a total finality that rocked Gavallan and McIver. "Banks may not charge interest. None. It is usury."

Gavallan glanced at McIver, then uneasily turned his full attention to the mullah. "If banks cannot charge interest, how will business operate internally and externally?"

"According to Islamic law. Only Islamic law. The Koran forbids usury." The mullah added distastefully, "What foreign banks do is evil—it's because of them Iran had many troubles. Banks are evil institutions and will not be tolerated. As to Iran Helicopter Company, the Islamic Revolutionary Komiteh has ordered all joint ventures suspended, pending review." The mullah waved the papers. "All these aircraft are Iranian, Iranian registry,

Iranian!" Again he peered at the paper. "Here in Tehran you have three 212s, four 206s, and one 47G4 here at the airport, haven't you?"

"They're spread around," McIver told him carefully, "here, Doshan Tappeh and Galeg Morghi."

"But they're all here, in Tehran?"

McIver had been gauging him while Gavallan had been talking, also trying to read upside down what the papers contained. The one in the mullah's hand listed all their airplanes with their registration numbers and was a copy of the manifest that was kept permanently in the tower, that S-G was obliged to keep permanently up to date. His stomach twisted nastily when he glimpsed EP-HBC ringed in red—Lochart's 212—also EP-HFC, Pettikin's 206.

"We've one 212 on loan to Bandar Delam," he said, deciding to play it safe, inwardly cursing Valik and hoping that Tom Lochart was either at Bandar Delam or safely on the way home. "The rest're here."

"On loan—that would be EP—EP-HBC?" the mullah said, very pleased with himself. "Now, wh—" The traffic controller's voice interrupted him: "EchoTangoLimaLima, request refused. Call Isfahan on 118.3—good day."

"Quite right—good." The mullah nodded, satisfied.

Gavallan and McIver cursed inwardly even more, and Sabolir, who had been silently watching and listening to the byplay, understanding very clearly how the two men were trying to manipulate the mullah, chortled to himself, carefully avoiding anyone's eyes, staring at the floor for safety. Once, a moment ago, when the mullah's attention was elsewhere, he had deftly caught McIver's eye and half smiled at him, encouragingly, pretending friendship, petrified McIver would misconstrue all those previous favors which were only repayment for his smoothing the way of inbound spares and outbound crews. On the radio this morning, a spokesman for the "Islamic Revolutionary Komiteh" had urged all loyal citizens to denounce anyone who had committed crimes "against Islam." During today three of his colleagues had been arrested which had sent a shudder of horror through the whole airport. Islamic Guards gave no specific reasons, just dragged the men away and put them into Evin Jail—the loathed SAVAK prison—where, it was rumored, half a hundred "enemies of Islam" had been shot today after summary trials. One of those arrested was one of his own men who had accepted the 10,000 rials and the three 5-gallon cans of gasoline from McIver's storeroom yesterday—the man had kept one, and the other two he himself had correctly taken home last night as was his due. Oh, God, let them not search my house.

Over the HF was Johnny Hogg, his voice still breezy: "EchoTango-

LimaLima, thank you. Up the revolution and good day." Then on their own channel, tersely: "HQ confirm."

McIver reached over and switched to their channel. "Standby One!" he ordered, deeply conscious of the mullah. "Do you thi—"

"Ah. You talk direct with the aircraft—a private channel?"

"Company channel, Excellency. It's normal practice."

"Normal. Yes. So EP-HBC is at Bandar Delam?" the mullah said and read from the paper: " 'Delivering spares.' Is that right?"

"Yes," McIver said, praying.

"When is this aircraft due to return?"

McIver could feel the weight of the mullah's attention on him. "I don't know. I haven't been able to raise Bandar Delam. As soon as I can, I'll tell you. Now, Excellency, about clearances for our various flights, do you th—"

"EP-HFC. EP-HFC is in Tabriz?"

"She's at the small Forsha airstrip," McIver said, not feeling very good at all, praying that the madness at the Qazvin roadblock had gone unreported and would be forgotten. Again he wondered where Erikki was—he was supposed to have met them at the apartment at three o'clock to come out to the airport but had never appeared.

"Forsha airstrip?"

He saw the mullah staring at him and concentrated with an effort. "EP-HFC went to Tabriz on Saturday to deliver spares and pick up a crew change. She returned last night. She'll be on the new manifest tomorrow."

The mullah was suddenly grim. "But any incoming or outgoing aircraft must be instantly reported. We have no record of any inward clearance yesterday."

"Captain Pettikin couldn't raise Tehran ATC yesterday. The military were in charge, I believe. He tried calling all the way inbound." McIver added quickly, "If we're to resume operations, who will authorize our IranOil flights? Mr. Darius as usual?"

"Er, yes, I would think so. But why wasn't its arrival reported today?"

Gavallan said with a forced brightness, "I'm very impressed with your efficiency, Excellency. It's a pity the military air traffic controllers on duty yesterday don't share it. I can see the new Islamic republic will far surpass any Western operation. It will be a pleasure to serve our new employers. Up the new! May we know your name?"

"I, I'm Mohammed Tehrani," the man said, diverted again.

"Then Excellency Tehrani, may I ask that you give us the benefit of your authority? If my Echo Tango Lima Lima could have your permission to land tomorrow, we could immeasurably improve our efficiency to parallel your own. I can then make sure our company gives the Ayatollah Khomeini and his personal assistants—like yourself—the service he and they have a right to expect. The spares ETLL will carry will put back two more 212s into operation and I can return to London to increase our support for the Great Revolution. Of course, you agree?"

"It's not possible. The komiteh w—"

"I'm sure the komiteh would take your advice. Oh, I noticed you've had the misfortune to break your glasses. Terrible. I can hardly see without mine. Perhaps I could have the 125 bring a new pair for you tomorrow from Al Shargaz?"

The mullah was unsettled. His eyes were very bad. The wish for new glasses, good glasses, almost overpowered him. Oh, it would be an unbelievable treasure, a gift from God. Surely God has put this thought into the foreigner's head. "I don't think . . . I don't know. The komiteh couldn't do what you ask so quickly."

"I know it's difficult, but if you'd intercede for us with your komiteh, surely they'd listen. It would help us immeasurably and we'd be in your debt," Gavallan added, using the time-honored phrase that in any language meant, what do you want in exchange? He saw McIver switch to the tower frequency, offer the mike. "You press the button to talk, Excellency, if you would honor us with your assistance. . . ."

The mullah Tehrani hesitated, not knowing what to do. As he looked at the mike, McIver glanced at Sabolir, pointedly.

Sabolir understood at once, his reflexes perfect. "Of course whatever you decide, Excellency Tehrani, your komiteh will agree," he said, his voice unctuous. "But tomorrow, tomorrow I understand you are ordered to visit the other airfields, to make sure where and how many civilian helicopters are in your area which is all Tehran? Yes?"

"Those are orders, yes," the mullah agreed. "I and some members of my komiteh have to visit the other airfields tomorrow."

Sabolir sighed heavily, pretending disappointment, and McIver had difficulty not laughing so overplayed was the performance. "Unfortunately it would not be possible for you to visit them all by car or foot and still be back to supervise, personally, the arrival and immediate turnaround of this single aircraft that has, through no fault of its own, been turned away because of arrogant traffic controllers in Kish and Isfahan who dared not to consult you first."

"True, true," the mullah agreed. "They were at fault!"

"Would 7:00 A.M. suit you, Excellency Tehrani?" McIver said at once. "We'd be glad to help our airport komiteh. I'll give you my best pilot and you'll be back in plenty of time to, er, to supervise the turnaround. How many men would come with you?"

"Six . . ." the mullah said absently, overwhelmed with the idea of being able to complete his orders—God's work—so conveniently and luxuriously, like a veritable ayatollah. "This . . . this could be done?"

"Of course!" McIver said. "At 7:00 A.M. here. Captain, er, Chief Captain Nathaniel Lane will have a 212 ready. Seven including yourself, and up to seven wives. You of course would fly in the cockpit with the pilot. Consider it arranged."

The mullah had only flown twice in his life—to England and university and home again, packed into a special, student-charter Iran Air flight. He beamed and reached for the mike: "At 7:00 A.M."

McIver and Gavallan did not betray their relief at their victory. Nor did Sabolir.

Sabolir was content that the mullah was entrapped. As God wants! Now if I'm falsely accused, now I have an ally, he told himself. This fool, this son of a dog false mullah, hasn't he accepted a bribe—clearly not pishkesh—two in fact, some new glasses and wasteful, unauthorized air travel? Hasn't he deliberately allowed himself to become the dupe of these glib and ever-devious English who still think they can seduce us with trinkets and steal our heritage for a few rials? Listen to the fool, giving the foreigners what they want!

He glanced at McIver. Pointedly. And caught his eye. Then once more looked back at the floor. Now you arrogant Western son of a dog, he thought, what valuable favor should you do for me in return for my assistance?

AT THE FRENCH CLUB: 7:10 P.M.   Gavallan accepted the glass of red wine from the uniformed French waiter, McIver, the white.

Both touched glasses and drank gratefully, tired after their journey from the airport. They were sitting in the lounge with other guests, mostly Europeans, men and women, overlooking the snow-covered gardens and tennis courts, the chairs comfortable and modern, the bar extensive—many other rooms for banquets, dancing, dining, cards, sauna in other parts of this fine building that was in the best part of Tehran. The French Club was the only expat club still functioning—the American Services Club, with its huge complex of entertainment facilities, sports field, and baseball pitch, as well as the British, Pars-American, German clubs, and most others had been closed, their bars and stocks of liquor smashed.

"My God, that's good," McIver said, the ice-cold, cleansing wine taking away the dross. "Don't tell Gen we stopped by."

"No need to, Mac. She'll know."

McIver nodded. "You're right, never mind. I managed to book here tonight for dinner—costs an arm and a leg but worth it. Used to be standing room only at this time of night . . ." He looked around at a burst of laughter from some Frenchmen in a far corner. "For a moment it sounded like Jean-Luc, seems years since we had his pre-Christmas party here—wonder if we'll ever have another."

"Sure you will," Gavallan said to encourage him, concerned that the fire seemed to be out of his old friend. "Don't let that mullah get to you."

"He gave me the creeps—so did Armstrong come to think of it. And Talbot. But you're right, Andy, I shouldn't let it get me down. We're in better shape than we were two days ago . . ." More laughter distracted him and he began thinking of all the great times he had had here with Genny and Pettikin and Lochart—won't think about him now—and all the other pilots and their many friends, British, American, Iranian. All gone, most gone. It used to be: "Gen, let's go over to the French Club, the tennis finals are this afternoon . . ." Or: "Valik's cocktail party's on from 8:00 P.M. at the Iranian Officers Club . . ." Or: "There's a polo match, baseball match, swimming party, skiing party . . ." Or: "Sorry, can't this weekend we're going to the ambassador's do on the Caspian . . ." Or: "I'd love to, Genny can't, she's shopping for carpets in Isfahan . . ."

"It used to be we had so much to do here, Andy, the social life was the best ever, no doubt about that," he said. "Now it's hard just trying to keep in touch with our ops."

Gavallan nodded. "Mac," he said kindly, "straight answer to a straight question: Do you want to quit Iran and let someone else take over?"

McIver stared at him blankly. "Good God, whatever gave you that idea? No, absolutely no! You mean you think because I was a bit down that . . . Good God, no," he said, but his mind was suddenly jerked into asking the same question, unthinkable a few days ago: are you losing it, your will, your grip, your need to continue—is it time to quit? I don't know, he thought, achingly chilled by the truth, but his face smiled. "Everything's fine, Andy. Nothing we can't deal with."

"Good. Sorry, I hope you didn't mind me asking. I think I was encouraged by the mullah—except when he was talking about 'our Iranian aircraft.'"

"The truth is that Valik and the partners've been acting like our aircraft were theirs ever since we signed that contract."

"Thank God it's a British contract, enforceable under British law." Gavallan glanced over McIver's shoulder and his eyes widened slightly. The girl coming into the room was in her late twenties, dark-haired, dark-eyed, and stunning. McIver followed his glance, brightened, and got up. "Hello, Sayada," he said, beckoning her. "May I introduce Andrew Gavallan? Andy, this's Sayada Bertolin, a friend of Jean-Luc. Would you like to join us?"

"Thanks, Mac, but no, sorry I can't, I'm just about to play squash with a friend. You're looking well. Pleased to meet you, Mr. Gavallan." She put out her hand and Gavallan shook it. "Sorry, got to dash, give my love to Genny."

They sat down again. "Same again, waiter, please," Gavallan said. "Mac, between you and me, that bird's made me feel positively weak!"

McIver laughed. "Usually it's the reverse! She's certainly very popular, works in the Kuwaiti embassy, she's Lebanese and Jean-Luc's smitten."

"My word, I don't blame him . . ." Gavallan's smile faded. Robert Armstrong was coming through the far doorway with a tall, strong-faced Iranian in his fifties. He saw Gavallan, nodded briefly, then continued with his conversation and led the way out and up the stairs where there were other lounges and rooms. "Wonder what the devil that man's g—" Gavallan stopped as recollection flooded his mind. "Robert Armstrong, chief superintendent CID Kowloon, that's who he is . . . or was!"

"CID? You're sure?"

"Yes, CID or Special Branch . . . wait a minute . . . he, yes, that's right, he was a friend of Ian's come to think of it, that's where I met him, at the Great House on the Peak, not at the races, though I might have seen him there too with Ian. If I remember rightly it was the night Quillan Gornt came as a very unwelcome guest . . . can't remember exactly, but I think it was Ian and Penelope's anniversary party, just before I left Hong Kong . . . my God, that's almost sixteen years ago, no wonder I didn't remember him."

"I had the feeling he remembered you the instant we met at the airport yesterday."

"So did I." They finished their drinks and left, both of them curiously unsettled.

TEHRAN UNIVERSITY: 7:32 P.M. The rally of over a thousand leftist students in the forecourt quadrangle was noisy and dangerous, too many factions, too many zealots, and too many of them armed. It was cold and damp, not yet dark, though already there were a few lights and torches in the twilight.

Rakoczy was at the back of the crowd, melded into it, haphazardly dressed like the others, looking like them though now his cover had been changed and he was no longer Smith or Fedor Rakoczy, the Russian Muslim, the Islamic-Marxist sympathizer, but here in Tehran had reverted to Dimitri

Yazernov, Soviet representative on the Tudeh Central Committee—a post he had had from time to time over the past few years. He stood in a corner of the quadrangle with five of the Tudeh student leaders, out of the sharpening wind, his assault rifle over his shoulder, armed and ready, and he was waiting for the first gun to go off. "Any moment now," he said softly.

"Dimitri, who do I take out first?" one of the leaders asked nervously.

"The mujhadin—that motherless bastard, the one over there," he said patiently, pointing at the black-bearded man, much older than the others. "Take your time, Farmad, and follow my lead. He's professional and PLO."

The others stared at him astonished. "Why him if he's PLO?" Farmad asked. He was squat, almost misshapen, with a large head and small intelligent eyes. "The PLO have been our great friends over the years, giving us training and support and arms."

"Because now the PLO will support Khomeini," he explained patiently. "Hasn't Khomeini invited Arafat here next week? Hasn't he given the PLO the Israeli mission headquarters as its permanent headquarters? The PLO can supply all the technicians that Bazargan and Khomeini need to replace the Israelis and the Americans—especially in the oil fields. You don't want Khomeini strong, do you?"

"No, but the PLO have been v—"

"Iran isn't Palestine. Palestinians should stay in Palestine. You won the revolution. Why give strangers your victory?"

"But the PLO have been our allies," Farmad persisted, and Rakoczy was glad that he had found the flaw before some measure of power was passed over to this man.

"Allies who have become enemies have no value. Remember the aim."

"I agree with Comrade Dimitri," another said, an edge to his voice, his eyes cold and very hard. "We don't want PLO giving orders here. If you don't want to take him out, Farmad, I will. All of them and all the Green Band dogs too!"

"The PLO're not to be trusted," Rakoczy said, continuing the same lesson, planting the same seeds. "Look how they vacillate and change positions even on their home ground, one moment saying they're Marxist, the next Muslim, the next flirting with the archtraitor Sadat then attacking him. We have documents to prove it," he added, the disinformation fitting in perfectly, "and documents that prove they plan to assassinate King Hussein, and take over Jordan and make a separate peace with Israel and America. They've had secret meetings with the CIA and Israel already. They're not truly anti-Israel . . ."

Ah, Israel, he was thinking as he let his mouth continue the well-thought-out lesson, how important you are to Mother Russia, set there so nicely in the cauldron, a perpetual irritant guaranteed to enrage all Muslims forever, particularly the oh so oil rich sheikdoms, guaranteed to set all Muslims against all Christians, our prime enemy—your American, British, and French allies —meanwhile to curb their power and keep them and the West off-balance while we consume vital prizes—Iran this year, Afghanistan also, Nicaragua next year, then Panama and others, always to the same plan: possession of the Strait of Hormuz, Panama, Constantinople, and the treasure chest of South Africa. Ah, Israel, you're a trump card for us to play in the world Monopoly game. But never to discard or sell! We'll not forsake you! Oh, we'll let you lose many battles but never the war, we'll allow you to starve but not to die, we'll permit your banking compatriots to finance us and therefore their own destruction, we'll suffer you to bleed America to death, we'll strengthen our enemies—but not too much—and assist you to be raped. But don't worry, we'll never let you disappear. Oh, no! Never. You're far too valuable.

"PLOs are arrogant and full of themselves," a tall student said darkly, "and never polite and never conscious of Iran's importance in the world and know nothing of our ancient history."

"True! They're peasants and they've parasited themselves throughout the Middle East and our Gulf, taking the best jobs."

"Yes," another agreed. "They're worse than the Jews . . ."

Rakoczy laughed to himself. He enjoyed his job very much, enjoyed working with university students—always a fertile field—enjoyed being a teacher. But that's what I am, he thought contentedly, a professor of terrorism, of power and the seizing of power. Perhaps I'm more like a farmer: I plant the seed, nurture it, guard it, and harvest it, working all hours and all seasons as a farmer must. Some years are good and some bad but every year a little further forward, a little more experienced, a little wiser about the land, ever more patient—spring summer autumn winter—always the same farm, Iran, always with the same aim: at best for Iran to become Russian soil, at worst a Russian satellite to protect the sacred motherland of Russia. With our foot on the Strait of Hormuz . . .

Ah, he thought, an unearthly, consuming religious glow pervading him, if I could give Iran to Mother Russia my life will not have been lived in vain.

The West deserves to lose, particularly the Americans. They're such fools, so egocentric, but most of all so stupid. It's inconceivable this Carter doesn't see the value of Hormuz in general and Iran in particular and what a catastrophe to the West their loss will be. But there it is; for all practical purposes he's given us Iran.

Rakoczy remembered the shock wave of disbelief that had soared to the very top when their innermost contacts in Washington had whispered that Carter was going to forsake the Shah. Ah, what an ally Carter has been to us. If I believed in God I'd pray: God is Great, God is Great, protect our best ally, President Peanut, and let him win a second term! With him in for a second term we'll own America and so rule the world! God is Great, God is . . .

Abruptly he felt chilled. He had been pretending to be Muslim for so long that sometimes his cover overcame his real self, and he began to question and have doubts.

Am I still Igor Mzytryk, captain KGB, married to my darling Delaurah, my oh so beautiful Armenian, who's waiting in Tbilisi for me to come home? Is she at home, she who oh so secretly believes in God—the God of the Christians that is the same as the God of the Muslims and of the Jews?

God. God who has a thousand names. Is there a God?

There is no God, he told himself like a litany, and put that thought back into its compartment and concentrated on the riot to be.

Around them tension was growing nicely among the massed students, angry cries raging back and forth: "We didn't spill our blood for mullahs to take all the power! Unite, brothers and sisters! Unite under the Tudeh banners . . ."

"Down with the Tudeh! Unite for the holy Islamic-Marxist cause, we mujhadin spilled our blood and we are the martyrs of Imam Ali, Lord of the Martyrs, and Lenin . . ."

"Down with the mullahs and Khomeini, archtraitor to Iran . . ."

Vast cheers greeted this shout and others took it up, then gradually, again the dominating voice was: "Unite, brothers and sisters, unite to the real leaders of the revolution, the Tudeh, unite to protect th—"

Rakoczy watched the crowd critically. It was still in pieces, formless, not yet a mob that could be directed and used as a weapon. Some bystanders, Islamics, watched and listened with varying degrees of contempt or rage. The few moderates shook their heads and walked away, leaving the stage to the vast majority who were deeply committed and anti-Khomeini.

Around them the buildings were tall, and brick, the university built by Reza Shah in the thirties. Five years ago Rakoczy had spent a few terms here pretending to be an Azerbaijani though the Tudeh knew him as Dimitri Yazernov and that he had been sent—continuing a pattern—to organize university cells. Since its beginning the university was always a place of dissension, anti-Shah, although Mohammed Shah, more than any monarch in Persia's history, had lavishly supported education. The Tehran students had been the vanguard of the rebellion, long before Khomeini had become the coalescing core.

Without Khomeini, we'd never've succeeded, he thought. Khomeini was the flame around which we could all cluster and unite to tip the Shah off the throne and the U.S. out. He's not senile or a bigot as many say but a ruthless leader with a dangerously clear plan, a dangerously great charisma, and dangerously huge power among the Shi'ites—so now it's time he joined the god that never was.

Rakoczy laughed suddenly.

"What is it?" Farmad asked.

"I was just thinking what Khomeini and all the mullahs will say when they discover there's no god and never was a god—there's no heaven, no hell, no houris, and it's all a myth."

The others laughed too. One didn't. Ibrahim Kyabi. There was no laughter left in him, just the wish for revenge. When he had gone home yesterday afternoon he had discovered his house in turmoil, his mother prostrate in tears, his brothers and sisters in anguish. The news had just arrived that his engineer father had been murdered by Islamic Guards outside his IranOil HQ at Ahwaz and that his body had been left to the vultures.

"For what?" he had screamed.

"For—for crimes against Islam," his uncle, Dewar Kyabi, who had brought home the terrible news, said through his own tears. "That's what they told us —his murderers. They were from Abadan, fanatics, illiterates mostly, and they told us that he was an American quisling, that for years he had cooperated with the enemies of Islam, allowing and helping them to steal our oil, th—"

"Lies, all lies," Ibrahim had shouted at him. "Father was anti-Shah, a patriot—a Believer! Who were those dogs? Who? I will burn them and their fathers. What were their names?"

"It was the Will of God, Ibrahim, that they did it. Insha'Allah! Oh, my poor brother! The Will of God . . ."

"There is no God!"

The others had stared at him, shocked. This was the first time Ibrahim had articulated a thought that had been building for many years, nurtured by student friends returning from overseas, friends at the university, fed by some of the teachers who had never said this openly, merely encouraging them to question anything and everything.

"Insha'Allah is for fools," he had said, "a curse of superstition for fools to hide under!"

"You mustn't say that, my son!" his mother had cried out, frightened. "Go to the mosque, beg God's forgiveness—that your father is dead is the Will of God, nothing more. Go to the mosque."

"I will," he had said, but in his heart he knew his life had changed—no God could have allowed this to happen. "Who were those men, Uncle? Describe them."

"They were just ordinary, Ibrahim, as I already told you, younger than you, most of them—there was no leader or mullah with them, though there was one in the foreigners' helicopter that came from Bandar Delam. But my poor brother died cursing Khomeini; if only he hadn't come back by the foreigners' helicopters, if only . . . but then, Insha'Allah, they were waiting for him anyway."

"There was a mullah in the helicopter?"

"Yes, yes, there was."

"You will go to the mosque, Ibrahim?" his mother had asked him again.

"Yes," he had said, the first lie he had ever told her. It had taken him no time to find the university Tudeh leaders and Dimitri Yazernov, to swear allegiance, to get a machine gun, and, most of all, to ask them to find the name of the mullah in the helicopter of Bandar Delam. And now he stood there waiting, wanting vengeance, his soul crying out against the outrage committed against his father in the name of the false god. "Dimitri, let's begin!" he said, his fury whipped by the shouting of the crowd.

"We must wait, Ibrahim," Rakoczy said gently, very pleased to have the youth with them. "Don't forget the mob is a means to an end—remember the plan!" When he had told it to them an hour ago they had been stunned.

"Raid the American embassy?"

"Yes," he had said calmly, "a quick raid, in and out, tomorrow or the next day. Tonight the rally will become a mob. The embassy's hardly a mile and a half away. It will be easy to send the mob rampaging that way as an experiment. What more perfect cover could we have for a raid than a riot? We let the enemy mujhadin and fedayeen go against Islamics and kill each other off while we take the initiative. Tonight we plant more seeds. Tomorrow or the next day we'll raid the U.S. embassy."

"But it's impossible, Dimitri, impossible!"

"It's easy. Just a raid, not an attempt at a takeover, that will come later. A raid will be unexpected, it's simple to execute. You can easily grab the embassy for an hour, hold the ambassador and everyone captive for an hour or so while you sack it. Americans do not have the will to resist. That's the key to them! Here are the plans of the buildings and the numbers of marines and I will be there to help. Your coup will be immense—it will hit world headlines and totally embarrass Bazargan and Khomeini, and even more the Americans. Don't forget who the real enemy is and that now you have to act fast to grab the initiative from Khomeini. . . ."

It had been easy to convince them. It will be easy to create the diversion, he thought. And it'll be easy to go straight to the CIA basement office and radio room, blow the safe, and empty it of all documents and cipher books, then up the back stairs to the second landing, turn left, into the third room on the left, the ambassador's bedroom, to the safe behind the oil painting hanging over the bed, blow that and empty it similarly. Sudden, swift, and violent—if there's any opposition.

"Dimitri! Look!"

Rakoczy spun around. Coming down the road were hundreds of youths— Green Bands and mullahs at the head. At once Rakoczy roared, "Death to Khomeini!" and fired a burst into the air. The suddenness of the shots whipped everyone into a frenzy, there were shouts and countershouts, simultaneously other guns went off all over the quadrangle, and everyone began to scatter, trampling over one another in their haste, the screams beginning.

Before he could stop him, he saw Ibrahim aim at the oncoming Green Bands and fire. Some men in the front rank went down, a howl of rage burst from them, and guns opened up in their direction. He dived to the ground, cursing. The torrent of bullets missed him but got Farmad and others nearby but not Ibrahim and the remaining three Tudeh leaders. He shouted at them and they all hugged the cement as panic-stricken students opened up with carbines and pistols.

Many were wounded before the big mujhadin Rakoczy had marked for execution rallied his men around him and led a charge at the Islamics and drove them back. At once others came to his aid and the retreat became a rout, a roar went through the students, and the rally became a mob.

Rakoczy grabbed Ibrahim who was just about to charge off mindlessly.

"Follow me!" he ordered, half shoved Ibrahim and the others farther into the lee of the building, then, when he was sure they were with him, took to his heels in a frantic, chest-hurting retreat.

At a junction of paths in the snow-covered gardens, he stopped a moment to catch his breath. The wind was chill and night on them now.

"What about Farmad?" Ibrahim gasped. "He was wounded!"

"No," he said, "he was dying. Come on!"

Again he led the rush unerringly through the garden, along the street near the scientific faculty, across the parking lot into the next, and he did not stop till the sound of the riot was distant. There was a stitch in his side and his breathing came in great pants, tearing at him. When he could speak, he said, "Don't worry about anything. Go back to your homes or your dormitories.

Get everyone ready for the raid, tomorrow or the next day—the committee will give the order." He hurried away into the gathering night.

AT LOCHART'S APARTMENT: 7:30 P.M. Sharazad was lying in a foam bath, her head propped on a waterproof pillow, eyes closed, her hair tied up in a towel. "Oh, Azadeh, darling," she said drowsily, perspiration beading her forehead, "I'm so happy."

Azadeh was also in the bath and she lay with her head at the other end, enjoying the heat and the intimacy and the sweet perfumed water and the luxury—her long hair also up in a pure white towel—the bath large and deep and comfortable for two. But there were still dark rings under her eyes, and she could not shake off the terrors of yesterday at the roadblock or in the helicopter. Outside the curtains, night had come. Gunfire echoed in the distance. Neither paid it any attention.

"I wish Erikki would come back," Azadeh said.

"He won't be long, there's lots of time, darling. Dinner's not till nine, so we've almost two hours to get ready." Sharazad opened her eyes and put her hand on Azadeh's slender thighs, enjoying the touch of her. "Don't worry, darling Azadeh, he'll be back soon, your redheaded giant! And don't forget I'm spending the night with my parents so you two can run naked together all night long! Enjoy our bath, be happy, and swoon when he returns." They laughed together. "Everything's wonderful now, you're safe, we're all safe, Iran's safe—with the Help of God the Imam has conquered and Iran's safe and free."

"I wish I could believe it, I wish I could believe it as you do," Azadeh said. "I can't explain how terrible those people near the roadblock were—it was as though I was being choked by their hate. Why should they hate us—hate me and Erikki? What had we done to them? Nothing at all and yet they hated us."

"Don't think about them, my dear one." Sharazad stifled a yawn. "Leftists are all mad, claiming to be Muslim and at the same time Marxist. They're anti-God and therefore cursed. The villagers? Villagers are uneducated as you know too well, and most of them simple. Don't worry—that's past, now everything is going to be better, you'll see."

"I hope, oh, how I hope you're right. I don't want it better but just as it was, normal, like it's always been, normal again."

"Oh, it will be." Sharazad felt so contented, the water so silky and so warm and womblike. Ah, she thought, only three more days to be sure and then Tommy tells Father that oh, yes, of course he wants sons and daughters, and then, the next day, the great day, I should know for certain though I'm certain now. Haven't I always been so regular? Then I can give Tommy my gift of God and he'll be so proud. "The Imam does the Work of God. How can it be otherwise than good?"

"I don't know, Sharazad, but never in our history have mullahs been worthy of trust—just parasites on the back of the villagers."

"Ah, but now it's different," Sharazad told her, not really wanting to discuss such serious matters. "Now we have a real leader. Now he's in control of Iran for the first time ever. Isn't he the most pious of men, the most learned of Islam and the law? Doesn't he do God's work? Hasn't he achieved the impossible, throwing out the Shah and his nasty corruption, stopping the generals from making a coup with the Americans? Father says we're safer now than we've ever been."

"Are we?" Azadeh remembered Rakoczy in the chopper and what he had said about Khomeini and stepping backward in history, and she knew he had spoken the truth, a lot of truth, and she had clawed at him, hating him, wanting him dead, for of course he was one of those who would use the simpleminded mullahs to enslave everyone else. "You want to be ruled by Islamic laws of the Prophet's time, almost fifteen hundred years ago—enforced chador, the loss of our hard-won rights of voting, working, and being equal?"

"I don't want to vote, or work, or be equal—how can a woman equal a man? I just want to be a good wife to Tommy, and in Iran I prefer the chador on the streets." Delicately Sharazad covered another yawn, drowsed by the warmth. "Insha'Allah, Azadeh, darling. Of course everything will be as before but Father says more wonderful because now we possess ourselves, our land, our oil, and everything in our land. There'll be no nasty foreign generals or politicians to disgrace us and with the evil Shah gone, we'll all live happily ever after, you with your Erikki, me with my Tommy, and lots and lots of children. How else could it be? God is with the Imam and the Imam is with us! We're so lucky." She smiled at her and put her arm around her friend's legs affectionately. "I'm so glad you're staying with me, Azadeh. It seems such a long time since you were in Tehran."

"Yes." They had been friends for many years. First in Switzerland where they had met at school, up in the High Country, though Sharazad had only stayed one term, unhappy to be away from her family and Iran, then later at the university in Tehran. And now, for a little over a year, because both had married foreigners in the same company, they had become even closer, closer than sisters, helping each other adapt to foreign idiosyncrasies:

"Sometimes I just don't understand my Tommy at all, Azadeh," Sharazad had said tearfully in the beginning. "He enjoys being alone, I mean quite alone, just him and me, the house empty, not even one servant—he even told me he likes to be alone by himself, just reading, no family around or children, no conversation or friends. Oh, sometimes it's just awful."

"Erikki's just the same," Azadeh had said. "Foreigners aren't like us— they're very strange. I want to spend days with friends and children and family, but Erikki doesn't. It's good that Erikki and Tommy work during the days—you're luckier, Tommy's off for two weeks at a time when you can be normal. Another thing, you know, Sharazad, it took me months to get used to sleeping in a bed an—"

"I never could! Oh, so high off the floor, so easy to fall off, always a huge dip on his side, so you're always uncomfortable and you wake up with an ache in your back. A bed's so awful compared with soft quilts on beautiful carpets on the floor, so comfortable and civilized."

"Yes. But Erikki won't use quilts and carpets, he insists on a bed. He just won't try it anymore—sometimes it's such a relief when he's away."

"Oh, we sleep correctly now, Azadeh. I stopped the nonsense of a Western bed after the first month."

"How did you do it?"

"Oh, I'd sigh all night long and keep my poor darling awake—then I'd sleep during the day to be fresh again to sigh all night long." Sharazad had laughed delightedly. "Seven nights and my darling collapsed, slept like a baby for the next three nights correctly, and now he always sleeps like a civilized person should—he even does so when he's at Zagros! Why don't you try it? I guarantee you'll be successful, darling, particularly if you also complain just a tiny bit that the bed has caused a backache and of course you would still adore to make love but please be a little careful."

Azadeh had laughed. "My Erikki's cleverer than your Tommy—when Erikki tried the quilts on our carpet *he* sighed all night and turned and turned and kept me awake—I was so exhausted after three nights I quite liked the bed. When I visit my family I sleep civilized, though when Erikki's at the palace we use a bed. You know, darling, another problem: I love my Erikki but sometimes he's so rude I almost die. He keeps saying 'yes' and 'no' when I ask him something—how can you have a conversation after yes or no?"

She smiled to herself now. Yes, it's very difficult living with him, but living without him now is unthinkable—all his love and good humor and size and strength and always doing what I want but only just a little too easily, so I have little chance to sharpen my wiles. "We're both very lucky, Sharazad, aren't we?"

"Oh, yes, darling. Can you stay for a week or two—even if Erikki has to go back, you stay, please?"

"I'd like to. When Erikki gets back . . . perhaps I'll ask him."

Sharazad shifted in the bath, moving the bubbles over her breasts, blowing them off her hands. "Mac said they'd come here from the airport if they were delayed. Genny's coming straight from the apartment but not before nine—I also asked Paula to join us, the Italian girl, but not for Nogger, for Charlie." She chuckled. "Charlie almost swoons when she just looks at him!"

"Charlie Pettikin? Oh, but that's wonderful. Oh, that's very good. Then we should help him—we owe him so much! Let's help him snare the sexy Italian!"

"Wonderful! Let's plan how to give Paula to him."

"As a mistress or wife?"

"Mistress. Well . . . let me think! How old is she? She must be at least twenty-seven. Do you think she'd make him a good wife? He should have a wife. All the girls Tommy and I have shown him discreetly, he just smiles and shrugs—I even brought my third cousin who was fifteen, thinking that would tempt him, but nothing. Oh, good, now we have something to plan. We've plenty of time to plan and dress and get ready—and I've some lovely dresses for you to choose from."

"It feels so strange, Sharazad, not to have anything—anything. Money, papers . . ." For an instant Azadeh was back in the Range Rover near the roadblock, and there before her was the fat-faced mujhadin who had stolen their papers, his machine gun blazing as Erikki rammed him against the other car, crushing him like a cockroach, blood and filth squeezed from his mouth. "Having nothing," she said, forcing the bad away, "not even a lipstick."

"Never mind, I've lots of everything. And Tommy'll be so pleased to have you and Erikki here. He doesn't like me to be alone either. Poor darling, don't worry. You're safe now."

I don't feel safe at all, Azadeh told herself, hating the fear that was so alien to her whole upbringing—that even now seemed to take away the warmth of the water. I haven't felt safe since we left Rakoczy on the ground and even that had only lasted a moment, the ecstasy of escaping that devil—me, Erikki, and Charlie unhurt. Even the joy of finding a car with gasoline in it at the little airstrip didn't take my fear away. I hate being afraid.

She ducked down a little in the tub, then reached up and turned on the hot-water tap, swirling the hot currents.

"That feels so good," Sharazad murmured, the foam heavy, and the water sensuous. "I'm so pleased you wanted to stay."

Last evening, by the time Azadeh, Erikki, and Charlie had reached McIver's apartment it was after dark. They had found Gavallan there, so no room for them—Azadeh had been too frightened to want to stay in her father's apartment, even with Erikki—so she had asked Sharazad if they could move in with her until Lochart returned. Sharazad had delightedly agreed at once, glad for the company. Everything had begun to be fine and then, during dinner, there was gunfire nearby, making her jump.

"No need to worry, Azadeh," McIver had said. "Just a few hotheads letting off steam, celebrating probably. Didn't you hear Khomeini's order to lay down all arms?" Everyone agreeing and Sharazad saying, "The Imam will be obeyed," always referring to Khomeini as "the Imam," almost associating him with the Twelve Imams of Shi'ism—the direct descendants of Mohammed the Prophet, near divinity—surely a sacrilege: "But what the Imam's accomplished is almost a miracle, isn't it?" Sharazad had said with her beguiling innocence. "Surely our freedom's a gift of God?"

Then so warm and toasty in bed with Erikki, but him strange and brooding and not the Erikki she had known. "What's wrong, what's wrong?"

"Nothing, Azadeh, nothing. Tomorrow I'll make a plan. There was no time tonight to talk to Mac or Gavallan. Tomorrow we'll make a plan, now sleep, my darling."

Twice in the night she had awakened from violent dreams, trembling and terrified, crying out for Erikki.

"It's all right, Azadeh, I'm here. It was only a dream, you're quite safe now."

"No, no, we're not. I don't feel safe, Erikki—what's happening to me? Let's go back to Tabriz, or let's go away, go away from these awful people."

In the morning Erikki had left her to join McIver and Gavallan, and she had slept some more but gathered little strength from the sleep. Passing the rest of the morning daydreaming or hearing Sharazad's news about going to Galeg Morghi, or listening to the hourly crop of rumors from her servants: many more generals shot, many new arrests, the prisons burst open by mobs, Western hotels set on fire or shot up. Rumors of Bazargan taking the reins of government, mujhadin in open rebellion in the south, Kurds rebelling in the north, Azerbaijan declaring independence, the nomad tribes of the Kash'kai and Bakhtiari throwing off the yoke of Tehran; everyone laying down their arms or no one laying down their arms. Rumors that Prime Minister Bakhtiar had been captured and shot or escaped to the hills or to Turkey, to America; President Carter preparing an invasion or Carter recognizing Khomeini's government; Soviet troops massing on the border ready to invade or Brezh-

nev coming to Tehran to congratulate Khomeini; the Shah landing in Kurdi-
stan supported by American troops or the Shah dead in exile.

Then going to lunch with Sharazad's parents at the Bakravan house near
the bazaar, but only after Sharazad had insisted she wear the chador, hating
the chador and everything it stood for. More rumors at the huge family
house, but benign there, no fear and absolute confidence. Abundance as
always, just as in her own home in Tabriz, servants smiling and safe and
thanks be to God for victory, Jared Bakravan had told them jovially, and now
with the bazaar going to open and all foreign banks closed, business will be
marvelous as it was before the ungodly laws the Shah instituted.

After lunch they had returned to Sharazad's apartment. By foot. Wrapped
in the chador. Never a problem for them and every man deferential. The
bazaar was crowded, with pitifully little for sale though every merchant fore-
told abundance ready to be trucked, trained, or flown in—ports clogged with
hundreds of ships, laden with merchandise. On the street, thousands walked
this way and that, Khomeini's name on every lip, chanting "Allah-u
Akbarrr," almost all men and boys armed—none of the old people. In some
areas Green Bands, in place of police, haphazardly and amateurishly directed
traffic, or stood around truculently. In other areas police as always. Two tanks
rumbled past driven by soldiers, masses of guards and civilians on them,
waving to the cheering pedestrians.

Even so, everyone was tense under the patina of joy, particularly the
women enveloped in their shrouds. Once, they had turned a corner and seen
ahead a group of youths surrounding a dark-haired woman dressed in Western clothes, jeering at her, abusing her, shouting insults, and making obscene
signs, several of them exposing themselves, waggling their penises at her. The
woman was in her thirties, dressed neatly, a short coat over her skirt, long legs
and long hair under a little hat. Then she was joined by a man who shoved
through the crowd to her. At once he began shouting that they were English
and to leave them alone, but the men paid no attention to him, jostling him,
concentrating on the woman. She was petrified.

There was no way for Sharazad and Azadeh to walk around the crowd that
grew quickly, hemming them in, so they were forced to watch. Then a
mullah arrived and told the crowd to leave, harangued the two foreigners to
obey Islamic customs. By the time they got home they were tired and both
felt soiled. They had taken off their clothes and collapsed on the quilt bed.

"I'm glad I went out today," Azadeh had said wearily, deeply concerned.
"But we women better organize a protest before it's too late. We better
march through the streets, without chador or veils, to make our point with

the mullahs: that we're not chattel, we have rights, and wearing the chador's up to us—not to them."

"Yes, let's! After all, we helped win the victory too!" Sharazad had yawned, half asleep. "Oh, I'm so tired."

The nap had helped.

Idly Azadeh was watching the bubbles of foam crackling, the water hotter now, the sweet-smelling vapor very pleasing. Then she sat up for a moment, smoothing the foam on her breasts and shoulders. "It's curious, Sharazad, but I was glad to wear chador today—those men were so awful."

"Men on the street are always awful, darling Azadeh." Sharazad opened her eyes and watched her, golden skin glistening, nipples proud. "You're so beautiful, Azadeh darling."

"Ah, thank you—but you're the beautiful one." Azadeh rested her hand on her friend's stomach and patted her. "Little mother, eh?"

"Oh, I do so hope so." Sharazad sighed, closed her eyes and gave herself back to the heat. "I can hardly imagine myself a mother. Three more days and then I'll know. When are you and Erikki going to have children?"

"In a year or two." Azadeh kept her voice calm as she told the same lie she had told so many times already. But she was deeply afraid that she was barren, for she had used no contraceptives since she was married and had wished, with all her heart, to have Erikki's child from the beginning. Always the same nightmare welling up: that the abortion had taken away any chance of children as much as the German doctor had tried to reassure her. How could I have been so stupid?

So easy. I was in love. I was just seventeen and I was in love, oh, how deeply in love. Not like with Erikki, for whom I will give my life gladly. With Erikki it is true and forever and kind and passionate and safe. With my Johnny Brighteyes it was dreamlike.

Ah, I wonder where you are now, what you're doing, you so tall and fair with your blue-gray eyes and oh, so British. Whom did you marry? How many hearts did you break like you broke mine, my darling?

That summer he was at school in Rougemont—the village next to where she was at finishing school—ostensibly to learn French. It was after Sharazad had left. She had met him at the Sonnenhof, basking in the sun, overlooking all the beauty of Gstaad in its bowl of mountains. He was nineteen then, she three days seventeen, and all that summer long they had wandered the High Country—so beautiful, so beautiful—up in the mountains and the forests, swimming in streams, playing, loving, ever more adventurous, up above the clouds.

More clouds than I care to think of, she told herself dreamily, my head in the clouds that summer, knowing about men and life, but not knowing. Then in the fall him saying, "Sorry, but I must go now, go back to university but I'll be back for Christmas." Never coming back. And long before Christmas finding out. All the anguish and terror where there should have been only happiness. Petrified that the school would find out, for then her parents would have to be informed. Against the law to have an abortion in Switzerland without parents' consent—so going over the border to Germany where the act was possible, somehow finding the kindly doctor who had assured her and reassured her. Having no pain, no trouble, none—just a little difficulty borrowing the money. Still loving Johnny. Then the next year, school finished, everything secret, coming home to Tabriz. Stepmother finding out somehow—I'm sure Najoud, my stepsister, betrayed me, wasn't it she who lent me the money? Then Father knowing.

Kept like a spiked butterfly for a year. Then forgiveness, a peace—a form of peace. Begging for university in Tehran. "I agree, providing you swear by God, no affairs, absolute obedience, and you marry only whom I choose," the Khan had said.

Top of her class. Then begging for the Teaching Corps, any excuse to get out of the palace. "I agree, but only on our lands. We've more than enough villages for you to look after," he had said.

Many men of Tabriz wanting to marry her but her father refusing them, ashamed of her. Then Erikki.

"And when this foreigner, this . . . this impoverished, vulgar, ill-mannered, spirit-worshiping monster who can't speak a word of Farsi or Turkish, who knows nothing of our customs or history or how to act in civilized society, whose only talent is that he can drink enormous quantities of vodka and fly a helicopter—when he finds out you're not a virgin, that you're soiled, spoiled, and perhaps ruined inside forever?"

"I've already told him, Father," she had said through her tears. "Also that without your permission I cannot marry."

Then the miracle of the attack on the palace and Father almost killed, Erikki like an avenging warrior from the ancient storybooks. Permission to marry, another miracle. Erikki understanding, another miracle. But as yet no child. Old Dr. Nutt says I'm perfect and normal and to be patient. With the Help of God soon I will have a son, and this time there will be only happiness, like with Sharazad, so beautiful with her lovely face and breasts and flanks, hair like silk and skin like silk.

She felt the smoothness of her friend beneath her fingers and it pleased her greatly. Absently she began to caress her, letting herself drift in the warmth and tenderness. We're blessed to be women, she thought, able to bathe together and sleep together, to kiss and touch and love without guilt. "Ah, Sharazad," she murmured, surrendering too, "how I love your touch."

IN THE OLD CITY: 7:52 P.M. The man hurried across the snow-covered square near the ancient Mehrid mosque and went through the main gate of the roofed bazaar, out of the freezing cold into the warm, crowded, familiar semi-darkness. He was in his fifties, corpulent, panting in his haste, his Astrakhan hat askew, his clothes expensive. A heavily laden donkey blocked his way in the narrow alley and he cursed, stood back to let the animal and its owner squeeze past, then hurried on again, turned left into a passage, then into the Street of the Clothes Sellers.

Take your time, he told himself over and over, his chest hurting and his limbs hurting. You're safe now, slow down. But his terror overcame his mind and, still in panic, he scuttled on to vanish in the vast labyrinth. In his wake, a few minutes behind him, a group of armed Green Bands followed. They did not hurry.

Ahead, the narrow street of the rice shops was blocked with bigger crowds than usual, all vying for the small amount for sale. He stopped for a moment and wiped his brow, then went on again. The bazaar was like a honeycomb, teeming with life, with hundreds of dirt lanes, alleys, and passages, lined on both sides with dimly lit open-fronted shops—some two-storied—and booths and cubbyholes, some barely more than niches scooped out of the walls, for goods or services of all kinds—from foodstuffs to foreign watches, from butchers to bullion, from moneylenders to munitions dealers—all waiting for a customer even though there was not much to sell or to do. Above the noise and clatter and bargaining the high-vaulted ceiling had skylights for ventilation and to let light in during the day. The air was heavy with the special smell of the bazaar—smells of smoke and rancid cooking fat, rotting fruit and roasting meat, food, spices, and urine and dung and dust and gasoline, honey and dates and offal, all mixed with the smells of bodies and the sweat of the multitude who were born, lived, and died here.

People of all ages and all kinds crammed the byways—Tehranis, Turkomans, Kurds, Kash'kai, Armenians and Arabs, Lebanese and Levantines —but the man paid no attention to them or to the constant entreaties to stop and buy, he just shoved and twisted his way through the crowds, darted across his own street of goldsmiths, down that of the spice sellers, the jewelry makers, onward ever deeper into the maze, his hair under his Astrakhan hat matted with sweat, his face florid. Two shopkeepers who noticed him laughed, one to another: "By God, I've never seen old Paknouri waddle so fast before—that old dog must be on his way to collect a ten-rial debt."

"More likely Miser Paknouri's got a succulent tribesboy waiting on a carpet, the lad's bum winking in the air!"

Their banter died quickly as the armed Green Bands passed. When they were safely out of sight, someone muttered, "What do those young motherless dogs want here?"

"They're looking for someone. It must be that. May their fathers burn! Didn't you hear they've been arresting folk all day?"

"Arresting people? What are they doing with them?"

"Putting them in jail. They've possession of jails now—didn't you hear they broke down the door of Evin Jail and set everyone free and locked up the jailers and now run it. They've set up their own firing squads and courts, I heard, and shot lots of generals and police. And there's a riot going on right now—at the university."

"God protect us! My son Farmad's at a rally there, the young fool! I told him not to go tonight."

Jared Bakravan, Sharazad's father, was in his upper-story, private inner room over the open-fronted shop in the Street of the Moneylenders that had been in his family for five generations and was in one of the best positions. His specialty was banking and financing. He was seated on thick pile carpets, drinking tea with his old friend, Ali Kia, who had managed to be appointed an official in the Bazargan government. Bakravan's eldest son, Meshang, sat just behind him, listening and learning—a good-looking clean-shaven man in his thirties, inclined to comfortable corpulence. Ali Kia was clean-shaven also, with glasses, Bakravan white-bearded and heavy. Both were in the sixties and had known each other most of their lives.

"And how will the loan be repaid, over what time period?" Bakravan asked.

"Out of oil revenues, as always," Kia said patiently, "just as the Shah would have done, the time period over five years, at the usual one percent per month. My friend, Mehdi, Mehdi Bazargan, says Parliament will guarantee the loan the moment it meets." He smiled and added, exaggerating slightly, "As I'm not only in Mehdi's cabinet but also in his inner cabinet as well, I can personally watch over the legislation. Of course you know how important the loan is, and equally important to the bazaar."

"Of course." Bakravan tugged at his beard to prevent himself guffawing. Poor Ali, he thought, just as pompous as ever! "It's certainly not my place to mention it, old friend, but some of the bazaaris have asked me what about the millions in bullion already advanced to support the revolution? Advanced to the fund for Ayatollah Khomeini—may God protect him," he added politely, in his heart thinking: May God remove him from us quickly now that we've won, before he and his rapacious, blinkered, parasitical mullahs do too much damage. As for you, Ali, old friend, bender of the truth, exaggerater of your own importance, you may be my oldest friend, but if you think I'd trust you further than a camel can cast dung . . . As if any one of us would trust any Iranian outside of immediate family—and then only with caution.

"Of course I know the Ayatollah never saw, needed, or touched a single rial," he said, meaning it, "but even so, we bazaaris advanced huge amounts of cash, bullion, and foreign exchange on his behalf, financing his campaign —of course for the Glory of God and our beloved Iran."

"Yes, we know. And God will bless you for it. So does the Ayatollah. Of course these loans will be repaid immediately we have the money—the very second! The Tehran bazaari loans are the first in line to be repaid of all internal debts—we, in government, realize how important your help has been. But, Jared, Excellency, old friend, before we can do anything we must get oil production going and to do this we must have some cash. The immediate 5 million U.S. we need will be like a grain of rice in a barrel now that all foreign banks will be curbed, controlled, and *most* cast out. The Pr—"

"Iran does not need any foreign banks. We bazaaris could do everything necessary—if we were asked. Everything. If we search diligently for the glory of Iran, perhaps, perhaps we might discover we have *all* the skills and connections in our midst." Bakravan sipped his tea with studied elegance. "My son Meshang has a degree from the Harvard Business School." The lie bothered none of them. "With the help of brilliant students like him . . ." He left the thought hanging.

Ali Kia picked it up immediately. "Surely you wouldn't consider lending his services to my Ministry of Finance and Banking? Surely he's far too important to you and your colleagues? Of course, he must be!"

"Yes, yes, he is. But our beloved country's needs should take precedence over our personal wishes—if of course the government wanted to use his unique talents."

"I will mention it to Mehdi in the morning. Yes, at my daily morning meeting with my old friend and colleague," Ali Kia said, wondering briefly when he would be allowed to have his first audience—long overdue—since he had been appointed deputy minister of finance. "I may tell him also you agree to the loan?"

"I will consult my colleagues at once. It would, of course, be their decision, not mine," Bakravan added with open sadness that fooled neither of them. "But I will press your case, old friend."

"Thank you." Again Kia smiled. "We in government, and the Ayatollah, will appreciate the help of the bazaaris."

"We're always ready to help. As you know, we always have," the older man said smoothly, remembering the massive financial support given by the bazaar to the mullahs, to Khomeini over the years—or to any political figure of integrity, like Ali Kia, who had opposed either of the Shahs.

God curse the Pahlavis, Bakravan thought, they're the cause of all our trouble. Curse them for all the trouble they've caused with their insistent, too hasty demand for modernization, for their insane disregard of our advice and influence, for inviting foreigners in, as many as fifty thousand Americans alone just a year ago, letting them take all the best jobs and all the banking business. The Shah spurned our help, broke our monopoly, strangled us, and tore away our historic heritage. Everywhere, all over Iran.

But we had our revenge. We gambled our remaining influence and treasure on Khomeini's implacable hatred and his hold over the unwashed and illiterate masses. And we won. And now, with foreign banks gone, foreigners gone, we'll be richer and with more influence than ever before. This loan will be easy to arrange but Ali Kia and his government can sweat a little. We're the only ones who can raise the money. The payment offered is not high enough yet, not nearly enough to compensate for the closing of the bazaar all those months. Now what should it be? he asked himself, highly satisfied with their negotiations. Perhaps the percentage shou—

The door burst open and Emir Paknouri rushed into the room. "Jared, they're going to arrest me!" he cried out, tears now running down his face.

"Who? Who's going to arrest you and for what?" Bakravan spluttered, the customary calm of his house obliterated, the faces of frightened assistants, clerks, teaboy, and managers now crowding the doorway.

"For . . . for crimes against Islam!" Paknouri wept openly.

"There must be some mistake! It's impossible!"

"Yes, it's impossible but they . . . they came to my house with my name . . . half an hour ago we—"

"Who? Give me their names and I'll destroy their fathers! Who came?"

"I told you! Guards, Revolutionary Guards, Green Bands, yes, them of course," Paknouri said and rushed on, oblivious of the sudden hush. Ali Kia blanched and someone muttered, God protect us! "Half an hour or so ago, with my name on a piece of paper . . . my name, Emir Paknouri, chief of the league of goldsmiths who gave millions of rials . . . they came to my house accusing me, but the servants . . . and my wife was there and I . . .

by God and the Prophet, Jared," he cried out as he fell to his knees, "I've committed no crimes—I'm an Elder of the Bazaar, I've given millions and—" Suddenly he stopped, seeing Ali Kia. "Kia, Ali Kia, Excellency, you know only too well what I did to help the revolution!"

"Of course." Kia was white-faced, his heart thumping. "There has to be a mistake." He knew Paknouri as a highly influential bazaari. Well respected, Sharazad's first husband, and one of his longtime sponsors. "There must be a mistake!"

"Of course there's a mistake!" Bakravan put his arm around the poor man and tried to calm him. "Fresh tea at once!" he ordered.

"A whisky. Please, do you have a whisky?" Paknouri mumbled. "I'll have tea afterward, do you have whisky?"

"Not here, my poor friend, but of course there's vodka." It came at once. Paknouri downed it and choked a little. He refused another. In a minute or two he became a little calmer and began again to tell what had happened. The first he had known that something was wrong were loud voices in the hallway of his palatial house just outside the bazaar—he had been upstairs with his wife, preparing for dinner. "The leader of the Guards—there were five of them—the leader was waving this piece of paper and demanding to see me. Of course the servants wouldn't dare disturb me or let such an ape in, so my chief servant said he'd see if I was in and came upstairs. He told us the paper was signed by someone called Uwari, on behalf of the Revolutionary Komiteh—in the Name of God, who're they? Who's this man Uwari? Have you ever heard of such a man, Jared?"

"It's a common enough name," Bakravan said, following the Iranian custom of always having a ready answer to something you don't know. "Have you, Excellency Ali?"

"As you say, it's a common name. Did this man mention anyone else, Excellency Paknouri?"

"He may have. God protect us! But who are they—this Revolutionary Komiteh? Ali Kia, surely you'd know?"

"Many names have been mentioned," Kia said importantly, hiding his instant unease every time "Revolutionary Komiteh" was uttered. Like everyone else in government or outside it, he thought disgustedly, I don't have any real information about its actual makeup or when or where it meets, only that it seemed to come into being the moment Khomeini returned to Iran, barely two weeks ago and, since yesterday when Bakhtiar fled into hiding, it's been acting like it was a law unto itself, ruling in Khomeini's name and with his authority, precipitously appointing new judges, most with no legal training whatsoever, authorizing arrests, revolutionary courts, and immediate executions, totally outside normal law and jurisprudence—and against our Constitution! May all their houses burn down and they go to the hell they deserve!

"Only this morning my friend Mehdi . . ." he began confidentially, then stopped, pretending to notice the staff still crowding the doorway for the first time, waved an imperious hand dismissing them. When the door was reluctantly closed, he dropped his voice, passing on the rumor as though it was private knowledge, "Only this morning, with, er, with our blessing, he went to the Ayatollah and threatened to resign unless the Revolutionary Komiteh stopped bypassing him and his authority and so put them in their place for all time."

"Praise be to God!" Paknouri said, very relieved. "We didn't win the revolution to let more lawlessness take the place of SAVAK, foreign domination, and the Shah!"

"Of course not! Praise be to God that now the government is in the best of hands. But please, Excellency Paknouri, please continue with your harrowing story."

"There's not much more to tell you, Ali," Paknouri said, calmer and braver now, surrounded by such powerful friends. "I, er, I went down to see these intruders at once and told them it was all a fatuous mistake, but this boneheaded, illiterate piece of dog turd just waved the paper in my face, said I was arrested, and that I was to go with them. I told them to wait—I told them to wait and went to fetch some papers but my wife . . . my wife told me not to trust them, that perhaps they were Tudeh or mujhadin in disguise, or fedayeen. I agreed with her and decided it would be best to come here to consult with you and the others." He put the real facts out of his mind, that he had fled the moment he had heard the leader call out in the name of Revolutionary Komiteh, and Uwari personally, that Paknouri the Miser submit to God for crimes against God.

"My poor friend," Bakravan said. "My poor friend, how you must have suffered! Never mind, you're safe now. Stay here tonight. Ali, directly after first prayer tomorrow, go to the prime minister's office and make sure this matter is dealt with and those fools are punished. We all know Emir Paknouri's a patriot, that he and all the goldsmiths supported the revolution and are essential to this loan." Wearily he closed his ears to all the platitudes that Ali Kia was uttering now.

He studied Paknouri, seeing his still-pallid face and sweat-matted hair. Poor fellow, what a shock they must have given him. What a shame, with all his riches and good name—connected as he is through Cousin Valik's wife Annoush to the Qajars—that all my work for Sharazad came to naught. What a shame he didn't sire children with her and so cement our families together, even one child, for then certainly there would never have been a divorce and my troubles wouldn't have been compounded with this Lochart foreigner. However much this foreigner tries to learn our ways he never will. And how expensive it is to keep him to uphold the family's reputation! I must talk to Cousin Valik and again ask him to arrange for Lochart to have extra monies—Valik and his greed-filled IHC partners can well afford to do that for me from the millions they earn, most of it in foreign currency now! What would it cost them? Nothing! The cost would be passed on to Gavallan and S-G. The partners owe me a thousand favors, I who for years have advised them how to gain so much control and wealth with so little effort!

"Pay Lochart yourself, Jared, Excellency," Valik had said to him rudely the last time he'd asked him. "Surely that's your own charge. You share everything we gain—and what's such a tiny amount to my favorite cousin and the richest bazaari in Tehran?"

"But it should be a partnership charge. We can use him when we have 100 percent control. With the new plan for the future of IHC, the partnership will be richer than ever an—"

"I will at once consult the other partners. Of course, it is their decision not mine. . . ."

Liar, the old man thought, sipping tea, but then, I would have said the same. He stifled a yawn, tired now and hungry. A nap before dinner would do me good. "So sorry, Excellencies, so sorry but I have urgent business to attend to. Paknouri, old friend, I'm glad everything is resolved. Stay here tonight, Meshang will arrange quilts and cushions, and don't worry! Ali, my friend, walk with me to the bazaar gate—do you have transport?" he asked thinly, knowing that the first perk of a deputy minister would be a car and chauffeur and unlimited gasoline.

"Yes, thank you, the PM insisted I arrange it, insisted—the importance of our department, I suppose."

"As God wants!" Bakravan said.

Well satisfied, they all went out of the room, down the narrow stairs and into the small passageway that led to the open-fronted shop. Their smiles vanished and bile filled their mouths.

Waiting there were the same five Green Bands, lolling on the desks and chairs, all armed with U.S. Army carbines, all in their early twenties, unshaven or bearded, their clothes poor and soiled, some with holed shoes, some sockless. The leader picked his teeth silently, the rest were smoking, carelessly dropping their ash on Bakravan's priceless Kash'kai carpets. One of these youths coughed badly as he smoked, his breath wheezing.

Bakravan felt his knees weakening. All of his staff stood frozen against one of the walls. Everyone. Even his favorite teaboy. Out in the street it was very quiet, no one about—even the owners of the moneylending shops across the alley seemed to have vanished.

"Salaam, Agha, the Blessing of God on you," he said politely, his voice sounding strange. "What can I do for you?"

The leader paid no attention to him, just kept his eyes boring into Paknouri, his face handsome but scarred by the parasite disease, carried by sandflies and almost endemic in Iran. He was in his early twenties, dark eyes and hair and work-scarred hands that toyed with the carbine. His name was Yusuf Senvar—Yusuf the bricklayer.

The silence grew and Paknouri could stand the strain no longer. "It's all a mistake," he screamed. "You're making a mistake!"

"You thought you'd escape the Vengeance of God by running away?" Yusuf's voice was soft, almost kind—though with a coarse village accent that Bakravan could not place.

"What Vengeance of God?" Paknouri screamed. "I've done nothing wrong, nothing."

"Nothing? Haven't you worked for and with foreigners for years, helping them to carry off the wealth of our nation?"

"Of course not to do that but to create jobs and help the econ—"

"Nothing? Haven't you served the Satan Shah for years?"

Again Paknouri shouted, "No, I was in opposition, everyone knows I . . . I was in oppo—"

"But you still served him and did his bidding?"

Paknouri's face was twisted and almost out of control. His mouth worked but he could not get the words out. Then he croaked, "Everyone served him —of course everyone served him, he was the Shah, but we worked for the revolution—the Shah was the Shah, of course everyone served him while he was in power . . ."

"The Imam didn't," Yusuf said, his voice suddenly raw. "Imam Khomeini never served the Shah. In the Name of God, did he?" Slowly he looked from face to face. No one answered him.

In the silence, Bakravan watched the man reach into his torn pocket and find a piece of paper and peer at it and he knew that he was the only one here who could stop this nightmare.

"By Order of the Revolutionary Komiteh," Yusuf began, "and Ali'allah Uwari: Miser Paknouri, you are called to judgment. Submit yo—"

"No, Excellency," Bakravan said firmly but politely, his heart pounding in his ears. "This is the bazaar. Since the beginning of time you know the bazaar has its own laws, its own leaders. Emir Paknouri is one of them, he

cannot be arrested or taken away against his will. He cannot be touched—
that is bazaari law from the beginning of time." He stared back at the young
man, fearlessly, knowing that the Shah, even SAVAK, had never dared to
challenge their laws or right of sanctuary.

"Is bazaari law greater than God's law, Moneylender Bakravan?"

He felt a wave of ice go through him. "No—no, of course not."

"Good. I obey God's law and do God's work."

"But you may not arres—"

"I obey God's law and do only God's work." The man's eyes were brown
and guileless under his black brows. He gestured at his carbine. "I do not
need this gun—none of us need guns to do God's work. I pray with all my
heart to be a martyr for God, for then I'll go straight to Paradise *without the
need to be judged, my sins forgiven me.* If it's tonight, then I will die blessing
him who kills me because I know I will die doing God's work."

"God is Great," one of the men said, the others echoed him.

"Yes, God is Great. But you, Moneylender Bakravan, did you pray five
times today as the Prophet ordered?"

"Of course, of course," Bakravan heard himself say, knowing his lie to be
sinless because of *taqiyah*—concealment—the Prophet's permission to any
Muslim to lie about Islam if he feels his life is threatened.

"Good. Be silent and be patient, I come back to you later." Another chill
racked him as he saw the man turn his attention back to Paknouri. "By order
of the Revolutionary Komiteh and Ali'allah Uwari: Miser Paknouri, submit
yourself to God for crimes against God."

Paknouri's mouth struggled. "I . . . I . . . you cannot . . . there . . ."
His voice trailed away. A little foam seeped from the corners of his lips. They
all watched him, the Green Bands without emotion, the others with horror.

Ali Kia cleared his throat. "Now, listen, perhaps it would be better to leave
this until tomorrow," he began, trying to keep his voice important. "Emir
Paknouri's clearly upset by the mista—"

"Who're you?" The leader's eyes bored into him as they had into Paknouri
and Bakravan. "Eh?"

"I'm Deputy Minister Ali Kia," Ali replied, keeping his courage under the
strength of the eyes, "of the Department of Finance, member of Prime
Minister Bazargan's cabinet and I suggest you wait u—"

"In the Name of God: you, your Department of Finance, your Cabinet,
your Bazargan has nothing to do with me or us. We obey the mullah Uwari,
who obeys the Komiteh, who obeys the Imam, who obeys God." The man
scratched absently and turned his attention back to Paknouri. "In the
street!" he ordered, his voice still gentle. "Or we'll drag you."

Paknouri collapsed with a groan and lay inert. The others watched help-lessly, someone muttered, "The Will of God," and the little teaboy began sobbing.

"Be quiet, boy," Yusuf said without anger. "Is he dead?"

One of the men went over and squatted over Paknouri. "No. As God wants."

"As God wants. Hassan, pick him up, put his head in the water trough, and if he doesn't wake up, we'll carry him."

"No," Bakravan interrupted bravely, "no, he'll stay here, he's sick an—"

"Are you deaf, old man?" An edge had crept into Yusuf's voice. Fear stalked the room. The little boy crammed his fist into his mouth to prevent himself from crying out. Yusuf kept his eyes on Bakravan as the man called Hassan, broad-shouldered and strong, lifted Paknouri easily and went out of the shop and up the alley. "As God wants," he said, eyes on Bakravan. "Eh?"

"Where . . . please, where will you be taking him?"

"To jail, of course. Where else should he go?"

"Which . . . which jail, please?"

One of the other men laughed. "What does it matter what jail?"

For Jared Bakravan and the others, the room was now stifling and cell-like even though the air had not changed and the open front onto the alley was as it had ever been.

"I would like to know, Excellency," Bakravan said, his voice thick, trying to mask his hatred. "Please."

"Evin."

This had been the most infamous of Tehran's prisons. Yusuf sensed an-other wave of fear. They must all be guilty to be so afraid, he thought. He glanced behind him at his younger brother. "Give me the paper."

His brother was barely fifteen, grubby and coughing badly. He took out half a dozen pieces of paper and shuffled through them. He found the one he sought. "Here it is, Yusuf."

The leader peered at it. "Are you sure it's the right one?"

"Yes." The youth pointed a stubby finger at the name. Slowly he spelled out the characters. "J-a-r-e-d B-a-k-r-a-v-a-n."

Someone muttered, "God protect us!" and in the vast silence Yusuf took the paper and held it out to Bakravan. The others watched, frozen.

Hardly breathing, the old man took it, his fingers trembling. For a moment he could not focus his eyes. Then he saw the words: "Jared Bakravan of the Tehran bazaar, by order of the Revolutionary Komiteh and Ali'allah Uwari, you are summoned to the Revolutionary Tribunal at Evin Jail tomorrow immediately after first prayer to answer questions." The paper was signed, Ali'allah, the writing illiterate.

"What questions?" he asked dully.

"As God wills." The leader shouldered his carbine and got up. "Until dawn. Bring the paper with you and don't be late." At that moment he noticed the silver tray and cut glasses and half-empty bottle of vodka that was on a low table almost hidden by a curtain in the dark hallway, glinting in some candlelight. "By God and the Prophet," he said angrily, "have you forgotten the laws of God?"

The shop people scattered out of his way as he upended the bottle, emptying the contents on the dirt floor, and hurled the bottle away. Some of the liquid ran onto one of the carpets. Instinctively the teaboy fell on his knees and began to mop it up.

"Leave it alone!"

Petrified, the boy scuttled away. With his foot, Yusuf carelessly diverted most of the flow. "Let the stain remind you of the laws of God, old man," he said. "If it stains." For a moment he studied the carpet. "What colors! Beautiful! Beautiful!" He sighed and scratched, then turned on Bakravan and Kia. "If you were to take all the wealth of all of us *pasadan* here, and add it to that of all our families, and our fathers' families, still we could not afford even a corner of such a carpet." Yusuf smiled crookedly. "But then, if I was as rich as you, Moneylender Bakravan—do you know usury is also against the laws of God?—even if I was so rich, still I wouldn't buy such a carpet. I have no need of such treasure. I have nothing, we have nothing, we need nothing. Only God."

He stalked out.

NEAR THE U.S. EMBASSY: 8:15 P.M. Erikki had been waiting for almost four hours. From where he sat in the first-floor window of his friend Christian Tollonen's apartment, he could see the high walls surrounding the floodlit U.S. compound down the road, uniformed marines near the huge iron gates stamping their feet against the cold, and the big embassy building beyond. Traffic was still heavy, snarled here and there, everyone honking and trying to get ahead, pedestrians as impatient and self-centered as usual. No traffic lights working. No police. Not that they'd make any difference, he thought, Tehranis don't give a damn for traffic regulations, never have, never will. Like those madmen on the road down through the mountains who killed themselves. Like Tabrizis. Or Qazvinis.

His great fist bunched at the thought of Qazvin. At the Finnish embassy this morning there had been reports of Qazvin in a state of revolt, that Azerbaijan nationalists in Tabriz had rebelled again and fighting was going on against forces loyal to the Khomeini government and that the whole oil-rich and vastly strategic border province had again declared its independence of Tehran, independence it had fought for over the centuries, always aided and abetted by Russia, Iran's permanent enemy and gobbler of her territory. Rakoczy and others like him must be swarming all over Azerbaijan.

"Of course the Soviets are after us," Abdollah Gorgon Khan had said angrily, during the quarrel, just before he and Azadeh had left for Tehran. "Of course your Rakoczy and his men are here in strength. We walk the thinnest tightrope in the whole world because we're their key to the Gulf and the key to Hormuz, the jugular of the West. If it hadn't been for us Gorgons, our tribal connections, and some of our Kurdish allies, we'd be a Soviet province now—joined to the other half of Azerbaijan that the Soviets stole from us years ago, helped as always by the insidious British—oh, how I hate the British, even more than Americans who are just stupid and ill-mannered barbarians. It's the truth, isn't it?"

"They're not like that, not the ones I've met. And S-G's treated me fairly."

"So far. But they'll betray you—the British betray everyone who's not British and even then they'll betray them if it suits them."

"Insha'Allah."

Abdollah Gorgon Khan had laughed without humor. "Insha'Allah! And Insha'Allah that in '46 the Soviet army retreated over the border and then we smashed their quislings, and stamped out their 'Democratic Azerbaijan Republic' and the 'Kurdish People's Republic.' But I admire the Soviets, they play only to win and change the rules to suit themselves. The real winner of your world war was Stalin. He was the colossus. Didn't he dominate everything at Potsdam, Yalta, and Tehran—didn't he outmaneuver Churchill and Roosevelt? Didn't Roosevelt even stay with him in Tehran in the Soviet embassy? How we Iranians laughed! The Great President gave Stalin the future when he had the power to stuff him behind his own borders. What a genius! Beside him your ally Hitler was a craven bungler! As God wills, eh?"

"Finland sided with Hitler only to fight Stalin and get back our lands."

"But you lost, you chose the wrong side and lost. Even a fool could see Hitler would lose—how could Reza Shah have been so foolish? Ah, Captain, I never understood why Stalin let you Finns live. If I'd been him I would have laid waste Finland as a lesson—as he decimated a dozen other lands. Why did he let you all live? Because you stood up to him in your Winter War?"

"I don't know. Perhaps. I agree the Soviets will never give up."

"Never, Captain. But neither will we. We Azerbaijanis will always outmaneuver them and keep them at bay. As in '46."

But then the West was strong, there was the Truman Doctrine toward the Soviets of hands off or else, Erikki thought grimly. And now? Now Carter's at the helm? What helm?

Heavily, he leaned forward and refilled his glass, impatient to get back to Azadeh. It was cold in the apartment and he still wore his overcoat—the central heating was off and the windows drafty. But the room was large and pleasant and masculine with old easy chairs, the walls decorated with small but good Persian carpets and bronze. Books, magazines, and journals were scattered everywhere, on tables and chairs and bookshelves—Finnish, Russian, Iranian—a pair of girl's shoes carelessly on one of the shelves. He sipped the vodka, loving the warmth it gave him, then looked out the window once more at the embassy. For a moment he wondered if it would be worth emigrating to the U.S. with Azadeh. "The bastions are falling," he muttered out loud. "Iran no longer safe, Europe so vulnerable, Finland on the sword's edge . . ."

His attention focused below. Now the traffic was totally blocked by swarms of youths collecting on both roads—the U.S. embassy complex was on the corner of Tahkt-e-Jamshid and the main road called Roosevelt. Used to be called Roosevelt, he reminded himself idly. What's the road called now? Khomeini Street? Street of the Revolution?

The front door of the apartment opened. "Hey, Erikki," the young Finn said with a grin. Christian Tollonen wore a Russian-style fur hat and fur-lined trench coat that he had bought in Leningrad on a drunken weekend with other university friends. "What's new?"

"Four hours I've been waiting."

"Three hours and twenty-two minutes and half a bottle of my best contraband Russian Moskava money can buy anywhere, and we agreed three or four hours." Christian Tollonen was in his early thirties, a bachelor, fair and gray-eyed, deputy cultural attaché at the Finnish embassy. They had been friends since he came to Iran, some years ago. "Pour me one, by God, I need it—there's another demonstration simmering, and I had a hell of a time getting through." He kept his trench coat on and went to the window.

The two sections of crowds had joined now, the people milling about in front of the embassy complex. All gates had been closed. Uneasily Erikki noticed that there were no mullahs among the youths. They could hear shouting.

"Death to America, death to Carter," Christian interpreted—he could speak fluent Farsi because his father too had been a diplomat here and he had spent five years of his youth at school in Tehran. "Just the usual shit, down with Carter and American imperialism."

"No Allah-u-Akbar," Erikki said. For a moment his mind took him back to the roadblock, and ice swept into his stomach. "No mullahs."

"No. I didn't see one anywhere around." In the street the tempo picked up with different factions swirling around the iron gates. "Most of them are university students. They thought I was Russian and they told me there'd been a pitched battle at the university, leftists versus the Green Bands—with perhaps twenty or thirty killed or wounded and it was still going on." While they watched, fifty or sixty youths began rattling the gates. "They're spoiling for a fight."

"And no police to stop them." Erikki handed him the glass.

"What would we do without vodka?"

Erikki laughed. "Drink brandy. Do you have everything?"

"No—but a start." Christian sat in one of the armchairs near the low table opposite Erikki and opened his briefcase. "Here's a copy of your marriage and birth certificates—thank God we had copies. New passports for both of you—I managed to get someone in Bazargan's office to stamp yours with a temporary residence permit good for three months."

"You're a magician!"

"They promised they'd issue you a new Iranian pilot's license but when they wouldn't say. With your S-G ID and the photocopy of your British license they said you were legal enough. Now, Azadeh's passport's temporary." He opened it and showed him the photograph. "It's not standard—I took a Polaroid of the photo you gave me—but it'll pass until we can get a proper one. Get her to sign it as soon as you see her. Has she been out of the country since you were married?"

"No, why?"

"If she travels out on a Finnish passport—well, I don't know how it will affect her Iranian status. The authorities have always been touchy, particularly about their own nationals. Khomeini seems even more xenophobic so his regime's bound to be tougher. It might look to them as though she'd renounced her nationality. I don't think they'll let her back."

A muted burst of shouting from the massed youths in the street diverted them for a moment. Hundreds were waving clenched fists and somewhere someone had a loudspeaker and was haranguing them. "The way I feel right now, as long as I can get her out, I don't care," Erikki said.

The younger man glanced at him. After a moment he said, "Perhaps she should be aware of the danger, Erikki. There's no way I can get her replacement papers or any Iranian passport, but it'd be very risky for her to leave without them. Why don't you ask her father to arrange them for her? He could get them for her easily. He owns most of Tabriz, eh?"

Bleakly Erikki nodded. "Yes, but we had another row just before we left. He still disapproves of our marriage."

After a pause Christian said, "Perhaps it's because you don't have a child yet, you know how Iranians are."

"Plenty of time for children," Erikki said, sick at heart. We'll have children in good time, he thought. There's no hurry and old Dr. Nutt says she's fine. Shit! If I tell her what Christian said about her Iranian papers she'll never leave; if I don't tell her and she's refused reentry she'll never forgive me, and anyway she'd never leave without her father's permission. "To get her new papers means we'll have to go back and, well, I don't want to go back."

"Why, Erikki? Usually you can't wait to get to Tabriz."

"Rakoczy." Erikki had told him everything that had happened—except the killing of the mujhadin at the roadblock and Rakoczy killing others during the rescue. Some details are best untold, he thought grimly.

Christian Tollonen sipped his vodka. "What's the real problem?"

"Rakoczy." Erikki held his gaze steady.

Christian shrugged. Two refills emptied the bottle. *"Prosit!"*

"Prosit! Thanks for the papers and passports."

Shouting outside distracted them again. The crowd was well disciplined though it was becoming noisier. In the American courtyard more floodlights were on now, and they could see faces clearly in the embassy windows. "Just as well they've their own generators."

"Yes—and their own heating units, gasoline pumps, PX, everything." Christian went over to the sideboard and brought out a fresh bottle. "That and their special status in Iran—no visas necessary, not being subject to Iranian laws—has caused a lot of the hatred."

"By God, it's cold in here, Christian. Don't you have any wood?"

"Not a damned bit. The damned heat's been off ever since I moved in here—three months, that's almost all winter."

"Perhaps that's just as well." Erikki motioned at the pair of shoes. "You have heat enough. Eh?"

Christian grinned. "Sometimes. I will admit Tehran is one of the—used to be one of the great places on earth for all sorts of pleasures. But now, now, old friend . . ." A shadow went over his face. "Now I think Iran won't be the paradise those poor bastards out there believe they've won, but a hell on earth for most of them. Particularly the women." He sipped his vodka. There was an eddy of excitement beside the compound wall as a youth, with his U.S. Army rifle slung, climbed on the shoulders of others and tried unsuccessfully to reach the top. "I wonder what I'd do if that was my wall and those bastards started coming over at me in strength."

"You'd blow their heads off—which'd be quite legal. Wouldn't it?"

Christian laughed suddenly. "Only if you got away with it." He looked back at Erikki. "What about you? What's your plan?"

"I don't have one. Not until I talk to McIver—there was no chance this morning. He and Gavallan were both busy trying to track down the Iranian partners, then they had meetings at the British embassy with someone called —I think they said Talbot . . ."

Christian masked his sudden interest. "George Talbot?"

"Yes, that's right. D'you know him?"

"Yes, he's second secretary." Christian did not add: Talbot's also covert chief of British Intelligence in Iran, has been for years, and is one very important operator. "I didn't know he was still in Tehran—I thought he'd left a couple of days ago. What do McIver and Andrew Gavallan want with him?"

Erikki shrugged and turned away, absently watching more youths trying to scale the wall, most of his mind concerned with what to do about Azadeh's papers. "They said something about wanting to know more about a friend of his they'd met at the airport yesterday—someone called Armstrong, Robert Armstrong."

Christian Tollonen almost dropped his glass. "Armstrong?" he asked, forcing calm, very glad that Erikki had his back toward him.

"Yes." Erikki turned to him. "Mean anything to you?"

"It's a common enough name," the younger man said, pleased to hear that his voice was matter-of-fact. Robert Armstrong, MI6, ex-Special Branch, who had been in Iran on contract for a number of years—supposedly on loan from the British government—supposedly chief adviser to Iran's highly classified Department of Inner Intelligence; a man rarely seen in public and known only to very few, most of whom would be in the intelligence community.

Like me, he thought and wondered what Erikki would say if he knew that he was an Iranian intelligence expert, that he knew a lot about Rakoczy and many other foreign agents, that his prime job was to try to know everything about Iran but to do nothing and never to interfere with any of the combatants, internal or external, just to wait and watch and learn and remember. What's Armstrong still doing here?

He got up to cover his disquiet, pretending to want to see the crowd better. "Did they find out what they wanted to know?" he asked.

Again Erikki shrugged. "I don't know. I never caught up with them. I was . . ." He stopped and studied the other man. "Is it important?"

"No—no, not at all. You hungry? Are you and Azadeh free for dinner?"

"Sorry, not tonight." Erikki glanced at his watch. "I'd better be getting back. Thanks again for the help."

"Nothing. You were saying about McIver and your Gavallan? They have a plan to change operations here?"

"I don't think so. I was supposed to meet them at 3:00 P.M. to go to the airport but seeing you and getting the passports was more important to me." Erikki stood up and put out his hand, towering over him. "Thanks again."

"Nothing." Christian shook hands warmly. "See you tomorrow."

Now in the street the shouting had ceased and there was an ominous silence. Both men ran for the window. All attention turned toward the main road once called Roosevelt. Then they heard the growing, "Allahhhh-uuuu Akbarrrr!"

Erikki muttered, "Is there a back way out of the building?"

"No. No, there isn't."

The new oncoming horde had mullahs and Green Bands in their front ranks, most of them armed like the following mass of the young men. All were shouting in unison, God is Great, God is Great, totally outnumbering the student demonstration in front of the embassy, though the men there were equally armed.

At once the leftists poured into well-chosen defensive positions in doorways and among the traffic. Men, women, and children trapped in cars and trucks began to scatter. The Islamics approached fast. As the front ranks flowed along the sidewalks and through the stalled vehicles and approached the floodlit walls, the tempo of their shouting increased, their pace quickened, and everyone readied. Then, astonishingly, the students began to retreat. Silently. The Green Bands hesitated, nonplussed.

The retreat was peaceful and so the horde became peaceful. Soon the protesters had moved away and now none of them threatened the embassy. Mullahs and Green Bands began directing traffic. Those bystanders who had fled or abandoned their vehicles breathed again, thanked God for His intercession and swarmed back. At once the hooting and cursing opened up in a growing frenzy as cars and trucks and pedestrians fought for space. The great iron gates of the embassy did not open, though a side door did.

Christian's throat felt dry. "I'd've bet my life there was going to be a pitched battle."

Erikki was equally astonished. "It's almost as though they'd expected the Green Bands and knew where they were coming from and when. It was almost as though it was a rehearsal for som—" He stopped and went closer to the window, his face suddenly flushed. "Look! Down there in the doorway, that's Rakoczy."

"Where? Wh— Oh, you mean the man in the flight jacket talking to the short guy?" Christian squinted into the darkness below. The two men were half in shadow, then they shook hands and came into the light. It was Rakoczy all right. "Are you sure that . . ."

But Erikki had already pulled the front door open and was halfway down the stairs. Christian had a fleeting glimpse of him as he pulled the great pukoh knife from his belt holster and slipped it into his sleeve, haft in his palm. "Erikki, don't be a fool," he shouted but Erikki had already vanished. Christian rushed back to the window and was just in time to see Erikki run out of the doorway below, shove through the crowds in pursuit, Rakoczy nowhere to be seen.

But Erikki had him in view. Rakoczy was half a hundred yards away and he just caught sight of him turning south into Roosevelt to disappear. When Erikki got to the corner, he saw the Soviet ahead, walking quickly but not too quickly, many pedestrians between them, the traffic slow and very noisy. Making a detour around a tangle of trucks, Rakoczy stepped out into the road, waited for a hooting, battered old Volkswagen to squeeze past and glanced around. He saw Erikki. It would have been almost impossible to miss him—almost a foot taller than most everyone else. Without hesitation Rakoczy took to his heels, weaving through the crowds, and cut down a side street, running fast. Erikki saw him go and raced after him. Pedestrians cursed both of them, one old man sent flying into the filthy dirt as Rakoczy shoved past into another turning.

The side street was narrow, refuse strewn everywhere, no stalls or shops open now and no streetlights, a few weary pedestrians trudging homeward with multitudes of doorways and archways leading to hovels and staircases of more hovels—the whole area smelling of urine and waste and offal and rotting vegetables.

Rakoczy was a little more than forty yards ahead. He turned into a smaller alley, crashing through the street stalls where families were sleeping—howls of rage in his wake—changed direction and fled into a passageway and into another, cut across it into an alley, quite lost now, into another, down this and into another. Aghast, he stopped, seeing that this was a cul-de-sac. His hand went for his automatic, then he noticed a passageway just ahead and rushed for it.

The walls were so close he could touch both of them as he charged down it, his chest heaving, going ever deeper into the curling, twisting warren.

Ahead an old woman was emptying night soil into the festering joub and he sent her sprawling as others cowered against the walls to get out of his way. Now Erikki was only twenty yards behind, his rage feeding his strength, and he jumped over the old woman who was still sprawled, half in and half out of the joub, and redoubled his efforts, closing the gap. Just around the corner his adversary stopped, pulled an ancient street stall into the way, and, before Erikki could avoid it, he crashed into it and went down half stunned. With a bellow of rage he groped to his feet, swayed dizzily for a moment, climbed over the wreckage, then rushed onward again, the knife now openly in his hand, and turned the corner.

But the passageway ahead was empty. Erikki skidded to a stop. His breath was coming in great, aching gasps and he was bathed in sweat. It was hard to see though his night vision was very good. Then he noticed the small archway. Carefully he went through it, knife ready. The passage led to an open courtyard strewn with rubble and the rusty skeleton of a ravaged car. Many doorways and openings led off this dingy space, some with doors, some leading to rickety stairways and upper stories. It was silent—the silence ominous. He could feel eyes watching him. Rats scuttled out of some refuse and vanished under a pile of rubble.

To one side was another archway. Above it was an ancient inscription in Farsi that he could not read. Through the archway the darkness seemed deeper. The pitted vaulted entrance stopped at an open doorway. The door was wooden and girt with bands of ancient iron and half off its hinges. Beyond, there seemed to be a room. As he went closer he saw a candle guttering.

"What do you want?"

The man's voice came out of the darkness at him, the hair on Erikki's neck twisted. The voice was in English—not Rakoczy's—the accent foreign, a gruff eeriness to it.

"Who—who're you?" he asked uneasily, his senses searching the darkness, wondering if it was Rakoczy pretending to be someone else.

"What do you want?"

"I—I want—I'm following a man," he said, not knowing where to talk to, his voice echoing eerily from the unseen, high-vaulted roof above.

"The man you seek is not here. Go away."

"Who're you?"

"It doesn't matter. Go away."

The candle flame was just a tiny speck of light in the darkness, making the darkness seem more strong. "Did you see anyone come this way—come running this way?"

The man laughed softly and said something in Farsi. At once rustling and some muted laughter surrounded Erikki and he whirled, his knife protectively weaving in front of him. "Who are you?"

The rustling continued. All around him. Somewhere water dripped into a cistern. The air smelled dank and rancid. Sound of distant firing. Another rustle. Again he whirled, feeling someone close by but seeing no one, only the archway and the dim night beyond. The sweat was running down his face. Cautiously he went to the doorway and put his back against a wall, sure now that Rakoczy was here. The silence grew heavier.

"Why don't you answer?" he said. "Did you see anyone?"

Again a soft chuckle. "Go away." Then silence.

"Why're you afraid? Who are you?"

"Who I am is nothing to you, and there's no fear here, except yours." The voice was as gentle as before. Then the man added something in Farsi and another ripple of amusement surrounded him.

"Why do you speak English to me?"

"I speak English to you because no Iranian or reader of the language of the Book would come here by day or by night. Only a fool would come here."

Erikki's peripheral vision saw something or someone go between him and the candle. At once his knife came on guard. "Rakoczy?"

"Is that the name of the man you seek?"

"Yes—yes that's him. He's here, isn't he?"

"No."

"I don't believe you, whoever you are!"

Silence, then a deep sigh. "As God wants," and a soft order in Farsi that Erikki did not understand.

Matches flickered all around him. Candles caught, and small oil lamps. Erikki gasped. There were ragged bundles against the walls and columns of the high-domed cavern. Hundreds of them. Men and women. The diseased, festering remains of men and women lying on straw or beds of rags. Eyes in ravaged faces staring at him. Stumps of limbs. One old crone was almost beside his feet and he leaped away in panic to the center of the doorway.

"We are all lepers here," the man said. He was propped against a nearby column, a helpless mound of rags. Another rag half covered the sockets of his eyes. Almost nothing was left of his face except his lips. Feebly he waved the stump of an arm. "We're all lepers here—unclean. This is a house of lepers. Do you see this man among us?"

"No—no. I'm—I'm sorry," Erikki said shakily.

"Sorry?" The man's voice was heavy with irony. "Yes. We are all sorry. Insha'Allah! Insha'Allah."

Erikki wanted desperately to turn and flee but his legs would not move. Someone coughed, a hacking, frightful cough. Then his mouth said, "Who—who are you?"

"Once I was a teacher of English—now I am unclean, one of the living dead. As God wants. Go away. Bless God for His mercy."

Numbed, Erikki saw the man motion with the remains of his arms. Obediently, around the cavern the lights began to go out, eyes still watching him.

Outside in the night air, he had to make a grim effort to stop himself from running away in terror, feeling filthy, wanting to cast off his clothes at once and bathe and soap and bathe and soap and bathe again.

"Stop it," he muttered, his skin crawling, "there's nothing to be afraid of."

WEDNESDAY
February 14

AT EVIN JAIL: 6:29 A.M. The jail was like any other modern jail—in good days or bad—gray, brooding, high-walled, and hideous.

Today the false dawn was strange, the glow below the horizon curiously red. No overcast or even clouds in the sky—the first time for weeks—and though it was still cold it promised to be a rare day. No smog. The air crisp and clean for a change. A kind wind took away the smoke from the still-burning wrecks of cars and barricades from last night's clashes between the now legal Green Bands and the now illegal loyalists, leftists, combined with suspect police and armed forces, as well as the smoke from countless cooking and heating fires of the Tehrani millions.

The few pedestrians who passed the prison walls and the huge door that was wrecked and broken off its hinges, and the Green Band guards who lolled there, averted their eyes and quickened their pace. Traffic was light. Another truck filled with Guards and prisoners ground its gears, stopped briefly at the main gate to be inspected. The temporary barricade opened and closed again. Inside the walls was a sudden volley of rifle fire. Outside the Green Bands yawned and stretched.

With the arrival of the sun the call of the muezzins from the minarets began—their voices mostly carried by loudspeakers, the voices on cassette. And wherever the call was heard, the Faithful stopped what they were doing, faced Mecca, knelt for first prayer.

Jared Bakravan had stopped the car just up the road. Now, with his chauffeur and the others, he knelt and prayed. He had spent much of the night trying to reach his most important friends and allies. The news of Paknouri's unlawful arrest and his own unlawful summons had swept through the bazaar. Everyone was instantly enraged, but no one came forward to marshal the thousands to stage a protest or strike or to close the bazaar. He had had plenty of advice: to protest to Khomeini personally, to Prime Minister Bazargan personally, not to appear at the court, to appear but to refuse to answer any questions, to appear and to answer some questions, to appear and answer all questions. "As God wants," but no one had volunteered to go with him, not even his great friend and one of the most important lawyers in Tehran who swore it was more important for him to be seeing the High Court judges on his behalf. No one volunteered, except his wife and son and three daughters who prayed on their own prayer mats behind him.

He finished praying and got up shakily. At once the chauffeur began to collect the prayer mats. Jared shivered. This morning he had dressed carefully and wore a heavy coat and suit and Astrakhan hat but no jewelry. "I . . . I will walk from here," he said.

"No, Jared," his tearful wife began, hardly noticing the distant gunfire. "Surely it is better to arrive as a leader should arrive. Aren't you the most important bazaari in Tehran? It wouldn't fit your position to walk."

"Yes, yes, you're right." He sat in the back of the car. It was a big blue Mercedes, new and well kept. His wife, a plump matron, her expensive coiffure hidden under a chador that also covered her long brown mink, got in beside him and held on to his arm, her makeup streaked by her tears. His son, Meshang, was equally tearful. And his daughters, Sharazad among them, all had chadors. "Yes . . . yes, you're right. God curse these revolutionaries!"

"Don't worry, Father," Sharazad said. "God will protect you—the Revolutionary Guards are only following the Imam's orders and the Imam only follows God's orders." She sounded so confident but looked so dejected that Bakravan forgot to tell her not to refer to Khomeini as "Imam."

"Yes," he told her, "of course it's all a mistake."

"Ali Kia swore on the Koran Prime Minister Bazargan would stop all this nonsense," his wife said. "He swore he would see him last night. Orders are probably already at the . . . already there."

Last night he had told Ali Kia that without Paknouri there could be no loan, that if he himself was troubled the bazaar would revolt and all funds stopped to the government, to Khomeini, to the mosques, and to Ali Kia personally. "Ali won't fail," he said grimly. "He daren't. I know too much about them all."

The car stopped outside the main gate. Idly the Green Bands stared at it. Jared Bakravan summoned his courage. "I won't be long."

"God protect you. We'll wait here for you—we'll wait here." His wife kissed him and so did the others and there were more tears and then he was standing in front of the Green Bands. "Salaam," he said. "I'm—I'm a witness at the court of Mullah Ali'allah Uwari."

The leader of the Guards took the paper, glanced at it upside down, gave it to one of the others who could read. "He's from the bazaar," the other youth said. "Jared Bakravan."

The leader shrugged. "Show him where to go." The other man led the way through the broken doorway. Bakravan followed, and as the barricade closed behind him, much of his confidence vanished. It was somber and dank in this small open dirt area between the walls and the main building complex. The air stank. Eastward, hundreds of men were crammed together, sitting or lying down, huddled miserably against the cold. Many wore uniforms—officers. Westward, the space was empty. Ahead was a tall iron-barred gate and it swung open to admit him. In the waiting room were dozens of other men, weary frightened men, sitting in rows on benches or standing or just sitting on the floor, some uniformed officers, and he noticed one full colonel. Some of the others he recognized, important businessmen, court favorites, administrators, deputies—but none he knew intimately. A few recognized him. There was a sudden hush.

"Hurry up," the Guard said irritably. He was a pockmarked youth and he shoved through to the desk, to the harassed clerk who sat there. "Here's another for Excellency Mullah Uwari."

The clerk accepted the paper and waved at Bakravan. "Take a seat—you'll be called when you're needed."

"Salaam, Excellency," Bakravan said, shocked at the man's rudeness. "When will that be? I was to be here just after fir—"

"As God wants. You'll be called when you're needed," the man said waving him away.

"But I'm Jared Bakravan of the baz—"

"I can read, Agha!" the man said more rudely. "When you're wanted you'll be called! Iran's an Islamic state now, one law for all, not one for the rich another for the people."

Bakravan was jostled by others being shoved toward the clerk. Weak with rage, he made his way toward a wall. To one side a man was using a latrine bucket that was already overfull, urine spilling onto the floor. Eyes watched Bakravan. A few muttered, "God's peace on you." The room smelled vile. His heart was pounding. Someone made a space for him on a bench and, thankfully, he sat down. "The Blessings of God upon thee, Excellencies."

"And on thee, Agha," one of them said. "You're accused?"

"No, no, I'm called as a witness," he said shocked.

"The Excellency is a witness in front of Mullah Uwari?"

"Yes, yes, I am, Excellency. Who is he?"

"A judge, a revolutionary judge," the man muttered. He was in his fifties, small, his face more lined than Bakravan's, his hair tufted. He twitched nervously. "No one here seems to know what's happening, or why they're called, or who this Uwari is, only that he's appointed by the Ayatollah and judges in his name."

Bakravan looked into the man's eyes and saw the terror and felt even more unnerved. "The Excellency is also a witness?"

"Yes, yes, I am, though why they should call me who was just a manager in the post office I don't know."

"The post office is very important—they probably need your advice. Do you think we'll be kept waiting long?"

"Insha'Allah. I was called yesterday after fourth prayer and I've been waiting ever since. They kept me here all night. We have to wait until we're called. That's the only toilet," the man said, pointing at the bucket. "The worst night I've ever had, terrible. During the night they . . . there was a great deal of firing; the rumor is three more generals and a dozen SAVAK officials were executed."

"Fifty or sixty," the man on the other side of him said, coming out of his stupor. "The number must be nearer sixty. The whole prison's crammed like bedbugs in a village mattress. All the cells're packed. Two days ago the Green Bands broke down the gates, overpowered the guards, and stuffed them in the dungeons, let most prisoners out and then started filling up the cells with locals"—he dropped his voice more—"all the cells are crammed, much more than in the Shah's time, God curse him for not . . . Every hour the Green Bands're bringing in more people, fedayeen and mujhadin and Tudeh all mixed up with us innocents, the Faithful . . ." He dropped his voice further, the whites of his eyes showing, "and good people who should never be touched and . . . when the mob broke the prison open they found electric probes and whips and . . . and torture beds and . . ." Foam collected at the corner of his mouth. ". . . they say the . . . the new jailers are using them and . . . and once you're here, Excellency, they keep you here." Tears began to well in his little eyes set in a pudgy face. "The food's terrible, the prison terrible, and . . . and I've got stomach ulcers and that son of a dog of a clerk, he . . . he won't understand I have to have special foods . . ."

There was a commotion on the far side and the door crashed open. Half a dozen Green Bands came into the room and began shoving a passage clear with their rifles. Behind them, other Guards surrounded an air force officer who walked proudly, his head high, his arms tied behind him, his uniform disheveled, epaulets half torn off. Bakravan gasped. It was Colonel Peshadi, commander of Kowiss Air Base—also a cousin.

Others recognized the colonel, for much had been made of the victorious Iranian expedition a few years ago to Dhofar in southern Oman, the successful smashing of the almost lethal Marxist attack by South Yemenis against Oman, and also of Peshadi's personal bravery leading Iranian tanks in a key battle. "Isn't that the hero of Dhofar?" someone said incredulously.

"Yes that's him . . ."

"God protect us! If they arrest him . . ."

Impatiently one of the Guards pushed Peshadi in the back, trying to force him to hurry up. At once the colonel lashed out at him, though badly hampered by his manacles. "Son of a dog," he shouted, his rage bursting, "I'm going as fast as I can. May your father burn!" The Green Band cursed him back, then shoved the butt of his rifle in the colonel's stomach. The colonel lost his balance and fell—at his mercy. But he still cursed his captors. And he cursed them as they pulled him to his feet, two on each arm, and frogmarched him outside into the western space between the walls. And there he cursed them, and Khomeini, and false mullahs, in all the names of God, then shouted, "Long live the Shah, there is no other God but G—" Bullets silenced him.

In the waiting room there was a ghastly silence. Someone whimpered. An old man began to vomit. Others began whispering, many started to pray, and Bakravan was sure all this was a nightmare, his tired brain rejecting reality. The fetid air was cold but he seemed to be in an oven and suffocating. Am I dying? he asked himself helplessly and pulled the neck of his shirt open. Then someone touched him and he opened his eyes. For a moment he could not focus them or fathom where he was. He was lying on the floor, the small man anxiously bending over him. "Are you all right?"

"Yes, yes, I think so," he said weakly.

"You fainted, Excellency. Are you sure you're all right?"

Hands helped him sit again. Dully he thanked them. His body seemed very heavy, his senses blunted, eyes leaden.

"Listen," the man with ulcers was whispering, "this's like the French Revolution, the guillotine and the Terror, but how can it happen with Ayatollah Khomeini in charge, that's what I don't understand?"

"He doesn't know," the small man said, equally fearfully. "He can't know, isn't he a man of God, pious and the most learned of all ayatollahs . . . ?"

Tiredness surged through Bakravan and he leaned against the wall, letting himself drift away.

Later a rough hand shook him awake. "Bakravan, you're wanted. Come on!"

"Yes, yes," he mumbled, and groped to his feet, finding it hard to talk, recognizing Yusuf, the leader of the Green Bands who had come to the bazaar last night. He stumbled after him, through the others, out of the room and into the corridor, up steps and along another heatless corridor lined with cells, peepholes in the doors, past guards and others who eyed him strangely, someone crying nearby. "Where—where are you taking me?"

"Save your strength, you'll need it."

Yusuf stopped at a door, opened it, and shoved him through. The room was small, claustrophobic, crammed with men. In the center was a wooden table with a mullah and four young men seated on either side of him, some papers and a large Koran on the table, a small barred window high up in the wall, a shaft of sunlight against the blue of the sky. Green Bands leaned against the walls.

"Jared Bakravan, the bazaari, the moneylender," Yusuf said.

The mullah looked up from the list he had been studying. "Ah, Bakravan, Salaam."

"Salaam, Excellency," Bakravan said shakily. The mullah was fortyish, with black eyes and black beard, white turban and threadbare black robes. The men beside him were in their twenties, unshaven or bearded, and poorly dressed, guns propped behind them. "How—how can I—I help you?" he asked, trying to be calm.

"I am Ali'allah Uwari, appointed by the Revolutionary Komiteh as a judge, and these men are also judges. This court is ruled by the Word of God and the Holy Book." The mullah's voice was harsh and his accent Qazvini. "You know this Paknouri, known as Miser Paknouri?"

"Yes, but may I say, Excellency, according to our Constitution and to ancient bazaari law th—"

"Better you answer the question," one of the youths interrupted, "we've no time to waste on speeches! Do you know him or don't you?"

"Yes, yes, of cour—"

"Excellency Uwari," Yusuf interrupted from the doorway. "Please, who do you want next?"

"Paknouri, then . . ." The mullah squinted at the list of names. "Then Police Sergeant Jufrudi."

One of the others sitting at the tables said, "That dog was judged by our other revolutionary court last night and shot this morning."

"As God wills." The mullah drew a line through the name. All the names above had lines through them. "Then bring Hassen Turlak—from cell 573."

Bakravan almost cried out. Turlak was a highly respected journalist and writer, half-Iranian–half-Afghani, a courageous and zealous critic of the Shah's regime who had even spent some years in jail because of his opposition.

The unshaven young man beside the mullah irritably scratched at the skin blemishes on his face. "Who's Turlak, Excellency?"

The mullah read from the list. "Newspaper reporter."

"It's a waste of time seeing him—of course he's guilty," another said. "Wasn't he the one who claimed the Word could be changed, that the Words of the Prophet weren't correct for today? He's guilty, of course he's guilty."

"As God wills." The mullah turned his attention to Bakravan. "Paknouri. Did he ever practice usury?"

Bakravan dragged his mind off Turlak. "No, never, and he w—"

"Did he lend money at interest?"

Bakravan's stomach churned. He saw the cold black eyes and tried hard to get his brain working. "Yes, but in a modern society int—"

"Isn't it written clearly in the Holy Koran that lending money at interest is usury and against the laws of God?"

"Yes. Usury is against the laws of God but in modern soc—"

"The Holy Koran is blemishless. The Word is clear and forever. Usury is usury. The law is the law." The mullah's eyes flattened. "Do you uphold the law?"

"Yes, yes, Excellency, of course, of course I do."

"Do you practice the Five Pillars of Islam?" These were obligatory to all Muslims: the saying of the Shahada; ritual prayer five times a day; the voluntary giving of Zakat, a year tax, a tenth part; fasting from dawn to dusk during the Holy Month of Ramadan; and last, making the Hajj, the ritual journey to Mecca once in a lifetime.

"Yes, yes, I do, except—except the last. I—I haven't yet made the pilgrimage to Mecca—not yet."

"Why not?" the young man with spots on his face asked. "You have more money than a dung heap has flies. With your money you could go in any air machine, any! Why not?"

"It's—it's my health," Bakravan said, keeping his eyes down and praying the lie sounded convincing. "My—my heart is weak."

"When were you last in the mosque?" the mullah said.

"On Friday, last Friday, at the mosque in the bazaar," he said. It was true that he was there, though not to pray but to have a business conference.

"This Paknouri, he practiced the Five Pillars as a true Believer?" one of the youths asked.

"I—I believe so."

"It's well known he didn't, well known he was a Shah supporter. Eh?"

"He was a patriot, a patriot who financially supported the revolution and supported Ayatollah Khomeini, the Blessings of God upon him, financially supported the mullahs over the years an—"

"But he spoke American and worked for Americans and the Shah, helping them exploit and steal our wealth from the soil, didn't he?"

"He, he was a patriot who worked with the foreigners for the good of Iran."

"When the Satan Shah illegally formed a party, Paknouri joined it, served the Shah in the Majlis, didn't he?" the mullah asked.

"He was a deputy, yes," Bakravan replied. "But he worked for the rev—"

"And he voted for the Shah's so-called White Revolution that took away land from the mosques, decreed equality of women, implanted civil courts and state education against the dictates of the Holy Koran . . ."

Of course he voted for it, Bakravan wanted to scream, the sweat trickling down his face and back. Of course we all voted for it! Didn't the people vote for it overwhelmingly and even many ayatollahs and mullahs? Didn't the Shah control the government, the police, the gendarmerie, SAVAK, the armed forces and own most of the land? The Shah was ultimate power! Curse the Shah, he thought, beside himself with rage, curse him and his White Revolution of '63 that started the rot, sent the mullahs mad, and continues to plague us, all his "modern reforms" that were directly responsible for the rise of the then obscure Ayatollah Khomeini to prominence. Didn't we bazaaris warn the Shah's advisers a thousand times! As if any of the reforms mattered. As if any of the reforms w—

"Yes or no?"

He was startled out of his reverie and cursed himself. Concentrate! he thought in panic. This vile son of a leprous dog is trying to trap you! What did he ask? Be careful—for your own life be careful! Ah, yes, the White Revolution! "Emir Pak—"

"In the Name of God, yes or no!" the mullah overrode him harshly.

"He—yes—yes, he voted for the, the White Revolution when he was a deputy in the Majlis. Yes, yes, he did."

The mullah sighed and the youths shifted in their seats. One yawned and scratched his groin, absently playing with himself.

"You are a deputy?"

"No—no, I resigned when Ayatollah Khomeini ordered it. The—"

"You mean when Imam Khomeini, the *Imam* ordered it?"

"Yes, yes," Bakravan said flustered. "I resigned, the, er, the moment the Imam ordered it, I—I resigned at once," he said, and did not add, We all resigned at Paknouri's suggestion when it was safe and certain the Shah had decided to leave and to pass over power to the moderate and rational Prime Minister Bakhtiar, but not for power to be usurped by Khomeini, he wanted to shriek, that was never the plan! God curse the Americans who sold us out, the generals who sold us out, the Shah who's responsible! "Everyone knows —knows how I supported the Imam, may he live forever."

"Yes, the Blessings of God on him," the mullah echoed with the others. "But you, Jared Bakravan of the bazaar. Have you ever practiced usury?"

"Never," Bakravan said at once, believing it, though fear racked him. I've loaned money all of my life but the interest's always been fair and reasonable, never usury, he thought, never. And all the times I acted as adviser to various people and ministers, arranging loans, private and public, transferring funds out of Iran, private and public, making money, a great deal of money, that was good business and not against the law. "I opposed the—I opposed the White Revolution and the Shah, wherever I could—it was well known that I opp—"

"The Shah committed crimes against God, against Islam, against the Holy Koran, against the Imam—God protect him—against the Shi'a faith. All those who helped him are equally guilty." The mullah's eyes were relentless. "What crimes have you committed against God and the Word of God?"

"None," he cried out, almost at the limit. "In God's name I swear, none!"

The door swung open. Yusuf came into the room with Paknouri. Bakravan almost fainted again. Paknouri's hands were manacled behind him. Muck and urine stained his trousers and vomit was on the front of his coat. His head was twitching uncontrollably, his hair matted and filthy, his mind gone. When he saw Bakravan, his face twisted into a grimace. "Ah, Jared, Jared, old friend and colleague, Excellency, have you come to join us all in hell?"

He shrieked with laughter for a moment. "It's not like I imagined, the devils haven't arrived yet, nor the boiling oil or flames but there's no air and just stink and you press against others and you can't lie down or sit so you stand and and then the screaming begins again and the firing and, all the time you're on an egg, packed like a caviar egg but but but—" The half-incoherent raving stopped as he saw the mullah. Terror swamped him. "Are you . . . are you God?"

"Paknouri," the mullah said gently, "you are charged with crimes against God. This witness against you says y—"

"Yes, yes, I've crimed against God, I'm guilty," Paknouri screamed. "Why else am I in hell?" He fell on his knees in a flood of tears, raving. "There is no God but God is no God there is no God and Mohammed is his Prophet of no God and . . ." Abruptly he stopped. His face was even more twisted when he looked up. "I'm God—you're Satan!"

One of the youths broke the shocked silence. "He's a blasphemer. He's possessed by Satan. He declared himself guilty. As God wants."

All the others nodded agreement. The mullah said, "As God wants." He motioned to a Green Band who pulled Paknouri to his feet and took him out and looked at Bakravan who stared after his friend, horrified how fast—just overnight—he had been destroyed. "Now, Bakravan, you w—"

"I've got this Turlak waiting outside," Yusuf said, interrupting him.

"Good," the mullah said. Then he turned his eyes back onto Bakravan and Bakravan knew he was as lost as his friend Paknouri was lost and that the sentence would be the same. The blood was rushing in his ears. He saw the lips of the mullah moving, then they stopped and everyone was looking at him. "Please?" he asked numbly. "I—I'm sorry, I didn't hear what you— what you said."

"You can leave. For the moment. Do God's work." Impatiently the mullah glanced at one of the Green Bands, a tallish, ugly man. "Ahmed, take him out!" Then to Yusuf, "After Turlak, Police Captain Mohammed Dezi, cell 917 . . ."

Bakravan felt a tug on his arm and turned and went out. In the corridor he almost fell, but Ahmed caught him and, strangely kind, propped him against the wall.

"Catch your breath, Excellency," he said.

"I'm—I'm free to go?"

"I'm certainly as surprised as you, Agha," the man said. "Before God and the Prophet I'm as surprised as you, you're the first to be let go today, witness or accused."

"I—is there—is there any water?"

"Not here. There's plenty outside. Best you leave," Ahmed dropped his voice even more. "Best to leave, eh? Lean on my arm."

Thankfully, Bakravan held on to him, hardly breathing. Slowly they went back the way he had come. He hardly noticed the other guards and prisoners and witnesses. In the corridor that led to the waiting room, Ahmed shouldered the way through a side door, out into the western space. The firing squad was there, three men tied to posts in front of them. One post was empty. Bakravan's bowels and bladder emptied of their own volition.

"Hurry up, Ahmed!" the man in charge said irritably.

"As God wants," Ahmed said. Happily, he half-carried Bakravan to the empty post that was next to Paknouri who was raving, lost in his own hell. "So you're not to escape after all. That's right, we all heard your lies, lies before God. We all know you, know your ways, know your lack of godliness, how you even tried to buy your way to heaven with gifts to the Imam, God protect him. Where did you get all that money if not through usury and theft?"

The volley was not accurate. The man in charge leisurely used a revolver to silence one of the condemned, then Bakravan. "I wouldn't have recognized him," the man said shortly. "It shows how foul and what liars newspapers are."

"This isn't Hassen Turlak," Ahmed said, "he comes next."

The man stared at him. "Then who's this one?"

"A bazaari," Ahmed said. "Bazaaris are usurers and godless. I know. For years I worked there for Farazan, collecting night soil like my father before me, until I became a bricklayer with Yusuf. But this one . . ." He belched. "He was the richest usurer. I don't remember much about him except how rich he was, but I remember everything about his women; he never curbed or taught his women who never wore chador, flaunting themselves. I remember everything about his devil daughter who'd visit the Street of the Moneylenders from time to time, half naked, skin like fresh cream, her hair flowing, breasts moving, buttocks inviting—the one called Sharazad who looks like the promised houris must look. I remember everything about her and how I cursed her for putting evil in my head, maddening me, how we all did—for tempting us." He scratched his scrotum, feeling himself hardening. God curse her and all women who disobey God's law and create evil thoughts in us against the Word of God. Oh, God, let me penetrate her or make me a martyr and go straight to heaven and do it there. "He was guilty of every crime," he said, turning away.

"But—but was he condemned?" the man in charge of the firing squad called out after him.

"God condemned him, of course He did. The post was waiting and you told me to hurry. It was the Will of God. God is Great, God is Great. Now I will fetch Turlak, the blasphemer." Ahmed shrugged. "It was the Will of God."

U.S.S.R.

KHOI

TABRIZ

MOUNT
SABALAN

BANDAR-E
PAHLAVI

Caspian Sea

U.S.S.R.

TURKEY

QAZVIN

★ TEHRAN

IRAQ

BAGHDAD
★

DEZ DAM

ZAGROS

•ISFAHAN

I R A N

BANDAR DELAM

AFGHANISTAN

Shatt-
al-Arab
Estuary

ABADAN

•ZAGROS THREE

KUWAIT

KHARG

•KOWISS

MOUNTAINS

JELLET

Persian Gulf

LENGEH

Strait of
Hormuz

PAKISTAN

BAHRAIN

SAUDI
ARABIA

QATAR

SIRI

Gulf of Oman

AL SHARGAZ

NEAR BANDAR DELAM: 11:58 A.M.   It was the time of noon prayer
and the ancient, rickety, overladen bus stopped on the shoulder of the road.
Obediently, following the lead of a mullah who was also a passenger, all
Muslims disembarked, spread their prayer mats and now were committing
their souls to God. Except for the Indian Hindu family who were afraid of
losing their seats, most of the other non-Muslim passengers had also disembarked—Tom Lochart among them—glad for the opportunity to stretch
their legs or to relieve themselves. Christian Armenians, Oriental Jews, a
nomadic Kash'kai couple who, though Muslim, were precluded by ancient
custom from the need of the noonday prayer, or their women from the veil or
chador, two Japanese, some Christian Arabs—all of them aware of the lone
European.

The day was warm, hazy, and humid from the nearby waters of the Gulf.
Tom Lochart leaned tiredly against the hood that was steaming, the engine

overheated, head aching, joints aching, muscles aching from his forced march
out from the Dez Dam—now almost two hundred miles to the north—and
from the cramped, bone-grinding, noisy discomfort of the bus. All the way
from Ahwaz where he had managed to talk himself past Green Bands and
onto the bus, he had been squeezed into a seat with barely enough room for
two, let alone three men, one of them a young Green Band who cradled his
M14 along with his child for his pregnant wife who stood in the narrow
corridor crammed against thirty others in space for fifteen. Every seat was
equally packed with men, women, and children of all ages. The air fetid,
voices babbling in a multitude of tongues. Overhead and underfoot, bags and
bundles and cases, crates packed with vegetables or half-dead chickens, a
small, undernourished, hobbled goat or two—the luggage racks outside on
the roof equally laden.

But I'm damned lucky to be here, he thought, his misery returning, half
listening to the lilting chant of the Shahada.

Yesterday, near sunset, when he had heard the 212 take off from Dez, he
had come out from under the little wharf, blessing God for his escape. The
water had been very cold and he was trembling, but he had picked up the
automatic, checked the action, and then gone up to the house. It was open.
There was food and drink in the refrigerator that still hummed nicely, pow-
ered by a generator. It was warm inside the house. He took off his clothes and
dried them over a heater, cursing Valik and Seladi and consigning them to
hell. "Sonsofbitches! What the hell'd I do to them but save their goddamn
necks?"

The warmth and the luxury of the house were tempting. His tiredness
ached him. Last night at Isfahan had been almost sleepless. I could sleep and
leave at dawn, he thought. I've a compass and I know the way more or less:
skirt the airfield Ali Abbasi mentioned, then head almost due east to pick up
the main Kermanshah-Ahwaz-Abadan road. Should be no trouble to get a bus
or hitch a ride. Or I could go now—the moon'll light my way and then I
won't be trapped here if the air base has sent a patrol—Ali was just as
nervous about that as Seladi and we could easily have been spotted. Easily.
But either way, when you get stopped, what's your story?

He thought about that while he fixed himself a brandy and soda and some
food. Valik and the others had opened two half-kilo cans of the best beluga
gray caviar and had left them carelessly on the sitting-room table, still partially full. He ate it with relish, then threw the cans into the garbage pail that
was outside the back door. Then he locked the house and left.

The forced march over the mountains had been bad but not as bad as he
had expected. Just after dawn he had come down to the main Kermanshah-

Ahwaz-Abadan road. Almost at once he had been given a ride by some Korean construction workers evacuating the steel mill they were building under contract at Kermanshah—it was almost custom that expats helped expats on the road. They were heading for Abadan Airport where they had been told transport to fly them back to Korea would be waiting for them. "Much fighting at Kermanshah," they had told him in halting English. "Everyone guns. Iranians killing each others. All mad, barbarians—worse than Japanese." They had dropped him off at the Ahwaz bus terminal. Miraculously he had managed to talk his way onto the next bus that went past Bandar Delam.

Yes. But now what? Gloomily he remembered how, after throwing the empty caviar cans into the garbage, on reflection he had retrieved them and buried them, then gone back and wiped the glass that he had used and even the door handle. You need your head examined, as if they'd check for fingerprints! Yes, but at the time I thought it best not to leave traces I'd been there.

You're crazy! You're on the flight clearance at Tehran, there's your unauthorized pickup of Valik and his family, the breakout from Isfahan, and flying "enemies of the state and helping them escape" to account for—whether it's from SAVAK or Khomeini! And how does S-G or McIver account for a missing Iranian helicopter that ends up in Kuwait or Baghdad or where the hell ever that's bound to be reported?

What a goddamn mess!

Yes. Then there's Sharazad . . .

"Don't worry, Agha," broke into his thoughts, "we're all in God's hands."

It was the mullah and he was smiling up at him. He was a youngish man, bearded, and he had joined the bus at Ahwaz with his wife and three children. Over his shoulder was a rifle. "The driver says you speak Farsi and that you're from Canada and a person of the Book?"

"Yes, yes, I am, Agha," Lochart replied, collecting his wits. He saw that prayer had finished and now everyone crowded the bus doorway.

"Then you too will go to heaven as the Prophet promised if you are found worthy, though not to our part." The mullah smiled shyly. "Iran will be the first real Islamic state in the world since the time of the Prophet." Again the shy smile. "You're—you're the first person of the Book that I've met or spoken to. You learned to speak Farsi at school?"

"I went to a school, Excellency, but mostly I had private teachers." Lochart picked up his flight bag that he had taken off with him for safety and moved to join the line. His own seat was already taken. Beside the road several passengers were relieving themselves or defecating, men, women, and children.

"And the Excellency works in the oil business?" The mullah moved into line beside him, and at once people stepped aside to let him take preference. Inside the bus passengers were already quarreling, a few shouting to the driver to hurry.

"Yes, for your great IranOil," Lochart said, very conscious that those nearby were listening also, jostling to get closer to hear better. Not long to go now, he thought, the airport can't be more than a few miles ahead. Just before noon he had caught a glimpse of a 212 heading in from the Gulf. She was too far away to see if she was civilian or military but she was heading in the general direction of the airport. It'll be great to see Rudi and the others, to sleep and . . .

"The driver says you were on holiday near Kermanshah?"

"In Luristan, south of Kermanshah." Lochart concentrated. He retold the story he had decided upon, the same that he had told the ticket seller at Ahwaz, and the Green Bands who also wanted to know who he was and why he was in Ahwaz. "I was on a hiking holiday north of Luristan, in the mountains, and got trapped there in a village by a snowfall—for a week. You are going to Shiraz?" This was the final destination of the bus.

"Shiraz is where my mosque is and the place of my birth. Come, we will sit together." The mullah took the nearest seat beside an old man, put one of his children on his knee, cradled his gun, and left Lochart just enough room on the aisle. Reluctantly Lochart obeyed, not wanting to sit beside a talkative and inquisitive mullah, but at the same time thankful for a place. The bus was filling up quickly. People shoved past, trying to get space or to move farther back. "Your country Canada borders the Great Satan, does it not?"

"Canada and America have common borders," Lochart said, his bile rising. "The vast majority of Americans are People of the Book."

"Ah, yes, but many are Jews and Zionists, and Jews and Zionists and Christians are against Islam, the enemy of Islam, and therefore against God. Isn't it true that Jews and Zionists rule the Great Satan?"

"If you mean America, no, Agha, no it is not."

"But if the Imam says it, it is so." The mullah was quite confident and gentle and quoted from the Koran, " 'For God is angry with them, and in torment shall they abide forever.' " Then he added, "If the Im—"

There was a flurry in the back of the bus, and they turned to see one of the Iranians angrily tug the turbaned Indian out of his seat to take his place. The Indian forced a smile and stayed standing. By custom it was always the first one seated who had the right to stay seated unharmed. The torrent of voices began again and now another man, jammed in the aisle, began cursing all foreigners loudly. He was roughly dressed, armed, and stood alongside the two Japanese who were crammed into a seat with a ragged old Kurd and glared down at them.

"Why should foreigner Infidels sit while we stand? With the Help of God, we're no longer lackeys of Infidels!" the man said even more angrily and jerked his thumb at them. "Move!"

Neither Japanese moved. One of them took off his glasses and smiled at the man. The man hesitated, began to bluster but thought better of it, then turned and shouted at the driver to hurry up. Just before the Japanese put back his glasses he caught Lochart's eye, nodded and smiled.

Lochart smiled back. At Ahwaz, while they were all pushing their way onto the bus, one of the Japanese had said to Lochart in passable English, "Follow us, sir, at rush hour Tokyo buses and trains are much worse." With a great display of politeness the two quickly cleared a path, found him a seat and places at the back for themselves. During the noon stop they had chatted briefly, telling him they were engineers coming back from leave, heading for Iran-Toda.

"Ah," the mullah said happily, seeing the driver squeeze back into his seat, "now we continue, thanks be to God."

With a great flourish the driver started the engine and the bus lumbered on its way. "Next stop Bandar Delam," he called out. "God willing."

"God willing." The mullah was very content. Once more he turned his attention to Lochart and shouted above the noise, "Agha, you were saying about the Great Satan?"

Lochart had his eyes closed and he pretended not to hear.

The mullah touched him. "You were saying, Agha, about the Great Satan?"

"I was saying nothing, Agha."

"What? I didn't hear you."

Lochart kept his face polite, knowing the danger he was in, and said louder, "I was saying nothing, Agha. Traveling is tiring, isn't it?" He closed his eyes again. "I think I will sleep a little."

"Why say nothing?" a young man standing alongside in the aisle shouted down at him over the grinding engine. "America is responsible for all our troubles. If it wasn't for America, there'd be peace in the whole world!"

Grimly Lochart kept his eyes closed and tried to shut his ears, knowing he was near snapping—half of him wishing he had the automatic in his pocket, the other half thankful it was in his bag. He felt the mullah shake him.

"Before you sleep, Agha, don't you agree the world would be much better without the American evil?"

Lochart fought down his anger and just kept his eyes closed. Another shake, much rougher, this time from the aisle, and the man shouted in his ear, "Answer His Excellency!"

He was suddenly sick to death of all the anti-American propaganda and lies continually fed to them. White with rage, he opened his eyes and shoved the man's hand away and exploded in English. "Well, I'll tell you, mullah, you'd better thank God America exists because without it there'd be goddamn nothing in the world and we'd all be in a goddamn gulag or under the goddamn ground, you, me, this jerk, and even Khomeini!"

"What?"

He saw the mullah gaping at him—and realized he had been speaking English. Taking a tight rein on his mouth, he said in Farsi, knowing there was no way he could explain logically, "I was quoting the Holy Bible in English," he said, making it up. "I was quoting Abraham when he was very angry. Didn't Abraham say: 'Evil stalks the earth in many guises—it is the duty of the Believer to . . . to guard against evil, any evil—all evil!' Isn't it?"

The mullah was looking at him strangely and quoted from the Koran: " 'And God said to Abraham, I will make you a leader to mankind, and Abraham said, of my offspring also! God said, My covenant embraceth not the evildoers.' "

"I agree," Lochart said. "And now I must think about God—the One God, the God of Abraham and Moses and Jesus and Mohammed, whose Name be praised!" Lochart closed his eyes. His heart was pounding. Any moment he expected the angry youth's rifle butt in his face or the mullah to shout for the bus to stop. He expected no mercy. But the moment passed and they left him to his supposed prayers.

The mullah sighed, lack of space pressing him against this Infidel. I wonder how an Infidel prays, he was thinking. What does he say to God—even a person of the Book? How pitiful they are!

AT BANDAR DELAM AIRPORT: 12:32 P.M. The Iranian Air Force car swung past the sleepy guards on the gate, its green Khomeini flag fluttering, and pulled up in a swirl of dust outside Rudi's office trailer. Two smartly uniformed officers got out. With them were three Green Bands.

Rudi Lutz went out to meet the officers—a major and a captain. When he recognized the captain, his face lit up. "Hello, Hushang. I've been wondering how you were do—"

The older officer interrupted him angrily. "I'm Major Qazani, Air Force Intelligence. What's an Iranian chopper under your control doing trying to leave Iranian airspace, repeatedly disobeying instructions from an intercept, and totally disregarding orders from ground control?"

Rudi stared at them blankly. "There's only one of my choppers airborne, and she's on a CASEVAC requested by Abadan radar control."

"What's her registration?"

"EP-HXX. What's this all about?"

"That's what I want to know." Major Qazani walked past him into the trailer and sat down. His Green Bands waited. "Come on!" the major said irritably. "Sit down, Captain Lutz."

Rudi hesitated, then sat at his desk. A few bullet holes in the wall let in light behind him. The Green Bands and the other officer came in and shut the door.

"What's HXX? A 206 or 212?" the major asked.

"It's a 206. What's th—"

"How many 212s have you here?"

"Two. HXX and HGC. Abadan radar cleared HXX on a CASEVAC yesterday to Kowiss with wounded from the fedayeen attack at dawn yester—"

"Yes, we heard about that. And that you helped the Guards blow them to the hell they deserve, for which many thanks. Is EP-HBC an S-G 212 registration?"

Rudi hesitated. "I don't know offhand, Major. I don't have records here of all our 212s, but I could find out—if I can raise our base in Kowiss. Radio's been out for a day. Now, please, I'll help all I can, but what's this about?"

Major Qazani lit a cigarette, offered one to Rudi who shook his head. "It's about a 212, EP-HBC, we believe an S-G-operated 212, with an unknown number of persons aboard that went over the Iraqi border just before sunset last night—with no clearances, disregarding, as I've said, disregarding explicit radio orders to land."

"I don't know anything about it." Rudi's mind was racing. Got to be someone making an escape, he thought. "She's not our bird. We can't even start engines without Abadan Control's okay. That's SOP."

"How would you explain HBC then?"

"She could be a Guerney aircraft taking some of their personnel away, or Bell, or any one of the other chopper companies. It's been hard, sometimes impossible, to file a flight plan recently. You know how, er, how fluid radar's been the last few weeks."

"Fluid's not a good word," Captain Hushang Abbasi said. He was a lithe, very handsome man with a clipped mustache and dark glasses, and wore wings on his uniform. All of last year he had been based at Kharg where he and Rudi had got to know each other. "And if she was an S-G aircraft?"

"Then there'll be a correct explanation." Rudi was glad that Hushang had weathered the revolution—particularly as he had always been an outspoken critic of mullahs meddling in government. "You're sure she was illegal?"

"I'm sure legal airplanes have clearances, legal airplanes obey air regulations, and legal airplanes don't take evading action and rush for the border," Hushang said. "And I'm almost sure I saw the S-G emblem on my first pass, Rudi."

Rudi's eyes narrowed. Hushang was a very good pilot. "You were flying the intercept?"

"I led the flight that scrambled."

The silence grew in the trailer. "Do you mind if I open a window, Major. The smoke—it gives me a headache."

The major said irritably, "If HBC's an S-G chopper someone's going to have more than a headache."

Rudi opened the window. HBC sounds like one of our registrations. What the hell's going wrong? We seem to be under a spell the last few days—first it was that psychopath Zataki and the murder of our mechanic, then poor old Kyabi, then the God-cursed leftist fedayeen dawn attack yesterday, damn nearly killing us and wounding Jon Tyrer—Christ, I hope Jon's all right!—and now more trouble!

He sat down again, feeling very weary. "Best I can do is to ask."

"How far north do you operate?" the major asked.

"Normally? Ahwaz. Dezful'd be about our extreme ra—" The base phone intercom rang. He picked it up and missed the look between the two officers. "Hello?"

It was Fowler Joines, his chief mechanic. "You okay?"

"Yes. Thanks. No sweat."

"Shout if you need help, old sport, and we'll all come arunning." The phone clicked off.

He turned back to the major, feeling better. Since he had stood up to Zataki, all of his men and pilots had treated him as though he were Laird Gavallan himself. And since yesterday when the fedayeen were beaten off, even the komiteh Green Bands had been deferential—all except Base Manager Yemeni who was still trying to give him a hard time. "Dezful's extreme range—one way. Once we flew . . ." He stopped. He had been going to say, Once we flew our area manager to Kermanshah. But then the memory of the brutal and senseless way Boss Kyabi had been murdered welled up and again he was sickened.

He saw the major and Hushang staring at him. "Sorry, I was going to say, Major, once we flew a charter to Kermanshah. With refueling, as you know, we're mobile."

"Yes, Captain Lutz, yes, we know." The major stubbed out his cigarette and lit another. "Prime Minister Bazargan, with of course the prior approval of Ayatollah Khomeini," he added cautiously, not trusting Abbasi or the Green Bands who also might secretly understand English, "has issued strict orders about all aircraft in Iran, particularly choppers. We'll call Kowiss now."

They went to the radio room. At once Yemeni protested that he could not approve the call without permission of the local komiteh, of which he had appointed himself a member as the only one who could read or write. One of the Green Bands went to fetch them but the major overrode Yemeni and got his way. Kowiss did not answer their calls.

"As God wants. It'll be better after dark, Agha," radio operator Jahan said in Farsi.

"Yes, thank you," the major said.

"What is it you need, Agha?" Yemeni said rudely, hating the encroachment, the Shah uniforms almost whipping him into a frenzy. "I will get it for you!"

"I don't need you for anything, son of a dog," the major shouted angrily, everyone jumped, and Yemeni was paralyzed. "If you give me trouble I'll haul you in front of our Tribunal for interfering with the work of the prime minister and Khomeini himself! Get out!"

Yemeni fled. The Green Bands laughed and one of them said, "Shall I beat his head in for you, Agha?"

"No, no, thank you. He's no more important than a fly eating a camel's turd." Major Qazani puffed his cigarette, surrounded with smoke, and glanced at Rudi thoughtfully. The news of how this German had saved Zataki, the most important Revolutionary Guard commander in this area, had flooded their air base.

He got up and went to the window. Beyond he could see his car and the green Khomeini flag and the Green Bands lolling around. Scum, he thought. Sons of dogs, all of them. We didn't get rid of American restraints and influence and help sack the Shah to give over control of our lives and beautiful planes to lice-covered mullahs, however brave some of them may be. "You wait here, Hushang. I'll leave two Guards with you," he said. "Wait here and make the call with him. I'll send the car back for you."

"Yes, sir."

The major looked at Rudi, his eyes hard. In English he said, "I want to know if HBC's an S-G chopper, where it was based, how it got to this area, and who was aboard." He gave the necessary orders and left in a swirl of dust.

Hushang sent the Guards to tell the others what was going on. Now the two of them were alone. "So," he said, and smiled and held out his hand. "I'm pleased to see you, Rudi."

"Me too." They shook hands warmly. "I wondered how you, er, how you fared."

Hushang laughed. "You mean if I'd been liquidated? Oh, don't believe all those stories, Rudi. No. Everything's great. When I left Kharg I spent a little time in Doshan Tappeh, then came down to Abadan Air Base."

Rudi waited. "And then?"

"And then?" Hushang thought a moment. "And then, when His Im— when the Shah left Iran, our base commander paraded us, everyone, and told us he considered our oath of allegiance canceled. All of us in the forces swore allegiance to the Shah personally but when he left, our oaths seemed repudiated somehow. Our commander asked us all to choose what we wanted to do, officers and men, to stay or to leave—but, he said finally, 'On this base the transfer of power to the new legal government will be orderly.' We were given twelve hours to decide." Hushang frowned. "A few left—they were mostly senior officers. What would you have done, Rudi?"

"Stayed. Of course. *Heimat ist immer Heimat.*"

"What?"

"Your homeland is always your homeland."

"Ah, yes. Yes, that's what I thought." A shadow went over Hushang. "After we had all chosen, our commander called in Ayatollah Ahwazi, our chief ayatollah, and formally made the transfer of power. Then he shot himself. He left a note saying, 'All my life I have served Mohammed Reza Shah, as my father served Reza Shah, his father. I cannot serve mullahs or politicians, or live with the stench of betrayal that pervades the land.' "

Rudi hesitated. "He meant the Americans?"

"The major thinks he meant the generals. Some of us think he meant . . . the betrayal of Islam."

"By Khomeini?" Rudi saw Hushang looking at him, brown eyes guileless, chiseled face, and for a second Rudi had the uneasy feeling that this was no longer his friend, but someone wearing the same face. Someone who might be ready to trap him. Trap him into what?

"To think that would be treason. Wouldn't it," Hushang said. It was a statement, not a question, and another shaft of caution went through Rudi. "I'm frightened for Iran, Rudi. We're so exposed, so valuable to either super-power, and hated and envied by so many nearby."

"Ah, but your forces are the biggest and best equipped around—you're the power in the Gulf." He went to the small built-in refrigerator. "How about splitting an ice-cold bottle of beer?"

"No thanks."

Usually they would share one with relish. "You on a diet?" Rudi asked.

The other shook his head, smiled strangely. "No. I've quit. It's my gift to the new regime."

"Then we'll have tea, like old times," Rudi said without missing a beat, went into the kitchen, and put on the kettle. But he was thinking, Hushang really has changed. But then, if you were him, you'd've changed too, his world's upside-down—like West Germany and East Germany but not as bad as that. "How's Ali?" he asked. Ali was Hushang's adored elder brother, a helicopter pilot, whom Rudi had never met but Hushang was always talking about, laughing about his legendary adventures and conquests in Tehran, Paris, and Rome in the old days—the good old days, he thought emphatically.

"Ali the Great's fine too," Hushang said with a delighted smile. Just before the Shah had left they had secretly discussed their options and had agreed, whatever happened, they would stay: "We're still the elite force, we'll still have leaves in Europe!" He beamed, so proud of him, not envious of his successes but wishing he could be a tenth as successful. "But he'll have to slow down now—at least he will in Iran."

The kettle began boiling. Rudi made the tea. "Mind if I ask you about HBC?" He glanced through the doorway into the other room. His friend was watching him. "That all right?"

"What do you want to know?"

"What happened?"

After a pause Hushang said, "I was leader of the duty flight. We were scrambled and told to intercept a helicopter that had been spotted sneaking through the area. It turned out to be civilian, ducking in and out of the valleys around Dezful. She wouldn't answer radio calls in Farsi or in English. We waited, trailing her. Once she was out in the open I buzzed her, that's when I thought I recognized the S-G emblem. But she completely disre-garded me, just turned for the border and poured on the coals. My wingman buzzed her but she took more evading action."

Hushang's eyes narrowed as he remembered the excitement that had possessed him, hunter and hunted, never having hunted before, his ears filled with the sweet scream of his jets, with static and with orders: "Arm missiles!" Hands and fingers obeying.

Pressing the trigger, the rocket missing the first time as the chopper pirouetted, darting this way and that, nimble as a dragonfly, his wingman also firing and missing by a fraction—the missiles not heat-seekers. Another miss. Now she was over the border. Over the border and safe but not safe from me, from justice, so going in with cannons blazing, impression of faces at the windows, seeing her dissolve into a ball of fire and when I came out of the G-wrenching turn to look again she had vanished. Only a puff of smoke remained. And the pleasure.

"I plastered her," he said. "Blew her out of the sky."

Rudi turned away to hide his shock. He had presumed HBC had escaped —whoever was flying. "There were no . . . no survivors?"

"No, Rudi. She exploded," Hushang said, wanting to keep his voice calm. And professional. "It was . . . it was my first kill—I never thought it would be so difficult."

Not much of a contest, Rudi thought, enraged and disgusted. Missiles and cannons against nothing, but I suppose orders are orders and HBC was in the wrong whoever flew her, whoever was aboard. She should have stopped—I would have stopped. Would I? If I'd been the fighter pilot and this was Germany and the chopper was fleeing toward the enemy-controlled border with God knows what aboard and I was on orders to . . . Wait a minute, did Hushang do it in Iraqi airspace? Well, I'm not going to ask him. As sure as God doesn't speak to Khomeini, Hushang wouldn't tell me if he did—I wouldn't.

Gloomily he filled the teapot from the kettle and was reminded of the other one from his childhood, then glanced out of the window. An old bus was stopping on the road outside the airport perimeter. He saw the tall man get out. For a moment he did not recognize him. Then, with a whoop of delight, he did, and said on the run, "Excuse me a moment . . ."

They met at the gate, Green Bands watching curiously. "Tom! *Wie geht's?* How are you? What the hell're you doing here? Why didn't you tell us you were coming? How's Zagros and Jean-Luc?" He was so happy he did not notice Lochart's fatigue, or the state of his clothes—dusty, torn, and travel-stained.

"Lot to tell, Rudi," Lochart said. "Lot to tell, but I'm bushed. I badly need some tea . . . and some sleep. Okay?"

"Of course." Rudi beamed at him. "Of course. Come on, and I'll open my last, secret bottle of whisky I even pretend to myself I haven't got and we'll h—" All at once he noticed the state of his friend and his smile left him. "What the hell's happened to you? You look like you've been dragged through a bush backward." He saw Lochart glance imperceptibly at the guards who stood nearby, listening.

"Nothing, Rudi, nothing at all. First a wash, eh?" he said.

"Sure—yes, of course. You, er, you can use my trailer." Very perturbed he walked alongside Lochart, heading into the airport. He had never seen him so old and so slow. He looks shaken up, almost—almost as though he's had an emergency and pranged badly . . .

Down by the hangar he saw Yemeni peering at them out of the office windows. Fowler Joines and the other mechanic had stopped work and were beginning to stroll over. Then, down at the far end of the encampment, he saw Hushang come out onto the step of his trailer and Rudi's head seemed to explode. "Oh, Christ," he gasped. "Not HBC?"

Lochart jerked to a stop, all color out of his face. "How the hell you know about her?"

"But he said HBC was plastered—blown out of the skies! How'd you get out? How?"

"Plastered?" Lochart was in shock. "Jesus, who—who said that?"

Reflexes helped Rudi, and without being obvious he turned his back on Hushang. "The Iranian officer in the doorway—don't look, for Christ's sake —he flew the intercept, F14—he blew her out of the sky!" He put a glassy smile on his face, grabbed Lochart by the arm, and again trying not to be obvious, steered him toward the nearest trailer. "You can bed down in Jon Tyrer's place," he said with forced joviality, and the moment he had closed the door behind them, he whispered in a rush, "Hushang said he shot down HBC near the Iraqi border at sunset yesterday! Totaled her. How'd you get out? Who was aboard? Quick, tell me what happened. Quick!"

"I—I didn't fly the last leg, I wasn't in her," Lochart said, trying to get his mind working and also keeping his voice down, for the walls of the trailer were very thin. "They left me at Dez Dam. I backpac—"

"Dez Dam? What the hell you doing there? Who left you?"

Lochart hesitated. Everything was happening so fast. "I don't know if I should . . . should say beca—"

"For Christ's sake, they're onto HBC, we've got to do something fast. Who was flying her, who was aboard?"

"All Iranians evacuating Iran—all air force from Isfahan—General Seladi, eight colonels and majors from Isfahan—I don't know their names—and General Valik, his wife and . . ." Lochart could hardly bring himself to say it, "and his two children."

Rudi was appalled. He had heard about Annoush and the two kids and he had met Valik several times. "That's terrible, terrible. What the hell'm I going to say?"

"What? About what?"

The words tumbled out, "Major Qazani and Hushang, they arrived barely half an hour ago—the major's just gone but I've been ordered to find out if HBC's S-G, where she was based, and who was aboard. I've been ordered to call Kowiss and find out and Hushang's going to be listening in and he's no fool, no fool, and he was sure he saw the S-G decal before he blew her to pieces. Kowiss'll have to say she was our bird, and they'll call Tehran and that's the end."

Lochart sat on one of the built-in bunks. Numb. "I warned them—I warned them to wait for nightfall! What the hell am I going to do?"

"Run for it. Maybe y—" A knock on the door and they froze.

"Skipper, it's me, Fowler. I brought you some tea, thought Tom could use some."

"Thanks, just a moment, Fowler," he said, then dropped his voice. "Tom, what's your story—do you have one?"

"Best I could do was I'm just coming back from a hiking holiday in Luristan, south of Kermanshah. I got caught in a village by a snowfall for about a week and eventually just hiked out."

"That's good. Where's your base?"

Lochart shrugged. "Zagros."

"Good. Anyone ask for your ID yet?"

"Yes. The ticket seller at Ahwaz and some Green Bands."

"*Scheisse!*" Rudi bleakly opened the door.

Fowler Joines brought the tea tray in. "How you doing, Tom?" he said with his toothless beam.

"Good to see you, Fowler. Still cursing?"

"Not as bad as Effer Jordon. How is my old mate?"

Tiredness enveloped Lochart and he leaned back against the wall. Zagros and Effer Jordon, Rodrigues, Jean-Luc, Scot Gavallan, and the others seemed so far away. "Still wearing his hat," he said with a great effort, accepted the tea gratefully, and swallowed it. Hot, thick, heavy, with sweet condensed milk—the greatest pick-me-up in the world. What did Rudi say? Run for it? I can't, he thought as sleep took him. Not without Sharazad . . .

Rudi finished telling Fowler Lochart's cover story. "Spread the word."

The mechanic blinked. "A hiking holiday? Tom Lochart? On his bleeding tod? With you know who in bleeding Tehran? Are you looped, Rudi, old cock?"

Rudi looked at him.

"Just as you say, old sport." Fowler turned to talk to Lochart but he was already asleep, his face sagged with exhaustion. "Cor! He's . . ." His shrewd blue eyes, set deep in the gnarled face, looked back at Rudi. "I'll spread the word like it was bleeding Genesis itself." He left.

Just before the door closed Rudi caught a glimpse of Hushang waiting by the trailer and he was sorry he had left him alone so long. He glanced at Lochart. Poor old Tom. What the hell was he doing in Isfahan? God in heaven what a mess! What the hell do I do now? Carefully he took the cup out of Lochart's hands, but the Canadian awoke startled.

For a moment Lochart did not know whether he was awake or in dream. His heart was pounding, he had a blinding headache, and he was back at the dam at the water's edge, Rudi standing against the light just like Ali, Lochart not knowing whether to dive at him or risk the water, wanting to shout, Don't shoot don't shoot . . .

"Christ, I thought you were Ali," he gasped. "Sorry, I'm all right now. No sweat."

"Ali?"

"The pilot, HBC's pilot, Ali Abbasi, he was going to kill me." Half asleep Lochart told him what had happened. Then he noticed Rudi had gone chalky. "What's the matter?"

Rudi jerked his thumb outside. "That's his brother—Hushang Abbasi—he's the one who totaled HBC. . . ."

TEHRAN: 4:17 P.M. Both men were staring anxiously at the telex machine in the S-G penthouse office. "Come on for God's sake!" McIver muttered and glanced again at his watch. The 125 was due at five-thirty. "We'll have to leave soon, Andy, you never know about traffic."

Gavallan was rocking absently in a creaky old chair. "Yes, but Genny's not here yet. Soon as she arrives we'll leave. If worst comes to worst I can call Aberdeen from Al Shargaz."

"*If* Johnny Hogg makes it through Kish and Isfahan airspace, and the clearance holds in Tehran."

"He'll arrive this time, I've a good feeling our mullah Tehrani wants the new glasses. Hope to God Johnny's got them for him."

"So do I."

This was the first day the komiteh had allowed any foreigners back into the building. Most of the morning had been spent cleaning up and restarting their generator that had, of course, run out of fuel. Almost at once the telex machine had chattered into life: "Urgent! Please confirm your telex is working and inform Mr. McIver I have an Avisyard telex for the boss. Is he still in Tehran?" The telex was from Elizabeth Chen in Aberdeen. "Avisyard" was a company code, used rarely, meaning a top classified message for McIver's eyes only and to operate the machine himself. It took him four tries to get the Aberdeen callback.

"So long as we haven't lost a bird," Gavallan said with an inward prayer.

"I was thinking that too." McIver eased his shoulders. "Any idea what could merit an Avisyard?"

"No." Gavallan hid his sadness, thinking about the real Avisyard, Castle Avisyard, where he had spent so many happy years with Kathy, who had suggested the code. Don't think about Kathy now, he told himself. Not now.

"I hate bloody telex machines—they're always going wrong," McIver was saying, his stomach churning, mostly because of the row that he had had last night with Genny, insisting that she go on the 125 today, also because there was still no news from Lochart. Added to that, again none of the Iranian office staff had reported for work, only the pilots who had come in this morning. McIver had sent them all away except Pettikin whom he had put on standby. Nogger Lane had wandered in around noon, reporting that his flight with the mullah Tehrani, six Green Bands, and five women went well. "I think our friendly mullah wants another ride tomorrow. He expects you 5:30 P.M. sharp at the airport."

"All right. Nogger, you relieve Charlie."

"Come on, Mac, old chap, I've worked hard all morning, above and beyond the call, and Paula's still in town."

"How well I know, 'old chap,' and the way things look she'll be here for the week!" McIver had told him. "You relieve Charlie, you get your hot little tail into a chair, bring our aircraft ledgers up to date, and one more bloody word out of you I'll post you to bloody Nigeria!"

They had waited, grimly conscious that telexes had to go part of the way through phone lines. "Bloody lot of wire between here and Aberdeen," McIver muttered.

Gavallan said, "Soon as Genny arrives we'll leave. I'll make sure she's all right in Al Shargaz before I go home. You're quite right to insist."

"I know, you know, and the whole of Iran knows but she bloody doesn't!"

"Women," Gavallan said diplomatically. "Anything else I can do?"

"Don't think so. Squeezing our two remaining partners helped a lot." Gavallan had tracked them down, Mohammed Siamaki and Turiz Bakhtiar— a common surname in Iran for those from the rich and powerful and multitudinous Bakhtiar tribe of which the ex-prime minister was one of the chiefs. Gavallan had extracted 5 million rials in cash—a little over $60,000, a pittance against what the partners owed—with promises for more every week, in return for a promise, and a handwritten note, to reimburse them personally "outside the country, should it be necessary, and passage on the 125 should it be necessary."

"All right, but where's Valik—how do I get hold of him?" Gavallan had asked, pretending to know nothing about his escape.

"We already told you: he's on vacation with his family," Siamaki had said, rude and arrogant as always. "He'll contact you in London or Aberdeen—there's the overdue matter of our funds in the Bahamas."

"Our joint funds, dear partner, and there's the matter of almost $4 million owing on work already completed, apart from our aircraft lease payments overdue, long overdue."

"If the banks were open you'd have the money. It's not our fault the Shah's pestilential allies ruined him and ruined Iran. We are not to blame for any of the catastrophes, none. As to the monies owed, haven't we paid in the past?"

"Yes. Usually six months late, but I agree, dear friends, eventually we have extracted our share. But if all joint ventures are suspended as the mullah Tehrani told me, how do we operate from now on?"

"*Some* joint ventures, not all—your information is exaggerated and incorrect, Gavallan. We are on notice to get back to normal as soon as possible—crews can leave once their replacements are safely here. Oil fields must be returned to full production. There will be no problems. But to forestall any trouble, once more we have bailed out the partnership. Tomorrow my illustrious cousin, Finance Minister Ali Kia, joins the board a—"

"Hold on a minute! I have prior approval of any change in the board!"

"You used to have that power, but the board voted to change that bylaw. If you wish to go against the board you can bring it up at the next meeting in London—but under the circumstances the change is necessary and reasonable. Minister Kia has assured us we'll be exempt. Of course Minister Kia's fees and percentage will come out of your share. . . ."

Gavallan tried not to watch the telex machine but he found it difficult, trying to think a way out of the trap. "One moment everything seems okay, the next it's rotten again."

"Yes. Yes, Andy, I agree. Talbot was today's clincher."

This morning, early, they had met Talbot briefly. "Oh, yes, old boy, joint ventures are definitely persona non grata now, so sorry," he had told them dryly. "The 'On High' have decreed that *all* joint ventures are suspended, pending instructions, though what instructions and from whom, they didn't impart. Or who the 'On High' are. We presume the Olympian decree is from the dear old Komiteh, whoever they are! On the other side of the coin, old chap, the Ayatollah and Prime Minister Bazargan have both said all foreign debts will be honored. Of course Khomeini overrides Bazargan and issues counterinstructions, Bazargan issues instructions which the Revolutionary Komiteh overrules, the local komitehs are vigilantes who're taking their own version of law as gospel, and not one rotten little urchin has yet handed in a weapon. The jails are filling up nicely, heads are rolling—and apart from the tumbrils it all has a jolly old tediously familiar ring, old boy, and rather suggests we should all retire to Margate for the duration."

"You're serious?"

"Our advice to evacuate all unessential personnel still stands the moment the airport opens which is God knows when but promised for Saturday—we've got BA to cooperate with chartered 747s. As to the illustrious Ali Kia, he's a minor official, very minor indeed, with no power and a good-weather friend to all sides. By the way, we've just heard that the U.S. ambassador in Kabul was abducted by anti-Communist, Shi'ite fundamentalist mujhadin who tried to exchange him for other mujhadin held by the pro-Soviet government. In the following shoot-out he was killed. Things are heating up rather nicely. . . ."

The telex clicked on, their attention zeroed, but the machine did not function. Both of them cursed.

"Soon as I get to Al Shargaz I can phone the office and find out what's the problem . . ." Gavallan glanced at the door as it opened. To their surprise it was Erikki—he and Azadeh had been due to meet them at the airport. Erikki was smiling his usual smile but there was no light behind it.

"Hello, boss, hi, Mac."

"Hi, Erikki. What's up?" McIver looked at him keenly.

"Slight change of plan. We're, er, well, Azadeh and I are going back to Tabriz first."

Yesterday evening Gavallan had suggested that Erikki and Azadeh take immediate leave. "We'll find a replacement. How about coming with me tomorrow? Perhaps we could get Azadeh replacement papers in London . . ."

"Why the change, Erikki?" he asked. "Azadeh's had second thoughts about leaving Iran without Iranian papers?"

"No. An hour ago we got a message—I got a message from her father. Here, read it for yourself." Erikki gave it to Gavallan, who shared it with McIver. The handwritten note said: "From Abdollah Khan to Captain Yokkonen: I require my daughter to come back here at once and ask you to grant her permission." It was signed, Abdollah Khan. The message was repeated in Farsi on the other side.

"You're sure it's his handwriting?" Gavallan asked.

"Azadeh's sure, and she also knew the messenger." Erikki added, "The messenger told us nothing else, only that there's lots of fighting going on there."

"By road's out of the question." McIver turned to Gavallan. "Maybe our mullah Tehrani'd give Erikki a clearance? According to Nogger, he was like a dog-eating wallah after his joyride this morning. We could fit Charlie's 206 with long-range tanks, and Erikki could take her, maybe with Nogger or one of the others to bring her right back?"

Gavallan said, "Erikki, you know the risk you're taking?"

"Yes." Erikki had not yet told them about the killings.

"You've thought it through—everything? Rakoczy, the roadblock, Azadeh herself? We could send Azadeh back alone and you could get on the 125 and we'd put her on Saturday's flight."

"Come on, boss, you'd never do that and neither will I—I couldn't leave her."

"Of course, but it had to be said. All right. Erikki, you take care of the long-range tanks, we'll try for the clearance. I'd suggest you both come back to Tehran as quickly as possible and take the 125 on Saturday. Both of you. It might be wise for you to transfer and do a tour somewhere else—Australia, Singapore, perhaps—or Aberdeen, but that might be too cold for Azadeh, you let me know." Gavallan cheerfully stuck out his hand. "Happy Tabriz, eh?"

"Thanks." Erikki hesitated. "Any news of Tom Lochart?"

"No, not yet—still can't raise Kowiss or Bandar Delam. Why? Sharazad's getting anxious?"

"More than that. Her father's in Evin Jail an—"

"JesusChrist," McIver exploded, Gavallan equally shocked, knowing the rumors of arrests and firing squads. "What for?"

"For questioning—by a komiteh—no one knows what for or how long he'll be held."

Gavallan said uneasily, "Well, if it's only for questioning . . . what happened, Erikki?"

"Sharazad came home half an hour or so ago in tears. When she went back last night after dinner to her parents' house all hell had broken loose. Apparently some Green Bands went into the bazaar, grabbed Emir Paknouri—you remember, her ex-husband—for 'crimes against Islam' and ordered Bakravan to appear at dawn for questioning—for what reason no one knows." Erikki took a breath. "They went with him to the prison this morning, she, her mother, sisters, and brother. They got there just after dawn and waited and waited and would be still waiting if they hadn't been told to clear off around 2:00 P.M. by Green Bands on guard there."

There was a stunned silence.

Erikki broke it. "Mac, try Kowiss. Get them to contact Bandar Delam—Tom should know about Sharazad's father." He noticed the look between the two men. "What's going on with Tom?"

"He's on a charter to Bandar Delam."

"Yes, you told me that. Mac's told me that and so has Sharazad. Tom told her he'd be back in a few days." Erikki waited. Gavallan just looked back at him. "Well," he said, "you must have good reasons."

"I think so," Gavallan said. Both he and McIver were convinced that Tom Lochart would not willingly have gone on to Kuwait, whatever bribe Valik offered him—both equally afraid that he had been forced.

"All right—you're the boss. Well, I'll be off. Sorry for bringing bad news but I thought you'd better know." Erikki forced a smile. "Sharazad wasn't in good shape. See you in Al Shargaz!"

"Sooner the better, Erikki."

McIver said, "If you bump into Gen—don't mention about Sharazad's father, eh?"

"Of course."

After Erikki had left, McIver said, "Bakravan's a pretty important bazaari to summarily arrest."

"I agree." After a pause Gavallan said, "Hope to God Erikki's not going into a trap. That message bit's very smelly, very sm—"

The telex chattering made them both jump. They read the telex, line by line, as it came through. Gavallan began cursing and continued to curse until the machine stopped. "God curse Imperial Helicopters to hell!" He ripped the telex out, Mac sent their call sign back and "Standby One." Gavallan reread it.

Again it was from Liz Chen: "Dear Boss, we've tried you every hour on the hour since we heard from Johnny Hogg you stayed in Tehran. Sorry to bring bad tidings but early Monday morning Imperial Air and Imperial Helicopters jointly announced 'new financial arrangements to revitalise their competitive position in the North Sea. IH have been allowed to write off 17.1 million sterling of taxpayers' money and have capitalised another 48 million of their 68 million debt by issuing paper to the head company in lieu of the debt.' We've just heard secretly that 18 of our 19 North Sea contracts due to be renewed by various companies have been awarded to IH *under real cost.* Thurston Dell of ExTex urgently needs to talk to you. Our ops in Nigeria urgently need 3 repeat 3 212s—can you provide from Iran redundancies? Presume you will go to Al Shargaz or Dubai with John Hogg today. Please advise! Mac—if Himself has already left, please advise. Love to Genny."

"We're buggered!" Gavallan said. "It's highway bloody robbery with tax-payers' money."

"Then, then take them to court," McIver said nervously, shocked at Gavallan's color. "Unfair competition!"

"I can't, for God's sake," then even louder and more angry, "unless the government screams there's bugger all I can do! Without having to service their legitimate debt they can bid way under even our cost! *Dew neh loh moh* on Callaghan and all his pinkos!"

"Come on, Andy, they're not all pinkos!"

"I know that, for God's sake," Gavallan roared, "but it sounds right!" Then his good nature overcame his fury and he laughed though his heart was still working hard. "Bloody government," he added sourly, "they don't know their arse from a hole in the ground."

McIver could feel his own hands shaking. "Christ, Andy, I thought you were going to bust a blood vessel." He was well aware of the implications of the telex. All his own nest egg was in S-G stocks and shares. "Eighteen contracts out of nineteen, that dents our whole North Sea ops!"

"It dents us everywhere. With those amounts of write-offs IH can under-cut us worldwide. And Thurston wanting me to call urgently? That's got to mean ExTex'll back out, the very least renegotiate, because of a new 'ad-justed' IH bid and I've signed the contract for our X63s." Gavallan took out his handkerchief and mopped his brow. Then he saw Nogger Lane gaping from the doorway. "What the hell do you want?"

"Er, er, nothing, sir, I thought the place was on fire. . . ." Nogger Lane hurriedly closed the door.

"Andy," McIver said softly when it was safe, "Struan's. Won't they pick up the slack for you?"

"Struan's could, though not easily this year—but Linbar won't." Gavallan kept his voice down equally. "When he hears about all this he'll dance a bloody jig. The timing couldn't be more perfect for him." He smiled wryly, thinking about Ian Dunross's call and his warnings. He had not told McIver about them—McIver was not part of Struan's though an old friend of Ian's too. Where the devil does Ian get his information?

He smoothed out the telex. This was the culmination of a number of problems with Imperial Helicopters. Six months ago IH had deliberately headhunted one of his senior executives who had taken with him many S-G secrets. Only last month Gavallan had lost a very important North Sea Board of Trade tender to IH—after a year of work and huge investment. The board of trade specifications were to develop electronic equipment for a helicopter air-sea rescue operation in all weather conditions, day or night, so that choppers could safely go out a hundred miles over the North Sea, hover, pick eight men out of the sea, and return safely—in zero-zero conditions and gale-force winds—fast. In winter months, even with a sea survival suit, about an hour was maximum life expectancy and endurance in those seas.

With Ian Dunross's private enthusiasm: "Don't forget, Andy, such knowledge and equipment would also fit perfectly into our projected China Seas endeavors," Gavallan had committed half a million pounds and a year of work developing the electronics and guidance systems with an electronics company. Then, on the great day, the official test pilot had found he couldn't work the equipment, even though six of S-G's line pilots, including Tom Lochart and Rudi Lutz, later had had no trouble. Even so, S-G could not get the necessary certification in time. "The unfairness of the whole rotten business," he had written McIver, "is that IH's got the contract using a Guerney 661 with noncertificated Danish equipment aboard. We get the runaround and they get dispensations. It's a bastard—by the way, of course I can't prove it, but I'd bet real money the test pilot was got at—he's been sent 'on a long rest.' Oh, we'll get the money back and the contract in a year or so because our equipment's better, safer, and British built. Meanwhile Imperial's operating at safety levels, I think, that can be improved."

That's what really counts, he thought, rereading the telex, safety—safety first and safety last. "Mac, would you send Liz a reply for me: 'Leaving for Al Shargaz now and will phone on arrival.' Telex Thurston and ask what deal he would offer if I double the number of X63s presently on order. S—"

"Eh?"

"Well, it costs nothing to ask; IH's bound to hear about our problems here and I'm not going to let those buggers start giving us the finger—better to keep them off-balance. In any event we could use two X63s here to service all the Guerney contracts—if things were different. Finish the telex, see you soon."

"Okay."

Gavallan sat back in the easy chair and let his mind drift, collecting his strength. I'm going to have to be very strong. And very clever. This is the one that can bury me and S-G and give Linbar everything he needs—this and Iran together. Yes, and it was stupid to lose your temper like that. What you need is Kathy's Shrieking Tree. . . . Ah, Kathy, Kathy.

The Shrieking Tree was an old clan custom, a special tree chosen by the oldest of the clan, somewhere nearby, that you could go out to, alone, when the deevil—as old Granny Dunross, Kathy's grandmother, called it—"when the deevil was upon you and there you could curse and rant and rave and curse some more until there were no more curses left. Then there would always be peace in the home and never a need to really curse a husband or wife or lover or child. Aye, just a wee tree, for a tree can bear all the curses even the deevil himself invented."

The first time he had used Kathy's Shrieking Tree was in Hong Kong. There it was a jacaranda in the garden of the Great House, the residence of the taipan of Struan's. Kathy's brother, Ian, was taipan then. Gavallan knew the date exactly: it was Wednesday, August 21, 1963, the night she told him.

Poor Kathy, my Kathy, he thought, loving her still—Kathy, born under an ill-set star. Swept off your feet by one of the Few—John Selkirk, flight lieutenant, DFC, RAF—married at once, not yet eighteen, widowed at once, not yet three months older, him torched out of the skies and vanished. Rotten war years and more tragedy, two beloved brothers killed in action—one your twin. Meeting you in Hong Kong in '46, at once in love with you, hoping with all my heart that I could make up for some of the unluck. I know Melinda and Scot did—they've turned out wonderfully, so grand. And then, in '63, before your thirty-eighth birthday, the multiple sclerosis.

Going home to Scotland as you'd always wanted—me to put Ian's plans into effect, you to regain your health. But that part not to be. Watching you die. Watching the sweet smile you used to cover the hell inside, so brave and gentle and wise and loving, but going, plateau by plateau. So slowly, yet so fast, so inexorably. By '68 in a wheelchair, mind still crystal, voice clear, the rest a shell, out of control and shaking. Then it was '70.

That Christmas they were at Castle Avisyard. And on the second day of the new year when the others had gone and Melinda and Scot were skiing in Switzerland, she had said, "Andy, my darling, I cannot endure another year, another month, or another day."

"Yes," he said simply.

"Sorry, but I'll need help. I need to go and I . . . I'm ever so sorry that it's been so long . . . but I need to go now, Andy. I have to do it myself but I'll need help. Yes?"

"Yes, my darling."

They had spent a day and a night talking, talking about good things and good times and what he should do for Melinda and Scot, and that she wanted him to marry again, and she told him how wonderful life had been with him and they laughed, one with another, and his tears did not spill till later. He held her palsied hand with the sleeping pills and held her shaking head against his chest, helped her with the glass of water—a little whisky in it for luck—and never let her go until the shaking had stopped.

The doctor had said kindly, "I don't blame her—if I'd been her I would have done it years ago, poor lady."

Going then to the Shrieking Tree. But shrieking no words, nothing—only tears.

"Andy?"

"Yes, Kathy?"

Gavallan looked up and he saw it was Genny, McIver by the door, both of them watching him. "Oh, hello, Genny, sorry, I was a million miles away." He got up. "It—I think it was the Avisyard that set me thinking."

Genny's eyes widened. "Oh, an Avisyard telex? Not a bird down?"

"No, no, thank God, just Imperial Helicopters up to their old tricks."

"Oh, thank God too," Genny said, openly relieved. She was dressed in a heavy coat and a nice hat. Her large suitcase was in the outer office where Nogger Lane and Charlie Pettikin waited. "Well, Andy," she said, "unless you override Mr. McIver, I suppose we should go. I'm as ready as I'll ever be."

"Come on, Gen, there's no n—" McIver stopped as she imperiously held up her hand.

"Andy," she said sweetly, "please tell Mr. McIver that battle is joined."

"Gen! Will y—"

"Joined, by God!" Imperiously she waved Nogger Lane away from her suitcase, picked it up, staggered a little under its weight, and swept out with an even more imperious, "I can carry my own suitcase, thank you very much."

There was a big hole in the air behind her. McIver sighed. Nogger Lane had a hard time keeping the laughter off his face. Gavallan and Charlie Pettikin thought it best to be noncommittal.

"Well, er, no need for you to drive out with us, Charlie," Gavallan said gruffly.

"I'd still like to, if it's all right," Pettikin said, not really wanting to but McIver had asked him privately for support with Genny. "That's a cute hat, Genny," he had told her just after a delightful breakfast with Paula. Genny had smiled sweetly. "Don't you try to butter me up, Charlie Pettikin, or I'll give you what for too. I've had men generally—in fact I'm very pissed off indeed. . . ."

Gavallan put on his parka. He picked up the telex and stuck it into his pocket. "Actually, Charlie," he said and some of his concern showed now, "if you don't mind I'd rather you didn't—I've got some unfinished stuff to chat with Mac about."

"Sure, of course." Pettikin stuck out his hand and hid the beam. Not going out to the airport would give him a few bonus hours alone with Paula. Paula the Fair, he had thought of her since breakfast even though she was brunette. To McIver he said, "I'll see you at home."

"Why not wait here—I want to raise all the bases as soon as it's dark and we can go back together. I'd like you to hold the fort. Nogger, you can quit." Nogger Lane beamed and Pettikin cursed silently.

In the car McIver drove, Gavallan was beside him, Genny in the back. "Mac, let's talk about Iran."

They went through their options. Each time they came back to the same gloomy conclusion: they had to hope the situation came back to normal, the banks reopened, they got the money owing to them, that their joint venture was exempt and they weren't nailed. "You just have to keep going, Mac. While we can operate, you'll have to continue, whatever the problems."

McIver was equally grave. "I know. But how do I operate without money —and what about the lease payments?"

"Somehow I'll get you operating money. I'll bring cash from London in a week. I can carry the lease payment on your aircraft and spares for another few months; I may even be able to do the same with the X63s if I can reschedule payments but, well, I hadn't planned on losing so many contracts to IH—maybe I can get some of them back. Whichever way, it'll be dicey for a while but not to worry. Hope to God Johnny gets in; just have to get home now, there's so much to do. . . ."

McIver narrowly avoided a head-on collision with a car that charged out of a side street, almost went into the joub, and came back onto the roadway again. "Bloody twit! You all right, Gen?" He glanced into the rearview window and winced, seeing her stony face.

Gavallan felt the icy blast too, started to say something to her but thought better of it. Wonder if I could get hold of Ian—perhaps he could guide me out of the abyss—and, thinking of that, reminded him of David MacStruan's tragic death. So many of them, the Struans, MacStruans, Dunrosses, their enemies the Gornts, Rothwells, Brocks of ancient days, had died violent deaths or vanished—lost at sea—or died in strange accidents. So far Ian's survived. But how much longer? Not many more times. "I think I'm up to my eighth, Andy," Dunross had said the last time they met.

"What now?"

"Nothing much. Car bomb went off in Beirut just after I'd passed by.

Nothing to worry about, I've said it before, there's no pattern. I just happen to have a charmed life."

"Like Macao?"

Dunross was an enthusiastic racer and had driven in many of the Macao Grand Prix. In '65—the race still amateur then—he had won the race but the right front tire of his E Type blew out at the winning post and shoved him into the barricade and sent him tumbling down the track, other cars taking evading action, one careening into him. They had cut him out of the wreckage, everything intact, unhurt but for his left foot missing.

"Like Macao, Andy," Dunross had said with his strange smile. "Just an accident. Both times." The other time his engine had exploded but he had been unscathed. Whispers had it that his engine had been tampered with— the finger pointed at his enemy Quillan Gornt, but not publicly.

Quillan's dead and Ian's alive, Gavallan thought. So am I. So's Linbar; that bastard will go on forever. . . . Christ Almighty, I'm getting morbid and stupid—got to stop it. Mac's worried enough as it is. Got to figure a way out of the vise. "In an emergency, Mac, I'll send messages through Talbot, you do the same. I'll be back in a few days without fail and by then I'll have answers—meanwhile I'll base the 125 until further notice—Johnny can be a courier for us. That's the best I can do for today. . . ."

Genny, who had not uttered a word and had politely refused to be drawn into the conversation though she listened attentively, was also more than a little worried. It's obvious there's no future for us here, and I'd be quite very glad to leave—provided Duncan comes too. Even so, we can't just meekly run away with our tails between our legs and let all of Duncan's work and life's nest egg be stolen, that'd kill him as certainly as any bullet. Ugh! I do wish he'd do what he's told—he should have retired last year when the Shah was still in power. Men! Bloody stupid, the whole lot of them! Christ Almighty! What fools men are!

Traffic was very slow now. Twice they had to divert because of barricades erected across the roads—both of them guarded by armed men, not Green Bands, who angrily waved them away. Bodies here and there among the piled refuse, burned-out cars and one tank. Dogs scavenging. Once there was sudden firing nearby and they took a side street, avoiding a pitched battle between what factions they never found out. A stray bazooka shell plastered a nearby building but without danger to them. McIver eased his way around the burned hulk of a bus, more than ever glad that he had insisted that Genny evacuate Iran. Again he glanced at her in the rearview mirror and saw the white face under the hat and his heart went out to her. She's damn good, he thought proudly, so much guts. Damn good, but so bloody-minded. Hate that bloody hat. Hats don't suit her. Why the hell won't she do what she's told without arguing? Poor old Gen, I'll be so relieved when she's not in danger.

Near the airport, traffic almost came to a standstill, hundreds of cars crammed with people, many Europeans, men, women, and children, going there on the rumor that the airport had been reopened—enraged Green Bands turning everyone away, crude signs scrawled in Farsi and misspelled English nailed to trees and to walls: AIRPRT FORBIDUN NOW. AIRPRT OPEN MUNDAY— IF TICKUT AND EXIT PURMIT.

It took them half an hour to talk their way through the barrier. It was Genny who finally managed it. Like most of the wives who had to shop and to deal with servants and day-to-day living, she could speak some Farsi—and though she had not said a word all the way, she leaned forward and spoke to the Green Bands pleasantly. At once they were waved through.

"My God, Gen, that was wonderful," McIver said. "What did you tell that bastard?"

"Andy," she said smugly, "please tell Mr. McIver I told them he was a suspected smallpox carrier who was being sent out of the country."

More Green Bands were on the gate that led to the freighting area and their office, but this time it was easier and clearly they were expected. The 125 was already on the runway, surrounded by armed Green Bands and trucks. Two motorcycle Green Bands motioned them to follow and roared off onto the tarmac, leading the way.

"Why are you late?" the mullah Tehrani said irritably, coming down the 125's steps, two armed revs following. Both Gavallan and McIver noticed he was wearing new glasses. They caught a glimpse of John Hogg inside the cabin, one of the revs at the head of the steps with a leveled submachine gun. "The aircraft must take off instantly. Why are you late?"

"So sorry, Excellency, the traffic—Insha'Allah! So sorry," McIver said carefully. "I understand from Captain Lane your work for the Ayatollah, may he live forever, was satisfactory?"

"There was not enough time to complete all my work. As God wants. It is, er, it is necessary to go tomorrow. You will arrange it please. For 9:00 A.M."

"With pleasure. Here is the passenger crew manifest." McIver gave him the paper. Gavallan, Genny, and Armstrong were on it, Armstrong as going on leave.

Tehrani read the paper easily now, openly ecstatic with his glasses. "Where is this Armstrong?"

"Oh, I presumed he was aboard."

"There's no one aboard but the crew," the mullah said irritably, the vast pleasure of being able to see overcoming his nervousness at having allowed the 125 to land. But he was glad he had, the glasses were a gift of God and the second pair promised by the pilot next week a protection against breakage and the third pair just for reading . . . Oh, God is Great. God is Great, all thanks to God for putting the thought into the pilot's head and for letting me see so well. "The aircraft must leave at once."

"It's not like Mr. Armstrong to be late, Excellency," Gavallan said with a frown. Neither he nor McIver had heard from him since yesterday—nor had he come to the flat last night. This morning Talbot had shrugged, saying that Armstrong had been delayed, but not to worry, he would be at the airport on time. "Perhaps he's waiting in the office," Gavallan said.

"There is no one there who should not be there. The aircraft will leave now. It will not wait. Aboard, please! The aircraft will leave now."

"Perfect," Gavallan said. "As God wants. By the way we'd like clearance for the 125 to come back Saturday and clearance for a 206 to go to Tabriz tomorrow." With great formality he handed him the papers, neatly filled out.

"The, er, the 125 may return but no flights to Tabriz. Perhaps Saturday."

"But, Excellency, don't y—"

"No," the mullah said, conscious of the others watching him. He ordered the truck blocking the runway out of the way and looked at Genny as she got out of the car and nodded approvingly. Gavallan and McIver were surprised to notice that now she had tucked her hair into the scarf part of her hat so none of her hair was showing and, with her long coat, almost gave the impression of being in chador. "Please to get aboard."

"Thank you, Excellency," she said in adequate Farsi that she had been rehearsing with the help of a dictionary all morning, with the necessary perfect amount of seriousness, "but with your permission I will stay. My husband is not as healthy in the head as he should be, temporarily, but you— being a man of such intelligence—you would understand that though a wife cannot go against her husband's wishes, it is written that even the Prophet himself had to be looked after."

"True, true," the mullah said and looked at McIver thoughtfully. McIver stared back perplexed, without understanding. "Stay if you wish."

"Thank you," Genny said, with great deference. "Then I stay. Thank you, Excellency, for your agreement and your wisdom." She hid her glee at her cleverness and said in English, "Duncan, the mullah Tehrani agrees I should stay." She saw his eyes cross and added hastily, "I'll wait in the car."

He was there before her. "You bloody get aboard that kite," he said, "or I'll bloody put you aboard."

"Don't be silly, Duncan, dear!" She was so solicitous. "And don't shout, it's so bad for your bloody pressure." She saw Gavallan coming over and some of her confidence vanished. Around her was rotten snow and rotten sky and sour youths gaping at her. "You know I really do love this place," she said brightly, "how could I leave?"

"You—you're bloody leaving an—" McIver was so angry he could hardly talk and for a second Genny was afraid she had gone too far.

"I'll leave if you leave, Duncan. Right now. I'm not repeat not going without you and if you try to force me I'll throw such a tantrum that it'll blow the 125 and the whole airport to kingdom come! Andy, explain to this —this person! Oh, I know you can both drag me aboard but if you do you'll both lose total face and I know you both too well! Andy!"

Gavallan laughed. "Mac, you've had it!"

In spite of his rage, McIver laughed too, and the mullah watching and listening shook his head with disbelief at the antics of Infidels.

"Gen, you . . . you've been planning this all along," McIver sputtered.

"Who me?" She was all innocence. "Perish the thought!"

"All right, Gen," McIver said, his jaw still jutting, "all right, you win, but you haven't just lost face, you've lost tail as well."

"Aboard!" the mullah said.

"What about Armstrong?" McIver said.

"He knows the rules and the time." Gavallan gave Genny a hug and shook hands with McIver. "See you soon and take care." He went aboard, the jet took off, and during the long drive back to the office neither Genny nor Duncan McIver noticed the time passing. Both were preoccupied. Genny sat in the front. She was very tired but very satisfied. "You're a good woman, Gen," he had said the moment that they were alone, "but you're not forgiven."

"Yes, Duncan," she had said meekly, as a good woman does—from time to time.

"You're not bloody forgiven at all."

"Yes, Duncan."

"And don't yes Duncan me!" He drove on for a while, then he said gruffly, "I'd rather have you safe in Al Shargaz but I'm glad you're here."

She said nothing, wisely. Just smiled. And put her hand on his knee. Both of them at peace now.

It was another foul drive, with many detours, more shootings, and more bodies and dogs and angry crowds, and garbage, the streets not cleaned for months now, the joubs long since clogged. Night came swiftly and the cold increased. Odd cars and some army trucks screamed by, careless of road safety, packed with men. "Are you tired, Duncan. Would you like me to drive?"

"No, I'm fine, thanks," he said, feeling very tired, and very glad when at length they turned into their street, dark and ominous like all the rest, the only light coming from their penthouse office. He would have preferred to leave the car on the street but he was sure by the time he came back the gasoline would have been siphoned out even though there was a lock on the tank—if the car itself was even still there. He drove into their garage, locked the car, locked the garage, and they climbed the stairs.

Charlie Pettikin met them on the landing, his face pasty. "Hi, Mac. Thank God y—" Then he saw Genny and he stopped. "Oh, Genny! What, what happened? Didn't the 125 get in?"

"She came in," McIver said. "What the hell's happened, Charlie?"

Pettikin closed the office door after them, glanced at Genny who said wearily, "All right, I'm going to the loo."

Christ Almighty, she thought, it's all so bloody stupid—will they never learn? Duncan'll tell me as soon as we're alone so I'll hear it anyway and I'd much rather have it from the source. Tiredly she plodded for the door.

"No, Gen," McIver said and she stopped, startled. "You chose to stay so . . ." He shrugged. She noticed something different in him and did not know if it was good or if it was bad. "Let's have it, Charlie."

"Rudi came in on the HF less than half an hour ago," Pettikin said in a rush. "HBC's been shot down, blown out of the skies, no survivors b—"

Both Genny and McIver went white, "Oh, my God!" She groped for a chair.

"I don't understand what's going on," Pettikin said helplessly. "It's all crazy, like a dream, but Tom Lochart hasn't been clobbered, he's at Bandar Delam with Rudi. H—"

McIver came back to life. "Tom's safe?" he burst out. "He got out?"

"You don't get out of a chopper if she was 'blown out of the skies.' Nothing makes any sense unless it's a cover-up. Tom was flying spares, no passengers, but this officer said she was full of people, and Rudi said, 'Tell Mr. McIver that Captain Lochart's back off leave.' I even talked to him!"

McIver gaped at him. "You talked to him? He's safe? You're sure? Off what leave, for God's sake?"

"I don't know but I did talk to him. He came on the blower."

"Wait a minute, Charlie. How'd Rudi reach us? Is he at Kowiss?"

"No, he said he was calling from Abadan Air Traffic Control."

McIver muttered an obscenity, so relieved about Lochart and at the same time appalled about Valik and his family. Full of people? Should've been only

four! There were fifty questions he wanted answered at once and knew there
was no way out of the trap that he and Tom were in. He had told no one of
Lochart's real mission or his own dilemma authorizing it, other than Gavallan. "Let's have it from the beginning, Charlie, exactly." McIver glanced at
Genny who was frozen. "You all right, Gen?"

"Yes, yes. I—I'll make a cuppa." Her voice seemed very small to both of
them and she went over to the kitchenette.

Shakily Pettikin sat on the edge of the desk. "As exactly as I can remem-
ber, Rudi said, 'I've got an officer from the Iranian Air Force here and have
to know officially . . .' Then this other voice came over the loudspeaker.
'This is Major Qazani, Air Force Intelligence! I require answer at once. Is
HBC an S-G 212 or isn't it?' To give myself time I said, 'Hang on a minute
I'll get the file.' I waited, hoping for a lead from Rudi but there wasn't one so
I figured it was all right. 'Yes, EP-HBC's one of our 212s.' At once Rudi blew
his stack and cursed as I've never heard him before and said something like,
'By God, that's terrible because HBC tried to escape into Iraq and the
Iranian Air Force rightly shot the ship down, blew her and all aboard to the
hell she deserved—who the hell was flying her and who the hell was
aboard?' "

Pettikin wiped away a dribble of sweat. "I think I swore myself, fell apart a
bit, can't remember exactly, Mac, then said something like, 'That's terrible!
Hold on—I'll get the flight book,' hoping like hell my voice sounded more or
less okay. I got it and saw Nogger's name crossed off, with 'reported sick'
alongside, then Tom Lochart's, and your signature authorizing the charter."
He looked up at McIver helplessly. "Clearly Rudi didn't want me to say Tom
so I just said, 'According to our flight book she's not checked out to anyone . . .' "

McIver went red. "But if you s—"

"It was the best I could do at the time, for God's sake. I said, 'She's not
checked out to anyone.' Rudi began cursing again but I thought his voice
sounded different now, more relieved. 'What the hell're you talking about?'
he said.

" 'I'm just telling you, Captain Lutz, according to the records here, HBC's
still hangared at Doshan Tappeh. If she's gone she must've been hijacked,' I
said, hoping my voice sounded convincing. Mac, I was groping and I still
don't understand what the problem is. Then this other voice said, 'This
matter will be taken up through channels at once. I require your flight clearance book at once.' I told him okay, where should I send it. That threw him a
little because of course there's no way we can get it to him at once. Eventu-

ally he said to keep our records safely and we'd get instructions later. Then Tom came on and said something like:

" 'Captain Pettikin, please give my apologies to Mr. McIver that I'm late off leave but I was trapped by a snowfall in a village just south of Kermanshah. Soon as I can I'll head for home.' " Pettikin exhaled, glanced at Genny then back at McIver. "That's it. That's all. What do you think?"

"About Tom? I don't know." McIver went over to the window heavily and both Pettikin and Genny saw the weight on him. Snow was on the sill and the wind had picked up a little. Sporadic gunfire sounded from the distance, rifle and automatic, but none of them noticed it.

"Genny?"

"I—it doesn't make any, any sense, Charlie, any sense at all about Tommy." Weakly she poured the boiling water into the teapot, the cups already laid out, glad to have had something to do with her hands, feeling helpless and wanting to cry, wanting to shout at the injustice of everything, knowing that Tom and Duncan were trapped—her Duncan had signed the flight plan—knowing she could not mention anything about Annoush or the children or Valik—*if* they were aboard, they must be aboard, but then who was flying if it wasn't Tommy? "The hijack . . . well, obviously Tommy's on the clearance here and so is Duncan. The authorities in Tehran still have the clearance. The clearance has Duncan's name on it so a hijack isn't . . . it doesn't make much sense."

"I can see that now but at the time the story sounded good." Pettikin felt awful. He picked up the clearance book. "Mac, how about if we lose this, get rid of it?"

"Tehran Control's still got the original, Charlie. Tom refueled, there'll be a record."

"In normal times, sure. Now? With all this mess going on?"

"Perhaps."

"Maybe we could retrieve the original?"

"Come on, for God's sake, not a hope till hell freezes."

Genny started pouring the tea into the three cups. The silence tightened. In misery Pettikin said, "I still don't see how if Tom started off from Doshan Tappeh and then . . . unless she was hijacked en route, or when he was refueling." Irritably he ran his fingers through his hair. "It's got to be a hijack. Where did he refuel? Kowiss? Maybe they could help?"

McIver did not answer, just stared out at the night. Pettikin waited, then leafed through the clearance book, found the right duplicate, and looked at the back. "Isfahan?" he said surprised. "Why Isfahan?"

Again McIver did not answer.

Genny added condensed milk to the tea and gave one cup to Pettikin. "I think you did very well, Charlie," she said, not knowing what else to say. Then she took the other cup to McIver.

"Thanks, Gen."

She saw the tears and her own tears spilled. He put an arm around her, thinking about Annoush and the Christmas party he and Genny had given for all the kids of their friends, such a short time ago—little Setarem and Jalal, the stars of all the games, such wonderful kids, now cinders or meat for scavengers.

"It's good about Tommy, dear, isn't it?" she said through her own tears, Pettikin forgotten. Embarrassed, Pettikin went out and shut the door behind him and neither of them noticed his going. "It's good about Tommy," she said again. "That's one good thing."

"Yes, Gen, that's one good thing."

"What can we do?"

"Wait. We wait and see. We hope to God they didn't buy it but . . . somehow I know they were aboard." Tenderly he brushed away her tears. "But come Sunday, Gen, when the 125 goes you're on it," he told her gently. "I promise only until we sort this all out—but this time you must go."

She nodded. He drank the tea. It tasted very good. He smiled down at her. "You make a damn good cuppa, Gen," he said, but that did not take away her fear or her misery—or her fury at all the killing and uselessness and tragedy and the blatant usurping of their livelihood, or the age that it was putting on her husband. The worry's killing him. It's killing him, she thought with growing rage. Then all at once the answer came to her.

She looked around to make sure Pettikin wasn't there. "Duncan," she whispered, "if you don't want those bastards to steal our future, why don't we leave and take everything with us?"

"Eh?"

"Planes, spares, and personnel."

"We can't do that, Gen, I've already told you fifty times."

"Oh, yes, we can if we want to and if we have a plan." She said it with such utter confidence it swept him. "There's Andy to help. Andy can make the plan, we can't. You can carry it out, he can't. They don't want us here, so be it, we'll leave—but with our planes and our spares and our self-respect. We'll have to be very secretive but we can do it. We can do it. I know we can."

BOOK TWO

SATURDAY
February 17

AT KOWISS: 6:38 A.M. The mullah Hussain was sitting cross-legged on the thin mattress checking the action of the AK47. With a practiced movement he snapped the new magazine into place. "Good," he said.

"Will there be more fighting today?" his wife asked. She was across the room, standing beside a wood-burning stove that was heating a pan of water for the first coffee of the day. Her black chador rustled as she moved, masking that she was heavy with child again.

"As God wants."

She echoed him, trying to hide her fear, afraid of what would become of them when her husband had obtained the martyrdom he sought so relentlessly, wanting in her most secret heart to scream from the minarets that it was too much to bear that God required such sacrifice of her and their children. Seven years of marriage and three live children and four dead children and the deep poverty of all those years—so great a contrast to her previous life with her own family who had owned a butcher's stall in the bazaar, always enough to eat and laughter and going out without chador, picnics, and even going to the cinema —had etched lines on her once attractive face. As God wants but it's not fair, not fair! We'll starve—who will want to support the family of a dead mullah?

Their eldest son, Ali, a little boy of six, squatted beside the door of this one-room hut that was beside the mosque, attentively following his father's every movement—his two little brothers, three and two years old, asleep on their straw mattress on the dirt floor, wrapped in an old army blanket. They were curled up like kittens. In the room was a rough wooden table and two benches, a few pots and pans, the big mattress and a small one on old carpets. An oil lamp for light. The joub outside was for washing and for waste. No decorations on the whitewashed, dried-mud walls. A tap for water that sometimes worked. Flies and insects. And in a niche, facing Mecca, the place of honor, the well-used Koran.

It was just after dawn, the day chill and overcast, and Hussain had already called for morning prayer in the mosque and had wiped the dirt off the gun and oiled it carefully, cleaned the barrel of spent cordite, and refilled the magazine. Now it's as good as ever, he thought contentedly, ready to do more of God's work and there's plenty of use for such a gun—the AK47 so much better than the M14, simpler, more rugged, and just as accurate at close quarters. Stupid Americans, stupid as ever to make an infantry gun that was complex and accurate at a thousand yards when most fighting was done at nearer to three hundred and you could drag the AK47 in the mud all day and it would still do what it was supposed to do: kill. Death to all enemies of God!

Already there had been clashes between Green Bands and the Marxist-Islamics and other leftists in Kowiss, and more at Gach Saran, a nearby oil refinery town to the northwest. Yesterday, after dark, he had led Green Bands against one of the secret Tudeh safe houses—the meeting betrayed by one of the members in return for the hope of mercy. There would be none. The battle was sudden, short, and bloody. Eleven men killed, he hoped some of the leaders. So far the Tudeh had not yet come out into the open in strength, but a mass demonstration had been called by them for tomorrow afternoon in support of the Tudeh demonstration in Tehran even though Khomeini had expressly warned against it. The confrontation was already planned. Both sides knew it. Many will die, he thought grimly. Death to all enemies of Islam!

"Here," she said, giving him the hot, sweet black coffee nectar, the one luxury he allowed himself except on Fridays—Holy Days—and other special days and all the Holy Month of Ramadan when he gave up coffee gladly.

"Thank you, Fatima," he said politely. When he had been appointed mullah here, his father and mother had found her for him and his mentor, Ayatollah Isfahani, had told him to marry so he had obeyed.

He drank the coffee, enjoying it very much, and gave her back the little cup. Marriage had not distracted him from his path, though from time to time he enjoyed sleeping against her, her buttocks large and warm in the chill of winter, sometimes turning her, joining, and then sleeping again, but never really at peace. I will only be at peace in Paradise, only then, he thought, his excitement growing, so soon now. God be thanked that I was named after Imam Hussain, Lord of the Martyrs, Imam Ali's second son, he of the Great Martyrdom, thirteen centuries ago at the Battle of Karbala.

We will never forget him, he thought, his ecstasy growing, reliving the pain of Ashura, the tenth day of Muharram—only a few weeks ago—the anniversary of that martyrdom, the Shi'as' most holy day of mourning. His back still bore the weals. That day he had been in Qom again, as last year and the year before that, taking part in the Ashura processions, the cleansing processions, with tens of thousands of other Iranians—whipping themselves to remind themselves of the divine martyrdom, scourging themselves with whips and chains, mortifying themselves with hooks.

It had taken him many weeks to recover, to be able to stand without pain. As God wants, he told himself proudly. Pain is nothing, this world is nothing, I stood against Peshadi at the air base and took over the air base and subdued it and brought him to Isfahan in bonds as I had been ordered. And now, today, first I will go again to the base to investigate the foreigners and curb them and this Sunni Zataki who thinks he's Genghis Khan, and this afternoon again I will lead the Faithful against the atheist Tudeh, doing God's work in obedience to the Imam who obeys only God. I pray that today I will gain admittance to Paradise, "there to recline on couches lined with brocade, and the fruit of the two gardens shall be within easy reach," the so familiar words of the Koran etched on his brain.

"We've no food," his wife said, interrupting his thought pattern.

"There will be food at the mosque today," he said, and his son Ali became even more attentive—momentarily distracted from scratching the fly sores and other insect bites. "From now on you and the children will not be hungry. We will be giving out daily meals of horisht and rice to the needy as we have done throughout history." He smiled at Ali, reached over, and tousled his head. "God knows we are among the needy." Since Khomeini had returned, the mosques had begun again this ancient role of giving daily meals of plain but nourishing food, the food donated as part of Zakat—the voluntary alms tax that all Muslims were subject to—or bought with money from

Zakat that was now again the sole prerogative of the mosques. Hussain heaped more curses on the Shah who had canceled the yearly subsidy to mullahs and mosques two years ago, causing them such poverty and anguish.

"Join the people waiting at the mosque," he told her. "When they are all fed, take enough for you and the children. Daily you will do this."

"Thank you."

"Thank God."

"I do, oh, yes I do."

He pulled on his boots and shouldered the gun.

"Can I come with you, Father?" Ali asked in his thin, piping voice. "I want to do God's work too."

"Of course, come along."

She closed the door after them and sat down on a bench, her stomach rumbling from hunger, feeling sick and weak, too tired to wave the flies away that settled on her face. She was eight months with child. The midwife had told her that this time would be harder than before because the baby was in a wrong position. She began to weep, remembering the tearing, screaming agony of the last birth and the one before and all of them. "Don't worry," the old midwife had said, complacently, "you're in the Hands of God. A little fresh camel dung spread on your stomach will take the pains away. It's a woman's duty to bear children and you're young."

Young? I'm twenty-two years old, and old, old, old. I know it, and know why, and I've a brain and have eyes and can even write my own name and know we can have better, as the Imam knows, once foreigners are expelled and the evil of foreign ways torn out. The Imam, God protect him, is wise and good and talks to God, obeys only God, and God knows that women are not chattel to be abused and cast back into the days of the Prophet as some fanatics want. The Imam will protect us from extremists, and won't allow them to repeal the Shah's Family Act that gave us the vote and protection against summary divorce—he won't allow our votes and rights and our freedoms to be taken away or our rights to choose if we want to wear chador or not, never when he sees how strongly we are against it. Not when he sees our staunch resolve. Throughout the land.

Fatima dried her tears and felt happier at the thought of the planned demonstrations in three days, and some of the pain left her. Yes, we women'll demonstrate through the streets of Kowiss, proudly supporting our sisters in the great cities of Tehran and Qom and Isfahan, except I shall of course wear chador by choice, because of Hussain. Oh, how wonderful to be able to show our solidarity both as women and for the revolution.

The news of the planned marches in Tehran had rushed throughout Iran, by what means no one was sure. But all women knew. Everywhere women decided to follow suit, and all women approved—even those who did not dare to say so.

AT THE AIR BASE: 10:20 A.M. Starke was in the S-G tower watching the 125 come in with full flaps to touch down and turn on full reverse thrust. Zataki and Esvandiary were also there with two Green Bands—Zataki cleanshaven now.

"Turn right at the end of the runway, Echo Tango Lima Lima," Sergeant Wazari, the young USAF-trained air traffic controller said throatily. He had on rough civilian clothes in place of his neat uniform. His face was badly bruised, nose mashed, three teeth missing, and his ears swollen from the public beating Zataki had given him. Now he could not breathe through the nose. "Park in front of main base tower."

"Roger." Johnny Hogg's voice came back over the loudspeaker. "I repeat we are cleared to pick up three passengers, to deliver urgently required spares, with immediate turnaround and departure for Al Shargaz. Please confirm."

Wazari turned to Zataki, his fear open. "Excellency, please excuse me but what should I say?"

"You say nothing, vermin." Zataki picked up his stubby machine gun. To Starke he said, "Tell your pilot to park, to stop his engines, then to put everyone in the aircraft onto the tarmac. The aircraft will be searched and if cleared by me, it may go onward, and if it is not cleared it will not go onward. You come with me, and you too," he added to Esvandiary. He went out.

Starke did as he was ordered and turned to follow, but for a second he and the young sergeant were alone. Wazari caught him by the arm and whispered pathetically, "For the love of God, help me get aboard her, Captain, I'll do anything, anything . . ."

"I can't—it's impossible," Starke said, sorry for him. Two days ago Zataki had paraded everyone and beaten the man senseless for "crimes against the revolution," brought him around, made him eat filth, and beat him senseless again. Only Manuela and the very sick had been allowed to stay away. "Impossible!"

"Please . . . I beg you, Zataki's mad, he'll k—" Wazari turned away in panic as a Green Band reappeared in the doorway. Starke walked past him, down the stairs, and out onto the tarmac, masking his disquiet. Freddy Ayre was at the wheel of a waiting jeep. Manuela was in it, along with one of his British pilots, and Jon Tyrer, a bandage around his eyes. Manuela wore loose pants, long coat, and her hair was tied up under a pilot's hat.

"Follow us, Freddy," Starke said and got in beside Zataki in the back of the waiting car. Esvandiary let out the clutch and sped off to intercept the 125 that now was turning off the main runway, an accompanying swarm of trucks of Green Bands and two motorcyclists weaving around dangerously. "Crazy!" Starke muttered.

Zataki laughed, his teeth white. "Enthusiasts, pilot, not crazy."

"As God wants."

Zataki glanced at him, no longer bantering: "You speak our language, you've read the Koran, and you know our ways. It is time you said the Shahada before two witnesses and became Muslim. I would be honored to be a witness."

"I, too," Esvandiary said at once, also wanting to help save a soul though not for the same reasons: IranOil would need expert pilots to get full production going while replacement Iranians were trained and a Muslim Starke could be one. "I too would be honored to be a witness."

"Thank you," Starke told them in Farsi. Over the years the thought had occurred to him. Once, when Iran was calm and all he had to do was fly as many missions as he could and look after his men and laugh with Manuela and the children—was that only half a year ago?—he had said to her, "You know, Manuela, there's so much in Islam that's great."

"Were you thinkin' of four wives, darlin'?" she had said sweetly and instantly he was on guard.

"C'me on, Manuela, I was being serious. There's a lot in Islam."

"For men, not for women. Doesn't the Koran say: 'And the Faithful'—all men by the way—'will lie on silken couches and there will be the houris whom neither man nor djinn hath touched'—Conroe, honey, I never could work that out, why should they be perpetual virgins? Does that do somethin' for a man? And do women get the same deal, youth and as many horny young men as they want?"

"Would you listen, for crissake! I meant that if you lived in the desert, the deep Saudi or Sahara desert—remember the time we were in Kuwait and we went out, just you and me, we went out into the desert, the stars as big as oysters and the quiet so vast, the night so clean and limitless, us insignificant, you remember how touched we were by the Infinite? Remember how I said, I can understand how, if you were a nomad and born into a tent, you could be possessed by Islam?"

"And remember, darlin', how I said we weren't born in no goddamn tent."

He smiled, remembering how he had caught her and kissed her under the stars and they had taken each other, their fill of each other, under the stars. Later he had said, "I meant the pure teaching of Mohammed, I meant how with so much space, so terrifying in its vastness, that you need a safe haven and that Islam could be such a haven, maybe the only one, his original teaching, not narrow, twisted interpretations of fanatics."

"Why, sure, darlin'," she had said in her most honeyed voice, "but we don't live in no desert, never will, and you're Conroe 'Duke' Starke, helicopter pilot, and the very moment you start afiguring on those four wives I'm off, me and the kids, and even Texas won't be big enough to escape the roasting you'll get from Manuela Rosita Santa de Cuellar Perez, honey sugar baby lamb. . . ."

He saw Zataki staring at him and inhaled the raw smell of gasoline and snow and winter. "Perhaps I will one day," he told Zataki and Esvandiary. "Perhaps I will—but in God's time, not mine."

"May God hurry the time. You're wasted as an Infidel."

But now all of Starke's concentration was on the 125 that was coming into its parking slot, and on Manuela who must leave today. Difficult for her, goddamn difficult, but she has to go.

This morning, early, McIver in Tehran had told Starke by HF they had permission for the 125 to stop off at Kowiss, provided it was also approved in Kowiss, that she would be bringing spares, and there'd be space for three passengers outbound. At length Major Changiz and Esvandiary had agreed but only after Starke had irritably told them in front of Zataki, "You know our crew changes are long overdue. One of our 212's waiting for spares, and two of the 206s are ready for their fifteen-hundred-hour checks. If I can't have fresh crews and spares, I can't operate, and you'll be responsible for not obeying Ayatollah Khomeini—not me."

The car stopped beside the 125, the engines whining down. The door was not yet open and he could see John Hogg peering out of the cockpit window. Trucks and guns ringed her, excitable Green Bands milling around.

Zataki tried to make himself heard, then, exasperated, fired a burst into the air. "Get away from the airplane," he ordered. "By God and the Prophet only my men will search it! Get away!" Sullenly the other Green Bands moved back a little. "Pilot, tell him to open the door quickly, and get everyone out quickly before I change my agreement!"

Starke gave the thumbs-up to Hogg. In a moment the door was opened by the second pilot. The steps came down. At once Zataki leaped up them and stood at the top, machine gun ready. "Excellency you don't need that," Starke told him. "Everybody out, quick as you can, okay?"

There were eight passengers—four of them pilots, three mechanics, and Genny McIver. "My God, Genny! I didn't expect to see you."

"Hello, Duke. Duncan thought it best and . . . well, never mind. Is Ma-

nuela going to co—" She saw her and went over to her. They embraced and
Starke noticed the age on Genny.

He followed Zataki into the empty, low-ceilinged aircraft. Extra seats had
been lashed in. At the back, near the toilet, were several crates. "Spares and
the spare engine you needed," Johnny Hogg called out from the pilot's seat,
handing him the manifest. "Hello, Duke!"

Zataki took the manifest and jerked a thumb at Hogg. "Out!"

"If you don't mind, I'm responsible for the aircraft, sorry," Hogg said.

"Last time. Out."

Starke said, "Get out of your seat a moment, Johnny. He just wants to see
if there are any guns. Excellency, it would be safer if the pilot was allowed to
stay in place. I will vouch for him."

"Out!"

Reluctantly John Hogg eased himself out of the small cockpit. Zataki
made sure nothing was in the side pockets, then waved him back into the
seat and studied the cabin. "Those are the spares you need?"

"Yes," Starke said, and politely made room on the landing where Zataki
shouted for some of his men to carry the crates onto the tarmac. The men
did this carelessly, banging the sides of the doorway and the steps, making
the pilots wince. Then Zataki searched the aircraft carefully, finding nothing
that irritated him. Except the wine on ice and the liquor in the cabinet.

"No more liquor into Iran. None. Confiscated!" He had the bottles
smashed on the tarmac and ordered the crates opened. One jet engine and
many other spares. Everything on the manifest. Starke watched from the
cabin doorway, trying to make himself inconspicuous.

Zataki said, "Who are these passengers?" The second officer gave him the
list of names. It was headed in English and Farsi: "Temporarily redundant
pilots and mechanic, all overdue leave and replacement." He began to scruti-
nize it, and them.

"Duke," Johnny Hogg said cautiously from the cockpit, "I've some money
for you and a letter from McIver. Is it safe?"

"For the moment."

"Two envelopes in my inside uniform pocket, hanging up. The letter's
private, Mac said."

Starke found them and stuffed them into his inner parka pocket. "What's
going on in Tehran?" he asked out of the side of his mouth.

"The airport's a madhouse, thousands trying to get on the three or four
planes they've allowed in so far," Hogg said rapidly, "with at least six jumbos
stacked in a holding pattern aimlessly waiting for permission to land. I, er, I
just jumped the queue, peeled in without a real clearance, and said, Oh, so

sorry, I thought I was cleared, picked up my lot, and scarpered. Hardly had time to chat with McIver—he was surrounded by trigger-happy revs and an odd mullah or two—but he seems okay. Pettikin, Nogger, and the others seemed okay. I'm based at Al Shargaz for at least a week to shuttle back and forth as I can." Al Shargaz was not far from Dubai, where S-G had its HQ that side of the Gulf. "We've permission from Tehran ATC to bring in spares and crew to match those we intend to take out—looks like they're going to keep us more or less one for one and up to strength—with flights scheduled Saturdays and Wednesdays." He stopped for breath. "Mac says for you to find excuses for me to come here from time to time—I'm to be kind of a courier for him and Andy Gavallan till normality re—"

"Watch it," Starke said, behind his hand, seeing Zataki glance up at the airplane. He had been watching him inspect the passengers and their documents. Then he saw Zataki beckon him and he went down the stairs. "Yes, Excellency?"

"This man has no exit permit."

The man was Roberts, one of the fitters, middle-aged, very experienced. Anxiety etched his already-lined face. "I told him I couldn't get one, Cap'n Starke, we couldn't get one, the immigration offices're still all closed. There was no problem at Tehran."

Starke glanced at the document. It was only four days past expiration. "Perhaps you could let it go this time, Excellency. It's true that the off—"

"No correct exit permit, no exit. He stays!"

Roberts went white. "But Tehran passed me and I've got to be in Lon—"

Zataki grabbed him by the parka and jerked him out of line to send him sprawling. Enraged, Roberts scrambled to his feet. "By God, I'm cleared an—" He stopped. One of the Green Bands had a rifle in his chest, another was behind him, both now ready to pull the triggers.

Starke said, "Wait by the jeep, Roberts. Goddamnit, wait by the jeep!"

One of the Green Bands roughly shoved the mechanic toward it as Starke tried to cover his own worry. Jon Tyrer and Manuela did not have up-to-date exit papers either.

"No exit permits, no exit!" Zataki repeated venomously and took the next man's papers.

Genny, next in line, was very frightened, hating Zataki and the violence and the smell of the fear surrounding her, sorry for Roberts who needed to be back in England as one of his children was very ill, polio suspected, and no mail or phones and the telex sporadic. She watched Zataki slowly going through the pilot's papers next to her. Rotten bastard! she thought. I've got to get on that plane, got to. Oh, how I wish we were all leaving. Poor

Duncan, he simply won't look after himself, won't bother to eat properly and he's bound to get his ulcers back. "My exit permit's not current," she said trying to sound timid, and let some tears glisten her eyes.

"Nor mine," Manuela said in a small voice.

Zataki looked at them. He hesitated. "Women are not responsible, men are responsible. You two women may leave. This time. Go aboard."

"Can Mr. Roberts come too?" Genny asked, pointing to the mechanic, "He's rea—"

"Get aboard!" Zataki shouted in one of his sudden, maniacal rages, blood in his face. The two women fled up the stairs, everyone else in momentary panic, and even his own Green Bands shifted nervously.

"Excellency, you were right," Starke said in Farsi, forcing himself to be outwardly calm. "Women should not argue." He waited and everyone waited, hardly breathing, the dark eyes boring into him. But he kept his gaze level. Zataki nodded and, sullenly, continued examining the papers in his hand.

Yesterday Zataki had come back from Isfahan and Esvandiary had authorized a flight for tomorrow afternoon to carry him back to Bandar Delam again. The sooner the better, Starke thought grimly.

And yet he felt sorry for Zataki. Last night he found him leaning against a helicopter, his hands pressed to his temples, in great pain. "What is it, Agha?"

"My head. I—it's my head."

He had persuaded him to see Dr. Nutt and taken him privately to the doctor's bungalow.

"Just give me aspirin, or codeine, Doctor, whatever you have," Zataki had said.

"Perhaps you'd let me examine you and th—"

"No examine!" Zataki had shouted. "I know what's wrong with me. SAVAK is wrong with me, prison is wrong with me . . ." And later, when the codeine had taken away some of the pain, Zataki had told Starke that about a year and a half ago he had been arrested, accused of anti-Shah propaganda. At the time he was working as a journalist for one of the Abadan newspapers. He had been jailed for eight months and then, just after the Abadan fire, released. He had not told Starke what they had done to him. "As God wants, pilot," he had said bitterly. "But since that day, I bless God every day for one more day of life to stamp out more SAVAKs and Shah men, his lackey police and lackey soldiers and any and all who assisted his evil— once I supported him, didn't he pay for my education, here and in England? But he was to blame for SAVAK! He was to blame! That part of my vengeance is just for me—I still haven't started on my revenge for my wife and sons murdered in the Abadan fire."

Starke had held his peace. The how or why or who of the arson that had caused almost five hundred deaths had never come to light.

He watched Zataki work slowly and laboriously down the line of would-be passengers—how many more with incomplete or not current papers Starke did not know, everyone tense, a brooding pall over them. Soon it would be Tyrer's turn and Tyrer *must* go. Doc Nutt had said to be safe Tyrer should be examined at Al Shargaz or Dubai as soon as possible where there were marvelous hospital facilities. "I'm sure he's all right, but it's best for him to rest his eyes for the time being. And listen, Duke, for the love of God, keep out of Zataki's way and warn the others to do the same. He's ripe to explode and God only knows what'll happen then."

"What's the matter with him?"

"Medically, I don't know. Psychologically he's dangerous, very dangerous. I'd say manic-depressive, certainly paranoiac, probably caused directly by his prison experiences. Did he tell you what they did to him?"

"No. No, he didn't."

"If it was up to me, I'd recommend he be under sedatives and absolutely nowhere near firearms."

Great, Starke thought helplessly, how the hell do I get that organized? At least Genny and Manuela're aboard and soon they'll be in Al Shargaz which's a paradise comp—

A warning shout distracted him. Beyond the 125, coming from behind the main tower exit was the mullah Hussain with more Green Bands and they looked very hostile.

At once Zataki forgot the passengers, unslipped his machine gun, and, carrying it loosely in one hand, moved between Hussain and the airplane. Two of his men moved alongside him, and the others moved nearer the airplane into defensive positions, covering him.

"Stone the bloody crows," someone muttered, "what's up now?"

"Get ready to duck," Ayre said.

"Cap'n," Roberts whispered brokenly, "I've got to get on that plane, I've got to, my little girl's sicker than anything, can you do something with that bastard?"

"I'll try."

Zataki was watching Hussain, hating him. Two days ago he had gone to Isfahan, invited there to consult with their secret komiteh. All eleven members had been ayatollahs and mullahs, and there, for the first time, he had found the real face of the revolution he had fought so hard to achieve and suffered so much for: "Heretics will be stamped into oblivion. We'll have only Revolutionary Courts. Justice will be quick and final with no appeal. . . ." The mullahs were so sure of themselves, so sure of their divine right to rule and administer justice as they alone interpreted the Koran and Sharia. Carefully Zataki had kept his horror and his thoughts to himself, but he knew that he was again betrayed.

"What do you want, mullah?" he said, the word a curse word.

"First I want you to understand that you have no power here—what you do in Abadan is up to the ayatollahs of Abadan—but here you have no power on this base, over these men, or this airplane." Surrounding Hussain were a dozen armed, hard-faced youths, all Green Bands.

"No power, eh?" Contemptuously Zataki turned his back and shouted in English, "The airplane will take off at once! All passengers get aboard!" Angrily he motioned at the pilot, waving him away, then faced Hussain again. "Well? What's second," he said as, behind him, the passengers hurried to obey and because the Green Bands were concentrating on Zataki and Hussain, Starke ordered Roberts to get aboard, then motioned to Ayre to help cover the escape of the mechanic. Together they helped Tyrer out of the jeep.

Zataki toyed with his gun, all his attention on Hussain. "Well? What's second?" he asked again.

Hussain was nonplussed, his men equally aware of the guns trained on them. The jets came to life. He saw the passengers hurrying aboard, Starke and Ayre helping a man with bandages over his eyes up the steps, then the two pilots beside the jeep again, the jet engines building, and the instant the last man was inside, the steps came up and the airplane taxied away.

"Well, Agha, what's next?"

"Next . . . next the komiteh of Kowiss orders you and your men to leave Kowiss."

Scornfully Zataki shouted to his men above the roar of the engines, his feet planted in the concrete, ready to fight if need be and die if need be, the superheated air from the fans passing him as the airplane moved toward the runway. "You hear, we are ordered to leave by the komiteh of Kowiss!"

His men began laughing, and one of Hussain's Green Bands, a beardless teenager on the far edge of the group, raised his carbine and died at once, almost cut in half by the accurate burst of gunfire from Zataki's men that neatly culled him. The silence was broken only by the distant jets. Momentarily Hussain was bewildered by the suddenness and by the pool of blood that flowed out onto the concrete.

"As God wants," Zataki said. "What do you want, mullah?"

It was then that Zataki noticed the petrified little boy peering out at him, hiding behind the mullah's robes, clutching them for protection, looking so much like his own son, his eldest, that for a moment he was taken back to the happy days before *the* fire when all seemed right and there was some form of a future—the Shah's White Revolution wonderful, the land reforms, curbing the mullahs, universal education, and other things—the good days when I was a father but never again. Never. The electrodes and pincers destroyed that possibility.

A violent stab of pain in his loins soared into his head at the remembrance and he wanted to scream. But he did not, just shoved the torment back, as usual, and concentrated on the killing at hand. He could see the implacability on the mullah's face and he readied. Killing with the machine gun pleased him greatly. The hot staccato, the gun alive in short stabbing bursts, acrid smell of cordite, the blood of the enemies of God and Iran flowing. Mullahs are enemy, and most of all Khomeini who commits sacrilege by allowing his photograph to be worshiped and his followers to call him Imam, and puts mullahs between us and God—against all the Prophet's teachings. "Hurry up," he bellowed, "I'm losing patience!"

"I—I want that man," Hussain said, pointing.

Zataki glanced around. The mullah was pointing at Starke. "The pilot? Why? What for?" he asked, perplexed.

"For questioning. I want to question him."

"What about?"

"About the escape of the officers from Isfahan."

"What should he know about them? He was with me in Bandar Delam hundreds of miles away when that happened, helping the revolution against the enemies of God!" Zataki added venomously, "Enemies of God are everywhere, everywhere! Sacrilege is everywhere, idol worship practiced everywhere—isn't it?"

"Yes, yes, enemies abound, and sacrilege is sacrilege. But he's a helicopter pilot, an Infidel was the pilot of the escape helicopter, he could know something. I want to question him."

"Not while I'm here."

"Why? Why not? Why won't y—"

"You won't, not while I'm here, by God! Not while I'm here! Later or tomorrow or the next day, as God wills, but not now."

Zataki had gauged Hussain and saw in his face and eyes that he had conceded and was no longer a threat. Carefully he looked from face to face of the Green Bands surrounding the mullah but no longer detected any danger —the quick and sudden death of one, he thought without guilt, as usual controls the others. "You will want to go back to your mosque now, it is almost time for prayer." He turned his back and walked to the jeep, knowing his men would be guarding him, beckoned Starke and Ayre, and got into the front seat, machine gun ready but not as overt as before. One by one his men retreated to their cars. They drove off.

Hussain was ashen. His Green Bands waited. One of them lit a cigarette, all of them conscious of the body at their feet. And the blood that still seeped.

"Why did you let them go, Father?" the little boy asked in his piping voice.

"I didn't, my son. We have more important things to do immediately, then we will return."

U.S.S.R.

TURKEY

KHOI

TABRIZ

Caspian Sea

U. S. S. R.

MOUNT
SABALAN

BANDAR-E
PAHLAVI

QAZVIN

★ TEHRAN

IRAQ

BAGHDAD

IRAN

DEZ DAM

ZAGROS

• ISFAHAN

AFGHANISTAN

BANDAR DELAM

Shatt-
al-Arab
Estuary

ABADAN

◎ ZAGROS THREE

• KOWISS

MOUNTAINS

KUWAIT

KHARG

JELLET

LENGEH

Strait of
Hormuz

Persian Gulf

PAKISTAN

BAHRAIN

SAUDI
ARABIA

QATAR

SIRI

Gulf of Oman

AL SHARGAZ

AT ZAGROS THREE: 12:05 P.M.   Scot Gavallan was staring down the barrel of a cocked Sten gun. He had just landed the 212 after the first trip of the day to Rig Rosa delivering another full load of steel pipe and cement, and the moment he had cut the engines, armed Green Bands had rushed out of the hangar to surround him.

Hating the fear that possessed him, he tore his gaze off the gun and looked at the black, malevolent eyes. "What's—what d'you want?" he croaked, then said it in halting Farsi, *"Cheh karbareh?"*

A flood of angry incomprehensible words came from the man with the gun.

He pulled off his headset. *"Man zaban-e shoma ra khoob nami danam, Agha!"* he shouted over the whine of the engines—I don't speak your language, Excellency—biting back the obscenity he wanted to add. More angry words and the man motioned him out of the cockpit. Then he saw Nasiri, the IranOil base manager, disheveled and bruised, being frog-marched out of the office toward the 212 by more of the Revolutionary Guards. He leaned out of the window a little. "What the hell's going on?"

"They—they want you out of the chopper, Captain," Nasiri called back. "They—please hurry!"

"Wait till I shut down!" Nervously Scot finished the procedure. The barrel of the Sten gun had not moved, nor had the enmity around him lessened. The rotors were slowing fast now, and when it was correct to leave, he unbuckled and got out. At once he was half shoved out of the way. Excited, shouting men pulled the cockpit door open farther, peered in, while others hauled the main cabin door open and scrambled aboard. "What the hell happened to you, Agha?" he asked Nasiri, seeing the extent of the bruises.

"The—the new komiteh made an error," Nasiri said, trying to maintain his dignity, "thinking I was . . . a Shah supporter and not a man of the revolution and the Imam."

"Who the hell're these men—they aren't from Yazdek."

But before Nasiri could answer, the Green Band with the Sten gun elbowed through the pack. "In office! NOW!" the man said in bad English, then reached out and grabbed Scot by the flight jacket sleeve to hurry him up. Automatically Scot jerked his arm away. A gun went into his ribs. "All right, for crissake," he muttered and stalked off toward the office, his face grim.

In the office Nitchak Khan, kalandar of the village, and the old mullah stood alongside the desk, their backs to the wall beside the open window. Both were set-faced. He greeted them and they nodded back, ill at ease. Behind him, many Green Bands crowded into the room after Nasiri.

"*Cheh karbareh, Kalandar?*" Scot asked. What's happening?

"These men are . . . claim to be our new komiteh," Nitchak Khan replied with difficulty. "They are sent from Sharpur to take over our . . . our village and our . . . airfield."

Scot was perplexed. What the village leader had said didn't make any sense. Though Sharpur was the nearest town and had nominal jurisdiction over the area, custom had always left the Kash'kai tribesmen of the mountains to govern themselves—so long as they acknowledged the suzerainty of the Shah and Tehran, obeyed the laws, and remained unarmed and peaceful. "But you always govern—"

"Quiet!" the leader of the Green Bands said, waving his Sten gun, and Scot saw Nitchak Khan flush. The leader was bearded, in his thirties, poorly dressed, with dark eyes that had something bad about them. He dragged Nasiri to the front of the group and rattled off more Farsi.

"I—I am to interpret, Captain," Nasiri said nervously. "The leader, Ali-sadr, says you are to answer the following questions. I've answered most but he wants . . ." Ali-sadr cursed him and began the questioning, reading from a prepared list, Nasiri translating.

"Are you in command here?"

"Yes, temporarily."

"What is your nationality?"

"British. Now what the h—"

"Any Americans here?"

"Not to my knowledge," Scot said at once and kept his face bland, hoping Nasiri, who knew that Rodrigues, the mechanic, was American with a false English ID, had not been asked that question. Nasiri translated without hesitation. One of the other Green Bands was writing down his answers.

"How many pilots are here?"

"At the moment I'm the only one."

"Where are the others, who are they, and what is their nationality?"

"Our senior pilot, Captain Lochart, Canadian, is in Tehran—he's on a charter out of Tehran, I think, expected back any day. The other, second in command, Captain Sessonne, French, had to go on an urgent charter for IranOil today to Tehran."

The leader looked up, his eyes hard. "What so urgent?"

"Rig Rosa's ready to log a new well." He waited while Nasiri explained what this meant and that the oil drillers needed the urgent help of Schlumberger experts, now based in Tehran. This morning Jean-Luc had called their local ATC at Shiraz on the off chance for clearance to go to Tehran. To his astonishment and delight Shiraz ATC gave an immediate approval. "The Imam has decreed that oil production will begin," they had said, "so it will begin."

Jean-Luc had been airborne within minutes. Scot Gavallan smiled to himself knowing the real reason why Jean-Luc did three cartwheels into the 206's cockpit was that now he could sneak an overdue visit to Sayada. Scot had met her once. "Has she got a sister?" he had said hopefully.

The leader listened impatiently to Nasiri, then cut in again and Nasiri flinched. "He, Ali-sadr, he says in future all flights will be cleared by him, or this man—" Nasiri pointed at the youthful Green Band who had been writing down Scot's answers. "In future all flights will have one of their men aboard. In future no takeoffs without advance permission. In about one hour you will take him and his men to all the rigs in the area."

"Explain to him that it's not possible to do that because we have to deliver more pipe and cement to Rig Rosa. Otherwise when Jean-Luc comes back tomorrow they won't be ready in time."

Nasiri began to explain. The leader interrupted him rudely, and got up. "Tell the Infidel pilot to be ready in about an hour and then . . . even better, tell him to come with us to the village where I can watch him. You come too. And tell him to be very obedient, for though the Imam wants oil production started quickly, all persons in Iran are subject to Islamic law if they're Iranian or not. We don't need foreigners here." The man glanced at Nitchak Khan. "Now we will return to our village," he said and strode out. Nitchak Khan flushed. He and the mullah followed.

"Captain, we are to go with him," Nasiri said, "to the village."

"What for?"

"Well, you're the only pilot here and you know the countryside," Nasiri said readily, wondering what the real reason was. He was very afraid. There had been no warning of any impending changes, nor were they even aware in the village that the road was open from the last snowfall. But this morning the truck with twelve Green Bands had arrived in the village. At once the leader of the "komiteh" had produced the piece of paper signed by the Sharpur Revolutionary Komiteh giving them jurisdiction over Yazdek and "all IranOil production and facilities and helicopters in that area." When, at Nitchak Khan's request, Nasiri had said he would radio IranOil to protest, one of the men had started beating him. The leader had stopped the man but had not apologized, nor had he shown Nitchak Khan the respect due to him as kalandar of this branch of the Kash'kai. More fear rushed through Nasiri and he wished he was back in Sharpur with his wife and family. God curse all komitehs and fanatics and foreigners and the Great American Satan who caused all our problems. "We'd . . . we'd better go," he said.

They went outside. The others were already well down the track that led to the village. As Scot passed the hangar, he saw his six mechanics collected under the watchful gaze of an armed guard. The guard was smoking and a twinge went through him. Signs in Farsi and English were everywhere: NO SMOKING—DANGER! To one side their second 212 was in its final stages of the fifteen-hundred-hour check, but without the two 206s that made up their present complement of airplanes the hangar seemed empty and forlorn. "Agha," he said to Nasiri, nodding back at their own guards, "tell them I've got to make arrangements about the chopper, and order that bugger not to smoke in the hangar."

Nasiri did as he was asked. "They said all right, but to hurry up." The guard who was smoking lazily flicked his cigarette onto the concrete. One of the mechanics hastily ground it out. Nasiri would have stayed but the guards motioned him onward. Reluctantly he left.

"Tank up FBC and ground-check her," Scot said carefully, not sure if any of the guards understood English. "In an hour I'm to take our komiteh for a state visit to the sites. It seems we've a new komiteh from Sharpur now."

"Oh, shit," someone muttered.

"What about the gear for Rig Rosa?" Effer Jordon asked. Beside him was Rod Rodrigues. Scot could see his anxiety.

"That'll have to wait. Just tank FBC, Effer, and everyone check her out. Rod," he said to encourage the older man, "now that we're getting back to normal, you'll soon get your home leave in London, *capito?*"

"Sure, thanks, Scot."

The guard beside Scot motioned him to go on. "*Baleh, Agha*—yes, all right, Excellency," Scot said, then added to Rodrigues, "Rod, do a careful ground check for me."

"Sure."

Scot walked off, his guards following. Jordon called out anxiously, "What's going on, and where're you going?"

"I'm going for a stroll," he said sarcastically. "How the hell would I know? I've been flying all morning." He trudged off feeling tired and helpless and inadequate, wishing that Lochart or Jean-Luc were there in his place. Bloody komiteh bastards! Bunch of bloody thugs.

Nasiri was a hundred yards ahead, walking quickly, the others already vanished around the bend in the track that meandered through the trees. It was just below freezing and the snow crunched underfoot, and though Scot felt warm in his flight gear, walking was awkward in his flying boots and he clomped along moodily, wanting to catch Nasiri but unable to. Snow was banked beside the path and heavy on the trees, clear skies above. Half a mile ahead, down the curling pathway was the village.

Yazdek was on a small plateau, nicely protected from the high winds. The huts and houses were made of wood, stone, and mud bricks and grouped around the square in front of the small mosque. Unlike most villages it was prosperous, plenty of wood for warmth in winter, plenty of game nearby, with communal flocks of sheep and goats, a few camels, and thirty horses and brood mares that were their pride. Nitchak Khan's home was a two-story, tile-roofed dwelling of four rooms, beside the mosque and bigger than all the others.

Next door was the schoolhouse, the most modern building. Tom Lochart had designed the simple structure and had persuaded McIver to finance it last year. Up to a few months ago the school had been run by a young man in the Shah's Teaching Corps—the village was almost totally illiterate. When the Shah left, the young man had vanished. From time to time Tom Lochart and others from the base had given talks there—more question-and-answer sessions—partially for good relations and partially for something to do when there was no flying. The sessions were well attended by adults as well as by children, encouraged to do so by Nitchak Khan and his wife.

As he came down the rise, Scot saw the others go into the schoolhouse. The truck that had brought the Green Bands was parked outside. Villagers were collected in groups, silently watching. Men, women, and children, none of them armed. Kash'kai women wore neither veils nor chador but multicolored robes.

Scot went up the stairs into the school. The last time he was here, just a few weeks ago, he had given a talk on the Hong Kong he knew when his father still worked there and he would visit from English boarding school during the holidays. It had been hard to explain what Hong Kong was like, with its teeming streets, typhoons, chopsticks and character writing, and foods and freebooting capitalism, the immensity of China overall. I'm glad we came back to Scotland, he thought. Glad the Old Man started S-G that I'm going to run one day.

"You are to sit down, Captain," Nasiri said. "There." He indicated a chair at the back of a low-ceilinged, crowded room. Ali-sadr and four other Green Bands were seated at the table where the teacher would normally sit. Nitchak Khan and the mullah sat in front of them. Villagers stood around.

"What's going on?"

"It's a . . . a meeting."

Scot saw the fear pervading Nasiri and wondered what he would do if the Green Bands started to beat him. I should've been a black belt or boxer, he thought wearily, trying to understand the Farsi that poured out of the leader.

"What's he saying, Agha?" he whispered to Nasiri.

"I . . . he's . . . he's saying . . . he's telling Nitchak Khan how the village will be run in future. Please, I will explain later." Nasiri moved away.

In time the tirade stopped. Everyone looked at Nitchak Khan. He got up slowly. His face was grave and his words few. Even Scot understood. "Yazdek is Kash'kai. Yazdek will remain Kash'kai." He turned his back on the table and began to leave, the mullah following.

At an angry command of the leader, two Green Bands barred his way. Contemptuously, Nitchak Khan brushed them aside, then others grabbed him, tension in the room soared, and Scot saw one villager slip out of the room unnoticed. Those Green Bands holding Nitchak Khan turned him around to face Ali-sadr and the other four who were on their feet, enraged, and shouting. No one had touched the old man who was the mullah. He held up his hand and began to speak, but the leader shouted him down and a sigh went through the villagers. Nitchak Khan did not struggle against the men pinioning him, just looked back at Ali-sadr, and Scot felt the hatred like a physical blow.

The leader harangued all the villagers, then pointed an accusing finger at Nitchak Khan and once more ordered him to obey and once more Nitchak Khan said quietly, "Yazdek is Kash'kai. Yazdek will remain Kash'kai."

Ali-sadr sat down. So did the four others. Again Ali-sadr pointed and said a few words. A gasp went through the villagers. The four men beside him nodded their agreement. Ali-sadr said one word. It cut through the silence like a scythe. "Death!" He got up and walked out, villagers and Green Bands frog-marching Nitchak Khan after him, Scot forgotten. Scot ducked down to one side, trying to make himself scarce. Soon he was alone.

Outside, the Green Bands dragged Nitchak Khan to the wall of the mosque and stood him there. The square was empty now of villagers. As the other villagers came out of the schoolhouse into the square, they too hurried off. Except the mullah. Slowly he walked over to Nitchak Khan and stood beside him, facing the Green Bands who, twenty yards away, readied their guns. On Ali-sadr's orders, two of them pulled the old man away. Nitchak Khan waited by the wall silently, proudly, then he spat in the dirt.

The single rifle shot came out of nowhere. Ali-sadr was dead before he slumped to the ground. The silence was sudden and vast, and the Green Bands whirled in panic, then froze as a voice shouted, "Allah-u Akbarr, put down your guns!"

No one moved, then one of the firing squad jerked his gun around at Nitchak Khan but died before he could pull the trigger.

"God is Great, put down your guns!"

One of the Green Bands let his gun clatter to the ground. Another followed suit, another rushed for the truck but died before he got ten yards. Now all other guns were on the ground. And all who stood stayed motionless.

Then the door of Nitchak Khan's house opened and his wife came out with the leveled carbine, a young man following, also with a carbine. She was fierce in her pride, ten years younger than her husband, the jingling of her earrings and chains and the swish of her long tan and red robes the only sound in the square.

Nitchak Khan's narrow eyes in his high-cheekboned face narrowed even more, and the deep lines at the corners crinkled. But he said nothing to her, just looked at the eight Green Bands who remained. Mercilessly. They stared back at him, then one of them grabbed for his gun, and she shot him in the stomach and he screamed, writhing on the snow. She left him to howl for a moment. A second shot and the screaming stopped.

Now there were seven.

Nitchak Khan smiled silently. Now, out of the houses and huts, the grown men and women of the village came into the square. All were armed. He turned his attention back to the seven. "Get in the truck, lie down, and put your hands behind you." Sullenly the men obeyed. He ordered four of the villagers to guard them, then he turned to the young man who had come out of his house. "There's one more at the airfield, my son. Take someone with you and deal with him. Bring his body back but cover your faces with scarves so the Infidels won't recognize you."

"As God wants." The young man pointed at the schoolhouse. The door was still open, but no sign of Scot. "The Infidel," he said softly. "He's not of our village." Then he went off quickly.

The village waited. Nitchak Khan scratched his beard thoughtfully. Then his eyes went to Nasiri who cowered beside the schoolhouse stairs.

Nasiri's face drained. "I—I saw—I saw nothing, nothing, Nitchak Khan," he croaked, and got up and stepped around the bodies. "I've always—for the two years I've been here I've always done everything I could for the village. I —I saw nothing," he said louder, abjectly, then his terror crested and he took to his heels out of the square. And died. A dozen had fired at him.

"It's true the only witness to these men's evil should be God." Nitchak Khan sighed. He had liked Nasiri. But he was not one of their people. His wife came up beside him and he smiled at her. She took out a cigarette and gave it to him and lit it for him, then put the cigarettes and matches back in her pocket. He puffed thoughtfully. Some dogs barked among the houses and a child cried, quickly to be hushed.

"There will be a small avalanche to break the road where it was swept away before, to keep all others out until the thaw," he said at length. "We will put the bodies into the truck, and pour gasoline over it and them and let it fall off the road into the Ravine of the Broken Camels. It seems that the komiteh decided we could govern ourselves as always and that we should be left in peace as always, then they went away and took Nasiri's body with them. They shot Nasiri here in the square, as all saw, when he tried to escape justice. Unfortunately they had an accident going back. It is a very dangerous road as all know. Probably they took Nasiri's body to prove they had done their duty and cleansed our mountains of a known Shah supporter and shot him as he tried to escape. Certainly he was a Shah supporter when the Shah had power and before the Shah ran away." The villagers nodded agreeably and waited. All wanted to know the answer to the final question: what about the last witness? What about the Infidel still in the schoolhouse?

Nitchak Khan scratched his beard. It always helped him to make difficult decisions.

"More Green Bands will come soon, drawn by the magnet of the flying machines, made by foreigners and flown by foreigners for the benefit of foreigners because of the oil that is gathered from our earth for the benefit of enemy Tehranis and enemy tax collectors and more foreigners. If there were no wells there would be no foreigners, therefore there would be no Green Bands. The land is rich in oil elsewhere, easy to gather elsewhere. Ours is not. Our few wells are not important and the eleven bases difficult of access and dangerous—did they not have to explode the mountaintop to save one from avalanche only a few days ago?"

There was general agreement. He puffed the cigarette leisurely. The people watched him confidently—he was kalandar, their chief who had ruled wisely for eighteen years in good times and bad. "If there were no flying machines there could be no wells. So if these foreigners departed," he continued in the same gruff, unhurried voice, "I doubt if other strangers would venture here to repair and reopen the eleven bases, for surely the bases would quickly fall into disrepair, perhaps even be looted by bandits and damaged. So we would be left in peace. Without our benevolence no one can operate in our mountains. We Kash'kai seek to live in peace—we will be free and ruled by our own ways and own customs. Therefore the foreigners must go, of their own free will. And go quickly. So must the wells. And everything foreign." Carefully he stubbed his cigarette into the snow. "Let us begin: Burn the school."

He was obeyed at once. A little gasoline and the tinder dry wood soon made it into a conflagration. Everyone waited. But the Infidel did not appear, nor when they searched the rubble did they find any remains.

NEAR TABRIZ: 11:49 A.M. Erikki Yokkonen was climbing the 206 through the high pass that led at length to the city, Nogger Lane beside him with Azadeh in the back. She wore a bulky flight jacket over her ski clothes, but in the carryall beside her was a chador: "Just for safety," she had said. On her head was a third headset that Erikki had rigged for her.

"Tabriz One, do you read?" he said again. They waited. Still no answer and well within range. "Could be abandoned, could be a trap, like with Charlie."

"Best take a jolly good look before we land," Nogger said uneasily, his eyes scanning the sky and the land.

The sky was clear. It was well below freezing, the mountains heavy with snow. They had refueled without incident at an IranOil depot just outside Bandar-e Pahlavi by arrangement with Tehran ATC. "Khomeini's got everything by the short and curlies, with ATC helpful and the airport opened up again," Erikki had said, trying to shove away the depression that sat heavily on all of them.

Azadeh was still badly shaken by the news of Emir Paknouri's execution for "crimes against Islam" and by the even more terrible news about Sharazad's father. "That's murder," she had burst out, horrified, when she had heard. "What crimes could he commit, he who has supported Khomeini and mullahs for generations?"

None of them had had any answer. The family had been told to collect the body and now were in deep and abject mourning, Sharazad demented with grief—the house closed even to Azadeh and Erikki. Azadeh had not wanted to leave Tehran but a second message had arrived from her father to Erikki, repeating the first: "Captain, I require my daughter in Tabriz urgently." And now they were almost home.

Once it was home, Erikki thought. Now I'm not so sure.

Near Qazvin he had flown over the place where his Range Rover had run out of gas and Pettikin and Rakoczy had rescued Azadeh and him from the mob. The Range Rover was no longer there. Then over the miserable village where the roadblock had been, and he had escaped to crush the fat-faced mujhadin who had stolen their papers. Madness to come back, he thought.

"Mac's right," Azadeh had pleaded with him. "Go to Al Shargaz. Let Nogger fly me to Tabriz and fly me back to get on the next shuttle. I'll join you in Al Shargaz whatever my father says."

"I'll take you home and bring you back," he had said. "Finish."

They had taken off from Doshan Tappeh just after dawn. The base was almost empty, with many buildings and hangars now burned-out shells, wrecked Iranian Air Force airplanes, trucks, and one fire-gutted tank with the Immortals emblem on its side. No one cleaning up the mess. No guards. Scavengers taking away anything burnable—still hardly any fuel oil for sale, or food, but many daily and nightly clashes between Green Bands and leftists.

The S-G hangar and repair shop were hardly damaged. Many bullet holes in the walls but nothing had been looted yet and it was operating, more or less, with a few mechanics and office staff about their normal work. Some back salary from the money McIver had squeezed from Valik and the other partners had been the magnet. He had given some cash to Erikki to pay the staff at Tabriz One: "Start praying, Erikki! Today I've an appointment at the Ministry to iron out our finances and the money we're owed," he had told them just before they took off, "and to renew all our out-of-date licenses. Talbot at the embassy fixed it for me—he thinks there's a better than good chance Bazargan and Khomeini can get control now and disarm the leftists. We've just got to keep our bottle, keep our cool."

Easy for him, Erikki thought.

Now they crested the pass. He banked and came down fast. "There's the base!" Both pilots concentrated. The wind sock was the only thing that moved. No transport parked anywhere. No smoke from any of the cabins. "There should be smoke." He circled tightly at seven hundred feet. No one came out to greet them. "I'll take a closer look."

They whirled in quickly and out again. Still nothing moved so they went back up to a thousand feet. Erikki thought a moment. "Azadeh, I could set her down in the forecourt of the palace or just outside the walls."

At once Azadeh shook her head. "No, Erikki, you know how nervous his guards are and how, how sensitive he is about anyone arriving unasked."

"But we're asked, at least you are. Ordered is the real word. We could go over there, circle, and take a look, and if it seems all right, we could land."

"We could land well away and walk in t—"

"No walking. Not without guns." He had been unable to obtain one in Tehran. Every damned hooligan has as many as he wants, he thought irritably. Have to get one. Don't feel safe anymore. "We'll go and look and then I'll decide." He switched to the Tabriz Tower frequency and called. No answer. He called again, then banked and went for the city. As they passed over their village of Abu Mard, Erikki pointed downward and Azadeh saw the little schoolhouse where she had spent so many happy hours, the glades nearby and there, just by the stream, was where she had first seen Erikki and thought him a giant of the forest and had fallen in love, miracle of miracles, to be rescued by him from a life of torment. She reached forward and touched him through the small window.

"You all right? Warm enough?" He smiled at her.

"Oh, yes, Erikki. The village was so lucky for us, wasn't it?" She kept her hand on his shoulder. The contact pleased both of them.

Soon they could see the airport and the railroad that went north to Soviet Azerbaijan a few miles away, then on to Moscow, southeast it curled back to Tehran, three hundred and fifty miles away. The city was large. Now they could pick out the citadel and the Blue Mosque and polluting steel factories, the huts and hovels and houses of the six hundred thousand inhabitants.

"Look over there!" Part of the railway station was smoldering, smoke billowing. More fires near the citadel and no answer from Tabriz Tower and no activity on the airfield apron, though some small, feeder airplanes were parked there. A lot of activity at the military base, trucks and cars coming and going, but as far as they could see, no firing or battles or crowds in the streets, the whole area near the mosque curiously empty. "Don't want to go too low," he said, "don't want to tempt some trigger-happy crackpot."

"You like Tabriz, Erikki?" Nogger asked, to cover his disquiet. He had never been here before.

"It's a grand city, old and wise and open and free—the most cosmopolitan in Iran. I've had some grand times here, the food and drink of all the world cheap and available—caviar and Russian vodka and Scottish smoked salmon and once a week, in the good times, Air France brought fresh French breads and cheeses. Turkish goods and Caucasian, British, American, Japanese—anything and everything. It's famous for its carpets, Nogger, and the beauty of its girls . . ." He felt Azadeh pinch his earlobe and he laughed. "It's true, Azadeh, aren't you Tabrizi? It's a fine city, Nogger. They speak a dialect of Farsi which is more Turkish than anything else. For centuries it's been a big trading center, part Iranian, part Russian, part Turkish, part Kurd, part Armenian, and always rebellious and independent and always wanted by the tsars and now the Soviets . . ."

Here and there knots of people stared up at them. "Nogger, see any guns?"

"Plenty, but no one's firing at us. Yet."

Cautiously Erikki skirted the city and headed eastward. There the land climbed into close foothills and there was the walled palace of the Gorgons on a crest with the road leading up to it. No traffic on the road. Many acres of land within the high walls: orchards, a carpet factory, garages for twenty cars, sheds for wintering herds of sheep, huts and outhouses for a hundred-odd servants and guards, and the sprawling main cupolaed building of fifty rooms and small mosque and tiny minaret. A number of cars were parked near the main entrance. He circled at seven hundred feet.

"That's some pad," Nogger Lane said, awed.

"It was built for my great-grandfather by Prince Zergeyev on orders of the Romanov tsars, Nogger, as a pishkesh," Azadeh said absently, watching the grounds below. "That was in 1890 when the tsars had already stolen our Caucasian provinces and once more were trying to split Azerbaijan from Iran and wanted the help of the Gorgon Khans. But our line has always been loyal to Iran though they have sought to maintain a balance." She was watching the palace below. People were coming out of the main house and some of the outhouses—servants and armed guards. "The mosque was built in 1907 to celebrate the signing of the new Russian-British accord on their partitioning of us, and spheres of infl— Oh, look, Erikki, isn't that Najoud and Fazulia and Zadi . . . and, oh, look, Erikki, isn't that my brother Hakim—what's Hakim doing there?"

"Where? Oh, I see him. No, I don't th—"

"Perhaps . . . perhaps Abdollah Khan's forgiven him," she said excitedly. "Oh, wouldn't that be wonderful!"

Erikki peered at the people below. He had only met her brother once, at their wedding, but he had liked him very much. Abdollah Khan had released Hakim from banishment for this day only, then sent him back to Khoi in the northern part of Azerbaijan near the Turkish border where he had extensive mining interests. "All Hakim has ever wanted was to go to Paris to study the piano," Azadeh had told him. "But my father wouldn't listen to him, just cursed him and banished him for plotting . . ."

"It's not Hakim," Erikki said, his eyes much better than hers.

"Oh!" Azadeh squinted against the wind. "Oh." She was so disappointed. "Yes, yes, you're right, Erikki."

"There's Abdollah Khan!" There was no mistaking the imposing, corpulent man with the long beard, coming out of the main door to stand on the steps, two armed guards behind him. With him were two other men. All were dressed in heavy overcoats against the cold. "Who're they?"

"Strangers," she said, trying to get over her disappointment. "They haven't guns and there's no mullah, so they're not Green Bands."

"They're Europeans," Nogger said. "You have any binoculars, Erikki?"

"No." Erikki stopped circling and came down to five hundred feet and hovered, watching Abdollah Khan intently. He saw him point at the chopper and then talk with the other men, then go back to watching the chopper again. More of her sisters and family, some wearing chador, and servants had collected, bundled against the cold. Down another hundred feet. Erikki slipped off his dark glasses and headset and slid the side window back, gasped as the freezing air hit him, stuck his head out so they could see him clearly, and waved. All eyes on the ground went to Abdollah Khan. After a pause the Khan waved back. Without pleasure.

"Azadeh! Take your headset off and do what I did."

She obeyed at once. Some of her sisters waved back excitedly, chattering among themselves. Abdollah Khan did not acknowledge her, just waited. *Matyeryebyets*, Erikki thought, then leaned out of the cockpit and pointed at the wide space beyond the mosaic, frozen pool in the courtyard, obviously asking permission to land. Abdollah Khan nodded and pointed there, spoke briefly to his guards, then turned on his heel and went back into the house. The other men followed. One guard stayed. He walked down the steps toward the touchdown point, checking the action of his assault rifle.

"Nothing like a friendly reception committee," Nogger muttered.

"No need to worry, Nogger," Azadeh said with a nervous laugh. "I'll get out first, Erikki, safer for me to be first."

They landed at once. Azadeh opened her door and went to greet her sisters and her stepmother, her father's third wife and younger than she. His first wife, the Khanan, was of an age with him but now she was bedridden and never left her room. His second wife, Azadeh's mother, had died many years ago.

The guard intercepted Azadeh. Politely. Erikki breathed easier. It was too far away to hear what was said—in any event, neither he nor Nogger spoke Farsi or Turkish. The guard motioned at the chopper. She nodded then turned and beckoned them. Erikki and Nogger completed the shutdown, watching the guard who watched them seriously.

"You hate guns as much as I do, Erikki?" Nogger said.

"More. But at least that man knows how to use one—it's the amateurs that scare me." Erikki slipped out the circuit breakers and pocketed the ignition key.

They went to join Azadeh and her sisters but the guard stood in the way. Azadeh called out, "He says we are to go to the Reception Room at once and wait there. Please follow me."

Nogger was last. One of the pretty sisters caught his eye, and he smiled to himself and went up the stairs two at a time.

The Reception Room was vast and cold and drafty and smelled of damp, with heavy Victorian furniture and many carpets and lounging cushions and old-fashioned water heaters. Azadeh tidied her hair at one of the mirrors. Her ski clothes were elegant and fashionable. Abdollah Khan had never required any of his wives or daughters or household to wear chador, did not approve of chador. Then why was Najoud wearing one today? she asked herself, her nervousness increasing. A servant brought tea. They waited half an hour, then another guard arrived and spoke to her. She took a deep breath. "Nogger, you're to wait here," she said. "Erikki, you and I are to go with this guard."

Erikki followed her, tense but confident that the armed peace he had worked out with Abdollah Khan would hold. The touch of his pukoh knife reassured him. The guard opened a door at the end of the corridor and motioned them forward.

Abdollah Khan was leaning against some cushions, reclining on a carpet facing the door, guards behind him, the room rich, Victorian, and formal—and somehow decadent and soiled. The two men they had seen on the steps were seated cross-legged beside him. One was European, a big, well-preserved man in his late sixties with heavy shoulders and Slavic eyes set in a friendly face. The other was younger, in his thirties, his features Asiatic and the color of his skin yellowish. Both wore heavy winter suits. Erikki's caution soared and he waited beside the doorway as Azadeh went to her father, knelt in front of him, kissed his pudgy, jeweled hands, and blessed him. Impassively her father waved her to one side and kept his dark, dark eyes on Erikki who greeted him politely from the door but stayed near it. Hiding her shame and fear, Azadeh knelt again on the carpet, and faced him. Erikki saw both of the strangers flick their eyes over her appreciatively, and his temperature went up a notch. The silence intensified.

Beside the Khan was a plate of halvah, small squares of the honey-rich Turkish delicacies that he adored, and he ate some of them, light dancing off his rings. "So," he said harshly, "it seems you kill indiscriminately like a mad dog."

Erikki's eyes narrowed and he said nothing.

"Well?"

"If I kill it's not like a mad dog. Whom am I supposed to have killed?"

"One old man in a crowd outside Qazvin with a blow from your elbow, his chest crushed in. There are witnesses. Next, three men in a car and one outside it—he an important fighter for freedom. There are more witnesses. Farther down the road five dead and more wounded in the wake of the helicopter rescue. More witnesses." Another silence. Azadeh had not moved though the blood had left her face. "Well?"

"If there are witnesses you will know also that we were peacefully trying to get to Tehran, we were unarmed, we were set upon by a mob and if it hadn't been for Charlie Pettikin and Rakoczy, we'd probably be—" Erikki stopped momentarily, noticing the sudden glance between the two strangers. Then, even more warily, he continued, "We'd probably be dead. We were unarmed —Rakoczy wasn't—we were fired on first."

Abdollah Khan had also noticed the change in the men beside him. Thoughtfully, he glanced back at Erikki. "Rakoczy? The same with the Islamic-Marxist mullah and men who attacked your base? The Soviet Muslim?"

"Yes." Erikki looked at the two strangers, hard-eyed. "The KGB agent, who claimed he came from Georgia, from Tbilisi."

Abdollah Khan smiled thinly. "KGB? How do you know that?"

"I've seen enough of them to know." The two strangers stared back blandly; the older wore a friendly smile and Erikki was chilled by it.

"This Rakoczy, how did he get into the helicopter?" the Khan said.

"He captured Charlie Pettikin at my base last Sunday—Pettikin's one of our pilots and he'd come to Tabriz to pick us up, Azadeh and me. I'd been asked by my embassy to check with them about my passport—that was the day most governments, mine too, had ordered nonessential expats out of

Iran," he said, the exaggeration easy. "On Monday, the day we left here, Rakoczy forced Pettikin to fly him to Tehran." He told briefly what had happened. "But for him noticing the Finnish flag on the roof we'd be dead."

The man with Asiatic features laughed softly. "That would have been a great loss, Captain Yokkonen," he said in Russian.

The older man with the Slavic eyes said, in faultless English, "This Rakoczy, where is he now?"

"I don't know. Somewhere in Tehran. May I ask who you are?" Erikki was playing for time and expected no answer. He was trying to decide if Rakoczy was friend or enemy to these two, obviously Soviet, obviously KGB or GRU —the secret police of the armed forces.

"Please, what was his first name?" the older man asked pleasantly.

"Fedor, like the Hungarian revolutionary." Erikki saw no further reaction and could have gone on but was far too wise to volunteer anything to KGB or GRU. Azadeh was kneeling on the carpet, stiff-backed, motionless, her hands at rest in her lap, her lips red against the whiteness of her face. Suddenly he was very afraid for her.

"You admit killing those men?" the Khan said and ate another sweetmeat.

"I admit I killed men a year or so ago saving your life, Highness, an—"

"And yours!" Abdollah Khan said angrily. "The assassins would have killed you too—it was the Will of God we both lived."

"I didn't start that fight or seek it either." Erikki tried to choose his words wisely, feeling unwise and unsafe and inadequate. "If I killed those others it was not of my choosing but only to protect your daughter and my wife. Our lives were in danger."

"Ah, you consider it your right to kill any time you consider your life to be in danger?"

Erikki saw the flush in the Khan's face, and the two Soviets watching him, and he thought of his own heritage and his grandfather's stories of the olden days in the North Lands, when giants walked the earth and trolls and ghouls were not myth, long long ago when the earth was clean and evil was known as evil, and good as good, and evil could not wear the mask.

"If Azadeh's life is threatened—or mine—I will kill anyone," he said evenly. The three men felt ice go through them. Azadeh was appalled at the threat, and the guards who spoke neither Russian nor English, shifted uneasily, feeling the violence.

The vein in the center of Abdollah Khan's forehead knotted. "You will go with this man," he said darkly. "You will go with this man and do his bidding."

Erikki looked at the man with the Asiatic features. "What do you want with me?"

"Just your skills as a pilot, and the 212," the man said, not unfriendly, speaking Russian.

"Sorry, the 212's on a fifteen-hundred-hour check and I work for S-G and Iran-Timber."

"The 212 is complete, already ground-tested by your mechanics, and Iran-Timber has released you to . . . to me."

"To do what?"

"To fly," the man said irritably. "Are you hard of hearing?"

"No, but it seems you are."

Air hissed out of the man's mouth. The older man smiled strangely. Abdollah Khan turned on Azadeh, and she almost jumped with fright. "You will go to the Khanan and pay your respects!"

"Yes . . . yes . . . Father," she stuttered and jumped up. Erikki moved half a step but the guards were ready, one had him covered and she said, near tears, "No, Erikki, it's . . . I . . . I must go . . ." She fled before he could stop her.

The man with the Asiatic face broke the silence. "You've nothing to fear. We just need your skills."

Erikki Yokkonen did not answer him, sure that he was at bay, that both he and Azadeh were at bay and lost, and knowing that if there were no guards here he would have attacked now, without hesitation, killed Abdollah Khan now and probably the other two. The three men knew it.

"Why did you send for my wife, Highness?" he said in the same quiet voice, knowing the answer now. "You sent two messages."

Abdollah Khan said with a sneer, "She's of no value to me, but she is to my friends: to bring you back and to make you behave. And by God and the Prophet, you will behave. You will do what this man wants."

One of the guards moved his snub-nosed machine gun a fraction and the noise he made echoed in the room. The Soviet with the Asiatic features got up. "First your knife. Please."

"You can come and take it. If you wish it seriously."

The man hesitated. Abruptly Abdollah Khan laughed. The laugh was cruel, and it edged all of them. "You will leave him his knife. That will make your life more interesting." Then to Erikki, "It would be wise to be obedient and to behave."

"It would be wise to let us go in peace."

"Would you like to watch your copilot hung up by his thumbs now?" Erikki's eyes flattened even more. The older Soviet leaned over to whisper to the Khan whose gaze never left Erikki. His hands played with his jeweled dagger. When the man had finished, he nodded. "Erikki, you will tell your copilot that he is to be obedient too while he is in Tabriz. We will send him to the base, but your small helicopter will remain here. For the moment." He motioned the man with the Asiatic features to leave.

"My name is Cimtarga, Captain." The man was not nearly as tall as Erikki but strongly built with wide shoulders. "First we g—"

"Cimtarga's the name of a mountain, east of Samarkand. What's your real name? And rank?"

The man shrugged. "My ancestors rode with Timour Tamburlaine, the Mongol, he who enjoyed erecting mountains of skulls. First we go to your base. We will go by car." He walked past him and opened the door, but Erikki did not move, still looked at the Khan.

"I will see my wife tonight."

"You will see her when—" Abdollah Khan stopped as again the older man leaned forward and whispered. Again the Khan nodded. "Good. Yes, Captain, you will see her tonight, and every second night. Providing." He let the word hang. Erikki turned on his heel and walked out.

As the door closed after them, tension left the room. The older man chuckled. "Highness, you were perfect, perfect as usual."

Abdollah Khan eased his left shoulder, the ache in the arthritic joint annoying him. "He'll be obedient, Petr," he said, "but only as long as my disobedient and ungrateful daughter is within my reach."

"Daughters are always difficult," Petr Oleg Mzytryk answered. He came from north of the border, from Tbilisi—Tiflis.

"Not so, Petr. The others obey and give me no trouble but this one—she infuriates me beyond words."

"Then send her away once the Finn has done what's required. Send them both away." The Slavic eyes crinkled in the good face and he added lightly, "If I were thirty years younger and she was free I would petition to take her off your hands."

"If you'd asked before that madman appeared, you could have had her with my blessing," Abdollah Khan said sourly, though he had noted the underlying hope, hid his surprise, and put it aside for later consideration. "I regret giving her to him—I thought she'd drive him mad too—regret my oath before God to leave him alive—it was a moment of weakness."

"Perhaps not. It's good to be magnanimous, occasionally. He did save your life."

"Insha'Allah! That was God's doing—he was just an instrument."

"Of course," Mzytryk said soothingly. "Of course."

"That man's a devil, an atheist devil who stinks of bloodlust. If it hadn't been for my guards—you saw for yourself—we would be fighting for our lives."

"No, not so long as she's in your power to be dealt with . . . improperly." Petr smiled strangely.

"God willing, they'll both be soon in hell," the Khan said, still infuriated that he had had to keep Erikki alive to assist Petr Oleg Mzytryk, when he could have given him to the leftist mujhadin and thus been rid of him forever. The mullah Mahmud, one of the Tabriz leaders of the Islamic-Marxist mujhadin faction that had attacked the base, had come to him two days ago and told him what happened at the roadblock. "Here are their papers as proof," the mullah had said truculently, "both of the foreigner who must be CIA and of the lady, your daughter. The moment he returns to Tabriz we will stand him before our komiteh, sentence him, take him to Qazvin and put him to death."

"By the Prophet you won't, not until I give you approval," he had said imperiously, taking their papers. "That mad dog foreigner is married to my daughter, is not CIA, is under my protection until I cancel it, and if you touch so much as one foul red hair or interfere with him or the base until I approve it, I'll withdraw all my secret support and nothing will stop the Green Bands from stamping out the leftists of Tabriz! He'll be given to you in my time, not yours." Sullenly the mullah had gone away and Abdollah had at once added Mahmud to his list of imperatives. When he had examined the papers carefully and found Azadeh's passport and ID and other permits, he had been delighted, for these gave him an added hold over her, and her husband.

Yes, he thought, looking up at the Soviet, she will do whatever I require of her now. Anything. "As God wants, but she may be a widow very soon."

"Let's hope not too soon!" Mzytryk's laugh was good and infectious. "Not until her husband's finished his assignment."

Abdollah Khan was warmed by the man's presence and wise counsel and pleased that Mzytryk would do what was required of him. But I'll still have to be a better puppeteer than ever before, he thought, if I'm to survive, and Azerbaijan to survive.

All over the province and in Tabriz the situation now was very delicate, with insurrections of various kinds and factions fighting factions, with tens of thousands of Soviet soldiers poised just over the border. And tanks. And nothing between them and the Gulf to hinder them. Except me, he thought. And once they possessed Azerbaijan—with Tehran indefensible as history's proved time and time again—then Iran will fall into their hands like the rotten apple Khrushchev forecast. With Iran, the Gulf, the world's oil, and Hormuz.

He wanted to howl with rage. God curse the Shah who wouldn't listen, wouldn't wait, hadn't the sense to crush a minor mullah-inspired rebellion not twenty years ago and send Ayatollah Khomeini into hell as I advised and so put into jeopardy our absolute, unstoppable, inevitable stranglehold over the entire world outside of Russia, tsarist or Soviet—our real enemy.

We were so close: the U.S. was eating out of our hands, fawning and pressing on us their most advanced weapons, begging us to police the Gulf and so dominate the vile Arabs, absorb their oil, make vassals of them and their flyblown, foul Sunni sheikdoms from Saudi to Oman. We could have overrun Kuwait in a day, Iraq in a week, the Saudi and Emirate sheiks would have fled back to their deserts screaming for mercy! We could get whatever technology we wanted, whatever ships, airplanes, tanks, arms for the asking, even the Bomb, by God!—our German-built reactors would have made them for us!

So close to doing God's will, we Shi'as of Iran, with our superior intelligence, our ancient history, our oil, and our command of the strait that must eventually bring all the People of the Left Hand to their knees. So close to gaining Jerusalem and Mecca, control of Mecca—Holy of Holies.

So close to being First on Earth, as is our right, but now, now all in jeopardy, and we have to start again, and again outmaneuver the satanic barbarians from the north and all because of one man.

Insha'Allah, he thought, and that took some of his anger away. Even so, if Mzytryk had not been in the room he would have ranted and raved and beaten someone, anyone. But the man was here and had to be dealt with, the problems of Azerbaijan arranged, so he controlled his anger and pondered his next move. His fingers picked up the last of the halvah and popped it into his mouth.

"You'd like to marry Azadeh, Petr?"

"You'd like me, older than you, as a son-in-law?" the man said with a deprecating laugh.

"If it was the Will of God," he replied with the right amount of sincerity and smiled to himself, for he had seen the sudden light in his friend's eyes, quickly covered. So, he thought, the first time you see her you want her. Now if I really gave her to you when the monster's disposed of, what would that do for me? Many things! You're eligible, you're powerful, politically it would be wise, very wise, and you'd beat sense into her and deal with her as she should be dealt with, not like the Finn who fawns on her. You'd be an instrument of revenge on her. There are many advantages . . .

Three years ago Petr Oleg Mzytryk had taken over the immense dacha and lands that had belonged to his father—also an old friend of the Gorgons— near Tbilisi where, for generations, the Gorgons also had had very important business connections. Since then Abdollah Khan had got to know him intimately, staying at the dacha on frequent business trips. He had found Petr Oleg like all Russians, secretive, volunteering little. But, unlike most, extremely helpful and friendly—and more powerful than any Soviet he knew, a widower with a married daughter, a son in the navy, grandchildren—and rare habits. He lived alone in the huge dacha except for servants and a strangely beautiful, strangely venomous Russian-Eurasian woman called Vertinskya, in her late thirties, whom he had brought out twice in three years, almost like a unique private treasure. She seemed to be part slave, part prisoner, part drinking companion, part whore, part tormentor, and part wildcat. "Why don't you kill her and have done with her, Petr?" he had said when a raging violent quarrel had erupted and Mzytryk had physically whipped her out of the room, the woman spitting and cursing and fighting till servants hauled her away.

"Not . . . not yet," Mzytryk had said, his hands trembling, "she's far . . . far too valuable."

"Ah, yes . . . yes, now I understand," Abdollah Khan had said, equally aroused, having almost the same feeling about Azadeh—the reluctance to cast away such an object until she was truly cowed, truly humbled and crawling—and he remembered how he had envied Mzytryk that Vertinskya was mistress and not daughter so the final act of revenge could be consummated.

God curse Azadeh, he thought. Curse her who could be the twin of the mother who gave me so much pleasure, who reminds me constantly of my loss, she and her evil brother, both patterns of the mother in face and manner but not in quality, she who was like a houri from the Garden of God. I thought both of our children loved me and honored me, but no, once Napthala had gone to Paradise their true natures came to pass. I know Azadeh was plotting with her brother to murder me—haven't I the proof? Oh, God, I wish I could beat her like Petr does his nemesis, but I can't, I can't. Every time I raise my hand against her I see my Beloved, God curse Azadeh to hell . . .

"Be calm," Mzytryk said gently.

"What?"

"You were looking so upset, my friend. Don't worry, everything will be all right. You will find a way to exorcise her."

Abdollah Khan nodded heavily. "You know me too well." That's true, he thought, ordering tea for himself and vodka for Mzytryk, the only man he had ever felt at ease with.

I wonder who you really are, he thought, watching him. In years gone by, in your father's time at the dacha when we met, you used to say you were on leave, but you'd never say on leave from what, nor could I ever find out, however much I tried. At first I presumed it was the Soviet army, for once when you were drunk you told me you'd been a tank commander during World War II at Sebastopol, and all the way to Berlin. But then I changed my mind and thought it more likely you and your father were KGB or GRU, for no one in the whole USSR retires to such a dacha with such lands in Georgia, the best part of the empire, without very particular knowledge and influence. You say you're retired now—retired from what?

Experimenting to find out the extent of Mzytryk's power in the early days, Abdollah Khan had mentioned that a clandestine Communist Tudeh cell in Tabriz was plotting to assassinate him and he would like the cell stamped out. It was only partially true, the real reason being that a son of a man he hated secretly and could not attack openly was part of the group. Within the week all their heads were stuck on spikes near the mosque with a sign, THUS WILL ALL ENEMIES OF GOD PERISH, and he had wept cold tears at the funeral and laughed in privacy. That Petr Mzytryk had the power to eliminate one of their own cells was power indeed—and also, Abdollah knew, a measure of his own importance to them.

He looked at him. "How long will you need the Finn?"

"A few weeks."

"What if the Green Bands prevent him flying or intercept him?"

The Soviet shrugged. "Let's hope he will have finished the assignment. I doubt if there would be any survivors—either him or Cimtarga—if they're found this side of the border."

"Good. Now, back to where we were before we were interrupted: you agree there'll be no massive support for the Tudeh here, so long as the Americans stay out and Khomeini doesn't start a program against them?"

"Azerbaijan has always been within our frame of interest. We've always said it should be an independent state—there's more than enough wealth, power, minerals, and oil to sustain it and . . ." Mzytryk smiled, "and enlightened leadership. You could lift the flag, Abdollah. I'm sure you'd get all the support you need to be president—with our immediate recognition."

And then I'd be assassinated the next day while the tanks roll over the borders, the Khan told himself without venom. Oh, no, my fine friend, the Gulf is too much temptation even for you. "It's a wonderful idea," he said earnestly, "but I would need time—meanwhile I can count also on the Communist Tudeh being turned on the insurrectionists?"

Petr Mzytryk's smile remained the same but his eyes changed. "It would be curious for the Tudeh to attack their stepbrothers. Islamic-Marxism is advocated by many Muslim intellectuals—I hear even you support them."

"I agree there should be a balance in Azerbaijan. But who ordered leftists to attack the airfield? Who ordered them to attack and burn our railway station? Who ordered the blowing up of the oil pipeline? Obviously no one sensible. I hear it was the mullah Mahmud of the Hajsta mosque." He watched Petr carefully. "One of yours."

"I've never heard of him."

"Ah," Abdollah Khan said with pretended joviality, disbelieving him. "I'm glad, Petr, because he's a false mullah, not even a real Islamic-Marxist, a rabble-rouser—he's the one who invaded Yokkonen's base. Unfortunately he has as many as five hundred fighters supporting him, equally ill-disciplined. And money from somewhere. And helpers like Fedor Rakoczy. What does Rakoczy mean to you?"

"Not much," Petr said at once, his smile the same and voice the same, far too clever to avoid the question. "He's a pipeline engineer from Astara, on the border, one of our Muslim nationals who is believed to have joined the mujhadin as a Freedom Fighter, strictly without permission or approval."

Petr kept his face bland but inside he was swearing obscenely, wanting to shout, My son, my son, have you betrayed us? You were sent to spy, to infiltrate the mujhadin and report back, that's all! And this time you were sent to try to recruit the Finn, then to go to Tehran and organize university students, not to ally yourself to a mad dog mullah or to attack airfields or kill scum beside a road. Have you gone mad? You stupid fool, what if you'd been wounded and caught? How many times have I told you they—and we—can break anyone in time and empty him or her of their secrets? Stupid to take such risks! The Finn's temporarily important but not important enough to disobey orders, to risk your future, your brother's future—and mine!

If the son's suspect, so is the father. If the father's suspect, so is the family. How many times have I told you that the KGB works by the Book, destroys those who won't obey the Book, who think for themselves, take risks, and exceed instructions.

"This Rakoczy's unimportant," he said smoothly. Be calm, he ordered himself, beginning the litany: There's nothing to worry about. You know too many secrets to be touched. So does my son. He's good, they must be wrong about him. He's been tested many times, by you and by other experts. You're safe. You're strong, you've your health, and you could beat and bed that little beauty Azadeh and still rape Vertinskya the same day. "What's important is that you are the focus of Azerbaijan, my friend," he said in the same soothing voice. "You will get all the support you need and your views on the Islamic-Marxists will reach the right source. The balance you require, you will have."

"Good. I will count on it," the Khan said.

"Meanwhile," Mzytryk said, coming back to the main reason for his sudden trip here. "What about the British captain? Can you help us?"

The day before yesterday a top secret, priority-coded telex from Center had arrived at his home near Tbilisi telling him that the CIA's covert radar listening post on Sabalan's north face had been blown up by saboteurs just before friendly local teams sent to remove all cipher books, cipher machines, and computers had arrived. "See Ivanovitch personally at once," the telex had continued, using Abdollah Khan's undercover name. "Tell him that the saboteurs were British—a captain and two Gurkhas—and an American CIA agent Rosemont (code name Abu Kurd), guided by one of our mercenaries who was murdered by them before he could lead them into an ambush. One soldier and the CIA agent were killed during their escape and the two survivors are believed to be heading toward Ivanovitch's sector—arrange his cooperation. Section 16/a. Acknowledge." The Section 16 command meant: this person or persons are priority enemies who are to be intercepted, detained, and brought back for interrogation by whatever means necessary. The added "/a" meant: if this cannot be done, eliminate them without fail.

Mzytryk sipped the vodka, waiting. "We would appreciate your help."

"You've always got my help," Abdollah said. "But to find two expert saboteurs in Azerbaijan who are certain to be disguised by now is almost an impossibility. They're bound to have safe houses to go to—there's a British consulate in Tabriz, and dozens of routes out of the mountains that would bypass us." He got up and went to the window and stared out of it. From here he could see the 206 parked in the forecourt under guard. The day was still cloudless. "If I'd been leading that operation I'd pretend to head for Tabriz, but then I'd double back and go out by the Caspian. How did they go in?"

"Caspian. But they were tracked this way. Two bodies were found in the snow, and tracks of the two others headed this way."

The failure of the Sabalan venture had sent a tremor of rage up the line. That there was so much CIA top secret equipment so near at hand had been a magnet for covert acquisition and infiltration for many years. In the last two weeks information that some of the radar posts had been evacuated but not destroyed in the retreat and panic they had helped foster, had had the hawks ready to move in immediately, in strength. Mzytryk, senior counselor in this area, had advised caution, to use locals rather than Soviet teams so as not to antagonize Abdollah Khan—his exclusive contact and prize agent—nor risk an international incident.

"It's totally unwise to risk a confrontation," he had said, keeping to the Book—and his private plan. "What do we gain by immediate action—if we've not been fed disinformation and Sabalan's not one great booby trap which is probable? A few cipher books that we may or may not already have. As to the advanced computers—our whole Operation Zatopek has that well in hand."

This was a highly controversial and innovative KGB covert operation—named after the Czech long-distance runner—set up in '65. With an initial budget of $10 million of terribly scarce foreign currency, Operation Zatopek was to acquire a continuing supply of the most advanced and best Western technology *by simple purchase through a network of bogus companies* and not by the conventional and very expensive method of theft and espionage.

"The money is nothing compared to the gains," his top secret initial report to Center had said when he had first returned from the Far East in '64. "There are tens of thousands of corrupt businessmen and fellow travelers who will sell us the best and the most up to date for a profit. A huge profit to any individual would be a pittance to us—because we will save billions in research and development which we can spend on our navy, air force, and army. And, just as important, we save years of sweat, toil, and failure. At almost no cost we maintain parity with anything their minds can conceive. A few dollars under their rotten little tables will get us all their treasures."

Petr Mzytryk felt a glow when he remembered how his plan had been accepted—though naturally and rightly taken over by his superiors as their idea, as he had taken it from one of his own deep-cover agents in Hong Kong, a French national called Jacques de Ville in the big conglomerate of Struan's who had opened his eyes: "It's not against U.S. law to ship technology to France or West Germany or a dozen other countries, and not against these countries' laws for a company to ship it on to other countries where there are no Swiss laws against shipping goods to the Soviet Union. Business is business, Gregor, and money makes the world go around. Through Struan's alone we could supply you tons of equipment the U.S. has forbidden you. We service China—why not you? Gregor, you seafarers don't understand business. . . ."

Mzytryk smiled to himself. In those days he had been known as Gregor Suslev, captain of a small Soviet freighter that plied from Vladivostok to Hong Kong, his cover for his top secret job of deputy controller for Asia for the KGB's First Directorate.

Over the years since '64, when I first proposed the scheme, he thought so proudly, with a total outlay so far of $85 million, Operation Zatopek has saved Mother Russia billions and provided a constant, ever-growing flow of NASA-, Japanese-, and European-developed gadgetry, electronic marvels, hardware, software, plans, robots, chips, micros, medicines, and all manner of magic to duplicate and manufacture at our leisure—with equipment developed by the same enemy, and bought and paid for with loans they provide that we'll never repay. What fools they are!

He almost laughed out loud. Even more important, Zatopek gives me a free hand to continue to operate and maneuver as I choose in this area, to play the Great Game the stupid British let slip from their grasp.

He watched Abdollah Khan standing at the window, waiting patiently for him to decide on the favor he wanted in return for catching the saboteurs. Come on, Bad Fats, he thought grimly, using his secret nickname for him, we both know you can catch those *matyeryebyets* if you want to—if they're still in Azerbaijan.

"I'll do what I can," Abdollah Khan said, still with his back to him, and Mzytryk did not hide his smile. "If I intercept them, what then, Petr?"

"Tell Cimtarga. He will make all arrangements."

"Very well." Abdollah Khan nodded to himself and came and sat down again. "That's settled, then."

"Thank you," Petr said, very satisfied. Such finality from Abdollah Khan promised quick success.

"This mullah we were discussing, Mahmud," the Khan said, "he's very dangerous. Also his band of cutthroats. I think they're a threat to everyone. The Tudeh should be directed to deal with him. Covertly, of course."

Mzytryk wondered how much Abdollah knew about their secret support for Mahmud, one of their best and most fanatic converts. "The Tudeh must be guarded, and their friends too." He saw the immediate flash of irritation, so he compromised and added at once, "Perhaps this man could be moved and replaced—a general split and fratricide would only help the enemy."

"The mullah's a false mullah and not a true believer in anything."

"Then he should go. Quickly." Petr Mzytryk smiled, Abdollah Khan didn't.

"Very quickly, Petr. Permanently. And his group broken."

The price was steep, but the Section 16/a gave him authority enough. "Why not quickly and permanently, since you say it's necessary? I agree to, er, pass on your recommendation." Mzytryk smiled and now Abdollah Khan smiled, also satisfied.

"I'm glad we agree, Petr. Become a Muslim for your eternal soul."

Petr Mzytryk laughed. "In time. Meanwhile, become a Communist for your earthly pleasure."

The Khan laughed, leaned forward, and refilled Petr's glass. "I can't persuade you to stay for a few days?"

"No, but thanks. After we've eaten, I think I'll start back for home." The smile broadened. "There's a lot for me to do."

The Khan was very content. So now I can forget the troublesome mullah and his band and another tooth's been drawn. But I wonder what you would do, Petr, if you knew your saboteur captain and his saboteur soldier were on the other side of my estate, waiting for safe passage out? But out to where? To Tehran or to you? I haven't yet decided.

Oh, I knew you'd come to beg my help, why else did I keep them safe, why else did I meet them secretly in Tabriz two days ago and bring them here secretly if not for you? Perhaps. Pity Vien Rosemont got killed, he was useful. Even so, the information and warning contained in the code he gave the captain for me is more than useful. He'll be difficult to replace.

Yes, and also true that if you receive a favor you must return a favor. The Infidel Erikki is only one. He rang a bell and when the servant appeared, he said, "Tell my daughter Azadeh she will join us for food."

AT TEHRAN: 4:17 P.M. Jean-Luc Sessonne banged the brass knocker on the door of McIver's apartment. Beside him was Sayada Bertolin. Now that they were off the street and alone, he cupped her breasts through her coat and kissed her. "I promise we won't be long, then back to bed!"

She laughed. "Good."

"You booked dinner at the French Club?"

"Of course. We'll have plenty of time!"

"Yes, *chérie.*" He wore an elegant, heavy raincoat over his flying uniform and his flight from Zagros had been uneasy, no one answering his frequent radio calls though the airwaves were filled with excitable Farsi which he did not speak or understand.

He had kept at regulation height, and made a standard approach to Tehran's International Airport. Still no answer to his calls. The wind sock was full and showed a strong crosswind. Four jumbos were on the apron near the terminal along with a number of other jets, one a burned-out wreck. He saw some were loading, surrounded by too many men, women, and children with no order to them, the fore and aft steps to the cabins dangerously over-crowded, discarded suitcases and luggage scattered everywhere. No police or traffic wardens that he could see, nor at the other side of the terminal building where all approach roads were clogged with standstill traffic that was jammed nose to tail. The parking lot was solid but more cars were trying to squeeze in, the sidewalks packed with laden people.

Jean-Luc thanked God that he was flying and not walking and he landed at the nearby airfield of Galeg Morghi without trouble, bedded the 206 in the S-G hangar, and organized an immediate ride into town with the help of a $10 bill. First stop at the Schlumberger office and a dawn date fixed to fly back to Zagros. Then to her apartment. Sayada had been home. As always the first time after being so long apart was immediate, impatient, rough, selfish, and mutually explosive.

He had met her at a Christmas party in Tehran a year and two months and three days ago. He remembered the evening exactly. The room was crowded and the moment he arrived, he saw her as though the room was empty. She was alone, sipping a drink, her dress sheer and white.

"*Vous parlez français, madame?*" he had asked, stunned by her beauty.

"Sorry, m'sieur, only a few words. I would prefer English."

"Then in English: I am overjoyed to meet you but I have a dilemma."

"Oh? What?"

"I wish to make love to you immediately."

"Eh?"

"You are the manifestation of a dream . . ." It would sound so much better in French but never mind, he had thought. "I've been looking for you forever and I need to make love to you, you are so desirable."

"But . . . but my . . . husband is over there. I'm married."

"That is a condition, madam, not an impediment."

She had laughed and he had known she was his. Only one thing more would make everything perfect. "Do you cook?"

"Yes," she had said with such confidence that he knew she would be superb, that in bed she would be divine, and that what she lacked he would teach her. How lucky she is to have met me, he thought happily, and banged on the door again.

Their months together had flown by. Her husband rarely visited Tehran. He was a Lebanese banker in Beirut, of French extraction, "and therefore civilized," Jean-Luc had said with total confidence, "so of course he would approve of our liaison, *chérie,* should he ever find out. He is quite old compared to you, of course he would approve."

"I'm not so sure, *chéri,* and he's only fifty and you're f—"

"Divine," he had said, helping her. "Like you." For him it was true. He had never known such skin and silky hair and long limbs and a sinuous passion that was a gift of heaven. *"Mon Dieu,"* he had gasped one night, kept lingering on the summit by her magic, "I die in your arms." Later she had kissed him and brought him a hot towel and slid back into bed. This was on a holiday in Istanbul in the fall of last year, and the utter sensuality of that city had surrounded them.

For her the affair was exciting, but not an affair to end all affairs. She had discussed Jean-Luc with her husband the night of the party. "Ah," he had said, amused, "so that was why you wanted to meet him!"

"Yes. I thought him interesting—even though French and totally self-centered as always—but he excited me, yes, yes, he did."

"Well, you'll be here in Tehran for two years, I can't be here more than a few days a month—too dangerous—and it would be a shame for you to be alone, every night. Wouldn't it?"

"Ah, then I have your permission?"

"Where is his wife?"

"In France. He's in Iran for two months, then has one month with her."

"Perhaps it would be a very good idea, this liaison—good for your soul, good for your body, and good for our work. More importantly, it would divert attention."

"Yes, that occurred to me too. I told him I did not speak French and he has many advantages—he's a member of the French Club!"

"Ah! Then I agree. Good, Sayada. Tell him I'm a banker of French extraction, which is partially true—wasn't my great-great-grandfather a foot soldier with Napoleon on his Middle East drive toward India? Tell your Frenchman we're Lebanese for many generations, not just a few years."

"Yes, you are wise as always."

"Get him to make you a member of the French Club. That would be perfect! A great deal of power there. Somehow the Iran-Israel entente must be broken, somehow the Shah must be curbed, somehow we have to split Israel from Iran oil or the archfiend Begin will be tempted to invade Lebanon to cast our fighters out. With Iranian oil he'll succeed and that will be the end of another civilization. I'm tired of moving."

"Yes, yes, I agree . . ."

Sayada was very proud. So much accomplished in the year, unbelievable how much! Next week Leader Yasir Arafat was invited to Tehran for a triumphal meeting with Khomeini as a thank-you for his help to the revolution: oil exports to Israel were finished, the fanatically anti-Israel Khomeini installed —and the pro-Israel Shah expelled into ignominy. So much progress since she had first met Jean-Luc. Inconceivable progress! And she knew that she had helped her husband who was highly placed in the PLO, by acting as a special courier taking messages and cassettes to and from Istanbul, to and from the French Club in Tehran—oh, how much intrigue to persuade the Iraqis to allow Khomeini to leave for the safe harbor of France where he would no longer be muzzled—to and from all sorts of places escorted by my handsome lover. Oh, yes, she thought contentedly, Jean-Luc's friends and contacts have been so useful. One day soon we will get back to Gaza and regain our lands and houses and shops and vineyards . . .

McIver's door swung open. It was Charlie Pettikin. "Good God, Jean-Luc, what the hell're you doing here? Hi, Sayada, you look more beautiful than ever, come on in!" He shook hands with Jean-Luc and gave her a friendly kiss on both cheeks and felt the warmth of her.

Her long, heavy coat and hood hid most of her. She knew the dangers of Tehran and dressed accordingly: "It saves so much bother, Jean-Luc; I agree it's stupid and archaic but I don't want to be spat on, or have some rotten thug wave his penis at me or masturbate as I pass by—it's not and never will be France. I agree it's unbelievable that now in Tehran I have to wear some form of chador to be safe, yet a month ago I didn't. Whatever you say, *chéri*, the old Tehran's gone forever. . . ."

Pity in some ways, she thought, going into the apartment. It had had the best of the West and best of the East—and the worst. But now, now I pity Iranians, particularly the women. Why is it Muslims, particularly Shi'as, are so narrow-minded and won't let their women dress in a modern way? Is it because they're so repressed and sex-besotted? Or is it because they're frightened they'd be shown up? Why can't they be open-minded like us Palestinians, or Egyptians, Shargazi, Dubaians, or Indonesians, Pakistanis, or so many others? It must be impotence. Well nothing's going to keep me from joining the Women's Protest March. How dare Khomeini try to betray us women who went to the barricades for him!

It was cold inside the apartment, the electric fire still down to half power, so she kept her coat on, just opened it to be more comfortable, and sat on one of the sofas. Her dress was warm and Parisian and slit to the thigh. Both men noticed. She had been here many times and thought the apartment drab and uncomfortable though she liked Genny very much. "Where's Genny?"

"She went to Al Shargaz this morning on the 125."

"Then Mac's gone?" Jean-Luc said.

"No, just her, Mac's out at th—"

"I don't believe it!" Jean-Luc said. "She swore she'd never leave without old Dirty Duncan!"

Pettikin laughed. "I didn't believe it either but she went like a lamb." Time enough to tell Jean-Luc the real reason why she went, he thought.

"Things've been bad here?"

"Yes, and getting worse. Lots more executions." Pettikin thought it better not to mention Sharazad's father in front of Sayada. No point in worrying her. "How about tea? I've just made some. You hear about Qasr Jail today?"

"What about it?"

"A mob stormed it," Pettikin said, going into the kitchen for extra cups. "They broke down the door and released everyone, strung up a few SAVAKs and police, and now the rumor is Green Bands have set up shop with kangaroo courts and they're filling the cells with whom the hell ever and emptying them as quickly in front of firing squads."

Sayada would have said that the prison had been liberated and that now enemies of the revolution, enemies of Palestine, were getting their just punishment. But she held her peace and listened attentively as Pettikin continued: "Mac went to the airport with Genny early, then to the Ministry, then here. He'll be back soon. How was the traffic at the airport, Jean-Luc?"

"Jammed for miles."

"The Old Man's stationed the 125 at Al Shargaz for a couple of weeks to get all our people out—if necessary—or bring in fresh crews."

"Good. Scot Gavallan's overdue for leave and also a couple of our mechanics—can the 125 get clearance to stop at Shiraz?"

"We're trying next week. Khomeini and Bazargan want full oil production back, so we think they'll cooperate."

"You'll be able to bring in new crews, Charlie?" Sayada asked, wondering if a British 125 should be allowed to operate so freely. Damn British, always conniving!

"That's the plan, Sayada." Pettikin poured more boiling water into the teapot and did not notice the grimace on Jean-Luc's face. "We've been more or less ordered by the British embassy to evacuate all nonessential personnel —we got out a few redundancies, and Genny, and then Johnny Hogg went to pick up Manuela Starke at Kowiss."

"Manuela's at Kowiss?" Sayada was as surprised as Jean-Luc.

Pettikin told him how she had arrived and McIver had sent her down there. "So much going on it's difficult to keep tabs on everything. What're you doing here and how're things at Zagros? You'll stay for dinner—I'm cooking tonight."

Jean-Luc hid his horror. "Sorry, *mon vieux*, tonight is impossible. As to Zagros, at Zagros things are perfect, as always; after all it is the French sector. I'm here to fetch Schlumberger—I return at dawn tomorrow and will have to bring them back in two days—how can I resist the extra flying?" He smiled at Sayada and she smiled back. "In fact, Charlie, I'm long overdue a weekend—where's Tom Lochart, when's he coming back to Zagros?"

Pettikin's stomach twisted. Since they had had the call three days ago from Rudi Lutz at Abadan Tower reporting that HBC had been shot down trying to sneak over the border and that Tom Lochart was "back off leave," they had had no further information other than one formal call relayed through Kowiss that Lochart had started back for Tehran by road. No official inquiries, yet, about the hijack.

I wish to God Tom was back, Pettikin thought. If Sayada wasn't here I'd tell Jean-Luc about it, he's a bigger friend of Tom's than I am, but I don't know about Sayada. After all, she's not family, she works for Kuwaitis and this HBC business could be called treason.

Absently he poured a cup and handed it to Sayada, another to Jean-Luc, hot, black, with sugar and goat's milk which neither of them liked but accepted out of politeness. "Tom's done what he had to do," he said carefully, making it sound light. "He started back from Bandar Delam day before yesterday by road. God knows how long he'll take but he should've been here last night. Easy. Let's hope he arrives today."

"That would be perfect," Jean-Luc said. "Then he could take the Schlumberger team back to Zagros and I'd take a few days' leave."

"You've just had leave. And you're in command."

"Well, at the very least he can come back with me, take over the base, and I'll return here Sunday." Jean-Luc beamed at Sayada. "*Voilà*, it's all fixed." Without noticing it, he took a sip of tea and almost choked. "*Mon Dieu*, Charlie, I love you like a brother but this is *merde*."

Sayada laughed and Pettikin envied him. Still, he thought, his heart picking up a beat, Paula's Alitalia flight's due back any day . . . what wouldn't I give to have her eyes light up for me like Sayada's do for M'sieur Seduction himself.

Better go easy, Charlie Pettikin. You could make a damn fool of yourself. She's twenty-nine, you're fifty-six, and you've only chatted her up a couple of times. Yes. But she excites me more than I've been excited in years and now I can understand Tom Lochart going overboard for Sharazad.

The warning buzzer went on the High Frequency transmitter-receiver on the sideboard. He got up and turned up the volume. "HQ Tehran, go ahead!"

"This is Captain Ayre in Kowiss for Captain McIver. Urgent." The voice was mixed with static and low.

"This is Captain Pettikin, Captain McIver's not here at the moment. You're two by five." This was a measure, one to five, of the signal strength. "Can I help?"

"Standby One."

Jean-Luc grunted. "What's with Freddy and you? Captain Ayre and Captain Pettikin?"

"It's just a code," Pettikin said absently staring at the set, and Sayada's attention increased. "It just sort of developed and means someone's there or listening in who shouldn't. A hostile. Replying with the same formality means you got the message."

"That's very clever," Sayada said. "Do you have lots of codes, Charlie?"

"No, but I'm beginning to wish we had. It's a bugger not knowing what's going on really—no face-to-face contact, no mail, phones and the telex ropy with so many trigger-happy nutters muscling us all. Why don't they turn in their guns and let's all live happily ever after?"

The HF was humming nicely. Outside the windows, the day was overcast and dull, the clouds promising more snow, the late afternoon light making all the city roofs drab and even the mountains beyond. They waited impatiently.

"This is Captain Ayre at Kowiss . . ." Again the voice was eroded by static and they had to concentrate to hear clearly. ". . . first I relay a message received from Zagros Three a few minutes ago from Captain Gavallan." Jean-Luc stiffened. "The message said exactly: 'Pan pan pan' "—the international aviation distress signal just below Mayday—" 'I've just been told by the local komiteh we are no longer persona grata in Zagros and to evacuate the area with all expatriates from all our rigs within forty-eight hours, or else. Request immediate advice on procedure.' End of message. Did you copy?"

"Yes," Pettikin said hastily, jotting some notes.

"That's all he said, except he sounded chocker."

"I'll inform Captain McIver and call you back as soon as possible." Jean-Luc leaned forward and Pettikin let him take the mike.

"This's Jean-Luc, Freddy, please call Scot and tell him I'll be back as planned tomorrow before noon. Good to talk to you, thanks, here's Charlie again." He handed the mike back, all of his bonhomie vanished.

"Will do, Captain Sessonne. Nice to talk to you. Next: the 125 picked up our outgoings along with Mrs. Starke, including Captain Jon Tyrer who'd been wounded in an aborted leftist counterattack at Bandar Delam . . ."

"What attack?" Jean-Luc muttered.

"First I've heard of it." Pettikin was just as concerned.

". . . and, according to plan, will bring back replacement crews in a few days. Next: Captain Starke." They all heard the hesitation and underlying anxiety and the curious stilted delivery as though this information was being read: "Captain Starke has been taken into Kowiss for questioning by a komiteh . . ." Both men gasped. ". . . to ascertain facts about a mass helicopter escape of pro-Shah air force officers from Isfahan on the thirteenth, last Tuesday, believed to have been piloted by a European. Next: air operations continue to improve under close supervision of the new management. Mr. Esvandiary is now our IranOil area manager and wants us to take over all Guerney contracts. To do this would require three more 212s and one 206. Please advise. We need spares for HBN, HKJ, and HGX and money for overdue wages. That's all for now."

Pettikin kept scribbling, his brain hardly working. "I've, er, I've noted everything and will inform Captain McIver as soon as he returns. You said, er, you said 'an attack on Bandar Delam.' Please give the details."

The airwaves were silent but for static. They waited. Then again Ayre's voice, not stilted now: "I've no information other than there was an anti-Ayatollah Khomeini attack that Captains Starke and Lutz helped put down. Afterward Captain Starke brought the wounded here for treatment. Of our personnel only Tyrer was creased. That is all."

Pettikin felt a bead of sweat on his face and he wiped it off. "What . . . what happened to Tyrer?"

Silence. Then: "A slight head wound. Dr. Nutt said he'd be okay."

Jean-Luc said, "Charlie, ask him what was that about Isfahan."

As though in dreamtime, Pettikin saw his fingers click on the sender switch. "What was that about Isfahan?"

They waited in the silence. Then: "I have no information other than what I gave you."

"Someone's telling him what to say," Jean-Luc muttered.

Pettikin pressed the sending button, changed his mind. So many questions to ask that Ayre clearly could not answer. "Thank you, Captain," he said, glad that his voice sounded firmer. "Please ask Hotshot to put his request for the extra choppers in writing, with suggested contract time and payment schedule. Put it on our 125 when they bring replacements. Keep . . . keep us informed about Captain Starke. McIver'll get back to you as soon as possible."

"Wilco. Out."

Now only static. Pettikin fiddled with the switches. The two men looked at

each other, oblivious of Sayada who sat quietly on the sofa, missing nothing.
" 'Close supervision'? That sounds bad, Jean-Luc."

"Yes. Probably means they have to fly with armed Green Bands." Jean-Luc
swore, all his thinking on Zagros and how young Scot Gavallan would cope
without his leadership. "*Merde!* When I left this morning everything was five
by five with Shiraz ATC as helpful as a Swiss hotelier off-season. *Merde!*"

Pettikin was suddenly reminded of Rakoczy and how close he had come to
disaster. For a second he considered telling Jean-Luc, then decided against it.
Old news! "Maybe we should contact Shiraz ATC for help?"

"Mac might have an idea. *Mon Dieu,* doesn't sound too good either for
Duke—these komitehs're breeding like lice. Bazargan and Khomeini better
deal with them quickly before the two of them're bitten to death." Jean-Luc
got up, very concerned, and stretched, then saw Sayada curled up on the sofa,
her untouched cup of tea on the small table beside her, smiling at him.

At once his bonhomie returned. There's nothing more I can do for young
Scot at the moment, or for Duke, but there is for Sayada. "Sorry, *chérie,*" he
said with a beam. "You see, without me there are always problems at Zagros.
Charlie, we'll leave now—I've got to check the apartment but we'll return
before dinner. Say 8:00 P.M.; by then Mac should be back, eh?"

"Yes. Won't you have a drink? Sorry, we've no wine. Whisky?" He offered
it halfheartedly as this was their last three quarters of a bottle.

"No thanks, *mon vieux.*" Jean-Luc got into his coat, noticed in the mirror
that he was looking as dashing as ever, and thought of the cases of wine and
the tins of cheese he had had the wisdom to tell his wife to stock in their
apartment. "*À bientôt,* I'll bring you some wine."

"Charlie," Sayada said, watching both of them carefully as she had done
since the HF came to life, "what did Scotty mean about the helicopter
escape?"

Pettikin shrugged. "All sorts of rumors about all sorts of escapes, by land,
sea, and air. Always 'Europeans' supposed to be involved," he said, hoping he
sounded convincing. "We're blamed for everything."

And why not, you are responsible, Sayada Bertolin thought without malice.
Politically, she was delighted to see them both sweating. Personally, she
wasn't. She liked both of them and most of the pilots, particularly Jean-Luc
who pleased her immensely and amused her constantly. I'm lucky to be
Palestinian, she told herself, and Coptic Christian—of ancient lineage. That
gives me strengths they don't have, an awareness of a heritage back to biblical
times, an understanding of life they could never reach, along with the capacity to dissociate politics from friendship and the bedchamber—as long as it is

necessary and prudent. Haven't we had thirty centuries of survival training? Hasn't Gaza been settled for three thousand years?

"There's a rumor Bakhtiar's slipped out of the country and fled to Paris."

"I don't believe that, Charlie," Sayada said. "But there's another that I do," she added, noticing he had not answered her question about the Isfahan helicopter. "It seems your General Valik and his family fled to join the other IHC partners in London. Between them they're supposed to have salted away millions of dollars."

"Partners?" Jean-Luc said contemptuously. "Robbers, all of them, whether here or London, every year worse than before."

"They're not all bad," Pettikin said.

Jean-Luc said, "Those *crétins* steal the sweat of our brow, Sayada. I'm astounded Old Man Gavallan lets them get away with it."

"Come off it, Jean-Luc," Pettikin said. "He fights them every inch of the way."

"Every inch of our way, old friend. We do the flying, he doesn't. As for Valik . . ." Jean-Luc shrugged with Gallic extravagance. "If I was an Iranian of wealth, I would have gone months ago with all I could collect. It's been clear for months that the Shah was out of control. Now it's the French Revolution and the Terror all over again but without our style, sense, civilized heritage, or manners." He shook his head disgustedly. "What a waste! When you think of all the centuries of teaching and wealth we French've put in trying to help these people crawl out of the Dark Ages and what have they learned? Not even how to make a decent loaf of bread!"

Sayada laughed and, on tiptoe, kissed him. "Ah, Jean-Luc, I love you and your confidence. Now, *mon vieux*, we should go, you've lots to accomplish!"

After they had left, Pettikin went to the window and stared out at the rooftops. There was the inevitable sporadic gunfire and some smoke near Jaleh. Not a big fire but enough. A stiff breeze scattered the smoke. Clouds reached down the mountains. The cold from the windows was strong, ice and snow on the sills. In the street below were many Green Bands. Walking or in trucks. Then from minarets everywhere muezzins began calling to afternoon prayer. Their calls seemed to surround him.

Suddenly he was filled with dread.

AT THE MINISTRY OF AVIATION: 5:04 P.M. Duncan McIver was sitting wearily on a wooden chair in a corner of the crowded antechamber of the deputy minister. He was cold and hungry and very irritable. His watch told him he had been waiting almost three hours.

Scattered around the room were a dozen other men, Iranians, some French, American, British, and one Kuwaiti wearing a *galabia*—a long-flowing Arabian robe—and headband. A few moments ago the Europeans had politely stopped chatting as, in response to the muezzins' calls that still came through the tall windows, the Muslims had knelt, faced Mecca, and prayed the afternoon prayer. It was short and quickly over and once more the desultory conversation picked up—never wise to discuss anything important in a government office, particularly now. The room was drafty, the air chilly. They all still wore their overcoats, were equally weary, a few stoic, most seething, for all, like McIver, had long overdue appointments.

"Insha'Allah," he muttered but that didn't help him.

With any luck Gen's already at Al Shargaz, he thought. I'm damned glad she's safely out, and damned glad she came up with the reason herself: "I'm the one who can talk to Andy. You can't put anything into writing."

"That's true," he had said, in spite of his misgivings, reluctantly adding, "Maybe Andy can make a plan that we could carry out—might carry out. Hope to God we don't have to. Too bloody dangerous. Too many lads and too many planes spread out. Too bloody dangerous. Gen, you forget we're not at war though we're in the middle of one."

"Yes, Duncan, but we've nothing to lose."

"We've people to lose, as well as birds."

"We're only going to see if it's feasible, aren't we, Duncan?"

Old Gen's certainly the best go-between we could have—if we really needed one. She's right, much too dangerous to put in a letter: "Andy, the only way we can safely extract ourselves from this mess is to see if we can come up with a plan to pull out all our planes—and spares—that're presently under Iranian registry and technically owned by an Iranian company called IHC . . ."

Christ! Isn't that a conspiracy to defraud!

Leaving is not the answer. We've got to stay and work and get our money when the banks open. Somehow I've got to get the partners to help—or maybe this minister can give us a hand. If he'll help, whatever it costs, we could wait out the storm here. Any government's got to have help to get their oil up, they've got to have choppers and we'll get our money . . .

He looked up as the inner door opened and a bureaucrat beckoned one of the others into the inner room. By name. There never seemed to be a logic to the manner of being called. Even in the Shah's time it was never first come, first served. Then it was only influence. Or money.

Talbot of the British embassy had arranged the appointment for him with the deputy prime minister and had given him a letter of introduction. "Sorry, old boy, even I can't get into the PM, but his deputy Antazam's a good sort, speaks good English—not one of these rev twits. He'll fix you up."

McIver had got back from the airport just before lunch and had parked as near as he could to the government offices. When he had presented the letter, in English and Farsi, to the guard on the main door in plenty of time, the man had sent him with another guard down the street to another building and more inquiries and then, from there, down another street to this building and from office to office until he arrived here, an hour late and fuming.

"Ah, don't worry, Agha, you're in plenty of time," the friendly reception clerk said, to his relief, in good English, and handed back the envelope containing the introduction. "This is the right office. Please go through that door and take a seat in the anteroom. Minister Kia will see you as soon as possible."

"I don't want to see him," he had almost exploded. "My appointment's with Deputy Prime Minister Antazam!"

"Ah, Deputy Minister Antazam, yes, Agha, but he's no longer in Prime Minister Bazargan's government. Insha'Allah," the young man said pleasantly. "Minister Kia deals with everything to do with, er, foreigners, finances, and airplanes."

"But I must insist th—" McIver stopped as the name registered and he remembered what Talbot had said about Kia and how remaining IHC partners had implanted this man on the board with an enormous retainer and no guarantees of assistance. "Minister Ali Kia?"

"Yes, Agha. Minister Ali Kia will see you as soon as possible." The receptionist was a pleasant, well-dressed young man in a suit and white shirt and blue tie, just like in the old days. McIver had had the foresight to enclose a pishkesh of 5,000 rials in the envelope with the introduction, just like in the old days. The money had vanished.

Perhaps things are really getting back to normal, McIver thought, went into the other room, and took a chair in the corner and began to wait. In his pocket was another wad of rials and he wondered if he should refill the envelope with the appropriate amount. Why not, he thought, we're in Iran, minor officials need minor money, high officials, high money—sorry, pishkesh. Making sure no one observed him, he put some high denomination notes into the envelope, then added a few more for safety. Maybe this bugger can really help us—the partners used to have the court buttoned up, perhaps they've done the same to Bazargan.

From time to time harassed bureaucrats hurried importantly through the anteroom into the inner room, papers in their hands, and came out again.

Occasionally, one of the men waiting would be politely ushered in. Without exception they were inside for just a few minutes and emerged taut-faced or red-faced, furious, and obviously empty-handed. Those who still waited felt more and more frustrated. Time passed very slowly.

"Agha McIver!" The inner door was open now, a bureaucrat beckoning him.

Ali Kia was seated behind a very large desk with no papers on it. He wore a smile, but his eyes were hard and small and McIver instinctively disliked him.

"Ah, Minister, how kind of you to see me," McIver said, forcing bonhomie, offering his hand. Ali Kia smiled politely and shook hands limply.

"Please sit down, Mr. McIver. Thank you for coming to see me. You have an introduction I believe?" His English was good, Oxford-accented, where he had gone to university just before World War II on a Shah grant, staying for the duration. He waved a tired hand at the bureaucrat beside the door. The man left.

"Yes, it, er, it was to Deputy Minister Antazam, but I understand it should have been directed to you." McIver handed him the envelope. Kia took out the introduction, noticed the amount of the notes exactly, tossed the envelope carelessly onto the desk to indicate more should be forthcoming, read the handwritten note with care, then put it down in front of him.

"Mr. Talbot is an honored friend of Iran though a representative of a hostile government," Kia said, his voice smooth. "What particular help can I give the friend of such an honored person?"

"There're three things, Minister. But perhaps I may be allowed to say how happy we are at S-G that you've considered giving us the benefit of your valuable experience by joining our board."

"My cousin was most insistent. I doubt I can help, but, as God wants."

"As God wants." McIver had been watching him carefully, trying to read him, and could not explain the immediate dislike he took great pains to hide. "First, there's a rumor that all joint ventures are suspended, pending a decision of the Revolutionary Komiteh."

"Pending a decision of the government," Kia corrected him curtly. "So?"

"How will that affect our joint company, IHC?"

"I doubt if it will affect it at all, Mr. McIver. Iran needs helicopter service for oil production. Guerney Aviation has fled. It would seem the future looks better than ever for our company."

McIver said carefully, "But we haven't been paid for work done in Iran for many months. We've been carrying all lease payments for the aircraft from Aberdeen and we're heavily overcommitted here in aircraft for the amount of work we have on the books."

"Tomorrow the banks . . . the Central Bank is due to open. By order of the PM—and the Ayatollah, of course. A proportion of the money owed will, I'm sure, be forthcoming."

"Would you conjecture how much we can expect, Minister?" McIver's hope quickened.

"More than enough to . . . to keep our operation going. I've already arranged for you to take out crews once their replacements are here." Ali Kia took a thin file from a drawer and gave him a paper. It was an order directed to Immigration at Tehran, Abadan, and Shiraz airports to allow out accredited IHC pilots and engineering crews, one for one, against incoming crew. The order was badly typed but legible, in Farsi and English, and signed on behalf of the komiteh responsible for IranOil and dated yesterday. McIver had never heard of him.

"Thank you. May I also have your approval for the 125 to make at least three trips a week for the next few weeks—of course only until your international airports are back to normal—to bring in crews, spares, and equipment, replacement parts, and so on, and," he added matter-of-factly, "to take out redundancies."

"It might be possible to approve that," Kia said.

McIver handed him the set of papers. "I took the liberty of putting it into writing—to save you the bother, Minister—with copies addressed to Air Traffic Control at Kish, Kowiss, Shiraz, Abadan, and Tehran."

Kia read the top copy carefully. It was in Farsi and English, simple, direct, and with the correct formality. His fingers trembled. To sign them would far exceed his authority but now that the deputy prime minister was in disgrace, as well as his own superior—both supposedly dismissed by this still mysterious Revolutionary Komiteh—and with mounting chaos in the government, he knew he had to take the risk. The absolute need for him, his family, and his friends to have ready access to a private airplane, particularly a jet, made the risk worthwhile.

I can always say my superior told me to sign it, he thought, keeping his nervousness away from his face and eyes. The 125 is a gift from God—just in case lies are spread about me. Damn Jared Bakravan! My friendship with that bazaari dog almost embroiled me in his treason against the state; I've never lent money in my life, nor engaged in plots with foreigners, nor supported the Shah.

To keep McIver off balance he tossed the papers beside the introduction almost angrily. "It might be possible for this to be approved. There would be a landing fee of $500 per landing. Was that everything, Mr. McIver?" he asked, knowing it was not. Devious British dog! Do you think you can fool me?

"Just one thing, Excellency." McIver handed him the last paper. "We've three aircraft that're in desperate need of servicing and repair. I need the exit permit signed so I can send them to Al Shargaz." He held his breath.

"No need to send valuable airplanes out, Mr. McIver; repair them here."

"Oh, I would if I could, Excellency, but there's no way I can do that. We don't have the spares or the engineers—and every day that one of our choppers're not working costs the partners a fortune. A fortune," he repeated.

"Of course you can repair them here, Mr. McIver, just bring the spares and the engineers from Al Shargaz."

"Apart from the cost of the aircraft there're the crews to support and pay for. It's all very expensive; perhaps I should mention that's the Iranian partners' cost—that's part of their agreement . . . to supply all the necessary exit permits." McIver continued to wheedle. "We need to get every available piece of equipment ready to service all the new Guerney contracts if the Ay — if, er, the government's decree to get oil production back to normal is to be obeyed. Without equipment . . ." He left the word hanging and again held his breath, praying he'd chosen the right bait.

Kia frowned. Anything that cost the Iranian partnership money came partially out of his own pocket now. "How soon could they be repaired and brought back?"

"If I can get them out within a couple of days, two weeks, maybe more, maybe less."

Again Kia hesitated. The Guerney contracts, added to existing IHC contracts, helicopters, equipment, fixtures, and fittings were worth millions of which he now had a sixth share—for no investment, he chortled deep inside. Particularly if everything was provided, without cost, by these foreigners! Exit permits for three helicopters? He glanced at his watch. It was Cartier and bejeweled—a pishkesh from a banker who, two weeks ago, had needed a private half an hour access to a working telex. In a few minutes he had an appointment with the chairman of Air Traffic Control and could easily embroil him in this decision.

"Very well," he said, delighted to be so powerful, an official on the rise, to be able to assist the implementation of government oil policy, and save the partnership money at the same time. "Very well, but the exit permits will only be valid for two weeks, the license will"—he thought a moment—"will be $5,000 per aircraft in cash prior to exit, and they must be back in two weeks."

"I, I can't get that money in cash in time. I could give you a note, or checks payable on a Swiss bank—for $2,000 per aircraft."

They haggled for a moment and settled on $3,100. "Thank you, Agha McIver," Ali Kia said politely. "Please leave downcast lest you encourage those rascals waiting outside."

When McIver was once more in his car he took out the papers and stared at the signatures and official stamps. "It's almost too good to be true," he muttered out loud. The 125's legal now, Kia says the suspension won't apply to us, we've exit permits for three 212s that're needed in Nigeria—$9,310 against their value of 3 million's more than fair! I never thought I'd get away with it! "McIver," he said happily, "you deserve a Scotch! A very large Scotch!"

IN THE NORTHERN SUBURBS: 6:50 P.M. Tom Lochart got out of the battered old cab and gave the man a $20 note. His raincoat and flight uniform were crumpled and he was very tired and unshaven and dirty and felt soiled, but his happiness at being outside his own apartment building and near Sharazad at long last took away all of it. A few flakes of snow were falling but he hardly noticed them as he hurried inside and up the staircase—no need to try the elevator, it had not worked for months.

The car that he had borrowed from one of the pilots at Bandar Delam had run out of gas yesterday, halfway to Tehran, the gas gauge defective. He had left it at a garage and fought onto the next bus and then another and, after breakdowns and delays and diversions, had reached the main terminal in Tehran two hours ago. Nowhere to wash, no running water, the toilets just the usual festering, clogged, flyblown holes in the ground.

No cabs at the cab rank or on the streets. No buses running anywhere near his home. Too far to walk. Then a cab appeared and he stopped it even though it was almost full, following custom, he pulled open a door and forced his way in, beseeching the other passengers to allow him to share their transport. A reasonable compromise was reached. They would be honored if he would stay and he would be honored to pay for all of them, and be last, and to pay the driver in cash. American cash. It was his last bill.

He got out his keys and turned the lock but the door was bolted from the inside, so he pressed the bell, waiting impatiently for the maid to open the door; Sharazad would never have opened it herself. His fingers drummed a happy beat, his heart filled with love for her. His excitement grew as he heard the maid's footsteps approach, the bolts being pulled back, the door inched open. A strange chadored face stared at him. "What do you want, Agha?" Her voice was as coarse as her Farsi.

His excitement vanished and left a sickening hole. "Who're you?" he said, as rudely. The woman started to close the door, but he put his foot out and shoved it open. "What're you doing in my house? I'm Excellency Lochart and this is my house! Where's Her Highness, my wife? Eh?"

The woman glowered at him, then padded away across his hallway toward his living room door and opened it. Lochart saw strangers there, men and women—and guns leaning against his wall. "What the hell's going on?" he muttered in English and strode into his living room. Two men and four women stared up at him from his carpets, cross-legged or leaning against his cushions, in the middle of a meal in front of his fireplace, a fire burning merrily, eating off his plates that were spread carelessly, their shoes off, their feet dirty. One man older than the other, in his late thirties, had his hand on an automatic that was stuck in his belt.

Blinding rage soared through Lochart, the presence of these aliens a rape and a sacrilege. "Who're you? Where's my wife? By God, you get out of m—" He stopped. The gun was pointing at him.

"Who're you, Agha?"

With a supreme effort Lochart dominated his fury, his chest hurting him. "I'm—I'm—this is—is my house—I'm the owner."

"Ah, the owner! You're the owner?" the man called Teymour interrupted with a short laugh. "The foreigner, the husband of the Bakravan woman? Yo—" The automatic cocked as Lochart readied a lunge at him. "Don't! I can shoot quickly and very accurately. Search him," he told the other man who was on his feet instantly. Expertly this man ran his hands over him, pulled the flight bag out of his hands, and looked through it.

"No guns. Flight manuals, compass—you're the pilot Lochart?"

"Yes," Lochart said, his heart pumping.

"Sit down over there! Now!"

Lochart sat in the chair, far away from the fire. The man put the gun on the carpet beside him and took out a paper. "Give it to him." The other man did as he was told. The paper was in Farsi. They all watched him carefully. It took Lochart a little time to decipher the writing: "Confiscation Order. For crimes against the Islamic State, all property of Jared Bakravan is confiscated except his family house and his shop in the bazaar." It was signed on behalf of a komiteh by a name he could not read and dated two days ago.

"This's—this's ridiculous," Lochart began helplessly. "His—His Excellency Bakravan was a huge supporter of the Ayatollah Khomeini. Huge. There must be some mistake!"

"There isn't. He was jailed, found guilty of usury, and shot."

Lochart gaped at him. "There . . . there's got to be a mistake!"

"There's none, Agha. None," Teymour said, his voice not unkind, watching Lochart carefully, seeing the danger in him. "We know you're Canadian, a pilot, that you've been away, that you're married to one of the traitor's daughters and not responsible for his crimes, or hers if she's committed any." His hand went to the gun, seeing Lochart flush. "I said 'if,' Agha, control your anger." He waited and did not pick up the dull, well-kept Luger, though completely ready. "We're not untrained rabble, we're Freedom Fighters, professionals, and we've been given these quarters to guard for VIPs who arrive later. We know you're not a hostile, so be calm. Of course this must be a shock to you—we understand, of course we understand, but we have the right to take what is ours."

"Right? What right do y—"

"Right of conquest, Agha—has it ever been different? You British should know that more than any." His voice stayed level. The women watched with cold, hard eyes. "Calm yourself. None of your possessions have been touched. Yet." He waved his hand. "See for yourself."

"Where is my wife?"

"I don't know, Agha. There was no one here when we arrived. We arrived this morning."

Lochart was nearly demented with worry. If her father's been found guilty, will the family suffer? Everyone? Wait a minute! Everything confiscated ". . . except his family house," wasn't that what the paper said? She's got to be there . . . Christ, that's miles away and I've no car . . .

He was trying to get his mind working. "You said, you said nothing's been touched—'yet.' You mean it will be touched soon?"

"A wise man protects his own possessions. It would be wise to take your possessions to a safe place. Everything of Bakravan stays here, but your possessions?" He shrugged. "Of course you may take them, we're not thieves."

"And my wife's possessions?"

"Hers too. Of course. Personal things. I told you we aren't thieves."

"How—how long do I have?"

"Until 5:00 P.M. tomorrow."

"That's not enough time. Perhaps the day after?"

"Until 5:00 P.M. tomorrow. Would you like some food?"

"No, no, thank you."

"Then good-bye, Agha, but first please give me your keys."

Lochart flushed in spite of his resolve. He took them out and the other man who was nearby accepted them. "You said VIPs. What VIPs?"

"VIPs, Agha. This place belonged to an enemy of the state; now it is the property of the state for whomever it chooses. Sorry, but of course you understand."

Lochart looked at him, then at the other man and back again. His weariness weighed him down. And his helplessness. "I, er, before I leave I want to change and—and shave. Okay?"

After a pause Teymour said, "Yes. Hassan, go with him."

Lochart walked out, hating him and them and everything that was happening, the man Hassan following him. Along the corridor and into his own room. Nothing had been touched though all the cupboards were open, and the drawers, and there was a smell of tobacco smoke but no sign of a hasty departure or of violence. The bed had been used. Get yourself together and make a plan. I can't. All right, then shave and shower and change and go to Mac, he's not far away, and you can walk there and he'll help you, he'll lend you money and a car and you'll find her at her family house—and don't think of Jared, just don't.

NEAR THE UNIVERSITY: 8:10 P.M. Rakoczy moved the oil lamp nearer to the bundle of papers, diaries, files, and documents he had stolen from the upstairs safe in the U.S. embassy, continuing to sort them out. He was alone in a small tenement room—one of a warren of similar rooms, mostly for students, that had been rented for him by Farmad, the student Tudeh leader who had been killed the night of the riot. The room was dingy, without heat, just a bed and rickety table and chair and one tiny window. The panes were cracked and half covered with cardboard.

He laughed out loud. So much achieved and at so little cost. Such good planning. Our covering riot perfectly staged outside the embassy gates—then sudden firing from the opposite rooftops, creating panic, quickly breaking down the gates and rushing the compound—our only opposition marines armed with shotguns and even then ordered not to fire—just enough time before Khomeini supporters could arrive to subdue the riot, kill us, or capture us. Covered by the pandemonium, rushing around the back of the building, smashing the side door, then up the back stairs alone while my cadre outside created more diversions, firing into the air, shouting, careful not to kill anyone but lots of noise and screaming. One landing and then the next, then running along the corridor shouting at the Americans, two frightened old women and a young man, "Get on the floor, lie down, or you'll all be killed!"

Frantically they obeyed and all the others—I don't blame them, the attack so sudden and they unprepared, unarmed, and carefully panicked. Into the bedroom. Empty but for a paralyzed Iranian servant, arms over his head, half under the bed. Blowing the safe quickly, everything into the carryall, then out again and down the stairs three at a time, then away into the milling crowds, Ibrahim Kyabi and the others covering me, retreating perfectly, every objective achieved.

Source's got to be impressed, he thought again, my promotion to major's got to be assured, and Father'll be so proud of me. "By God and the Prophet of God," he said involuntarily as another surge of ecstasy swept him—not noticing what he had said. "I've never felt so fulfilled."

Happily he went back to his work. So far the safe had revealed no treasures, but lots of documents about CIA involvement in Iran, some private ambassador rubber stamps, one cipher book that could be special, private accounts, some jewelry of little value, a few ancient coins. Never mind, he thought. There's lots to go through yet, diaries and personal papers.

Time passed for him easily. Soon Ibrahim Kyabi would be here to discuss the Women's March. He wanted to know how to disrupt it to further Tudeh objectives and to damage Khomeini and Shi'ism. Khomeini's the real danger, he thought, the only danger. That strange old man, him and his granite inflexibility. The quicker he's brought before the No God the better.

A current of freezing air came through the broken panes. It did not disturb him. He was warm for he wore his heavy leather jacket and sweater and shirt and underwear and good socks and strong shoes: "Always have good socks and shoes in case you've got to run," his teachers had said. "Always be prepared to run. . . ."

He remembered, amused, running away from Erikki Yokkonen, leading him into the maze and losing him near the Deathhouse of the Lepers. I'm sure I'm going to have to kill him one day, he thought. And his hellcat wife. What about Azadeh? What about the daughter of the Abdollah Khan, Abdollah the Cruel who though valuable as a double agent, is becoming too arrogant, too independent, and too important for our safety? Yes, but now I'd like both husband and wife back in Tabriz, doing what we require of them. And as for me, I'd like to be on leave again, once more home again, safe again, Igor Mzytryk, captain KGB again, safe at home with Delaurah, my arms around her, in our fine bed with the finest linens from Ireland, her green eyes sparkling, skin like cream, and oh so beautiful. Only seven more weeks and our firstborn arrives. Oh, I hope it's a son. . . .

With half an ear—as always most of his hearing tuned to detect danger—he heard the muezzins calling for evening prayer. He began clearing the little table. Very soon now Ibrahim Kyabi would be here and there was no need for the young man to know what did not concern him. Everything went quickly into the carryall. He lifted the floorboard and put the carryall into the hollow beneath that also contained a loaded, spare automatic, carefully wrapped in oilcloth, and half a dozen British fragmentary grenades. A little dirt scuffed into the cracks and now no sign of a hiding place. He doused the oil lamp until the wick was just alight and pulled the curtains back. A little snow had collected on the inside of the sill. Contentedly he began to wait. Half an hour passed. Not like Kyabi to be late.

Then he heard footsteps. His automatic covered the door. The code of the knock was flawless; even so when he unlocked the door he slid into ambush in the comparative safety of the wall and swung the door open, ready to blast the hostile if it was a hostile. But it was Ibrahim Kyabi, bundled up and pleased to be here. "Sorry, Dimitri," he said, stamping his feet, a little snow in his curling black hair, "but buses are almost nonexistent."

Rakoczy relocked the door. "Punctuality's important. You wanted to know who the mullah was in the Bandar Delam helicopter when your father was murdered, poor man—I've got his name for you." He saw the youth's eyes light up and hid a smile. "His name's Hussain Kowissi and he's the mullah of Kowiss. Do you know it?"

"No, no, I've never been there. Hussain Kowissi? Good, thank you."

"I checked him out for you. He appears to be a fanatic anti-Communist, fanatic for Khomeini, but in reality, he's secretly CIA."

"What?"

"Yes," Rakoczy said, the disinformation perfectly justified. "He spent a number of years in the U.S., sent there by the Shah, speaks fluent English, and was secretly turned by them when he was a student. His anti-American-ism's as false as his fanaticism."

"How d'you do it, Dimitri? How do you know so much so fast—without phones, or telex, or anything?"

"You forget every bus contains some of our people, every taxi, truck, village, post office. Don't forget," he added, believing it, "don't forget the Masses are on our side. We are the Masses."

"Yes."

He saw the young man's zeal and he knew Ibrahim was the correct instru-ment, and ready. "The mullah Hussain ordered the Green Bands to shoot your father, accusing him of being a plant and dupe of foreigners."

All color left Kyabi's face. "Then—then I want him. He's mine."

"He should be left to professionals. I'll arrange a t—"

"No. Please. I must have revenge."

Rakoczy pretended to think about that, hiding his content. Hussain

Kowissi had been marked for extinction for some time. "In a few days I'll arrange weapons, a car, and a team to go with you."

"Thank you. But all I need will be this." Kyabi pulled out a pocket knife, his fingers shaking. "This, and an hour or two, and some barbed wire and I'll show him the extent of a son's revenge."

"Good. Now the Women's March. It's definitely scheduled in three days. Wh—" He stopped aghast, abruptly leaped for the side wall, pulled a half-seen knot. A section of the wall swung open to give access to the unlit rickety fire-exit staircase. "Come on," he ordered and raced down it to freedom, Kyabi blindly following in a panic run. At that moment without warning the door burst open, almost torn off its hinges, and the two men who had shouldered it open almost fell into the room, others on their heels. All were Iranian, all wore Green Bands, and they charged in pursuit, guns out.

Down the stairs three at a time, hunted and hunters, stumbling and almost falling, scrambling up and rushing out into the street and the night, into the crowds and then Rakoczy went straight into the ambush and into their arms. Ibrahim Kyabi did not hesitate, just changed direction and fled across the street and into the crowded alley and was swallowed up in the darkness.

In an old parked car across the street from the side exit, Robert Armstrong had seen their men go in and Rakoczy caught and Kyabi escape. Rakoczy had been quickly bundled into a waiting van before many people in the street knew what was happening. Two of the Green Bands strode over toward Armstrong, both better dressed than usual. Both had holsters on their belts for their Mausers. People moved out of their way uneasily, watching without watching, wanting no trouble. The two men got into the car and Armstrong let out the clutch and eased away, the remaining Green Bands mixing with the pedestrians.

In moments Robert Armstrong was part of the rush-hour traffic. The two men slid off their green armbands and pocketed them. "Sorry we lost that young bastard, Robert," the older of the two said in fluent English, American-accented. He was a clean-shaven man in his fifties—Colonel Hashemi Fazir, deputy chief of Inner Intelligence, U.S. trained and SAVAK before the separate secret service department was formed.

"Not to worry, Hashemi," Armstrong said.

The younger man in the backseat said, "We've got Kyabi on film at the embassy riot, Agha. And at the university." He was in his twenties, with a luxuriant mustache and his lips twisted cruelly. "We'll pick him up tomorrow."

"Now that he's on the run, I wouldn't if I were you, Lieutenant," Armstrong said, driving carefully. "Since he's pegged, just tail him—he'll lead you to bigger fish. He led you to Dimitri Yazernov."

The others laughed. "Yes, yes, he did."

"And Yazernov'll lead us to all sorts of interesting people and places." Hashemi lit a cigarette, offered them. "Robert?"

"Thanks." Armstrong took a puff and grimaced. "My God, Hashemi, these are awful, they'll really kill you."

"As God wants." Then Hashemi quoted in Farsi, " 'Wash me in wine when I die,/At my funeral use a text concerning wine,/Would you wish to find me on the Day of Doom,/Look for me in the dust at the wineshop's door.' "

"Cigarettes, not wine'll kill you," Armstrong said dryly, the lilt of the Farsi words beautiful.

"The colonel was quoting from the *Rubáiyát of Omar Khayyám*," the young man in the back said helpfully in English. "It means th—"

"He knows what it means, Mohammed," Hashemi interrupted. "Mr. Armstrong speaks perfect Farsi—you've a lot to learn." He puffed his cigarette for a while, watching the traffic. "Pull over for a moment, will you, Robert?"

When the car stopped, Hashemi said, "Mohammed, go back to the HQ and wait for me there. Make sure no one—no one—gets at Yazernov before me. Tell the team just to make sure everything's ready. I want to start at midnight."

"Yes, Colonel." The younger man left them.

Hashemi watched him vanish into the crowds. "I could use a large whisky and soda. Drive on for a while, Robert."

"Sure." Armstrong let out the clutch, glanced at him, hearing an undercurrent. "Problem?"

"Many." Hashemi studied the traffic and the pedestrians, his face set. "I don't know how long we'll be allowed to operate, how long we're safe, or who to trust."

"What else's new?" Armstrong smiled mirthlessly. "That's an occupational hazard," he said—the lesson well learned from eleven years as adviser to Inner Intelligence, and twenty years before that in the Hong Kong police.

"You want to be present when Yazernov's interrogated, Robert?"

"Yes, if I'm not in the way."

"What does MI6 want with him?"

"I'm just an ex-CID, Special Branch, on private contract to help you fellows set up the equivalent service, remember?"

"I remember very well. Two five-year contracts, the last happily extended until next year when you retire with a pension."

"Fat chance," Armstrong said disgustedly. "Khomeini and the government'll pay my pension? Fat chance." It was very much on his mind that now all his Iranian service was wasted, and with the devaluation of the Hong Kong dollar since he retired in '66, his real retirement would be scratchy. "My pension's had it."

The dark eyes hardened. "Robert, what does MI6 want with this bastard?"

Armstrong frowned. Something was very wrong tonight. The youth Kyabi should not have escaped the net and Hashemi's as nervous as a rookie agent on his first drop behind the lines. "Far as I know they don't. I'm interested in him. Me," he said casually.

"Why?"

Such a long story, Armstrong thought. Should I tell you that Dimitri Yazernov's a cover for Fedor Rakoczy, the Russian Islamic-Marxist you've been trying to catch for months? Should I tell you the real reason I was told to help you grab him tonight is that, quite by chance, MI6's just discovered through a Czech defector his real name is Igor Mzytryk, son of Petr Oleg Mzytryk who back in my Hong Kong days used to be known as Gregor Suslev, master spy, we thought long since dead.

No, we don't want Yazernov but we do want—I want—the father who's supposed to live just north of the border somewhere, within reach, oh, God, let him be alive and within reach, for we would dearly like to debrief that sod by any means possible—ex-intelligence chief, Far East, senior lecturer in espionage at Vladivostok University, senior Party member and God knows what since.

"I think—we think—Yazernov's more important than just Tudeh liaison with students. He's a dead ringer for your Kurdish dissident, Ali bin Hassan Karakose."

"You mean he's the same man?"

"Yes."

"Impossible."

Armstrong shrugged. He had thrown him a bone; if he didn't want to gnaw it that was his problem. The traffic was snarled again, everyone hooting and cursing. The big man shut his ears to the noise, stubbed out the local Iranian cigarette.

Hashemi frowned, watching him. "What's your interest in Karakose and the Kurds—if what you say's true?"

"Kurds straddle all the borders, Soviet, Iraqi, Turkish, and Iranian," he said easily. "The whole Kurdish national movement's very sensitive and easy for the Soviets to exploit—with heavy international implications throughout Asia Minor. Of course we're interested."

The colonel stared out of the window, lost in thought, snow falling lightly. A cyclist squeezed past, carelessly banging the side of the car. To Armstrong's surprise—usually Hashemi was well tempered—he furiously wound down his window and cursed the youth and all his generations. Grimly he stubbed his cigarette out. "Drop me here, Robert. We'll begin with Yazernov at midnight. You're welcome." He started to open the door.

"Hang on, old son," Armstrong said. "We've been friends a long time. What the hell's up?"

The colonel hesitated. Then he closed the door. "SAVAK's been outlawed by the government, so have all intelligence departments, including us, and ordered disbanded at once."

"Yes, but the prime minister's office has already told you to continue, undercover. You've nothing to fear, Hashemi. You're not tainted. You've been told to smash the Tudeh, the fedayeen, and the Islamic-Marxists . . . you showed me the order. Wasn't tonight's operation following this line?"

"Yes. Yes, it was." Again Hashemi paused, his face set and his voice thick. "Yes, it was—but! What do you know about the Islamic Revolutionary Komiteh?"

"Only that it's supposed to consist of men personally selected by Khomeini," Armstrong began honestly. "Its powers are loose, we don't know the who, how many, where, or when they meet or even if Khomeini presides or what."

"I now know for a fact that, with Khomeini's approval, in future ultimate power is to be invested in this komiteh, that Bazargan is only a momentary figurehead until the komiteh issues the new Islamic Constitution which will put us back to the time of the Prophet."

"Bloody hell!" Armstrong muttered. "No elected government?"

"None." Hashemi was beside himself with rage. "Not as we know the term."

"Perhaps the Constitution'll be rejected, Hashemi. The people'll have to vote it in, not everyone's a fanatic support—"

"By God and the Prophet, don't fool yourself, Robert!" the colonel said harshly. "The vast majority are fundamentalist, that's all they've got to hang on to. Our bourgeois, rich, and middle classes are Tehranis, Tabrizis, Abadanis, Isfahanis, all Shah-sponsored, a handful compared to the other thirty-six million of us, most of whom can't even read or write. Of course whatever Khomeini approves will be voted in! And we both know what his vision of Islam, the Koran, and Sharia is."

"How soon will . . . how soon will they have the Constitution ready?"

"Do you understand so little about us, after all this time?" Hashemi said irritably. "The moment we seize power we use it before it slips away. The new Constitution went into effect the moment that poor bastard Bakhtiar was betrayed by Carter, betrayed by the generals, and forced to flee. As to Bazargan, pious, honest, fair, and democratically inclined, Khomeini-appointed, legal prime minister pending elections, the poor bastard's just a dupe for anything and everything that goes wrong between now and then."

"You mean he'll be the scapegoat—be put on trial?"

"Trial? What trial? Haven't I told you what the komiteh considers a trial? If they charge him, he's shot. Insha'Allah! Last, and why I can't think straight and I'm so angry I need to get drunk, I heard this afternoon, very privately, I heard that SAVAK's been secretly reorganized, it's going to be rechristened SAVAMA—and Abrim Pahmudi's been made director!"

"Christ Almighty!" Armstrong felt as though he'd been smashed in the stomach. Abrim Pahmudi was one of three lifelong friends of the Shah who had been to school with him in Iran and later in Switzerland, who had risen to become high in the Imperial council, SAVAK, and, it was rumored, after the Shah's family, his most-sought-after counselor—and who right now was supposed to be in hiding, waiting an opportunity to negotiate with the Bazargan government on the Shah's behalf a constitutional monarchy and the Shah's abdication in favor of his son Reza. "Christ Almighty! That explains a lot."

"Yes," Hashemi said bitterly. "For years that bastard's been part of almost every crucial military or political meeting, every head of state conference, every secret agreement, and in the last days part of every important meeting with the U.S. ambassador, U.S. generals, every important decision of the Shah, of our generals, and present every time a coup d'état was discussed—and turned down." He was so angry that tears ran down his cheeks, "We're all betrayed. The Shah, the revolution, the people, you, me, everyone! How many times have we reported to him over the years together, and me dozens of other times? With lists, names, bank accounts, liaisons, secrets that only we could find out and know. Everything—everything in writing but one copy only—wasn't that the rule? We're all betrayed."

Armstrong felt chilled. Of course Pahmudi knew all about his involvement with Inner Intelligence. Pahmudi had to know everything of value about George Talbot, about Masterson, his CIA opposite number, Lavenov, his Soviet opposite number, all our short and long contingency planning, invasion planning, operations to neutralize the CIA's top secret radar sites with men like young Captain Ross.

"Bloody hell," he muttered, at the same time furious that their own sources had not forewarned them. Pahmudi, suave, intelligent, trilingual, and discreet. Never once over the years had there been the slightest suspicion against him. Never. How could he have escaped cleanly, even from the Shah who was constantly having his top associates checked and double-checked and rechecked. With every right, he thought. Five assassination attempts against him, bullets in his body and face, wasn't he ruler of a people known for violence toward and from their rulers?

Christ! Where will it all end?

IN THE SAME TRAFFIC: 9:15 A.M.   McIver was inching along, well to the south, heading for the bazaar area where Jared Bakravan's family house was, Tom Lochart beside him.

"It'll all work out," McIver said, sick with worry.

"Sure, Mac. No sweat."

"Yes, not to worry." When McIver had got back home to his apartment from Ali Kia and the Ministry, elated, Tom Lochart was there, arrived just moments before. His even greater joy at finding Tom Lochart safe was dashed at once by the look of him and by the news Pettikin gave him about Freddy Ayre's relayed radio call from Scot Gavallan at Zagros, and about Starke being taken by the Kowiss komiteh for questioning about "the Isfahan escape."

"It's all my goddamn fault, Mac, all of it," Tom Lochart had said.

"No, not your fault, Tom. We were both trapped—anyway I okayed the flight, not that it helped Valik. Were they all aboard; how the hell did you get out? Tell us what happened, then I'll call Freddy—you'd like a drink?"

"No, no, thanks. Listen, Mac, I've got to find Sharazad. She wasn't home, I'm hoping she's at her folks' house and I've got t—"

"She's there, I know she's there, Tom. Erikki told me just before he left this morning for Tabriz. Did you hear about her father?"

"Yes, I have, awful, bloody awful! You're sure she's there?"

"Yes." McIver walked heavily over to the sideboard and fixed himself a drink as he continued: "She hasn't been at your flat since you left and she was fine until . . . Erikki and Azadeh saw her day before yesterday. Yesterday they . . ."

"Did Erikki say how she was?"

"He said she was as well as could be expected—you know how close Iranian families are. We don't know anything about her dad other than what Erikki told us—that he had been ordered to the jail as a witness, and the next thing the family was told to pick up his body, he'd been shot for 'crimes against Islam.' Erikki said they picked up the, er, the body and, well, yesterday they were in mourning. Sorry, but there you are." He took a deep swallow of the lovely, peat-tasting drink and felt a little better. "She's safe at home—first tell us what happened to you, then I'll call Freddy and we'll go and find Sharazad."

Quickly Lochart did so. They listened, appalled. "When Rudi told me that this Iranian Air Force officer, Abbasi, was the one who shot down HBC I almost went mad. I, I kinda collapsed and the next thing I remember was the next day. Abbasi and the others had gone by then and it was all SOP. Mac, Charlie's idea about a 'hijack'—that's not going to stand up—no way!"

"We know that, Tom," McIver had said. "First finish your story."

"I couldn't get a clearance to fly back so I borrowed a car, just got back a couple of hours ago and went straight to the apartment. The bastard of it is it's been confiscated by Green Bands, along with all Mr. Bakravan's property, except the shop in the bazaar and his family home."

Lochart told them what had happened, adding, "I'm—I'm a waif in the storm. I've nothing now, we've nothing, Sharazad and I." He laughed and it was a bad laugh and McIver could see that he was dying inside. "It's true it was Jared's building, the apartment and everything in it, though . . . though part of Sharazad's, er, dowry. . . . Let's go, huh, Mac?"

"First let me call Freddy. Th—"

"Oh, of course, sure, sorry. I'm so worried I can't think straight."

McIver finished his drink and went to the HF. He stared at it. "Tom," he said sadly, "what do you want to do about Zagros?"

Tom Lochart hesitated. "I could take Sharazad there with me."

"Too dangerous, laddie. Sorry, but there it is." McIver saw Lochart look into himself and measure himself, and sighed, feeling very old.

"If Sharazad's okay I'll go back with Jean-Luc tomorrow morning and we'll sort out Zagros, and she goes on the next shuttle to Al Shargaz," Lochart said. "Depending on what we find at Zagros . . . if we have to close down, Insha'Allah, we'll ferry all our riggers to Shiraz to go out by regular flights— their company'll tell them where they're to go—and we'll move everything to Kowiss, airplanes, spares, and personnel. Okay?"

"Yes. Meanwhile I'll get on to the Ministry first thing tomorrow and see if I can straighten it out." McIver clicked on the sender. "Kowiss, this is HQ. Do you read?"

Almost instantly: "HQ this is Kowiss, Captain Ayre, go ahead please, Captain McIver."

"First, about Zagros Three: Tell Captain Gavallan that Captains Lochart and Sessonne will be back tomorrow around noon with instructions. Meanwhile prepare plans to obey the komiteh." Rotten bloody sods, he thought, then went on for the benefit of those who were listening in: "The Zagros IranOil base manager should remind the komiteh that the Ayatollah and the government have specifically ordered oil production back to normal. Closing down Zagros will severely interfere with orderly production in that area. Inform Captain Gavallan I will take this up at once with Minister Kia personally who, an hour ago, confirmed this to me, and gave me written approvals to take out and replace crew by our own 125 until . . ."

"Christ, Mac, that's great news," came over the airwaves involuntarily.

"Yes . . . by our own 125 until regular service resumes. Crew replacements and replacement aircraft to service all the extra work and Guerney contracts the government are asking us to service, so I cannot understand the actions of the local komiteh. Got it, Captain Ayre?"

"Yessir. Message received five by five."

"Has Captain Starke returned yet?"

A long silence, then: "Negative, HQ."

McIver's voice became even colder. "Call me at once when he does. Captain Ayre, just between you and me and to go no further: if he has any problems whatsoever and isn't safe back at base by dawn, I will ground all our aircraft throughout Iran, close down all our operations, and order 100 percent of all our personnel out of Iran."

"Good, Mac," Pettikin said softly.

McIver was too concentrated to hear him. "Did you get that, Kowiss?"

Silence, then: "Affirmative."

"As far as you're concerned," McIver added, developing his sudden thought, "inform Major Changiz and Hotshot from me, I'm ordering you right now to cease all operations including all CASEVACs until Starke's back on the base. Got that?"

Silence, then: "Affirmative. The message will be relayed at once."

"Good. But only the information that applies to your base. The rest's private until dawn." He smiled grimly, then added, "I'll be making an inspection trip as soon as the 125 returns so make sure all manifests are up to date. Anything else?"

"No, sir. Not for the present. We'll look forward to seeing you and we'll listen out as usual."

"HQ over and out."

Pettikin said, "That should do it, Mac, that'll put a hornet up their arses."

"Maybe, maybe not. We can't stop CASEVACs—apart from humanitarian reasons that makes us illegal and they can steal everything." McIver finished his drink, glanced at his watch. "Come on, Tom, we won't wait for Jean-Luc, let's go and find Sharazad."

The traffic had lessened a little now but was still inching along, snow griming the windshield. The road was slippery and banked with dirty snow.

"Turn right at the next corner," Lochart said.

"Okay, Tom." They drove in silence again. McIver turned the corner. "Tom, did you sign for the fuel at Isfahan?"

"No, no, I didn't."

"Anyone interview you, ask for your name, that sort of thing? Green Bands? Anyone?"

Lochart pulled his mind off Sharazad. "No, not that I remember. I was just 'Captain' and part of the scenery. Far as I remember I wasn't introduced to anyone. Valik and . . . and Annoush and the kids, they went off for lunch as soon as we landed with the other general—Christ, I can't even remember his name—ah, yes, Seladi, that was it. Everyone called me 'Captain'—I was just a piece of the scenery. Matter of fact I stayed with the chopper at the hangar all the time we were there, watching the refueling and checking her out—they even brought me some food on a tray and I ate sitting in the cabin. I stayed there all the time until those goddamn Green Bands fell on me and dragged me off and locked me in the room. I had no warning, Mac. They just enveloped the base, they must've been helped lavishly from inside, had to be. The bastards that grabbed me were all hopped up, shouting I was CIA, American—they kept on about that, but they were more concerned about subduing the base than about me. Take the left fork, Mac. It's not far now."

McIver drove on uneasily, the area very run down and passersby glaring at them. "Maybe we could get away with it—pretend HBC was hijacked from Doshan Tappeh by someone unknown. Maybe they won't follow it up from Isfahan."

"Then why did they grab Duke Starke?"

"Routine." McIver sighed heavily. "I know it's a long shot but it might work. Maybe the 'American CIA' will stick and that's all. Grow a mustache, or beard, just in case."

Lochart shook his head. "That's no help. I'm on the first clearance. We both are . . . that's the kicker."

"When you took off from Doshan Tappeh, who saw you off?"

Lochart thought a moment. "No one. I think it was Nogger who supervised the fueling the day before. Th—"

"That's right, I remember now, he was bitching, said I was giving him too much work with young Paula in town. Were there any Iranian staff, guards there? Did you pay anyone baksheesh?"

"No, there was no one. But they could have me on their automatic recorders . . ." Lochart peered out of the side window. His excitement picked up and he pointed. "There's the turning, not far now."

McIver steered into the narrow street, just room for two cars to pass. Snow banked the sides up to the high walls—doors and doorways either side. McIver had never been here before and was surprised that Bakravan, so rich, would live in an area so clearly poor. Was rich, he reminded himself with an involuntary shiver, and now very dead for "crimes against the state"—and what constitutes a crime against the state? Again he shivered.

"There's the door, there on the left."

They stopped beside the snowbank heavy with refuse. The nondescript doorway was cut into the high, mildewed wall. The door was iron-banded, the iron rusty. "Come on in, Mac."

"I'll wait for a moment, then if all's well I'll leave. I'm pooped." There's only one solution, McIver thought, and he reached out and stopped Lochart. "Tom, we've permission to fly out three 212s. You take one. Tomorrow. The hell with Zagros, Jean-Luc can cope with that. I don't know about Sharazad, if they'll let her go or not, but you'd better get out, fast as you can. It's the only thing to do, get out while you can. We'll put her on the next 125 flight."

"And you, what about you, Mac?"

"Me? Nothing to worry about. You get out—if they'll let her go, take her too. Jean-Luc can handle Zagros—looks like we'll have to close down there anyway. All right?"

Lochart looked at him. "Let me think about that one, Mac. But thanks." He got out. "I'll be by just after dawn—don't let Jean-Luc go without me. We can decide then, okay?"

"Yes." McIver watched his friend use the old-fashioned knocker. The sound was loud. Both men waited, Lochart nauseous with anxiety, preparing for the family surrounding him, the tears and the welcome and the questions, having to be polite when all he wanted was to take her off to their own rooms and hold her and feel safe and all the nightmare gone. Waiting in front of the door. Then knocking again, louder. Waiting. McIver switching off to save gasoline, the silence making the waiting worse. Snowflakes on the windshield building up. People passing like wraiths, everyone suspicious and hostile.

Muffled footsteps approached and the grilled peephole opened a fraction. The eyes that peered at Lochart were cold and hard and he did not recognize the little part of the face he could see.

"It's me, Excellency Lochart," he began in Farsi, trying to sound normal. "My wife, the Lady Sharazad is here."

The eyes peered closer to see if he was alone or accompanied, examining the car behind him and McIver in the driving seat. "Please wait, Agha."

The peephole closed. Again waiting, stamping his feet against the cold, waiting, then impatiently using the knocker again, wanting to smash the door down, knowing he couldn't. More footsteps. The peephole opened again. Different eyes and face. "What's your name, Agha?"

Lochart wanted to shriek at the man but he did not. "My name is Agha Pilot Thomas Lochart, husband of Sharazad. Open the door. It is cold and I'm tired and I have come for my wife."

Silently the peephole closed. A moment of agonized waiting, then to his relief he heard the bolts being pulled back. The door swung open. The servant held an oil lamp on high. Beyond him was the high-walled courtyard, an exquisite fountain in the center, trees and plants winter-protected. On the far side was another door, iron-studded. This door was open and he saw her silhouetted against the lamplight; he rushed forward and she was in his arms, weeping and moaning.

The door on the street slammed closed and the bolts shoved home. "Wait!" Lochart called out to the servant, remembering McIver. Then he heard the car start up and drive off.

"What is it, Agha?" the servant asked.

"Nothing," he said and helped Sharazad into the house and into the warmth. When he saw her in the light, his happiness vanished and his stomach filled with ice. Her face was puffy and dirty, her hair limp and dirty, eyes sightless, her clothes were crumpled.

"Jesus Christ . . ." he muttered but she paid no attention, just clung to him demented, moaning a mixture of Farsi and English, tears running down her cheeks. "Sharazad, it's all right, all right now . . ." he said, trying to gentle her. But she just continued with her monotonous gibberish.

"Sharazad, Sharazad, my darling. I'm back now . . . it's all right . . ." He stopped. It was almost as though he hadn't said anything and, suddenly, he was petrified that her mind had gone. He started to shake her gently but that had no effect either. Then he noticed the old servant standing by the staircase, waiting for orders. "Where's—where's Her Highness Bakravan?" he asked, Sharazad's arms tight around his neck.

"She's in her rooms, Agha."

"Please tell her I'm here and . . . and that I'd like to see her."

"Oh, she'll see no one now, Agha. No one. As God wants. She hasn't seen anyone since the day." Tears glistened in the old eyes. "Your Excellency has been away, perhaps you won't know that His Ex—"

"I heard. Yes, I heard."

"Insha'Allah, Agha, Insha'Allah, but what crimes could the Master commit? Insha'Allah that he should be chosen, Insh—"

"Insha'Allah. Please tell Her Highness . . . Sharazad, stop it! Come on, darling," he said in English, her moans maddening him, "stop it!" Then in Farsi to the servant, "Please ask Her Highness to see me."

"Oh, yes, I'll ask her, Agha, but Her Highness won't open the door nor answer me nor see you but I'll go at once and do your bidding." He began to leave.

"Wait, where is everyone?"

"Who, Agha?"

"The family? Where's the rest of the family?"

"Ah, the family. Her Highness is in her rooms, the Lady Sharazad is here."

Again Lochart felt his rage scourged by her moaning. "I mean where's Excellency Meshang and his wife and children and my sisters-in-law and their husbands?"

"Where else would they be but in their homes, Agha?"

"Then tell Excellency Meshang I'm here," he said. Meshang, the eldest son, and his family were the only ones semipermanently in residence here.

"Certainly, Agha. As God wants, I'll go to the bazaar myself."

"He's at the bazaar?"

The old man nodded. "Of course, Agha, tonight he is, he and his family. Now he is the Master and has to run the business. As God wants, Agha, he is head of the house of Bakravan now. I'll go at once."

"No, send someone else." The bazaar was close by and it would be no imposition. "Is there anyone . . . Sharazad, Sharazad, stop it!" he said roughly, but she did not seem to have heard him. "Is there hot water in the house?"

"There should be, Agha. The furnace is very good but it's not on."

"You've no fuel?"

"Oh, there should be fuel, Agha. Would you like me to make sure?"

"Yes, put the furnace on and bring us some food, and tea."

"Certainly, Agha. What is it His Excellency's pleasure to have?"

Lochart held on to his sanity with difficulty, her whimperings setting him even more on edge. "Anything—no, rice and horisht, chicken horisht," he said, correcting himself, naming a common and easy dish. "Chicken horisht."

"If you wish it, Agha, but the cook prides himself on his chicken horisht and it will take him hours to make it to your satisfaction." Politely the old man waited, eyes going from Lochart to the girl and back again.

"Then . . . then, oh, for the love of God, just fruit. Fruit and tea, whatever fruit you have . . ." Lochart could stand it no longer and he lifted Sharazad into his arms and went up the staircase and along the corridors to the rooms they usually used in this three-story, flat-roofed house that was palatial, rich, and meandering. He opened the door and kicked it closed.

"Sharazad, listen to me . . . Sharazad, listen! For Christsake listen!"

But she just leaned against him, gibbering and moaning. He carried her into the stuffy inner room, windows tight shut and shutters closed, and forced her to sit on the unmade bed, then rushed into the bathroom that was modern—most of the plumbing modern—except the toilet.

No hot water. The cold water ran and it did not seem too brackish. He found some towels and soaked one and went back again, his chest hurting, knowing he was out of his depth. She had not moved. He tried to wash her face but she resisted and began to blubber, making herself even more ugly. Saliva seeped out of the sides of her mouth.

"Sharazad . . . Sharazad, my darling, for the love of God, my darling . . ." He lifted her and held her closer but nothing touched her. Only the moans remained constant, pushing him nearer and nearer his limit. "Get hold of yourself," he said helplessly out loud, and got up, but her hands caught his clothes and tried to drag him back.

"Oh, God give me strength . . ." He saw his hand smash her across the face. For a moment the moaning stopped, she stared at him incredulously, then her eyes went blank again, the gibberish started once more, and she clawed at his clothes. "God help me," he said brokenly, then began to smack her face, harder and harder, open-handed, desperately trying to be hard but not too hard and then he shoved her face downward on the bed and belted her hard on the buttocks, hit her till his palm ached and hand ached and all at once he heard screams that were real screams and not gibberish: "Tommyyyy . . . stop oh please Tommy please stopppppp . . . Tommy, you're hurting me what have I done? I swear I've not thought about anyone oh God Tommy please stopppp . . ."

He stopped. Sweat was in his eyes, his clothes wringing, and he stumbled panting off the bed. She was writhing in pain, her buttocks scarlet and face scarlet, but her tears were real tears now and her eyes her own now and her brain her own.

"Oh, Tommyyyyyy, you hurt me, you hurt me," she sobbed as a whipped child would sob. "Whyyyyy? Whyyyy? I swear I love you . . . I've never done anything . . . anything to . . . to hurt you and make you . . . make you hurt me . . ." Racked with pain and shame that she had enraged him, not understanding why but only that she must help him out of his rage, she crawled off the bed and fell at his feet, begging his forgiveness through her tears.

Her tears stopped as her mind flooded with reality and she looked up at him. "Oh, Tommy," she said brokenly, "Father's dead . . . murdered . . . murdered by Green Bands . . . murdered . . ."

"Yes . . . yes, my darling, I know, oh, I know . . . I'm so sorry . . ."

He lifted her up and his tears mixed with hers and he held her tight and gave her of his strength and made her whole as she gave him of her strength and made him whole. Then they slept fitfully—waking sometimes, but sleeping again peacefully, gathering life, the flame of the oil lamp casting kind shadows. Just before midnight he awoke. Her eyes were watching him. Tentatively she moved to kiss him but a shaft of pain stopped her.

"Oh, you all right?" His arms at once around her.

"Oh, be careful . . . sorry, yes . . . it's . . ." Painfully she tried to look at her back, then found she was in soiled clothes. She grimaced. "Ugh, these clothes, please excuse me, my darling . . ." She stood awkwardly and tore them off. Painfully she picked up the damp towel and cleaned her face and brushed her hair. Then, when she went closer to the light, he saw that one of her eyes was already slightly black and her buttocks badly bruised. "Please forgive me . . . what did I . . . I do to offend you?"

"Nothing, nothing," he said appalled, and told her how he had found her.

She stared at him blankly. "But . . . you say that I . . . I don't remember any of that only . . . only being . . . only being beaten."

"I'm so sorry but it was the only way I could . . . I'm so sorry."

"Oh, I'm not, not now, my darling." Trying to recollect she came back and carefully lay on the bed on her stomach. "But for you . . . As God wants but if I was as you say . . . strange, and I remember nothing, nothing from the time I . . ." Her voice broke a little, then she continued, trying to be firm, "But for you, perhaps I would have been mad forever." She squirmed closer and kissed him. "I love you, Beloved," she said in Farsi.

"I love you, Beloved," he told her, possessed.

After a moment she said in a strange voice, "Tommy, I think what sent me mad . . . I saw Father . . . saw him yesterday, the day before . . . I can't remember . . . was that he looked so small dead, so tiny, dead, with all those holes in him, in his face and head—I never remembered him so small but they had made him small, they'd taken away his . . ."

"Don't," he said, gently, seeing the tears brimming. "It's Insha'Allah. Don't think about it."

"Certainly, husband, if you say so," she said at once, formally, in Farsi. "Of course it's as God wants, yes, but it's important for me to tell you, to remove the shame from me, you finding me like this . . . I would like to tell you one day."

"Then tell me now, Sharazad, and we can put it behind us forever," he told her, equally formally. "Please tell me now."

"It was that they had made the biggest man in the world—after you—had made him insignificant. For no reason. He was always against the Shah when he could be and a great supporter of this mullah Khomeini." She said it calmly and he heard the word "mullah" and not Ayatollah or Imam or far-mandeh and a warning rushed through him. "They murdered my father for no reason without trial and outside the law and made him small, they took away everything that he had as a man, a father, as a beloved father. As God wants, I should say and I will try. But I cannot believe it is what God wants. It may be what Khomeini wants. I don't know. We women will soon find out."

"What? What do you mean?"

"In three days we women march in protest—all the women of Tehran."

"Against what?"

"Against Khomeini and mullahs who are against women's rights—when he sees us marching without chador he will not do what is wrong."

Lochart was half listening, remembering her a few days ago—was it only a few days ago that all this nightmare began?—Sharazad so content with herself and wearing chador, so happy to be just wife and not a modern like Azadeh. He saw her eyes and read her resolve and knew that she had committed herself. "I don't want you to take part in this protest."

"Yes, of course, husband, but every woman in Tehran will march and I am sure you would not wish me shamed before the memory of my father—against the representatives of his murderers, would you?"

"It's a waste of time," Lochart said, knowing he was going to lose but impelled onward. "I'm afraid, my love, a protest march of every woman in Iran or all Islam will not touch Khomeini a little bit. Women in his Islamic state will have nothing not granted in the Koran, nothing. Nor will anyone else. He's inflexible—isn't that his strength?"

"Of course you are right—but we will march in protest and then God will open his eyes and make all clear to him. It's as God wants, not as Khomeini wants—in Iran we have historic ways of dealing with such men."

His arms were around her. Marching is not the answer, he thought. Oh, Sharazad, there's so much to decide, to say, to tell, now not the time. But there's Zagros and a 212 to ferry out. But that leaves Mac alone to carry the ball, if there's a ball to carry. What if I took him too? I couldn't, unless by force. "Sharazad, I might have a ferry to do. To take a 212 to Nigeria. Would you come too?"

"Of course, Tommy. How long would we be gone?"

He hesitated. "A few weeks—perhaps longer." He felt her change in his arms, imperceptibly.

"When would you want to leave?"

"Very soon. Perhaps tomorrow."

She moved out of his embrace without moving. "I wouldn't be able to leave Mother, not for a while. She's . . . she's torn apart with grief, Tommy, and . . . and if I went I'd be afraid for her. And then there's poor Meshang—he has to run the business, he has to be helped—there's so much to do and to look after."

"Do you know about the confiscation order?"

"What order?"

He told her. Tears filled her eyes again and she sat up, her pain for the moment forgotten. She stared at the oil flame and at the shadows it cast. "Then we've no home, nothing. As God wants," she said dully. Then almost at once in a different voice, "No, not as God wants! As Green Bands want. Now we have to join together to save the family, otherwise they will have beaten Father—we cannot allow them to murder him and then beat him as well, that would be terrible."

"Yes, I agree, but this ferry'd solve our problems for a few weeks . . ."

"You're right, Tommy, as always, yes, yes, it would if we needed to leave but this is our home just as much if not more, oh, how happy we'll be here! In the morning I will get servants and bring everything of ours from the apartment—pah! what are a few carpets and trinkets when we have this house and ourselves. I will arrange everything—oh, we will be happy here."

"But if y—"

"This theft makes it even more important for us to be here, to resist, to protest—it makes the march, oh, so much more important." She put a finger on his lips as she saw him start to speak. "If you must do this ferry—and of course you must do your work—then go, my darling, but hurry back quickly. In a few weeks Tehran will be normal and kind again and I know that is what God wants."

Oh, yes, she thought confidently, her happiness overcoming the pain, by then it will be my second month and Tommy will be so proud of me and meanwhile it will be wonderful to live here, surrounded by family, Father avenged, the house filled with laughter again. "Everyone will help us," she said, lying back in his arms, so tired but so happy. "Oh, Tommy, I'm so glad you're home, we're home, it will be so wonderful, Tommy." Her words became slower as waves of sleep washed over her. "We'll all help Meshang . . . and those abroad will come back, Aunt Annoush and the children . . . they'll help . . . and Uncle Valik will guide Meshang . . ."

Lochart did not have the heart to tell her.

SUNDAY
February 18

AT THE KHAN'S PALACE, TABRIZ: 3:13 A.M. In the darkness of the small room Captain Ross opened the leather cover of his watch and peered at the luminous figures. "All set, Gueng?" he whispered in Gurkhali.

"Yes, sahib," Gueng whispered, glad that the waiting was over.

Carefully and quietly both men got off their pallets that lay on old, smelly carpets on the hard-packed, earthen floor. They were fully dressed, and Ross picked his way across to the window and peered out. Their guard was slumped down beside the door, fast asleep, his rifle in his lap. Two hundred yards away beyond the snow-covered orchards and outbuildings was the four-story palace of the Gorgon Khan. The night was dark and cold with some clouds, a nimbus around the moon that came through brightly from time to time.

More snow, he thought, then eased the door open. Both men stood there, searching the darkness with all their senses. No lights anywhere. Noiselessly

Ross moved over to the guard and shook him but the man did not wake from the drugged sleep that was good for at least two hours. It had been easy to give him the drug in a piece of chocolate, kept for just that purpose in their survival kit—some of the chocolate drugged, some poisoned. Once more he concentrated on the night, waiting patiently for the moon to go behind a cloud. Absently he scratched at the bite of a bedbug. He was armed with his kookri, and one grenade. "If we're stopped, Gueng, we're only going for a stroll," he had told him earlier. "Better to leave our weapons here. Why have kookris and one grenade? It's an old Gurkha custom—an offense against our regiment to be unarmed."

"I think I would like to take all our weapons now and slip back into the mountains and make our way south, sahib."

"If this doesn't work, we'll have to but it's a rotten gamble," Ross had said. "It's a rotten gamble. We'll be trapped in the open—those hunters're still searching and they won't give up till we're caught. Don't forget we only just made it to the safe house. It was only the clothes that saved us." After the ambush where Vien Rosemont and Tenzing had been killed, he and Gueng had stripped some of their attackers and put tribesmen's robes over their uniforms. He had considered dumping their uniforms entirely but thought that unwise. "If we're caught we're caught and that's the end of it."

Gueng had grinned. "Therefore better you become a good Hindu now. Then if we get killed, it's not an end but a beginning."

"How do I do that, Gueng? Become a Hindu?" He smiled wryly, remembering the perplexed look on Gueng's face and the vast shrug. Then they had tidied the bodies of Vien Rosemont and Tenzing and left them together in the snow according to the custom of the High Lands: "This body has no more value to the spirit, and because of the immutability of rebirth, it is bequeathed to the animals and to the birds that are other spirits struggling in their own karma toward Nirvana—the place of Heavenly Peace."

The next morning they had spotted those who followed relentlessly. When they came down out of the hills into the outskirts of Tabriz, their pursuers were barely half a mile behind. Only their camouflage had saved them, allowing them to be lost in the crowds, many tribesmen as tall as he and with blue eyes, many as well armed. More luck was with them and he had found the back door of the filthy little garage the first time, used Vien Rosemont's name, and the man there had hidden them. That night Abdollah Khan had come with his guards, very hostile and suspicious. "Who told you to ask for me?"

"Vien Rosemont. He also told us about this place."

"Who is this Rosemont? Where is he now?"

Ross had told him what had happened at the ambush and noticed something new behind the man's eyes now, even though he remained hostile.

"How do I know you're telling me the truth? Who are you?"

"Before Vien died he asked me to give you a message—he was delirious and his dying bad, but he made me repeat it three times to make sure. He said: 'Tell Abdollah Khan that Peter's after the Gorgon's head and Peter's son is worse than Peter. The son plays with curds and whey and so does the father who'll try to use a Medusa to catch the Gorgon.' " He saw the other man's eyes light up at once but not happily. "So it means something to you?"

"Yes. It means you know Vien. So Vien's dead. As God wants, but that's a pity. Vien was good, very good, and a great patriot. Who are you? What was your mission? What were you doing in our mountains?"

Again he hesitated, remembering that Armstrong had told him at his briefing not to trust this man too far. Yet Rosemont whom he had trusted had said in his dying, "You can trust that old bastard with your life. I have, half a dozen times, and he's never failed me. Go to him, he'll get you out. . . ."

Abdollah Khan was smiling, his mouth cruel like his eyes. "You can trust me—I think you have to."

"Yes." But not very far at all, he added silently, loathing the word, the word that costs millions their lives, more millions their freedom and every adult on earth peace of mind at some time or another. "It was to neutralize Sabalan," he said and told him what had happened there.

"God be praised! I will pass word to Wesson and Talbot."

"Who?"

"Ah, doesn't matter. I'll get you south. Come with me, it's not safe here— the hue and cry's out, with a reward, for 'two British saboteurs, two enemies of Islam.' Who are you?"

"Ross. Captain Ross and this is Sergeant Gueng. Who were the men chasing us? Iranians—or Soviets? Or Soviet-led?"

"Soviets don't operate openly in my Azerbaijan—not yet." The Khan's lips twisted into a strange smile. "I have a station wagon outside. Get into it quickly and lie down in the back. I'll hide you and when it's safe, get you both back to Tehran—but you have to obey my orders. Explicitly."

That was two days ago, but then the coming of the Soviet strangers and the arrival of the helicopter had made everything different. He saw the moon go behind a cloud and he tapped Gueng on the shoulder. The small man vanished into the orchard. When the all-clear signal came out of the night, he followed. They leapfrogged each other, moving very well until they were beside the corner of the north wing of the great house. No guards or guard dogs yet though Gueng had seen some Doberman pinschers chained up.

It was an easy climb up a balustrade to the first-floor balcony. Gueng led. He hurried down half its length, passed the corridor of shuttered windows to the staircase that climbed to the next balcony. At the top he waited, getting his bearings. Ross came alongside. Gueng pointed at the second set of windows and took out his kookri but Ross shook his head and motioned to a side door that he had noticed, deep in shadow. He tried the handle. The door squeaked loudly. Some night birds skeetered out of the orchard, calling to one another. Both men concentrated on where the birds had come from, expecting to see a patrol. None appeared. Another moment to make sure, then Ross led the way inside, adrenaline heightening his tension.

The corridor was long, many doors either side, some windows to the south. Outside the second door he stopped, warily tried the handle. This door opened silently and he went in quickly, Gueng following, his kookri out and grenade ready. The room seemed to be an anteroom—carpets, lounging pillows, old-fashioned Victorian furniture and sofas. Two doors led off it. Praying it was the correct choice, Ross opened the door nearest the corner of the building and went in. The curtains were drawn but a crack of moonlight to one side showed them the bed clearly and the man he sought and a woman asleep there under the thick quilt. It was the right man but he had not expected a woman. Gueng eased the door closed. Without hesitation they went to either side of the bed, Ross taking the man and Gueng the woman. Simultaneously they clapped the bunched handkerchiefs over the mouths of the sleepers, holding them down with just enough pressure under their noses to keep them from crying out.

"We're friends, pilot, don't cry out," Ross whispered, close to Erikki's ear, not knowing his name or who the woman was, only recognizing him as the pilot. He saw the blank fright of the sudden awakening transformed into blinding rage as sleep vanished and the great hands came up to rip him apart. He avoided their grasp, increasing the pressure just under Erikki's nose, holding him down easily. "I'm going to release you, don't cry out, pilot. We're friends, we're British. British soldiers. Just nod if you're awake and you understand." He waited, then felt more than saw the huge man nod, watching his eyes. The eyes shouted danger. "Keep her gagged, Gueng, until we're all set this side," he said softly in Gurkhali, then to Erikki, "Pilot, don't be afraid, we're friends."

He released the pressure and leaped out of the way as Erikki lunged at him, then squirmed in the bed to get at Gueng but stopped rigid. Moonlight glinted off the curved kookri held near her throat. Azadeh's eyes were wide open and she was petrified.

"Don't! Leave her alone . . ." Erikki said hoarsely in Russian, seeing only Gueng's Oriental eyes, thinking it must be one of Cimtarga's men, still confused and in panic. He was heavy with sleep, his head aching from hours of flying, mostly on instruments in bad conditions. "What do you want?"

"Speak English. You're English, aren't you?"

"No, no, I'm Finnish." Erikki peered at Ross, little more than a silhouette in the shaft of moonlight. "What the hell do you want?"

"Sorry to wake you like this, pilot," Ross said hastily, coming a little closer, keeping his voice down. "Sorry, but I had to talk to you secretly. It's very import—"

"Tell this bastard to let my wife go! Now!"

"Wife? Oh, yes . . . yes, of course, sorry. She . . . she won't scream? Please tell her not to scream." He watched the huge man turn toward the woman who lay motionless under the heavy quilt, her mouth still covered, the kookri unwavering. He saw him reach out warily and touch her, eyes on the kookri. His voice was gentle and encouraging but he did not speak English or Farsi but another language. In panic Ross thought it was Russian and he was further disoriented, expecting a British S-G pilot, without a bed partner, not a Finn with a Russian wife, and he was petrified he had led Gueng into a trap. The big man's eyes came back on him and more danger was there.

"Tell him to let my wife go," Erikki said in English, finding it hard to concentrate. "She won't scream."

"What did you say to her? Was it Russian?"

"Yes, it was Russian and I said, 'This bastard's going to release you in a second. Don't shout out. Don't shout out, just move behind me. Don't move quickly, just behind me. Don't do anything unless I go for the other bastard, then fight for your life.'"

"You're Russian?"

"I told you, Finnish, and I tire quickly of men with knives in the night, British, Russian, or even Finnish."

"You're a pilot with S-G Helicopters?"

"Yes, hurry up and let her go whoever you are or I'll start something."

Ross was not yet over his own panic. "Is she Russian?"

"My wife's Iranian, she speaks Russian and so do I," Erikki said icily, moving slightly to get out of the narrow beam of moonlight into shadows. "Move into the light, I can't see you, and for the last time tell this little bastard to release my wife, tell me what you want, and then get out."

"Sorry about all this. Gueng, let her go now."

Gueng did not move. Nor did the curved blade. In Gurkhali he said, "Yes, sahib, but first take the knife from under the man's pillow."

In Gurkhali Ross replied, "If he goes for it, brother, even touches it, kill her, I'll get him." Then in English he said pleasantly, "Pilot, you have a knife under your pillow. Please don't touch it, sorry, but if you do until this is all okay . . . please be patient. Let her go, Gueng," he said, his attention never leaving the man. With the side of his eyes he saw the vague shape of a face, long hair touseled and half covering her, then she moved behind the great shoulders, bunching her long-sleeved, winter nightclothes closer. Ross had his back to the light and he saw little of her, only the hatred in her half-seen eyes, even from the shadows. "Sorry to arrive like a thief in the night. Apologies," he said to her. She did not answer. He repeated the apology in Farsi. She still did not answer. "Please apologize to your wife for me."

"She speaks English. What the hell do you want?" Erikki felt a little better now that she was safe, still very aware how close the other man with the curved knife was.

"We're sort of prisoners of the Khan, pilot, and I came to warn you and to ask your help."

"Warn me about what?"

"I helped one of your captains a few days ago—Charles Pettikin." He saw the name register at once so he relaxed a little. Quickly he told Erikki about Doshan Tappeh and the SAVAK attack and how they had escaped, describing Pettikin accurately so there could be no mistake.

"Charlie told us about you," Erikki said, astonished, no longer afraid, "but not that he'd dropped you off near Bandar-e Pahlavi—only that some British paratroopers had saved him from a SAVAK who'd have blown his head off."

"I asked him to forget my name. I, er, we were on a job."

"Lucky for Charlie you, we—" Ross saw the woman whisper in her husband's ear, distracting him. The man nodded and turned his eyes back again. "You can see me, I can't see you, move into the light—as to Abdollah, if you were his prisoners, you'd be chained up, or in a dungeon, not loose in the palace."

"I was told the Khan would help us if we had trouble. We had trouble and he said he'd hide us until he could get us back to Tehran. Meanwhile he put us in a hut, out of sight, across the estate. There's a permanent guard on us."

"Hide you from what?"

"We were on a, er, classified job, and being hunted an—"

"What classified job? I still can't see you, move into the light."

Ross moved but not enough. "We had to blow some secret American radar stuff to prevent it being pinched by Soviets or their supporters. I rec—"

"Sabalan?"

"How the hell did you know that?"

"I'm being forced to fly a Soviet and some leftists to ransack radar sites near the border, then take the stuff down to Astara on the coast. One of them was wrecked on the north face—they got nothing out of that one and so far the rest haven't produced anything worthwhile—as far as I know. Go on—warn me about what?"

"You're being forced?"

"My wife's hostage to the Khan and the Soviets—for my cooperation and good behavior," Erikki said simply.

"Christ!" Ross's mind was working overtime. "I, er, I recognized the S-G decal when you were circling and came to warn you Soviets were here, they came here early this morning, and they're planning to kidnap you with the friendly help of the Khan—it seems he's playing both ends against the middle, double agent." He saw Erikki's astonishment. "Our people should know that quickly."

"Kidnap me to do what?"

"I don't know exactly. I sent Gueng on a recce after your chopper arrived —he slipped out of a back window. Tell them, Gueng."

"It was after they had eaten lunch, sahib, the Khan and the Soviet, and they were beside the Soviet's car when he was leaving—I was in the undergrowth near and could hear well. At first I could not understand them, but then the Khan said, Let's talk English—there are servants nearby. The Soviet said, Thanks for all the information and the offer. The Khan said, Then we have an agreement? Everything, Patar? The Soviet said, Yes I'll recommend everything you want. I'll see the pilot never bothers you again. When he's finished here he'll be brought north . . ." Gueng stopped as the air hissed out of Azadeh's mouth. "Yes, memsahib?"

"Nothing."

Gueng concentrated, wanting to get it perfect for them: "The Soviet said, I'll see the pilot never bothers you again. When he's finished here he'll be brought north, permanently. Then . . ." He thought a moment. "Ah, yes! Then he said, The mullah won't trouble you again and in return you'll catch the British saboteurs for me? Alive, I'd like them alive if possible. The Khan said, Yes, I'll catch them, Patar, do y—"

"Petr," Azadeh said, her hand on Erikki's shoulder. "His name was Petr Mzytryk."

"Christ!" Ross muttered as it fell into place.

"What?" Erikki said.

"I'll tell you later. Finish, Gueng."

"Yes, sahib. The Khan said, I'll catch them, Patar, alive if I can. What's my favor if they're alive? The Soviet laughed. Anything, within reason, and mine? The Khan said, I'll bring *her* with me on my next visit. Sahib, that was all. Then the Soviet got into his car and left."

Azadeh shuddered.

"What?" Erikki said.

"He means me," she said, her voice small.

Ross said, "I don't follow."

Erikki hesitated, the tightness in his head greater than before. She had told him about being summoned for lunch by her father, and about Petr Mzytryk inviting her to Tbilisi—"and your husband, of course, if he's free; I would love to show you our countryside. . . ." and how attentive the Soviet had been. "It's . . . it's personal. Not important," he said. "It seems you've done me a big favor. How can I help?" He smiled tiredly and stuck out his hand. "My name's Yokkonen, Erikki Yokkonen and this is my wife, Az—"

"Sahib!" Gueng hissed warningly.

Ross jerked to a stop. Now he saw Erikki's other hand was under the pillow. "Don't move a muscle," he said, kookri suddenly out of its scabbard. Erikki recognized the tone and obeyed. Cautiously Ross moved the pillow aside but the hand was not near the knife. He picked the knife up. The blade glinted in the shaft of moonlight. He thought a moment, then handed it back to Erikki, haft first. "Sorry, but it's better to be safe." He shook the outstretched hand that had never wavered and felt the enormous strength. He smiled at him and turned slightly, the light now on his face for the first time. "My name's Ross, Captain John Ross, and this's Gueng . . ."

Azadeh gasped and jerked upright. They all looked at her and now Ross saw her clearly for the first time. It was Azadeh, his Azadeh of ten years ago, Azadeh Gorden as he had known her then, Azadeh Gorden of the High Country staring up at him, more beautiful than ever, eyes bigger than ever, still heaven-sent. "My God, Azadeh, I didn't see your face . . ."

"Nor I yours, Johnny."

"Azadeh . . . good God," Ross stammered. He was beaming and so was she, and then he heard Erikki and looked down and saw him staring up at him, the great knife in his fist, and a shaft of fear rushed through him and through her.

"You're 'Johnny Brighteyes'?" Erikki said it flat.

"Yes, yes, I'm . . . I had the privilege of knowing your wife years ago, many years ago . . . Good Lord, Azadeh, how wonderful to see you!"

"And you . . ." Her hand had not left Erikki's shoulder.

Erikki could feel her hand and it was burning him but he did not move, mesmerized by the man in front of him. She had told him about John Ross and about their summer and the result of the summer, that the man had not known about the almost child, nor had she ever tried to find him to tell him, nor did she want him ever to know. "The fault was mine, Erikki, not his," she had told him simply. "I was in love, I was just a few days seventeen and he nineteen—Johnny Brighteyes I called him; I had never seen a man with such blue eyes before. We were deeply in love but it was only a summer love, not like ours which is forever, mine is, and yes, I will marry you if Father will allow it, oh, yes, please God, but only if you can live happily with knowing that once upon a time, long long ago, I was growing up. You must promise me, swear to me you can be happy as a man and a husband for perhaps one day we will meet him—I will be happy to meet him and I will smile at him but my soul will be yours, my body yours, my life yours, and all that I have . . ."

He had sworn as she had wished, truly and with all his soul, happily brushing aside her concern. He was modern and understanding and Finnish —wasn't Finland always progressive, hadn't Finland been the second country on earth after New Zealand to give women the vote? There was no worry in him. None. He was only sad for her that she had not been careful, for she had told him of her father's anger—an anger he could understand.

And now here was the man, fine and strong and young, far nearer her size than he, far nearer her age than he. Jealousy ripped him apart.

Ross was trying to collect his wits, her presence possessing him. He pulled his eyes off her and the memory of her and looked back at Erikki. He read his eyes clearly. "A long time ago I knew your wife, in Switzerland at . . . I was at school there for a short time."

"Yes, I know," Erikki said. "Azadeh told me about you. I'm . . . I'm . . . it's a . . . it's a sudden meeting for all of us." He got out of bed, towering over Ross, the knife still in his hand, all of them aware of the knife. He saw that Gueng, on the other side of the bed, still had his kookri out. "So. Again, Captain, again thanks for the warning."

"You said you're being forced to fly the Soviets?"

"Azadeh's hostage for my good behavior," Erikki said simply.

Thoughtfully Ross nodded. "Not much you can do about that if the Khan's hostile. Christ, that's a mess! My thought was that as you were threatened too, you'd want to escape too and that you'd give us a ride in the chopper."

"If I could I would, yes . . . yes, of course. But I've twenty guards on me all the time I'm flying and Azadeh . . . my wife and I are watched very closely when we're here. There's another Soviet called Cimtarga who's like my shadow, and Abdollah Khan's . . . very careful." He had not yet decided what to do about this man Ross. He glanced at Azadeh and saw that her smile was true, her touch on his shoulder true, and that clearly this man meant nothing more than an old friend to her now. But this did not take away his almost blinding urge to run amok. He made himself smile at her. "We must be careful, Azadeh."

"Very." She had felt the surge under her hand when he had said "Johnny Brighteyes" and knew that, of the three of them, only she could control this added danger. At the same time, Erikki's jealousy that he sought so hard to hide excited her, as did the open admiration of her long-lost love. Oh, yes, she thought, Johnny Brighteyes, you are more wonderful than ever, slimmer than ever, stronger than ever—more exciting, with your curved knife and unshaven face and filthy clothes and man smell—how could I not have recognized you? "A moment ago when I corrected this man's 'Patar' to 'Petr' it meant something to you, Johnny. What?"

"It was a code message I had to give the Khan," Ross said, achingly aware she still bewitched him. " 'Tell Abdollah Khan that Peter'—that could be Gueng's Patar or Petr, the Soviet—'that Peter's after the Gorgon's head and Peter's son is worse than Peter. The son plays with curds and whey and so does the father, who'll try to use a Medusa to catch the Gorgon.' "

Azadeh said, "That's easy. Erikki?"

"Yes," Erikki said, distracted. "But why 'curds and whey'?"

"Perhaps this," she said, her excitement rising. "Tell Abdollah Khan that Petr Mzytryk, KGB, is after his head, that Mzytryk's son—let's presume also KGB—is worse than his father. The son plays at curds and whey—perhaps that means the son is involved with the Kurds and their rebellion that threatens Abdollah Khan's power base in Azerbaijan, that the KGB, the father, and the son are also involved—and that Petr Mzytryk will use a Medusa to catch the Gorgon." She thought a moment. "Could that be another pun and mean 'use a woman,' perhaps even an evil woman to catch my father?"

Ross was shocked. "The Khan's . . . My God, the Khan's your father?"

"Yes, I'm afraid so. Gorgon's my family name," Azadeh said, "not Gorden. But the principal of the school at Château d'Or told me the first day I could hardly have a name like Gorgon—I would get teased to death—so I was to be just Azadeh Gorden. It was fun for me, and the principal thought it better for me that I was just plain Azadeh Gorden and not the daughter of a Khan."

Erikki broke a silence. "If the message's correct, the Khan won't trust that *matyeryebyets* at all."

"Yes, Erikki. But my father trusts no one. No one at all. If Father's playing both sides as Johnny thinks—there's no telling what he'll do. Johnny, who gave you the message to give to him?"

"A CIA agent who said I could trust your father with my life."

Erikki said witheringly, "I always knew the CIA were . . . were crazy."

"This one was all right," Ross said more sharply than he meant. He saw Erikki flush and her smile vanish.

Another silence. More jagged. The moonlight in the room faded as the moon went behind a bank of cloud. It was uneasy in the gloom. Gueng who had watched and listened felt the increased disquiet and he silently called on all gods to extricate them from Medusas, the pagan devil with snakes for hair that the missionaries had taught about in his first school in Nepal. Then his special sense felt the approaching danger, he hissed a warning and went to the window and peered out. Two armed guards with a Doberman pinscher on a leash were coming up the staircase opposite.

The others were equally rigid now. They heard the guards pad along the terrace, the dog sniffing and straining on the leash. Then go toward the outside door. Again it creaked open. The men came into the building.

Muffled voices outside the door of the bedroom and the sound of the dog snuffling. Then near the door of the anteroom. Gueng and Ross moved into ambush, kookris ready. In time the guards moved down the corridor, out of the building and down the staircase again. Azadeh shifted nervously. "They don't come here normally. Ever."

Ross whispered back hastily, "Maybe they saw us coming up here. We'd better leave. If you hear firing, you don't know us. If we're still free tomorrow night, could we come here, say just after midnight? We could perhaps make a plan?"

"Yes," Erikki said. "But make it earlier. Cimtarga warned me we might have to leave before dawn. Make it around 11:00 P.M. We'd better have several plans ready—to get out is going to be very difficult, very."

"How long will you be working for them—before you're finished?"

"I don't know. Perhaps three or four days."

"Good. If we don't make contact with you—forget us. Okay?"

"God protect you, Johnny," Azadeh told him anxiously. "Don't trust my father, you mustn't let him . . . mustn't let him or them take you."

Ross smiled and it lit up the room, even for Erikki. "No problem—good luck to all of us." He waved a devil-may-care salute and opened the door. In a few seconds he and Gueng were gone as quietly as they had arrived. Erikki watched out of the window and saw them only as shadows going down the steps, noting how cleverly and silently the two men used the night, envying Ross his careless elegance of manner and movement.

Azadeh was standing alongside him, a head smaller, her arm around his waist, also watching. After a moment, his arm went around her shoulders. They waited, expecting shouting and firing, but the night remained undisturbed. The moon came out from the clouds again. No movement anywhere. He glanced at his watch. It was 4:23.

He looked at the sky, no sign of any dawn yet. At dawn he had to leave, not to the north face of Sabalan but to other radar sites farther west. Cimtarga had told him that the CIA still operated certain sites nearer the Turkish border but that today the Khomeini government had ordered them closed, evacuated, and left intact. "They'll never do that," Erikki had saiᵈ "Never."

"Perhaps, perhaps not." Cimtarga had laughed. "The moment we get orders, you and I will just fly there with my 'tribesmen' and hurry them up. . . ."

Matyer! And *matyer* Johnny Brighteyes arriving to complicate our lives. Even so, thank all gods for the warning he brought. What's Abdollah planning for Azadeh? I should kill that old swine and have done with it. Yes, but I can't, I swore by the ancient gods an oath that may not be broken, not to touch her father—as he himself swore by the One God not to hinder us though he'll find a way to break that oath. Can I do the same? No. An oath is an oath. Like the one you swore to her that you could live happily with her, knowing about him—*him*—didn't you? His mind blackened and he was glad of the darkness.

So the KGB plan to kidnap me. If it's a real plan I'm done for. Azadeh? What's that devil Abdollah planning for her now? And now this Johnny arrives to harass us all—I never thought he'd be so good-looking and tough and no man to mix with, him with that sodding great knife, killing knife . . .

"Come back to bed, Erikki," she said. "It's very cold, isn't it?"

He nodded and followed and got in his side, greatly troubled. When they were back under the great quilt, she snuggled against him. Not enough to provoke a reaction but just enough to appear normal and untouched. "How extraordinary to find it was him, Erikki! John Ross—in the street I certainly wouldn't have recognized him. Oh, that was such a long time ago, I'd forgotten all about him. I'm so pleased you married me, Erikki," she said, her voice calm and loving, sure that his mind was grinding her long-lost love to dust. "I feel so safe with you—if it hadn't been for you I would have died of fright."

She said it as though expecting an answer. But I don't expect one, my darling, she thought contentedly and sighed.

He heard her sigh and wondered what it meant, feeling her warmth against him, loathing the rage that possessed him. Was it because she's sorry she had smiled at her lover as she did? Or is she furious with me—she must have seen my jealousy. Or is she saddened that I have forgotten my oath, or is she hating me because I hate that man? I swear I'll exorcise him from her. . . .

Ah, Johnny Brighteyes, she was thinking, what ecstasy I enjoyed in your arms, even the first time when it was supposed to hurt, but it never did. Just a pain that became a burning that became a melting that tore away life and gave life back to me again, better than before, oh, how so much better than before! And then Erikki . . .

It was much warmer now under the quilt. Her hand went across his loins. She felt him move slightly and she hid her smile, sure that her warmth was reaching him now, so easy to warm him further. But unwise. Very unwise, for then she knew he would only take her with Johnny in the forefront of his mind, taking her to spite Johnny and not to love her—perhaps even thinking that in her acquiescence she was feeling guilty and was trying to make up for her guilt. Oh, no, my love, I'm not a foolish child, you're the guilty one, not me. And though you'd be stronger than usual and more rough, which would normally increase my pleasure, this time it would not, for, like it or not, I would resist even more than you, aware of my other love. So, my darling, it is ten thousand times better to wait. Until the dawn. By then, my darling, if I'm lucky you will have persuaded yourself that you are wrong to hate and be jealous and you will be my Erikki again. And if you haven't? Then I will begin again—there are ten thousand ways to heal my man. "I love you, Erikki," she said and kissed the cloth that covered his chest, turned over, and settled her back against him and went into sleep, smiling.

AT KOWISS AIR BASE: 8:11 A.M.   Freddy Ayre bunched his fists. "No, by God! You heard McIver's orders: If Starke's not back by dawn all flights are grounded. It's past eight o'clock and Starke's not back so all fl—"

"You will obey *my* flight orders!" Esvandiary, the IranOil manager, shouted at him, his voice echoing around the S-G base. "I've ordered you to deliver a new mud tank and pipe under Guerney's contract to Rig Si—"

"No flying until Captain Starke's back!" Ayre snarled. They were on the flight line near the three 212s that Esvandiary had scheduled for today's operations, the three pilots geared and ready since dawn, the rest of the expats watching in varying degrees of nervousness or anger. Around them were a truckload of hostile Green Bands and servicemen from the base who had just arrived with Esvandiary. Four of Zataki's men squatted near the choppers but none of them had moved since the quarrel had erupted though all of them were watching closely. "All flights are grounded!" Ayre repeated.

Furiously Esvandiary called out in Farsi, "These foreigners refuse to obey legitimate orders of IranOil." A mutter of anger went through his supporters, guns covered the expats, and he stabbed a finger at Ayre. "They need an example!"

Without warning rough hands grabbed Ayre, and the beating began. One of the pilots, Sandor Petrofi, rushed forward to intervene but he was shoved back, slipped, and was kicked back to the others who were helpless under the guns.

"Stop it!" Pop Kelly, the tall captain, shouted out, his face chalky. "Leave Ayre alone, we'll fly the missions!"

"Good." Esvandiary told his men to stop. They dragged Ayre to his feet. "Get all flights under way. At once!"

When the flights were airborne he dismissed the expats roughly. "There'll be no more mutinies against the Islamic state. By God, all orders of IranOil will—will—be obeyed instantly." Very satisfied with himself that he had put down the mutiny as he had promised the camp commandant, he strode into the main office, down the corridor into Starke's office that he had commandeered, and stood at the window surveying his domain.

He saw two choppers well away now, the third was hovering twenty feet over the mud tank a hundred yards away, waiting for the ground crew to link its skyhook into the big steel ring that topped the hawsers. In front of the office Ayre, surrounded by other expats, was being succored by Doc Nutt. Rotten bastard to give me so much trouble, Esvandiary thought, and glanced at his watch, admiring it. It was a gold Rolex that he had bought on the black market this morning as befitted his increased stature, the money pishkesh from a bazaari who wanted his son to join IranOil.

"Do you need anything, Excellency?" Pavoud asked unctuously from the doorway. "May I add my congratulations for the way that you handled the foreigners. For years they've all needed a good beating to put them in their places, how wise you were."

"Yes. From now on the base *will* run smoothly. The moment there's a problem, whoever's in charge will be made an example of. Praise God that son of a dog Zataki leaves in an hour with his thugs for Abadan."

"That's one flight that will leave on time, Excellency." Both men laughed.

"Yes. Bring me some tea, Pavoud." Deliberately Esvandiary left out the normal politeness and noted the man's humility increase. He stared out of the window again. Doc Nutt was dabbing a cut over Ayre's eye. I enjoyed watching Freddy being beaten, he thought. Yes, yes, I did.

In the chill wind Doc Nutt had wrapped a spare parka around Ayre. "You'd better come over to the surgery, laddie," he said.

"I'm all right," Ayre said, hurting all over. "Don't think . . . don't think anything's damaged."

"Bastards," someone said. "Freddy, we'd better figure how we're going to get to hell out of here."

"It's me on the first plane out. . . . I'm not going to risk an—"

They all looked off as the jet engines of the chopper hovering over the mud tank picked up tempo. Getting such a heavy load airborne was tricky—particularly in this wind—but no problem for a professional like Sandor. The hook went in first time and the moment the ground crew had their hands clear, he increased power, the engines screamed at a higher pitch, taking the strain, then chopper and load eased into the sky. The guard in the front seat beside Sandor waved excitedly—as did the one in the cabin.

"You're doing fine, Captain . . . no sweat," came into Sandor's headphones from Wazari in their tower, Sandor estimating the distance, gaining height, his hands and feet perfectly coordinated—seeing only Esvandiary at the office window, still maddened by Ayre's savage beating by many armed men at the orders of a coward. It took him back in time to his childhood in Budapest during the Hungarian Revolution. He had been helpless then—but not now.

"You're okay, HFD, but kinda close." Wazari's voice cautioned him. "You're kinda close, ease south . . ."

Sandor increased power, moving toward the tower that topped the office building. "Is the load okay?" he asked. "Feels strange."

"Looks fine, no sweat, but ease south as you climb. Everything five by five . . . ease south, do you read me?"

"You sure, for crissake? She feels sluggish as all hell. . . ." The needle climbed through a hundred feet. Sandor's face closed and his hand snapped the stick right, at the same time he gave her hard right rudder. At once the chopper reeled sickeningly, the guard in the seat beside him was thrown off balance; he bashed against the door, then grabbed Sandor, trying to steady himself, and tangled with the controls. Again Sandor overcorrected, cursing the guard as though the petrified man was a real hazard.

For a moment it seemed that the gathering swing would take the chopper out of the sky, then Sandor shoved the frantic guard away. "Mayday—load's shifted," he shouted, his ears shut to Wazari, eyes concentrating below, oblivious of everything except the need for revenge. "Load's shifted!"

His hand pulled the Emergency Load Release, the hook freed, the steel tank plummeted out of the sky directly onto the office. The ton and a half of steel smashed through the roof, pulverizing rafters and walls and glass and metal and desks, obliterating the whole corner, and came to rest upended against the remains of the inner wall.

A moment of appalled silence took the whole camp, then the screaming engines filled the sky as, released suddenly from its load, the chopper had careened upward out of control. Sandor's reflexes fought the controls, his mind not caring whether he dominated them or not, whether he landed or not, just knowing that he had had vengeance on one brute. Beside him the guard was vomiting and his earphones were filled with, "Jesuschrist . . . Jesuschrist . . ." from the tower.

"Christ, look outttttt!" someone shouted as the chopper whirled down at them. Everyone scattered but Sandor's reflexes cut engines and went for the impossible emergency landing. The skids hacked into the snow of the grass verge, did not buckle, and the chopper skeetered forward to come to rest unharmed forty yards away.

Ayre was the first at the cockpit. He jerked the door open. Sandor was sheet white, numb, staring ahead. "Load shifted . . ." he croaked.

"Yes," was all Ayre could say, knowing it to be a lie, then others joined them and they helped Sandor, his limbs momentarily uncontrollable, out of the cockpit. Behind him, near the building, Ayre saw Green Bands gaping at the wreckage, then Pavoud and the other clerk totter out of the front door in shock, the window and corner where Esvandiary had been standing was rubble. Doc Nutt pushed through the crowd and hurried toward the ruins as Wazari came down the emergency steps outside the tower that were twisted precariously, half off the side of the building. Christ, Ayre thought, Wazari must've seen everything. He knelt beside his friend. "You all right, Sandy?"

"No," Sandor said shakily. "I think I went crazy. I couldn't stop."

Wazari was shoving through the people toward the cockpit, still panicked from seeing the tank hurtling down on him, knowing the pilot had deliberately disregarded his instructions. "You crazy, goddamnit?" he exploded at Sandor over the wind-down scream of the engines.

Ayre's temper snapped. "Goddamnit, the load shifted! We all saw it and so did you!"

"You're goddamn right I saw it and so did you." Wazari's eyes were frantically darting this way and that, watching for Green Bands, but none were near—then he saw Zataki approaching from one of the bungalows. His dread escalated. He was still badly bruised from the beating Zataki had given him, his nose mashed, his mouth still aching where three teeth had been knocked out, and he knew he would admit anything to prevent another beating. He knelt beside Sandor, half pulling Ayre with him. "Listen," he whispered desperately, "you swear by God you'll help me? You promise, huh?"

"I said I'd do what I could!" Angrily Ayre jerked his arm away, the pain of bending very bad. He stood upright and found he was looking into Zataki's face. The suddenness chilled him—and the eyes. Everyone else had backed away from them.

"Pilot, you did that to kill Esvandiary. Eh?"

Sandor stared up at him from the snow. "The load shifted, Colonel."

Zataki put his eyes on Ayre who remembered what Doc Nutt had said about the man, his own head aching, his groin, and pain everywhere. "The, er, the operation's difficult, it was the wind. The load shifted. An Act of God, Excellency . . ."

Wazari went back a pace as Zataki turned on him. "It's true, Excellency," he said at once. "The winds aloft're gust—" He cried out as Zataki's fist rammed into his stomach and he doubled up in agony, then Zataki grabbed him and shoved him against the chopper. "Now tell me the truth, vermin!"

"It's the truth," Wazari whimpered, barely able to talk through his nausea. "It's the truth! It was Insha'Allah!" He saw Zataki's fist ready again and he cried out in a jumble of Farsi and English, "If you hit me I'll say anything you want, anything, I can't stand another beating and I'll swear to anything you want, anything, but the load shifted—by God, the load shifted, I swear by God the load shifted. . . ."

Zataki stared at him. "God will put you into the fiery vats for all eternity if you've sworn a lie by His Name," he said. "You swear it was God's will alone? That the load shifted? You swear it was an Act of God?"

"Yes, yes, I swear it!" Wazari was trembling, helpless in his grasp. He tried to keep his eyes guileless, knowing that his only chance for life lay with Ayre, proving his value to him. "I swear by God and the Prophet it was an accident, an . . . an Act of God. Insha'Allah . . ."

"As God wants." Zataki nodded, absolved, and released him. Wazari slid to the snow, retching, and all the others were thanking God or joss or heaven or karma that, for the moment, this crisis had passed. Zataki jerked a thumb at the wreckage. "Get what remains of Esvandiary out of there."

"Yes . . . yes, at once," Ayre said.

"Unless the captain returns, you will fly me and my men to Bandar Delam." Zataki walked off. His Green Bands went with him.

"Christ!" someone muttered, all of them almost sick with relief. They helped Sandor to stand and Wazari. "You okay, Sergeant?" Ayre asked.

"No, goddamnit, no, I'm not!" Wazari spat out some vomit. When he saw the Green Bands had gone with Zataki his face twisted with hatred. "That bastard! I hope he fries!"

Ayre pulled Wazari aside and dropped his voice. "I won't forget I said I'd try to help you. When Zataki leaves you'll be okay. I won't forget."

"Nor me," Sandor said weakly. "Thanks, Sergeant."

"You owe me your goddamn life," the younger man said and spat again, his knees weak and chest hurting. "You could've killed me too with that goddamn tank!"

"Sorry." Sandor stuck out his hand.

Wazari looked at the hand, then up into his face. "I'll shake hands with you when I'm safe out of this goddamn country." He limped off.

"Freddy!" Dr. Nutt was at the wreckage with a couple of mechanics, lifting off rafters and mess, beckoning him. Green Bands stood around watching. "Give us a hand here, will you?"

All of them went to help. None of them wishing to be the first one to see Esvandiary.

They found him crumpled in a pocket under one side of the tank. Dr. Nutt squeezed down beside him, examining him awkwardly. "He's alive," he cried out, and Sandor's stomach turned over. Quickly they all helped get the last of the splintered rafters and the remains of Starke's desk out of the way and gently eased the man out. "I think he's all right," Dr. Nutt said, hoarsely. "Get him over to the infirmary—nasty bonk on the head but limbs seem okay and nothing crushed. Someone get a stretcher." People rushed to do his bidding, the pall off them now, all of them hating Hotshot but all of them hoping he'd be all right. Unnoticed, Sandor went behind the building, so relieved he could have wept, and was very sick.

When he came back only Ayre and Nutt were waiting. "Sandy, you'd better come along too, let me give you the once-over-lightly," Nutt said. "Bloody casualty ward, that's what we've got now."

"You're sure Hotshot'll be okay?"

"Pretty sure." The doctor's eyes were watery and pale blue and a little bloodshot. "What went wrong, Sandy?" he asked quietly.

"Don't know, Doc. All I wanted was to get that bastard an' at the time dumping the tank seemed the perfect way to do it."

"You know that would have been murder?"

Uneasily Ayre said, "Doc, don't you think it'd be better to leave it?"

"No, no, I don't." Nutt's voice hardened. "Sandy, you know that was a deliberate attempt at murder."

"Yes." Sandor looked back at him. "Yes, I understand that and I'm sorry."

"You're sorry he's not dead?"

"Swear to God, Doc, I thank God he's alive. I still think he's become vile and evil and everything I detest and I can't forgive him for . . . for ordering Freddy's beating but that's no excuse for what I did. Doing what I did was crazy, and no excuse, and I really thank God he's alive."

"Sandy," Nutt said, his voice even quieter, "you'd better not fly for a day or two. You were pushed beyond the limit—nothing to worry about, laddie, so long as you understand. Just take it easy for a day or so. You'll get the shakes tonight but don't worry. You too, Freddy. Of course this's all between the three of us and the load shifted. I saw it shift." He brushed the threads of hair over his bald pate that the wind toyed with. "Life's strange, very strange, but just between us three, God was with you today, Sandy, if there is such a thing." He walked off, crumpled like an old sack of potatoes.

Ayre watched him. "Doc's right, you know, we were bloody lucky, so near to disaster, so n—"

There was a shout and they looked off. One of the pilots near the main gate shouted again and pointed. Their hearts leaped. Starke was coming down the road from the direction of the town. He was alone. As far as they could see from there, he was unhurt, walking tall. They waved excitedly and he waved back, the word flashed throughout the camp and Ayre was already running to meet him, oblivious of his pain. Maybe there's a God in heaven after all, he was thinking happily.

AT LENGEH: 2:15 P.M. Scragger was sunbathing on the big raft that was moored a hundred yards offshore, a small rubber dinghy attached to it. The raft was made with planks lashed to empty oil drums. In the dinghy was fishing equipment and the walkie-talkie, and below it hung a strong wire cage with the dozen fish that he and Willi Neuchtreiter had already caught for dinner—the Gulf being abundant with shrimp, Spanish mackerel, tuna, sea bass, rock cod, and dozens of others species.

Willi, another pilot, was swimming lazily in the warm shallow water nearby. On the shore was their base—half a dozen trailers, cookhouse, dormitories for the Iranian staff, office trailer with attached radio tower and antenna, hangars with space for a dozen 212s and 206s.

The present complement was five pilots, including himself, seven mechanics, fifteen Iranian staff, day laborers, cooks and houseboys, and the IranOil manager Kormani, presently sick. Of the other pilots two were British, the last, Ed Vossi, American.

On base now were three 212s—with just enough work for one at the moment—and two 206 Jet Rangers with hardly any work at all. Apart from the French Consortium with their Siri contracts from Georges de Plessey, all other contracts had been canceled or held up pending the end of the troubles. There were still rumors of bad trouble at the big naval base of Bandar Abbas eastward and of fighting all along the coast. Two days ago trouble had spilled over to the base for the first time. Now they had a permanent komiteh of Green Bands, police, and one mullah: "To protect the base against leftists, Excellency Captain."

"But, Excellency Mullah, old sport, we don't need protection."

"As God wants, but our vital Siri island oil installations were attacked and hurt by those sons of dogs. Our helicopters are vital to us and will not be hurt. But don't be concerned, nothing will be changed by us—we understand your nervousness about flying with guns so none of us will be armed though one of us will fly with you every time—for your protection."

Scragger and the others had been reassured by the presence on the komiteh of their local police sergeant, Qeshemi, with whom they had always had good relations. The troubles of Tehran, Qom and Abadan had hardly touched them here on the Strait of Hormuz. Strikes had been minimal and orderly. De Plessey was paying EPF's bills, so everything had been fine, except for the lack of work.

Idly Scragger glanced shoreward. The base was tidy and he could see men about their tasks, cleaning, repairing, a few of the komiteh idly sitting around in the shade. Ed Vossi was near the duty 206 doing his ground check.

"Just not enough work," Scragger muttered. It had been the same for months and he knew only too well how costly and disastrous that could be. It was the lack of steady charters and the need to get modern equipment that had persuaded him to sell his Sheik Aviation to Andrew Gavallan so many years ago.

But I've no regrets, he thought. Andy's a beaut, he's been straight with me, I've a little piece of the company, and I can fly so long's I'm fit. But Iran's terrible for Andy now—not even getting paid for work done or for current work, excepting here, and that's a pittance. It must be four or five months the banks've been closed, so he's been carrying Iran ops out of his own swag bag. Something's got to go. With only Siri working, that's not enough to half pay our way.

Three days ago, when Scragger had brought Kasigi back from the Iran-Toda plant near Bandar Delam, Kasigi had asked de Plessey if he could

charter a 206 to go to Al Shargaz or Dubai. "I need to be in immediate
telephone-telex touch with my head office in Japan to confirm arrangements
I've made with you for your spot price, and about uplifting future supplies."
De Plessey had agreed immediately. Scragger had decided to do the charter
himself and was glad he had. While he was in Al Shargaz he had met up with
Johnny Hogg and Manuela. And Genny.

In private she had brought him up to date, particularly about Lochart.

"Gawd Almighty!" he had said, shocked how rapidly their ops were falling
apart and the revolution was embroiling them personally. "Poor old Tom."

"Tom was due from Bandar Delam the day before I left but he never
arrived so we still don't know what really happened—at least I don't," she
said. "Scrag, God knows when we can talk privately again but there's something else: just between us?"

"Cross my heart and cut my throat!"

"I don't think the government's ever going to get back to normal. I
wanted to ask you: even if it does, could the partners—with or without
official help—or IranOil force us out and keep our planes and equipment?"

"Why should they do that? They've got to have choppers . . . but, if
they wanted to, sure, too right they could," he had said and whistled, for that
possibility had never occurred to him before. "Bloody hell, if they decided
they didn't need us, Genny, that'd be dead easy, dead easy. They could get
other pilots, Iranian or mercenaries—isn't that what we are? Sure they could
order us out and keep our equipment. And if we lost everything here, that'd
gut S-G."

"That's what Duncan thought. Could we leave with our planes and spares
—if they tried to do that?"

He had laughed. "It'd be a bonzer heist and that's wot it'd be. But it
couldn't be done, Genny. If we tried and they caught us, they'd throw the
book at us. There's no way we could do it—not without Iran CAA approval."

"Say this was Sheik Aviation?"

"It'd make no difference, Genny."

"You'd just let them steal your life's work, Scrag? Scrag Scragger, DFC
and Bar, AFC and Bar? I don't believe it."

"Nor do I," he said at once, "though wot I'd do God only knows."

He saw the nice face looking at him, dark glasses perched on her head,
anxiety behind the eyes, knowing her concern was not only for McIver and
all that he had built, not only for their own stock and pension that, like his,
was tied to S-G—but also for Andy Gavallan and all the others. "Wot'd I
do?" he said slowly. "Well, we've almost as much in spares in Iran as birds.
We'd have to start getting them out, though how to do it without making the

locals suspicious I don't know. We couldn't get 'em all out, but we could dent the amount. Then we'd all have to leave at the same time—everyone, all choppers—from Tehran, Kowiss, Zagros, Bandar Delam, and here. We'd . . ." He thought a moment. "We'd have to make for here, Al Shargaz . . . But, Genny, we'd all have different distances to go and some'd have to refuel once, maybe twice, and even if we got to Al Shargaz they'd still impound us without proper clearances." He studied her. "Andy believes that's wot the partners're going to do?"

"No, no, he doesn't, not yet, nor does Duncan, not for certain. But it is a possibility and Iran's getting worse every day—that's why I'm here, to ask Andy. You . . . you can't put that in a letter or telex."

"You phoned Andy?"

"Yes, and said as much as I dared—Duncan said to be careful—and Andy told me he'd try to check in London and when he arrived in a couple of days he'd decide what we should plan to do." She pushed her glasses back on her nose. "We should be prepared, shouldn't we, Scrag?"

"I wondered why you'd left the Dunc. He sent you?"

"Of course. Andy'll be here in a couple of days."

Scragger's mind was buzzing. If we do a bunk, someone's bound to get hurt. What'd I do about Kish, Lavan, and Lengeh radar who could scramble twenty fighters in minutes to catch us before we were into friendly skies if we took off without clearance? "Dunc thinks they're going to do us proper?"

"No," she had said. "He doesn't—but I do."

"In that case, Genny, just between us, we'd better make a plan."

He remembered how her face had lit up, and thought again what a lucky man Duncan McIver was even though he was as ornery and opinionated as a man could be.

His eyes were watching the sea when he heard the 206 wind up and saw it neatly airborne. Ed's a bonzer pilot, he thought.

"Hey, Scrag!"

"Yes, Willi?"

"You swim and I'll watch." Willi climbed onto the raft.

"Good on you, mate." Along with abundant edible fish there were also predators, sharks and stingrays, and others—with occasional poisonous jellyfish—but few here in these shallows, and provided you kept your eyes open you could see their shadows a long way off with plenty of time to make the raft. Scragger touched wood, as always, before he dived into the six feet of water that was lukewarm.

Willi Neuchtreiter was also naked. He was a short stocky man of forty-eight with brown hair and more than five thousand hours in helicopters, ten years with the German Army and eight with S-G—working Nigeria, the North Sea, Uganda, and here. His peaked cap was on the raft and he put it on and his sunglasses, squinted at the 206 that was heading out into the Gulf, then watched Scragger. In moments the sun had dried him. He enjoyed the sun and swimming and being at Lengeh.

So different from home, he thought. Home was in Kiel in northern Germany on the Baltic where the climate was harsh and mostly cold. His wife and three children had gone home last year because of his children's educational needs, and he had elected to do two months here and one in Kiel, and had got a transfer back to the North Sea to be closer. Next month, after his leave, he would not return to Lengeh.

Shit on the North Sea with its foul moods and constant danger, on the crummy quarters and the vast boredom of two weeks flying off a rig a hundred miles offshore to earn one week at home in Kiel and barely enough money to pay the mortgage and schooling and stay ahead with a little to spare for holidays. But you'll be near the kids and Hilda and Ma and Pa, your homeland is always your homeland. Yes, it is, and with any luck, some day soon, all Germans will mix freely with all Germans, Ma can visit her family in Schwerin whenever she wants—and Schwerin and all our other Schwerins won't be occupied anymore. Oh, God, let me live to see that day.

"Scrag, a shadow's coming in."

Scragger had seen it almost at the same time, and he swam back to the raft and got aboard. The shadow came in fast. It was a shark. "Stone the crows," he gasped. "Look at her size!"

The shark slowed, then leisurely began to circle, its large dorsal fin cutting the calm surface. Dull gray, lethal and unhurried. Both men watched silently, awed. Then Scragger chuckled. "How about it, Willi?"

"Yes, by God Harry, he's not Jaws but he's the biggest beetch I've ever seen so I think we get him, by God!" Gleefully, he got the fishing tackle that was in the dinghy. "What about bait? What you think for bait?"

"The sea bass, the big one!"

Laughing, Willi reached down into the cage and pulled out the squirming fish and baited the steel shark hook. There was blood on his hands now and he washed them off in the water, watching the prey. Then he got up, checked the short length of chain attached to the hook, knotted it carefully to the heavy nylon fishing line that was on the reel of the rod. "Here you are, Scrag."

"No, cobber. You spotted her first!"

Excitedly Willi wiped the sea salt off his forehead with the back of his hand, settled his cap jauntily, and looked at the shark that still circled twenty yards away. With great care he threw the bait directly into its path, gently tightened the line. The shark passed the bait and continued circling. Both men cursed. Willi reeled in. The sea bass danced and kicked spasmodically, dying fast. A thin trail of blood was in its wake. Again Willi cast perfectly. Again nothing happened.

"Goddamn," Willi said. This time he left the bait where it was, watching it settle lower and lower until it lay on the bottom, keeping just enough tension on the line. The shark came around, passed over it, almost touching it with its belly, and continued circling.

"Maybe he's not hungry."

"Those sonsofbeetches're always hungry. Maybe he knows we're waiting for him—or he's going to trick us. Scrag, get a smaller fish and throw it just where the bait is as he comes around."

Scragger chose a rock cod. He threw it deftly. The fish fell into the water ten yards ahead of the shark, sensed the danger, and fled for the sandy bottom. The shark paid no attention to it, or to the sea bass so close by, just flicked its tail and circled. "Let the bait stay where it is," Scragger said. "That bugger can't've not got its scent."

Now they could see the yellow eyes and the three small pilot fish hovering over its head, the thin line of the vast mouth under the blunt nose, the sleek skin and power of the great tail. Another circuit. A little closer this time. "Betcha he's nearer eight feet than six, Willi."

"That sonofabeetch's watching us, Scrag," Willi said uneasily, his excitement gone now, a hollowness in its place.

Scragger frowned, having the same feeling. He looked away from the eyes to the dinghy. No weapons there of any value, just a small sheath knife, a light aluminum three-pronged fishing spear and some oars. Even so, he tugged on the painter to bring the dinghy closer, knelt down, and reached for the knife and fishing spear. Wish I had a gun, he thought.

A sudden warning cry from Willi made him jump back and he just had time to see the shark coming straight for him at full speed. It smashed against the side of the rubber dinghy, its ugly head now out of the water, jaws gaping as it lunged at him, crashing against the oil drums, making the bow of the dinghy rear up out of the water. Then it was gone, both men aghast.

"By God Harry . . ." Willi shouted and pointed. The shark was charging toward the bait. They saw it take it and the hook into its mouth and swim away, the line singing off the reel. Willi held his breath, tightened the line, then with both hands on the rod, he struck hard. "Gotttt heemmm!" he shouted, taking the strain, the reel shrieking as the line rushed out, the hook deeply embedded now.

"Bloody bastard near did me," Scragger said, his heart racing, watching the taut line. "Don't let the bugger cheat you."

Willi put more strain on the line and began to fight him, the line taut.

"Watch him, Willi, he'll turn and come back fast . . ." But the shark did not, just slowed and fought the line and hook in a frenzy, boiling the water around it, half in and out of the water, rolling over and turning. But the hook held and the line was strong enough and Willi gave the fish just enough leeway, allowing it to swim off a way, then once more began to reel in. Minutes passed. The strain of fighting such a fish without a harness or chair, unable to use his legs to help him, was overwhelming. But Willi held on. Abruptly the shark stopped fighting, beginning to circle again. Slower.

"Good on you, Willi, you got him, Willi."

"Scrag, if he comes in fast see if you can keep the line from fouling, and when I get him near enough, jab him with the harpoon." Willi felt the pain in his back and hands but now he was exhilarated, waiting for the next move. It came quickly.

The shark swirled and headed for them. Frantically Willi reeled in to take up the slack lest the shark turn again and snap the line, but it kept barreling in and went directly under the raft. Miraculously the line did not foul and when the shark came out on the other side to charge off toward deeper water, Willi let him take line with him and gradually got the tension back. Once more the shark tried to shake off the hook in a paroxysm of rage, churning the water white, and once more Willi held him. But his muscles were weakening, he knew he would not be able to hold him alone and swore silently. "Give me a hand, Scrag."

"Okay, mate."

Together the two men held the rod now, Willi working the reel, pulling the shark in, playing him, closer and closer. The shark was slowing. "He's tiring, Willi." Inch by inch they pulled him in. Now the shark was thirty yards out from the raft just making headway, its great tail waving slowly back and forth, almost wallowing in the water. To breathe, a shark must have forward motion. If it stops it drowns.

Patiently they fought it, its huge weight hurting them. Now they could see its great size, the yellow eyes, jaws tight shut, the pilot fish. Twenty-five yards, twenty, eighteen, seventeen . . .

Then it happened. The shark came to life and tore away from them for fifty yards at incredible speed, line screeching off the reel, then turned ninety degrees at full speed and was going away but Willi somehow got tension back on the line, forcing the fish to circle, but he could not bring it nearer. Another circuit, Willi using all his strength on the reel to no avail. On the next circuit he gained a little. Another inch. Another, then both men lurched and nearly fell overboard as the line came free. "Lost heem by God Harry . . ."

Both were panting and aching and bitterly disappointed. There was no sign of the shark now. "God cursed line," Willi said, reeling in, swearing in two languages. But it wasn't the line. It was the chain. The links nearest the hook were mashed. "That bugger must've just chewed through it!" Scragger said, awed.

"He was playing with us, Scrag," Willi said disgustedly. "He could have bust it any time he wanted. He was giving us the finger." They searched the water all around but there was no sign of it. "He could be on the bottom, waiting," he said thoughtfully.

"More likely he's two miles away, mad as a rabid dingo."

"I betcha he's mad, Scrag. That hook'll do him no good at all." Both men searched the sea. Nothing. Then they noticed the rubber dinghy was listing by the bow and half submerged. Scragger bent down and carefully examined it, his eyes on the sea and under the raft.

"Look," he said. There was a great rip in one of the air chambers. "The bugger must've done it when he came charging in." The air was escaping fast. "No problem. We can make the shore in time. Let's go."

Willi looked at the raft, then at the sea. "You go, Scrag. Me I wait for the wood dinghy with someone up front with a machine gun."

"There's no problem, for God's sake. C'me on."

"Scrag," Willi said sweetly, "I love you like a brother but I'm not moving. That beetch frightened me to death." He sat down in the center of the raft and put his arms around his knees. "That motherless beetch's lurking somewhere, bottoming. You want to go, okay, but me, I know the Book says when in doubt, duck. Order up the other boat on the walkie-talkie."

"I'll bring her myself." The dinghy squelched as Scragger stepped carefully into it, nearly capsized, and he scrambled back on the raft cursing, quicker than he wanted to. "Wot the hell're you laughing about?"

"You got out of there like you got jellyfish on your bum." Willi was still laughing. "Scrag, why don't you swim home?"

"Get stuffed." Scragger looked at the shore, heart pounding. Today it seemed far away when most days it was so close.

"You swim and you're crazy," Willi said, seriously now. "Don't do it."

Scragger paid no attention to him. You know something? he was thinking.

You're scared fartless. That bugger was a small one and you hooked him and he got away and now he's miles out in the Gulf. Yes, but where?

He put a tentative toe in the water. Something below caught his eye. He knelt on the side of the raft and pulled up the cage. It was empty. The whole side was torn off. "Stone the crows!"

"I'll call up the boat," Willi said, reaching for the walkie-talkie. "With a machine gun."

"No need for that, Willi," Scragger said with a show of bravado. "Race you to the shore."

"Not on your Nelly! Scrag, for God's sake don't . . ." Willi was appalled as Scragger dived over the side. He saw him surface and strike out strongly, then all at once turn back and scramble back onto the raft, spluttering and choking with laughter.

"Fooled you, huh? You're right, me son, anyone who swims ashore's crazy! Call up the boat, I'm fishing for more dinner."

When the boat came, one of the mechanics was on the tiller with two excited Green Bands in the bow, others watching from the beach. They were halfway back to shore when the shark appeared out of nowhere and began circling. The Green Bands started firing and, in their excitement, one fell overboard. Scragger managed to grab his gun and opened up on the shark that raced for the petrified man now standing in the shallow water. The bullets went into the shark's head and into the eyes and though the shark was dead it did not believe it, just rolled over thrashing, its jaws working and tail working, then went driving ahead for its prey. But without the guidance of scent or eyesight it missed the man and went on up the sloping bottom until it beached itself and thrashed around, half in and half out of the water.

"Scrag," Willi said, when he could talk, "you've the luck of the devil. If you'd swum in he'd've got you. You've the luck of the devil."

AT RIG ROSA—ZAGROS: 3:05 P.M.   Tom Lochart got out of the 206 stiffly and shook hands with Mimmo Sera, the "company man" who greeted him warmly. With Lochart was the Schlumberger expert, Jesper Almqvist, a tall young Swede in his late twenties. He carried his special case with the necessary down-hole tools—all his other equipment already here, on site. "*Buon giorno*, Jesper, good to see you. She's waiting for you."

"Okay, Mr. Sera, I'll go to work." The young man walked off toward the rig. He had logged most of the wells in the field.

"Come inside for a moment, Tom." Sera led the way through the snow to the office trailer. Inside it was warm and a pot of coffee was on the big-bellied, iron, wood-burning furnace near the far wall. "Coffee?"

"Thanks, I'm bushed, the trip from Tehran was boring."

Sera handed him a cup. "What the hell's going on?"

"Thanks. I don't know exactly—I just dropped off Jean-Luc at the base, had a brief word with Scot, then thought it best to bring Jesper at once and come see you myself. Haven't seen Nitchak Khan yet; I'll do that soon as I get back but Scot was quite clear: Nitchak Khan told him the komiteh had given us forty-eight hours to leave. McI—"

"But why? Mamma mia, if you leave we'll have to close down the whole field completely."

"I know. My God, the coffee's good! Nitchak's always been reasonable in the past—you heard this komiteh shot Nasiri and burned the schoolhouse?"

"Yes, terrible. He was a fine fellow, though pro-Shah."

"So were we all—when the Shah was in power," Lochart said, thinking of Sharazad and Jared Bakravan and Emir Paknouri and HBC—always back to HBC, and Sharazad. At dawn he had left her, hating to leave her. She was still deep in sleep. He had thought about waking her but there was little to say. Zagros was his responsibility—and she looked so exhausted, the bruise on her face vivid. His note said: "Back in a couple of days. Any problem see Mac or Charlie. All my love." He looked back at Sera. "McIver's got an appointment this morning with a top official in the government, so with any luck he can straighten everything out. He said he'd get a message to us soon as he got back. Your radio's working?"

Sera shrugged. "As usual: from time to time."

"If I hear anything I'll get word to you, either tonight or first thing. I hope it's all a storm in a bucket of shit. But if we have to clear out, McIver told me temporarily to base out of Kowiss. There's no way in hell we can service you from there. What do you think?"

"If you're forced out, we'll have to evacuate. You'll have to ferry us to Shiraz. We've company HQ there; they can put us up or fly us out until we're allowed back. Madonna, there would be eleven bases to close, double shifts."

"We could use both 212s, no sweat."

"Plenty of sweat, Tom." Sera was very worried. "There's no way to close down and get the men out in forty-eight hours. No way at all."

"Maybe it won't be necessary. Let's hope, huh?" Lochart got up.

"If we have to evacuate, most of the crew'll cheer—we haven't had a replacement in weeks and they're all overdue leave." Sera got up and glanced out of the window. They could just see the afternoon sun glinting off the crest over Rig Bellissima. "You heard what a fine job Scot did, with Pietro?"

"Yes. The lads call him Bomber Pietro now. Sorry about Mario Guineppa."

"*Che sarà, sarà!* Doctors're all *stronzi*—he had a medical last month or so. It was perfect. *Stronzo!*" The Italian looked at him keenly. "What's up, Tom?"

"Nothing."

"How was Tehran?"

"Not good."

"Did Scot tell you anything I don't know?"

"A reason for the komiteh's order? No. No, he didn't. Maybe I can get something out of Nitchak Khan." Lochart shook hands and went off. Once he was airborne, he thought of the story Scot had told him, Jean-Luc, and Jesper about what happened in the village after the komiteh had sentenced Nitchak Khan to death:

"The moment they marched Nitchak Khan out of the schoolhouse and I was alone, I slipped out the back window and sneaked into the forest as quietly as I could. A couple of minutes later I heard a lot of firing and rushed back to base as fast as possible—must admit I was scared fartless. It took me quite a time, bloody snow's in ten-foot drifts in places. Not long after I got back old Nitchak Khan and the mullah and some of the villagers came up here—my God, I was so relieved! I thought for certain Nitchak and the mullah'd been shot and I guess they were just as relieved because they stared at me pop-eyed, thinking me dead too."

"Why?" Tom had asked.

"Nitchak said that just before the komiteh left they fired the schoolhouse, supposedly with me still in it. He said they had ordered all foreigners out of the Zagros. Everyone—particularly us with our choppers, out by tomorrow night."

Lochart was watching the land below, the base not far off, the village nearby. The afternoon sun was sliding off it, going behind the mountains. There was plenty of daylight left but no longer the sun to warm them. Just before he had left with Jesper for Rig Rosa and no one was near, Scot had told him really what happened. "I saw it all, Tom. I didn't run off when I said I did. I haven't dared tell anyone but I was watching out of the schoolhouse window, frightened to bloody death, and saw it all. Everything happened so fast. My God, you should've seen old Nitchak's wife with the rifle, talk about a tigress. And tough! She shot a Green Band in the belly, then left him to scream a bit and . . . banggg! stopped it. I'll bet she was the one who shot the first bastard, the leader, whoever the hell he was. Never seen such a woman, never'd believe she could be like that."

"What about Nasiri?"

"Nasiri never had a chance. He just ran off and they shot him. I'm sure they shot him just because he was a witness and not a villager. That got my wits working, and my legs, and I sneaked out of the window like I said, and when Nitchak came up here I pretended to believe his story. But I swear to

God, Tom, all those komiteh bastards were dead before I left the village, so Nitchak must've ordered the schoolhouse burned."

"Nitchak Khan wouldn't do that, not with you in it. Someone must've seen you sneak out."

"I hope to Christ you're wrong because then I'm a living threat to the village—the only witness."

Lochart landed and walked down to the village. He went alone. Nitchak Khan and the mullah were waiting for him in the coffeehouse as arranged. And many villagers, no women. The coffeehouse was the meeting house, a one-room hut made from logs and mud wattle with a sloping roof and crude chimney, the rafters black from years of the wood fire's smoke. Rough carpets to sit on.

"Salaam, Kalandar, peace be upon you," Lochart said, using the honorific title to imply that Nitchak Khan was also leader of the base.

"Peace be upon you, Kalandar of the Flying Men," the old man said politely. Lochart heard the slap and saw there was none of the friendliness of olden times within the eyes. "Please sit here in comfort. Your journey was beneficent?"

"As God wants. I missed my home here in the Zagros, and my friends of the Zagros. You are blessed by God, Kalandar." Lochart sat on the uncomfortable carpet and exchanged the interminable pleasantries, waiting for Nitchak Khan to allow him to come to the point. The room was claustrophobic and smelled rancid, the air heavy with body odors and goat smells and sheep smells. The other men watched silently.

"What brings Your Excellency to our village?" Nitchak Khan said and a current of expectancy went through the closeness.

"I was shocked to hear that strangers came to our village and had the impertinence to lay evil hands on you."

"As God wants." Nitchak's eyes narrowed slightly. "Strangers came to *our* village but they went away leaving our village as it has always been. *Your* camp, unfortunately, is not to be the same."

"But why, Kalandar? We have been good for the village and employ many of your peo—"

"It is not for me to question *our* government or these komitehs of *our* government or *our* Commander of the People, the Ayatollah himself. The young flier saw and heard, so there is nothing more to be said."

Lochart perceived the trap. "The young flier heard and saw only what happened in the schoolhouse, Kalandar. I ask that we, as old but known guests . . ." he chose the word carefully, "that we be allowed time to seek a change in a ruling that appears to go against the interests of the Zagros."

"The Zagros extends a thousand miles and crosses Kash'kai lands into Bakhtiari and the lands of a hundred other tribes. Yazdek is Yazdek," Nitchak rasped, then quoted from the *Rubáiyát*, " 'Resign your body to fate and put up with pain,/Because what the Pen has written for you,/It will not unwrite.' "

"True, but did not Omar Khayyám also write: 'The good and evil that are in man's heart,/The joy and sorrow that are our fortune and destiny,/Do not impugn them to the wheel of heaven because, in the light of reason,/The wheel is a thousand times more helpless than you.' "

A rustle went through the villagers. The old mullah nodded, pleased, and said nothing. Nitchak Khan's eyes smiled though his mouth did not and Lochart knew the meeting would be better now. He blessed Sharazad who had opened his ears and eyes and senses to the *Rubáiyát* that, in Farsi, was beyond elegance.

Everyone waited. Nitchak Khan scratched his beard, reached into his pocket, and found a pack of cigarettes. Lochart casually brought out the pishkesh, a gold-plated Dunhill lighter he had bought from Effer Jordon for just this purpose: "Effer, I'll goddamn kill you if it doesn't work first time!" He caressed the flint. The wick ignited and he breathed again. His hand was very steady as he leaned forward and held the light for the old man.

Nitchak Khan hesitated, then puffed and took a deep drag of smoke. "Thank you." His eyes narrowed as Lochart put the lighter on the carpet in front of him.

"Perhaps you would accept this gift from all of us in our camp who are grateful for your guidance and protection. After all, didn't you break down the gates and take possession of the base in the name of the People? Didn't you win the toboggan race, beating the best of us, through the quality of your courage?"

Another rustle in the room, everyone waited filled with delight as the contest stiffened, though all knew the Infidel had said only what was true. The silence grew, then the Khan reached over and picked up the lighter and looked at it closely. His gnarled thumb clicked up the lid as he had seen others in the camp do. With hardly any motion it lit the very first time and everyone was as pleased as he was with the quality of the pishkesh.

"What guidance does His Excellency need?"

"Nothing in particular, not really, Excellency Kalandar," Lochart said deprecatingly, continuing the game according to ancient custom.

"But there must be something that might make His Excellency's lot better?" The old man stubbed his cigarette into the earth.

At length Lochart allowed himself to be persuaded. "Well, since Your

Excellency has the magnanimity to ask, if Your Excellency would intercede for us with the komiteh to give us a little more time, I would be very grateful. Your Excellency, who knows these mountains like the inside of his own eating bowl, knows we cannot obey the orders of strangers who obviously don't know we cannot clear the rigs of personnel, nor safeguard the rigs—the Zagros property of the illustrious Yazdek branch of the Kash'kai—nor take away our machines and spares by tomorrow sunset."

"True, strangers know nothing," Nitchak Khan said agreeably. Yes, he thought, strangers know nothing and those sons of dogs who dared to try to implant their filthy strangers' ways were quickly punished by God. "Perhaps the komiteh would grant an extra day."

"That would be more than I would dare ask. But, Kalandar, it would hardly be enough to show them how little they know about your Zagros. Perhaps they need to be taught a lesson. They should be told at least two weeks—after all, you are kalandar of Yazdek and of all eleven rigs and the whole Zagros knows of Nitchak Khan."

Nitchak Khan was very proud and so were the villagers, pleasantly swept along with the Infidel's logic. He took out his cigarettes and his lighter. It lit the first time. "Two weeks," he said and everyone was very satisfied, including Lochart. Then he added, to give himself time to consider if two weeks was too long, "I will send a messenger and ask for two weeks."

Lochart got up and thanked the Khan profusely. Two weeks would give McIver time. Outside, the air tasted like wine and he filled his lungs gratefully, pleased with the way he had handled the delicate negotiation. "Salaam, Nitchak Khan, peace be upon you."

"And upon you."

Across the square was the mosque, and beside it the ruined schoolhouse. The other side of the mosque was Nitchak Khan's two-storied house and, at the door, his wife and two of his children with some other village women also colorfully dressed.

"Why was the schoolhouse burned, Kalandar?"

"One of the komiteh was heard to say, 'Thus should perish everything foreign. Thus will perish the base and all that it contains—we need no foreigners here, want no foreigners here.'"

Lochart was saddened. That's what most of you believe, if not all of you, he thought. And yet lots of us try to be part of Iran, speak the language, want to be accepted but never will be. Then why do we stay, why do we try? Perhaps for the same reason Alexander the Great stayed, why he and ten thousand of his officers married Iranian women in one vast ceremony—

because there's a magic to them and to Iran that is indefinable, totally obses-
sive, that consumes as I am consumed.

A burst of laughter came from the women surrounding Nitchak Khan's
wife at something she had said.

"It's better when wives are happy, eh? That's God's gift to men, eh?" the
Khan said jovially, and Lochart nodded, thinking how fantastically lucky
Nitchak Khan had been and what a gift of God his wife was—like Sharazad
was to him and, thinking of her, once more the horror of last night welled up,
his terror of almost losing her, her madness and unhappiness, then hitting her
and seeing the bruises when all he wanted was her happiness in this world
and the next, if there was a next.

"And lucky for me, God made her such a fine shot, eh?"

"Yes," Lochart said before he could stop himself. His stomach heaved and
he cursed himself for letting his attention wander. He saw the shrewd eyes
watching him and added hastily, "Shot? Your wife's a fine shot? Please excuse
me, Excellency, I didn't hear you clearly. You mean with a rifle?"

The old man said nothing, just studied him, then nodded thoughtfully.
Lochart kept his gaze steady and looked back across the square, wondering if
it had been a deliberate trap. "I've heard that many Kash'kai women can use
a rifle. It would seem that, er, that God has blessed you in many ways,
Kalandar."

After a moment Nitchak Khan said, "I will send word to you tomorrow,
how much time the komiteh agrees. Peace be upon you."

Going back to the base Lochart asked himself, Was it a trap I fell into? If
the remark was involuntary, made from pride in her, then perhaps, perhaps
we're safe and Scot's safe. In any event we've time—perhaps we have, but
perhaps Scot hasn't.

The sun had gone from this part of the plateau and the temperature had
quickly fallen below freezing again. The cold helped to clear his head but did
not eliminate his anxiety or overcome his weariness.

A week, two weeks, or a few days, you've not much time, he thought. In
Tehran, McIver had told him about getting export licenses for three 212s to
go to Al Shargaz "for repairs." "Tom, I'll send one of yours, one from here,
and one from Kowiss—thence to Nigeria, but for God's sake keep that part
to yourself. Here're the exit papers dated for Wednesday next. I think you
should go yourself, and get out while you can. You get out and stay at Al
Shargaz—there're plenty of pilots there to take the 212 onwards."

Mac just doesn't understand, he thought. He came up out of the trees and
saw the base, Scot and Jean-Luc waiting for him beside a 212.

I'll send Scot on the ferry whatever happens, Lochart thought, and having made the decision, some of his concern left him. The main decision's do we start the evacuation or not? To decide that, you have to decide how far to trust Nitchak Khan. Not very far at all.

CHAPTER 38

AT INNER INTELLIGENCE HQ: 6:42 P.M. It was barely twenty-three hours since Rakoczy had been captured, but he was already broken and babbling the third level—the truth. The first two levels were cover stories of partial truths rehearsed and rerehearsed by all career agents until they were deeply embedded into the subconscious in the hope that these partial truths would deflect questioners from probing deeper, or make them believe they already had all the truth. Unfortunately for Rakoczy, his interrogators were expert and anxious to probe ever deeper. Their problem was to keep the torment from killing him first. His problem was how to die quickly.

When he had been caught yesterday evening, he had at once tried to get his teeth into the point of his collar where the poison vial was sewn—a trained reflex action. But his captors had forestalled him, held his head backward while they chloroformed him, then carefully stripped him, probed his mouth for a false tooth of poison and his anus for a capsule.

He had expected beating and psychedelic drugs: "If they use those on you, Captain Mzytryk, you're finished," his teachers had said. "Nothing much to do but to try to die before giving secrets away. Better to die before they break you. Never forget we'll avenge you. Our reach can span fifty years and we'll get those who betrayed you."

But he had not expected the level of agony to which they had taken him so fast, or the unspeakable things they had done to him, electrodes inside him, in his nose mouth stomach rectum, on his testicles and eyeballs—with drug injections to put him to sleep, to wake him up, minutes only between sleep wake sleep wake, disoriented, upside down, inside out.

"For Christ's sake, Hashemi," Robert Armstrong had said, sickened, long long ago in the beginning, "why don't you just give him the truth drugs, you've got them, no need for all this shit."

Colonel Hashemi Fazir had shrugged. "A little cruelty is good for the soul. By Allah, you've seen the files, you've seen what the KGB's done to some of our citizens who weren't even spies."

"That's no excuse."

"We need his information quickly, by God. We need to reach the third level you're always harping about. I've no time for your twisted ethics, Robert. If you don't want to stay, leave."

Armstrong had stayed. He had muffled his ears against the screams, loathing the brutality. No need for that, not nowadays, he had said to himself, knowing he would have died long since.

He watched the two men through the one-sided mirror as they worked Rakoczy over again in the small, well-equipped chamber, sorry for him in an oblique way—after all, Rakoczy was a professional like him, a brave man who had held out against them extraordinarily.

Abruptly the screams stopped and Rakoczy was again inert. Hashemi spoke into the mike that fed into the earphones of the man below. "Is he dead? I told you stupid sons of dogs to be careful!"

One of the two men was a doctor. The headset he wore cut out all sound except instructions from the interrogators. Irritably he lifted Rakoczy's eyelids and peered at his eyes, then, with his stethoscope, listened to his heartbeat.

"He's alive, Colonel. He's . . . there's still a way to go yet."

"Give him five minutes, then wake him up. And don't kill him until I say so." Angrily, Hashemi clicked off the mike and cursed the man. "Don't want him dead when we're so close to cleaning him out." He glanced at Armstrong, eyes glittering. "He's the best we've ever had, ever, eh? By God, Robert, he's a gold mine."

Rakoczy had babbled out his two covers long since and then his real name, KGB number, where he was educated, born, married, lived, his known superiors in Tbilisi, their involvement in Iran, the Tudeh, the mujhadin, how and where they supported the Kurdish independence movement, who his contacts were.

"Who's the top KGB Azerbaijani?"

"I . . . no more please . . . pleasestoppppp it's Abdollah Khan of Tabriz . . . him, only him of importance and he . . . he was . . . is to to to be the first President when Azer . . . Azerbaijan be . . . becomes independent but now he's too big and inde . . . independent so . . . so now he's a Section 16/a . . ."

"You're not telling us all the truth—teach him a lesson!"

"Oh I amIamIampleaseeeeee . . ."

Then reviving him and his babbling again, about Ibrahim Kyabi, Ibrahim's father, the mullah Kowissi, who the Tudeh student leaders were, about his own wife, about his father and where he lived in Tbilisi, and about his grandfather who was in the tsar's secret police before being a founding member of the Cheka, then OGPU, NKVD, and finally the KGB—founded in '54 by Khrushchev after Beria had been shot as a Western spy.

"You believe Beria was a spy for us, Mzytryk?"

"Yes . . . yes . . . yes he was, the KGB had proof oh yes . . . please stoppppp . . . please stopppppp I'll tell you anyththingggggg . . ."

"How could they have proof to that lie?"

"Yes it was a lie but we were to believe it we were . . . we had to had to had to . . . please stoppppppp I begggggg you . . ."

"Stop hurting him, you devils." Armstrong's voice came in on cue. "No need to hurt him if he's cooperating—how many times do I have to tell you! So long as he tells the truth don't touch him. Give him a glass of water. Now, Mzytryk, tell us all you know about Gregor Suslev."

"He's . . . he's a spy I think."

"You're not telling us the truth!" Hashemi roared at him, on cue. "Teach him a lesson!"

"No . . . no . . . noplease stoppppppppppohGodplease stopppppp he's he's Petr Oleg Mzytryk my father my father . . . Suslev was his . . . his cover name in the in the Far East based out of Vlad . . . Vladivostok and and and another cover's Brodnin . . . and and and he lives in in Tbilisi and he's commissar and senior ad . . . adviser Iranian affairs and con controller of Abdollah Abdollah Khan . . ."

"You're lying again. How could you know such secrets? Teach him a les—"

"Please no I swearrrrrr I'm not lying I . . . read his secret dossier and I know it's true . . . Brodnin was last and then he . . . Allah helppppp meeeeee . . ." Again he fainted again. Again they revived him.

"How does Abdollah Khan contact his controller?"

"He . . . my . . . they meet when whenever . . . some . . . sometimes at the . . . at the dacha sometimes at Tabriz . . ."

"Where in Tabriz?"

"At . . . at the Khan's palace . . ."

"How do they arrange a meeting?"

"By code . . . coded telex from Tehran . . . from HQ . . ."

"What code?"

"The . . . G16 . . . G16 . . ."

"What's Abdollah Khan's code name?"

"Ivanovitch."

"And his controller's?" Armstrong was careful not to agitate the helpless man by reminding him he betrayed his father.

"Ali . . . Ali Khoy . . ."

"Who were Brodnin's contacts?"

"I . . . I don't . . . I don't rememb remember . . ."

"Help him remember!"

"Pleaseplease oh God oh Goddddddd wait let me think I can't remember it was it was . . . wait he told me there were there were three . . . it was something like like like one of them was a color a color . . . wait, yes, Grey yes Grey that was it . . . and and an another was . . . and another was Broad something . . . Broad something . . . I think . . . you it was Julan Broad something . . ."

"Who else?" Armstrong asked, hiding his shock. "The third?"

"I . . . I cant remem . . . no waitttttttt let me thinkkkk . . . there was there was anoth . . . told me there were he told me about . . . about four . . . one . . . one was . . . Ted . . . Ever . . . Ever something . . . Everly . . . and and another there were . . . if . . . I . . . pleaseeee if I think let me think and it was it was Peter . . . no Percy . . . Percy Smedley yes Smedey Tailler or Smidley . . ."

The color left Armstrong's face.

". . . that was all that was all that he that he told me . . ."

"Tell us all you know about Roger Crosse!"

No answer.

Through the mirror they saw the man writhing on the operating table, heaving against the wires as more pain was fed into him and, mixed with the moans, the words poured out again: "He he . . . stopppppppppppppp he was was head no assistant head of MI6 and almost our top English secret agent

for for for . . . twenty or more years for us and . . . and Brodnin Brod my
father found . . . found out he was a double . . . triple agent and ordered
him Section 16/a . . . Crosse cheated us for years cheated cheated
cheated . . ."

"Who tipped Brodnin about Crosse?"

"Idontknow I swearIdontknow I can't know everything everything only
what was in his dossier and and what he told me. . ."

"Who was Roger Crosse's controller?"

"I don't know, don't know, how could I know I only know what I read
secretly in my father's doss . . . you've got to believe mmmmm-
meeeeeee . . ."

"Tell me everything in the dossier," Hashemi said, as vitally interested
now as Armstrong.

They listened, sifting the words from the screams. At times the almost
incoherent mixture of Russian and Farsi as Rakoczy continued to bring forth
more names and addresses and covers and ranks in answer to their questions,
his memory prompted by new levels of pain, until he was spent and repeating
and now confused, himself confused and no longer of value. Then mixed
with the gibberish ". . . Pah . . . mud . . . Pah . . . mudi . . ."

"What about Pahmudi?" Hashemi said abruptly.

"I . . . he's . . . helppp meeee . . ."

"What about Pahmudi? Is he a Soviet agent?"

Now only gibberish and weeping and confusion.

"Better give him a rest, Hashemi. His memory's too good to blow—we can
get what Pahmudi means tomorrow and go back over the stuff." Armstrong
was equally drained, secretly marveling at the knowledge Rakoczy had provided. "I advise a rest period, let him sleep for five hours, then we could
begin again."

In the chamber the two men were waiting for instructions. The doctor
glanced at his watch. He had been at it for six hours without a break, his back
ached and so did his head. But he was a long-term SAVAK specialist and very
pleased that he had brought Rakoczy to the level of truth without drugs.
Atheist son of a burnt father! he thought disgustedly.

"Let him sleep for four hours, then we begin again," came over the loudspeaker.

"Yes, Colonel. Very good." He peered at the eyes under the lids, then said
carefully to his assistant who was a deaf-mute but could lip-read, "Leave him
as he is—that'll save time when we come back. He'll need a wake-up injec-
tion." The man nodded and, when the door was opened from the outside,
both men left.

In the room behind the mirror the air was smoky and dry.

"What about Pahmudi?"

"He has to be connected with Mzytryk, Petr Oleg." Armstrong was sifting all Rakoczy's information, awed.

Hashemi took his eyes off the man lying on the table and switched off the cassette recorder, pressed the rewind button. In a half-opened drawer were seven other cassettes.

"Can I have copies?" Armstrong asked.

"Why not?" Hashemi's eyes were red-rimmed and the stubble of his heavy beard showed darkly even though he had shaved only a few hours ago. "What was so important about Brodnin and those other names, Grey, Julan Broad something, Ted Ever something, and Percy Smedley or Smidley Tailler?"

Armstrong got up to ease the pain in his shoulders, also to give himself a little time to think. "Brodnin was a Soviet businessman, KGB, but a double agent for us. There was never a suspicion he was duping us. Julan Broad something has got to mean Julian Broadhurst. We've never had anything on him, never a whisper, nothing. He's a leading light of the Fabian Society, a highly respected member of the Labour party, in or out of the cabinet at his whim, adviser and confidant of prime ministers." He added disgustedly, "Patriot."

"So now you have him. Traitor. So put him on a table for a few hours, milk him dry, then drown him in the Thames. Grey?"

"Lord Grey, firebrand of the Left, ex–trades unionist, rabid leader of the anti-China anti–Hong Kong lobby, politely anti-Communist, sent up to the Lords a few years ago to create more trouble. We did an investigation on him a few years ago but he came up clean as a whistle—nothing except his politics." My God, Armstrong was thinking, if they're both spies and traitors —and we could prove it—that would rip Labour apart, let alone the explosion Percy'd cause the Tories. But how to prove it and stay alive? "We've had nothing on him ever."

"So now you have him too. Traitor. Clean him out and shoot him. Ted Ever something?"

"Everly—golden boy of the TUC being groomed for high office. Impeccable centrist politics. Never a smell of pink let alone Communist."

"Now you have him. Rack him. Smedley or Smidley Tailler?"

Robert Armstrong offered his cigarettes. Percy Smedley-Taylor: landed gentry, rich, Trinity College—an apolitical deviate who manages to keep his aberrations out of the press when he's caught—well-known ballet critic, publisher of erudite magazines, with impeccable, untouchable connections into the highest and most delicate sources of English power. Christ Almighty, if he's a Soviet spy . . . It's impossible! Don't be bloody silly, you've done too many years, know too many secrets to be surprised about anyone. "Doesn't mean beans, but I'll check him out, Hashemi," he said, not wanting to share the knowledge until he had thought through what he should do.

The cassette clicked off as the rewind finished. Hashemi took it out, put it with the others in the lower drawer and locked the drawer carefully. "Then deal with them in our fashion: send an emissary to them, Robert, to them and their lousy high-blown friends. They'll soon give you plenty of pishkesh to compensate for your loss of pension." Hashemi laughed mirthlessly, inserting a new cassette. "But don't go yourself or you'll end up in a back alley with a knife in your back or poison in your beer—these high-blown bastards are all the same." He was very tired but his elation at all the marvelous knowledge Rakoczy had given them pushed away the need for sleep. "We've already got enough from him to dynamite the Tudeh, control the Kurds, stop the insurrection in Azerbaijan, make Tehran safe, Kowiss safe—and cement Khomeini into power," he said to himself.

"Is that what you want? What about Abrim Pahmudi?"

Hashemi's face darkened. "Allah let me deal with him properly! Rakoczy's given me a golden key perhaps even to him." He looked at Armstrong. "Gold for you too, eh? This Suslev—Petr Oleg—who murdered the great Roger Crosse? Eh?"

"Yes. You too. Now you know who's your top enemy."

"What's Mzytryk, this Suslev, to you?"

"I had a run-in with him years ago in Hong Kong." Armstrong sipped some cold coffee, baiting the hook. "He could provide you—and me—with more gold than his son. He could peg Abrim Pahmudi, and if him, Christ only knows who else—perhaps the Revolutionary Komiteh? I'd give a lot to debrief Suslev. How can we do that?"

Hashemi tore his concentration off Pahmudi and put it back on the personal danger he himself and his family were in. "In return you will arrange me a British passport, safe passage out, and a substantial pension—if I need it?"

Armstrong put out his hand. "Done," he said. The two men shook hands, neither believing the gesture had any value other than as a politeness, both knowing they would deliver if they could, but only so long as it was then to their own advantage.

"If we get him, Robert, I control the briefing and I ask what I want first."

"Of course, you're the boss." Armstrong's eyes veiled his excitement. "Could you get him?"

"Perhaps I could persuade Abdollah Khan to arrange a meeting this side of the border. Rakoczy's given us enough on him to make even him squirm though I'd have to be careful . . . he's one of our best agents too!"

"Barter the knowledge of the Section 16/a—I bet he doesn't know they've betrayed him."

Hashemi nodded. "If we get Petr Oleg over the border, no need to bring him here. We could clean him out in our place in Tabriz."

"I didn't know you had a place there."

"Lots of things you don't know about Iran, Robert." Hashemi stubbed out his cigarette. How much time have I got? he asked himself nervously, totally unused to feeling like the hunted and not the hunter. "On second thought, give me the passport tomorrow."

"How soon could you 'persuade' Abdollah Khan?"

"We'd still have to be careful—that bastard's all-powerful in Azerbaijan." They both glanced at Rakoczy as he stirred momentarily, moaned, then went back into nightmare again. "Have to be very careful."

"When?"

"Tomorrow. Soon as we've finished with Rakoczy we'll visit Abdollah. You provide the plane—or chopper. You're very friendly with IHC, aren't you?"

Armstrong smiled. "You know everything, don't you?"

"Only about Tehran things, Islamic things, Iranian things." Hashemi wondered what McIver and the other oil support foreigners would do if they knew that Deputy Minister Ali Kia, newly appointed to the ATC board, had, some days ago, recommended immediate nationalization of all foreign oil-based companies, all Iran-registered airplanes, airplane companies, and the expulsion of all foreign pilots and personnel. "How are you going to service the oil fields, Excellency Minister?" he had asked when he had been told.

"We don't need foreigners. Our own pilots will service our own fields—haven't we hundreds of pilots who need to prove their loyalty? I presume you have secret files on all foreign pilots, executives and so on. The, er, the komiteh requires them."

"I don't think we have anything, Excellency. Those files were SAVAK-instigated," Hashemi had said smoothly. "I presume you know those terrible people have an extensive file on Your Excellency?"

"What file? Me? SAVAK? You must be mistaken."

"Perhaps. I've never read it, Excellency, but I was told of its existence. I was told it goes back over twenty years. Probably it contains nothing but lies. . . ."

He had left a badly shaken Deputy Kia with the promise that he would try to obtain the file secretly and give it to him and had laughed all the way back to Inner Intelligence HQ. The file on Ali Kia—his file—really did go back twenty years and contained unshakable proof of all sorts of smelly business deals, usury, pro-Shah voting and informing, together with highly ingenious —photographed—sexual practices that would send conservative fundamentalists into a frenzy.

"What's the joke?" Armstrong asked.

"Life, Robert. A couple of weeks ago I had at my disposal a whole air force if need be, now I must ask you to arrange the charter. You arrange the charter, I'll arrange the clearance." He smiled. "You'll give me the British passport, very bloody valid, as Talbot might say, prior to takeoff. Agreed?"

"Agreed." Armstrong stifled a yawn. "While we're waiting, can I hear the last cassette?"

Hashemi reached for his key, stopped at the knock on the door. Tiredly he got up and opened it. His fatigue vanished. Four men were outside. One of his own men, white-faced, and three Green Bands. Armed. He knew the oldest of them. "Salaam, General," he said politely, his heart grinding. "Peace be upon you."

"Salaam, Colonel. Peace be upon you." General Janan was hard-faced with a thin line for a mouth. SAVAK. He looked at Armstrong coldly, then took out a paper, offered it to Hashemi. "You are to hand over the prisoner Yazernov to me at once."

Hashemi took the paper, thanking God he had risked everything to capture Rakoczy and ram him through to the third level fast. "To Colonel Hashemi Fazir, Inner Intelligence. Immediate. By authority of the Revolutionary Komiteh: The Department of Inner Intelligence is disbanded and all personnel absorbed into this organization at once under the command of General Janan. You are suspended from all duties pending further orders. You will hand over to General Janan the prisoner Yazernov and all interrogation tapes at once. [signed] Abrim Pahmudi, Director, SAVAMA."

"The spy's still on the second level and you'll have to wait. It's dangerous to remove him an—"

"He's no longer your responsibility." The general motioned to one of his men who went out, beckoned to others in the corridor, then walked down the steps and into the chamber below, the doctor, white-faced and very nervous, now with them. When the Green Bands saw the naked man on the table and the instruments and the way he was wired, their eyes glittered. The doctor began to unwire him.

In the interrogation room above, Hashemi looked back at the general. "I formally tell you it's dangerous to move him. You're responsible."

"Insha'Allah. Just give me the tapes."

Hashemi shrugged and unlocked the top drawer and gave him the dozen, almost useless tapes from the first and second level.

"And the others! Now!"

"There aren't any."

"Open the other drawer!"

Again Hashemi shrugged, selected a key, and used it carefully. If turned correctly, the key set the magnetizer into operation and wiped the tapes. Only he and Armstrong knew the secret—and about the secret installation of duplicate cassette recorders: "You never know, Hashemi, when you might be betrayed or by whom," Armstrong had told him years ago when, together, they had installed the devices. "You might want to wipe tapes, then use the secret ones to barter for your freedom. You can never be too careful in this game."

Hashemi slid the drawer open, praying that both devices were operating. Insha'Allah, he thought, and gave over the eight cassettes. "They're empty, I tell you."

"If they are, accept my apologies, if they're not . . . Insha'Allah!" The general looked at Armstrong, his eyes granite. "Better you leave Iran quickly. I give you a day and a night for past services."

AT THE BAKRAVAN HOUSE, NEAR THE BAZAAR:

8:57 P.M. Sharazad was lying on her stomach on the bed, being massaged, and she groaned with pleasure as the old woman caressed oil into her bruises and into her skin. "Oh, be careful, Jari . . ."

"Yes, yes, my princess," Jari crooned, her hands softly strong, easing the pain away. She had been nursemaid and servant to Sharazad ever since her birth, and had given her suck when her own baby, born a week earlier, had died. For two years she suckled Sharazad and then, because Jari was a quiet and gentle woman, now widowed, she had been given full charge of her. When Sharazad married Emir Paknouri she accompanied her into his house and then, the marriage finished, happily they had returned home. Stupid to marry such a flower to one who prefers boys, however much money he has, Jari had always thought but never said out loud. Never never never. Dangerous to go against the head of the house—any head of a family—even more so with a money-grubbing miser like Jared Bakravan, she thought, not sorry he was dead.

When Sharazad had married the second time, Jari had not gone to stay in the apartment. But that did not matter, for Sharazad spent the days here when the Infidel was away. All the household called him that and tolerated him because of her happiness that only women understood.

"Eeeee, what devils men are," she said and hid her smile, understanding very well. They had all heard the screams last night and the sobbing, and though they all knew a husband was entitled to beat his wife and that God had allowed the Infidel's blows to shake their mistress out of her fit, she herself had heard the different cries, just before dawn this morning, the cries of her and him in the Garden of God.

Never had she been there herself. Others had told her about being transported, so had Sharazad, but the few times her own husband had lain with her had been for his pleasure and not hers. Her share had been pain and six children before she was twenty, four dying in infancy. Then him dying to release her from the childbirth death that she knew, for her, would otherwise have been inevitable. As God wants! Oh, yes, she told herself so contentedly, God rescued me and made him die and now, surely, he burns in hell, for he was a foul blasphemer who barely prayed once a day. God also gave me Sharazad!

She looked down on the beautiful, satin body and long, dark-dark hair. Eeeee, she told herself, how blessed to be so young, so moist, so resilient, so ready to do God's work at long last.

"Turn over, Princess, an—"

"No, Jari, it hurts so."

"Yes, but I must knead your stomach muscles and condition them." Jari chuckled. "They must be very strong soon."

At once, Sharazad turned and looked up at her, pain forgotten "Oh, Jari, are you sure?"

"Only God is sure, Princess. But have you ever been late before? Isn't your time overdue—and a son long overdue?"

The two women laughed together, then Sharazad lay back and gave herself to the hands and to the future and to the happy time she would have when she told him: Tommy, I'm honored to tell . . . no, that's no good. Tommy, God has blessed us . . . no, that's no good either though it's true. If only he was Muslim and Iranian it'd be so much easier. Oh, God, and Prophet of God, make Tommy Muslim and so save him from hell, make my son strong and let him grow up to have sons and daughters and them sons . . . oh, how blessed we are by God . . .

She let herself drift. The night was calm, still a little snow falling and not much gunfire. Soon they would have their evening meal and then she would play backgammon with her cousin Karim or with Zarah, her brother Meshang's wife, then to sleep contentedly, the day well spent.

The morning when Jari had awakened her the sun was up, and though she had wept a little from the pain, oil and massage soon took most of it away. Then the ritual washing and first prayer of the day, kneeling in front of the little shrine in a corner of the bedroom and its *sajadeh*, the small square of lovely wrought tapestry with its bowl of sacred sand from Cabella and, beyond that, the string of prayer beads and her copy of the Koran, beautifully decorated. A quick breakfast of tea, fresh bread still hot from the kiln oven, butter and honey and milk, a boiled egg as always—rarely a shortage even during the bad troubles—then quickly to the bazaar, veiled and chadored, to see Meshang, her adored brother.

"Oh Meshang, my darling, you look so tired. Did you hear about our apartment?"

"Yes, yes, I did," he said heavily, dark shadows around his eyes. The four days since their father had gone to Evin Jail had aged him. "Sons of dogs, all of them! But they're not our people. I heard they're PLO acting on instructions of this Revolutionary Komiteh." He shuddered. "As God wants."

"As God wants, yes. But my husband said a man called Teymour, the leader, this man said we had until afternoon prayer today to take our things away."

"Yes, I know. Your husband left a message for me before he left this morning for Zagros. I've sent Ali and Hassan and some of the other servants, told them to pretend they were movers and to collect everything they could."

"Oh, thank you, Meshang, how clever you are." She was greatly relieved. It would have been unthinkable for her to have gone herself. Her eyes filled with tears. "I know it's the Will of God but I feel so empty without Father."

"Yes, yes, it's the same for me . . . Insha'Allah." There was nothing more he could do. He had done everything correctly, overseeing the washing of the body, binding it with the best muslin, and then the burial. Now the first part of mourning was over. On the fortieth day would be another ceremony at the cemetery when once more they would weep and rend their clothes and all would be inconsolable. But then, as now, each would once more take up the weight of living, there was the Shahada to say five times a day, the Five Pillars of Islam to obey to ensure you went to heaven and not to hell—your only important reason for life. I will certainly go to Paradise, he thought with total confidence.

They sat silently in the small room over the shop that such a short time ago was the private domain of Jared Bakravan. Was it only four days since Father was negotiating with Ali Kia for the new loan—that we still somehow have to provide—and Paknouri burst in and all our troubles began? Son of a dog! It's all his fault. He led the Green Bands here. Yes, and he's been a curse for years. If it hadn't been for his weakness, Sharazad would have had five or six children by now and we wouldn't be saddled with the Infidel who makes us the butt of a thousand bazaari sneers.

He saw the bruise around her left eye and did not comment. This morning he had thanked God and agreed with his wife that the beating had brought her out of her fit. "No harm to a good beating from time to time, Zarah," he had said with relish, and thought, All women need a good beating now and then with their constant nagging and nattering and crying and bickering, and jealousies and interference and all this ungodly talk of voting and marches and protests. Against what? Against the laws of God!

I'll never understand women. Still, even the Prophet, whose Name be praised, he, the most perfect man that ever lived, even he had problems with women and ten more wives after Khadija, his first, had died after having given him six children—how sad that no sons survived him, only his daughter Fatima. Even after all this experience with women it's written that even the Prophet, even he, would have to take himself aside for peace from time to time.

Why can't women be content to stay in the home, be obedient, keep quiet, and not meddle?

So much to do. So many threads to pick up and to find, secrets to unlock, accounts and promissory notes and debts to uncover, and so little time. All our property stolen, villages, the estate on the Caspian, houses and apartments and buildings all over Tehran—all the ones the devils know about! Devils! The Revolutionary Komiteh and mullahs and Green Bands are devils on earth. How am I going to deal with them all? But I must, somehow. I must, then next year I will make the pilgrimage to Mecca.

"As God wants," he said and felt a little better. And it's as God wants that I am put in charge long before I expected it, even though I'm as well trained as any son could be to take over an empire, even the Bakravan empire.

It's also as God wants that I already know where most of the secrets are, whispered to me by Father over the last few years when he discovered I was to be trusted, cleverer than he had ever expected. Didn't I suggest the numbered Swiss bank accounts nearly seven years ago, and explain about U.S. Treasury bills, real-estate investment in America, and most of all about the Seven Sisters? We made millions, all of it safe from these sons of dogs, thanks be to God! Safe in Switzerland in gold, land, blue chips, dollars, deutsche marks, yen, and Swiss francs . . .

He saw Sharazad looking at him, waiting. "The servants will do everything before sunset, Sharazad, don't worry," he said, loving her though wanting her to leave so that he could continue his work. But it was time to gather in other strings: "This husband of yours, he agreed to become a Muslim, didn't he?"

"How kind of you to remember, dear Meshang. My husband agreed to consider it," she said defensively. "I've been teaching him whenever I can."

"Good. When he returns please tell him to come to see me."

"Yes, of course," she said at once. Meshang was head of the family now, and, as such, was to be obeyed without question.

"The year and a day is overdue, is it not?"

Sharazad's face lit up. "I'm honored to tell you, darling Meshang, that perhaps God has blessed us, I am overdue one or two days."

"God be praised. Now that is worth celebrating! Father would have been so pleased." He patted her hand. "Good. Now, what about him—your husband? This would be the perfect time to divorce, wouldn't it?"

"No! Oh, how could you say such a thing?" she burst out before she could stop herself. "Oh, absolutely not, oh, no, that would be terrible, I would die, it would be terr—"

"Be quiet, Sharazad! Think!" Meshang was astonished by her bad manners. "He's not Iranian, not Muslim, he has no money, no future, he's hardly worthy to be part of the Bakravans, wouldn't you agree?"

"Yes, yes, of course I . . . I agree to everything you say but if I may add . . ." she said hastily, keeping her eyes lowered to cover her shock, cursing herself for not being aware how much Meshang was opposed to her Tommy, that therefore he was enemy, to be guarded against. How could I have been so naive and so stupid? "I agree there may be problems, my darling, and agree with everything you say . . ." she heard herself tell him in her most honeyed voice, her mind working with the speed of light, analyzing, discarding, trying to make a plan—for now and for the future—for without Meshang's benevolence, life would be very difficult. "You're the wisest man I know . . . but perhaps I may be allowed to say that God put him into my path, Father agreed to my marriage, so until God takes him out of my path and guides m—"

"But now I am head of the family and everything's changed—the Ayatollah's changed everything," he said curtly. He had never liked Lochart, resented him as an Infidel, the cause of all their present and past troubles, despised him as an interloper and an unwarranted expense, but because he had had no power to interfere and because of their father's tacit agreement he had always kept it hidden. "Don't worry your pretty little head, but the revolution's changed everything. We live in a different world, and in the light of this I must consider your future and the future of your son."

"You're perfectly right, Meshang, and I bless you for thinking of me and my child, how wonderful you are and how fortunate that you're here to take care of us," she said, back in control now. She continued to flatter, cajole, being penitent for her lack of manners, using all of her guile, allowing him no opening and turning their conversation to other things. Then at the perfect time she said, "I know you must be very busy." She got up, smiling. "Will you and Zarah be home for dinner? Cousin Karim's coming if he can get away from the base, won't that be fun? I haven't seen him since . . ." She stopped herself in time. "For at least a week, but most important, Meshang, cook is making your favorite horisht, just the way you like it."

"Oh? He is? Oh, well, yes, yes, we will—but tell him not to use too much garlic—now concerning your husb—"

"Oh that reminds me, darling Meshang," she said, playing her last card— for the moment. "I heard that Zarah now has your permission to go on the Women's March, the day after tomorrow, how sensitive of you." She saw the sudden flush and laughed to herself, knowing that Zarah was as adamant about going as he was adamant against it. His fury soared. She listened patiently, her eyes guileless, nodding in agreement from time to perfect time.

"My husband agrees with you totally, darling Meshang," she said with suitable fervor. "Yes, totally, dearest brother, and I'll certainly remind Zarah, if she asks me, about your feelings . . ." Not that this will make the slightest difference to her, or to me, because on this protest march we *will* go. She kissed him lightly. "Good-bye, my darling, try not to work too hard. I'll make sure about the horisht."

Then she had gone at once to Zarah and had warned her that Meshang was still furious against the march: "Ridiculous! All our friends will be there, Sharazad. Does he want us shamed before our friends?" Together they had made a plan. By this time it was late afternoon and she had rushed home to command horisht, "just as the Master likes it and if you use too much garlic and it's not perfect I'll . . . I'll get old Ashabageh the Soothsayer to put the evil eye on you! Go to the market and buy the melon he adores!"

"But, mistress, there haven't been any melons for s—"

"Get one!" she had screeched and stamped her foot. "Of course you can get one!"

Then supervising Jari tidying away all her clothes and Tommy's clothes, shedding a tear now and then, not for the loss of their apartment that he had wanted and enjoyed more than she, but only from happiness to be home again. A rest, last prayer, and then a bath and now the massage.

"There, Princess," Jari said, her arms tired. "Now you should dress for dinner. What would you like to wear?"

Wearing the dress that would please Meshang the most, the multicolored woolen skirt and blouse he admired. Then once more checking on the horisht and the polo—the golden-crusted, mouth-watering Iranian way of cooking rice—and the other Meshang specialty, the melon, sweet-smelling and juicy and perfectly sculptured.

Waiting for her cousin Karim Peshadi to arrive—loving him, remembering their lovely times growing up, their families always intermingled, summers on their Caspian estates, swimming and sailing and, in the winter, skiing near Tehran, nothing but parties and dances and laughter, Karim tall like his father, the colonel commandant at Kowiss, and as fine. Always associating Karim with that first September evening she had seen the strange tall foreigner with the blue-gray eyes—eyes that had glowed with the heavenly fire the ancient poets wrote about, the instant he had seen her . . .

"Highness, His Excellency your cousin Captain Karim Peshadi requests permission to see you."

Joyfully running to greet him. He was staring out of a window in the smaller of the reception rooms, the walls all small mirrors and windows set into an artistic Persian design, the only furniture the usual low, continuous sofa around the walls, a few inches off the close-sheared carpet, soft-padded and upholstered with the finest Persian fabric—like the backrest that was attached to the walls.

"Darling Karim, how wonder—" She stopped. This was the first time she had seen him since the day, a week ago, when they had gone together to the riot of Doshan Tappeh, and now she was looking at a stranger—stretched skin over the high cheekbones, the dreadful pallor, dark rings around his eyes, stubbled beard, untidy clothes when usually he was impeccably dressed and groomed. "Oh, Karim, what is it?"

His lips moved but no sound came out. He tried again. "Father's dead, shot for crimes against Islam, I'm suspect and suspended and may be arrested any moment," he said bitterly. "Most of our friends are suspect, Colonel Jabani's vanished, accused of treason—you remember him, the one who led the people against the Immortals and had most of his hand blown off . . ."

Numbed, she sat listening, watching him.

". . . but there's worse to come, darling Sharazad. Uncle . . . Uncle Valik and Annoush and little Jalal and Setarem are all dead, killed trying to escape to Iraq in a civilian 212 . . ."

Her heart seemed to stop and doom began.

". . . they were intercepted and shot down near the Iraqi border. I was at HQ today, waiting to answer our komiteh's questions when the telex came in from our base at Abadan—those komiteh sons of dogs can't read so they asked me to read it out, not knowing I had any connection with Valik, that we were related. The telex was marked secret and it said the traitors General Valik and a General Seladi had been identified in the 212's wreckage from identity cards, along with others and . . . and a woman and two children . . . and asked us to check out the chopper, supposedly one of Tom's company that'd been hijacked, EP-HBC . . ."

She fainted.

When she came to, Jari was patting her forehead with a cold towel, other servants anxiously grouped around, Karim, white-faced and apologetic in the background. Blankly she stared at him. Then what he had said flooded back, what Erikki had said flooded back, and Tommy's strangeness. And once again the three mixed, another wave of terror started to engulf her. "Has . . . has Excellency Meshang arrived yet?" she asked weakly.

"No, no, Princess. Let me help you to bed, you'll feel bett—"

"I'm . . . no, thank you, Jari, I'm . . . I'm fine. Please leave us alone."

"But, Prin—"

"Leave us alone!"

They obeyed. Karim was filled with anguish. "Please excuse me, darling Sharazad, I shouldn't have worried you with all these problems, but I'm . . . I only discovered about . . . about Father this morning, I'm so sorry, Sharazad, it's not a woman's place to worry about wh—"

"Karim, listen to me, I beg you," she interrupted with growing desperation. "Whatever you do, don't mention about Uncle Valik, don't mention to Meshang about him and . . . and the others, not yet, please, not yet! Don't mention about Valik!"

"But why?"

"Because . . . because . . ." Oh God oh God what do I do? she was thinking, wanting to cry out, I'm sure Tommy was flying HBC, oh God let me be wrong but I'm sure that's what Erikki said when I asked him how long Tommy'd be away. Didn't Erikki say: "Don't worry, Tommy's charter's to Bandar Delam—HBC with spares—that shouldn't take but a day or two." Isn't Bandar Delam beside Abadan that's beside the border? Didn't Uncle Valik come to see Tommy late at night, much too late unless the matter was very urgent, and then, after he'd left, wasn't Tommy changed, in misery, staring into the fire? "Family must look after family," wasn't that what he muttered? Oh God help me . . .

"What is it, Sharazad, what is it?"

I daren't tell you, Karim, even though I'd trust you with my life, I've got to protect Tommy . . . if Meshang finds out about Tommy that'll be the end of us, the end of everything! He'll denounce him, he won't risk any more trouble . . . or crimes against God! I can't oppose the family, Meshang will make me divorce. God help me, what shall I do? Without Tommy I'll . . . I'll die, I know I will, I'll . . . what was it Tommy said about taking a helicopter on a ferry? A ferry to Al Shargaz? Was it there or to Nigeria? I daren't tell you, Karim, I daren't . . .

But when her eyes saw the enormity of his concern, her mouth opened, and she blurted out everything that she had not dared to tell.

"But it's impossible," he stuttered, "impossible, the telex said there were no survivors, impossible he should be flying it."

"Yes, but he was he was, I'm sure of it, I'm sure of it. Oh, Karim, what am I going to do? Please help me, please, I beg you, please help meeeeee!" The tears were running down her cheeks and he held her, trying to comfort her. "Please don't tell Meshang, please help me, if my Tommy . . . I'd die."

"But Meshang's bound to find out! He's got to know."

"Please help me. There must be something you can do, there must be som—"

The door opened and Meshang hurried in, Zarah with him. "Sharazad, my dear, Jari said you fainted, what happened, are you all right? Karim, how are you?" Meshang stopped, astonished at Karim's ill-kempt appearance and pallor. "What on earth's happened?"

In the silence Sharazad put her hand to her mouth, petrified she would blurt everything out again. She saw Karim hesitating. The silence worsened, then she heard him say in a rush, "I've terrible news. First . . . first about my . . . my father. He's been shot, shot for . . . for crimes against Islam . . ."

Meshang burst out. "That's not possible! The hero of Dhofar? You must be mistaken!"

"Excellency Jared Bakravan wasn't possible but he's dead and Father's dead like him, and there's other news, all bad . . ."

Helplessly Sharazad began to cry, Zarah put her arms around her, and Karim's heart went out to her and he buried Valik and his wife and children for others to bring forth.

"Insha'Allah," he said, loathing the excuse that he could no longer accept for blasphemous crimes committed by men in the Name of God that such men would never know. The Ayatollah's truly a gift from God. We need only to follow him to cleanse Islam of these foul blasphemers, he thought. God will punish them after death as we, the living, must punish them into death.

"My news is all bad, I'm suspect, most of my friends, the air force's being put on trial. Foolishly I told Sharazad . . . I wanted you to know, Meshang, but foolishly I told her and that was the reason she . . . she fainted. Please excuse me, I'm so sorry, I won't stay, I can't, I've got to . . . got to get back. I just came to tell you about . . . I had to tell someone . . ."

AT McIVER'S OFFICE: 10:20 P.M. McIver was alone in the penthouse offices, sitting in his creaking chair, feet comfortably on his desk, reading—the light good and the room warm thanks to their generator. The telex was on, and the HF. It was late but there was no point in going home yet where it was cold and damp and no Genny. He looked up. Footsteps were hurrying up the outside stairs. The knock was nervous. "Who is it?"

"Captain McIver? It's me, Captain Peshadi, Karim Peshadi."

Astonished, McIver unlocked the door, knowing the young man quite well, both as a helicopter student and favored cousin of Sharazad. He stuck out his hand, covering his further surprise at the youth's appearance. "Come in, Karim, what can I do for you? I was terribly sorry to hear about your father's arrest."

"He was shot two days ago."

"Oh, Christ!"

"Yes. Sorry, none of this is going to be pleasant." Hurriedly Karim closed the door and dropped his voice. "Sorry, but I've got to hurry, I'm already hours overdue but I've just come from Sharazad—I went to your apartment but Captain Pettikin said you were here. Tonight I read a secret telex from our base in Abadan." He told him what it said.

McIver was appalled and tried to cover it. "Did you tell Captain Pettikin?"

"No, no, I thought I should tell only you."

"Far as we know HBC was hijacked. None of our pilots were invol—"

"I'm not here officially, I just came to tell you because Tom's not here. I didn't know what else to do. I saw Sharazad tonight and found out, also quite by chance, about Tom." He repeated what Sharazad had told him. "How could Tom be alive and them all dead?"

McIver felt the hurt in his chest begin again. "She's mistaken."

"In the Name of God, tell me the truth! You must know! Tom must've told you, you can trust me," the young man exploded, beside himself with worry. "You've got to trust me. Perhaps I can help. Tom's in terrible danger, so's Sharazad and all our families! You've got to trust me! How did Tom get out?"

McIver felt the knot tightening around them all—Lochart, Pettikin, him. Don't lose your wits, he ordered himself, be careful. You daren't admit anything. Don't admit anything. "Far as I know Tom was nowhere near HBC."

"Liar!" the young man said enraged and spilled out what he had concluded all the way here, walking, fighting on a bus, walking again, snow falling and cold and desperate—the komiteh still to appear before. "You must've signed the clearance, you or Pettikin, and Tom's name's got to be on the clearance —I know you all too well, you and your hammering into us about flying by the book, signing forms, always have a form signed. You did, didn't you? Didn't you?" he shouted.

"I think you'd better go, Captain," McIver said curtly.

"You're as involved as Tom, don't you see? You're in trouble as mu—"

"I think you'd better leave it. I know you're overwrought and it's terrible about your father," he said kindly. "I'm truly, terribly sorry."

There was no sound but the gentle hum of the HF and the generator that was above on the roof. McIver waited. Karim waited. Then the young man half nodded. "You're right," he said crestfallen, "why should you trust me? Trust's gone away from us. Our world's become hell on earth and all because of the Shah. We trusted him but he failed us, gave us false allies, muzzled our generals, ran away and left us in the pit, shamed, left us to false mullahs. I swear by God you can trust me but what difference does that make to you or anyone? Trust's gone from us." His face twisted. "Perhaps God's gone from us." The HF in the other room crackled gently, static from an electrical storm somewhere. "Can you get Zagros? Sharazad said Tom went back this morning."

"I tried earlier but can't raise them," McIver said truthfully. "This time of the year it's almost impossible but I heard they arrived safely. Our base in Kowiss relayed a report just after noon."

"You'd . . . you'd better tell Tom, tell him what I told you. Tell him to get out." Karim's voice was dulled. "You're all blessed, you can all go home." Then his despair burst and tears spilled down his cheeks.

"Oh, laddie . . ." Compassionately McIver put an arm around his shoulders and gentled him, the youth of an age with his own son safe in England, safely born English, safe on the ground, a doctor and nothing to do with flying, safe . . . God in heaven, who the hell is ever safe?

In a little while he felt the heaving of the youth's chest lessen. To save Karim's face, he backed off and turned and looked at the kitchenette. "I was just going to have some tea, will you join me?"

"I'll . . . just have some water and then, then I'll go, thank you."

At once McIver went to fetch some. Poor lad, he was thinking, how terrible about his father—such a wonderful fellow, tough, hard-line but straight and loyal and never a fiddle on the side. Terrible. God Almighty, if they'll shoot him, they'll shoot anyone. We'll all be dead soon, one way or another. "Here," he said, sickened, giving Karim the glass.

The youth accepted it, embarrassed that he had lost control in front of a foreigner. "Thank you. Good night." He saw McIver staring at him strangely. "What is it?"

"Just a sudden idea, Karim. Could you get access to Doshan Tappeh Tower?"

"I don't know. Why?"

"If you could, without anyone knowing what you wanted, maybe you could get HBC's clearance—it's got to be in the takeoff book, if they were using one that day. Then we could see, couldn't we, who was flying her. Eh?"

"Yes, but what good would that do?" Karim watched the pale eyes set in the craggy face. "They'd have the automatic tape recorders on."

"Maybe, maybe not. There'd been fighting there—maybe they were not so efficient. Far as we know, whoever took HBC didn't have verbal clearance to or from the tower. He just took off. Maybe in all the excitement they didn't even record any clearance." McIver's hope grew as he developed his thought. "Only the book'd tell, the takeoff clearance book. Wouldn't it?"

Karim tried to see where McIver was leading him. "And what if it says Tom Lochart?"

"I don't see how it could, because then it'd have my signature on it, and then it'd, er, it'd have to be a forgery." McIver loathed the falsehoods, his hastily made-up story sounding weaker every minute. "The only clearance I signed was for Nogger Lane to take some spares to Bandar Delam but canceled it and him before he could go. The spares were unimportant and what with one thing and another, by that time HBC'd been hijacked."

"The clearance's the only proof?"

"Only God knows that for certain. If the clearance says Tom Lochart and it's signed by me, it's a forgery. A forgery like that could cause lots of troubles. As such it shouldn't exist. Should it?"

Slowly Karim shook his head, his mind already taking him to the tower, past the guards—would there be guards?—finding the book and the right page and seeing . . . seeing the Green Band in the doorway but killing him, taking the book and hurrying away, as silently and secretly as he had entered, going to the Ayatollah, telling him about the monstrous crime committed against his father, the Ayatollah wise and listening and not like the dogs who abused the Word, at once ordering revenge in the Name of the One God. Then going to Meshang and telling him the family was saved, but more important, knowing the Sharazad he loved to distraction and wanted to dis-

traction but never possible in this life—first cousin and against Koranic law—
was also saved.

"The clearance shouldn't exist," he said, very tired now. He got up. "I'll
try. Yes, I'll try. What happened to Tom?"

Behind McIver the telex began to chatter. Both jumped. McIver put his
attention back on Karim. "When you see him ask him, that's the right thing
to do. Isn't it? You ask Tom."

"Salaam."

They shook hands and he left and McIver relocked the door. The telex was
from Genny in Al Shargaz: "Hello number one child. Talked at length with
Chinaboy who arrives tomorrow night, Monday, and will be on the 125 to
Tehran, Tuesday. He says imperative you meet him for conference at airport.
All arrangements made here for repairs on the 212s and fast turnaround.
Acknowledge. Talked to kids in England and all's well. I'm having a wonder-
ful time here, whooping it up and on the town, glad you're not here, why
aren't you? MacAllister."

MacAllister was her maiden name and she used it only when she was very
pissed off with him. "Good old Gen," he said aloud, the thought of her
making him feel better. Glad she's safe and out of this mess. Glad she called
the kids, that'll make her happy. Good old Gen. He reread the telex. What
the hell's imperative with Andy? I'll know soon enough. At least we're in
touch through Al Shargaz. He sat at the secretary chair and began to type out
the acknowledgment.

At dusk he had got a telex from HQ in Aberdeen, but it had arrived
garbled. Only the signature was legible: Gavallan. At once he had telexed for
a repeat and had been waiting ever since. Tonight radio reception was also
bad. There were rumors of big snowstorms in the mountains and the BBC
World Service, fading badly and worse than usual, told of huge storms across
all of Europe and the East Coast of America, terrible floods in Brazil. News
had been generally rotten: strikes continuing in Britain, heavy fighting inside
Vietnam between Chinese and Vietnamese armies, a Rhodesian airliner
coming in to land shot down by guerrillas, Carter expected to order gasoline
rationing, Soviets testing a fifteen-hundred-mile cruise missile, and in Iran,
"Chairman Yasir Arafat met Ayatollah Khomeini in a tumultuous welcome,
the two leaders embraced publicly, and the PLO took over Israeli Mission
Headquarters in Tehran. Four more generals were reported shot. Heavy fight-
ing continues in Azerbaijan between pro- and anti-Khomeini forces, Prime
Minister Bazargan ordered the U.S. to close two radar listening posts on the
Iran-Soviet border, and arranged a meeting with the Soviet ambassador and

Ayatollah Khomeini in the next few days to discuss outstanding differ-
ences . . ."

Depressed, McIver had turned the set off, the strain of trying to sift the
news from the static had given him a worse headache. He had had one all
day. It had started after his meeting this morning with Minister Ali Kia. Kia
had accepted the notes on a Swiss bank, "license fees" for the three 212
departures, and also for six landings and takeoffs for the 125 and had promised to find out about the Zagros expulsions: "Tell the Zagros komiteh meanwhile their order is overruled by this department pending investigation."

Fat lot of good that'll do when you're looking down the barrel of a gun! he
thought. Wonder how Erikki and Nogger are doing now? This afternoon a
telex relayed by Tabriz ATC from Iran-Timber had come in: "Captains
Yokkonen and Lane are required here for emergency work for three days.
Usual terms for the charter. Thanks." It was signed as usual by the area
manager and a normal request. Better for Nogger than sitting on his butt,
McIver had thought. Wonder what Azadeh's father wanted her for?

Promptly at 7:30 P.M. Kowiss had come through but transmission was
barely two by five, just enough to be partially audible, and heterodyning
badly. Freddy Ayre reported that Starke had returned unharmed.

"Thank God for that!"

"Say ag . . . I'm read . . . g you one by five, Cap . . . . . . ver."

"I say again," he said slowly and carefully. "Tell Starke I'm very glad he's
back. He's okay?"

". . . . . . . tain Starke . . . swered ques . . . . . iteh . . . .
orily."

"Say again, Kowiss."

"I say again, Capt . . . . . arke answ. . . . .uestions of the . . . . iteh
sa . . ."

"You're one by five. Try again at 9:00 A.M.; even better I'll be here late and
I'll try around eleven."

"Understand yo . . . . .ry later . . ound . . leven tonight?"

"Yes. Around eleven tonight."

"Capt . . . . hart and Jean-Luc arriv . . . Zagro . . . .ree
safely . . ."

The rest of the transmission was incomprehensible. Then he had settled
back to wait. While he waited he slept a little and read a little and now,
sitting at the telex machine, again he glanced at his watch: 10:30 P.M.

"Soon as this's done, I'll call Kowiss," he said out loud. Carefully he finished the telex to his wife adding for Manuela's sake that everything was fine

at Kowiss—it is, he thought, so long as Starke's back and he's okay, and the lads okay.

He fed the hole-punched tape into the cogged sender, typed the number for Al Shargaz, waited interminably for the answer back, then pressed the transmit button. The tape chattered through the cogs. Another long wait but the Al Shargaz accept code came up.

"Good." He got up and stretched. In the desk drawer were his pills and he took the second of the day. "God-cursed blood pressure," he muttered. His pressure was 160 over 115 at his last medical. The pills brought it down to a comfortable 135 over 85: "But listen, Mac, that doesn't mean you can swill the whisky, wine, eggs, and cream—your cholesterol's up too . . ."

"What bloody whisky and cream, for Christ's sake, Doc? This's Iran . . ."

He remembered how foul-tempered he had been and when Genny said, "How was it?" "Great," he had said, "better than last time and don't bloody nag!" The hell with it! Nothing I can do that I'm not doing but I certainly could use a large whisky and soda and ice and then another one. Normally there would be a bottle in the safe and ice and soda in the little refrigerator. Now there was none. Supplies zero. He made a cup of tea. What about Karim and HBC? I'll think about that later: 11:00 P.M.

"Kowiss, this is Tehran, do you read?" Patiently he called and recalled and then stopped. In a quarter of an hour he tried again. No contact. "Got to be the storm," he said, out of patience now. "To hell with it, I'll try from home."

He put on his heavy coat and went up the spiral staircase to the roof to check the level of generator fuel. The night was very black and quiet, hardly any gunfire and what there was was deadened by the snow. No lights anywhere that he could see. Snow still fell gently, almost five inches since dawn. He brushed it off his face and shone the flashlight on the gauge. The level of fuel was all right but somehow they'd have to get another supply in the next few days. Bloody nuisance. What about HBC? If Karim could get the book and the book could be destroyed, there'd be no evidence, would there? Yes, but what about Isfahan, refueling at Isfahan?

Lost in thought, he went back, locked up, and, using the flash to light his way, started down the five flights of stairs. He did not hear the telex chatter into life behind him.

In the garage he went to his car and unlocked it. His heart leaped as he saw a tall figure approaching. SAVAK and HBC jumped into his head; he almost dropped the flash but the man was Armstrong, dark raincoat and hat.

"Sorry, Captain McIver, I didn't mean to startle you."

"Well, you bloody did," he said furiously, heart still pounding. "Why the hell didn't you announce yourself or come up to the office instead of hiding in the bloody shadows like a bloody villain?"

"You might have had more visitors—I saw one come out so I thought I'd just wait. Sorry. Please put the flash down."

Angrily McIver did as he was asked—since Gavallan had pinpointed Armstrong, he had searched his own memory but had no recollection of ever meeting him. "Special Branch and CID" did nothing to ease his dislike. "Where the hell've you been? We expected you at the airport but you didn't show."

"Yes, sorry about that. When does the 125 come back to Tehran?"

"Tuesday, God willing. Why?"

"Approximately when?"

"Noon, why?"

"Excellent. That would be perfect. I need to go to Tabriz; could I and a friend charter her?"

"No way. I could never get a clearance and who's the friend?"

"I'll guarantee the clearance. Sorry, Captain, but it's very important."

"I heard there's heavy fighting in Tabriz; it was on the news tonight. Sorry, couldn't authorize that, it'd be an unnecessary risk to air crew."

"Mr. Talbot will be glad to add his request for assistance," Armstrong said in the same quiet, patient voice.

"No. Sorry." McIver turned away but was stopped at the sudden venom.

"Before you go shall I ask you about HBC and Lochart and your partner Valik and his wife and two children?"

McIver was shock-still. He could see the chiseled face and the hard mouth and eyes that glittered in the reflected light from the flash. "I—I don't know what you mean."

Armstrong reached into his pocket and pulled out a piece of paper and held it up to McIver's face. McIver directed the circle of light onto it. The paper was a photocopy of an entry in a clearance book. The writing was neat. "EP-HBC cleared at 0620 for an IHC charter to Bandar Delam, delivery of spares; pilot Captain T. Lochart, flight authorized by Captain McIver." The lower half of the paper was a photocopy of the actual clearance, signed by him with Captain N. Lane crossed out "sick," and Captain T. Lochart substituted. "A present, with my compliments."

"Where did you get it?"

"When the 125 gets into Tehran airspace, radio Captain Hogg that he's got an immediate charter to Tabriz. You'll have the clearance in good time."

"No. I'll not se—"

"If you don't arrange everything happily, and keep it all rather quiet—just between us," Armstrong said with such finality that McIver was quite frightened, "the originals of these go to SAVAK—renamed SAVAMA."

"That's blackmail!"

"It's barter." Armstrong shoved the paper into his hand, began to leave.

"Wait! Where—where are the originals?"

"Not in their hands, for the moment."

"If—if I do what you say, I get them back, all right?"

"You must be joking! Of course you get nothing."

"That's not fair—that's not bloody fair!"

Armstrong came back and stood over him, his face a mask. "Of course it's not fair. If you get these back you're out of the vise, aren't you? All of you. So long as these exist, you will do what's required of you, won't you?"

"You're a bloody bastard!"

"And you're a fool who should look after his blood pressure."

McIver gasped. "How d'you know about that?"

"You'd be astounded what I know about you and Genevere MacAllister and Andrew Gavallan and the Noble House and lots of other things that I haven't begun to use yet." Armstrong's voice became rougher, his tiredness and anxiety taking away his control. "Don't you bloody understand there's the very strong probability of Soviet tanks and aircraft permanently stationed this side of Hormuz and Iran a bloody Soviet province? I'm tired of playing silly buggers with you ostriches—just do what I ask without arguing and if you don't I'll shop the bloody lot of you."

TUESDAY
February 20

TABRIZ: 5:12 A.M.   In the small hut on the edge of the Khan's estate, Ross was suddenly awake. He lay motionless, keeping his breathing regular but all of his senses concentrated. Seemingly nothing untoward, just the usual insects and closeness of the room. Through the window he could see that the night was dark, the sky mostly overcast. Across the room on the other pallet, Gueng slept curled up, breathing normally. Because of the cold, both men had gone to bed with their clothes on. Noiselessly Ross went to the window and searched the darkness. Still nothing. Then, close to his ear, Gueng whispered, "What is it, sahib?"

"I don't know. Probably nothing."

Gueng nudged him and pointed. There was no guard in the seat outside on the veranda.

"Perhaps he's just gone to take a leak." There had always been at least one guard. By day or night. Last night there had been two so Ross had made a mock dummy in his bed and left Gueng to divert them and had slipped out of the back window and gone to see Erikki and Azadeh alone. Coming back he had almost stumbled into a patrol but they had been sleepy and unattentive so he had passed them by.

"Take a look out the back window," Ross whispered.

Again they watched and waited. Dawn in about an hour, Ross thought.

"Sahib, perhaps it was just a spirit of the mountain," Gueng said softly. In the Land Atop the World it was a superstition that by night, spirits visited the beds of sleeping men and women and children, for good purposes or ill, and that dreams were the stories they whispered.

The little man kept his eyes and ears feeling out the darkness. "I think perhaps we'd better pay attention to the spirits." He went back to his bed and pulled on his boots, put the talisman he had kept under his pillow back into his uniform pocket, then put on the tribesman robes and turban. Nimbly he checked his grenades and carbine and settled the rough backpack that contained ammunition, grenades, water, and a little food. No need to check his kookri, that was never out of reach, always oiled and cleaned nightly—and sharpened nightly—just before sleep.

Now Ross was equally ready. But ready for what? he asked himself. It's hardly five minutes since you awoke and here you are, kookri loose in the scabbard, safety catch off and for what? If Abdollah meant you harm, he would've already taken away your weapons—or tried to take them.

Yesterday afternoon they had heard the 206 take off and shortly afterward Abdollah Khan had visited them. "Ah, Captain, sorry for the delay but the hue and cry is worse than ever. Our Soviet friends have put a very large price on your heads," he had said jovially. "Enough even to tempt me, perhaps."

"Let's hope not, sir. How long will we have to wait?"

"A few days, no more. It seems the Soviets want you very much. I've had another deputation from them asking me to help capture you, the first was before you arrived. But don't worry, I know where the future of Iran lies."

Last night Erikki had confirmed about the reward: "Today I was near Sabalan, cleaning out another radar site. Some of the workers thought I was Russian—lots of Russian speakers among the border people—and said they hoped they'd be the ones to catch the tall British saboteur and his helper. The reward's five horses and five camels and fifty sheep. That's a fortune, and if they know about you that far north you can bet they're looking here."

"Were Soviets supervising you?"

"Only Cimtarga, but even then he didn't seem to be in charge. Just of me and the aircraft. The Russian speakers kept asking me when we were coming over the border in strength."

"My God—did they have anything to base that on?"

"I doubt it, just more rumors. People here feed on them. I said, 'Never,' but this man scoffed and said he knew we had 'leagues' of tanks and armies waiting, that he'd seen them. I can't speak Farsi so I don't know if he was another KGB plant disguised as a tribesman."

"The 'stuff' you're carrying? Is it anything important?"

"I don't know. Some computers and lots of black boxes and papers—they keep me away from it but none of it's dismantled by experts, just pulled out of walls, wires cut, and hanging loose and stacked carelessly. The only thing the workers're interested in is stores, cigarettes particularly."

They had talked about escaping. Impossible to make plans. Too many imponderables. "I don't know how long they want me to keep flying," Erikki had said. "This bastard Cimtarga told me Prime Minister Bazargan has ordered the Yanks out of two sites, far to the east, near Turkey, the last they've got here, ordered them to evacuate at once and to leave the equipment intact. We're supposed to fly up there tomorrow."

"Did you use the 206 today?"

"No. That was Nogger Lane, one of our captains. He came here with us—to take the 206 back to Tehran. Our base manager told me they've co-opted Nogger to look at some places where fighting's going on. When McIver doesn't hear from us he'll go into shock and send out a search party. That might give us another chance. What about you?"

"We might sneak off. I'm getting very nervous in that rotten little hut. If we evacuate, we might head for your base and hide out in the forest. If we can, we'll contact you—but don't expect us. All right?"

"Yes—but don't trust anyone at the base—except our two mechanics, Dibble and Arberry."

"Anything I can do for you?"

"Could you leave me a grenade?"

"Of course, have you ever used one?"

"No, but I know how they work."

"Good. Here. Pull the pin and count to three—not four—and heave it. Do you need a gun?"

"No, no thanks. I've my knife—but the grenade might come in handy."

"Remember they can be rather messy. I'd better be going. Good luck."

Ross had been looking at Azadeh when he had said it, seeing how beautiful she was, so very aware that their time was already written among the stars or on the wind or in the chimes of the bells that were as much a part of the summer High Country as the peaks themselves. Wondering why she never replied to his letters, then the school telling him she had gone. Gone home.

Gone. On their last day she had said, "All this that has come to pass may not come to pass again, my Johnny Brighteyes."

"I know. If it doesn't, I can die happy because I know what love is. Truly. I love you, Azadeh."

Last kiss. Then down to his train and waving good-bye, waving until she was lost. Lost forever. Perhaps we both knew that it was forever, he thought, waiting here in the darkness of the little hut, trying to decide what to do, to wait more, to sleep or to flee. Maybe it's as the Khan said and we're safe here —for the moment. No reason to mistrust him completely. Vien Rosemont was no fool and he said to trust h—

"Sahib!"

He had heard the stealthy footsteps at the same instant. Both men moved into ambush, one covering the other, both of them glad that the time for action had arrived. The door opened quietly. It was a ghoulish spirit of the mountain standing there peering into the greater darkness of the hut—a shape and vague face. To his astonishment he recognized Azadeh, the chador blending her with the night, her face puffy from crying.

"Johnny?" she whispered anxiously.

For a moment Ross did not move, gun still leveled and expecting enemies. "Azadeh, here, beside the door," he whispered back, trying to adjust.

"Quick, follow me, you're both in danger! Hurry!" At once she ran off into the night.

He saw Gueng shake his head uneasily and he hesitated. Then he decided, grabbed his backpack. "We go." He slid out of the doorway and ran after her, the moonlight small, Gueng following, flanking, automatically covering him. She was waiting beside some trees. Before he reached her, she beckoned him to follow, unerringly led the way through the orchard and around some farm buildings. The snow muffled their way but left tracks and he was very aware of them. He was ten paces behind her, watching the terrain carefully, wondering what danger and why had she been crying and where's Erikki?

Clouds were toying with the moon, hiding it mostly. Whenever it came clear, she would stop and motion him to stop and to wait, then she would move on again, using cover well, and he wondered where she had learned woodsmanship then remembered Erikki and his great knife and Finns and Finland—land of lakes and forests and mountains and trolls and hunting. Concentrate, fool, time enough to let your mind wander later, not now when you're endangering everyone! Concentrate!

His eyes searched, expecting trouble, wanting it to begin. Soon they were near the perimeter wall. The wall was ten feet high and made of hewn stone, with a wide, empty swath between it and the trees. Again she motioned him to stop in cover and walked forward into the open, seeking a special place. Finding it without trouble, she beckoned him. Before he was beside her she was already climbing, her feet fitting easily into the notches and cracks with sufficient handholds, some natural, some cleverly embedded to make the climb easy. The moon came into a bare patch of sky and he felt naked and climbed more quickly. When he reached the top she was already halfway down the other side. He slithered over and found some footholds, ducked down to wait for Gueng. His anxiety mounted until he saw the shadow darting over the ground, reaching the wall safely.

The climb down was more difficult and he slipped and fell the last six feet, cursed and looked around to get his bearings. She was already across the boundary road and heading for a rocky outcrop on the steep mountainside two hundred yards away. Below and to the left he could see part of Tabriz, fires on the far side of the city near the airport. Now he could hear distant guns.

Gueng landed neatly beside him, grinned and motioned him onward. When he reached the outcrop she had vanished.

"Johnny! Here!"

He saw the small crack in the rock and went forward. Just enough room to squeeze through. He waited until Gueng came up, and then went through the rock into darkness. Her hand came out and guided him to one side. She beckoned Gueng and did the same for him, then moved a heavy leather curtain across the crack. Ross reached into his pack for his flash but before he could pull it out the match flamed. Her hand was cupped around it. She was kneeling and lit the candle that was in a niche. Quickly he looked around. The curtain over the entrance seemed lightproof, the cave spacious, warm and dry, some blankets, old carpets on the ground, a few drinking and eating utensils—some books and toys on a natural shelf. Ah, a child's hideout, he thought, and looked back at her. She had stayed kneeling by the candle, her back to him, and now, as she pulled the chador away from her head, she became Azadeh again.

"Here." He offered her some water from his water bottle. She accepted it gratefully but avoided his eyes. He glanced at Gueng and read his mind. "Azadeh, do you mind if we put the light out—now that we see where we are —then we can pull the curtain back and keep watch and hear better. I've a flash if we need it."

"Oh, oh, yes . . . yes, of course." She turned back to the candle. "I . . . oh, just a minute, sorry . . ." There was a mirror on the shelf he had not noticed. She picked it up and peered at herself, hated what she saw, the streaks of sweat and puffy eyes. Hastily she brushed away some smudges, picked up the comb and tidied herself as best she could. A final check in the mirror and she blew out the candle. "Sorry," she said.

Gueng moved the curtain away and went through the rock and stood there listening. More gunfire from the city. A few buildings burning beyond the single runway of the airfield below and to the right. No lights there and very few on in the city itself. A few car headlights in the streets. The palace still dark and silent and he could sense no danger. He came back and told Ross what he had seen, speaking Gurkhali, and added, "Better I stay outside, safer, there's not much time, sahib."

"Yes." Ross had heard disquiet in his voice but did not comment. He knew the reason. "You all right, Azadeh?" he asked softly.

"Yes. Yes I am now. It's better in the dark—sorry I looked such a mess. Yes, I'm better now."

"What's this all about—and where's your husband?" He used the word deliberately and heard her move in the darkness.

"Just after you left last night, Cimtarga and a guard came and told Erikki he had to dress at once and leave—this man Cimtarga said he was sorry but there'd been a change of plan and he wanted to leave at once. And I, I was summoned to see my father. At once. Before I went into his room I overheard him giving orders for you both to be captured and disarmed, just after dawn." There was a catch to her voice. "He was planning to send for you both to discuss your departure tomorrow, but you would be led into ambush near the farmhouses and bound up and put into a truck and sent north at once."

"Where north?"

"Tbilisi." Nervously she hurried onward: "I didn't know what to do, there was no way to warn you—I'm watched as closely as you and kept away from the others. When I saw my father, he said Erikki wouldn't be back for a few days, that today he, my father, he was going on a business trip to Tbilisi and that . . . that I would be going with him. He . . . he said we would be away two or three days and by that time Erikki would be finished and then we would go back to Tehran." She was almost in tears. "I'm so frightened. I'm so frightened something's happened to Erikki."

"Erikki will be all right," he said, not understanding about Tbilisi, trying to decide about the Khan. Always back to Vien: "Trust Abdollah with your life and don't believe the lies about him." And yet here was Azadeh saying the opposite. He looked across at her, unable to see her, hating the darkness, wanting to see her face, her eyes, thinking that perhaps he could read something from them. Wish to Christ she'd told me all this the other side of the bloody wall or at the hut, he thought, his nervousness increasing. Christ, the guard! "Azadeh, the guard, do you know what happened to him?"

"Oh, yes, I . . . I bribed him, Johnny, I bribed him to be away for half an hour. It was the only way I could get . . . it was the only way."

"God Almighty," he muttered. "Can you trust him?"

"Oh, yes. Ali is . . . he's been with Father for years. I've known him since I was seven and I gave him a pishkesh of some jewelry, enough for him and his family for years. But, Johnny, about Erikki . . . I'm so worried."

"No need to worry, Azadeh. Didn't Erikki say they might send him near to Turkey?" he said encouraging her, anxious to get her back safely. "I can't thank you enough for warning us. Come on, first we'd better get you back an—"

"Oh, no, I can't," she burst out. "Don't you understand? Father'll take me north and I'll never get away, never—my father hates me and he'll leave me with Mzytryk, I know he will, I know he will."

"But what about Erikki?" he said shocked. "You can't just run away!"

"Oh, yes, I have to, Johnny, I have to. I daren't wait, I daren't go to Tbilisi, it's much safer for Erikki that I run away now. Much safer."

"What're you talking about? You can't run away just like that! That's madness! Say Erikki comes back tonight and finds you gone? Wh—"

"I left him a note—we made an arrangement that in an emergency I'd leave a note in a secret place in our room. We had no way of telling what Father would do while he was away. Erikki'll know. There's something else. Father's going to the airport today, around noon. He has to meet a plane, someone from Tehran, I don't know who or what about but I thought perhaps you could . . . you could persuade them to take us back to Tehran or we could sneak aboard or you . . . you could force them to take us."

"You're crazy," he said angrily. "This's all crazy, Azadeh. It's madness to run off and leave Erikki—how do you know it's not just as your father says, for God's sake? You say the Khan hates you—my God, if you run off like this, whether he does or doesn't he'll blow a gasket. Either way you put Erikki into more danger."

"How can you be so blind? Don't you see? So long as I'm here Erikki has no chance, none. If I'm not here he has to think only of himself. If he knows I'm in Tbilisi he'll go there and be lost forever. Don't you see? I'm the bait. In the Name of God, Johnny, open your eyes! Please help me!"

He heard her crying now, softly but still crying, and this only increased his fury. Christ Almighty, we can't take her along. There's no way I could do that. That'd be murder—if what she says about the Khan's true the dragnet'll be out for us in a couple of hours and we'll be lucky if we see sunset—the dragnet's already out for God's sake, think clearly! Bloody nonsense about running away! "You have to go back. It's better," he said.

The crying stopped. "Insha'Allah," she said in a different voice. "Whatever you say, Johnny. It's better you leave quickly. You've not much time. Which way will you go?"

"I—I don't know." He was glad for the darkness that hid his face from her. My God, why must it be Azadeh? "Come on, I'll see you safely back."

"There's no need. I'll . . . I'll stay here for a while."

He heard the falsehood and his nerves jangled even more. "You're going to go back. You've got to."

"No," she said defiantly. "I can never go back. I'm staying here. He won't find me, I've hidden here before. Once I was here two days. I'm safe here. Don't worry about me. I'll be all right. You go on. That's what you've got to do."

Exasperated, he managed to control his urge to drag her to her feet, and instead sat back against the wall of the cave. I can't leave her, can't carry her back against her will, can't take her. Can't leave her, can't take her. Oh you can take her with you but for how long and then, when she's captured, she's mixed up with saboteurs and Christ only knows what else they'd accuse her of and they stone women for that. "When we're found missing—if you are too—the Khan'll know you tipped us off. If you stay here, eventually you'll be found and anyway the Khan'll know you gave us the tip and that'll make it worse than ever for you, and worse for your husband. You must go back."

"No, Johnny. I'm in the Hands of God and not afraid."

"For God's sake, Azadeh, use your head!"

"I am. I'm in God's hands, you know that. Didn't we talk about that in our High Country a dozen times? I'm not afraid. Just leave me a grenade like the one you gave to Erikki. I'm safe in God's hands. Please go now."

In the other time they had talked about God often. On a Swiss mountaintop it was easy and ordinary and nothing to be shy about—not with your beloved who knew the Koran and could read Arabic and felt very close to the Infinite and believed in Islam absolutely. Here in the darkness of the small cave it was not the same. Nothing was the same.

"Insha'Allah it is," he said and decided. "We'll go back, you and I, and I'll send Gueng on." He got up.

"Wait." He heard her get up too and felt her breath and nearness. Her hand touched his arm. "No, my darling," she said, her voice as it used to be. "No, my darling, that would destroy my Erikki—and you and your soldier. Don't you see, I'm the lodestone to destroy Erikki. Remove the lodestone and he has a chance. Outside my father's walls, you too have a chance. When you see Erikki, tell him . . . tell him."

What should I tell him? he was asking himself. In the darkness he took her hand in his and, feeling its warmth, was back in time again in the darkness together in the great bed, a vast summer storm lashing the windows, the two of them counting the seconds between the lightning flashes and the thunder that bounced off the sides of the high valley—sometimes only one or two seconds, oh, Johnny it must be almost overhead, Insha'Allah if it hits us, never mind we're together—holding hands together just like this. But not like this, he thought sadly. He put her hand to his lips and kissed it. "You can tell him yourself," he said. "We'll give it a go—together. Ready?"

"You mean go on—together?"

"Yes."

After a pause she said, "First ask Gueng."

"He does what I say."

"Yes, of course. But please ask him. Another favor. Please?"

He went to the neck of the cleft. Gueng was leaning against the rocks outside. Before he could say anything Gueng said softly in Gurkhali, "No danger yet, sahib. Outside."

"Ah, you heard?"

"Yes, sahib."

"What do you think?"

Gueng smiled. "What I think, sahib, has no weight, affects nothing. Karma is karma. I do what you say."

AT TABRIZ AIRPORT: 12:40 p.m. Abdollah Khan stood beside his bulletproof Rolls on the snow-covered concrete apron near the airport terminal. He was flushed with rage, watching the 125 turn onto final, praying it would crash. Yesterday a telex relayed through police HQ had been brought by his nephew, Colonel Mazardi, the chief of police. "Please meet jet G-ETLL, ETA 1240 tomorrow Tuesday. [signed] Colonel Hashemi Fazir." The name had sent an immediate shudder through him and everyone else who had access to the message. Inner Intelligence had always been above the law and Colonel Hashemi Fazir its grand inquisitor, a man whose ruthlessness was legend even in Iran where ruthlessness was expected and admired.

"What does he want here, Highness?" Mazardi had asked, very afraid.

"To discuss Azerbaijan," he had said, hiding his dread and seething at the curtness of the telex, completely thrown by this unexpected and unwanted arrival. "Of course to ask how he can assist me—he's been a secret friend for years," he added, lying automatically.

"I'll order an honor guard and welcoming komiteh and ma—"

"Don't be a fool! Colonel Fazir likes secrecy. Do nothing, don't go near the airport, just make sure the streets are quiet and . . . ah, yes, increase pressure on the Tudeh. In fact, implement Khomeini's orders to crush them. Burn their headquarters tonight and arrest their known leaders." That will be a perfect pishkesh should I need one, he had thought, delighted with his cleverness. Isn't Fazir fanatically anti-Tudeh? God be thanked that Petr Oleg gave his approval.

Then he had sent Mazardi away and cursed everyone near him and sent them away too. Now what does that son of a dog Fazir want with me?

Over the years they had met several times and had exchanged information, to their mutual advantage. But Colonel Hashemi Fazir was one of those who believed that Iran's only protection lay in absolute centralized government, ruled from Tehran, and that tribal chieftains were archaic and a danger to the state—and also Fazir was a Tehrani with the power to uncover too many secrets, secrets that could be used against him. God curse all Tehranis and send them to hell. And Azadeh, and her God-cursed husband!

Azadeh! Did I truly sire that demon? It's not possible! Someone must have . . . God forgive me that I suspect my Beloved Napthala! Azadeh's Satan-possessed. But she won't escape, oh no, I swear I'll take her to Tbilisi and I'll let Petr use her . . .

Blood began roaring in his ears again and the clawing started in his chest again, a grasping pain. Stop it, he told himself desperately, calm yourself. Put her aside, you'll get your revenge later. Stop it or you'll kill yourself! Stop it and put her aside and think of Fazir, you'll need all your cunning to deal with him. She can't escape.

When, just after dawn, petrified guards had rushed in to tell him the two prisoners had vanished and, almost at the same time she was also discovered missing, his violence had known no bounds. At once he had sent men to search her hiding place in the rocks that he had known about for years and ordered them not to come back without her or the saboteurs. He had had the nose of the night guard cut off, the rest of the guards flogged and shoved into jail, charged with conspiracy, her maids whipped. At length he had stormed off to the airport, leaving a pall of terror over the whole palace.

God curse them all, he thought, making a great effort to calm himself, his eyes never leaving the jet. The sky was patchy blue with ominous clouds and a bad wind that swept the snow-covered runway. He wore an Astrakhan hat and fur-collared winter coat and fur-lined boots, the cold misting his glasses.

In his pocket was a small revolver. Behind him, the small terminal building was empty but for his men who had secured it and the access road beyond. Above, on the roof, he had put a sniper into ambush with instructions to shoot Fazir if he took out a white handkerchief and blew his nose. I've done all I can, he thought, now it is up to God. Crash, you son of a burnt father!

But the 125 made a perfect touchdown, snow flaring from her wheels in a vast spray. His dread increased. And the sound of his own heartbeat. "As God wants," he muttered and got into the back of the car, partitioned from the chauffeur and Ahmed, his most trusted counselor and bodyguard, by the movable, bulletproof glass. "Intercept it," he ordered and checked the revolver, leaving the safety off.

The 125 came off the far end of the runway into the feeder area, turned into the wind and stopped. It was bleak here, just snowdrifts and empty space. The big black Rolls pulled up alongside, and the door of the jet swung open. He saw Hashemi Fazir standing there, beckoning him, "Salaam! Peace be upon you, Highness, come aboard."

Abdollah Khan opened the window and called back, "Salaam, peace be upon you, Excellency, join me here." You must think me a fool to put my head in such a trap, he thought. "Ahmed, go aboard, go armed and pretend you don't speak English."

Ahmed Dursak was a Muslim Turkoman, very strong, very quick with a knife or gun. He got out, the submachine gun loose in one hand, and ran nimbly up the steps, the wind pulling at his long coat. "Salaam, Excellency Colonel," he said in Farsi, standing outside on the top step. "My Master begs you to please join him in the car—cabins of small jets make him disquieted. In the car you can talk in private and in peace, totally alone if you wish. He asks if you will honor his poor house and stay with him during your stay here."

Hashemi was shocked that Abdollah had had the effrontery—and confidence—to send the emissary armed. Going to the car did not suit him either, too easy to be bugged, or booby-trapped. "Tell His Highness I sometimes have car sickness and I beg him to come here. Here we can speak in private, be alone also and it would be a favor to me. Of course you should search the cabin in case a foul alien sneaked aboard."

"My Master would prefer, Excellency, that you j—"

Hashemi came closer to him and now his lips were a thin line and his voice as tight. "Search the airplane! Now! And do it quickly, Ahmed Dursak, three times murderer—one a woman called Najmeh—and do what I order or you will not last one more week on this earth."

"Then all the sooner I will be in Paradise because serving the Khan I do

God's work," Ahmed Dursak said, "but I will search as you wish." He stepped through the doorway and saw the two pilots in the cockpit. In the cabin was Armstrong. His eyes narrowed but he said nothing, just went past politely and opened the lavatory door making sure it was empty. There was nowhere else that anyone could hide. "Should what you suggest be possible, Excellency, the pilots will leave?"

Earlier Hashemi had asked the captain, John Hogg, if he would oblige, should it become necessary.

"Sorry, sir," Hogg had said, "but I don't like that idea at all."

"It would only be for a few minutes. You can take the ignition key with you—and the circuit breakers," Robert Armstrong had said. "I will personally guarantee no one gets into the cockpit or touches anything."

"I still don't like that idea, sir."

"I know," Armstrong had said. "But Captain McIver told you you were to do what we asked. Within reason. And this's within reason."

Hashemi saw the arrogance in Ahmed's face and he wanted to smash it off. That comes later, he promised himself. "The pilots will wait in the car."

"And the Infidel?"

"This Infidel speaks better Farsi than you, lice, and if you're wise, lice, you'll be polite to him and call him Excellency for I can assure you and your dog Turkoman ancestors he has as long a memory as me and can be more cruel than you can imagine."

Ahmed's mouth smiled. "And His Excellency, the Infidel, he waits on the runway also?"

"He stays here. The pilots wait *in* the car. Should His Highness want one guard with him—to make sure no assassins wait in ambush—he is of course welcome. If this arrangement does not suit him, then perhaps we should meet in police headquarters. Now take your foul manners away."

Ahmed thanked him politely and strode back and told the Khan what had been said, adding, "I think that dog's turd must be very sure of himself to be so rude." And in the airplane Hashemi was saying in English, "Robert, that son of a dog must be very sure of himself to have such arrogant servants."

"You'd really haul the Khan of all the Gorgons down to police HQ?"

"I could try." Hashemi lit another cigarette. "I don't think I'd succeed. His nephew Mazardi's still chief of police and police here still hold most of their power—Green Bands and komitehs aren't dominant. Yet."

"Because of Abdollah?"

"Of course Abdollah. For months, on his orders, the Tabrizi police covertly supported Khomeini. The only difference from Shah days to Khomeini days is that Shah pictures have been replaced with Khomeini pictures, Shah emblems taken off all uniforms, and now Abdollah's grasp is tighter than ever." A chill draft came through the half-open door. "Azerbaijanis are a treacherous breed, and cruel—the Qajar Shahs came from Tabriz—so did Shah Abbas, who built Isfahan and tried to ensure his longevity by murdering his eldest son and blinding another . . ."

Hashemi Fazir was watching the car out of the window, willing Abdollah Khan to concede. He was feeling better now and more confident that he would see Holy Day this week than he had been on Sunday evening when General Janan had burst into his HQ with orders for the dissolution of Inner Intelligence and had taken possession of the cassettes and Rakoczy. All that night he had been at his wits' end, then at dawn yesterday when he had left his house he had found men tailing him and, during the morning, his wife and children were jostled on the streets. It had taken him until early afternoon to lose those who followed him. By that time one of his secret Group Four leaders was waiting at a safe house and that evening when General Janan got out of his bulletproof limousine to go into his home, a nearby parked car filled with plastic explosive blew him and two of his most trusted assistants to pieces, totally wrecking his house, obliterating his wife and three children and seven servants—and his elderly, bedridden father. Men shouting leftist mujhadin slogans were heard running away. In their wake they left crudely written pamphlets: "Death to SAVAK now SAVAMA."

In the early hours of this morning, half an hour after Abrim Pahmudi had discreetly left the bed of his very secret mistress, cruel men had paid her a visit. More leftist slogans were heard and the same message daubed on her walls, using her blood and vomit and feces for paint. At nine this morning he had gone by appointment to give his condolences to Abrim Pahmudi for both tragedies—of course Inner Intelligence had informed him of them. As a pishkesh he brought part of Rakoczy's testimony as though it was information that had come into his hands from another source—just enough to be of value. "I'm sure, Excellency, if I were allowed to resume my work I could gather much more. And if my department was to be honored with your confidence and allowed to operate as before—but to report solely to you and no other power—I could prevent such foul deeds and perhaps smash these terrorist dogs off the earth."

While he was there an aide had rushed in, distraught, to say that more terrorists had assassinated one of the most important ayatollahs in Tehran—another car bomb—and the Revolutionary Komiteh required Pahmudi's immediate presence. At once Pahmudi had got up but before he left he rescinded his previous order. "I agree, Excellency Colonel. For thirty days. You have thirty days to prove your value."

"Thank you, Excellency, your confidence overwhelms me, you may be sure of my loyalty. May I have Rakoczy back, please?"

"That dog, General Janan, allowed him to escape."

Then he had gone to the airport and joined Robert Armstrong at the 125, and, once airborne, had laughed and laughed. It was the first time that a car bomb with a remote detonator had been used in Iran. "By God, Robert," he had said jovially, "it's totally efficient. From a hundred yards away you wait until you're sure it's him, then you just touch the switch on the sender that's no bigger than a pack of cigarettes and . . . boom! another enemy gone forever—and his father!" He wiped the tears out of his eyes, his laughter infectious. "That's what really got to Pahmudi. Yes, and without Group Four it would've been me and my family."

Group Four had grown out of a suggestion of Armstrong's that he had taken and elaborated: small teams of very select bands of men and women, highly trained in the most modern antiterrorist tactics, very highly paid and carefully protected—all non-Iranian, none of whom knew any of the other cells—and all known and loyal only to Hashemi. Their anonymity meant that some could be used against the others if necessary, individually they were expendable and easily replaceable—in the Middle and Near East there was too much poverty, too many betrayed causes, too much hatred, too many beliefs, too many homeless not to provide a ready ocean of men, and women, desperate for such a job.

Over the years his Group Four team had prospered, its coups secret, the vast majority secret even from Armstrong. He looked at him and smiled. "Without them I'd be dead."

"Me too, probably—I was very bloody frightened when that bugger Janan said, 'I give you a day and a night for past services.' That bugger'd never've let me get out."

"True." A few thousand feet below them the land was deep in snow and the jet already high over the mountains, the journey to Tabriz little more than half an hour.

"What about Rakoczy? You believe what Pahmudi said about him escaping?"

"Of course not, Robert. Rakoczy was a trade, a pishkesh. When Pahmudi found the tapes empty and the state Rakoczy was in he had no value—other than as a payment for past favors—he couldn't possibly know the connection with your Petr Oleg Mzytryk. Or could he?"

"Not likely—I'd say impossible."

"It's probable he's in Soviet HQ—if he's not already dead. Soviets'd want to know what he gave away . . . could he tell them anything?"

"I doubt it—he was on the brink." Armstrong shook his head. "Doubt it. What'll you do now that you're Mr. Big again? Feed Pahmudi more of his info within the thirty days—if he's alive in thirty days."

Hashemi smiled thinly and did not reply. I'm not your Mr. Big yet, he thought, or even safe until Pahmudi's in hell—with many others. I may still have to use your passport. Armstrong had given it to him before takeoff. He had checked it very carefully.

Then he had closed his eyes and settled back, enjoying the luxury and convenience of the private jet that was already over Qazvin, just a quarter of an hour out of Tabriz. But he did not nap. He spent the time considering what to do about SAVAMA, Pahmudi, and Abdollah Khan, and what to do about Robert Armstrong who knew too much.

Through the cabin window, he continued to watch the Rolls, big, immaculate, and possessed by so few on earth. By God and the Prophet, what riches, he thought, awed at this proof of the Khan's position and power. What power to flaunt such a possession so fearlessly in the faces of the komitehs, and mine. Abdollah Khan won't be easy to bend.

He knew that here in the airplane they were dangerously exposed—easy targets if Abdollah ordered his men to fire on them—but he had dismissed that possibility, certain that even Abdollah Khan would not dare such an open murder of three Infidels and one jet, and him. But just in case the Khan arranged an "accident," two Group Four teams were already en route by road, one for Abdollah personally, the other for his family, to be stopped only by code word from him personally. He smiled. Once Robert Armstrong had told him that a Chinese punishment for an important person in olden days was "death—*and all his generations.*"

"I like that, Robert," he had said. "That has style."

He saw the front side door of the car open. Ahmed got out, carrying the submachine gun oddly, then walked to the back door and opened it for Abdollah.

"You win the first round, Hashemi," Armstrong said and went forward as agreed. "All right, Captain. We'll be as quick as we can."

Reluctantly the two pilots squeezed out of the little cockpit, pulled on their parkas, and hurried out into the cold and down the steps. They saluted the Khan politely. He motioned them into the back of the car, began to climb the gangway, Ahmed following him.

"Salaam, Highness, peace be upon you," Hashemi said warmly, greeting him at the door, a concession that Abdollah noted at once.

"And upon you, Excellency Colonel." They shook hands. Abdollah walked past him into the cabin, his eyes on Armstrong, and sat in the chair nearest the exit.

"Salaam, Highness," Armstrong said. "Peace be upon you."

"This is a colleague of mine," Hashemi said, sitting opposite the Khan. "An Englishman, Robert Armstrong."

"Ah, yes, the Excellency who speaks Farsi better than my Ahmed and is famous for his memory—and cruelty." Behind him Ahmed had closed the heavy curtain over the outside door and stood with his back to the cockpit, on guard, gun ready but not impolitely so. "Eh?"

Armstrong smiled. "That was a pleasantry of the colonel, Highness."

"I don't agree. Even in Tabriz we've heard of the Special Branch expert, twelve years in service of the Shah, and running dog of his running dogs," Abdollah said scornfully in Farsi. The smile vanished from Armstrong's face, and both he and Hashemi tensed at the blatant bad manners. "I've read your record." He turned his black eyes on Hashemi, completely sure that his plan would work: Ahmed would kill them at his signal, booby-trap the airplane, send the pilots back aboard and into a hasty takeoff and fiery death—nothing to do with him, as God wants, and he, himself, after such a wonderful discussion where he had promised "complete support for the central government," would be filled with sadness.

"So, Excellency," he said, "we meet again. What can I do for you—I know your time is, unfortunately, short with us."

"Perhaps, Highness, it is what I can do for you? Per—"

"Come to the point, Colonel," the Khan said harshly, now in English, totally sure of himself. "You and I know each other, we can dispense with flattery and compliments and get to the point. I'm busy. If you'd had the courtesy to come to my car, alone, I would have been more comfortable, we could have spoken in private, leisurely. Now come to the point!"

"I want to talk to you about your controller, Colonel General Petr Oleg Mzytryk," Hashemi said as harshly, but suddenly petrified that he'd been trapped and that Abdollah was a secret Pahmudi supporter, "and about your long-term KGB connection through Mzytryk, code name Ali Khoy."

"Controller? What controller? Who's this man?" Abdollah Khan heard himself say, but his head was shrieking, You can't know that, impossible, not possible. And through the torrent of his own heartbeat he saw the colonel's mouth open and say other things that made everything worse, much worse, and worst of all it tore his plan to shreds. If the colonel spoke such secrets so openly in front of this foreigner and Ahmed, the secrets would be recorded elsewhere in a safe place to be read by the Revolutionary Komiteh and his enemies in case of an "accident."

"Your controller," Hashemi slammed at him, seeing the change, and pressed home his advantage. "Petr Oleg, whose dacha is beside Lake Tzvenghid in the Place of Hidden Valley, east of Tbilisi, code name Ali Khoy, yours is Iv—"

"Wait," Abdollah said throatily, his face livid—not even Ahmed knew that, must not know that. "I—I—give me some water."

Armstrong began to get up but froze as Ahmed's gun covered him. "Please sit, Excellency. I will get it. Fasten your belt, both of you."

"There's no n—"

"Do it," Ahmed snarled and waved the gun, aghast at the Khan's change in face and tactic, and quite prepared to put the other plan into operation himself. "Fasten them!"

They obeyed. Ahmed was near the water fountain and he filled a plastic cup and gave it to the Khan. Hashemi and Armstrong watched unbalanced. Neither had expected such an immediate capitulation from the Khan. The man seemed to have shrunk before their eyes, his pallor and breathing bad.

The Khan finished the water and looked at Hashemi, his small eyes bloodshot behind his glasses. He took them off and polished them absently, trying to regain his strength. Everything seemed to be taking more time than normal. "Wait for me beside the car, Ahmed."

Uneasily, Ahmed obeyed. Armstrong unsnapped his belt and closed the curtain again. For a moment the Khan felt better, the chill air that came in momentarily helping to clear his head. "Now, what do you want?"

"Your code name's Ivanovitch. You've been a KGB spy and helper since January 1944. In that time y—"

"All lies. What do you want?"

"I want to meet Petr Oleg Mzytryk. I want to question him seriously. In secret."

The Khan heard the words and considered them. If this son of a dog knew Petr's code name and his own code name and about Hidden Valley and January '44 when he went secretly to Moscow to join the KGB, he would know other more punishable matters. That he himself was playing both sides for the good of his Azerbaijan would make little difference to the assassins of the Right or of the Left. "In return for what?"

"Freedom to maneuver in Azerbaijan—so long as you do what is good for Iran—and a firm working relationship with me. I will give you information that will put the Tudeh, the leftists, *and* the Kurds into your hands—and give you evidence how the Soviets are thwarting you. For example, you're declared Section 16/a."

The Khan gaped at him. His ears began roaring. "I don't believe it!"

"Immediate. Petr Oleg Mzytryk signed the order," Hashemi said.

"Pr . . . proof, I . . . I want proof," he choked out.

"Entice him this side of the border, alive, and I'll give you proof—at least he will."

"You're . . . you're lying."

"Haven't you planned to go to Tbilisi today or tomorrow, at his invitation? You would never have returned. The story would be that supposedly you had fled Iran. You'd be denounced, your possessions confiscated and family disgraced—and fed to the mullahs." Now that Hashemi knew he had Abdollah in his grasp, the only thing that worried him was the state of the man's health. His head now had a slight twitch to it, the normally swarthy face was pallid with a strange reddishness around the eyes and temples, the vein in his forehead prominent. "You'd better not go north, and double your guards. I could barter Petr Oleg—even better I could allow you to rescue him and . . . well, there are many solutions if I had possession of him."

"What . . . what do you want with him?"

"Information."

"I would . . . I would be party to it?"

Hashemi smiled. "Why not? Then it's agreed?"

The Khan's mouth moved soundlessly. Then he said, "I will try."

"No," the colonel said roughly, judging the time for the coup de grace had come. "No. You have four days. I will return Saturday. At noon Saturday I will be at your palace to take delivery. Or if you prefer, you can deliver him secretly to this address." He put the piece of paper on the table between them. "Or, third, if you give me the time and place he comes over the border I will take care of everything." He unsnapped his seat belt and stood up. "Four days, Ivanovitch."

Abdollah's rage almost burst his eardrums. He tried to get up but failed. Armstrong helped him to stand and Hashemi went to the curtain but before he opened it, he took his automatic out of his shoulder holster. "Tell Ahmed not to trouble us."

Weakly the Khan stood in the open doorway and did as he was ordered. Ahmed was at the foot of the steps, his gun leveled. The wind had changed direction, now blowing toward the far end of the runway, and had picked up considerably.

"Didn't you hear His Highness?" the colonel called down. "Everything's all right but he needs help." He kept his voice reassuring. "He should perhaps see his doctor as soon as possible."

Ahmed was flustered, not knowing what to do. There was his Master, clearly worse than before, but here were the men who caused it—who were to be killed.

"Help me into the car, Ahmed," the Khan said with a curse and that settled everything. At once he obeyed. Armstrong took his other side and together they went down the stairs. Hastily the pilots got out and hurried into the airplane as Armstrong helped the sick man into the backseat. Abdollah settled himself with difficulty, Armstrong feeling more naked than he had ever been, him out in the open alone, Hashemi standing up there safely in the cabin door. The jet's engines fired up.

"Salaam, Highness," he said. "I hope you're all right."

"Better you leave our land quickly," the Khan said, then to the driver, "Go back to the palace."

Armstrong watched the car hurrying away, then turned. He saw Hashemi's strange smile, the half-concealed automatic in his hand, and for a moment thought the man was going to shoot him.

"Hurry up, Robert!"

He ran up the steps, his legs chilled. The copilot had already stabbed the Steps Retract button. The steps came up, the door closed, and they were moving. In the warmth and closeness he came to life again. "It's cold out there," he said.

Hashemi paid no attention to him. "Quick as you can, Captain, take off," he ordered, standing behind the pilots.

"I'll have to taxi back, sir. I daren't take off this way with this wind up our tails."

Hashemi cursed and peered through the cockpit windows. The other end of the runway looked a million miles away, the wind whisking snow off the drifts. To use the proper exit ramp would take them close to the terminal parking area. They would have to cross it and use the opposite ramp to the takeoff point. Over toward the terminal the Rolls was speeding along. He could see armed men collecting to meet it. "Taxi back along the runway and do a short-field takeoff."

"That's highly irregular without tower clearance," John Hogg said.

"Would you prefer a bullet in your head or a SAVAK jail? Those men there are hostiles. Do it!"

Hogg could see the guns. He clicked on his transmit button. "ECHO TANGO LIMA LIMA requesting permission to backtrack," he said, not expecting any answer—after they had cleared Tehran airspace there had been none all the way here, and no contact with this tower. He swung the jet back onto the runway, skidding, and opened the throttle some more, keeping to the left side, paralleling their landing tracks. "Tower, this is Echo Tango

Lima Lima, backtracking." Gordon Jones, the copilot, was checking every-thing, setting up for their Tehran inbound. The wind was tugging at them, their wheels uncertain. Over at the terminal he saw the Rolls stop and men surround it.

"Quick as you can—turn around, there's plenty of runway," Hashemi said.

"Soon as I can, sir," John Hogg said politely, but he was thinking, bloody twit, Colonel whoever you are, I'm more than a little anxious to be up in the Wild Blue myself but I've got to get a run at it. He had seen the hostility of the men in the car and, at Tehran, McIver's nervousness. But Tehran Tower had cleared him instantly, given him priority as though he were carrying Khomeini himself. Bloody hell, what we do for England and a pint of beer! His hands and feet were feeling the snow and the ice and the slipperiness of the surface. He eased off the throttles a little.

"Look!" the copilot said. A jet helicopter was crossing the airspace, low down a mile or so ahead. "A 212, isn't she?"

"Yes. Doesn't look like she's inbound here," Hogg said, his eyes sweeping constantly. At the terminal another car had joined the men near the Rolls; ahead to the left was a glint of light; now the 212 had gone behind a hill; to the right was a flock of birds; all needles safe in the Green; more men near the Rolls and someone on the roof of the terminal building; fuel fine; snow not too deep, sheet ice underneath; watch the drift ahead; go right a little; radio's correctly tuned; wind's still up our tail; thunderclouds building up to the north; back a hair on the left engine!

Hogg corrected the lurching swing, the airplane overresponsive on the icy surface. "Perhaps you'd better go back to your seat, Colonel," he said.

"Get airborne as fast as possible." Hashemi went back. Armstrong was peering out of the windows toward the terminal. "What're they doing there, Robert? Any problem?" he asked.

"Not yet. Congratulations—you handled Abdollah brilliantly."

"If he delivers." Now that it was over, Hashemi felt a little sick. Too close to death that time, he thought. He fastened his seat belt, then undid it, took the automatic from his side pocket, put the safety on, and slipped it into the shoulder holster. His fingers touched the British passport in his inner pocket. Perhaps I won't need it after all, he thought. Good. I'd hate having to disgrace myself by using it. He lit a cigarette.

"Do you think he'll last till Saturday? I thought he was going to have a fit."

"He's been that fat and that foul for years."

Armstrong heard the violent undercurrent. Hashemi Fazir was always dan-gerous, always on the edge, his fanatic patriotism mixed with his contempt for most Iranians. "You handled him wonderfully," he said and looked out of the window again. The Rolls and the other car and the men surrounding them were quite far and half-hidden by the snow dunes, but he could see many guns among them and from time to time someone would point in their direction. Come on, for God's sake, he thought, let's get aloft.

"Colonel"—Hogg's voice came over the intercom—"could you come forward, please?"

Hashemi unlocked his belt and went to the cockpit.

"There, sir," Hogg said pointing off to the right, past the end of the runway, to a clump of pines in front of the forest. "What do you make of that?" The tiny fleck of light began winking again. "It says SOS."

"Robert," Hashemi called out, "look ahead and to the right."

The four men concentrated. Again the light repeated the SOS. "No mistaking it, sir," Hogg said. "I could signal them back." He pointed to the heavy-duty signal flash that was for emergency use to give a Green or a Red light in case their radios failed.

Hashemi called back into the cabin. "What do you think, Robert?"

"It's SOS all right!"

The 125 was hurrying down the runway toward the signal. They waited, then saw three tiny figures come out from the trees, two men and a woman in chador. And they saw their guns.

"It's a trap," Hashemi said at once, "don't go any closer, turn around!"

"I can't," Hogg said, "haven't got enough runway." He eased the throttles a little more open. The jet was taxiing very fast, paralleling their landing tracks. They could see the figures waving their guns.

Armstrong called out, "Let's get to hell out of here!"

"Soon as I can, sir. Colonel, perhaps you'd better get back to your seat, this might be kind of bumpy," Hogg said, his voice nerveless, then dismissed them both from his mind. "Gordon, keep your eye on those buggers out there and on the terminal."

"Sure. No sweat."

The captain turned momentarily to check the other end of the runway, judged they were not quite far enough yet, but eased back on the throttle and touched the brakes. The skid began so he loosed them, keeping the jet as straight as he could, the wind shifting. The figures near the trees were larger now.

"They look a ropy lot, tribesmen, I'd say. Two automatic carbines." Gordon Jones squinted at the terminal. "Rolls's gone but a car heading our way along the ramp."

Pulling off the throttles now. Still too fast to turn.

"Christ, I think . . . I think one of the tribesmen fired a gun," Jones said, his voice picking up.

"Here we go," Hogg said into the intercom mike, braked, felt her slide, held it, then began his right turn onto the width of the runway, their momentum skidding them and the wind still hostile.

In the cabin Armstrong and Hashemi were hanging on grimly, peering out of the windows. They could see one of the figures running toward them, brandishing his gun. Armstrong muttered, "We're bloody sitting ducks." He felt the jet sliding in the turn, no traction, and he cursed.

In the cockpit Hogg was whistling tonelessly. The jet surged over their landing tracks, still skidding, the far side of the runway banked by solid, heavy dunes. He did not dare to gun her yet and waited, mouth dry, willing her to come around faster and into the wind. But she didn't, just continued to slide, wheels useless, brakes dangerous, engines growling, the subsurface ice.

Inexorably the snow dunes came closer and closer. He could see the jagged ice edges that would tear their thin skin asunder. Nothing to do but wait. Then a gust took her tail section and buffeted it around and now, though she was still sliding, she faced into the wind. Delicately he gunned both engines, felt the slide slowing, and at once began inching the throttles forward until he had some forward speed, more open and faster, and more control and now complete control and he shoved the throttles hard against the gate. The 125 surged ahead, his wheels left the surface, he touched the undercart retract, and they were soaring.

"You may smoke if you wish," he said laconically into the intercom, totally pleased with himself.

On the airfield, not far from the trees, Ross had stopped running and waving, his chest hurting him. "Bloody bastard," he shouted at the airplane. "Haven't you any bloody eyes?"

Bitterly disappointed, he started walking back to the others who had obediently waited on the edge of the forest. Over all of them was a deep gloom. So near, he thought. Through his binoculars he had seen the Khan arrive, then go aboard, then, later, Armstrong come down the steps with the Khan, helping him. "Oh, let me look, Johnny." Azadeh had said anxiously and refocused the lenses to suit her eyes. "Oh, dear, Father looks sick—I hope he's all right," she had said. "The doctor's always telling him to diet and take his life easier."

"He's doing just fine, Azadeh," he had said, trying to keep the sarcasm out of his voice. But she had heard it and flushed and she said, "Oh so sorry, I didn't mean . . . I know he's . . ."

"I meant nothing," he had said and refocused on Armstrong, ecstatic that it was Armstrong, devising a plan how to get aboard. So easy. An S-G airplane—easy to see the decal—and Armstrong. We're safe! But now we're not safe, we're in a mess, he told himself even more bitterly, trudging back in the snow, feeling filthy and wanting a bath and helpless with rage. They've got to have seen the SOS. Were their heads in their arses? Why the hell didn't th—

He heard Gueng's keening danger signal and he whirled. A car was a few hundred yards away, heading their way. He ran back and pointed into the forest. "That way!"

Earlier he had made a plan. First the airport, then, if that didn't work, they would head for Erikki's base. The base was about four miles away, southeast of Tabriz. Covered by the trees, he paused and looked back. The car stopped at the end of the runway and men got out, started after them, but found the going too heavy through the drifts. They climbed back into the car and headed away. "They won't catch us now," Ross said. He led the way deeper into the forest, of necessity keeping to the crude path.

On the edge of this clump of forest were frozen fields that in the summer would be abundant with crops, most of them belonging to a few landowners, in spite of the Shah's land reforms. Beyond the fields were the outlying slums of Tabriz. They could see the minarets of the Blue Mosque and smoke from many fires, pulled away by the wind. "Can we skirt the city, Azadeh?"

"Yes," she said, "but it's . . . it's quite a long way."

They heard her underlying concern. So far she had moved quickly and without complaint. But she was still a hazard. They wore their tribesmen's clothes over their uniforms. Their scrubby boots would pass. So would their weapons. And her chador. He looked at her, still not used to the ugliness that it made of her. She felt his glance and tried to smile. She understood. Both about the chador and about being a burden.

"Let's go through the town," she said. "We can stay in the side streets. I have some . . . some money and we can buy food. Johnny, you could pretend to be Caucasian from, say, from Astara, I could pretend to be your wife. Gueng, you speak Gurkhali or a foreign tongue and be rough and arrogant like the Turkomans from the north—you'd pass for one of them—they were descended from the Mongols, many Iranians are. Or perhaps I could buy some green scarves and make you Green Bands . . . That's the best I can do."

"That's good, Azadeh. Perhaps we'd better not stay bunched up. Gueng, you tail us."

Azadeh said, "In the streets Iranian wives follow their husbands. I . . . I will stay a pace behind you, Johnny."

"It's a good plan, memsahib," Gueng said. "Very good. You guide us."

Her smile thanked him. Soon they were in the markets and the streets and alleys of the slums. Once a man shoved into Gueng carelessly. Without hesitation Gueng slammed his fist into the man's throat, sending him sprawling into the joub senseless, cursing him loudly in a dialect of Ghurkali. There was a moment's silence in the crowd, then noise picked up again and those nearby kept their eyes down and passed onward, a few surreptitiously making a sign against the evil eye that all those who came from the north, the descendants of the hordes who knew not the One God, were known to possess.

Azadeh bought food from street vendors, fresh bread from the kilns, charcoaled lamb kebab and bean and vegetable horisht, heavy with rice. They sat on rough benches and gorged, then went on again. No one paid any attention to them. Occasionally someone would ask him to buy something but Azadeh would intervene and protect him well, coarsening her voice and talking the local Turkish dialect. When the muezzins called for afternoon prayer, she stopped, afraid. Around them, men and women searched for a piece of carpet or material or newspaper or cardboard or box to kneel on and began to pray. Ross hesitated, then following her pleading look, pretended to pray also and the moment passed. In the whole street only four or five remained standing, Gueng among them, leaning against a wall. No one bothered those who stood. Tabrizi came from many races, many religions.

They continued onward, making their way southeast and now were in the outlying suburbs, shantytowns filled with refuse and mangy, half-starved dogs, the joub the only sewer. Soon the hovels would end, the fields and orchards would begin, then the forest and the main Tehran road that curled upward to the pass that would lead them to Tabriz One. What he would do when they got there, Ross did not know, but Azadeh had said that she knew of several caves nearby where they could hide until a helicopter landed.

They went through the last of the slums, out onto the crude, snow-banked track. The snow of the surface was stained from mule and donkey droppings, pitted and treacherous, and they joined others who trudged along, some leading burdened donkeys, others bent over under the weight of their loads, others relieving themselves, men and women and children—a handful of snow with the left hand, then on again—a polyglot of people, tribesmen, nomads, townspeople—only their poverty in common, and their pride.

Azadeh was feeling very tired, the strain of crossing the city heavy on her. She had been afraid she would make a mistake, afraid they would be spotted,

frantic with worry over Erikki and worried how they would get to the base
and what then? Insha'Allah, she told herself, over and over. God will look
after you and after him and after Johnny.

When they came near the junction of the track and the Tehran road they
saw Green Bands and armed men standing beside a makeshift roadblock,
peering into vehicles and watching the people filing past. There was no way
to avoid them.

"Azadeh, you go first," Ross whispered. "Wait for us up the road—if we
get stopped, don't interfere, just go on—head for the base. We'll split up,
safer." He smiled at her. "Don't worry." She nodded, her fear making her
face more pale, and walked off. She was carrying his rucksack. Coming out of
the town she had insisted: "Look at all the other women, Johnny. If I don't
carry something, I'll stand out terribly."

The two men waited, then went to the side of the track and urinated into
the snowbank. People plodded by. Some noticed them. A few cursed them as
Infidels. One or two wondered about them—unknowingly, they were relieving themselves toward Mecca, an act no Muslim would ever do.

"Once she's through, you next, Gueng. I'll follow in ten minutes."

"Better you next," Gueng whispered back. "I'm a Turkoman."

"All right, but if I'm stopped—do not interfere. Sneak by in the fracas and
get her to safety. Don't fail me!"

The little man grinned, his teeth very white. "Don't you fail, sahib. You
have much yet to do before you're a Lord of the Mountain." Gueng looked
past him toward the roadblock, a hundred yards away. He saw that Azadeh
was in line now. One of the Green Bands said something to her, but she kept
her eyes averted, replied, and the man waved her through. "Don't wait for
me on the road, sahib. I may cross the fields. Don't worry about me—I'll
track you." He pushed through the pedestrians and joined the stream going
back toward the town. After a hundred yards or so, he sat on an upturned
crate and unlaced his boot as though it was hurting him. His socks were in
shreds but that did not matter. The soles of his feet were like iron. Taking his
time, he relaced his boots, enjoying being a Turkoman.

At the roadblock Ross joined the line of those leaving Tabriz. He noticed
police standing around with the Green Bands, watching the people. The
people were irritable, hating any authority as always and any infringement of
their right to go where and how and when they pleased. Many were openly
angry and a few almost came to blows. "You," a Green Band said to him,
"where are your papers?"

Angrily Ross spat on the ground. "Papers? My house is burned, my wife
burned, and my child burned by leftist dogs. I have nothing left but this gun

and some ammunition. God's will—but why don't you go and burn Satanists and do the Work of God instead of stopping honest men?"

"We're honest!" the man said angrily. "We're doing the Work of God. Where do you come from?"

"Astara. Astara on the coast." He let the anger come out. "Astara. And you?"

The next man in line and the one behind him began cursing and telling the Green Band to hurry up and not cause them to wait around in the cold. A policeman was edging over toward them, so Ross decided to chance it and he shoved past with another curse, the man behind followed, and the next, and now they were out in the open. The Green Band sullenly shouted an obscenity after them, then went back to watching others file through.

It took Ross a little while to breathe easier. He tried not to hurry and his eyes searched ahead. No sign of Azadeh. Cars and trucks were passing now, grinding up the incline or coming down too fast, people scattering from time to time with the inevitable stream of curses. The man who had been behind him at the roadblock came up alongside, pedestrians thinning out now, turning off into the side paths that led to hovels beside the road or to villages within the forest. He was a middle-aged man with a lined, very strong face, poorly dressed, his rifle well serviced. "That Green Band son of a dog," he said with a thick accent. "You're right, Agha, they should be doing God's work, the Imam's work, not Abdollah Khan's."

Ross was instantly on guard. "Who?"

"I come from Astara and from your accent I know you don't come from Astara, Agha. Astaris never piss toward Mecca or with their backs to Mecca —we're all good Muslims in Astara. From your description you must be the saboteur the Khan's put a price on." The man's voice was easy, curiously friendly, the old Enfield rifle over his shoulder.

Ross said nothing, just grunted, not changing his pace.

"Yes, the Khan's put a good price on your head. Many horses, a herd of sheep, ten or more camels. A Shah's ransom to ordinary folk. The ransom's better for alive than dead—more horses and sheep and camels then, enough to live forever. But where's the woman Azadeh, his daughter, the daughter that you kidnapped, you and another man?"

Ross gaped at him and the man chuckled. "You must be very tired to give yourself away so easily." Abruptly the face hardened, his hand went into the pocket of his old jacket, pulled out a revolver and shoved it into Ross's side. "Walk ahead of me a pace, don't run or do anything or I shall just shoot you in the spine. Now where's the woman—there's a reward for her too."

At that moment a truck coming down from the pass careened around the bend ahead, lurched to the wrong side of the road, and charged them, hooting loudly. People scattered. Ross's reflexes were faster and he sidestepped, shoved his shoulder into the man's side and sent him reeling into the truck's path. Its front wheels went over the man and the back wheels. The truck skidded to a stop a hundred feet below.

"God protect us, did you see that?" someone said. "He lurched into the truck."

Ross dragged the body out of the road. The revolver had vanished into the snow.

"Ah, is the sacrifice of God your father, Agha?" an old woman said.

"No . . . no," Ross said with difficulty, everything so fast, in panic. "I . . . he's a stranger. I've never seen him before."

"By the Prophet, how careless walkers are! Have they no eyes? Is he dead?" the truck driver called out, coming back up the hill. He was a rough, bearded, swarthy man. "God witness that he moved into my path as all could see! You," he said to Ross, "you were beside him, you must have seen it."

"Yes . . . yes, it is as you say. I was behind him."

"As God wants." The trucker went off happily, everything correct and finished. "His Excellency saw it. Insha'Allah!"

Ross pushed away through the few who had bothered to stop and walked up the hill, not fast, not slow, trying to get himself together, not daring to look back. Around the bend in the road, he quickened his pace, wondering if it was right to react so quickly—almost without thought. But the man would have sold her and sold them. Put him away, karma is karma. Another bend and still no Azadeh. His anxiety increased.

Here the road was twisting, the grade steep. He passed a few hovels half hidden in the forest edge. Mangy dogs were scavenging. The few that came near him he cursed away, rabies usually rampant among them. Another bend, sweat pouring off him, and there she was squatting beside the road, resting like any of a dozen other old crones. She saw him at the same moment, shook her head cautioning him, got up, and started off up the road again. He fell into place twenty yards behind her. Then there was firing below them. With everyone else, they stopped and looked back. They could see nothing. The roadblock was far behind, around many corners, half a mile or more away. In a moment the firing ceased. No one said anything, just began climbing more hurriedly.

The road was not good. They walked on for a mile or so, stepping aside for traffic. Occasionally a bus groaned past but always overloaded and none would stop. These days you could wait a day or two even at a correct stop before there was space. Trucks sometimes would stop. For payment.

Later one chugged past him and as it came alongside Azadeh, it slowed to her pace. "Why walk when those who are tired can ride with the help of Cyrus the trucker—and God," the driver called out, leering at her, nudging his companion, a dark-bearded man of his own age. They had been watching her for some time, watching the sway of her hips that not even a chador could hide. "Why should a flower of God walk when she could be warm in a truck or on a man's carpet?"

She looked up at him and gave him a gutter curse and called back to Ross, "Husband, this leprous son of a dog dared to insult me and made lewd remarks against the laws of God . . ." Ross was already alongside her, and the driver found himself looking into the barrel of a gun. "Excellency . . . I was asking if . . . if you and she would . . . would like to ride," the driver said in panic. "There's room in the back . . . if his Excellency would honor my vehicle . . ."

The truck was half filled with scrap iron, but it would be better than walking. "On your head, driver, where do you go?"

"To Qazvin, Excellency, Qazvin. Would you honor us?"

The truck did not stop but it was easy for Ross to help her climb up over the tailgate. Together they ducked down out of the wind. Her legs were shaking and she was chilled and very nervous. He reached out and put his arms around her and held her.

"Oh, Johnny, if you hadn't been there . . ."

"Don't worry, don't worry." He gave her of his warmth. Qazvin. Qazvin? Isn't that halfway to Tehran? Of course it is! We'll stick with the truck until Qazvin, he told himself, gathering strength. Then we can get another ride, or find a bus, or steal a car, that's what we'll do.

"The turnoff to the base is two or three miles ahead," she said, shivering in his arms. "To the right."

Base? Ah, yes, the base. And Erikki. But more important, what about Gueng? What about Gueng? Get your mind working. What are you going to do?

"What's the . . . what's the land like there, open and flat or a ravine or what?" he asked.

"It's fairly flat. Our village is soon, Abu Mard. We pass our village, then shortly afterward, the land flattens into a kind of wooded plateau where our own road is. Then the main road climbs again up to the pass."

Ahead he could see the road curling away, occasionally coming into view as it wound precariously along the mountainside. "We'll get off the other side of the village, before the flat, circle through the forest, and get to the base. That possible?"

"Yes. I know the country very well. I . . . I taught in the village school and used to take the children for . . . for walks. I know the paths." Again she trembled.

"Keep down out of the wind. You'll soon be warm."

The old truck was laboring on the incline not much faster than walking but better than walking. He kept his arm around her and in time she stopped trembling. Over their tailgate, he noticed a car overtaking them fast, gears shrieking, followed by a mottled green semi. The driver of the car kept his hand on the horn. There was nowhere for their truck to pull over, so the car swung over to the wrong side of the road and charged ahead. Hope you bloody kill yourself, he thought, angered by the noise and the incredible stupidity. Idly he had noticed that it had been filled with armed men. So was the following semi, though all these men stood in the back, hanging onto metal stanchions, the tailgate down and banging wildly. As it roared past, he caught a glimpse of a body slumped under their feet. At first he thought it was the old man. But it wasn't. It was Gueng. No mistaking the remains of the uniform. Or the kookri one of the men had stuck in his belt.

"What is it, Johnny?"

He found himself beside her, not feeling her or anything, only that he had failed the second of his men. His eyes were filled with tears.

"What is it, what's the matter?"

"Nothing. It's just the wind." He brushed the tears away, then knelt and looked ahead. Curling away, the road disappeared and appeared again. So did the car and semi. He could see the village now. Beyond it the road climbed again, then flattened, just as she had said. The car and semi went through the village full tilt. In his pocket were his small but very powerful binoculars. Steadying himself against the rocking of the truck, he focused on the car. Once the car came up onto the flat it speeded up, then turned right onto the side road to the base and disappeared. When the semi reached the intersection it stopped, blocking most of the road outward bound. Half a dozen of the men jumped down, spread out across the road, and stood facing Tabriz. Then, the semi turned right and vanished after the car.

Their truck slowed as the driver shifted noisily into bottom gear. Just ahead was a short, steeper grade, a path nearby, no pedestrians on this section of road. "Where does that go, Azadeh?"

She got onto her knees and looked where he pointed. "Toward Abu Mard, our village," she said. "It wanders this way and that but that's where it ends."

"Get ready to jump out—there's another roadblock ahead."

At the right moment he slipped over the side, helped her down, and they scrambled into hiding. The truck did not stop nor the driver look around. Soon it was well away. Hand in hand, they fled into the trees.

AT ZAGROS THREE: 4:05 P.M.   Lochart leaned against the cockpit of the 212 waiting to go again to Rig Rosa with another load of pipe—sky cloudless, the mountains so clean and sharp he felt he could almost reach out and touch them. He was watching Rodrigues, his mechanic, who knelt in the snow and peered into a belly inspection panel. "It's an afternoon for skiing or tobogganing, Rod, not grinding away."

"It's a day to get the hell outta here, Tom."

"Maybe we won't have to," Lochart said. Since Sunday when he had had his confrontation with Nitchak Khan he had heard nothing more from him or anyone in the village. "Maybe the komiteh will change their minds or Mac'll get the order canceled. Crazy for us to be shoved out when they need all the oil they can get and Rosa's new well's a bonanza—Jesper Almqvist said he figured it'd pump eighteen thousand barrels a day when it was put on stream. That's almost $360,000 a day, Rod."

"Mullahs don't give a shit for oil or anything but Allah, the Koran, or Paradise, you said it a million times." Rodrigues wiped an oil streak away. "We should've all gone with Jesper to Shiraz—then out. We're not wanted. Nasiri got his head blown off, right? For what? He was one nice guy. Never hurt no one. We've been told to get out—what the hell're we waiting for?"

"Maybe the komiteh changed its mind. We've eleven rigs to service."

"The rigs are down to minimums, crews all itchy to get the hell out and anyway they've had no replacements for weeks." Rodrigues got up, knocked the snow off his knees, and began wiping the oil off his hands. "Crazy to stay where you're not wanted. Young Scot's acting mighty strange—so're you, come to think of it."

"Bull," Lochart said. He had told no one what Scot said had really happened in the village square. His anxiety returned—for Scot, the base, Sharazad, HBC, and always back to Sharazad again.

"Bull nothing," Rodrigues was saying, "you've been itchy as hell since you got back from Tehran. You wanna stay in Iran, Tom, okay, that's different— you're married to Iran. Me, I want out."

Lochart took his mind off Sharazad. He saw the fear in his friend's face. "What's the problem, Rod?"

The heavyset man pulled his belt over the beginnings of his paunch, and closed his parka again. "I'm nervous as all hell about my false IDs, Tom. Shit, soon's I open my mouth, they gotta know I'm not a Brit. All my permits're outta date. So it's the same with some of the other guys, but I'm the only American here, I gave a talk in the school on the States, and goddamn mullahs and Khomeini say I'm Satan—me a goddamn good Catholic for crissake! I'm not sleeping nights."

"Why the hell didn't you say so before? No need for you to stay, Rod. The 212's due out tomorrow. How about going with Scot? Once you get to Al Shargaz you can transfer to Nigeria, Kenya, or where the hell ever."

For a moment Rodrigues said nothing, his face bleak. "I'd like that, Tom. Sure, if you can okay it, that'd be one helluva load off my back."

"It's done. We've got to send a mechanic—why not you, you're senior."

"Thanks. Yeah, thanks, Tom." Rodrigues beamed. "I'll just tighten the foot pedal, and then you're as good as new."

Down by the supply helipad Lochart saw that the load of pipe was ready for pickup. Two Iranian laborers were waiting to guide the skyhook into the ringbolt. He began to get into the cockpit, stopped on seeing two men striding up the village path a hundred yards away, Nitchak Khan, and another man carrying a carbine. Even from this distance it was easy to see the green armband.

Lochart went to meet them, preparing his mind to think and speak Farsi. "Salaam, Kalandar, salaam, Agha," he said to the other man, also bearded but much younger.

"Salaam," Nitchak said. "You have been granted until the fifth sunset."

Lochart tried to hide his shock. Today was Tuesday, the fifth day would be Sunday. "But, Excellency, th—"

"Until the fifth sunset," the Green Band said without politeness. "You may not work or fly on Holy Day—better you give thanks to God—and on the fifth sunset from tonight if all foreigners and their airplanes have not left, the base will be fired."

Lochart just looked at him. Behind the man was the cookhouse and he saw Jean-Luc come out, then walk over toward them. "Four working days will be very difficult, Agha, and I don't th—"

"Insha'Allah."

"If we go, all the rigs will have to stop. Only we can supply them and their men. That will hurt Iran, that w—"

"Islam does not *need* oil. Foreigners *need* oil. Five sunsets. Be it on your own heads if you stay."

Nitchak Khan looked sideways at the man. Then to Lochart he said, "Agha, I wish to go with this man to see the kalandar of the Italian foreigners. I would like to go now, please."

"It is my honor, Kalandar," Lochart said, and he was thinking, Mimmo Sera's been in the mountains for years, he'll know what to do. "I've a load of pipe to deliver to Rig Rosa; we can go at once."

"Pipe?" the youth said rudely. "No need for pipe. We go straight. No pipe."

"IranOil says pipe and the pipe goes or you don't," Lochart said angrily. "Ayatollah Khomeini ordered oil production to come back to normal—why does the komiteh disobey him?"

Sullenly the youth looked at the Khan, who said quietly, "As God wills. The Ayatollah is the Ayatollah, komitehs obey only him. Let us go, Agha."

Lochart took his eyes off the youth. "All right. We will go at once."

"Salaam, Kalandar," Jean-Luc said, joining them. "Tom, what's the answer?" he asked in English.

"Sunset Sunday. We have to be out by then and can't fly Friday."

Jean-Luc swallowed a curse. "No negotiation?"

"None. Unless you want to argue with this mother."

Insolently the youth with the gun stared back at Jean-Luc. "Tell this son of a dog he smells vile."

Lochart had caught a faint whiff of the garlic. "He says your cooking smells great, Jean-Luc. Listen, they want to go to see Mimmo Sera—I'll be back as quick as I can, then we'll decide what to do. Kalandar, we will go now," he said in Farsi and opened the cabin door.

"Lookit!" Rodrigues said suddenly and pointed northward high into the mountains. Smoke was billowing into the sky. "That Maria?"

"Might be Bellissima," Jean-Luc said.

Nitchak Khan was squinting into the distance. "That is near where we should go. Yes?"

"Not far off course, Kalandar."

The old man appeared very worried. "Perhaps it would be better to take the pipe on your next flight, pilot. For days now we heard that leftists were infiltrating the hills, wanting to sabotage and create trouble. Last night one of my shepherds had his throat cut and genitals hacked off—I have men out searching for the murderers." Grim-faced, he got into the cabin. The Green Band followed.

"Rod," Lochart said, "get the 206 out. Jean-Luc, stand by on the HF—I'll radio you."

"*Oui. Pas problème.*" Jean-Luc looked back at the smoke.

Lochart left the load of pipe at the base and hurried northward. It was Bellissima and it was on fire. From quite far out he could see flames spouting thirty feet from one of the trailers that, tinder dry in the moistureless air, was now almost gutted. Off to one side near the drilling rig was another fire, near the dynamite shed a body lay in the snow. Above the base, the snowcap of the mountain, re-formed by Pietro's explosion and the resultant avalanche, was benign. Below, the ravine fell seventy-five hundred feet.

As he got closer he noticed half a dozen figures running down the winding path that led at length into the valley—all of them armed. Without hesitation he banked and went after them, seeing them ahead now, directly ahead, cursing that he wasn't a gunship—no problem to blast them all. Six men, bearded, in nondescript tribesman clothes. Then he saw one man stop and aim and then the familiar sparks from the muzzle of the gun and he peeled away, taking evading action, and when he was around again, higher and safer, the figures had disappeared.

He looked back into the cabin. Nitchak Khan and the Green Band were staring down out of the side windows, noses pressed against them. He shouted but could not make himself heard, so he banged the side of the cabin to attract their attention and beckoned Nitchak Khan. The old man came forward, holding on, ill at ease flying.

"Did you see them?" he shouted.

"Yes—yes," Nitchak Khan shouted back. "Not mountain people—they're the terrorists."

Lochart went back to flying. "Jean-Luc, do you read?"

"Loud and clear, Tom, go ahead."

He told him what he had seen and to stay on the radio, then concentrated on the landing—in over the immensity of the ravine as usual, updrafts bad and a stiff wind today. This was the first time he had been to Bellissima since he had come back from Tehran. With the death of Guineppa, Bellissima was down to a minimum, one shift only. As he touched down he saw Pietro, now senior in Guineppa's place, leave the fire near the rig and hurry toward them.

"Tom! We need help," he shouted into the pilot's window, almost in tears. "Gianni's dead and a couple hurt in the fire . . ."

"Okay. No sweat." Lochart began shutdown. "Nitchak's in the back with a Green Band—don't worry, okay?" He twisted in his seat again and pointed at the door. The old man nodded. "What the hell happened, Pietro?" he asked, his fingers finding the switches.

"Don't know . . . I don't know, *amico*." Pietro put his head close to the cockpit window. "We were having lunch when this *stronzo* bottle with gasoline and a burning rag came through the *stronzo* window and we were on fire . . ." He looked back as flames caught a half-full oil drum and leaped into the sky, choking black smoke billowing. The four men fighting the fire backed off. "*Sì*, we were on fire quickly in the dining room and when we rushed out there were these men, tribesmen, *banditos* . . . Mamma mia, they started shooting so we scattered and took cover. Then later Gianni saw them starting a fire in the generator room, near where the dynamites are and . . . and he just ran out to warn them but one of them shot him. Mamma mia, no reason to shoot him! *Bastardi, stronzi bastardi* . . ."

Quickly Lochart and the others climbed out of the airplane. The only sound was that of the wind and the flames and the single fire pump—Pietro had cut the generators and pumps and done an emergency closedown of the whole rig. The roof of the trailer collapsed and sparks and embers soared, many falling on nearby roofs, but these were heavy with snow and no danger to them. The fire was still out of control near the rig, fed by waste oil and oil fumes, and highly dangerous. The men sprayed foam, but flames still reached toward the dynamite shed, licking a corrugated iron wall.

"How much is in there, Pietro?"

"Too much."

"Let's get it out."

"Mamma mia . . ." Pietro followed Lochart, their hands over the faces against the flames, and forced the door open—no time to find the key. The

dynamite was in neat boxes. A dozen of them. Lochart picked up a box and
went out, felt the blast of heat, and then he was clear. One of the other men
took the box from him and hurried it to safety while Lochart returned for
another.

Near the helicopter Nitchak Khan and the Green Band stood in the lee of
the wind out of danger. "As God wants."

"As God wants," the Green Band echoed. "What shall we do now?"

"There are the terrorists to consider. And the dead man."

The young man looked across the snow at the figure lying like a broken
doll. "If he hadn't come to our hills he would not be dead. It's his fault he's
dead—no one else's."

"True." Nitchak Khan watched the fire and the men fighting it and by the
time Lochart and Pietro had cleared the shed of dynamite, the others had the
fire contained.

Lochart leaned against a trailer wall to catch his breath. "Pietro, we've
only got till Sunday sunset. Then it's get out or else."

Pietro's face closed. He glanced at the Green Band and Nitchak Khan who
was near the helicopter. "Five days? That saves me a decision, Tom. We
evacuate to Shiraz—via Rig Rosa or direct." Pietro gestured at the fire with
his clenched left fist, his other hand on the bicep. "For the moment Bellissima is ruined. I'll need Almqvist to plug the wells. Mamma mia, that's a lot
of men to transport. What a waste! I'm glad old Guineppa's not here to see
the foulness of the day. Best I come to see Mimmo."

"At once, with those who're hurt. What about Gianni?"

Pietro glanced at the body. "We'll leave him until last, my poor blood
brother," he said sadly. "He won't rot."

AT RIG ROSA: Mimmo Sera was sitting opposite Nitchak Khan and the
Green Band in the mess hall, Lochart, Pietro, and the three senior riggers
also at the table. For half an hour Mimmo, who spoke good Farsi, had tried
to persuade the komiteh Green Band to extend the time, or to allow him to
leave skeleton crews while he and Lochart went with him to see the chief of
IranOil in Shiraz.

"In the Name of God, enough!" the Green Band said irritably.

"But Excellency, without the helicopters we'll have to shut down the
whole field and start evacuating at once. Surely, Excellency, because the
Ayatollah, bless him, and your Prime Minister Bazargan want oil production
back to normal we should consult IranOil in Sh—"

"Enough! Kalandar," the Green Band added to Nitchak Khan, "if these mosquito brains disobey, it's on your head, you're finished, Yazdek is finished and all your people! If one foreigner or one flying machine remains on the fifth sunset and you haven't fired the base, we will! Then we will burn the village, by hand or by air force. You," the Green Band snarled at Lochart, "start up the airplane. We go back. Now!" He stormed out.

They all stared after him dismayed. Lochart felt sad for all those who had found the oil and developed the field and put so much energy, money, talent, gamble, and risk into it. Scandalous, he thought, but we've no option. Nothing else to do. We evacuate. I cancel Scot leaving and use all airplanes and do the job. We work like hell for five days and forget Tehran and Sharazad and that today's the day of the Protest March she's forbidden.

"Kalandar," he said. "Without your benevolence, and assistance, we must leave."

Nitchak Khan saw all the eyes turn to him. "I have to choose between the base and my village," he said gravely. "That is no choice. I will try to find the terrorists and bring them to justice. Meanwhile, best that you take no chances. These hills are full of hiding places."

With great dignity he got up and walked out, quite sure that now he would not have to burn the base, though, if God wanted, he knew he would do it without a moment's hesitation, whether it be full or empty.

He allowed himself the shadow of a smile. His plan had worked impeccably. All the foreigners had accepted Hassan the Goatherd as a genuine Green Band whose pretended arrogance and temper were marvelous to see; the foreigners had swallowed his fabrication about "terrorists" murdering a shepherd and he had seen their fear; these same "terrorists" had mutilated the oil rig, the most difficult to reach of all eleven and, in the black hours tonight, these same "terrorists" would fire part of the Rig Rosa and then would vanish forever—back into the village life stream from which they came. And by dawn tomorrow, he thought with satisfaction, terror will be widespread, all foreigners will be falling over themselves to leave, their evacuation is assured, and peace will come to Yazdek.

Fools to play games where only we know the rules! But there is still the problem of the young pilot. Was he a witness, or wasn't he? The elders have advised an "accident" to be safe. Yesterday would have been perfect when the young man was hunting alone. So easy to slip and fall on your gun. Yes. But my wife advised against an "accident."

"Why?"

"Because the schoolhouse was a marvelous thing," she had said. "Wasn't it the first we have ever had? Without the pilots it would never have been. But now we *know* and can easily build another of our own; because the pilots have been good for us, without them we would not know much that we now know, nor would we have such a rich village; because I think that young man told the truth. I commend that you should let him go, don't forget how that young man made us laugh with his fairy stories about this place called Kong in the land called China, where there are a thousand times a thousand times a thousand times a thousand people, where all their hair is black, all eyes black, and they eat with pieces of wood."

He remembered how he had laughed with her. How could there be so many people in one land, all the same? "There is still the danger he lied."

"Then test him," she had said. "There's still time."

Yes, he thought, there are four days to uncover the truth—five including Holy Day.

TEHRAN: 5:16 P.M.   Now the Women's March was over.

It had begun that morning with the same air of expectancy that had enveloped Tehran for two days—when incredibly, for the first time in history, women by themselves as a group were about to take to the streets in protest, to show their solidarity against any encroachment of their hard-earned rights by the new rulers, even by the Imam himself.

"The proper dress for a woman is the hijab *that requires them to cover their hair and arms and legs and* zinaat—*their enticing parts."*

"I chose to wear the chador as a protest against the Shah, Meshang," Zarah, his wife, had screeched at him. "I chose it! I did! I'll never wear a veil or chador or scarf against my will, never never never . . ."

"Coeducation introduced by the Satan Shah a few years ago will cease as in practice it has turned many of our schools into houses of prostitution."

"Lies, all lies! Ridiculous!" Sharazad had told Lochart. "The truth must be shouted from the rooftops. It's not the Imam saying these things, it's the zealots surrounding him . . ."

"*The Satan Shah's heinous Marriage Protection Act is disapproved.*"

"Surely that's a mistake, Hussain," the mullah's wife had said carefully. "The Imam can't be saying that. It protects us against rejection by a husband, against polygamy, and grants us the right of divorce, gives us the vote and protects a wife's property . . ."

"*In our Islamic nation everyone will be governed only by the Koran and the Sharia. Women should not work, they must return to the home, stay in the home, to do their blessed, God-ordained duty to bear and bring up children and look after their Masters.*"

"By the Prophet, Erikki, as much as I wish to have your children and be the best wife to you," Azadeh had said, "I swear I cannot sit idly by and watch my less fortunate sisters be forced back into the Dark Ages without any freedom, or rights. It's the fanatics, the zealots, not Khomeini, who are trying to do this. I will march wherever I am . . ."

All over Iran women had prepared sympathy marches—in Qom, Isfahan, Meshed, Abadan, Tabriz, even small towns like Kowiss—but never in the villages. All over Iran there had been arguments and quarrels between most fathers and their daughters, most husbands and their wives, most brothers and their sisters, the same fights, pleadings, cursing, demands, promises, beggings, forbiddings and, God protect us, even rebellions—covert and overt. And all over Iran was the same secret resolve of the women.

"I'm glad my Tommy's not here, that makes it so much easier," Sharazad had told her reflection in the mirror this morning, the march due to begin at noon. "I'm glad he's away because whatever he said, eventually I'd disobey him." A tremor of excitement, pleasing and at the same time painful.

She was checking her makeup in the mirror a last time, just to make sure that the bruise around her left eye was well covered with powder. It hardly showed at all now. She smiled at herself, pleased with what she saw. Her hair was curled and flowing and she wore a warm green sweater and green skirt and nylons and Russian suede boots, and when she went out she had decided to wear a matching fur-lined coat and hat. Isn't green the color of Islam? she thought happily, all her soreness forgotten.

Behind her the bed was littered with ski clothes and other clothes that she had considered and discarded. After all, women have never protested as a group before so we should certainly look our best. What a pity it's not spring, then I could wear my light yellow silk dress and yellow hat and . . .

A sudden sadness took her. Her father had given her that dress for her birthday present last year, and the lovely pearl choker necklace. Poor dear

Father! she thought, her anger welling. God curse the evil men who murdered him. God cast them into the pit forever! God protect Meshang and all the family and my Tommy and let not zealots take away our freedoms.

Now there were tears in her eyes and she brushed them away. Insha'Allah, she thought. Father's in Paradise where the Faithful belong so there's no real reason to mourn. No. Only the wish to see justice done to the foul murderers. Murder! Uncle Valik. HBC. Annoush and the children. HBC! How I hate those letters! What's happened to Karim? She had heard nothing since Sunday and did not know if he was denounced, dead or free, or anything more about the telex—nothing to do but pray.

So she did. Again. And swept those problems out of her mind onto the shoulders of God and felt cleansed. As she put on her little fur-lined hat, the door opened, and Jari hurried in, also dressed in her best. "It's time, Princess. Her Highness Zarah has arrived, oh, how pretty you look!"

Filled with excitement, Sharazad picked up her coat and ran down the corridor, skirts flying, down the stairs to greet Zarah who waited for her in the hallway. "Oh, you look beautiful, Zarah darling," she said embracing her. "Oh, I thought Meshang'd stop you at the last minute!"

"He never had a chance," Zarah said with a laugh, a cute fur hat jauntily on her head, "I started on him yesterday at breakfast and continued all day and all night and this morning about the new sable coat that was absolutely necessary, that I absolutely must have or I would die of shame in front of my friends. He fled to the bazaar to escape and forgot all about the march. Come along, we mustn't be late, I've a taxi waiting. It's stopped snowing, the day promises to be fair, though it's chilly."

There were already three other women in the taxi, friends and cousins, two proudly wearing jeans and high heels and ski jackets, hair free, one with a ski hat, and they were all as excited as if they were going to a barbecue picnic in the old days. None of them noticed the muttering disapproval of the taxi driver, or cared about him. "To the university," Zarah ordered, and then they all chattered together like so many birds. When they were still two streets away from the university gates where the march was to assemble, the taxi had to stop, the crush was so huge.

Where a few hundred had been expected, there were thousands and more arriving every minute from all points of the compass. Young old, highborn lowborn, literate illiterate, peasant patrician, rich poor—jeans, skirts, pants, boots, shoes, rags, furs—and over all the same fervor, even from those who had come wearing chador. Some of the more militant were already making speeches and a few were shouting slogans:

"No chador by force . . ."

"Unity, struggle, victory . . ."

"Women unite, we refuse to be forced into *purdah* or chador . . ."

"I was at Doshan Tappeh against the Immortals—we didn't fight and suffer to give ourselves over to despotism . . ."

"Death to despotism by any name . . ."

"Yessssss! Hooray for women," Sharazad shouted, "down with enforcing the chador and veils and scarves!" Like the others she was caught up in the excitement. Zarah paid the man and gave him a good tip, turned back joyfully, linking arms with Sharazad and Jari, and none of them heard the taxi driver call out, "Whores, all of you," as he drove away.

The crowds were milling around, not knowing what to do, most of them overwhelmed by the enormous numbers and variety of women and costumes and ages—even a few men joining them enthusiastically. "We're protesting, Zarah, we're really here, aren't we?"

"Oh, yes, Sharazad! And there're so many of us . . ."

Shouting in the noise, listening to a well-dressed woman, a well-known Tehrani lawyer and activist and champion of women's rights, Namjeh Lengehi—a few groups of men, students and teachers, for and against, along with a few mullahs, all against, also listening: "Some mullahs say we women can't be judges, should not be educated and must wear chador. For three generations we have been unveiled, for three generations we have had the right of education and for one generation the right to vote. God is Great . . ."

"God is Great," a thousand echoed her.

"Some of us are more fortunate than others, some better educated than others, some even better educated than some men. Some of these know modern law better, even Koranic law better than some men—why shouldn't those women be judges? Why?"

"No reason! Those women for judges," Zarah called out with a hundred others, drowning the mullahs and their supporters who shouted, "Sacrilege!"

When she could make herself heard, Namjeh Lengehi continued: "We supported the Ayatollah with all our hearts . . ." More cheers interrupted her, a great outpouring of affection. "We bless him for what he did and we fought as best we could, side by side with men, shared their suffering and the prisons and helped win the revolution and threw out the despot and now we are free, Iran is free from his yoke and from foreign yoke. But that does not give anyone, mullahs, even the Ayatollah, the right to turn back the clock . . ."

Huge cries of, "No! No! No! No despots. Votes for women! No to despo-

tism under any cover! Lengehi for the Majlis! Lengehi for minister of education!"

"Oh, Zarah, isn't this wonderful?" Sharazad said. "Have you ever voted?"

"No, darling, of course not. But that doesn't mean I don't want the right
to if I wanted to. A hundred times I told Meshang that of course I'd ask him
who to vote for, but I still want to go into the booth myself, by myself, if I
choose to!"

"You're right!" Sharazad turned and shouted, "Up the revolution. God is
Great! God is Great! Lengehi for the High Court! Women for judges! We
insist on our rights . . ."

Teymour, the PLO-trained Iranian who had taken over Sharazad's apartment and had been sent to monitor the march and identify the militants,
recognized her from photographs he had seen there. His anger increased.
"Women to obey God's law," he shouted. "No women judges! Women to do
God's work!" But he was drowned by the thousands and no one paid any
attention to him.

No one knew how the march began. They just seemed to set off and soon
they massed the avenues, wall to wall, stopping all traffic, surging happily
along, an irresistible force. Those at the stalls and at the windows and balconies of houses adjoining stared at the marchers open-mouthed.

Most men were shocked. "Look at that one, the young whore with the
green coat that flaps open in the front to show her cleft, look, look there!
God curse her for tempting me . . ."

"Look at that one with the pants like an outer skin."

"Where! Ah, I see her, the blue pants! God protect us! You can see every
ripple of her *zinaat*! She's inviting it! Like the one she's linking arms with—
the green coat! Harlot! Hey, harlot down there, you just want a cock—that's
what you all want . . ."

Men watched and seethed. Lust followed the march.

Women watched and wondered. More and more forgot their shopping or
their stalls and joined their sisters, aunts, mothers, grandmothers, fearlessly
removing their head scarves and veils and chador—wasn't this the capital,
weren't they Tehranis, the elite of Iran, no longer villagers? It was different
here, not like back in the village where they would never have dared to shout
slogans and pull away veils and scarves and chadors. "Women unite, God is
Great, God is Great! Victory, unity, struggle. Equality for women! The vote!
No to despotism, any despotism . . ."

Ahead of the marchers, behind them, around them, on highways and in
the side streets, groups of men began forming. Those for and those against.
Arguments became more and more violent—Koranic law demanded that

Muslims resist any attempt against Islam. A few scuffles began. One man pulled a knife and died, another man's knife in his back. A few guns and woundings. Many clashes. Scattered riots between liberals and fundamentalists, between leftists and Green Bands. A few heads broken, another man dead and, here and there, children caught in the crossfire, some dead, others cowering behind parked cars.

Ibrahim Kyabi, the student Tudeh leader who had escaped the ambush the night Rakoczy had been caught, ran into the street and picked up one of the petrified children while his friends gave him covering fire. He made the safety of the corner. Once he was sure the little girl was unhurt, he shouted to his friends, "Follow me," knowing they were outnumbered here, and took to his heels. There were six of them and they ran into the alleys and side streets. Soon they were safe and heading for Roosevelt Avenue. The Tudeh had been ordered to avoid open clashes with Green Bands, to march with the women, to infiltrate the ranks and to proselytize. He was glad to be active again after being in hiding.

Within half an hour of Rakoczy's being captured, he had reported the betrayal to his controller at Tudeh HQ. The man had told him not to go home, to shave off his beard and keep out of sight in a safe house near the university: "Do nothing until the Women's Protest on Tuesday. Join that with your cell as planned, then leave for Kowiss the next day—that should keep you safe for a while."

"What about Dimitri Yazernov?"—the only name he knew Rakoczy by.

"Don't worry, we'll get him away from the scum. Tell me again what the men looked like."

Ibrahim had told them the little he had remembered about the Green Bands and the ambush. And then he had asked, "How many men will come with me to Kowiss?"

"You and two others should be enough for one rotten mullah."

Yes, he thought again, but I don't need anyone—soon my father will be avenged. His hands tightened on the M16 that had been stolen a week ago from Doshan Tappeh's armory. "Freedom!" he shouted, and hurried into Roosevelt to join the front ranks of the protest, his friends spreading out.

A hundred yards farther back, an open truck filled with youths trundled along slowly, surrounded by the thousands, waving and shouting encouragement. These were airmen out of uniform. Among them was Karim Peshadi. For hours he had been searching the marchers for Sharazad but had not seen her. He and the others were stationed at Doshan Tappeh where order and discipline were almost nonexistent, komitehs holding sway, issuing orders and counterorders, others coming from the High Command subservient to Prime

Minister Bazargan, others from the Revolutionary Komiteh—and others over the radio where, from time to time, Ayatollah Khomeini would speak and set the law.

As all other pilots and officers throughout the land, Karim had been ordered before a komiteh to be cross-examined on his record, his political beliefs, and his pre-revolutionary connections. His record was good, and he could truthfully swear he supported Islam, Khomeini and the revolution. But the specter of his father hung over him and he had carefully buried his desire for revenge in his most secret heart. So far he had been untouched.

The night before last he had tried to sneak into the Doshan Tappeh Tower to find the HBC clearance book but had been turned back. Tonight he was going to try again—he had sworn to himself not to fail. I mustn't fail, he thought, Sharazad depends on me . . . oh, Sharazad, thou who gives my life meaning even though thou art forbidden.

Anxiously he hunted for her among the marchers, knowing she was somewhere here. Last night he and a group of his friends heard a violently incendiary broadcast by an ayatollah fundamentalist, opposing the Women's Protest and demanding there be counterprotests by "Believers." He had become gravely concerned for Sharazad, his sisters, and relations who he knew would also be marching. His friends were equally concerned for theirs. So this morning they had taken the truck and had joined the protest. With guns.

"Equality for women," he shouted. "Democracy forever! Islam forever! Democracy and law and Islam forev—" The words died.

Ahead of the march men had formed a thick barrier across the road now, barring progress. The women to the forefront saw their anger and raised fists. Instinctively the women in the first half-dozen ranks tried to slow but could not. The swell of the thousands pushed them inexorably forward.

"Why're those men so angry?" Sharazad asked, her happiness evaporating, the crush increasing.

"They're just misguided, villagers mostly," Namjeh Lengehi said bravely. "They want us as slaves, slaves, don't be afraid! God is Great . . ."

"Link arms," Zarah shouted, "they can't stop us! Allahhhh-u Akbarrr . . ."

Among the men blocking the road was the man who had, at Evin Jail, led Jared Bakravan to slaughter. He had recognized Sharazad in the vanguard. "God is Great," he muttered in ecstasy, his words drowned by the shouting, "God made me an instrument to send the evil bazaari to hell and now God has given into my hands the harlot daughter." His eyes gloated over her, seeing her naked on the couch, spread, breasts proud, eyes filled with lust, mouth moist, lips moist, hearing her begging him, "Take me, take me, quick, for you no money, let me have it, all of it, quick, quick, fill me, stretch me, for you anything, quick quick . . . oh, Satan, help me suck God out of his organ . . ."

He jerked out his knife, loins throbbing, manhood proud, and hurled himself at her, "God is Greatttt . . ." His rush was sudden and he went across the space separating him from the women, knocked down half a dozen, reaching for her, but slipped and fell in his excitement, his knife flailing. Those he wounded were screaming and he fought to his feet and groped for her, seeing only her, her eyes wide, terror-stricken, knife in his fist ready to gut her, now only three paces away, two paces, one . . . his head filled with her perfume, the stench of the Devil Incarnate. The death blow began but never touched her and he knew Satan had sent an evil djinn his way—there was a monstrous burning in his chest, his eyes became sightless, and he died with the Name of God on his lips.

Sharazad stared down at the crumpled figure, Ibrahim beside her now, the gun in his hand, shouts and more screams and a roar of rage from a thousand women pressing behind them.

Another shot, another man fell screaming. "Forward for God!" Lengehi cried over her own fear, her shout taken up by Ibrahim who tugged at Sharazad: "Don't be afraid, forward for women . . ."

She saw his confidence and for a moment mistook him for her cousin Karim so similar in height and build and face, then her terror and hatred at what had happened burst and she shouted, "Forward for my father . . . Down with zealots and Green Bands . . . down with murderers!" She grabbed Zarah. "Come on! Forward!" and she linked arms with her and with Ibrahim, her savior, so like Karim they could be brothers, and they started off again. More men were running to the front in support, the truck with the airmen among them.

Another knife wielder came at them screaming.

"God is Great . . ." Sharazad shouted, the horde with her, and before he was neutralized the screaming youth had slashed Namjeh Lengehi's arm. Inexorably, the front ranks pressed forward, both sides roaring "God is Great," both sides equally sure they were right. Then the opposition crumpled.

"Let them march," a man shouted. "Our women are there too, some of them, there're too many of them . . . too many . . ." Those men in the way backed off, others stood aside and now the way was clear. A roar of triumph from the marchers: "Allahhh-u Akbarrr . . . God is with us, sisters!"

"Forward," Sharazad shouted again and the march continued again. Those who were wounded were carried or helped to the side, the others streaming onward. Now the protest became orderly again. No more opposition barred their way though many men watched sullenly from the sidelines, Teymour and others photographing the militants.

"It's a success," Namjeh Lengehi said weakly, still walking in the front rank, a scarf staunching the flow of blood from her arm. "We're a success—even the Ayatollah will know of our resolution. Now we can go home to our husbands and families. We've done what we wanted and now we can go home."

"No," Sharazad said, her face pale and dirt-stained, not yet over her fright. "We must march tomorrow and tomorrow and tomorrow until the Imam agrees publicly to no enforced chador and to our rights."

"Yes," Ibrahim said, "if you stop now the mullahs will crush you!"

"You're right, Agha, oh how can I thank you for saving us?"

"Yes," Zarah said, still shaken. "We will march tomorrow or those . . . those madmen will destroy us!"

The march proceeded without more trouble and this was the pattern in the cities, initial trouble then the peaceful protest continuing.

But in the villages and small towns the march was stopped before it began and far to the south, in Kowiss, there was silence in the town square except for the sound of the lash and the screams. When the march had formed the mullah Hussain had been there. "This protest is forbidden. All women not dressed according to the *hijab* are liable to sentencing for public nakedness against the dictates of the Koran." Only half a dozen women among two hundred were dressed in overcoats and Western dress.

"Where does it say in the Koran we disobey God if we don't wear chador?" one woman shouted. She was the bank manager's wife, and had been to Tehran University. Her appearance was modest, she wore an overcoat and a skirt but her hair was free.

" 'Oh, Prophet, say to thy wives and daughters and believing women, that they draw their veils closer to them . . .' Iran is an Islamic state . . . the first in history. The Imam has decreed *hijab*. It is *hijab*. Go and dress properly at once!"

"But Believers in other lands aren't required chador, nor do their leaders or husbands force them into it."

" 'Men are managers of the affairs of women, for that God has preferred in bounty one of them over another . . . righteous women are therefore obedient . . . Those that you fear may be rebellious, admonish; banish them to their couches and beat them. If they then obey you, look not for any way against them.' Go and cover your hair!"

"I will not. For more than forty years Iranian women have been unveiled an—"

"Forty lashes will curb your disobedience! God is Great!" Hussain motioned to one of his acolytes. Others grabbed the woman and pinioned her. The whip soon ripped through the material on her back to the jeers of the men who watched. When it was over, the senseless woman was carried away. By other women. The rest went back to their homes. In silence.

There Hussain looked at his wife, her stomach huge with child. "How dare you join a protest of harlots and loose women?"

"It . . . it was an error," she said, petrified. "It was a great error."

"Yes. You will have no food, only water for two days to remind you. If you weren't with child you would have had the same, in the square."

"Thank you for being merciful, God bless you and keep you. Thank you . . ."

AT TEHRAN AIRPORT: 6:40 P.M. With Andrew Gavallan beside him, McIver drove out of the freight area onto the feeder road heading for their 125, ETLL, that was parked on the freight apron a quarter of a mile away. She had been back from Tabriz for about an hour and was refueled and ready for the return flight across the Gulf. When she had landed, Armstrong had thanked them profusely for allowing them the use of the airplane. So had Colonel Hashemi Fazir.

"Captain Hogg says the 125 returns on Saturday, Mr. Gavallan," Hashemi had said politely. "I wonder if you'd be kind enough to give us a ride to Tabriz. Just one way this time, no need to wait, we can make our own way back."

"Of course, Colonel," Gavallan had said pleasantly, not feeling pleasant about either of the men. When he had arrived from Al Shargaz this morning McIver had told him at once, in private, why it was necessary to cooperate. "I'll deal with that right smartly with Talbot, Mac," he had said, furious at the blackmail. "CID or Special Branch notwithstanding!"

They all held their hands over their ears as a giant USAF transport taxied past on its way to the distant takeoff point—one of the many U.S. government charters arranged to evacuate remaining American service and embassy personnel except for a skeleton staff. Superheated air from the jets tore up snow and washed over them. When Gavallan could make himself heard, he said, "Talbot left a message for you, Mr. Armstrong, and asked if you'd see him as soon as possible." He saw the glance between the two men and wondered what it meant.

"Did he say where, sir?"

"No, just to see him as soon as possible." Gavallan was distracted by a big black limo hurrying toward them, the official Khomeini flag on the fender. Two hard-faced men got out and saluted Hashemi deferentially, held the door open for him.

"Until Saturday—thank you again, Mr. Gavallan." Hashemi got into the back.

"How do we contact you, Colonel—in case there's a change in plan?"

"Through Robert. He can get a message to me. Is there anything I can do for you? Here at the airport?"

McIver said quickly, "About refueling—thanks for arranging it—if you could see we get the same rapid service every time I'd appreciate it. And also our clearances serviced."

"I'll take care of it. You *will* have priority for Saturday's flight. If there's anything else, please ask Robert. Come on, Robert!"

Robert Armstrong said, "Thanks again, Mr. Gavallan, see you Saturday, if not before."

When Talbot had come by earlier to find out Armstrong's arrival time back from Tabriz, Gavallan had taken him aside and almost howled with rage over the blackmail. "Bless my soul," Talbot had said, shocked. "What a ghastly accusation, terribly un-British, Andrew, if I may say so! I understand Robert went to a considerable amount of trouble to try to extricate you, your company, Duncan, and Lochart—good man that, lovely wife, sad about her father—from a disaster that can raise its ugly head at any moment. Couldn't it?" He smiled sweetly. "I understand Robert *asked*, only asked for a modest favor, easy to provide, no skin off the old nose, Andrew."

"He's Special Branch, ex-CID Hong Kong, isn't he?"

Talbot's smile had never lost its sweetness. "I wouldn't know. But he does seem to want to do you a favor. Rather nice of him. Isn't it?"

"Does he have the clearance book?"

"I wouldn't know anything about that sort of thing."

"Who's this Colonel Fazir anyway?"

Talbot had lit a cigarette. "Just a friend. Good man to have as a friend."

"I can see that. He arranged refueling and immediate priority clearance as though he was God All bloody Mighty."

"Oh, he's not, by no means not. Near it, but not God. God's English," Talbot had chuckled. "And a woman. No masculine intelligence could balls up the world so satisfactorily. A word to the wise, old chap: I hear, following the advice of your fellow board member, Ali Kia, *they* intend nationalizing all foreign aircraft companies, particularly yours, if ever they can get the piece of paper together."

Gavallan was shocked. "Who're *'they'*?"

"Does it matter?"

After Talbot had driven off, Gavallan had stalked back into the office that was well staffed today. Not back to normal yet but getting there—radio op, telex op, office manager, stores men and some secretaries, no women present today as all had requested permission to go on the Protest March. "Mac, let's take a walk."

McIver glanced up from a pile of reports. "Sure," he said, seeing the gravity.

They had had no time to talk privately yet, impossible in or near the office, the walls all thin and ears wide open everywhere. From the moment Gavallan had arrived hours ago, the two of them had been busy going through the cash ledgers, contracts still in service, contracts held up or canceled, and the current status of each base—all of them reporting, guardedly, minimum work and maximum harassment—the only good piece of news McIver's permission to export the three 212s and even that was not sure. Yet.

The two men went out onto the freight apron. A JAL jumbo roared into the sky. "They say there're still two to three thousand Japanese techs kicking their heels at Iran-Toda," McIver said absently.

"Their consortium's taking a hell of a beating. Today's *Financial Times* said their override's already half a billion dollars, no way they can get finished this year and no way to pull out—that and the world shipping glut must be hurting Toda badly." Gavallan saw there was no one near. "At least our capital investment's mobile, Mac, most of it."

McIver looked up at him, seeing the craggy face, gray bushy eyebrows, brown eyes. "That's the reason for the 'imperative conference'?"

"One of them." Gavallan told him what Talbot had said. " 'Nationalized'! That means we lose the lot—unless we do something about it. Genny's right, you know. We've got to do it ourselves."

"I don't think it's possible. Did she tell you that?"

"Of course, but I think we can. Try this on for size: Say today's Day One. All nonessential personnel begin to quit Iran for reassignment or on leave; we get out all the spares we can—either by our 125 or on regular airlines when they start up again—as obsolete, redundant, for repair or as personal baggage. Zagros Three retreats to Kowiss, Tabriz closes 'temporarily' and Erikki's 212 goes to Al Shargaz, then to Nigeria along with Tom Lochart from Zagros, and one 212 from Kowiss. You close HQ in Tehran and relocate at Al Shargaz to run operations and control our three remaining bases of Lengeh, Kowiss and Bandar Delam 'pending return to normality' from there—we're all still under our government orders to evacuate all nonessential personnel."

"Right, but th—"

"Let me finish, laddie. Say we can do the prep and planning and all that in thirty days. Day Thirty-one's D day. At an exact time on D day—or D plus one or two depending on weather or Christ knows what—we radio a code word from Al Shargaz. Simultaneously all remaining pilots and choppers take off, head across the Gulf for Al Shargaz. There we remove the rotors, stow the choppers into 747 freighters I've chartered from somewhere, they'll fly to Aberdeen and Bob's your bloody uncle," Gavallan ended with a beam.

McIver stared at him blankly. "You're crazy! You're stark raving bonkers, Chinaboy. It's got so many holes in it . . . you're bonkers."

"Name one hole."

"I can give you fifty, firs—"

"One at a time, laddie, and remember your bloody pressure. How is it by the way—Genny asked me to ask?"

"Fine, and don't you bloody start. First, the same takeoff time: choppers from the different bases'll take vastly different times because of the distances they have to go. Kowiss'll have to refuel—can't make it in one hop, even across the Gulf."

"I know that. We make separate subplans for each of the three bases. Each base commander makes his own plan how to get out—we're responsible for them on arrival. Scrag can zip across the Gulf easily, so can Rudi from Bandar De—"

"He can't. Neither Rudi from Bandar Delam nor Starke from Kowiss can make it in one hop all along the Gulf to Al Shargaz—even if they can get across the Gulf in the first place. They'll have to go through Kuwait, Saudi, and Emirate airspace and God only knows if they'd impound us, jail, or fine us—Al Shargaz too, no reason why they should be any different." McIver shook his head. "The sheikdoms can't do anything without proper Iranian clearances—rightly they're all scared fartless Khomeini's revolution'll spread to them, they've all got big Shi'a minorities, they're no match for Iranian armed forces if he decides to get mean."

"One point at a time," Gavallan said calmly. "You're right about Rudi's and Starke's planes, Mac. But say they have permission to fly through all those territories?"

"Eh?"

"I telexed all Gulf ATC's individually for permission and I've got telex confirms that S-G choppers in transit can go through."

"Yes, but—"

"But one point at a time, laddie. Next, say all our planes were back on British registry—they are British, they *are* our planes, we're paying for them, we own them whatever the partners try to pull. On British registry they're not subject to Iran or anything to do with them. Right?"

"Once they're out, yes, but you won't get Iran Civil Aviation Authority to agree to the transfer, therefore you can't get them back to British."

"Say I could get them onto British registry regardless."

"How in the hell would you do that?"

"Ask. You ask, laddie, you ask the registry lads in London to do it. In fact I did before I left London. 'Things are kind of ropy in Iran,' says I. 'Totally snafu, old boy, yes,' says they. 'I'd like you to put my birds back on British registry, temporarily,' says I, 'I may bring them out until the situation normalizes—of course, the powers that be in Iran'd approve but I can't get a bloody piece of paper signed there at the moment, you know how it is.' 'Certainly, old boy', says they, 'same with our bloody government—any bloody government. Well, they are your kites, no doubt about that, it's a tiny bit irregular but I imagine it might be all right. Are you going to the Old Boys' beer-up?' "

McIver had stopped walking and stared at him in wonder. "They agreed?"

"Not yet, laddie. Next?"

"I've got a hundred 'nexts' but!" Irritably McIver started walking again, too cold to stand still.

"But?"

"But if I give them one at a time, you'll give me an answer—and a *possible* solution but they still won't all add up."

"I agree with Genny, we have to do it ourselves."

"Maybe, but it has to be feasible. Another thing: We've permission to take three 212s out, maybe we could get out the rest."

"The three aren't out yet, Mac. The partners, let alone ICAA, won't let us out of their grasp. Look at Guerney—all their choppers are impounded. Forty-eight, including all their 212s—maybe $30 million rotting, they can't even service them." They glanced at the runway. An RAF Hercules was landing. Gavallan watched it. "Talbot told me by the end of the week all British army, navy, and air force technicians and training personnel'll be out and at the embassy they'll be down to three, including him. It seems that in the fracas at the U.S. embassy—someone sneaked in under cover of it, blew open safes, grabbed ciphers . . ."

"They still had secret stuff there?" McIver was appalled.

"Seems so. Anyway, Talbot said the infiltration caused every diplomatic sphincter in Christendom—and Sovietdom—and Arabdom—to palpitate. All embassies are closing. The Arabs are the most fractured of all—not one of the oil sheiks wants Khomeinism across the Gulf and they're anxious, willing and able to spend petro dollars to prevent it. Talbot said: 'Fifty pounds against a bent hat pin that Iraq privately now has an open checkbook, the Kurds likewise, and anyone else who's Arab, pro-Sunni and anti-Khomeini. The whole Gulf's poised to explode.' "

"But meanwhile th—"

"Meanwhile, he's not so bullish as he was a few days ago and not so sure that Khomeini's going to quietly retire to Qom. 'It's jolly old Iran for the Iranians, old boy, so long as they're Khomeini and mullahs,' he said. 'It's in with Khomeinism if the leftists don't assassinate him first and out with the old. That means us.' " Gavallan banged his gloved hands together to keep the circulation going. "I'm bloody frozen. Mac, it's clear from the books we're in dead trouble here. We've got to look after ourselves."

"It's a hell of a risk. I think we'd lose some birds."

"Only if luck's against us."

"You're asking a lot from luck, Andy. Remember those two mechanics in Nigeria who've been jailed for fourteen years just for servicing a 125 that was flown out illegally?"

"That was Nigeria, the mechanics stayed behind. We'd leave no one."

"If just one expat gets left behind, he'll be grabbed, tossed into jail, and become a hostage for all of us and all the birds—unless you're prepared to let him take the flak. If you're not, they'll use him to force us back and when we come back they'll be plenty bloody irritated. What about all our Iranian employees?"

Doggedly Gavallan said, "If luck's against us it'll be a disaster whatever we do. I think we should come up with a proper plan with all the final details, *in case.* That'll take weeks—and we'd better keep the planning super secret, just between us."

McIver shook his head. "We'll have to consult Rudi, Scragger, Lochart, and Starke, if you want to be serious."

"Just as you say." Gavallan's back was aching and he stretched. "Once it's properly planned . . . We don't have to press the final tit until then."

They walked for a while in silence, snow crunching loudly. Now they were almost at the end of the apron. "We'd be asking a hell of a lot from the lads," McIver said.

Gavallan did not appear to have heard him. "We can't just leave fifteen years of work, can't toss away all our savings, yours, Scrag's, and everything," he said. "Our Iran's gone. Most of the fellows we've worked with over the years have fled, are in hiding, dead—or against us if they like it or not. Work's at a minimum. We've got nine choppers working out of twenty-six here. We're not being paid for the little we do, or any back money. I think that's all a write-off."

Doggedly McIver said, "It's not as bad as you think. The partn—"

"Mac, you've got to understand I can't write off the money we're owed *plus our birds and spares* and stay in business. I can't. Our thirteen 212s are worth $13 million, nine 206s another $1.3 odd million, three Alouettes another $1.5 million, and 3 million of spares—$20 million give or take a few dollars. I can't write that off. Ian warned me Struan's needs help this year, there's no spare cash—Linbar's made some bad decisions and . . . well you know what I think of him and he of me. But he's still taipan. I can't write off Iran, can't get out of the new contracts for the X63s, can't battle Imperial who're presently clobbering us in the North Sea with their unfair bloody bookkeeping with taxpayers' money. Can't be done."

"You'd be asking a hell of a lot from the lads, Chinaboy."

"And from you, Mac, don't forget you. It'd be a team effort, not just for me, for them too—because it's that or go under."

"Most of our lads can get jobs with no problem. The market's desperate for trained chopper pilots who're oilers."

"So what? Bet you all of them'd rather be with us, we look after them, pay top dollar, we've the best safety record—S-G's the best chopper company on earth, and they know it! You and I know we're part of the Noble House, by God, and that means something too." Gavallan's eyes suddenly lit up with his irrepressible twinkle. "It'd be a great caper if we pulled it off. I'd love to shove Linbar's nose in it. When the time comes we'll ask the lads. Meanwhile all systems go, eh, laddie?"

"All right," McIver said without enthusiasm. "For the planning."

Gavallan looked at him. "I know you too well, Mac. Soon you'll be raring to go and I'll be the one saying, Hold it, what about so-and-so . . ."

But McIver wasn't listening. His mind was trying to formulate a plan, despite the impossibility of it—except for the British registry. Could that make the difference?

"Andy, about the plan. We'd better have a code name."

"Genny said we should call it 'Whirlwind'—that's what we're mixed up in."

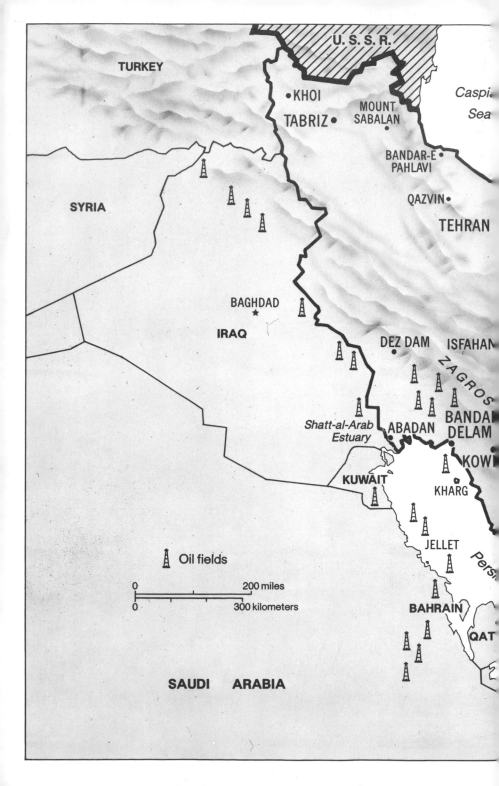